# The CSA Trilogy

An Alternate History/Historical Novel about Our Vast and Beautiful Confederate States of America – A Happy Story in Three Parts of What Might Have Been – 1861 to 2011

Part 1 -- How the Confederate States Won Independence and Expanded Westward to Southern California -- 1861 and 1862

Part 2 – How the Confederate States Expanded to Include the State of Cuba, Six States out of Northern Mexico, the State of Russian America, and the State of Hawaii – 1862 to 1877

Part 3 – How Confederates Retained their Cherished Principles of State Sovereignty and Respect for Population Diversity while Developing the World's Greatest Economy – 1878 to 2011

By Howard Ray White

Note to Reader: This alternate history/historical novel is a happy, non-violent, non-racial, story of what might have been. So, please enter into the pages of this historical novel knowing that you will be experiencing far less of the violence, racial hatred and political hatred than exists in the truthful history of mankind. Just set aside notions of American politically correct thought, open your mind, and live through a refreshing historical novel about the Southern people as they expand in territory and progress across 150 years of alternate history, along the way enjoying a diverse society and creating the "Greatest Country on Earth."

### Other Books by Howard Ray White

Truthful history books by Howard Ray White include the following, still available on Amazon:

*Bloodstains, An Epic History of the Politics that Produced and Sustained the American Civil War and the Political Reconstruction that Followed.* Four volumes: Volume 1: *The Nation Builders* (Ancient British Isles to March 1848), published in 2002; Volume 2: *The Demagogues* (March 1848 to April 1861), published in 2003; Volume 3: *The Bleeding* (April 1861 to May 1865), published in 2007; and Volume 4: *Political Reconstruction and the Struggle for Healing* (May 1865 to March 1885), published in 2012.

*Understanding the War Between the States, A Supplemental Booklet . . .* , by 16 authors in The Society of Independent Southern Historians, Howard Ray White, editor and contributing author, published in 2015.

*Understanding Abe Lincoln's First Shot Strategy (Inciting Confederates to Fire First at Fort Sumter)*, published in 2011.

*Understanding "Uncle Tom's Cabin" and "The Battle Hymn of the Republic" – How Novelist Harriet Beecher Stowe and Poet Julia Ward Howe Influenced the Northern Mind*, published in 2003.

*American History for Home Schools, with a Focus on Our Civil War*, by 16 authors in The Society of Independent Southern Historians, Howard Ray White, editor and contributing author, published in 2018.

*Understanding Creation and Evolution*, published in 2018.

A future Historical Novel by Howard Ray White.

*Who Are Our True Friends?*, to be published in late 2019.

### Reviews by Readers of *The CSA Trilogy*

Eight people who are skilled in writing and reading history related to the South read *The CSA Trilogy* manuscript prior to publication. Of these, the assessment by Dr. Fred Moss of Alabama is thought to be the most helpful:

"It was my privilege to review this fascinating series prior to publication! . . . In this fun and informative read, Howard Ray White turns his considerable writing skill to a unique combination of fiction and historical non-fiction composition. His Trilogy is what I call a 'two by two' read! The fictional story of a group of twelve impressive young people of diverse backgrounds coming together for a special four-week-long seminar provides the framework that carries the storyline. . . . The included historical material will be new to many readers. . . They will love reading the revealed truth – truth all nicely documented with excellent clarifying footnotes, less fiction be confused with non-fiction. It also contains several accounts of the twelve engaged in outside weekend adventures with physical dangers, rescues, and at least one budding romance. Something for everyone! I highly recommend this most impressive, informative, and enjoyable series of three parts! *The CSA Trilogy* offers a new model for alternate histories of the American Civil War and what followed afterward. The South fought for what it believed to be a new classical Greek type of democracy. Thus, the war was for state's rights and democracy, not slavery."

# Preface

This alternate history/historical fiction novel, is presented as a trilogy: 150 years of the Confederate States of America, from its formation in early 1861, to the 2011 celebration of the sesquicentennial of what has become the "Greatest Country on Earth" -- A trilogy, because it climaxes three times:

Part 1 -- This alternate history of years 1861 and 1862 differs remarkably from truthful history. Herein you learn how Confederates won recognition of their independence, accepted the North's African Americans, and negotiated a boundary separating the two countries. At this point, the CSA gave up northern and western Virginia in exchange for Indian Territory (Oklahoma) and very arid land west of Texas, out to Southern California. The story proceeds to Part 2.

Part 2 -- Our alternate history next explains how, beyond those original boundaries, nine new States are subsequently added to the Confederacy:

- Six States from the northern region of Mexico,
- Cuba,
- Russian America (known to us as Alaska), and
- The Hawaiian Islands.

All slaves are soon emancipated, embarking on happy, successful lives for them and future generations. These rapid events, remarkably consistent with truthful history of those regions and times, tantalize the reader concerning what might have been. The story proceeds to Part 3.

Part 3 – Confederates create a vibrant modern economy, accelerated by the immigration of men and families of remarkable talent, thereby facilitating a rapid industrial expansion -- accomplished without losing the cherished principle of State Sovereignty.

When Japan attacks the Confederate State of Hawaii, the country is again drawn into war. Confederates succeed in winning that one, too, and Asia is far different as a result.

The story concludes with the heart-warming celebration of the Confederate Sesquicentennial at the University of the South in Sewanee, Tennessee.

But *The CSA Trilogy* is more than an alternate history. It is also an historical novel, where twelve prominent and especially capable young men and women participate in the Sewanee Project at The University of the South in Tennessee. Here their leader and the twelve, learn and discuss Confederate history, and enjoy personal relationships and experiences over a four week time of togetherness. *The CSA Trilogy* concludes with each of the twelve presenting their essay before worldwide television, each essayist addressing, from twelve different perspectives, why the CSA is the "Greatest Country on Earth."

So, the reader enjoys an alternate history, a historical novel, a clear understanding of truthful, versus alternate history, a novel involving twelve amazing young men and women, weekend adventures, and a bit of romance. Is that not "something for everyone?"

4

# Acknowledgements

I wish to acknowledge and thank the many people who taught me important lessons about how to study history and write about it, in such a way that others can learn to enjoy a broader understanding of our past.

Perhaps I should start with James A. Michener of Texas, who began with *Hawaii* and wrote many, many comprehensive historical novels that hooked me into a love of history -- a love of learning history through the lives of his carefully crafted characters, and through his skillful story-telling involving several generations, thereby covering the time span of a century or two. He taught me that, "to understand history you have to live it." And it was through his characters that I and other readers enjoyed "living" the history as if I or they were there.

In my previous books, which are non-fiction histories, I wrote to enable the reader to "understand the history by living it." I have attempted to continue that goal in this, my first historical novel, *The CSA Trilogy*.

I am especially thankful for the help of Dr. Clyde N. Wilson, of South Carolina, who had encouraged me in my previous histories, including *Bloodstains*, and has further encouraged me in the writing of *The CSA Trilogy*.

Together, Dr. Wilson and I co-founded the Society of Independent Southern Historians, and it is to members of this Society that I wish to express additional thanks.

At Dr. Wilson's suggestion, Tom G. Moore, of South Carolina, read Part 1 of the manuscript and made helpful suggestions. Following that, Dr. Wilson invited other members of our Society to read copies of the manuscript and offer suggestions. I am honored that seven members volunteered and did read much of the manuscript, often all of it, while, along the way, marking helpful comments in the margins and cataloging further suggestions in written response back to me. To these I am grateful.

Dr. Fred M. Moss of Alabama.

Bertil Haggman, LLM of Sweden.

Barbara Marthal of Tennessee.

Carleton Wilkes of Texas.

Jonathan Varnell of North Carolina.

Herbert Bing Chambers of South Carolina.

Valerie Protopapas of New York.

# The CSA Trilogy

## An Alternate History/Historical Novel about Our Vast and Beautiful Confederate States of America

## A Happy Story, in Three Parts, of What Might Have Been

## 1861 to 2011

## The CSA Trilogy, Part 1 -- How the Confederate States Won Independence and Expanded Westward to Southern California -- An Alternate History – 1861 and 1862

### Foreword

Thanks for your interest in this alternate history, presented as a trilogy, which covers 150 years of the Confederate States of America, from its formation in early 1861, to the celebration of the sesquicentennial of what has become the Greatest Country on Earth. The three parts of this trilogy match the three major stories of the Confederate States.

### Part 1

Our alternate history of the years 1861 and 1862 differ remarkably from truthful history. In our alternate history you learn how Confederates won recognition of their independence, guaranteed by a peace treaty between the United States and the Confederate States. Confederates did not fire on Fort Sumter, instead allowing Federal tax collection agents to operate in Charleston harbor. By choosing a campaign of passive resistance, Confederates gained many months of time to build military strength and to organize a brilliant defense. You will learn how Confederates influenced Northern political thought in their secret service campaign aimed at weakening support among the people, and among Republican governors and state militia, for an invasion of the seceded states. You will learn how Confederates used propaganda to encourage people of the North to fear that a Federal conquest of the Confederate States would result in free people of color migrating into their states and communities and becoming their neighbors. Of course, in 1861, in the Southern States, free people of color, with very few exceptions, had no desire to migrate into the Northern States and suffer the abuse prevalent there -- but Confederates cleverly encouraged fear in the North that a war of conquest would produce that result. Furthermore, people of African ancestry, whether slave or free, were a valuable resource in the South -- providing skilled labor in agriculture and animal husbandry – many with the obvious potential to farm land on their own.

When the North eventually invaded the Confederacy in May 1862, you will learn how Confederates overwhelmed the first wave of Federal invaders and forced the Lincoln

Administration to agree to peaceful separation. Stated another way, you will read herein the alternate history of that remarkable Confederate success -- made possible by employing tools of passive resistance, propaganda, political activism and military preparedness, thereby preventing the Lincoln Administration from gathering sufficient military strength to conquer the seceded Confederate States. The negotiated treaty settlement between the United States and the Confederate States involved giving the portion of Virginia along the Potomac and the Ohio rivers to the United States in exchange for the arid land west of Texas – New Mexico Territory, Arizona Territory and Southern California. An important feature of the settlement agreement was the Federal demand that Confedcrates accept all free people of color who were living at that time in the states and territory that remained within the United States. This resettlement south, into the Confederacy, was forced upon people of color by the northern states, for the White people of the Republican states were insisting that all people of color no longer be their neighbors. Federals also demanded the emancipation and deportation of all slaves who lived in what remained of the United States -- Delaware, Maryland, the transferred portion of Virginia, the remaining portion of Kentucky and the remaining portion of Missouri. Confederates agreed, and these emancipated free people of color were rounded up by Federals, handed over to Southern officials at the border, and resettled in various areas within the Confederate States as free people. This agreement satisfied several major objectives: it gave the remaining United States full control over the valleys of the Potomac and Ohio River; it allowed Northern white people to forevermore prohibit free people of color or slaves from living among them; it allowed the Confederacy to expand westward to the Pacific and to transfer into their country a small amount of southern Kentucky and southern Missouri. [1]

### Part 2

With the Confederate States now established and unchallenged, we proceed to Part 2. Here our alternate history follows, to a remarkable extent, truthful history of the subsequent 1860's and early 1870's. What makes our alternate history possible is the presence of the Confederate States as a new and prosperous country. It is really amazing to understand how the successful defense of the Confederate States quickly snow-balled into successful independence movements in Cuba, in the northern region of Mexico, in Russian America (known at Alaska in truthful history) and in the Hawaiian Islands. With Confederate help and encouragement, these successful independence movements resulted in the addition of nine more states within the Confederacy – the State of Cuba, 6 states out of Northern Mexico, the State of Russian America and the State of Hawaii. These rapid events, to a great extent consistent with truthful history of those regions in those times, will tantalize the reader -- elevate his or her imagination concerning what might have been. All of this takes place between 1863 and 1877.

### Part 3

With the Confederate States now expanded in territory to span from mid-Virginia to Hawaii, and from Russian America to Cuba, we enter into Part 3. Here we witness the alternate history of how Confederates created a vibrant modern economy in the subsequent 134 years, to the sesquicentennial celebration of 2011. Most importantly, we learn the history of how Confederates encouraged immigration into their country of men and families of remarkable talent, thereby

---

[1] In truthful history, the political movement in the Republican Party to free slaves did not gain traction until after two years of war and over one hundred thousand Federal military deaths. Remember that the "underground railroad" did not help slaves find homes in the northern States; it kept moving them north into Canada. The New York City draft riots of July 1863 illustrated the hatred whites of the north held toward free people of color. And several states, including Illinois and Oregon, by constitutional law, prevented free people of color from moving into their state to live there. Excluding free people of color from Northern communities was the dominant passion in the Republican States. The Northern passion was not a crusade to force the emancipation of slaves who lived far away in the South.

facilitating a rapid industrial expansion. We also learn how Confederates accomplished that remarkable achievement without losing the cherished principle of State Rights, while continuing to encourage respect for the country's very diverse population. Regulations over slavery remained the prerogative of each State, but that does not impede a rather rapid transition from slavery to independent living for families of African descent – a complete emancipation that included education, full citizenship and equal rights. Part 3 concludes with the heart-warming celebration of the Confederate Sesquicentennial at the University of the South in Tennessee.

The industrial expansion within the Confederate States was remarkably complete and far more rapid than we recall in the truthful history of the South. Much credit goes to immigrants who brought terrific scientific and industrial skills – men like Thomas Edison (father was Canadian), Cyrus McCormick (of Chicago, but originally of Virginia), Henry Ford (from Michigan, father Irish), Antonio Luchic (Croatia), Orville and Wilbur Wright (Ohio), Paul Heroult (France), Nikola Tesla (Serbia) and Guglielmo Marconi (Italy).

The Confederate States became engaged in the Pacific and maintained good relations with China, so, when Hawaii, a Confederate State, was attacked by Japanese Imperialists in 1941, Confederates are drawn into a Pacific War and the outcome is remarkably different than we recall in truthful history.

Although this trilogy is primarily an alternate history of 150 years of the Confederate States, the writer has overlaid a novel upon this story, which presents twelve individuals of remarkable ancestry who are studying these 150 years and preparing essays to explain "Why the Confederate States are the Greatest Country on Earth." In the closing chapter, these twelve will be reading their essays before you and a before a world-wide television audience on the evening of the Sesquicentennial Celebration. You will be following and getting to know these fictional characters – impressive and accomplished young people – through the three parts of this trilogy. The reader will enjoy following them, their interactions, and their experiences, over the four weeks that they are together, including some thrilling weekend adventures. You will also enjoy getting to know their professor, who is guiding their studies and essay preparations.

This trilogy is a happy story, so much happier that the truthful history of the conquest of the Seceded States -- a four-year military nightmare that resulted in the death of approximately one million people, about half from the United States and about half from the Confederate States.

Let us ask ourselves, "Did this calamity have to happen?" This writer submits that the answer is "No!!" Alternate futures are always possible in the course of human events. Looking back from our vantage point today, we realize that a change in certain historic circumstances could have frequently and dramatically changed the course of human history, and, moving forward, even to redefining the world as we know it today.

Drawing upon his knowledge as an historian of the Civil War and mid-1800's American political events, the writer has reflected upon numerous plausible alternate circumstances that might have gained prominence during that era, storing away a "tool-kit" of possible historical alternatives. From this "tool-kit", he has picked a set of alternatives he believes would have been the most likely to result in successful independence for the Confederate States, agreement on a boundary between the two countries, and transfer southward of emancipated African Americans who lived north of that boundary. He believes the resulting alternate history is a tribute to what mankind is capable of achieving when goodness is allowed to prevail.

*The CSA Trilogy* is also a story about the bonds of friendship between whites and people of color, whether free or slave. My friend, of African descent, wrote the following to help you, as a reader, understand why black people would have been successful living in the Confederacy over the course of 150 years:

"The truth is that most free people of African descent knew and understood that the South offered the greatest opportunities for success and did not look to the North as the Promised Land. There are accounts of free people of color who wrote to their friends and families in the North encouraging them to move south before the Civil War because free people of color enjoyed economic success in the Colonial and Antebellum South. Our readers need to know this history to understand why black people would have been able to be successful in the CSA. They need to know that this is real history and not based upon our having to imagine what could have been." [2]

And you are invited to join this writer, Howard Ray White, within the pages of this book -- invited to set aside existing prejudices and historical knowledge, toss a bit of magic dust before your eyes, and engage with him in a happy novel -- a story of the Confederate States surviving as an independent country; a story of African Americans transitioning from living as slaves to living as free, productive, prosperous and moral people; a country expanding many-fold in land area and population; a people encouraging talented immigrants and thereby experiencing unprecedented inventiveness and industrial expansion; a land belonging to a great and diverse people who are recognized world-wide as being fortunate to be living in the "Greatest Country on Earth."

If your interest is primarily of a military nature, hoping to herein read about many battles over many years, "*The CSA Trilogy*" may disappoint, because in this alternate history you read that success in defending State Secession was greatly enabled by declining to fire on Fort Sumter; engaging in passive resistance and deception; dispensing propaganda among people of the North, and using the months thereby gained to modernize and expand weaponry to be better prepared to successfully defend against the anticipated military invasion. Only through such political efforts, the writer believes, could success have been achieved by the Secessionists. Again, why not toss a bit of magic dust before your eyes and engage with him in a happy historical novel?

Today, many writers tell stories called fantasies. This is not one of these, but as a reader, you might choose to think so. This is a good-feelings story of a fictional country, viewed as of 2011, celebrating its sesquicentennial and its great and successful population diversity -- a might-have-been country celebrating how it had remained successful without giving up "Individual Liberties" and the people's right to govern themselves at the state level. Yes, those two guiding principles have remained and continued to work for 150 years -- for the benefit of all Confederates. How was this accomplished in today's complex, modern world? You have to read further to find out. If you are more comfortable thinking of this story as a fantasy, you need not apologize.

Near the beginning of this Foreword, you were told that this book is, to a significant degree, a novel. Although most of this *Trilogy* reads like an alternate history, parts read like a novel. Enjoy the experiences and interpersonal relationships developed during these four weeks at the University of the South, Sewanee, Tennessee. And enjoy the story of three weekend trips away from Sewanee: the adventure of six engaged in an overnight sailing adventure off the coast of Cuba; the adventure of two exploring an historic cave west of Sewanee, and the adventure of five enjoying a weekend overnight backpacking trip on the remote Fiery Gizzard trail east of Sewanee.

A list of the thirteen characters follows:

- Joseph Evan Davis IV, 64, professor of history, University of the South, Sewanee, Tennessee.
- Isaiah Benjamin Montgomery, 27, corporate farmer, of Mississippi.

---

[2] This account of relations between Southern whites and free people of color is the result of studies by Barbara G. Marthal of Tennessee, the author of the book, *Fighting for Freedom, A Documented Story*.

- Marie Saint Martin, 23, beginning her career in business, of Louisiana.
- Emma Cathrine Lunalilo, 22, working toward her Ph. D., of Hawaii.
- Carlos Jose Cespedes, 24, cane sugar farmer, of Cuba.
- Chris Withers Memminger, 22, veterinary medicine student, of South Carolina.
- Benedict Christian Juárez, 27, Ph. D. in Philosophy, teaching professor, Costa Este (of former Mexico).
- Allen Bruce Ross, 26, bison rancher, Sequoyah (in truthful history the US State of Oklahoma).
- Conchita Marie Rezanov, 23, working on her Ph. D. in political science, Russian America (in truthful history, Alaska).
- Robert Edward Lee, IV, 23, BA degree in political science, of Alabama.
- Andrew Houston, 23, BS petroleum engineering, of South Texas.
- Tina Kathleen Sharp, 26, nuclear engineer, of North Texas.
- Amanda Lynn Washington, 25, working on her Ph. D. in Education, Virginia.

You will read about the ancestry of these 13 people and discover that they are descended from men who played major roles in the success of the Confederate States, including Cuba, northern Mexico, Russian America and Hawaii. You will enjoy the past family connections of these thirteen and appreciate how those relationships enabled them to tell the story of our Confederate States from the perspective of especially meaningful family experiences.

In the final chapter of Part 3 of this trilogy, you will arrive at a dramatic conclusion, the celebration of the sesquicentennial, July 4, 2011. Here you will read the twelve essays presented before a world-wide television audience by the twelve young Sewanee Project team members, each, from a different perspective answering the question, "Why are the Confederate States the Greatest Country on Earth?"

We conclude the Foreword here. To learn more, one must read on.

The narrative presented within *The CSA Trilogy* is in the voice of Joseph Davis, 64, professor of history at the University of the South – a truthful and lovely college setting from which our story is told. We now go to Sewanee, Tennessee to hear our fictional character, Professor Davis, begin what is called the "Sewanee Project." He will explain. Hope you enjoy this alternative history presented with a novel overlay.

# Table of Contents

# THE CSA TRILOGY, PART 3, HOW CONFEDERATES RETAINED THEIR CHERISHED PRINCIPLE OF STATE SOVEREIGNTY AND RESPECT FOR POPULATION DIVERSITY WHILE DEVELOPING THE WORLD'S GREATEST ECONOMY, AN ALTERNATE HISTORY – 1878 TO 2011          277

## Part 1, Chapter 1, Day 1 – The Sewanee Project Introduction -- at the University of the South, Sewanee, Tennessee, CSA, Monday Morning, June 6, 2011

### A Quick Orientation for the Readers of this Book

Professor Davis: "This year, 2011, all across the Confederacy, citizens are celebrating the 150th aniversary of the founding of our country, The Confederate States of America. But first, perhaps I should introduce myself. My name is Joseph Evan Davis, IV, age 64, professor of history and political studies at the University of the South at Sewanee, Tennessee, CSA. You may have not heard of me, but I am confident that you have heard of my great-great-grandfather, Jefferson Davis, the first President of our country, so I need not say much about him as we begin. Instead, a few words about our University are now appropriate.

"We are renouned at the University of the South for our excellence in educating past and future leaders of our country, and in providing academic advice to governments both here and abroad, because the CSA is the recognized world leader:

- In political anaylsis and synthesis,
- In building successful governmental structures that are broadly beneficial to a diverse citizenship, and,
- In advising governments around the world concerning improvements that will help them sustain themselves and beneficially govern their diverse populations.

"Sewanee is located on the top of the southern Cumberland Plateau, and although remote by some measures of geography, we are only 150 miles east-north-east of our country's capital at Davis and 20 miles north of the Alabama State line. I presume you know that the capital of our country, Davis, is located on land donated by Tennessee, Mississippi and Alabama, at the junction of the boundaries of those three States, at the point where the Tenn-Tom waterway joins the Tennessee River, thereby providing water transport from the Gulf of Mexico into Alabama, Mississippi and Middle Tennessee. Davis, named for Jefferson Davis, is surprisingly small for the capital of such a huge country as ours, but here, unlike countries elsewhere, government reponsibilities are decentralized to such an extent that obligations at Davis, at the Confederate level, are far smaller than obligations at the State and local levels. And here, at the University of the South, we have historically advocated for government that is heavily decentralized and have witnessed rewarding results over the past 150 years. I suppose it was toward ensuring such a governmental structure that the Southern States seceded in late 1860 and early 1861, and as late as early 1862.

"Furthermore, it is here today, on June 6, 2011, that we begin the "Sewanee Project" in support of our sesquicentennial celebration and toward a better understanding of the question put to us, which I repeat here:

By analysis of our history and our culture, answer the question: "**Why are the Confederate States of America the greatest country on Earth?**"

"We anticipate that this inquiry will result in 12 essays, each authored by a visiting guest, who is noteworthy because of his or her descent from particularly influencial leaders in our history, and because he or she has been recognized for his or her exceptional power of analysis and keen judgment – in spite of the fact that all twelve are yet young and unmarried."

## Our Story Now Begins

So, dear readers, having finished the brief orientation via Professor' Davis's voice, we begin telling the story of the CSA. Just pretend you are there in the Confederate States of America in the year 2011 witnessing it all yourself. Here we go. . .

Professor Davis is addressing the twelve young men and women who have been selected to spend four weeks at studying assigned aspects of our history in preparation for delivering their relevant essay. We now listen in on that first meeting, an oreintation.

Professor Davis:

"It is so good to see all twelve of you assembled here this morning. Yes, it is today, Monday June 6, 2011, that we are beginning our work together, which, for no better name, I am calling "The Sewanee Project." Consider this Orientation Day. But, before we break up this morning for lunch, we will also engage in our first study, that being the history of the Nation-State of Sequoyah, located west of Arkansas and north of Texas. The program we begin this morning will last four weeks and one day. The last day, Monday, July 4, will be the main objective that all of us will be shooting for, that being presenting your essays, the twelve essays you will be writing and presenting as part of the televised Confederate Day Celebration event, which will be held here on the campus, be televised throughout the Confederate States and be seen by many around the world. Since you and your essays will be featured on the event schedule, take your work seriously and good luck to all.

"I will present nineteen lectures, one each morning, starting tomorrow and continuing on Mondays through Fridays until concluding on Wednesday, June 29. The schedule for these lectures follows:

1. Tuesday, June 7: Secession of Seven States.
2. Wednesday, June 8: The Confederacy's First 10 months.
3. Thursday, June 9: Confederates Decline to Fire on Fort Sumter, Choose Passive Resistancce.
4. Friday, June 10: U. S. Congress Chooses War – Four More States Secede.
5. Monday, June 13: Federal Invasion and Victorious Confederate Defense.
6. Tuesday, June 14: Montreal Treaty Negotiations.
7. Wednesday, June 15: Boundary Settlement.

   This concludes the first of three climaxes in our history. We continue.

8. Thursday, June 16: French Intervention and Mexican State Secession.
9. Friday, June 17: The Heroic Story of Russian America.
10. Monday, June 20: Hawaii – From Kingdom to Republic to Confederate State.
11. Tuesday, June 21: Cuba Wins Independence from Spain, becomes Confederate State.
12. Wednesday, June 22: The Great Confederate Expansion.

    This concludes the second of three climaxes in our history. We again continue.

13. Thursday, June 23: Early Confederate Industrialization Studies.
14. Friday, June 24: Confederate Population Studies.
15. Monday, June 27: Overview of Confederate History 1870 to 1890.
16. Tuesday, June 28: Overview of Confederate History 1891 to 1920.
17. Wednesday, June 29: Overview of Confederate History 1921 to 1938.
18. Thursday, June 30: Fascist Japan, Emerging China. Pearl Harbor, and the War Against Japan.
19. Friday, July 1: Overview of Underlying Confederate Principles.

20. Saturday and Sunday, July 2 and 3: Events leading up to the Sesquicentennial Day Celebration.
21. Monday, July 4: Televised Sesquicentennial Celebration Event and Presentation of Twelve Essays.

This concludes the third of three cliimaxes in our history.

"Before proceeding any further, let us get to know a bit about each other. I will begin with a brief story about myself."

## Professor Joseph Evan Davis, IV

At this point, with all twelve essayists before him in the lecture room, professor Joseph Evan Davis, IV, age 64, begins the round of introductions. As a reader of *The CSA Trilogy*, you will be involved with Professor Davis and the twelve young men and women throughout the three parts of this work, all the way to the final pages, where you get to read the twelve essays as presented to the worldwide television audience at the close of the celebration of the Confederacy's 150 years. So use this opportunity, dear reader, to begin to get to know theses characters, which represent the novel that overlays this alternate history of 150 years of the Confederate States. Joseph Davis is the senior professor of history and political studies at the University of the South at Sewnaee, Tennessee, CSA. He now begins to address the twelve:

"My great-great-grandfather, Jefferson Finis Davis, was born in Kentucky in 1808, attended West Point, and served in the United States army both in the upper Mississippi Valley and in the War Against Mexico. He and his brother Joseph raised cotton on large adjacent farms alongside the Mississippi River in the State of Mississippi in a region called 'Davis Bend.' He was elected United States Senator from Mississippi and lived in Washington several months of each year from 1847 to 1851 and from 1857 to 1861. Soon after returning home, he was asked to accept the position of Provisional President of the Confederate States of America, later confimed by the votes of the people. The rest of the story is too well known to repeat here.

"My great-great-grandmother, wife of Jefferson, was Varina Anne Howell Davis, born in 1828. She was of Natchez, Mississippi, a river town of notable Native American heritage, stretching back many centuries. My great-grandfather was Joseph "Joe" Evan Davis, born in 1859, son of Jefferson and Varina, named for Jefferson's brother, Joseph and his grandfather, Evan.[3] My grandfather was Joseph Evan Davis, Jr., who spent most of his life in the Confederate State of Virginia. My father was Joseph Evan Davis, III, who spent most of his life in South Texas, where I was born and raised.

"I received my bachelor's degree in history at Houston University and my doctorate in 1976, here at Sewanee, at the age of 29 years. I have been married to my lovely wife Judith for 40 years. She is a professional musician, playing first chair, French horn section, in the Nashville Symphony, and often backing up country music stars at recording sessions. That keeps her away from Sewanee some days and nights, but she does love her music and I am glad that she has a career she enjoys. We have four children, Varina, Billy, Evan and

---

[3] In truthful history little Joe Davis died in an accident on April 30, 1864, apparently falling from a balcony at the Confederate White House in Richmond, Virginia. The little boy fell thirty feet to a brick-paved walk below, dying within moments. The conquest of the Confederacy would occur only 12 months into the future, and prospects for defending the new country's independence were already dismal. It may not have been an accident. It may have been murder by a Federal spy. The truth was never firmly established. But the father continued with all his might to preserve the country he was charged with defending. Little Joe's death was a terrible blow. In her *Memoir*, Varina Davis would write, "On Joe [Jefferson Davis] set his hope. This child was the greatest joy of his life." In our alternate history, the Confederacy is not struggling for survival in April 1864 and little Joe Davis does not suffer this fall.

Mary Katheryn and are expecting our first grandchild soon. Oh yes, we stopped the Joseph naming convention at me, the fourth. There are no plans for the fifth.

"What are my interests? Although I am not accomplished I do play a banjo and sing. Several of us in my church get together regularly. I still play tennis, was rather good in my former years, but age has trimmed my game. Our family likes to hike the ridges and mountains, back packing and camping out occasionally. Sewanee, here atop the Cumberland Plateau, is a great jumping off point for hiking and backpacking. I have researched and written a few non-fiction books about history and political struggles.

"So that's a little story about me and my Davis ancestors."

## The Twelve Visiting Guests

"So, at this time, let me welcome each of you, our essayists. Perhaps each would like to take turns telling about yourself and your relevant ancestry, and the area of our history which each of you has been charged with analyzing and reporting upon.

"Isaiah perhaps you will lead off for the twelve visiting guests. Your essay will concern **Understanding Human Diversity**. Mr. Montgomery, please come forward and tell us about yourself."

## Isaiah Benjamin Montgomery

At this point Isaiah Montgomery came forward. Six foot one inch tall, 170 pounds, muscular, athletic, and of three-fourths African ancestry, Isaiah is both handsome and intelligent – a young man who people quickly learn to admire – a man who others look to for leadership. Isaiah began to introduce himself:

"I am 27 years old and presently reside in Mound Bayou, Mississippi, where I am a field supervisor for Section 8 of the Mound Bayou Corporate Plantation. Overall, MBCP farms 110,000 acres. Section 8 contains 3,400 acres. I received my BS degree in Agricultural Science at the Montgomery Agricultural Institute, named for my ancestors, located in Oxford, Mississippi. In Section 8 we grow cotton, field peas, various legumes, soybeans, alfalfa and sweet potatoes. Cotton covers about 35 percent of the land most years. My ancestry is three-forths African and one-forth European. Played quarterback on football teams in high school and college. Had a lot of fun, but I am rather small for the pros and, to be honest, I love the land and the farm life. I am not just an employee at MBCP. Like many with a long family tradition of working there, I am a significant stockholder. Continued success for our corporation will be more meaningful to me than the salary I make working there. I expect you all understand.

"My great-great-great-grandfather was Isaiah Thornton Montgomery, son of Benjamin (Ben) Thornton Montgomery, both slaves owned by Joseph Davis, the brother of President Jefferson Davis. Both Davis brothers owned large cotton plantations along the Mississippi River between Vicksburg and Natchez. The Montgomery family was remarkable, including the father, my ancestor Isaiah, and his brother Thornton. Although a little white blood does flow through my veins, my ancestor Isaiah's parents were born in America as were his parents and grandparents. Yet, by blood, they were of pure African ancestry. Ben, the patriarch of this family, was self-educated and exceptionally enterprising, even though a slave -- the result of his remarkable ability and steady encouragement from the Davis brothers. He set up a mercantile store, soon gaining enough money to buy emancipation for the family. The store grew into a major business, Montgomery and Sons. In 1887 Isaiah founded the community of Mound Bayou, which grew to 800 African American inhabitants and 30,000 acres of farmland, which, after years of hard work, was well protected from Mississippi River flooding by an amazing span of high dikes. [4] There, in upstate Mississippi, over the generations, Colored people built a huge farming cooperative that benefitted from the most advanced agriculture science. This is now a corporate farm that owns and manages 110,000 acres of upstate Mississippi farmland. The stockholders in the Mound Bayou corporation, this closely held enterprise, are all farmers, are all working the land, and are all former slaves."

Professor Davis:

"Thank you, Mr. Montgomery. Now, Miss Saint Martin, your essay will concern **ensuring State Rights and Individual Liberty.** Please come forward and introduce yourself."

## Marie Saint Martin

Several young women are among the twelve. Marie Saint Martin will be the first lady introduced to you as a reader of *The CSA Trilogy*. She may have a slight degree of African ancestry, but it is not very noticable. Attractive and tall at five foot eleven inches, tanned from days at the beach, her long black hair is easily spotted in the crowd. Her athletic build might be deceiving in that she is also both smart and an accomplished musician. In fact, as *The CSA Trilogy* unfolds, it will be Marie that organizes and leads the musical endeavors that several of the twelve discover they enjoy as the course of the four weeks of togetherness moves forward. Marie:

"I am 23 years old and mostly of South Louisiana French Creole ancestry, very close to 100 percent European blood. I tan really well and spend time at the beaches east of my home in New Orleans. Love to swim. Played volley ball and ran cross country in high school and do love tennis. But do not consider myself exceptionally athletic. Love to sing country music, New Orleans style. Five of us have a band in my home town: two guitars, a string base and drummer, and I sing lead. We do have a CD, which can be my gift to you all. Love the band, but doubt we will ever become popular enough to make it our career. Like they say in the music business, we will need to "find a day job to earn a living." Anyway, the passions mentioned above are secondary to my major career ambition. I want to be an entrepeneur, to start up and run my own business. I want to work for myself. That goal dovetails into my essay topic rather well. State Rights and Individual Liberty are the foundation that makes successful entrepreneurship achieveable. In the way of preparation, I have earned a degree in accounting and business administration at the Benjamin School of Business at New Orleans and am working various entry-level jobs to gain hands-on experience while I save every penny I can and consider business ideas as they materialize. My mom and dad send me ideas on occasion and I network with others of my persuasion. Glad to be here. Have an idea for a venture? I'm all ears.

"Jules Saint Martin, my great-great-great-grandfather, was Judah Benjamin's nephew who worked alongside him during his term as Attorney General in the Davis Administration and as the leader of the Confederate Secret Service during the successful Defense of Independence. My Study and subsequent essay will concern the **importance of ensuring State Rights and Individual Liberty**. You see, the Confederate Constitution ensures State Rights and Individual Liberty, because those limits on Confederate power are unassailable. Of course, there is much more to our story."

---

[4] In truthful history, Mound Bayou, Mississippi was founded as an independent black community in 1887 by former slaves led by Isaiah Montgomery and other slaves from Davis Bend. Its founders envisioned an all-black, self-sufficient farming community.

Professor Davis:

"Thank you Miss Saint Martin. Emma Cathrine Lunalilo will be presenting the third essay. It will concern **how State and local governments compete for citizen loyalty**. Miss Lunalilo, please come forward and introduce yourself."

## Emma Cathrine Lunalilo

Emma Cathrine Lunalilo is the Hawaiian member of the team of twelve essayists. At barely under six feet tall, her powerful 129-pound suntanned swimmer's physique reminds you of a confident life guard on a beach where the scarry big waves come crashing in. As a reader of *The CSA Trilogy*, you are getting to know a little about each of the twelve characters who will be along with you from the beginning to the end. Enjoy getting to know them. Although, exceptionally intelligent and capable in many ways, these twelve represent the diversity for which the Confederate States are known. Emma:

"I am 22 years old and call home the Big Island, Hawaii. Attended Hawaiian Cultural, a private school, through 12$^{th}$ grade. Received a BA in Political Science and Diversified Government at Qween Emma University in Honolulu and am presently at Guadalajara University in the State of Costa del Sur. I am there working toward my Ph. D. in Politics and Government Affairs. Friends sometime call me "Surfer Girl," because so much of my free time growing up in Hawaii was spent on the beach and out in the big surf. Of course I greatly miss having access to the surf in Guadalajara. Can get to the ocean only about once a month. My ancestry is about half and half, mixture of European and Hawaiian. I really do feel passionate about the importance of maintaining individual liberty in the modern world. So I purposely chose to diversify my living experiences by going to a former Mexican State to study for my doctorate. Friends sometimes complain that I talk too much and have trouble settling down to serious study. Let me know if you see me bouncing around too much. But if you want to really get my attention and my focus, just holler "Surf's up!

"My great-great-great-grandfather was William Charles Lunalilo, former King of Hawaii and grandnephew of Kamehameha I, the king who united the Islands in the early 1800s. As you know, with help from Russian Americans and Confederates, the the Hawaiian Islands – the group of mid-Pacific islands so important to the early days of marine shipping and whaling – we Hawaiians overcame take-over schemes by New England missionary families, traders and businessmen, to peacefully emerge as an independent democratic republic. Soon thereafter, the Republic of Hawaii accepted statehood in the Confederate States of America. We know it now as simply Hawaii. My Study and subsequent essay will concern the **importance of ensuring that each individual State compete for the loyalty of her citizens**, for citizenship is first to the State, second to the country. That is the Confederate way. We insist that local governments retain important control over all local matters that require government oversight."

Professor Davis:

"Thank you Miss Lunalilo. Carlos Jose Cespedes will be presenting the fourth essay, which concerns the principle that a citizen's **right to vote is defined by the State where he or she lives**. Mr. Cespedes, please come forward and introduce yourself."

## Carlos Jose Cespedes

Carlos Cespedes is the Cuban member of the team of twelve essayists. He is no athelete, but, at six feet one inch and 165 pounds, he will tell you he is "rugged enough." He is a good sailor of the Gulf of Mexico waters off the northern side of the island. Handles his family's ocean-capable sailboat well and has a bit of a windswept, suntanned complextion, even at this young age. Let us hear what he has to say:

"At 24 years old, I fall in the middle of the pack here today. My ancestry is European, mostly of Spanish origin. I don't play sports, but it seems everybody loves to hear me play Spanish and Classical music on my guitar. Sing along, too. I have CD's for sale, but each of you will receive one as a gift. I have been an ocean sailor since becoming a teenager. Hey! Good news! Dad has promised that he will send up our company airplane and take six of us down to Matanzas, Cuba for a twenty-four hour, overnight sailing trip. More on what should be a great week-end adventure later. My family home is there, in Central Cuba, on the north coast in the seaport city of Matanzas. We have been sugar producers for 167 years. How sweet it has been. No, not really; like all agricultural enterprises, owners and workers encounter ups and downs. World sugar prices historically fluctuate -- occasionally so wildly that large losses must be sustained and then overcome. But Confederate trade policy has been a leveling force over the years. Neither the Confederate Government nor the State of Cuba hands out price supports in needy years, but the Confederate Sugar Association does step in with occasional voluntary quotas to balance supply to demand, and the Confederate Government will retaliate against countries that suppress world sugar prices by subsidizing their inefficient growers. But I love farming and, although the sugar business is not always sweet, I love every year, both the good and the bad. Confederates love their cane sugar as well. Soft drinks and store-bought deserts that are sweetened with processed corn syrup, so common in the United States, are shunned in the Confederacy. I think we are healthier as a result. I sought a double major at Zulueta and Poey University in Havana, Cuba. One was Governmental Philosophy and Political Science. The other was Comparative North American History.

"Carlos Manuel Cespedes, my great-great-great-grandfather, was the leader of the successful Cuban Revolution of 1868 which led to independence from Spain, admission into the Confederacy as the State of Cuba and the first, step-by-step emancipation program for people of African descent who were held as slaves. My study and subsequent essay, concerns the **importance of ensuring that the right to vote, as defined in each State, results in governments that are sufficiently reflective of the voices of their citizens, who facilitate their existences.**"

Professor Davis:

"Thank your Mr. Cespedes. Now, our next essay will be by Chris Withers Memminger. It will concern **the importance of low tariffs and vigerous international trade**. Mr. Memminger, please come forward and introduce yourself and your subject."

### Chris Withers Memminger

Chris Memminger is a South Carolinian as were his Memminger ancestors. Growing up on a farm with fine thoroughbred race horses, he knows that life well. At five feet eleven inches and 143 pounds and looking every bit the part of a White South Carolinian, he is as confident and capable on a horse as his background would suggest. He now tells his brief story:

"Good morning, you all. I am 22 years old and call Aiken, South Carolina home. Going back four generations we Memminger's have been engaged in corporate farming and raising and racing prime thoroughbred horses. We are proud of our five championships at the Confederacy's premier annual race: the Old Hickory Stakes, run the second Saturday in May at the Hermitage Race Track near Nashville, Tennessee. I do love horses and the seasonal swings and struggles that farmers contend with year after year. I earned my B.S. in Agricultural Science at The Citadel in Charleston, South Carolina, and am presently working toward a degree in Veterinary Medicine at Davidson University in Nashville, Tennessee. Love being close to those Middle Tennessee thoroughbreds. Amazing horses.

"About my essay. Confederate farmers understand the importance of vibrant and balanced international trade. Much of the passion in the late 1850s and early 1860s for State Secession came from a determination to enjoy low-tariff, balanced export-import trade. I look forward to addressing the importance of vigorous international trade.

"Christopher Gustavus Memminger of South Carolina, my great-great-great-grandfather, was Secretary of the Treasury during the Davis Administration. My study and subsequent essay will concern the **importance of ensuring that international trade and our tariff structure contribute to a vibrant economy**. We believe that the United States, just to our north, suffers from heavy reliance on high tarrifs on imports. Here in the Confederate States, tariffs are low to zero, and international trade is fair to both importers and to exporters, and also vibrant and profitable."

Professor Davis:

"Thank you Mr. Memminger. The sixth essay in the Project is the responsibility of Benedict Christian Juárez who has accepted the essay assignment converning **what makes a wise immigration policy**. Mr. Juárez, please come forward and tell us about yourself, your illustrious ancestor and the subject of your forthcoming essay."

### Benedict Christian Juárez

From Costa Este, one of the Seceded Mexican States, Benedict Juárez complements the team of twelve by virture of his mostly Native American ancestry. He is the shortest of the men, at five feet eight inches, but his broad, muscular body proves he is no pushover. On the other hand, his mild mannered, easygoing temperment suggests everything will be just fine. Benedict:

"I am 27 years old, and my ancestry is seven-eights Native American and one-eighth European. My home is at Monterrey, a large manufacturing city in the State of Costa Este. Our motto is, "If it can be made, we can make it best." Jobs are abundant for folks of all walks of life, but I am particularly proud of the great job opportunities for people of largely Native ancestry. Opportunities are there for Native Americans from entry level positions to upper levels of management. I completed my B.A. degree in World History and then my Ph. D. degree in Philosophy at Juárez University in Ciudad Juárez, in the State of Central Norte. My thesis, completed two years ago, was titled, "Quantifying the Distribution of Human Talents, Strengths and Weaknesses within Races and Ethnic Groups." I have just begun teaching in the Philosophy Department at Freedom University in Queretaro in the State of Central del Sur. My family has been active in government service and education ever since Mexican State Secession. So, I have just followed in their footsteps, I suppose. What are my other activities? I like to make things, and should have been an engineer, but my family ghosts must have pulled me toward the career I have undertaken. On the side, I do construction work for myself and other family members. Have just about completed a small house that is becoming my bachelor pad, I suppose. I am always looking for ways to be more effiient at whatever I undertake. Seems like that is the Monterrey way. What did I say? "If it can be made, we can make it best."

"Benito Juárez of Mexico, my great-great-great-grandfather, was the recognized leader of the northern Mexican States in their 1865 War of Mexican State Secession. During the fight against dictatorial rule from Mexico City, many northern Mexican states, then reduced to mere departments within the autocratic Mexican government, rose up and proclaimed State Secession. With Confederate help and the resolve and determination of northern Mexico secessionists, independence from dominantion by Mexico City was secured. This resulted in the admission of six Mexican States into the Confederate States of America. My study and subsequent essay will concern **Confederate immigration policy.**"

Professorn Davis:

"Thank you Mr. Juárez. Our next essay will be by Allen Bruce Ross. His will be explaining **what makes the Confederate electorate exceptional**. Mr. Ross, please come forward and tell us about yourself and your subject."

## Allen Bruce Ross

Allen Bruce Ross adds knowledge of, and ancestry from, the Cherokee Nation to the twelve essayists. He is not a cowboy, for his herds are bison, not cattle. The Confederate State of Sequoyah, the location of his family ranch, is just north of the four Texas states. Allen introduces himself:

"I am 26 years old, and a little over one-fourth Cherokee in ancestry. My Ross family have been ranchers in Sequoyah for three generations. Ross Brothers Buffalo Ranch consists of 4,500 acres of Native-leased prairie grassland in upper Sequoyah upon which 1,900 head of bison are raised for market. Our animals are 100 percent grass-fed and the meat is among the top choice and healthiest anywhere in the world. As a teenager I worked the fences and looked over the herds in summer and winter, including that heavy snow we suffered in 1999. I love ranching, but I have three brothers and two sisters and it does not need all of us. So I have struck out on a career in Native American Law. I completed by B.A. in government studies, history and creative writing at The Cherokee Nation University in Cherokee City, Sequoyah. I then received my law degree using interdisciplinary exchange, attending Cherokee National for two years and here at Sewanee for the other two years. The interdisciplinary exchange program is popular with Native Americans seeking to become lawyers because our challenge is to be competent in law in typical Confederate states, such as Georgia or Texas, as well as competent in the Native American law issues within the State of Sequoyah. Interdisciplinary exchange is also popular for aspiring lawyers in Russian America and Hawaii. I passed the Sequoyah bar last year and am just starting to practice law. I am 6 feet tall and as rugged as one would expect for a man of my background. Folks don't call us "cowboys." We are known as "bisonboys." Bisonboys are tougher than cowboys because it takes a tougher man to manage a herd of bison and keep the fences in repair. I participated in rodeo contests in earlier years, but, after sustaining a bad fall, I have reasoned, "been there; done that." So I just play a guitar and sing country music ballads. I am looking forward to my essay, "**Because the Two Political Parties Compete by Appealing to an Informed Electorate**." I come from a strong, self-reliant and freedom-loving family. I am grounded in a firm faith and rock-solid code of morality. I have benefited from great teachers and mentors. I abhor biased education of our youth and efforts to mislead voters through political demagoguery. So do not be surprised if my essay is focused on those themes. By the way, Ross Brothers buffalo will be featured for dinner this coming Sunday. You will love it!

"My ancestors and I have lived in the Nation-State of Sequoyah going back over 160 years, and before that, for many generations, near or not far from the Great Smoky Mountains. My great-great-great-great-grandfather was Principle Chief of the Cherokee Nation, Koo-wi-s-gu-wi, known often by his English name, John Ross. He was the leader of the Cherokee Nation from 1828 until his death in 1868. His wife, Quatie, was my great-great-great-grandmother. John's father was Scottish and his mother was three-fourths Scottish, so John Ross was only one-eighth Cherokee, but he was a great leader of the

Cherokee people during very difficult times. I am a bit more than one-quarter Cherokee myself, being descended down through the male Ross line (William Allen Ross to Robert Bruce Ross, and so forth). My study and subsequent essay will concern the political parties over the 150-year history of the Confederacy and the extent to which citizens have demanded and secured for themselves **an electorate that is excceptional.**"

Professor Davis:

"Thank you Mr. Ross. Our next essay is being undertaken by Conchita Marie Rezanov. Her subject answers the question: **Is Davis no bigger than it ought to be?** Please come forward Miss Rezanov and tell us about yourself and the question your essay will answer."

### Conchita Marie Rezanov

You now know a bit about seven of the twelve essayists. All are young men and women. So far, none are married or in serious romatic relationships. This will be the situation for the remaining five, suggesting that a budding romance may just flower during the upcoming four weeks in beautiful Sewanee. Of the five remaining, one of the most interesting is Conchita Marie Rezanov of the Confederate State of Russian America. [5] Tall at six feet two inches, athletic, a blue-eyed blond and lovely to look at, Conchita is both smart and extremely difficult to beat on the tennis court. Conchita is beginning to speak:

"I am 23 years old and presently residing in San Diego, South California. B.A., History, Baranov University, Sitka, Russian America. Presently in second year of a Ph. D. program at Argüello University in San Diego. Captain of the Argüello tennis team. Some of you may know that I am among the top 50 Confederate amateur female tennis players. Born in Sitka. At age 13 moved with family to San Diego, South California where Dad became a professor with the designation of Professor of Political Philosophy, the Baranov Chair. My Ph.D. thesis will concern a comparative study of human consequences of limited federal government power, as enjoyed by Confederate citizens, versus the centralized government power experienced by other nations of similar human, financial, and natural resources. What am I passionate about? Resisting the world-wide movement toward very powerful centalized governments. Hey, it seems like we Confederates are the world's last great hope. Tennis, anyone?

"My great-great-great-grandfather was Nikolai Rezanov, an important leader in the settlement of Russian America as was his wife Concepción, their son Jose Rezanov, and their grandson, also named Nikolai. The Aleksandr Baranov and the Rezanov families were the most important leaders in Russian America over the generations, and key in arranging for Mother Russia to expand settlement of the region and then to grant independence in exchange for payment in gold, a payment that the Confederate States advanced on our behalf. You see, these Russian American leaders knew where the gold was and the Emperor of Russia did not. We know this vast region as the State of Russian America, the largest of all Confederate states in land area. My study and subsequent essay will concern the limited growth of the Confederate Government at our capital city of Davis, and the question: **'Is Davis no bigger than it ought to be'?**"

Professor Davis:

"Thank you Miss Rezanov. Our ninth essay is the task of Robert Edward Lee, IV. Mr. Lee's essay will concern **how Councils of Confederate Governors ensure**

---

[5] In truthful history the Confederate State of Russian America is known as Alaska.

**cooperation among neighboring States**.  Mr. Lee, please come forward and tell us about yourself, your  famous ancestor, and about your important subject."

## Robert Edward Lee, IV

Robert Edward Lee, IV is of the Virginia Lee family that is well known to Confederates for his leadership in the defeating the Federal invasion of his State.  Of the five commanders that led the defense against the Federal's simultaneous invasion launched on May 1, 1862, General Lee is considered by military historians to have been the most capable.  The fourth Robert calls himself a regular sized fellow: six feet tall, 150 pounds.  Let us listen in:

"I am 23 years old and recently began working at the Department of Interstate Affairs in the Confederate Government at Davis, in the Confederate District.  Going back four or five generations, my Lee family hails from Virginia, North Carolina, Tennessee and Alabama.  My home is in Montgomery, Alabama, where my family has been in the insurance business for over 100 years.  But insurance is not for me.  I love studying people, especially leaders in government, commerce and industry.  I constantly am asking myself:

- In government, what makes a statesman?
- In commerce, what is the source of long-term success?
- And in industry, how do winnners emerge from the competitive struggle?

"I want to become a writer, but not a college professor.  Just want to focus on the study of an issue that moves me and then write effectively to move my readers.  Just want to be a positive force for the good of our country.  As you know, it is not easy to navigate a hierachy of government from the bottom up -- from local to state, to Confederate -- in a manner where interstate conficts can be resolved and progress can be sustained.  In other nations, government is far more centralized and politicians at the top level decree what lower level governments will be doing, and how individuals are expected to comply.  It is far different here, and, in reality, far more difficult to manage for the good of the people.  So I have prepared myself for this career by gaining a B.A. degree in Political Science at Jefferson Davis University in Jackson, Mississippi, and a Masters at the Calhoun School of Government Studies in Athens, Georgia.  I chose both schools because of their historical depth.  But, I consider my education just beginning.  I love to read and observe and analyse events and people, their actions and reactions.  What makes them tick.

"But I do love the outdoors.  I love taking my horse on mountain pack trips and camping out wherever it suits me.  Do love the Great Smoky Mountains and the rugged landscapes in West Texas and Costa Sudoeste.  Back at my family's home, my collection of mounted hunting trophies is modest, but growing.  I am a caver, too.  I enjoy exploring caves in northern Alabama and the Cumberland Plateau here in Tennessee.  By the way, there are some big caves near here that some of us might like to explore.  It's a thought.

"Robert Edward Lee of Virginia, my great-great-great-grandfather commanded the Confederate army that defeated the Federal invasion force attempting to conquer Richmond, Virginia.  I am descended from his son, Robert, Jr., and so on down the line.

"My study and subsequent essay will concern the **importance of State Cooperative Commissions as effective governmental organizations,** created to ensure that each State retains its constitutional rights, while, as technology and populations expand, to ensure that effective coordination is maintained among the necessary State and Local government regulations and programs, thereby keeping such coordination out of the hands of the Confederate Government at Davis and within the authority of the various States, jointly acting through coordinating bodies."

Professor Davis:

"Thank you Mr. Lee. Mr. Andrew Houston has agreed to address the next essay, which concerns **the excellence in our Confederate Transportation Network**."

## Andrew Houston

We now move west to Austin, South Texas, and learn about Andrew Houston, a descendant of the most important leader in the struggle by Texans to win independence from Mexico and in the subsequent ten-year era of the Republic of Texas, an independent nation. Like the sterotypical Texan, Andrew is tall at six feet, six inches, and muscular. With his height and red hair Andrew is easy to spot in a crowd, and resembles a rugged outdoorsman, which he enjoys being when time permits. He now describes himself to the other eleven:

"Hello folks, here I am in a nutshell. Twenty-three years old and presently residing in Austin, South Texas. [6] Have a B.S. in Petroleum Engineering from Hughes-Sharp School of Science and Engineering, Houston, South Texas. Graduated two years ago. Presently on leave of absence from Texas Oil Company while working on my Masters of Business Administration at The University of Austin, South Texas. I love to hunt, hike, kayak, crew on ocean sailboat adventures. Played on the Hughes-Sharp tennis team. An avid student of Confederate history, have published a study guide for high school students titled, *Making Confederate History Easy to Comprehend – A Concise Study Guide*. Rather unusual for a 23 year old engineer to put time into publishing a history study guide. But I began work on it at age 17 and over the course of 5 years polished it off. With the internet, e-books and print-on-demand publishing, I found getting the final booklet out to students was not all that difficult. I sure learned a lot in the process. That old saying is true: 'you never really know a subject until you teach it to others.'

"Sam Houston, my great-great-great-great-grandfather, is best known for his leadership in Texas. He was commander over the Texas military force that captured Santa Anna and forced the Mexican Government to grant independence to the Mexican state of Tejas. Subsequently, he was twice President of the Republic of Texas. After merger into the United States he was, for ten years, a Senator in Washington City, after that the Governor of the State of Texas. Before arriving in Texas, Houston had spent three years as a teenager with Eastern Cherokees and had as a young man become a military and political leader in Tennessee, for a time being the state's governor. Late in life, following his service in Texas, he lived again with the Cherokee people where he helped facilitate the union of the Five Civilized Tribes and their acceptance as the Nation-State of Sequoyah. His wife, my great-great-great-great-grandmother, was Tiana Rogers Houston, of the Cherokee Nation. I am descended from their son Andrew. [7] My Study and subsequent essay will concern the **importance of excellence in our country's transportation network**."

Professor Davis:

"Thank your Mr. Houston. Miss Tina Kathleen Sharp will be researching, writing and presenting our eleventh essay. It concerns the **importance of excellence in our country's energy production and distribution**. Miss Sharp, please come forward and introduce yourself and your subject."

---

[6] You are coming to realize that the Texas of truthful history is divided into four States in our alternate history.

[7]-In truthful history Tiana Rogers was Sam Houston's wife for a few years while he lived with Cherokee in what is now Oklahoma, but there is no record of a child named Andrew. Andrew is a fictional character in our alternate history.

## Tina Kathleen Sharp

Two young women complete the group of twelve essayists. Next to last is Tina Kathleen Sharp, also from one of the Texas states and also pursuing an energy-related field. To that extent, she and Andrew Houston have complementary careers. He is in pertoleum; she is in nuclear power. A real smart lady, for sure, and her ancestor was very important to launching the original Texas oil boom. Let us listen in:

"I am 26 years old and working as a nuclear power engineer at the Comanche Peak Nuclear Station, north of Fort Worth in the State of North Texas. Because Comanche Peak was built over 35 years ago, I am helping with design and planning to upgrade the plant for reliable performance over the next 25 years. Five years from now I will probably be working on the design of a new nuclear station in the State of Russian America. I am proud that we Confederates have never suffered a nuclear power plant failure such as Three Mile Island in the United States, the Soviet's Chernobyl reactors, and Japan's Fukushima Daiichi Nuclear Station. No other country in the world generates more electricity with nuclear power than ours. I grew up in West Texas, and earned my B.S. degree in nuclear engineering at the Confederate Science and Engineering Institute in Atlanta, Georgia. I went on to earn a Master's degree there. So, now I am working in my field and happy to be here in Sewanee this summer. Other interests? It has to be history. I am a nut about Confederate history. Would have majored in that, but felt I could contribute more to our country in the field I chose. Music. I play the French horn rather well. West Texas State Youth Orchestra, Atlanta Civic Orchestra and the Comanche Peak Brass Quintet. Love to cook great meals from scratch. Learned a lot from Mom and Dad as well as my high school Home Economics teacher.

"Walter Benona Sharp, my great-great-grandfather, of Tennessee and Texas, was a leading Texas oil man and inventor of the Sharps-Hughes hardrock drill bit. His pioneering work made possible the Texas oil boom, which began with the Spindletop gusher in 1901 and helped make the Hughes Tool Company a leader in oil field drilling equipment. [8] His son, my Great Grandfather Dudley, was Sectretary of the Confederate Air Force from 1956 to 1960. My study and subsequent essay will concern the **importance of excellence in our country's energy production and distribution**. In the Confederacy our electricity generation is 60 percent nuclear. No nation produces and distributes electricity as cheaply as we do. Furthermore, our oil and gas reserves mean our petroleum and petrochemical industries are by far the most efficient on earth. The price of our gasoline? People who are not Confederates appear to be, how should I say, jealous?"

Professor Davis:

"Thank your Miss Sharp. Our final essay is the task of Amanda Lynn Washington. Her subject will concern the **importance of excellence in our country's schools, colleges and universities**. Miss Washington, please come forward and tell us your story."

## Amanda Lynn Washington

Amanda Washington completes the team of twelve essayists, and is probably destined to become the team's most important contributor. Her appearance clearly shows her ancestry is about 50-50, from Africa and from Europe. Athletic, five feet eleven inches and 135 pounds, she looks the part of a former high school basketball guard. She wraps up the intoductions:

---

[8] The history of the Sharps-Hughes hardrock drill bit and its importance is truthful history. The story of Walter Benona Sharp is truthful.

"I am 25 and presently residing in Lynchburg, Virginia and expect to complete my Ph.D. in Public Education late next year. I earned a joint B.A./B.S. degree in Education at Jefferson Davis University in Jackson, Mississippi three years ago. After one year of classroom teaching experience I came to Lynchburg to Washington University to earn my Ph. D. My thesis is titled, 'Achieving Excellence in Educating a Diverse Population.' My ancestry is close to 50 percent African, 40 percent European and 10 percent Native American. I have participated in athletics in several ways in public school and college. I love to run. Played a rather good game of basketball, mostly as point guard. I love to sing and have a great deal of experience in chorus and piano. Gospel music is a favorite. Love jazz. Want to race me in the 100 yard dash?

"Booker T. Washington of Virginia and Alabama, my great-great-grandfather was a leading educator of students of full or partial African ancestry, notably at the Tuskegee Institute, which he founded. My father, Dr. Larry Washington, a physician, is the son of Booker T. Washington, III. My great-great-grandfather's pragmatic approach to teaching studens of color and his advocacy for similar educational programs all across the Confederacy had much to do with the successful training of our people to succeed in technical work in many fields, ranging from agriculture, to manufacturing, to transportation, to construction, to medicine, and so forth. And, as we all know, the pragmatic training of which he pioneered has been a major contribution to the excellence our Confederacy has enjoyed in intelligent and capable craftmanship across diverse fields of endeavor.

"My study and subsequent essay will concern the **importance of excellence in our country's schools, colleges and universities**, to ensure that a non-political educational culture is sustained and that the brightest students are encouraged to study and succeed in the important fields of business, technology, medicine, science and engineering -- fields key to the economic progress of everyone in our country. Our high schools are very good and we realize that a college education is not worthwhile for well over three-quarters of Confederate young men and women.

"Entrepreneurship is very strong in our country, and college does not help much with that. Unlike to our north in the United States, we see very few college graduates flipping hamburgers. There is a good reason for that."

Professor Davis:

"Thank you, Miss Washington. This completes the introductions."

### Our Plans for the Next Two Weeks

With the introductions complete, Professor Davis begins to tell the twelve essayists about the schedule for the next four weeks at the University of the South, all leading to their presentations of essays before the worldwide television audience on July 4, 2011. Professor Davis:

"Personally speaking, I could not be more pleased with the way the Sewanee Project is lifting off the ground this morning. You are here as individuals and also as part of a team that is designed to be greater than its indiviuals. By that I mean by personal interactions and discussion among yourselves, I anticipate much greater outcomes will resullt from interpersonal associations and comaradary within this team. You inspire me and I hope each other as well. Thanks go to each of you, our twelve Sewanee Project Essayists. Each of you is charged with the task of studying relevant facts and relevant history, analyzing what you find, and writing your essay, each answering from the chosen perspective the burning question that seems to so puzzle the world: 'What has made the CSA the greatest country on Earth.'

"Now about some ground rules for the next four weeks that we will be together.

"Saturday and Sunday are days for free time, but Monday through Friday you will be fully engaged in the project from the time you wake in the morning until you go to sleep. The following are the rules for those five days.

"Breakfast will be eaten together at 7:00 am each morning. We will be together at the big round 12-seat breakfast table in Davis Hall and you will note that rotating seat assignments will be in place to facilitate getting to know one another and to talk together about experiences and progress on writing individual essays. Eat a full breakfast because lunch will not be served until 1:15.

"Class will begin at 8:00 am and conclude at 1:00 pm."

"Lunch will began at the big round table at 1:15 pm and conclude at 2:00 pm. Seating will be reassigned each day. Get to know each other a bit more and use this time to hit upon some discussion inspired by the morning's class.

"From 2:00 pm to 4:00 pm you are expected to be in the library engaged in independent study to improve your understanding of the Confederacy and the essay subject which you have been assigned. Four library assistants have come in from summer break to be here for you over the next four weeks, so please use their talents to help with your individual research. The library at Sewanee is among the world's best and our staff there is eager and qualified to help.

"You will have two hours in late afternoon for free time and exercise, from 4:30 pm to 6:30 pm. I know you will enjoy that. I hear talk of tennis and other endeavors.

"You are to be at supper from 6:30 pm to 8:00 pm. Here the seating is different, for you will not be eating together at the big round table. You will find a nice spread of traditional Southern Cooking on that table. But you will not be seated there to eat. You will serve your plate, choosing from among the nice spread of offerings. Then you will move to your assigned private dining table to eat and to better get to know another person among the eleven, one-on-one. Every evening the pairings will be changed. No one looking over your shoulder, no one else talking, just the two of you alone to share whatever interests you. Of course, part of your conversation ought to be discussing the day's events. Using portable sound-deadening high-profile partitions, our campus maintenance men have set up 6 private dining tables near the big round table, so everything will be convenient and easy to maneuver. Every evening you will be assigned a two person table for supper, table one, two, three, four, five or six. Over the course of 11 days, you will have held a supper-time discussion with every other essayist. Then the table assignment scheme goes into repeat mode.

"After supper, there will be time for relaxing, and music, and further conversation. There are several musicians among us. Something might emerge from that interest.

"Before retiring for the night one more task remains. That is completing your private diary. On the table at the back of the room are 13 bound, 7-inch-by-10-inch diary books containing 150 pages of blank ruled paper. Every day I want you to make a diary entry before retiring. I will be starting my diary book, the thirteenth one, as well. I will begin each day's entry on a fresh page listing the day and the date, followed by "Joe to diary." From there the diary notes will flow. Now, I want you to make your diary entries at the close of the day, not the next morning or some later time. Why? Folks, your next four weeks will be greatly exciting and stimulating. But you need a good night's sleep more than ever before. Believe me when I tell you that recording notes about the day just closing and about possible plans and ideas for the day to come will help you relax and go to sleep. Those who do not do that will often toss and turn and mull over experiences and ideas for an hour or so, failing to slow down the brain and put it to sleep. I have this on high authority, so trust me on this.

"We shall make an exception in our schedule this afternoon. Instead of library time, please return here after lunch for a presentation on The Scquoyah Story. Allen Ross and Andrew Houston have agreed to help me with it, so I know it will be special for all of us."

The just-before-bedtime-diary-note assignment surely made sense to Professor Davis. He believed that putting notes on paper just before bed would prevent such issues from interferring with sleep. But there will be an additional benefit. As readers of *The CSA Trilogy*, you will have an opportunity to see a few selected diary notes at the close of each chapter (each day will be a chapter). Through this sampling of diary notes, you, as a reader, will get to better know the twelve essayists – their thoughts about the day's lecture – their thoughts about each other – plans for weekend adventures – musical interests -- occasional romatic notions – and so forth. For that reason you should enjoy reading a page of diary notes at the end of each chapter.

You may wonder why the twelve essayists selected for the Sewanee Project were descended from notable leaders in the early days of the Confederates States. "Why not include some young people whose ancestry is not notable?", you may ask. Well, as it turns out, Professor Davis and the administration of the University of the South had decided that it was not necessary to showcase young people whose ancestry was not noteworthy. All Confederates in the year 2011 knew that opportunity for success in their country was open to all. That fact did not need to be illustrated through the selection of the twelve. So, what was special about the twelve? They were specially positioned to tell about important leaders and accomplishments in Confederate history from the viewpoint of **family history** as well as public history – a very special addition – an addition that enhanced the popularity of the project.

Part 1, Chapter 2, Day 1 – The Sequoyah Story -- Monday Afternoon, June 6, 2011

Professor Davis continues: "Now, your are in for a special treat. Among you are descendants of perhaps the two most important men in the history of the Cherokee Nation and in the founding of the Nation-State of Sequoyah. I personally know of no more heroic and charitable event in the history of the Confederate States of America than the story of Sequoyah. Three of us will be presenting this history over the next two hours. I will present the core history, Allen Bruce Ross will present that part that relates directly to his ancestor Principle Chief John Ross, and Andrew Houston will present that part that relates directly to his ancestors Sam Houston and Tiana Rodgers Houston. I will now begin."

### How the Nation-State of Sequoyah Came to Be

As we all know, the Nation-State of Sequoyah is today's homeland for Confederates of Native American ancestry. How did that come about? How did Native Americans persevere through broken treaty, after broken treaty, after broken treaty to retain a part of North America as their national homeland? First we need to understand that those broken treaties had been made between Natives and earlier governments -- during colonial days with certain European nations (England, Great Britain, France, Spain and the Netherlands) – and afterward, with the United States government. Most of these had been broken prior to State Secession and, in truthful history, would be broken by the United States in subsequent years.

But in our own history, following the creation of the Confederate States of America, treaties between Natives and Confederates have always been honored. The Five Civilized Tribes, between 1817 and 1840, had been forced by treaty and/or the U. S. Army to relocate to the land west of Arkansas and North and east of Mexican Tejas. Those resettled had been promised that a large stretch of land west of Arkansas would be their national land forever, and there they would be free to operate a government of their own creation.[9] This land, promised to the Five Civilized Tribes, was a region of 64,273 square miles -- a vast area for the relatively small Native population to occupy. An example for comparison is helpful. The land granted to these five tribes was twenty-six times the size of little Delaware, which would be supporting a population of 112,216 people in 1860. Soon after Secession, the Confederate Government promised to honor the former commitment by the United States to support a Native American nation across those 64,273 square miles. Confederates promised to support a Native nation-state if the Five Civilized Tribes living there would support the cause of secession for the adjacent Southern States and fight, if necessary, to defend it against attack from Kansas, northern Missouri and elsewhere.

The Five Civilized Tribes of Southeastern North America consisted of the Cherokees, the Choctaws, the Chickasaws, the Creeks and the Seminoles. Living east of the Mississippi River and south of Virginia and Kentucky, they had been farmers who raised beans, squash and corn in field crops and acquired meat by fishing and hunting. Most advanced were the Cherokees. For a long time Whites had occasionally married native women and the children of those mothers were called mixed blood and were perceived as citizens of the relevant native Nation, be it Choctaw, Chickasaw, Cherokee, Creek or Seminole. Mixed blood citizens were most prevalent in the Cherokee Nation, and by 1861 a significant number of Cherokees were far more White than Native. The people of the Civilized Tribes were remarkably different from the Woodland Indians to the north and the Plains Indians to the north-west.

---

[9] This large stretch of land resembled what in truthful history is today called Oklahoma, but without the western "panhandle" appendage that was carved out of the Republic of Texas.

Before arrival of Europeans and the diseases they brought to the Americas, people in the Civilized Tribes had numbered in the millions and many lived in towns, some of them being very large towns on raised mounds. But by 1861, the Native population had been drastically reduced. So the land exchanged with them, lying west of Arkansas, was large enough to support their remnant population for many generations into the future.

Meanwhile, to the North, during the 1850s, across the Northern States, the Republican Party was new, was becoming powerful, and was promoting an attitude that the land being settled in the Plains, the Rocky Mountains and the Pacific Northwest was exclusively for White people of European ancestry. This extreme racial attitude, encouraged by Republican leaders, portended dangerous times for Native Americans living in those regions – a future without bison, being restricted onto so-called reservations, onto the worst, driest land available. Sadly, Confederates would refuse to accept Natives seeking to flee the North's wide-spread passion for ethnic cleansing with regard to Natives -- its negotiators would insist on prohibiting southward immigration of Native Americans from United States land, unless invited by leaders of the Five Civilized Tribes. Northern Natives would remain on assigned reservations.

In mid-1861, President Davis had appointed Albert Pike to negotiate alliances with the Five Civilized Tribes and with any other smaller native groups then living in Indian Territory. Assisting Pike was General Ben McCulloch, commander of Confederate troops in the region. Pike and McCulloch first won an alliance with the Creek Nation, the Chickasaw Nation and the Choctaw Nation at a gathering of chiefs and headmen at North Fork Village. Subsequently, the Seminole Nation agreed at its council house gathering. Pike even won support from small bands of Wichitas, Kiowas and Comanches who were then living in the western part of the territory. Finally, on October 1, 1861, at a great mass meeting of the Cherokee Nation, the decision was reached to also make an alliance:

> "All of the treaties which Pike signed with the Indians were very much alike. The Indians agreed to join the South, and the Confederacy agreed to take the position toward the Indians that the United States had held. It agreed to pay them their annuities, to guarantee to them their lands, to furnish them with arms, and to protect them against attack by the North. The Indians were to have delegates in the Confederate Congress, and they were encouraged to believe that eventually they might become a State within the Confederacy."

Essentially, Confederates promised the Five Civilized Tribes: if you support the Confederacy against anticipated aggression by the United States and the Lincoln Administration, we will support you. If we are successful, after the immediate danger passes, we will recognize a Native American nation that will encompass the land west of Arkansas, south of Kansas and north and east of Texas. Furthermore, we will negotiate an arrangement whereby this Native American nation can become a special nation-state with voting power in the political structure of the Confederate States of America. And we will support your right to control immigration into your nation-state.

Warriors of the Five Civilized Tribes fought bravely and heroically in Defense of the Confederacy, earning a place of deep gratitude in the hearts of fellow Confederates. And the Confederate Government did keep its promise: Indian Territory would become a Nation-State reserved for Native Americans and controlled, with regard to all internal matters, by Native Americans living under their rules of government.

The boundaries of what would become the State of Sequoyah are easy to define. The eastern boundary was the westward boundary of the State of Arkansas. The northern boundary was the southern boundary of Kansas, a State in the United States. The southern boundary was the Red River westward to where the headwaters fork and from there further westward along the northern branch. The southern and western boundaries were shared with Texas. Within what would become the State of Sequoyah, the initial Tribal boundaries were as follows (these were not rigidly observed, and would be less so as the years advanced):

> The Choctaws settled in the southeastern part; the Chickasaws settled west of the Choctaws; the Cherokee settled the northeastern part; the Creeks settled southwest of the Cherokee, and the Seminoles, a small population, settled in a modest region just beyond their Creek kinsmen. Land west of these allocations was not clearly allocated, but the inference was clear that all land to the west was for the use of the Five Civilized Tribes, and they would be empowered to control immigration into it and the governance of it "as long as the waters run." [10]

Sam Houston played a major role in bringing together leaders among Choctaw, Chickasaw, Cherokee, Creek and Seminole and winning their agreement to give up each Tribe's authority in exchange for collective sovereignty for the whole. By this agreement, the Choctaw-Chickasaw-Cherokee-Creek-Seminole Unification Treaty of July, 1864, Houston's supporters elevated the authority of the Union of the Five Civilized Tribes into a bulwark of unquestioned United Authority. This led to the Sequoyah Constitutional Convention of 1865, where the Sequoyah Nation-State Constitution was drafted and signed. It provided for a bicameral legislature, a House and a Senate, an Executive headed by a Governor (Joint Principle Chief) and a system of tribal courts, district courts and a supreme court. The Secretary of Native Immigration was a powerful position, for, by agreeing to allow Sequoyah to become a homeland for Natives further west in the Confederacy, the Five Civilized Tribes gained the good will essential to winning approval of its bid for admittance as a Nation-State under the Confederate States Government. Leaders of the Five Civilized Tribes started from a disadvantaged position, for Sequoyah was large in land mass but small in population. This is where Sam Houston was most influential.

Before the Confederate Congress, on April 5, 1866, Sam Houston, speaking as ambassador for the Choctaw-Chickasaw-Cherokee-Creek-Seminole Alliance, explained the great benefit to both Confederate Native Americans and Confederates of European ancestry who were settling near-vacant lands from west Texas to the Pacific.

> "Andrew Houston, please step forward and read the portion of you ancestor's address to Congress which gives us a flavor of what he said.

> "I have read this many times before and am always thrilled each time I do so."

The words of Sam Houston as read by Andrew:

> "My fellow Confederates, it is my belief -- and I encourage you to share it with me – that no matter from what lands a people's ancestry originated, our Lord understands that they have a right, even an obligation, to occupy underutilized land, to make it fruitful and to multiply upon it. This God-given right exists even though the existing occupiers have resided upon that land for many, many generations. That is a God-given right to mankind,

---

[10] In truthful history, most of the natives in the Five Civilized Tribes supported the Confederacy and suffered greatly during repeated Federal invasions of their lands during and after the War Between the States. In our alternate history, because peace was achieved in 1862, after only one great battle west of the Mississippi, the Five Civilized Tribes avoided the massive destruction and death among the population that was suffered in truthful history. This enabled the Five Civilized Tribes to move forward toward unifying under a nation-state government -- first under the protection of the Confederate States and eventually as a nation-state government with all the rights of statehood -- plus an additional right to control immigration and preserve Sequoyah for settlement by Native Americans from within the boundaries of the Confederacy, such as from the Upper Rio Grande and the Lower Colorado rivers.

the right to occupy underutilized land and build a flourishing God-fearing society upon it. Some have called this our 'Manifest Destiny.'

"But that right carries with it a serious obligation to deal fairly with those who had long been living on that underutilized land. Our Lord wants us to be gracious and helpful to those less fortunate than ourselves, and that, too, is our obligation. The Natives living in this hemisphere were living as stone-age people (did not possess metals technology except for gold and silver) when Europeans first arrived. We brought diseases and chaos that severely decimated the tribes of Native peoples; in some regions hardly a remnant remains living today. My friends, we cannot change the past, but we can change the future. We can give Native Americans a home in a nation-state of Sequoyah. Choctaw, Chickasaw, Cherokee, Creek and Seminole are already there. These we call the "Five Civilized Tribes." These we have come to know well, for they were farmers, hunters and fishermen living in what became North Carolina, South Carolina, Georgia, Florida, Tennessee, Alabama, Mississippi and eastern Louisiana, where so many of our ancestors settled. No Native peoples in North America are more advanced than the Choctaw, Chickasaw and Cherokee. Believe me. I know them well. These and the two others have united under the Choctaw-Chickasaw-Cherokee-Creek-Seminole Unification Treaty of July, 1864. They have named their region Sequoyah, to honor the Cherokee who invented the easily learned Cherokee system of writing. They have approved a Sequoyah Nation-State Constitution, establishing a government well suited to their needs, which promises to enable Native advancements not dreamed of just a few years ago.

"My friends, Natives deserve their Nation-State under the Confederate States Government. Our Lord beseeches us to grant it to them. Not just for their sake – also for everyone living in the Confederacy today and tomorrow. Under the tutelage of Sequoyah's leaders, other Native Americans will migrate to this new Nation-State and benefit from opportunities found there. From east of the Mississippi, most remaining Choctaw, Chickasaw, Cherokee, Creek and Seminole will come, as well as Lumbee from North Carolina. From western Louisiana, Houma will come. But most importantly, from west Texas to the Pacific will come Apache, Navaho, Pueblo and smaller groupings from the southwest, including Cheyenne, Comanche, Paiute, Pima, Shoshone, Tohono O'odham and Yaqui. But Natives presently living to the north, in the United States, shall remain there and this will be enforced. The government of Sequoyah will grant migration rights and oversee the process. We believe Natives are best at such oversight and guidance. I stand today embarrassed, so greatly embarrassed, over the suffering and lives lost in the Cherokee Nation during its forced westward migration known as the "Trail of Tears." That alone tells me that Choctaw, Chickasaw and Cherokee are bound to do a better job than can we. We only have to let them do it!"

### The Nation-State of Sequoyah

After thanking Andrew Houston, Professor Davis launched into the history of the Nation State of Sequoyah: [11]

"The Confederate Congress admitted the Nation-State of Sequoyah into the Confederate States of America on July 4, 1870. This decision was one of the most beneficial decisions Confederates have ever made. The 2010 Census has shown that 1,352,941 people of full or partial

---

[11] We are departing from truthful history with regard to Sam Houston – in our alternate history, Sam Houston and his family would play a major role in uniting the Five Civilized Tribes around a decision to denounce the United States and team up with the Confederacy, and later to help unify the tribal leaders to cooperate in creating a Nation-State government for Sequoyah.

Native ancestry live in Sequoyah. During 2010, a little over 100,000 people of no Native ancestry also lived in Sequoyah at some point, being permitted to be there because of work or visitation permits. Today, Sequoyah remains a Nation-State where only its government can grant the right of residence. And the Sequoyah constitution stipulates that only persons with at least 1/16 native ancestry are permitted to live there (children who fall below 1/16 must move out upon reaching adulthood).

"The story of the Sequoyah prairie grassland deserves inclusion. In the early years, the 1840's and 1850's, the population of the Five Civilized Tribes was too small and the business/ranching skills too marginal to successfully develop the economic potential of the vast prairie grassland in the western half of Indian Territory. This region promised to be sustainable prairie grassland when properly managed and not overgrazed. Leasing grazing land in the western region of the Indian Territory began with many leases from the Cherokee Nation to Texas Ranchers, who moved large herds of their longhorn cattle north into what was called the prairie grassland of the Cherokee Outlet, allowing them to gain weight, then moving them further north through western Kansas to railroad heads from which they were shipped to Chicago and points east. Lease revenue served to strengthen the Cherokee economy, and taught Cherokees valuable lessons about the longhorn cattle ranching business and the importance of moving cattle to top-dollar markets. By the 1850s, ambitious mixed-blood Cherokees were operating a few cattle ranches and hiring Texans to move Cherokee longhorns through Kansas to railheads. After the Montreal Treaty, Cherokees could no longer market longhorns to the north. So, they were soon moving cattle to river ports on the Mississippi and Red rivers. From there Cherokee cattle went by riverboat to New Orleans and Mobile, and by rail across Tennessee and on to North Carolina and Virginia, and by rail across Alabama, Georgia and South Carolina. Choctaws and Chickasaws were quick learners. Cattle ranching soon developed into a major industry for the Natives and part-bloods living in what would become the Nation-State of Sequoyah and beyond. And cattle ranching diversified into Bison ranching in the Native Game Lands. Native cattlemen became bison ranchers, managing the growing herds as those amazing animals thrived on the Native Game Lands. The key was herd population management and grassland conservation. When the historic drought would strike the Native Game Lands in the 1930s, laying waste to the plowed lands elsewhere in that part of North America, Native management of the virgin prairie grassland paid off. During those "dust bowl days," many bison were moved east to pasture in Arkansas and Louisiana and the population was thinned moderately. Recovery was excellent after the rains returned, and today Cherokee grass-fed bison is considered the finest red meat available anywhere in the world.

"Moving rapidly forward to present days, the story of the Nation-State of Sequoyah is a picture worth painting. Let us look at population, industry, education, nature of the people, political organization, tourism, racial mix and race relations, immigration rules, and influence in Confederate politics. [12]

---

[12] In truthful history, Native Americans have no nation-state and many live on reservations. Apache, Navaho, Pueblo and others in the southwestern United States live on reservations. After Federal forces defeated the Confederacy, many northern tribes were relocated to Indian Territory, which became Oklahoma Territory. Then Oklahoma Territory was opened to "Land Rush" settlement by people of European ancestry. The Federal Government made sure that, when Oklahoma was granted statehood, Native American residents would be forever a minority unable to protect themselves against the demands of the White majority. Whites plowed up the prairie to grow cotton, etc. The drought years arrived in the 1930's, the top soil blew away, and Oklahoma became a "Dust Bowl," a land of great sorrow. It recovered but slowly. The population in 2010 was 3,762,000 persons, of which 321,687 were of full or partial Native ancestry. In our alternate history, Native Americans are gathered together on the land as citizens of the Nation-State of Sequoyah, most of the prairie remained intact as grazing land, the population grew more slowly, and the Native residents controlled their destiny and prospered.

"At this point I am going to ask Allen Bruce Ross to step forward and tell us about four Cherokee families: Sequoyah, the Major Ridge family, the John Ross family, and the John Rogers family."

## Major Cherokee Leaders: Sequoyah and the Ross and Rogers Families

At this point, Allen Bruce Ross continued the history:

"The story of the State's namesake, Sequoyah, although familiar to most, needs telling again. A Cherokee, Sequoyah was born about 1770 to Wut-teh -- a full-blood Cherokee of the Red Paint Clan and related to Chief Old Tassel and Chief Doublehead. The baby's father was Nathaniel Gist, a half-blood Cherokee fathered by an Englishman or Scot by the name of Gist or Guess. So Sequoyah was three-fourths Cherokee. He spent his youth in the Cherokee village named Tuskegee. As an adult, he fathered four children with wife Sally Waters and three with wife Utiyu. Like many Cherokees who allied with Andrew Jackson's militia, he fought the "Red Sticks" in the Battle of Horseshoe Bend (the 'Red Sticks" were a faction of Creek warriors who were aligned with the British during the War of 1812). Later he became a silversmith and found that Whites were often his customers. Frequent contact with Whites and his business experience inspired him to tackle the task of teaching members of the Cherokee Nation to read and write. Finding the Cherokee language difficult to express through the 26-symbol alphabet of English-speaking neighbors, he resolved to create an alphabet of 86 characters, each of which represented a syllable in the Cherokee language. Stringing together these syllables created words and then sentences. Use of this alphabet enabled many Cherokee to communicate by written messages. In 1825 the Cherokee Nation officially adopted Sequoyah's writing system. The *Cherokee Phoenix*, the first regular newspaper for the Cherokee Nation, subsequently began publication using a special type face of 86 characters. Afterward Sequoyah travelled west to join the Western Cherokees in Arkansas; later further west into Indian Territory. There, he established a business as a blacksmith and periodically represented Cherokees in negotiation between his people and American authorities. Later in life, he visited other Native tribes west of Texas, learning their language and striving to adapt his alphabet to their tongue. He crossed into Mexico to engage with Cherokees who were experimenting with relocating there. Sometime in 1843, 1844 or 1845, he died when engaged in this last mission. Although a powerful concept of writing, the only language to successfully adapt his method was the Cherokee's. The story of Sequoyah and the Cherokee system of writing is important to our understanding of why and how the Cherokee rose to become the most capable leaders of all the Native Nations of North America.

"There are three prominent names in Cherokee history, each of which deserves mention. These names are "Ridge," "Ross," and "Rogers." We can call them the three "R's." We now turn to the first of the "R's," Major Ridge.

"Major Ridge (also known as Nunnehidihi) was born about 1771, near the Great Smokies in a Cherokee town along the Hiwassee River in what would become Tennessee. He was three-fourths Cherokee, his maternal grandfather being of Scottish ancestry. Ridge helped lead Cherokees in joining with General Andrew Jackson at the Battle of Horseshoe Bend. He grew rather prosperous, developing a sizable plantation of nearly 300 cleared acres, planted in tobacco and cotton and worked by 30 African-American slaves. Furthermore he operated a profitable ferry service and trading post.

"Along with several other Cherokee leaders, Major Ridge, without proper authorization, signed (made his mark) on the Treaty of New Echota, which allegedly bound all Cherokee to accept removal to new lands west of Arkansas. Principle Cherokee Chief

John Ross declared Ridge's treaty illegal and resisted Cherokee removal with all the force he could muster.

"We now turn to the second "R," John Ross. John Ross was the longest serving Principle Chief of the Cherokee Nation. Born in 1790 near the head of the Coosa River in northern Alabama, John Ross was the son of a one-fourth Cherokee mother, Mollie McDonald, and father Daniel Ross, of Scottish descent. Since all babies born to Cherokee mothers were deemed full members of the tribe, the baby's Cherokee ancestry was derived from his mother's mother, Anna, who had been born to Ghigooie, a full-blood Cherokee, and her husband, John McDonald, also of Scottish ancestry. Such marriages of Cherokee women to men of European ancestry were common in the Cherokee Nation and history would show that children born to these unions would become a great strength in the Cherokee people. This tradition would enable them to become the most advanced and most politically capable of all Native populations. John Ross grew up in the vicinity of what would become Chattanooga, Tennessee. As a young man, he was with Cherokees allied with Andrew Jackson at the Battle of Horseshoe Bend. He became a farmer, raising tobacco on 170 acres in Tennessee with the help of 20 African slaves. And he ran a ferry across the Tennessee River at Ross's Landing, which would become the city of Chattanooga. [13]

"Elected to the Cherokee National Council, Ross, being the most fluent in English, became a major leader in negotiations on behalf of the Cherokee Nation at discussions in Washington City that took place between 1818 and 1824. He was elected Principle Chief of the Cherokee Nation in 1828, which had organized under a constitutional National Government, complete with judicial, legislative and executive branches. At Washington City, Principle Chief Ross encouraged recognition of the Cherokee people as belonging to a distinct Nation, appealing to major United States government leaders and filing a claim in the U. S. Supreme Court (*Cherokee Nation v. Georgia*). Chief Justice John Marshall agreed that the Cherokee were of a sovereign nation, and that the State of Georgia could not impose laws upon Cherokee people, but President Andrew Jackson held the trump card. He persuaded Congress to pass the Indian Removal Act of May 1830, which ordered Cherokee, Chickasaw, Choctaw and Creek to relocate to Indian Territory west of Arkansas. Of the four, only the Cherokee refused to comply. Ross led the resisters, but as mentioned earlier, others, led by Major Ridge, chose to negotiate the best possible removal deal outside of Cherokee authority. Ignoring that the Ridge group had no authority to speak for the Cherokee Nation, the U. S. Government closed a deal with them at New Echota (a trick), creating a great feud within the Nation. Principle Chief John Ross had been circumvented. Sadly, signers of the so-called Treaty of New Echota would be charged with treason, condemned by a Cherokee court and sentenced to death. Ridge, his son and a nephew would be executed two years later.

"Ross did persuade U. S. General Winfield Scott to let him take charge of the final 1838 Cherokee removal to Indian Territory, but the extremely cold weather that winter and scarcity of provisions resulted in many deaths, including Ross's wife Quatle, who died of pneumonia near Little Rock. John Ross continued as Principle Chief for many years, and, on August 21, 1861 he advocated an alliance with the Confederate States of America.

"We now turn to the story of the third "R," John Rogers, Jr., who, for the years 1839 and 1840, was Principal Chief of the Cherokee Nation West, the name given to Cherokees who had migrated west long before the final "Removal" mentioned above. He was born in

---

[13] The Ross house can still be seen, as of 2011.

1876 near the Great Smokies to John Rogers, Sr., of European ancestry, and Alice Vann, of partial Cherokee ancestry. His full brother was James Rogers. His half-sister was Tiana Rogers, the daughter of John Rogers, Sr. and Jennie Due. The Rogers clan is important to Cherokee history. By the way, the great American entertainer, Will Rogers, is descended from this family. But it is now time to tell about Tiana Rodgers, John Roger's half-sister.

"Tiana Rogers would become the wife of (General, Governor, President, Senator) Sam Houston of Texas fame. The story of Houston's Cherokee wife, Tiana, is both epic and heroic, so let us spend a few pages on that. We start with Tiana, daughter of Captain John James Rogers and Jennie Due, born about 1800 within view of the majestic Smoky Mountains. The baby's father was one of the most prominent White men in the Cherokee Nation and her mother was the part Cherokee sister of two prominent Cherokee Chiefs: Chief Tah-lhon-tusky and Chief Oo-loo-te-ka, the latter taking the name John Jolly when dealing with Whites. Also the baby was related to Sequoyah, who would create the Cherokee alphabet. The baby had been named "Diana Rogers" but Cherokee's had trouble making the "D" sound, so they called her "Tiana." Captain Rogers and his family lived among Chief Oo-loo-te-ka's clan of about 300 Cherokees on Hiwassee Island, a large island in the Tennessee River where the Hiwassee River rushes in from the Great Smokies. Rogers had two wives and many children. Sons John Rogers, William Rogers, and Charles Rogers were destined to become prominent among Cherokees. Sons John Rogers and James Rogers were to become teenage friends of Sam Houston, now to be introduced."

Professor Davis:

"Allen, we thank you for those splendid family stories.

## Sam Houston and the Cherokee Nation

"Now, Andrew Houston, please come forward to tell us the rest. Tell us the relevant Houston family story." Andrew began:

"About 50 miles to the east of Hiwassee Island, where Cherokees and the Rogers family lived, was the pioneer town of Maryville, Tennessee. Near Maryville, with a splendid view of the Cherokee Nation's Great Smokies, was the new farm of Elizabeth Houston, a vigorous pioneer widow and mother of an energetic family of 6 sons and 3 daughters, all born in Virginia. The Houston's had recently relocated to Tennessee, arriving in 1807. The fifth son, born in 1793, was named Sam for his late father, Captain Samuel Houston, who had died just before the family's pioneering immigration of 1807. Having purchased a 400 acre tract of raw Tennessee land, and, with 6 males, age 11, 14 and older, and some money left from selling the family farm in Virginia, the Houston family seemed destined to become successful Tennesseans. But one of the males, 14-year-old Sam, was not inspired toward farm work. He loved to read and explore the woods. At age 16 he did rather rebel against his stern, hard-driving older brothers, and he ran away, with books in tow, to the Cherokee Nation, to live the playful life of Cherokee natives based at Hiwassee Island. He stayed a long time – three years except for a few short visits back home. He loved spending time on the island with the Roger's family, especially brothers John and James Rogers. He also noticed their little half-sister, Tiana Rogers, seven years younger than he. Chief Oo-le-te-ka's clan welcomed Sam Houston, for the growing teenager was a popular companion and a source of useful learning. Handsome, ruggedly built, tall at six-foot two and intelligent, Sam Houston impressed as a potential important future leader of the Cherokee people. Chief Oo-le-te-ka decided to adopt Sam Houston as his son and gave him the Cherokee name, "The Raven," obviously a name suggesting greatness to come. Of his three teenage years with the Cherokee, Sam would much later write:

" 'It was the molding period of life when the heart, just charmed into the feverish hopes and dreams of youth, looks wistfully around on all things for light and beauty – 'when every idea of gratification fires the blood and flashes on the fancy -- when the heart is vacant to every fresh form of delight, and has not rival engagements to draw it from the importunities of a new desire.' The poets of Europe, fancying such scenes, have borrowed their sweetest images from the wild idolatry of the Indian maiden. . . . There's nothing half so sweet to remember as this sojourn [I] made among the untutored children of the forest'.

"But would 19-year-old Sam Houston take charge of the family mercantile store in Maryville? Would he work the family farm alongside his brothers? Neither. He would join the army.

"We now fast-forward to January 22, 1829. Oo-le-te-ka's Cherokees are now living west of Arkansas on land given by treaty exchange to the Western branch of the Cherokee Nation, and Tiana Rogers, now 29 and widowed, is living there with her people. Meanwhile, Sam Houston is now Governor of Tennessee and getting ready to marry. His career had been illustrious. He had risen to the rank of colonel in the 39th regiment of the United States Army; then become a prominent Nashville lawyer and close associate of Tennessean Andrew Jackson, now President of the United States. He was also Major-General of the Tennessee militia and had served two terms in Congress. Yes, Sam Houston, now 35 and the Governor of Tennessee, is to be betrothed to Eliza Allen, 18, the daughter of Colonel John Allen, head of a prominent, wealthy and ambitious Middle Tennessee family. They were married, but in three short months, the marriage crumbled. Eliza returned to her parents. The problem is not well understood. Governor Houston loved young Eliza to be sure. But had the father pushed his young daughter into a marriage that she did not want in order to gain prestige and advantage for his family? Governor Sam Houston, a sensitive man who held honor at the loftiest heights, was emotionally crushed and felt unable to faithfully carry on his duties as Tennessee's Governor. He resigned. He headed west to the land of the Western Cherokee Nation, to Oo-loo-te-ka's people who had been his happy refuge during his latter teenage years. The Raven flew toward the sunset, flew to his other home, where he had known happiness.

"With an adventurous male companion, Sam Houston rode a steamboat up the Cumberland River and down the Ohio to Cairo, Illinois, where the pair employed a flatboatman to take them on a drifting course down the Mississippi River to the mouth of the Arkansas River. From there the party poled upstream to Little Rock. There Houston bought a horse and rode 140 miles further up the Arkansas River Valley to Fort Smith, then further to the westernmost Federal outpost, Cantonment Gibson. From there he boarded a small steam packet to Webber Falls, where navigation terminated. Word of the Raven's journey had already reached Chief Oo-loo-te-ka and a large Cherokee welcoming group was on hand to greet the emotionally devastated traveler:

" 'My son', said Oo-loo-te-ka, 'I have heard you were a great chief among your people . . . I have heard that a dark cloud has fallen on the White path you were walking . . . I am glad of it – it was done by the Great Spirit . . . We are in trouble and the Great Spirit has sent you to us to give us counsel. My wigwam is yours – my home is yours -- my people are yours – rest with us.'

"Of his June 1829 arrival, using the third person story-telling style, the Raven would many years later write: 'when he laid himself down to sleep that night, he felt like a weary wanderer returned at last to his father's house.'

"For three and one half years Sam Houston would live among the Western Cherokees, among Oo-loo-te-ka's people. He quickly found himself 'in a position of leadership over 7,000 Native Americans who controlled the country from Missouri to Texas and westward to the Great Plains.' During the first ten months, Houston kept busy helping Cherokee leaders make peace with the Osage, a plains-culture tribe which lived in the western region of what would be called Indian Territory; improving cooperation with the other four Civilized Tribes; dealing with Federal agents and military officers on behalf of the Cherokees and the Creeks; surviving a terrible case of malaria that almost killed him; traveling to Washington to personally appeal to President Andrew Jackson to honor the commitments Federals were attempting to make with the Five Civilized Tribes in exchange for their removal from east of the Mississippi to west of Arkansas; and, somewhat in secret, giving support to Chief Oo-loo-te-ka's dream of a Native American Nation within North America.

"In April 1830, 12 months following his resignation as Governor, Houston was back in Middle Tennessee seeking Eliza's final decision on reconciliation of their marriage. Bad news. Eliza and, or her family refused to consider reconciliation. What was Sam Houston to do? He had fulfilled his commitment to "honor." He had gone down onto his knees, professed his love and apologized profusely. He could do no more. The beautiful Tiana Rogers was waiting for him in the Cherokee Nation. He now felt free to do what he had wanted to do for the past ten months, since renewing his life with those Cherokees he had known and loved in his late teenage years. He would return to Oo-loo-te-ka's people and take Tiana as his wife. He had no divorce paper, but he and Tiana would be living together as man and wife anyway. That summer of 1830, The Raven, 37, took as his wife Tiana Rogers, 30. The bride was tall, slender, intelligent, beautiful, and no family contained more important Cherokee leaders than did the Rogers. Sam selected land near the Neosho River, 30 miles from Oo-loo-te-ka's lodge and a little above Cantonment Gibson. He built or bought a large log house, set out an apple orchard, lived in style and entertained his friends.

"But, after two and a half years with Tiana; after two and a half years dealing with Federal agents, persuading Federals and President Andrew Jackson to honor the commitments made in past treaties, Sam Houston was drawn to a new field of opportunity -- Mexican Texas! He felt he must cross the southern boundary of Indian Territory, enter Mexican Texas and search out the opportunities it afforded. He needed to understand the relations between recent Anglo immigrants recently arrived in Mexican Texas and officials at Mexico City, opportunities for Texas Independence, and how future events might affect relations with the adjacent Five Civilized Tribes in Indian Territory. He could not take Tiana with him on this adventure; she would be safer at their Cherokee home where she would be protected and provided for. But he could send for her when it made sense for her to join him. Sam Houston was heading for Texas. But he knew not that he was to become the most important political and military leader that huge land would ever know. [14]

---

[14] In truthful history Talahina (Tiana) would die of pneumonia in 1838. As she had waited for her husband's return, Sam, still needing official divorce papers from Tennessee, would be busy leading the Texas Independence fight and then serving his first term as President of the Republic of Texas. In truthful history, after finishing his first term as President, having learned of Talahina's untimely death, and after, about the same time, receiving divorce papers, Sam would marry Margaret Lea, 21, of Alabama on May 9, 1840 and bring his bride to Texas where the couple would eventually have seven children. In truthful history, Tiana would not give birth to a son fathered by Sam Houston.

"The story of the fight for Texas independence from Mexico, the Alamo, the capture of Mexican President Santa Anna, the creation of the Republic of Texas, and the election of Sam Houston as the Nation's president, is well known to most. However, there is insufficient time today to retell it. So I proceed to describe Sam Houston's return visit to Tiana and the Cherokee people."

"Sam Houston, no longer President, and with divorce papers from Tennessee finally in hand, is in Cherokee Territory by January 1839. While he is re-uniting with Tiana, she explains that he is the father of a son, Sam Houston III, who is 6 years old. Upon hearing this surprising news, Houston exclaimed, 'Why had you not sent word to me in Texas that you had given birth to our son? I never knew you were pregnant!' Tiana explained, 'I had not shown when you left. And I know you are a man of rigid honor, a man who, if he had known, would have returned, abandoning his calling to help the people of Texas. So I did not want you to know until after you were free to return to me.' Happily, Sam married Tiana Rogers, 39, in the Cherokee Nation on March 1, 1839.

"The Houston family returned to Texas in August, but not in time to prevent his successor, Texas President Mirabeau Buonaparte Lamar, from ordering Texas militia to drive Cherokee settlers out of Texas, in the process killing a great Cherokee chief, The Bowl, in the Battle of Neches. Houston was furious. And his open support for the right of Native Americans to live in Texas would cost him political support from this point forward. But, you see, few men in history have been more stubborn than was Sam Houston. He had told Texans that Tiana, a part-blood Cherokee, was his wife and Sam, Jr. was their son: 'You people of Texas, my friends, had better get used to it, for I will never abandon my family.'

"And in time Texans respected Sam Houston as a man of his word, a man who stood by honorable principles. They elected him to a second term as President of the Republic of Texas. Tiana stood by his side as Sam was inaugurated; Texans had grown to admire his beautiful and intelligent Cherokee wife. After Texas merged with the United States, Texans elected Houston to the Federal Senate to represent the new State of Texas from February 1846 to March 1859. From time to time, Tiana was in Washington City with her husband, but people of the Northern culture seemed far less congenial. Political sectionalism and racial exclusionism were passions too strong in the North. Also, from time to time, while Sam was in Washington, Tiana and their sons, Sam III and Andrew, spent time with their Cherokee relatives, thereby preparing them for positions of future leadership among the Cherokee people." [15]

"By the summer of 1859, as news of political sectionalism in the Northern States became ever more worrisome, Texans asked Sam Houston to leave the Senate and become their Governor. Sam had been Governor for 11 months when Abe Lincoln was elected President, 12 months before South Carolina seceded.

"We now proceed to March 16, 1861. Twelve days earlier, on March 4, the same day that President Abraham Lincoln was inaugurated, a Texas Constitutional Convention had declared the State of Texas an independent nation, seceded from the Federal Government of the United States. Union under the Confederate States of America followed and all Texas government officials were now compelled to swear allegiance to it. But, when the

---

[15] In truthful history Sam Houston did serve a second term as President of the Republic of Texas and did serve as a Senator for the State of Texas as reported above. But Tiana was not with him, of course.

Secretary of the Convention called for Governor Sam Houston to swear his allegiance, he did not come forth. He was at home writing his letter of resignation. Like a replay of the scene in Nashville, Tennessee, Governor Houston was again stepping down from the office of Governor, handing the office to Lieutenant-Governor Edward Clark. How could this be? Sam Houston was Texas! He had been, by far, the most important leader in the Texas struggle to secure independence from Mexico -- as Commander-in-Chief of the Armies of the Republic of Texas, he had brilliantly led his troops to a resounding victory over Mexican General and President Santa Anna in April 1836 at San Jacinto and there received the defeated Mexican leader's admission that Texas was an independent nation -- he had twice served as President of the Republic of Texas -- he had encouraged the union of the Republic of Texas and the United States, thus transforming vast Texas into a State with the promise that it could divide itself into as many as five States in the future -- for thirteen years he had represented the State of Texas in the United States Senate. On the other hand, having been elected Governor in August 1859, during the tumultuous sectional political turmoil of 1860, Houston had tried to calm enthusiasm for Texas Secession. [16]

"Sam knew what he planned to do, and Tiana understood it for sure. The family, Sam, 68, Tiana, 61, Samuel, III, 29, and Andrew, 20, would leave Texas for the Cherokee Nation in Indian Territory. Sam felt unable to help seceded Texas. But Sam knew without a doubt, that he, Tiana and their two sons would be useful in the land of the Five Civilized Tribes."

Professor Davis then stepped forward and said:

"Thank you Andrew.

"That about wraps up our story about the Nation-State of Sequoyah. There is so much to tell, but so little time allocated to it. There are many good books and biograhies and studies that you ought to read when time permits in the years ahead.

"Now, we are wrapping up Orientation Day for all of you. Enjoy supper together. Spend valuable time at the library at any time over the next four weeks and get to know the staff there. They have agreed to remain at their work through July 1 to be at your service. Regarding time there, I am handing each of you a suggested personalized reading list which is directed at studies for the essay to which each of you has been assigned. In addition to the essay-targeted list, at the library you will pick up your package of readings that all will find useful. They include the Confederate Constitution, double-spaced to allow ample edit notes; the first inaugural addresses of Presidents Davis and Lincoln; the Montreal Treaty; Secretary Benjamin's famous essay on the "Great Confederate Expansion"; The last annual report to Czar Alexsandr II by the Russian American Company and the Russian America Independence Acceptance Treaty; the Declaration of Independence for Seceded Mexican States and the Treaty of Saltillo; The Declaration of Independence of the Cuban People and the Spanish Accord signed at Havanah; the essay by Samuel Kipi, "How Hawaiian people became Confederates"; the Confederate Declaration of War against Japan, the Japanese Surrender Accord, and the Plan for Reconstructing Japan, its Government and its People," and, finally, *A Comprehensive History of the Confederacy*, by David Herbert Donald of Mississippi, which was published last year.

"All are now dismissed, but I will remain here to answer any questions you may have. Oh, yes! Please do not forget to make your diary entry every evening before going to sleep.

---

[16] All of the above is truthful history except for Tiana. Our story now proceeds to our alternate history.

"See you here in the morning."

Dear reader: I will be posting selected diary notes as recorded in the evening of each day by Professor Davis and our 12 Sewanee Project analysts. The selections below were from Monday, June 6:

## Monday Evening Selected Diary Postings

Diary note by Professor Davis said, "Near me at breakfast were four impressive fellows -- Allen Ross, a bison rancher of Sequoyah; Andrew Houston, a petroleum engineer of South Texas; Carlos Cespedes, a sugar farmer of Cuba; and Isiah Montgomery, an African American corporate farmer of Mississippi. I expect excellent contributions will come from these fine young men."

Diary note by Allen Ross said, "Had supper with Conchita Rezanov, of Spanish-Russian ancestry, born in Russian America and now living in South California working on a Ph. D. in history. A beautiful blond, a highly ranked tennis player, and a gifted conversationalist, the fellows will be competing for her attention. Being a simple bison rancher myself, I doubt I will have much of a chance with her. . . . . I was honored this afternoon to be able to tell much of the story of my Ross Cherokee ancestors in conjunction with Andrew Houston. What a wonderful afternoon, followed by a lovely evening."

Diary note by Emma Lunalilo said, "Supper with Carlos Cespedes. I can't believe it. He invited me to go sailing this coming weekend, off Matanzas, Cuba. Says there will be six of us. Will fly Saturday morning from Tennessee to Cuba on the Cespedes' private jet, then take an overnight sailing trip on the family 50-foot sailboat. He said, 'Emma, no one here is more skillful on the water than you. I will be so, so disappointed if you decline to join the group.' Obviously, I said 'yes.' We were matched for supper and had a great conversation: two islanders I suppose, Cuba and Hawaii."

Diary note by Andrew Houston said, "Amazing afternoon! Such a wonderful chance to tell the story of my ancestor Sam Houston's relationship with the Cherokee Nation."

Diary note by Marie Saint Martin said, "Hard to believe that, among the thirteen of us, there are five musicians: Professor Davis plays banjo and sings. Carlos Cespedes plays guitar in both Classical and Country style. Allen Ross plays guitar in Country and Western styles. Tina Sharp plays French horn and is talented at singing. Amanda Washington plays piano and sings, too. I intend to get all of us together for some jam sessions and to see what we can do well when playing together."

## Part 1, Chapter 3, Day 2 – The Secession of Seven States and The Confederate States Prior to Lincoln's Inauguration – Class Lecture, Tuesday, June 7, 2011

Professor Davis continued with his lectures as soon as the twelve were seated and ready to listen.

### The Story of Judah Benjamin and Jean Lafitte

Here's a helpful hint: as a reader, just pretend you are in the class room with Professor Davis and the twelve essayists, listening to the day's lecture. Professor Davis begins now.

Confederate actions prior to Abraham Lincoln's inauguration were in many ways key to eventual Confederate success in defending its independence. To be sure, Lincoln was determined to conquer the Seceded States [17] and his ploy to incite cannon fire at Charleston's Fort Sumter was designed to force Confederates to "fire the first shot." And he and fellow conspirators had every reason to believe the tactic would work. [18] But he had not figured on the influence of Jean Lafitte, his son Jean Pierre Lafitte and the son's relative by marriage, the exceptionally capable and savvy Judah Benjamin. [19] I am about to tell you the fascinating Benjamin-Lafitte story using lots of quoted conversation, which may not be entirely authentic, but let us not be fussy about such details as, together, we live this bit of important history as if we were there, listening in.

---

[17] The writer will be capitalizing more often than is considered proper style in the United States today. He is adopting style choices rather common during the mid-1800s, in situations where he believes the Confederate culture would have approved. For example, to stress that a State is sovereign over most matters in the CSA, he uses the capital "S". State Secession, like World War II, is an historic event deserving capital treatment. Much is said about race in *The CSA Trilogy*, and the White race and the Negro or Black race is capitalized. Also, the mixed race of White and Black is termed Colored people (today almost all Confederates of African ancestry are mixed race, so Black or Negro does not often apply). There are more examples. The writer thought you might like to know about the reasons for his style selections.

[18] In truthful history, President Lincoln was intent on implementing some scheme that would incite Confederates to fire first to initiate the war he planned to launch. That was a political tactic designed to support a propaganda campaign alleging that the United States was under attack and state militia must come forward to defend it. Any first shot might serve Lincoln's purpose, but Charleston was surely his preference. Fort Sumter was a partially completed large fortress in the middle of Charleston harbor. South Carolina had declared Secession on December 20 and, during the night of December 26, a small Federal garrison, under the command of Robert Anderson, had, under the cover of night, relocated from a shore fort, Moultrie, to the mid-harbor fort, Sumter, in violation of an understanding between U. S. President James Buchanan and the Nation of South Carolina -- an agreement stipulating that Anderson's garrison would make no aggressive move. Wishing to avoid any appearance of distrust, South Carolina troops had not been placed in Fort Sumter, allowing Anderson to sneak in at night and bring in cannon. A strict interpretation of international law infers that Anderson's action was an act of war.

[19] We deviate from truthful history when Jean Lafitte, 79, enters the story on Monday, February 18, 1861 at Montgomery, Alabama. Jean Lafitte and brother Pierre Lafitte were famous in history as the Barataria, Louisiana pirates during the early 1800's and for the pirates' important support of Andrew Jackson during the Battle of New Orleans in 1814. In true history, Jean Lafitte was killed in a naval attack off the coast of Honduras in 1823, two years after his brother Pierre had died in 1821, while on the run from authorities -- struck down by illness near Cancun, Mexico. The wives and children of both brothers had been safely secured in New Orleans in 1820, the year that Jean's son Jean Pierre was only 5 years old. In the alternate history presented in *The CSA Trilogy*, Pierre Lafitte does die as history recorded it in 1821, but Jean does not die. Jean spends a few years in South America and eventually returns to New Orleans in 1830. Charges of piracy are dropped at the request of President Andrew Jackson, and Jean Lafitte joins wife Catherine in New Orleans in raising son Jean Pierre from age 15 to adult years. Son Jean Pierre does not die of the epidemic that struck New Orleans in 1832, as truthful history tells us, but lives on to play an important role in this historical novel. In 1840, at age 25, Jean Pierre Lafitte marries a sister of Natalic St. Martin Benjamin, named Marie St. Martin (age 21), the fictional wife having been born in 1819, two years after the birth of Natalie St. Martin. Catherine Lafitte dies in 1858 in accordance with truthful history. Natalie Saint Martin, in conformance with truthful history, marries Judah Benjamin in 1833. Both Saint Martin sisters are of a rather prominent New Orleans Creole family. So, our story creates a brother-in-law relationship between Judah Benjamin and Jean Pierre Lafitte.

The scene is Montgomery, Alabama, February 18, 1861. Jefferson Davis has just completed delivering his remarks to the gathered crowd, accepting the office of President of the Confederate States of America. Immediately afterward, Jean Lafitte approached Judah Benjamin, both of Louisiana. They were related by marriage, for Jean's son Jean Pierre and Judah were married to sisters of New Orleans' rather prominent Saint Martin family. Jean Lafitte clasped Judah's hand and said, "That was a fine start to what ought to become a great nation, but we will need every trick we can muster to sustain it, Judah. What part will you play in the effort?"

Judah answered, "President Davis has spoken briefly to me about a position in the Cabinet, but only in generalities. I agreed to take any position where I could be useful. Attorney General was mentioned, among other possibilities. You look well. I did not know you were here. I know you miss your wife Catherine. It's been two years since she passed away. She was a fine lady. Your son Jean Pierre and his wife Marie are well I hope. Except for quickly passing through during my travels, I've not been in New Orleans for over a year; so busy in Washington and Mississippi."

Jean Lafitte then told Judah what he knew: "I arrived early this morning. My son Pierre had encouraged me to come and, well, I wouldn't miss this historic event for anything. Pierre had talked at some length with Mr. Davis when he was traveling from his farm, Brierfield, on Captain Leather's Mississippi paddle steamer, coming down from Davis Landing to New Orleans. Pierre is 46 years old now and, as you know, often captains Mississippi riverboats himself, mostly the long haul up to Wheeling and back to New Orleans, but on this trip Pierre was just an assistant to Leathers. Pierre advised me that Davis was a great choice for President but seemed too bent on doing the honorable thing. He said, 'Papa, you are a master at trickery and deceit when it is called for. Honorable men, such as Mr. Davis, seldom deal effectively with deceitful politicians. We have to be cunning and careful. Please go to Montgomery and see how you can help. You are better at circumventing deceit than any man I have ever met. If you mastered anything during your days of piracy, it was dealing with deceit. And talk to Judah. He can get you connected'."

Judah injected, "I don't see Pierre much these days. Since my wife Natalie spends all of her time in France, and I do so miss her, she does not get a chance to visit with her sister Marie and Marie's family. Tell me, do Pierre and Marie speak very often of Natalie and me?"

Understanding, Jean answered, "On occasion, but, although you and Pierre are brother-in-laws, the Atlantic Ocean keeps the wives apart and it seems like you and Pierre find little time to get together.

Then Jean continued with his report: "I am 79 years old, Judah -- blessed to have lived such a long life. Why, I was almost Pierre's age when my men and I, with our artillery, fought alongside Andrew Jackson in the Battle of New Orleans. That was 1815, 46 years ago. It was a massacre. The Redcoats were taken by surprise and slaughtered. And my men from Baratavia, with their cannon, were in the thick of it. If you had the right authorization papers for piracy on the high seas, there was some slight honor in being a pirate back then; at least I like to think so."

"But that was then, and this is now. Today, the rules governing right and wrong are altogether different. Which gets me to my worry over our new Confederacy: those damned Republicans -- way up north from Massachusetts and westward along the Great Lakes out to Chicago -- do not intend to obey the rules. Davis and our other leaders must not be deceived in hoping that the rules so clearly written in the Federal Constitution will protect each state's right to peaceably secede. We must not be overly focused on doing the 'right thing.' Honor among thieves is foolish thought, and Abe Lincoln and his cadre of thieves feel no need to be constrained by law or by 'honor.' And, I know that you know that -- when it comes to understanding the behavior of 'thieves' -- well, look me in the eye, now -- what do you see? -- Yes, Judah, you see me -- an expert at understanding the behavior of thieves. Perhaps you can introduce me to President Davis so we can talk and figure out how this old man and his nefarious connections can be of help."

About mid-day on the following day, Tuesday, January 18, 1861, Judah Benjamin gained a brief audience with President Davis for the purpose of introducing Jean Lafitte. "Mr. President, thank you for these few moments of your time and allow me to introduce you to a wise old man from Louisiana, long a friend of mine, and a relative by marriage, Jean Lafitte."

President David replied, "Jean Lafitte, I am so glad to meet you face to face for the first time. I well know the story of how your men and their artillery helped Andrew Jackson defeat the British at New Orleans. So I am eager to learn from a man with your wide range of experience. We face a most difficult situation, as you surely realize, and must use all available resources at hand. Talked with your son Pierre coming down the Mississippi on Captain Leather's riverboat and was most impressed with him. He updated me on family activities and alerted me that he was going to urge you to come to Montgomery and offer your help. That is wonderful. Have a seat."

Jean then began explaining how his family might help: "Mr. President, your warm reception of a man, far less honorable than you in his career of early years, speaks volumes of your eagerness to use all available resources. My family's network of connections ought to be helpful -- at least you have our full and eager support."

"Jean, my friend, anyone as helpful as you and your men were to General Jackson at the Battle of New Orleans is eagerly welcomed here. Tell me what you know."

"First, Mr. President, our Confederacy is up against men who have no respect for established law or personal honor. They have risen to power by agitating a majority of voting men in each Northern State to believe that the Democratic Party in each of those states is 'evil by association,' -- evil because of association with the Democratic Parties of each Southern State -- evil because the governments in each of those states permits slavery -- permits the bonding of people of full or partial African ancestry. Accordingly, as justified by their "holier than thou" manner of reasoning, they have deluded themselves into believing there is a 'higher law' which permits them to seize every power they deem useful in advancing their agenda. And, Mr. President, their agenda is firmly against letting any seceded state go its own way in peace. Is there honor in violating the limits on Federal power clearly and unquestionably imposed in the United States Constitution? Is there honor in violating those limits to merely advance their party's political agenda? In their minds, they say, 'yes', -- even in violating the highest law of the land, there is 'honor.' 'Yes,' because anything they do to conquer seceded states and force them back under the Federal Government imparts 'honor', -- is authorized by their view of a 'higher law'."

Carefully listening, President replied, "Jean, I understand clearly your point, and witnessed it repeatedly in the United States Senate over the past four years. Senator Seward of New York, repeatedly referred to a 'higher law,' as if it superseded the Constitution. And President-elect Lincoln seems to be taking the same view. He left Springfield, Illinois on February 11, 8 days ago, on an extended travel and speaking tour, which my associates call the 'Republican Railroad Rally,' -- all leading up to persuading voters in the Northern States to support some sort of military confrontation with our Seceded States. We get daily newspaper reports of his railroad stops and speeches, but have no person following the train to give us first hand reports."

Immediately seeing a way his family could help, Jean offered: "With your concurrence, Mr. President I believe I can have our man shadowing that train within two days. That is the nature of the help I wish to contribute to our cause of peaceful separation. My family, because of our operation of riverboats from New Orleans to Wheeling, have unusual ability to gather intelligence in the northern States, especially the important States of Missouri, Illinois, Indiana, Ohio and Pennsylvania, as well as Maryland and Washington."

Gratified that the conversation was becoming helpful, Judah injected: "Mr. President, Jean Lafitte and I talked at some length last night about his family's capabilities and his assertion that the Confederacy needs a secret service which is empowered to gather intelligence and distribute propaganda in support of our peaceful separation. For the most part, we Southerners have always sought to behave honorably and lawfully in our social and political lives. But Jean and I believe the time has come for dealing with our adversaries as we would deal with criminals. If I may suggest it, Mr. President, is there a time tomorrow evening when we can discuss this further? By then I am hopeful that Jean and I can lay out our thoughts in the form of a 2 to 4 page written policy proposal."

Davis concurred: "Mr. Lafitte, Mr. Benjamin, I would like to do just that. Say 5 o'clock at my hotel room. We will dine as we review your thoughts."

So, a very important strategy concept was being born during these first two days of the Confederate States Government -- a strategy concept that would grow into a successful program for the Defense of the Confederacy. Jean Lafitte and Judah Benjamin worked late into the night developing their recommendations. They were at it after breakfast and, for a few hours during the early afternoon, discussed their thoughts and sought advice from Robert Toombs and Stephen Mallory. Toombs, of Georgia, had excellent advice on how to persuade Confederate citizens (a proud bunch to say the least) that it was in their best interest to appear weak and avoid any aggressive action, even to let Federals take control of Fort Sumter if it meant avoiding firing the "first shot" that Lincoln coveted. Mallory had great knowledge of the strength of the U. S. navy and saw some wisdom in a strong priority on defense against invasion down the Mississippi and Tennessee rivers, viewing that as more important that defense along the seacoast and at the Confederate seaports.

### The Lafitte-Benjamin Position Paper and Preliminary Cabinet Debate

By 4 o'clock that afternoon, the first Lafitte-Benjamin position paper was written up. It consisted of four pages:

Mr. President, we see merit in basing the defense of the Confederacy on the following principles:

1. The strength of the Republican Party is in the Northern State governments that it controls and the governor of each of those states, each of whom controls his respective state militia. Collectively, those state Republican Parties and those Republican governors hold more power than President Abe Lincoln and the Republican political leaders in Washington City. Therefore, every effort must be made to persuade the people of each Northern state to support a policy of peaceful co-existence and to oppose calling up their militias to launch a War Between the States. Toward that goal, we must:

    a. Send our spies and propaganda agents into each northern state to gather intelligence and to spread our message.

    b. Send friendly delegations from each Confederate state to designated Republican northern states in search of friendly relations and settling differences (match up state assignments; Mississippi to Illinois and Michigan, Alabama to Indiana and Ohio, etc.).

2. While our Southern states are sending delegations and spies northward to designated "sister" Northern states, the Confederate Government must be doing likewise

with respect to activities in Washington City and the workings of the upcoming Lincoln Administration. In that effort we must be especially attentive to activities related to communications between the Lincoln Administration and the Republican governors, and related to future Federal military action against Fort Sumter and Fort Pickens, which we foresee as being for the purpose of instigating a conflict as an excuse for calling up Republican state militia.

3. We must appear peaceful and conciliatory toward the northern states. A few specifics are worthy of discussion:

a.   Promise to keep the Mississippi River open for the northern states, down to the Gulf of Mexico and back;

b.   Promise to help collect Federal tariffs imposed on goods moving across the boundary between the Confederacy and the United States;

c.   Promise to pay for any Federal property that resides in the Confederacy;

d.   Promise to operate an independent postal system;

e.   Place our defensive military fortifications 5 to 20 miles south of our northern border so they do not seem threatening to states to our north;

f.   Begin planning in each state for introducing a tentative program for gradual emancipation of slaves. We are speaking of a plan that does not commit anyone to action, but is to be widely broadcast northward to counter the holier-than-thou crowd of radical Abolitionists, for this is to be primarily a propaganda activity, and

g.   Encourage those among us of partial African ancestry to help in disseminating propaganda and collecting needed intelligence.

4. Also we should include in our propaganda messages the fact that the United States Constitution prohibits a state from using military force against a sister state and prohibits the Federal military from using military force against any of its states. We are dealing with criminals who will not obey the law and will use deceit to persuade the gullible that launching a military invasion force toward the South is not a violation of law.

5. Through state-to-state diplomatic efforts, we must encourage the Democrat-controlled states to our north (especially North Carolina, Tennessee, Arkansas, Virginia, Kentucky and Missouri) to support us in our independence and to join us in secession if forced to choose between 1), fighting against us, or, 2), joining in our mutual defense. Toward that end we should encourage them to:

a.   Establish secession conventions and keep them active so each can quickly choose between joining in a military attack upon Seceded States versus seceding their state and joining in the defensive effort.

b.   Prepare their State militia for any eventuality.

c.   Make no aggressive moves that would alarm Republican-controlled states to the north.

6. We must use every means at our disposal to avoid appearing to be aggressive toward the North. If they bring naval warships into our harbors, we must not shoot. If they bring soldiers onto our shores, we must not shoot. We must not shoot until we have drawn their forces far inland to such a place that we can cut them off, envelope them, and force

their surrender. Capturing prisoners is more important than defending every foot or our waterfront and soil. Toward that goal our strategy must be "Retreat, Envelope, Capture." The Lincoln Administration will probable try to coerce us into firing the "first shot." We must avoid doing that!

7. We must delay the foreseen invasion from the north as long as possible — hopefully until December of this year, 1861, when the Federal House and Senate are scheduled to convene. During these 10 months it is imperative that we strengthen all aspects of our defense.

8. We must take advantage of every month we put off facing a military invasion by using all possible means to enhance our preparations:

    a.    Using Confederate bonds, purchase the vast majority of the cotton crop in our country and expedite shipment to safe havens in Cuba and elsewhere in anticipation of a blockade by the U. S. Navy. Use this cotton revenue to pay for arms, steam engines, tooling for firearms and ammunition manufacture, iron for armoring ships and laying railroads, telegraph wires, etc. Seek the most modern rifles and pistols in large numbers, especially arms that rapidly fire repeated rounds. Maximize the size and effectiveness of Confederate cavalry and make every effort to maximize the mobility of all ground troops.

    b.    Our greatest vulnerability is invasion through armed river gunboats coming down the Mississippi and Tennessee rivers. Recognizing that the U. S. military will attempt to split our eastern States from our western States, priority should be toward defending against that line of attack as compared to defending against invasion from the seacoast.

9. An effective and dispersed Confederate Secret Service organization needs to be quickly established. It is suggested that the Service not be under the administration of the Confederate War Department, because their plate is too full to take on administration of such a large additional responsibility. We suggest, instead, that the Confederate Secret Service be under the Confederate Attorney General's office because legal issues are significant and because that department can give rapt attention to rapidly building and dispersing an effective Service.

One hour later, at 5 o'clock, Lafitte and Benjamin met with President Davis. Every word of the 4-page position paper was discussed and analyzed in depth. Davis saw a great advantage in avoiding firing the "first shot." He saw a great advantage in delaying the day the Confederates would have to defend against a major invasion force. A cotton farmer himself, he even saw merit in a program for purchasing cotton and expediting shipment out of the country. Much he liked, but much worried him as well. Every fiber of his being was naturally committed to honesty and straightforward interpersonal dealings. He detested deceit and demagoguery, and knew that Republicans, such as Senator Seward of New York, had no qualms about such behavior. "How," Davis mused, "can we persuade our people to appear weak and non-aggressive? Will they tolerate a retreating response to U. S. Navy occupation of Charleston harbor and Fort Sumter? Will England and France judge us as unworthy to join the nations of the world if we appear weak and let the Lincoln Administration push us around?" The meeting concluded at midnight.

Davis suggested the following plan: "In the morning, first thing, I will call a preliminary Cabinet meeting for 10 am on Friday, February 22. That gives us tomorrow to further develop our thoughts. By then I expect to appoint to the Cabinet Robert Toombs of Georgia, as Secretary of State; Christopher Memminger of South Carolina, as Secretary of the Treasury, and LeRoy Pope Walker, as Secretary of War, and all three should be able to join us by then. Furthermore, Judah, I have known you for several years based on our time together in the United States Senate and have admired your legal mind and your ability to grasp a situation and present a lucid analysis of what it means and what ought to be the best response to it. My Cabinet needs representation from Louisiana. Please give consideration to my invitation to you, now offered, to become our Attorney General. If the ideas you and Jean are advancing win approval, I can think of no better place from which to administer a large and active Confederate Secret Service than from the desk which you will command."

Prior to the Friday morning Cabinet meeting Benjamin handed a letter to Davis formally accepting the position of Attorney General. Davis eagerly accepted and asked Benjamin to attend the meeting, and suggested that Jean Lafitte be available in the hotel lobby if called upon to answer questions. Therefore, the Friday morning meeting involved President Davis of Mississippi; Vice President Alexander Stephens of Georgia; Secretary of State Robert Toombs also of Georgia; Secretary of the Treasury, Christopher Memminger of South Carolina, Secretary of War Leroy Walker of Alabama, and Judah Benjamin of Louisiana, Attorney General. Several topics were covered, but by far the greatest amount of time was spent discussing the position paper prepared by Benjamin and Jean Lafitte.

There was universal agreement that the Confederacy would greatly benefit by delaying the foreseen attack by the United States army and by state militia from the Republican states. Treasury Secretary Memminger said that delaying an attack "would give valuable time to raise money to support a military purchase program." Secretary of State Toombs said such a delay would "contribute to winning recognition from Great Britain and France," but warned that "an appearance of weakness might hurt our chances of winning recognition." So, he explained, the issue "could work for us or against us." War Secretary Walker agreed "more time would aid in building and equipping a Confederate army, especially with regard to obtaining rifles and artillery," but, he warned, the "same delay would help the North, but on balance the greater advantage would be ours." On the other hand, among the group, Walker was probably the most confident that the North would not attack. Vice President Stephens seemed not to offer any strong opinions, but did not object to a focus on building a "strong" Confederate Secret Service and placing the administration of the organization outside of the War Department. Davis explained that he "worried most of all about the Executive Department's ability to hold off the more militant" among those in the Confederate House and Senate -- and, within the Confederate States, the more militant among newspapermen and citizens. Davis supposed that, if and when a fleet of U. S. Navy warships and transports enters Charleston harbor and lands at Fort Sumter, "how can we hold back the eager young South Carolinians who will be determined to force them back out to sea, thereby giving the Lincoln Administration that 'first shot,' which we believe to be their strategy for rallying the people of the North? Turning such 'honorable men into timid tricksters' will be difficult, especially since most of our people live in rural areas, own a rifle, and 'half of those can shoot a squirrel perched in a tree 50 yards away'."

It would be only a few days before the full Cabinet would be appointed and the first full meeting would be held. That would be the time to strive for decisions pertaining to the suggestions in the Benjamin-Lafitte paper. The thoughts of the new Secretary of the Navy and the new Postmaster General could then be assayed.

Of the nature, character and agenda of one Abraham Lincoln, it was mostly a mystery. The Republican Railroad Rally Train had pulled out of Springfield, Illinois, 11 days previously, on February 11, taking the President-elect on a speaking tour across the Northern States. Realizing that the last known position of Mr. Lincoln and his train was New York City, where it had arrived two days ago, February 20, President Davis explained, "We know not what Mr. Lincoln is telling Republican leaders across the Northern States, but based on his public statements in speeches that we have seen reported, his agenda appears to be quite uncompromising and militant. It can be presumed he is rallying the people for military action and making arrangements with Republican governors to strengthen State militia and to be prepared for a call-up of troops." As he moved to close the meeting, Davis said, "As you leave, please, without raising suspicions, candidly introduce yourself to Jean Lafitte. You should spot him in the lobby of this hotel. Make whatever arrangements you choose so as to gain further knowledge of the man, his experiences, and how he proposes to help us. You can trust him to keep all secret, but make sure no one overhears you or becomes suspicious. Judah will be helpful in this regard. Keep your copies of the Benjamin-Lafitte paper for future contemplation but make sure to keep each sheet away from anyone outside of this Cabinet. Discuss strategy ideas among yourselves, but privately. This is Friday, February 22. Our next meeting will be on Monday, February 25. I expect we will have a full Cabinet present for that one. Let us target Wednesday, February 27 for decisions regarding the proposals in this paper. Oh, I am about to forget to make a special request of you, Secretary Memminger. You are of Charleston. At our next meeting I want a report from you on how you and other leaders of that important city can help us keep peace when, or if, the Federal navy moves in on Fort Sumter and attempts to incite our side to fire the coveted 'first shot'." With that the meeting adjourned.

## President Abraham Lincoln and his Railroad Rally

This day, February 22 was also the day of Mr. Lincoln's last Republican Railroad Rally speech, a speech he delivered to the Pennsylvania Legislature in Harrisburg. [20] Afterward, as evening arrived, Lincoln's "handlers" decided upon secretly sneaking him into Washington City on a night train, leaving the Railroad Rally Train at the Harrisburg station, which would, the following day, resume the published route with all other members of the entourage, a tactic designed to fool newspapermen and everyone else, and, we must suspect, to create the false impression that Southerners in Maryland were out to kill the President-elect. So Lincoln donned a disguise and boarded a special train from Harrisburg to Philadelphia, where he transferred to a scheduled night train down to Baltimore, where he switched to a scheduled night train from Baltimore to Washington City. Throughout this ruse during the night of February 22 and early morning of February 23, the future President was disguised in a long overcoat thrown over his shoulders, his long arms hidden within, the sleeves just dangling, and an uncharacteristic soft felt hat upon his head to minimize his height. He arrived with his bodyguard and, unknown to the public, entered into his room in Willard's Hotel. The Railroad Rally Train arrived without incident a few hours later. [21] By evening the ruse became known and news of it was telegraphed to Montgomery, Alabama. Jeff Davis read the report that evening and thought to himself: "What kind of a coward am I to be dealing with." In fact he went on to include that thought in a letter he wrote to wife Varina the following day. She was expected to arrive in Montgomery in a few days. A portion of the letter said:

Montgomery, Alabama, February 24, 1861,

My Dear Wife,

---

[20] Abraham Lincoln's travel to Washington City and his first weeks in office is truthful history, as will be his eagerness to force the Confederates to fire the first shot. It will be several more months into our narrative before the history of the Lincoln Administration deviates from truthful history, and that transformation will be footnoted for you at the point it takes place.

[21] In truthful history, President-elect Lincoln's bodyguards, of the Alan Pinkerton agency, alleged that some person or people in and around Baltimore planned to kill him while passing through Maryland. As a student of history and the writer of *The CSA Trilogy*, I believe the allegation was just propaganda to make the South look evil. President Davis' interpretation of the elaborate disguise is a reasonable reaction giving the circumstances.

I am taking a few moments this Sunday to add a bit to the letter I wrote on February 20. Have met with Judah Benjamin and Jean Laffite, both of New Orleans. You know Judah from our time together in the U. S. Senate. I think you know of Jean Laffite, although perhaps have never met him. He is 79 years old now. His son Pierre is married to Marie Saint Martin the sister of Judah's wife Natalie. As you recall, Natalie spends all of her time in France to her husband's great disappointment. By the way, I talked with Pierre on the way down the Mississippi on Leathers' boat and found his insight useful. Pierre is a river man who often captains a boat for Leathers, but he was just an assistant when we talked. I am trying to remember that many years ago you knew Natalie and perhaps her sister, too. Anyway, when you get to Montgomery we will have dinner with Judah and Jean and talk over things.

Last night I received a telegram from our people in Washington City reporting that on February 23, Mr. Lincoln snuck into town in disguise pretending to be escaping some phantom threat from Democrats in Maryland. Of course, there was no threat. What kind of coward, what kind of demagogue am I going to be dealing with? That is certainly a strike against his character. It makes me worry all the more. Looking forward to hearing your interpretation, for your instincts are sharp and useful to me. The Lafitte's (who ought to know what they are talking about) believe we should deal with the Lincoln Administration as if they are criminal personalities without regard to law -- and that we need to keep such behavior in mind as we arrive at our policy toward them.

Again, devoted love to you and the children,

Your Husband

## Davis, Benjamin and the Full Confederate Cabinet Meeting

The next day at noon, on February 25, President Davis held his first meeting with his full Cabinet. Postmaster General John Henninger Reagan of Texas had arrived and accepted his role, as had Secretary of the Navy Stephen Russell Mallory of Florida. So, all were present. Many topics were introduced and many opinions offered, but the topic that most concerns readers of *The CSA Trilogy* are the group's discussions centered on the four-page Benjamin-Lafitte position paper. President Davis, Vice President Stephens, Toombs of Georgia (State), Walker of Alabama (War) and Memminger of South Carolina (Treasury) had previously reviewed the paper and had engaged in discussions over the weekend, but the concerns and ideas presented were new to Reagan and Mallory.

As alternatives and opinions sparked across the makeshift conference table some basic positions were becoming clear: Toombs, Walker and Memminger felt more strongly that a response which delayed the anticipated calling up of militia in the Republican states would work to their advantage, even if achieved through a "timid trickster" strategy reeking of embarrassing weakness. Mallory of the Navy, new to the idea of purposeful timidity, reasoned that, because it was hopeless to challenge the United States Navy head-on, time gained for building a naval defense and inland river defense would be useful. Benjamin submitted:

"Jean Laffite tells me that he and his son have hopes that we can engage the talents of James Eads of Missouri, the most capable man in America at building Mississippi steamboats, including iron-clad gunboats. A project under his leadership would be most helpful in organizing a defense against attackers coming down the Mississippi and the Tennessee -- another benefit from winning delay." [22]

Several saw merit in expediting the shipment overseas of the remainder of the 1860 cotton crop through immediate government purchase and hastened shipping even though only about 20 percent of the crop remained to be shipped. A strategy to raise and export the 1861 crop was needed with a target of 90 percent picked, ginned, baled and exported by the first of December.

Without question, all agreed that efforts to appear non-aggressive should be stressed and reported widely in the northern states, such as free navigation of the Mississippi and Tennessee rivers and assistance in collecting U. S. tariff duties at the northern Confederate border.

Midway through the discussions, Memminger delivered the report that President Davis had requested in the previous meeting -- concerning how he and other leaders of Charleston can help keep peace when, or if, the Federal navy moves in on Fort Sumter, attempting to incite our side to fire the coveted "first shot". To that question Memminger offered the following suggestions:

"We should establish a Department of Confederate Communication tasked to frequently disseminate news throughout the Confederacy to inform our people about the reasons for future measured responses to potential attacks by northern states militia and by the U. S. Navy. I believe if we are candid and open, we can win our people over to a timid trickster tactic, and we can do that in a way that will deceive the Lincoln Administration to our advantage. If we engage Southern newspapermen and give them honest news, I believe they will report it out in persuasive language. We must send people from the Executive Department to the Confederate House and Senate and to the governors and State legislatures for the purpose of delivering the same message. Every aggressive move Mr. Lincoln presents must be analyzed and delivered to the communication network we ought to establish. The people will support us if we steadily teach them to know the character and methods of the enemy we face."

Other issues were discussed, as well, but there is insufficient space here to report them.

The Cabinet meeting lasted all afternoon. At the conclusion, President Davis asked each man to study the issues and be prepared to state final opinions on the questions on the table at the next meeting, which would be held in two days, on Wednesday, February 27. At that time, he said, "we will be casting votes that are intended to afford me your best advice."

The Cabinet meeting on February 27 was held as planned. Votes were cast and much in the Benjamin-Laffite paper was supported by the majority. President Davis directed Secretary of State Robert Toombs to add the Confederate Communications Department (CCD) to his oversight and to do what was needed to be sure the Executive Department's decisions and strategies were made known to the people for the purpose for encouraging their support, especially their support of a potential "timid trickster" response to a potential U. S. military reinforcement of Fort Sumter. He also directed Judah Benjamin to proceed with establishing a strong and extensive Confederate Secret Service (CSS) within the Department of Justice. He advised that money and resources intended for the War Department would be transferred to the Secret Service as needed and that he, Davis, would mediate between the financial needs of the War Department and the CSS. But, he said, communications by the CSS will always be in code.

---

[22] In truthful history, river gunboats built by James Eads of St. Louis, Missouri were greatly responsible for the Federal victories on the Cumberland River, the Tennessee River and the Mississippi River.

## The Confederate Secret Service

So the CCD and CSS were launched on February 27, 1861 in Montgomery, Alabama, two events that would play major roles in the successful defense of State Secession:

Toombs issued a press release to all newspapers in the Confederacy announcing the Confederate Communications Department (CCD) and how communications would flow back and forth. No coded messages here. To facilitate outgoing communications he recruited a team of 7 communications deputies, each a native of the state he was to serve; three surveillance deputies who were charged with gathering and cataloging readily obtainable intelligence; three secretaries, and two telegraph operators. Within two days new telegraph wires were run into the newly established CCD telegraph office and ample battery power was installed to ensure reliable electrical strength.

Benjamin began building his Confederate Secret Service personnel one person at a time, giving priority to people who had vision and resources to build and organize teams of their own. As the size of the department grew, he reasoned, he would add layers of supervision and chains of command. But for a start, he felt an urgency to recruit agents and get them out into the field as fast as possible. Mr. Lincoln was already in Washington City plotting strategy and would be taking office in less than a week. Benjamin's immediate staff, stationed in Montgomery, would be Jean Laffite and Jules Saint Martin. Saint Martin, also of New Orleans, was his wife's young brother, available and capable. Jules sent a message to Pierre Laffite to come to Montgomery immediately for discussions. With his steamboat traveling routinely back and forth between New Orleans and Wheeling, Virginia, Pierre would be valuable in transporting Secret Service agents and documents into the upper Mississippi states as well as Illinois, Indiana, Ohio and Pennsylvania. Over the next few weeks many other agents would be recruited.

Female Secret Service agents would number among the most effective, for Republican operatives generally considered the plantation Southern lady, with her charm and manner of speaking, too ignorant to be carrying secret Confederate messages. This misconception about the Southern lady was especially prevalent in the northeastern Yankee culture. They were wrong -- female agents would prove very effective in dispensing propaganda. Most helpful would be propaganda aimed at accusing President Lincoln of lying about his parentage, for there was substantial evidence in western North Carolina and eastern Kentucky that his father was North Carolinian Abraham Eloe, that he was two years old when his mother, Nancy Hanks married his step-father, Thomas Lincoln. In 1861, a man of illegitimate birth, who had lied about it, was not to be respected.

Men and women of color were also effective Secret Service agents. Although they sometimes had trouble with racial abuse in the Republican States because of their Negro ancestry, Republican operatives never suspected that they would be supporting State Secession. This freedom from suspicion allowed them to carry messages and report on observations in the North without interference. Most Secret Service agents of color were able to read and write, also not suspected by Republican operatives.

Confederate Secret Service agents would be lobbing politicians and newspapermen in Washington City and in Northern States capitals -- providing evidence that encouraged peaceful separation of the two countries.

### Early Preparations for a Military Defense of the Confederacy

From the first few days, efforts were underway to procure improved weaponry for the new Confederate army. Heavy guns were already in position at the seacoast forts along with powder and cannon balls. But there were little field artillery and it was mostly in the hands of arsenals that served State militia. Regarding small arms, the weapons and ammunition in the State arsenals, although in modest quantities, were at hand, as were the weapons and ammunition at Federal arsenals, which had been renamed as Confederate arsenals. [23]

Of the former Federal arsenals within the Confederacy, the small arms inventory totaled 117,010 pieces.[24]

A few weeks earlier, Secretary of War Leroy Walker had recruited United States Colonel Josiah Gorgas to become the Confederate Chief of Ordinance. Accepting, Gorgas had resigned his command over the U. S. Frankford Arsenal, an ammunition plant near Philadelphia, and come south. Born in Pennsylvania and graduated from West Point in 1841, Gorgas had married the daughter of former Alabama Governor John Gayle and thought of himself as a Southerner. In the meantime Confederate purchasing officers were already in the northern states seeking opportunities to procure arms and ammunition, among them Raphael Semmes of Alabama, who was in New York and finding good opportunities to buy ordinance stores in considerable quantity and ship them to the Confederate states. Another purchasing officer of note was Caleb Huse, also buying in the northern states. Born and raised in Massachusetts, Huse married a woman from Alabama and eventually called that state his home. He would soon be sent to Great Britain as general purchasing agent for the Confederacy. His want list was long: a variety of machinery to produce military stores in new Confederate factories; artillery for fortifications and field batteries; rifles of the newest design; brass shells for bullets of the new cartridge design, which was superior to paper; lead for bullets; percussion caps and copper and fulminate of mercury to produce them locally; gunpowder, and steam engines. Furthermore, there was early discussion of the need to seek out and recruit men in the northern states and in Europe who were skilled in the manufacture of military stores. Recruiters would be instructed to pay travel expenses for top recruits. This was the beginning of a long-standing Confederate tradition concerning emigration: always seek emigrants who would bring to the country skills and character capable of advancing Confederate goals. In other words, Confederate immigration resembled recruitment.

## Tuesday Evening Selected Diary Postings

Diary note by Professor Davis said, "At breakfast enjoyed conversation with Robert Lee of Alabama, an inspiring writer with a remarkable and inquiring mind; Marie Saint Martin of New Orleans, lovely to look at, athletic of build, and a musician of ability who aspires to become an entrepreneur; Andrew Houston, a petroleum engineer of South Texas, who impressed me the previous morning; and Chris Memminger of South Carolina, of a long-standing corporate farming family who loves to talk about his thorough-bred race horses and his work toward a degree in veterinary science. Chris and Marie seemed to be attracted to one another. Who knows? Romance may grow out of these four weeks of togetherness. All twelve of them are single and, as far as I have determined so far, none are seriously attached as of yet."

---

[23] The Baton Rouge Arsenal in Louisiana contained 47,372 arms of great variety, consisting of U. S. rifle muskets; caliber .69 rifle muskets; new and altered percussion muskets; flint muskets; Harper's Ferry rifles; Colt rifles; Hall rifles; various types of carbines, and Colt and percussion pistols. At the Mount Vernon Arsenal in Alabama, the inventory of all types of arms totaled 19,455. At Charleston, South Carolina, the small arms inventory totaled 22,469. The small arms total at Augusta, Georgia, was 27,714. Altogether there were about 2,000,000 cartridges for small arms and about 100,000 pounds of gun powder suitable for making about 900,000 more cartridges.

[24] Fortunately, there was an ample supply of percussion caps, about 2,000,000, in Montgomery, Alabama. All arms were single shot. There were no revolvers, either as pistols or rifles, in the inventories of Southern arsenals. However, the Le Mat revolver pistol, first produced in 1856, was, in truthful history, ordered by the Confederate military immediately after Lincoln proclaimed war and became an important weapon for cavalry.

Diary note by Marie Saint Martin said, "Supper with the Cuban sailor and grower of sugar cane -- none other than Carlos Cespedes himself. Surfing Emma Lunalilo of Hawaii, who ate supper with him Monday, told me today that 'Carlos might brag too much about his family's wealth and political influence in Cuba,' but she was thrilled that he had 'invited her on the sailing trip he is planning for this weekend.' Well, I did not mind the bragging, and perhaps to call his pride in his family 'bragging' is really not fair. That sailing trip this weekend – he invited me, too. Fantastic. Oh, he claims to play Spanish guitar and classical music as well. Have to include him in some jam sessions. Allan Ross plays country, cowboy music on his guitar and Amanda Washington sings and plays jazz piano. I am for forming a musical group!"

Diary note by Robert Lee said, "Really enjoyed this morning's lecture on the secession of the first seven states. Of course, my famous ancestor's State, Virginia, was not among these seven, but that "Mother of States" was holding open its secession convention in order to be ready if Virginians found it necessary to quickly secede. By the way, the Lincoln Administration, soon after Abe took office, asked my ancestor, Robert E. Lee, to take command of the Federal Army. Was an attempt to make the Federal Army look like it was not opposed to slavery or opposed to Southern slave owners, make it easier to retain Southerners in the Federal Army. Lee refused, resigned, and returned to Virginia to be of service to his State if called upon." [25]

Diary note by Benedict Juárez said, "Being descended from President Juárez, I so much admire the decision of those first seven American States to repudiate the oppressive agenda of that upstart Republican Party and simply exercise their individual constitutional right to secede from the United States Government. They were quick to join together to create the Confederate States of America, too."

---

[25] Lincoln's invitation to Robert E. Lee to take command of the Federal Army and Lee's refusal and resignation is truthful history.

## Part 1, Chapter 4, Day 3 – President Lincoln's Scheme to Draw the "First Shot" from Confederates at Charleston – Class Lecture, Wednesday, June 8, 2011

### President Lincoln's Scheme's for Fort Sumter and the Confederate's Response

Editor's note: As a reader you are about to witness the actions of President Abraham Lincoln and his Administration from the day he took office until the day that a Federal fleet of warships and transports arrived off the coast of Charleston, South Carolina. All that you will read below concerning the Lincoln Administration is true history up until the moment of the arrival of the fleet positioned in the Atlantic just beyond Charleston Harbor. The corresponding Confederate response, as portrayed by the actions of President Jefferson Davis, Judah Benjamin and others, is an alternate history, not a true history. So, although you may be surprised to learn the history of how President Lincoln maneuvered a Federal fleet to Charleston for the purpose of inciting the coveted "first shot," rest assured the history reported here is the truth of what really happened concerning events in the North -- spies, deception and all. Only the response by Confederates is an alternate history.

We listen in as Professor Davis continues with his lectures as soon as the twelve are seated and ready to go.

Five days after the February 27 Confederate Cabinet meeting, on March 4, 1861, Republican Abraham Lincoln of Illinois was inaugurated as President of the remaining United States. Except for recently admitted Kansas (of Bleeding Kansas notoriety), Lincoln was becoming President over seven fewer States than had existed prior to State Secession. He replaced Democrat James Buchanan of Pennsylvania, who rode off into the sunset, so to speak, with no intention to resume public life. Lincoln's address to the gathered crowd emphasized a twisted interpretation of the right to State secession and his intent to pursue Federal subjugation, by force if necessary, of the Seceded States, but minced his words just enough to not sound as militant as were obviously his intentions. Regarding the right to State secession he argued:

State secession "heretofore only menaced, is now formidably attempted. I hold that, in the contemplation of universal law and of the [Federal] Constitution, the union of these States is perpetual. Perpetuity is implied, if not expressed, in the fundamental law of all national governments. [26] . . . The [association of American States] is much older than the [Federal] Constitution. It was formed, in fact, by the Articles of Association in 1774. It was matured and continued by the Declaration of Independence in 1776. It was further matured . . . by the Articles of Confederation in 1778. And finally, in 1787, one of the declared objects for ordaining and establishing the [Federal] Constitution, was 'to form a more perfect union.' . . . It follows from these views that no State, upon its own mere motion, can lawfully get out [from under the Federal Government] -- that resolves and ordinances to that effect are legally void, and that acts of violence, within any [seceded] State or States, against the authority of the [Federal Government], are insurrectionary or revolutionary, according to circumstances. . . . Therefore, . . . to the extent of my ability . . . I shall take care . . . that the laws of the [Federal Government] be faithfully executed in all the States. . . . "

"In doing this there needs to be no bloodshed or violence; and there shall be none, unless it be forced upon the [Federal] authority. The power confided in me will be used to

---

[26] Lincoln's legal deception – at this time those United States were a federation of States, not a singular nation. The notion of a "fundamental law of all national governments" is not relevant.

hold, occupy, and possess the property and places belonging to the [Federal] Government, and to collect the [Federal] taxes; but beyond what may be necessary for these objects, there will be no invasion — no using of force against or among the people anywhere. . . . The mails, unless repelled, will continue to be furnished in all parts of the [former and present country]. . . . The course here indicated will be followed, unless current events and experience shall show a modification or change to be proper. . . ."

"In your hands, my dissatisfied fellow-countrymen, and not in mine, is the momentous issue of civil war. The [Federal] Government will not assail you. You can have no conflict without being yourselves the aggressors. You have no oath registered in heaven to destroy the [Federal] Government, while I shall have the most solemn one to "preserve, protect, and defend it."

The inaugural address clarified Lincoln's strategy: he intended to maneuver a few Confederates into firing the coveted "first shot." His method would involve occupying forts and buildings that were formerly considered Federal property and in forcing importers to pay Federal tariffs on taxed goods brought into the Seceded States from foreign countries. Republicans believed those tariff collections would amount to a lot of money, because the duties on imported goods, expressed as a percentage, had been raised by a very large amount the previous month -- the majority votes in the Federal House and Senate for the tariff tax hike having been enabled by the resignation of Representatives and Senators from the seven Seceded States (logically speaking a form of taxation without representation). And the vast majority of import taxes collected by the Federal Government had historically been collected in Southern seaports, giving the North a bit of a free ride. Details of Lincoln's address were quickly sped to Montgomery and elsewhere in the South.

President Davis convened the Confederate Cabinet at noon the following day, March 5, to study Lincoln's address and discuss the best corresponding strategy. Everyone read the text of the message once more and discussions began -- one paragraph at a time. After an hour two major elements of the address became their focus:

      1. Lincoln's convoluted argument that State secession was legally void, and
      2. "There needs to be no bloodshed or violence; and there shall be none, unless it be forced upon the [Federal] authority."

Secretary of State Robert Toombs submitted: "That means Lincoln will attempt to send a Federal military force against us soon and without advanced approval from the Federal House and Senate, which is not scheduled to convene until December 1, almost eight months into the future. Furthermore, Lincoln's address tells us that the Federal military objective will be to trick us into firing the coveted 'first shot.' The Federal army is far too small to subjugate us; he must call up many regiments of State militia from the Republican States to present a military threat to our vast country; and potential militiamen may not rally to his side and face possible death on the battlefield unless he can allege that their country has been attacked and must be "defended." His strategy requires that we fire the 'first shot.' I am now sure of it."

None could state the conclusion in more concise words. And none could present a logical alternative. In a way the discussions during the previous week concerning the Benjamin-Lafitte paper had conditioned the mind-set of Cabinet members to almost anticipate Lincoln's message. President Davis and all others agreed with Toombs's assessment. So, the discussion moved forward to the obvious issue: "How should the Confederate Government prepare to face this challenge?"

By the next day, March 6, the agreed strategy could be condensed into the following two directives:

First, if Lincoln succeeds in rallying vast hordes of State militia out of the Republican States, all under the control of compliant Republican governors, it is probable that we will be subjugated, that we will be defeated.  Therefore, it is imperative that we launch a propaganda campaign to teach the people -- both North and South -- that we only seek peaceful separation, that the Federal Constitution forbids Federal military and, or, State military making war on a state that is behaving peacefully.  The first message in that campaign is to be a letter to the people from President Davis.  Carriers of this message and supporting documents should include newspapermen, diplomats, and Secret Service agents.  We must ask our friends in the Democratic Parties of every Northern State and their respective newspapers to help us spread this message.  It is imperative that Republicans not succeed in conjuring up the idea among their people that going to war against us is morally right or justified in any way.  President Davis agreed and accepted the assignment of having a draft of a letter to the people ready for the Cabinet meeting the following day.

Second, it is to our advantage to delay as long as possible making any response that gives Lincoln an excuse for calling up State militia, such as refusing to pay Federal tariffs at seaports or firing against Federal military within view of witnesses.  So how do we organize our seaports and our military to comply when we must, and retreat when we must, yet retain our strength and build rapidly upon it toward the day when the anticipated war does erupt?  Toward those goals the following was outlined:

1.  Confederate artillery must be retained in any retreat and we anticipate that Charleston harbor is a likely target from which we will decide to retreat rather than give Lincoln his coveted "first shot."  Therefore, the fixed artillery around Charleston harbor that cannot be modified into mobile artillery must be withdrawn to safe, hidden locations inland but done so secretly to keep Federals unaware.  Where practical, fixed artillery should be converted to mobile artillery.  Full retreat with all other weapons and supplies should be planned so all can be brought out quickly, in one movement, when the order is given.  Similar plans should be made for the vicinity of Fort Pickens and other likely targets of the Federal Navy.  Our artillerymen must be nimble and quick, capable of escaping capture and capable of rapidly supporting cavalrymen and foot soldiers when the enemy, in large or small groups, ventures inland and becomes vulnerable to being cut off, surrounded and forced to surrender, hopefully out of view of witnesses.

2.  Our ground forces must be capable of rapid retreat.  We should consider building light personnel wagons that would enable one mule or one cavalryman upon his horse to evacuate several men with personal weapons rapidly down designated roads.  Look into a light personnel wagon for rapid retreat, made of wood, which our people can easily produce.  Maximize the percentage of our fighting men who are cavalry.  Procure horses and mules wherever possible, including to the north as far as Kentucky and Virginia.

3.  If we are successful in avoiding giving Lincoln his coveted "first shot," when he does move to make war against us with massive State militia reinforcements, we hope the support he enjoys from militiamen in the Republican states will be less in number and less enthusiastic than otherwise.  If we can delay the start of full-scale war until this winter, or even March, 1862, we must make the most of it so as to be best prepared.

4.  The suggestion in the Benjamin-Lafitte paper regarding purchasing the remainder of the last cotton crop and expediting export is worthy and should be pursued.  We need steam engines and skilled men to maintain and operate them on the railroads and on ships and riverboats.

5.    We need rifles and pistols capable of six shots or more per loading. We need to seek brass cartridge technology and employ it as best we can. We need to scour the world for that technology and bring it in as finished weapons and ammunition, and also bring in machining tools and raw materials needed to make such weapons and ammunition in our States.

6.    We need machinists and machine shop tools, so launch a recruiting effort to bring in immigrants with those skills and the tooling they will need, looking especially to the British Isles and Europe.

But all we do must enable greater mobility, for that will be most important when we face Federal incursions. And the list went on. More definitions of policy were noted that day, but space does not permit their inclusion here.

Just before the meeting broke up Secretary Memminger said, "I will contact authorities in Charleston immediately, and make sure that the good ladies of our city resume sending food out to Fort Sumter every day, and that newspapers report on that often. The last thing we need is for Lincoln to succeed at convincing the people of the Republican States that Federals at Fort Sumter are starving to death, for God's sake." And President Davis added, "Good, please see that is done. Furthermore, Robert Anderson of Kentucky, who commands the Federal garrison in the fort, was a friend of mine at West Point and afterward during my military career. I will consider going to Charleston myself and, perhaps, have a chat with him. Let us show good Southern hospitality where we can." [27]

Although the Confederate Executive had existed not quite one month, a plan for defending secession was taking place. This first month of the Jefferson Davis Administration would go down in history as one of the most effective government launches in recorded history.

Meanwhile, in Washington City, President Abraham Lincoln was selecting his Cabinet and moving forward toward his goal of inciting the "first shot." His Cabinet members were:

- Secretary of State: William Seward, Republican, of New York.
- Secretary of War: Simon Cameron, Republican, of Pennsylvania.
- Secretary of the Navy: Gideon Welles, Republican of Connecticut.
- Secretary of the Treasury: Salmon Chase, Republican of Ohio.
- Attorney General: Edward Bates, of what little Republican Party existed in Missouri.
- Postmaster General: Montgomery Blair, of what little Republican Party existed in Maryland.
- Secretary of the Interior: Caleb Smith, Republican of Indiana.

Prior to Abe Lincoln's inauguration, South Carolina Governor Francis Pickens had sent two Delegations to Washington City, both seeking to negotiate with leaders in the Buchanan Administration on the Fort Sumter crisis. But these Delegations had made no progress with those "lame ducks." And Republicans who were supposedly influential with Lincoln had given the South Carolinians no reason for hope. So, those Delegations had returned home with nothing but a stronger fear that Lincoln would stop at nothing in his quest to conquer the Seceded States.

---

[27] In truthful history, Charleston ladies did attempt to send food to soldiers in Fort Sumter, but Captain Anderson refused to accept it, and President Lincoln falsely alleged that Federal soldiers in the island fort were facing starvation, requiring that he send the U. S. Navy with relief supplies to Charleston Harbor, complete with armed warships and troop transports.

59

In February, President Jefferson Davis had taken over control of the South Carolina militia at Charleston, and had sent a Delegation of three men to Washington City to again seek an audience with President Lincoln to find a way to defuse the Fort Sumter crisis. These men had departed on February 27 and had arrived 3 days prior to Lincoln's inauguration. They had notified the new President that they were emissaries from President Davis and that they earnestly sought an audience with him to discuss the crisis at Fort Sumter and all other matters of interest to both parties. Lincoln had refused to see them, probably more than once, in that they were most likely quite insistent. They were seeking opportunities to talk with new Secretaries in Lincoln's Cabinet and Federal Representatives and Senators, but it was Lincoln whom they most wanted to see. These men would keep at their mission in Washington City through March and into April. They would be keeping in touch with President Davis by telegraph and letter. [28]

The morning of his first day on the job, March 5, President Lincoln started considering various plans for maintaining Federal troops at Fort Sumter in South Carolina and Fort Pickens in Florida. He read a report alleging that the Federals at Fort Sumter would run out of food supplies in six weeks. But that was an old report and the ladies of Charleston were persistently attempting to deliver lovely food daily. Federals only had to accept those wonderful and nourishing gifts. That same day, Lincoln issued a verbal Executive Order to the Federal Navy directing it to immediately land at Fort Pickens the 200 troops presently on the offshore warship, the *Brooklyn*. These men had been sent by former President James Buchanan to reinforce Fort Pickens, but had agreed in consultation with Florida officials to remain a short distance offshore. Confederate forces had taken over the substantial nearby navy yard at Pensacola, but had determined that it was not possible to take control of nearby Fort Pickens without a substantial fight. The Confederates already had the good stuff. They had the shipyard. Seeking to avoid bloodshed and recognizing their practical limitations, Confederates had promised not to attack the Federals under siege in Fort Pickens if the men on the warship Brooklyn made no move to reinforce the Fort. Lincoln thought that, by violating that agreement unilaterally, he was underway toward achieving his goal of inciting the "first shot." [29]

Three days earlier, Congress had passed an Amendment to the Federal Constitution, which, if ratified by three-fourths of the States, would become the law of the land. That Amendment would prohibit the Federal Government from passing any laws or enforcing any executive orders that would interfere with each State's right to regulated slavery. Clearly, incoming President Lincoln would have great difficulty mounting a moral outrage, an Abolitionist crusade against slavery in Delaware, Maryland, Kentucky, Missouri, Virginia, North Carolina, Tennessee or Arkansas, much less against the Seceded States. Freeing the slaves was totally off the table. But some figured that an Amendment to the Federal Constitution might encourage some Seceded States to return. [30]

Before long, Secretary of State William Seward agreed to talk, indirectly and unofficially, with the Confederate Commissioners through two Justices of the Federal Supreme Court, Samuel Nelson of New York and John Campbell of Alabama, the latter having chosen not to resign his lifetime appointment. Both Nelson and Campbell were totally against war. Claiming to be also speaking for Chief Justice Roger Taney of Virginia, Nelson was warning Seward, Salmon Chase

[28] The history of this Confederate Delegation is truthful.

[29] The history of Lincoln's first day in office is truthful.

[30] The referenced Amendment is known as the Corwin Amendment. It was never ratified by three-fourths of the States, so it never became law. In truthful history it passed Congress on March 2, 1861. It was sponsored in the House by Thomas Corwin of Ohio and in the Senate by William Seward of New York, who became Lincoln's Secretary of State.

and Edward Bates, all Secretaries in Lincoln's Cabinet, that Federal invasion of the seceded States would totally violate the Federal Constitution and be illegal use of armed force unless it was constructed as the invasion of a foreign nation, meaning the Confederate States had to first be recognized as a legitimate foreign government. Although negotiating with Seward through Nelson and Campbell was a far cry from the audience with Lincoln that the Commissioners were seeking, they shucked their pride and decided to work with whatever lines of communication they could pry open. They agreed to talk with Seward.

On the other hand, leading Democrats were anticipating a peaceful resolution to the secession crisis. Democrat Senator Stephen Douglas of Illinois, considered the leader of his party in the Northern States, was publicly praising what he alleged to be Lincoln's professed restraint -- alleging that Lincoln's inaugural message was a "peace offering rather than a war message," and claiming Lincoln gave "a distinct pledge that the policy of the Administration shall be conducted with exclusive reference to a peaceful solution of our national crisis."

But there is reason to suspect that Republican leaders were quietly letting Douglas have the spotlight, hoping that would retard the building secession movement in other Democrat-controlled States: Virginia, North Carolina, Tennessee, Maryland, Kentucky, Missouri, Arkansas and little Delaware. Keeping Douglas in the spotlight would buy time for Lincoln and his Cabinet to organize their Administration and complete their arrangements to wage war.

On March 11 Lincoln discovered that the Navy had not obeyed his order to direct the 200 men on the warship Brooklyn to land and reinforce Fort Pickens at Pensacola. Infuriated, he restated the order in writing, and, the next day, General Winfield Scott dispatched a vessel to steam to Florida and deliver the order directing the men to land at Fort Pickens. However, Captain Henry Adams, commander of the Federal naval forces in and offshore from Fort Pickens would not act on General Scott's order. The order would either be pocket vetoed somewhere down the chain of command or Adams would personally veto the thing. It would appear that Adams did not want to unilaterally violate the armistice in effect at Fort Pickens and was intentionally procrastinating. Adams' sense of personal responsibility was heightened by the fact he was personally in possession of the initial papers that documented the agreement between the Federals and Florida State officials.

On March 15, a mere 11 days into his new job, President Lincoln opened a Cabinet meeting discussion about plans to re-supply and re-enforce Fort Sumter by sea. The discussions carried over to March 16. Postmaster General Montgomery Blair of Maryland was a West Point graduate and his wife's brother-in-law, a former Navy man, had developed a proposal to do just that. Montgomery Blair thought the plan had merit and persuaded Lincoln to give it serious consideration. Two options were contained in the Postmaster General's wife's brother-in-law's plan to send Federal warships into Charleston harbor. The mission would be only to re-supply or it would be to re-supply and reinforce. Secretary of State William Seward of New York took the lead in opposing the plan to invade Charleston Harbor. At that time he was definitely against creating a military incident at Charleston. Seward argued that a Navy expedition to put more Federals into Fort Sumter would "provoke combat, and probably initiate a civil war." In his position statement Seward added: "Suppose the expedition successful, we have then a garrison in Fort Sumter that can defy assault for six months. What is it to do then? Is it to make war by opening its batteries and attempting to demolish the defenses of [Charleston]? . . . I would not initiate war to regain a useless and unnecessary position on the soil of the seceding States." Secretary of the Navy, Gideon Welles of Connecticut acknowledged that under different circumstances he might advocate initiating war, but the Fort Sumter plan was not one of those circumstances. Wells included in his written position paper: "By sending, or attempting to send provisions into Sumter, will not war be precipitated? It may be impossible to escape it under any course of polity that may be pursued, but I am not prepared to advise a course that would provoke hostilities." Secretary of War Simon Cameron of Pennsylvania and Secretary of the Interior Caleb Smith of Indiana agreed with Seward as well. Secretary of the Treasury Salmon Chase of Ohio disliked the plan for he feared it would ignite a war of invasion that the Treasury was ill-prepared to fund, but he reluctantly agreed to offer his support if Abe Lincoln was sure it would not be the prelude to war. Chase wrote: "If the attempt will so inflame civil war as to involve an immediate necessity for the enlistment of armies and the expenditure of millions, I cannot advise it in the existing circumstances of the [Federation] and in the present condition of the [Federal] finances." [31] Only Secretary Montgomery Blair of Missouri -- who, ironically, did not represent the political views of the vast majority of the people of his state, and was in charge of only the unrelated U. S. Postal Service -- strongly endorsed an invasion of Charleston harbor by the Federal Navy. Blair explained such action was needed to repudiate what he alleged to be southern States expectations that "Northern [States] men are deficient in the courage necessary to [force Seceded States back under] the [Federal] Government." Blair urged prompt action to "vindicate the hardy courage of [Northern States men] and the determination of the people and their President to [reinstall] the authority of the [Federal] Government." So at this time Lincoln did not have agreement on a course of military action within his Cabinet. Seward, Cameron, Welles and Smith were eager to avoid war, and Chase was quite cautious. Only Postmaster Blair was eager to launch a militant incident to elicit the coveted "first shot." In Lincoln's view, negotiating with the Confederacy or the Confederate State of South Carolina was definitely out and opening a dialogue with President Davis or his Commissioners was impossible. Lincoln would never recognize that the Confederate States of America even existed. Lincoln refused to accept his Cabinet's vote. He decided to postpone any decision on the matter.

Meanwhile in Montgomery, on the next day, March 16, Confederate Secretary of State Robert Toombs instructed three Confederate Commissioners who had been chosen to present Confederate policy to Great Britain, France and other European powers:

"They were to make clear the absolute right, as stipulated in the Federal Constitution, of the southern States to secede from the Federation. They were to stress the importance of tax-free trade with the Confederacy. They were to warn that, if the Lincoln Administration were to make war upon the Confederate States, the essential raw material, cotton, would be cut off from British mills. Since African American bonding might be a stumbling block to recognition, they were to touch the subject lightly, but emphasize two facts. The Confederate Constitution prohibited the importation of bonded Africans. Some were already emancipated free people of color, and a trend toward eventual emancipation of all was being discussed among state leaders. Commissioners should emphasize that, even now, more than half of the free people of color in North America were living in the Southern States and many of them were successful landowners, farmers, skilled laborers, and business men and women."

The March 18 issue of the Boston *Transcript* presented the underlying Republican argument for a Federal conquest of the Confederacy: specifically to keep prices of manufactured goods high by ensuring collection of Federal import taxes, not only in Seceded States, but in Federal States as well. African American bonding was not an issue. The newspaper argued, "It is apparent that the people of the principal seceding States are now for commercial independence." Believing it would be impossible to stop the smuggling of heavily taxed goods across the very long land boundary between the Confederate States and the United States, the newspaper alleged

[31] The editor of this book is substituting "federation" for "nation" to more accurately describe the country in 1861.

that Northern States west of the Appalachian Mountains would "find it to their advantage to purchase their imported goods at New Orleans [using smugglers] rather than at New York [City, where the Federal Tax could be efficiently collected]." Officials believed the high Federal import tax on foreign goods was only collectable in an efficient manner at established seaports. Yet, the Lincoln Administration could have obtained help from the Confederate Government in collecting import taxes had it been willing to talk to the Confederate Commissioners, who were patiently seeking an audience with Abe Lincoln.

Meanwhile, Commander-in-Chief General Winfield Scott presented the position of the Federal Army concerning Fort Sumter. He proposed the following message to the commander at Fort Sumter: "You will, after communicating your purpose to His Excellency, the Governor of South Carolina, engage suitable water transportation and peacefully evacuate Fort Sumter . . . [and] with your entire command embark for New York [City]." But Lincoln had other plans.

Ignoring Scott's recommendation, Lincoln proceeded to gather independent military information by personally sending spies to Charleston:

1.  Firstly, Lincoln personally sent Lieutenant Gustavus Fox to Charleston to check out the situation, alleging that Fox was going to Charleston to talk with the troops at Fort Sumter about evacuation plans. But in reality Fox was on a secret mission for the President to spy on Charleston's coastal defenses. Fox, a Massachusetts textile agent who had formerly been a naval officer, was Postmaster Montgomery Blair's wife's brother-in-law. Fox was the Navy man who had originally proposed the Navy reinforcement plan to Blair.

2.  Secondly, Lincoln personally sent Stephen Hurlbut to Charleston. Hurlbut was an old friend from Illinois who had been born in Charleston. Lincoln instructed Hurlbut to make connections with people who had been opposed to State secession – which Lincoln in his naivety expected to be numerous – and to assess their political strength. As a native-born South Carolinian, Hurlbut would be able to circulate among the State's influential people.

3.  Thirdly, Lincoln sent Ward Lamon to South Carolina to spy. Lamon was known in the southern States for his opposition to Abolitionism, so he would not be suspected of aiding the Republicans. Comfortable in bars and saloons, Lamon would be able to limber up loose tongues.

President Lincoln's deliberations about Fort Sumter were no secret. But most well informed people probably expected the Cabinet to have a dominating influence over the new President, simply because Lincoln was so inexperienced in Federal Government work, and in leading a large organization. [32] So, appeals for peace were directed at the Executive as a whole, not just at Lincoln himself. Just about every well-informed person in the Northern States, the remaining Southern States, and the Confederacy recognized that the Lincoln Administration was deliberating on reinforcement or withdrawal at Fort Sumter and Fort Pickens; and there was agreement that one path led to war while the other led to peaceful coexistence. Many well-informed Northern States people were concerned about Washington City becoming isolated between Maryland and Virginia, should secession spread to all Democrat-controlled States. But hardly anyone believed there was any real danger of the Confederacy launching an invasion of the Northern States. Many wise and powerful voices pleaded with the Lincoln Administration to let the Secessionists go in peace. These people did not want war, and they were hopeful that letting

---

[32] In truthful history the biggest organization that Lincoln had ever led was his two-man law office.

those seven States remain apart would deflate mounting State secession movements in the other Southern States. [33]

Horace Greeley, in his New York *Tribune*, a Republican newspaper which, among all newspapers, had been most influential in building the Republican Party throughout the Northern States, alleged that he opposed instigating war. In fact it was about this time that a newspaperman on the *Tribune* staff arrived in Charleston, encouraged by a joint invitation from Robert Toombs (State), Judah Benjamin (Attorney General), and Christopher Memminger (Treasury and a Charleston native). A second newspaperman had accepted a similar invitation. He was of the Cincinnati *Enquirer*, a very influential newspaper for southern Ohio and northern Kentucky, which was owned by Washington McLean, a Democrat. The third newspaper to accept an invitation to send a reporter to Charleston was a man from the New York *Herald*, a widely read staunchly Democrat newspaper edited by Frederic Hudson. The Davis Administration hoped the presence of these three newspapermen from three influential newspapers would be helpful in assuring the peaceful intent and friendly nature of the Confederate people. As each arrived in town, he was witness to the festive and friendly ladies of the city who, every day, prepared fine southern food and arranged for and attempted to deliver it to the Federal garrison holed up in Fort Sumter. [34]

Furthermore, the Confederate Commissioners in Washington City, although officially ignored by the Lincoln Administration, observed political opinion within their view, and reported back to Montgomery that it appeared that Northern States public opinion strongly favored peaceful coexistence.

The March 21 issue of the New York *Times* editorialized, "There is a growing sentiment throughout the [Northern States] in favor of letting the Gulf States go." But the Lincoln Administration had different ideas. On that same day, Abe Lincoln's first spy, Gustavus Fox, mentioned previously as the Postmaster General's wife's brother-in-law, was arranging to row out to Fort Sumter to sharpen his plans for an assault on Charleston Harbor by the Federal Navy. He explained to Governor Pickens that he had merely wished to peacefully visit the Fort Sumter garrison. Obviously suspicious of Fox's intent, Pickens asked that he join him for lunch to discuss further the nature of his business. Deftly, Pickens managed to get the New York *Tribune* reporter to join in the discussion. So Fox found himself uncomfortably contriving excuses on the spot regarding the purpose of his visit. Fox claimed "he had come on pacific purposes." Although Pickens probably suspected that Fox was lying, he granted the man permission to row out to the Fort and then dutifully reported Fox's visit to Montgomery to keep President Davis informed. Fox probably had little confidence in Major Anderson's loyalty to the new Republican Administration, because he also deceived the Federal garrison of his intent. Then Fox set about to thoroughly survey the Fort and its surroundings and mentally firm his plans for landing Federals from a flotilla of Navy ships, which would force their way into Charleston Harbor from the Atlantic. After completing his survey, and without explaining Lincoln's intent to Major Anderson, Fox rowed back across the harbor to Charleston and hurried back to Washington to report to President Lincoln. A report of the visit also reached the press room at the New York *Tribune*, and Horace Greeley made brief mention of it in the next issue, closing with the question: "What was the real mission of officer Fox, brother-in-law to the wife of Postmaster General Montgomery Blair?" [35]

---

[33] The foregoing is truthful history.

[34] This Confederate effort to influence three influential Northern newspapers is our alternate history.

[35] Lincoln's spying trip by Gustavus Fox is truthful history except for the witnessing by the *Tribune* reporter.

Lincoln's second spy, Stephen Hurlbut, did not visit Governor Pickens. Instead, he frequented a few bars about town and gathered a sense of the attitudes of South Carolinians for or against secession, and found that an opponent of secession was a rare bird indeed.

A few days later Abe Lincoln's third spy, Ward Lamon, a personal friend from Springfield Illinois, spoke with Governor Pickens about the intent of his trip. Lamon alleged to Pickens he "had come to try to arrange for a removal of the garrison." Pickens listened a bit and likewise extended an invitation to lunch. This time the reporter from the Cincinnati *Enquirer* was found and brought to the table. Lamon struggled to invent excuses, but Pickens permitted Lamon to row out to the fort. Then he wired Montgomery a report of the encounter. Meanwhile, Lamon rowed out to the fort and talked with Major Anderson about the politics surrounding Fort Sumter. Anderson, well aware that he and his men sat upon a powder keg that could launch a dreaded brother-against-brother war, told Lamon that he strongly favored a policy to evacuate his men and turn over Fort Sumter to the Confederacy. When Lamon rowed back from the fort, he again called on Governor Pickens, and asked if an armed Federal warship might be given clearance to enter the harbor and take away Major Anderson and the Federal garrison. Recognizing that there was no logical reason to assign such a sensitive task to an armed Federal warship, Pickens replied that no armed ship of the Federal Navy would be allowed in Charleston harbor. With that, Lamon replied that he believed Major Anderson would prefer a passenger steamship anyway. Lamon concluded his meeting with Governor Pickens with the upbeat allegation that he hoped to return to Charleston in a few days to help remove the Federal garrison. Then, Lincoln's spy likewise hastily traveled to Washington City to report back to his Commander-in-Chief. News of this visit soon reached the press room at the Cincinnati *Enquirer*. Editor Frederic Hudson, sensing a significant story, headlined the item: "Why Was Lincoln Confidant Ward Lamon Snooping Around Fort Sumter?" People knew of Ward Lamon and his work for the Lincoln campaign, including printing hundreds of counterfeit tickets so Lincoln supporters could pack the galleries that day in Chicago when Abe had won the Republican nomination for President, and the many days he had spent on the Republican Railroad Rally train acting as a bodyguard for Lincoln. The *Enquirer* story raised significant questions about what the new and inexperienced President was up to. Was he operating a personal spy network? [36]

On March 25 Stephen Douglas stood before the Senate, recognized the Confederate States of America and its capital in Montgomery, and advocated a Federal policy of peaceful coexistence. Douglas advocated "withdrawal of the [Federal] garrisons from all forts within the limit of the States which had seceded, except those of remote Key West and Dry Tortugas, needful to the United States for coaling stations." Declaring, "Anderson and his gallant band should be instantly withdrawn," Douglas argued that, unless the Federal Government intended to subjugate the seceded States, Fort Sumter rightfully belonged to Charleston and Fort Pickens rightfully belonged to Pensacola. So at this time Douglas claimed to stand opposed to a Federal invasion, declaring, "We cannot deny that there is a Southern Confederacy de facto, in existence, with its capital at Montgomery. We may regret it. I regret it most profoundly, but I cannot deny the truth of the fact, painful and mortifying as it is." Then Douglas concluded with, "I proclaim boldly the policy of those with whom I act. We are for peace." [37]

But not all people were advocating peace. Many Republican leaders were openly advocating an invasion. The Republican Party had come from nowhere to dominance throughout the Northern States in just six short years. Militant Republicans were peppered throughout the

---

[36] The spying trip by Ward Lamon is truthful history except for the witnessing by the Cincinnati *Enquirer* reporter.

[37] The Douglas speech is truthful history.

Northern States. Their recent political triumphs were rather intoxicating. Michigan Senator Zachariah Chandler argued, "Without a little blood-letting this [Federation] will not, in my estimation, be worth a rush." Pointing directly at Fort Sumter, Lyman Trumbull of Illinois introduced a resolution in the Senate stipulating, "It is the duty of the President to use all the means in his power to hold and protect the public property of the United States." Stooping to the exaggerated rhetoric typical of crisis-time politicians, a caucus of Republican Representatives warned the Lincoln Administration that failure to reinforce Fort Sumter would bring disaster to the Republican Party. But the March 4 through March 28 Special Session of the U. S. Congress would conclude soon.

About this time Secretary of State William Seward again met with the Confederate Commissioners who were hoping to win recognition and a pledge of peaceful co-existence. Apologizing for the delay, Seward, again with apparent confidence, alleged to the Commissioners that the Federal garrison would soon be withdrawn from Fort Sumter. But Seward was not in control!

Within a few days Lincoln's three spies were back in Washington City to report on their respective trips to Charleston. Lieutenant Fox advised Lincoln that, having seen the situation first hand, he was even more confident that his proposal to sneak Federals into the harbor by sea at night would work. Stephen Hurlbut, returning on March 27, exploded Lincoln's dream that opposition to State secession resided in the hearts of a significant remnant of South Carolinians. Hurlbut reported, "Separate nationality is a fixed fact; there is no attachment to the [past Federation of States] . . . positively nothing to appeal to." He reported that South Carolinians viewed themselves as citizens of a new nation. He believed they would protect their harbor from any ships that appeared intent on sustaining foreign occupation of their fort. Even "a ship known to contain only provisions for Sumter would be stopped and refused admittance," Hurlbut predicted. But all three reported that there would be no starvation at Fort Sumter, if the commander would accept the food that the ladies of Charleston were attempting to send out to the men every day. Although the "starvation" gambit was dead, the reports by Lincoln's spies bolstered his confidence that a military mission to re-supply Fort Sumter would be perceived as technically doable, and that such a mission would produce the desired result. South Carolinians would feel compelled to fire that useful "first shot," which Lincoln believed he needed to persuade the people of the Republican-controlled States and their respective State militia to support him when he began his war. Lincoln figured, with the "first shot" coming from Confederate cannon, Republican newspapers and politicians all over the northern States would, the next day, in orchestrated unison, cry out for patriotic men to take up arms against the alleged "aggressor." And Lincoln hoped that at least one soldier in Fort Sumter would be killed in the melee to properly get the blood flowing.

On March 28 Army Commander-in-Chief Winfield Scott recommended to Lincoln that both Fort Sumter and Fort Pickens be evacuated and turned over to the Confederacy. Scott told Lincoln that evacuating Fort Sumter, while continuing to occupy Fort Pickens, would be viewed as an aggressive move likely to influence other States, notably Virginia, to secede. Therefore, both forts should be evacuated and turned over to the Confederacy. Scott had been born on a large farm near Petersburg, Virginia, attended the College of William and Mary, studied law a bit and served as a Virginia militia cavalry corporal before embarking on a life-long military career with the United States Army. So he was of the Southern culture as were many of the Army's leading officers. The Army Chief's eagerness to avoid war troubled the President greatly.

Apparently, that very afternoon, Lincoln resolved within himself to move toward decisive military action as quickly as possible to arrest the growing peace sentiment. Coincidentally, that very night the President and First Lady held their first official state dinner at the White House.

Most members of the Cabinet attended.  At the conclusion of the affair, Lincoln asked the Cabinet to stay so he could speak with them about the forts.  Lincoln told them that the Army Chief recommended abandonment of both forts, but, he warned, a decision on the matter was his and his alone.  He directed the Cabinet to meet with him the next day to assist him in reaching a decision.

At noon, March 29, President Lincoln convened his Cabinet to press for their blessings to his plans to send warships, troops and transports to Fort Sumter and to unilaterally break the agreement not to reinforce Fort Pickens.  The earlier cover story, the imminent crisis story, the idea that those few Federals at Fort Sumter were running out of food, had been reduced to nonsense by the ladies of Charleston's attempted food delivery campaign, and newspaper coverage of their daily efforts.  The Confederate Secrete Service had made sure that story received wide coverage in Northern newspapers.  So a mercy mission to resupply was no longer considered.  The proposed mission would be to re-enforce and the stated object would be to collect taxes on imports. [38]

Gustavus Fox had completed his initial preparation and planning work at the New York Naval Yard, and he had returned back to Washington City to present directly to Lincoln a practical and executable list of ships, men and war material needed to reinforce both forts.  Fox told Lincoln that the flotilla could be assembled and made ready to steam south in about one week.  So, by circumventing the command structure in the Federal Army and Navy, and by working through Gustavus Fox, a navy man and the brother-in-law of the wife of his Postmaster General, Lincoln now had the specific details he needed to directly order that two armed fleets be quickly assembled, and that they invade the Confederate harbors at Charleston and Pensacola.  It is doubtful that, on March 29, Cabinet members fully comprehended the extent to which Gustavus Fox had already arranged for Lincoln's naval flotilla to be assembled at the New York Naval Yard.  They were about to be asked to express their opinions as if Lincoln was still undecided.

Lincoln submitted to the Cabinet his proposal to reinforce either fort, or both forts.  These were very serious proposals with great potential to propel the United States toward a military invasion of the Confederate States.  So Lincoln asked each man to submit his recommendations in writing, and that they did.

Secretary of State William Seward remained firmly opposed to reinforcing Fort Sumter because he firmly believed that such action would lead to the war of invasion he was striving to avoid.  However, Seward greatly feared Lincoln's militant attitude, and attempted to limit the President's aggression to the less politically sensitive Fort Pickens in hopes of maintaining peace at Fort Sumter.  Applying that psychology, Seward wrote that he favored reinforcing only Fort Pickens.  Caleb Smith agreed with Seward.  Edward Bates supported Seward on reinforcing Fort Pickens, but would not commit one way or the other on Fort Sumter.  Continuing to express hope such a move would not propel the United States toward war, Salmon Chase reservedly gave his blessing to reinforce both Fort Sumter and Fort Pickens.  Apparently changing his position on the issue, Navy Secretary Gideon Welles revealed he would support reinforcing both Fort Sumter and Fort Pickens.  As before, Montgomery Blair was insistent that both forts be reinforced.  In fact, Montgomery's father, Francis Blair, had come to the White House that morning and lectured Lincoln that turning over those forts to the Confederate States would be treason and would dangerously slow the Republican Party's momentum.  Secretary of War Simon Cameron was absent, but he had supported Seward's peace-making stance two weeks earlier.  So Lincoln's chief advisers, the Cabinet plus the Army Chief, were divided five-to-three on Fort Sumter: five opposed a mission (Army Chief Scott, Secretary of State Seward, Interior Secretary Smith,

---

[38] In truthful history Lincoln would stress that the Navy mission was to bring food to the Federal troops that occupied Fort Sumter.

Attorney General Bates, and Secretary of War Cameron) and three, to differing degrees, supported a Navy mission to Fort Sumter (Treasury Secretary Chase, Navy Secretary Welles and Postmaster General Blair). Lincoln read over the written opinions and heard the discussion. We must surmise that he was disappointed that so few blessed the invasion of Charleston Harbor. But Lincoln held the trump card. So, as he had seen courtroom judges do so many times in Illinois, Lincoln announced his decision: A Federal Navy fleet, to be under the direction of Navy Secretary Welles, would be ordered to Charleston Harbor with reinforcements, arms and supplies with the announced intention of placing them in Fort Sumter. Another Navy fleet, to be under the direction of War Secretary Cameron, would be ordered to Pensacola with reinforcements, arms and supplies also with the announced intention of placing them at Fort Pickens.

Abe Lincoln handed Navy Secretary Welles the following directive:

"I desire that an expedition, to move by sea, be got ready to sail as early as the 6th of April next, the whole according to memorandum attached, and that you cooperate with the Secretary of War for that object."

The directive further specified that the flotilla to Charleston Harbor include the warships *Pocahontas* and *Pawnee*, that it include a revenue collection cutter, and that 300 Federal seamen and 200 other Federal soldiers be sent to New York City with combat supplies to go aboard and provide troop support for the mission. He directed that the two fleets depart for Charleston and Pensacola, respectively, by April 6 at the latest. Secretary Welles handed the order to Gustavus Fox with instructions to speed it to New York. Then Lincoln told the Cabinet that as soon as Secretary of War Cameron could be reached, he would be assigned responsibility for the mission to reinforce Fort Pickens, and that ships leave New York no later than April 6. Lieutenant Fox, whose loyalty was to Lincoln, left immediately for New York to ensure that the orders for the Navy mission to Fort Sumter were speedily carried out. Welles obtained Lincoln's agreement that the Federal Navy's most powerful warship, the *Powhatan*, would be commanded by Samuel Mercer and would lead the Navy's mission to Fort Sumter.

Secretary of State Seward was horrified. His Fort Pickens diversionary psychology had failed to defuse the Navy mission against Fort Sumter. [39]

Meanwhile, Confederate Treasury Secretary C. G. Memminger was having great success in selling the Confederate's first offering of $5,000,000 in new government bonds. When all sales would be totaled, the issue would be oversubscribed to $8,000,000 in Confederate money. The Confederate Government was on a sound financial footing and her treasury notes were so well regarded that they could be exchanged for gold. [40]

On April 4, Lincoln wired Lieutenant Fox with final go-ahead orders to set out for Fort Sumter to reinforce it. If the fleet met resistance from shore batteries, the relief force was to retreat and leave those in the fort to defend for themselves. At the same time Lincoln arranged to get a secret message to the garrison in Fort Sumter to expect the fleet to arrive about April 12.

The next day, April 5, a Washington City dispatch to the Montgomery, Alabama *Daily Mail* announced: "The frigate *Powhatan* goes to sea tomorrow morning, fully equipped and provisioned, and will probably take three companies of troops. The impression at the [New York] Navy Yard is that Forts Sumter and Pickens are both to be re-enforced." So people in both countries knew that the Federal Navy armada was about to steam out of the New York Naval Yard for Charleston harbor and Fort Pickens. The fleet of warships and transports ordered to

---

[39] Lincoln's Cabinet votes and orders to Navy commanders are truthful history.

[40] The success of Confederate bond sales is truthful history.

enter Charleston harbor was very large, indeed, consisting of war-ships *Powhatan*, *Pawnee*, *Pocahontas*, and the revenue cutter *Harriet Lane*; steam-tugs *Uncle Ben*, *Yankee* and *Freeborn*, plus the merchant ship *Baltic* with 200 men and the necessary supplies. It was altogether a formidable little armada that was to enter Charleston Harbor consisting of 8 vessels carrying at least 26 guns, maybe more, and about 1,400 men.

At this time Seward warned Lincoln that he had earlier promised the three Confederate Commissioners -- who were still seeking an audience in Washington City -- that Fort Sumter "would not be reinforced without prior notice." So, apparently to accommodate Seward's sensitivities, and to further increase deception, Lincoln, on April 6, dispatched Robert Chew, a clerk in the Federal State Department, to Charleston with a letter to Governor Francis Pickens. Lincoln's order to Chew, dated April 6, said:

> "Sir – You will proceed directly to Charleston, South Carolina; and if, on your arrival there, the flag of the United States shall be flying over Fort Sumter, and the fort shall not have been attacked, you will procure an interview with Governor Pickens and read him as follows: 'I am directed by the President of the United States to notify you to expect an attempt will be made to supply Fort Sumter with provisions only; and that if such an attempt be not resisted, no effort to throw in men, arms, or ammunition will be made, without further notice, or in case of an attack upon the fort.'

> "After you shall have read this to Governor Pickens, deliver him the copy of it herein enclosed, and retain this letter yourself.

> "But if, on your arrival at Charleston, you shall ascertain that Fort Sumter shall have been already evacuated, or surrendered, by the United States force; or shall have been attacked by an opposing force, you will seek no interview with Governor Pickens, but return here forthwith."

On April 7, Robert Anderson received his first written order since the Republicans had taken over the Federal Government. Up until this day the few verbal communications that had come to him had been intended to deceive him. The new message, from Secretary of War Simon Cameron, commanded that he remain in Fort Sumter awaiting resupply by the Navy. He added: "You will therefore hold out, if possible, until the arrival of the expedition." But Lincoln Administration had no real intention of holding Fort Sumter for the long term. Once the "first shot," was drawn, they intended to get Anderson and his men out of Charleston. A few killed Federals would be fine, but a fight to the last man might draw unnecessary criticism. So Cameron advised: "Whenever, if at all, in your judgment, to save yourself and command, a capitulation becomes a necessity, you are authorized to make it."

The same day, April 7, the Secretary of State William Seward answered a "strong letter" from Supreme Court Justice John Campbell demanding to know if past assurances of evacuation at Fort Sumter had been truthful or deceptive. Seward, rarely inclined to be truthful when a lie better served his purposes, replied in writing to Campbell: "Faith as to Sumter fully kept. Wait and see." Judge Campbell forwarded the "promise" to Montgomery, but Jefferson Davis was not deceived, for he personally knew about Seward's propensity to lie for best effect.

The next day, April 8, Robert Anderson, the commander in Fort Sumter, wrote a "distressed letter" to the Adjutant General, Colonel Lorenzo Thomas, in which he appealed for recall of the Federal Navy fleet. Clearly, Anderson did not want war. Yet he was the man who Lincoln had chosen to draw the "first shot." Anderson wrote a postscript asking Thomas to destroy the letter after reading it, for Anderson, a career officer who abhorred insubordination, knew his letter damned the Lincoln Administration. However, Thomas would never receive Anderson's letter, for Confederates in Charleston intercepted the dispatch and sent it to President Davis. Anderson had written:

> "Colonel: . . . I had the honor to receive, by yesterday's mail, the letter of the honorable Secretary of War, dated April 4, and confess that what he there states surprises me very greatly. . . . I trust that this matter will be at once put in a correct light, as a movement made now, when the [Confederacy] has been erroneously informed that none such would be attempted, would produce most disastrous results throughout our [country]. . . . We shall strive to do our duty, though I frankly say that my heart is not in the war, which I see is to be thus commenced. That God will still avert it, and cause us to resort to pacific means to maintain our rights, is my ardent prayer."

When Anderson's letter reached Jefferson Davis, he read it with considerable feeling, because they had been close friends during Jeff's military career. They had been together at West Point. Although Jeff had chosen to retire after 7 years of military service and settle down on a farm, Robert had chosen to make the military his life's career. [41]

On the evening of April 8, Lincoln's agent, Robert Chew, arrived in Charleston and called on Governor Pickens. Chew was the Federal State Department employee Lincoln had picked to attempt to deceive Pickens into believing that the fleet steaming for Charleston harbor was merely going to re-supply the Federal garrison with food, water and lamp oil. Chew read aloud to Pickens the following statement from Lincoln:

> "I am directed by the President of the United States to notify you to expect an attempt will be made to supply Fort Sumter with provisions only; and that if such an attempt be not resisted, no effort to throw in men, arms, or ammunition will be made, without further notice, or in case of an attack upon the fort."

Of course this letter was merely an attempt at further deception. The Federal Navy fleet was far more than would be necessary to deliver supplies to the few well-fed men within Fort Sumter.

By April 9, it was obvious to the Confederate Commissioners that the Lincoln Administration was intent on invasion. Lincoln had repulsed every effort they had made to open up dialogue. He continued to be fervent about ignoring them as if the slightest recognition of their existence might knock the underpinnings from the flimsy legal argument he would make to justify his invasion. The dejected Commissioners – Roman, Crawford and Forsyth – wrote President Lincoln their final letter. They also prepared a copy and sent it to President Davis. Excerpts from their letter to Lincoln follow:

> "Your refusal to entertain these overtures for a peaceful solution, the active naval and military preparations, and the formal notice . . . that the President intends to provision Fort Sumter by forcible means, if necessary . . . can only be received by the world as a declaration of war . . . . The undersigned are not aware of any Constitutional power in the President of the United States to levy war, without the consent of [the Federal House and Senate], upon a foreign People, much less upon any portion of the People of the United States. . . . Whatever may be the result, impartial history will record the innocence of the Government of the Confederate States, and place the responsibility of the blood and mourning that may ensue upon those who have denied the great fundamental doctrine of American liberty, that 'Governments derive their just powers from the consent of the

---

[41] The story of Robert Anderson is truthful history.

governed,' and who have set naval and land armaments in motion to subject the people of one portion of this land to the will of another portion."

## Confederate Response to Lincoln's Aggressive Plans

The three Confederate Commissioners had been kept in the dark about the Davis Administration's plans to refuse to give Lincoln his coveted "first shot." It had seemed best to keep that a secret. So, they were left to assume that Southern pride would compel Confederates to repulse an attempt by Federals to enter Charleston harbor with a fleet of warships. Before departing, the Commissioners forwarded to Montgomery news from that day's issue of the New York *Tribune*: "The *Tribune* of today declares the main object of the expedition to be the relief of Sumter, and that a force will be landed which will overcome all opposition." That same day the New York *Herald* – in defiance of Republican pressures -- courageously charged, "Our only hope now against civil war of an indefinite duration seems to lie in the overthrow of the demoralizing, disorganizing and destructive sectional Party, of which 'honest Abe Lincoln' is the pliant instrument." Lincoln Administration censors, backed by the Federal military, would eventually silence the *Herald* and other newspapers that editorialized against the Republican Party. But for the moment, the men in charge of the *Herald*, dared to defy the Republicans. [42]

From Charleston, General Beauregard telegraphed Montgomery that he was assured by informants that the Federal fleet would soon be at Charleston Harbor, attempting to land men and war materials into Fort Sumter. [43]

Night fell in Montgomery while President Davis conferred with his Cabinet on organizing the Confederate States response to the Federal fleet's imminent arrival in Charleston harbor. A decision to avoid firing the "first shot" had been made two weeks previously, pending unexpected developments -- and nothing unexpected had taken place. But Robert Anderson and his command, holed up in Fort Sumter, did not know that. Intentionally restrained from entering the city and receiving visitors without the approval of the Governor, the soldiers only knew that they were not starving, even though their commander was refusing the daily meal deliveries persistently attempted by the good ladies of the city. They did not know that heavy artillery had been removed and only easily withdrawn field artillery remained at various points around the harbor (some excuses had been published that a few heavy guns were being temporarily moved out of the city for repairs or were being relocated elsewhere along the harbor, giving the impression around town that, although movements were noted, defenses were still in place). The essence of the Confederate response, agreed to that night, was as follows:

To prevent a trigger-happy artilleryman from firing an artillery piece, all cannon loads of gun powder was to be removed from the city a few hours before the fleet arrived.

When the fleet was spotted, the following was to rapidly take place:

1.　　To ensure accurate reporting of the event, all newspapermen in the city (especially those from the Republican States, were to be encouraged to advance to the Battery to witness the proceedings (the Battery was the waterfront edge of the city, giving a fine view of Fort Sumter). The Confederate photographer would set up on the Battery to record the event.

2.　　The field artillery surrounding the harbor was to be withdrawn.

---

[42] The *Herald* editorial is truthful history.

[43] The above history of Lincoln Administration activity is truthful. The Confederate non-militant response is our alternate history.

3.       Confederate army troops and South Carolina State militiamen were to be gathered around their commander and read the message from President Davis, which would explain the importance of the strategy to avoid firing the coveted "first shot." All would be ordered to stack their arms and take positions to watch the proceedings until further orders.

4.       The mayor of the city was to speak to the citizens to explain the strategy of avoiding firing the coveted "first shot" and to seek their cooperation, ensuring them that the wisest councils had been consulted in arriving at this political decision, and that this decision is a sign of strength and wise council, not a sign of foolishness and weakness. They would be told that import and export activity would largely be diverted to other Confederate seaports and coastal places where landing and shipping out goods was workable, because the Federals would be intent on collecting Federal tariffs on goods within their grasp. He would ensure them that Confederate financial aid would compensate importers and exporters for taxes paid, but the major effort would be to relocate import and export activity elsewhere.

There had been a switch of assignments while the Federal fleet was steaming to Charleston: The most powerful Federal warship, the *Powhatan*, was directed to bypass Charleston and proceed to Florida. Command of the Charleston mission was to transfer to the Federal warship *Pawnee*. [44] According to plan, on the morning high tide of April 12, the Federal warship *Pawnee* led the Federal fleet into Charleston harbor, guns at the ready, expecting shore batteries to open fire at any second. *Pawnee* was followed by *Pocahontas*, then the revenue cutter *Harriet Lane*, this being three warships in total. After them came the merchant ship *Baltic* with "brother-in-law" Gustavus Fox on board. The last three to enter Charleston harbor and anchor near Fort Sumter were the steam-tugs, *Uncle Ben*, *Yankee* and *Freeborn*. From shore, people just watched. General Beauregard stood at the ready to engage with any Federal official who came ashore. Newspaper men -- both those representing newspapers to the north and those representing newspapers within the Confederate States -- wrote their stories and headed off to the telegraph office. The Confederate photographer took photographs every hour to ensure he got the best lighting available that day. Some of the rougher sort about town complained loudly that Southerners were just cowards for letting the "damn Yankees" into our harbor. But, overall, the crowds were under control.

Meanwhile, the situation at Florida's Fort Pickens was becoming more grave. When Washington Gwathmey had been ordered to carry Lincoln's message to Fort Pickens, that Navy officer had refused and tendered his resignation. Navy Secretary Welles had then selected John Worden to act as messenger, who had arrived at Pensacola on the afternoon of April 11. Without delay he had sought out the Confederate Commander, Braxton Bragg, and falsely alleged that his mission was to deliver a "verbal message of a pacific nature" to Henry Adams. Eager to maintain a posture of peaceful coexistence, Bragg had agreed to let Worden take a boat out to Fort Pickens. So, on the morning of April 12, Worden took a boat out to Fort Pickens, wrote out Lincoln's order based on his memorization of the thing, and handed the order to Henry Adams, Commander of Federal forces at Pickens and of the Navy ships anchored further offshore. This order personally commanded Henry Adams to violate the standing truce and off-load soldiers, artillery and military supplies from the warship Brooklyn into Fort Pickens. This order undoubtedly demanded that the movement be undertaken secretly at first nightfall and without notifying the Confederates in any way. But word had reached Montgomery that Worden was delivering an

---

[44] We now depart for truthful history with regard to the Federal fleet. In true history the fleet bobbed about off-shore watching the artillery duel it had incited. In this alternate history, the fleet enters the harbor and no artillery is fired.

order to unilaterally break the truce at Fort Pickens, and Confederate Secretary or War Leroy Walker rushed a telegram to Bragg advising him to intercept Worden. But Bragg was tipped off too late. He telegraphed Montgomery, "Mr. Worden had communicated with fleet before your dispatch received."

During the darkness of the Florida night, Federal artillerymen, artillery guns and military equipment were transferred from the Navy warships into Fort Pickens, in violation of the agreement between the Federal Government and what had been at that time the Nation of Florida, for, then, she had just seceded and not yet entered into the Confederacy. [45] The *Powhatan*, which had steamed on beyond Fort Sumter toward Florida was still 5 days away, but Henry Adams had finally decided he had no choice but to obey Abe Lincoln's order to unilaterally violate the armistice. The next day Secretary of War Leroy Walker would show Jeff Davis the telegram from Pensacola reporting the Federals "have violated their agreement. Reinforcements thrown into Fort Pickens last night by small boats from the outside. The movement could not even be seen from our side, but was discovered by a small boat reconnoitering." Worden would be detained when the train he was riding north passed through Montgomery, but he carried no incriminating papers and was released for lack of evidence. [46]

Editor's note:

From this point forward, the history you will be reading is not truthful, but involves historically correct individuals placed in historically correct offices of authority and reacting to events forced upon them in ways consistent with their prior thought processes and biases.

## Wednesday Evening Selected Diary Postings

Diary note by Benedict Juárez said, "I really enjoyed supper with Tina Sharp. She grew up in West Texas and is presently a nuclear engineer working at the Comanche Peak Nuclear Station north of Fort Worth. I appreciated the sincere interest she showed in stories about my Juárez ancestor, but I was more interested in learning about her heritage, which is in Texas oil. Got a short course in ancestor Walter Benona Sharp and how the Sharps-Hughes hardrock drill bit launched the famous Texas Oil Boom at Spindletop in 1901. Her career also involves producing energy. Not with petroleum, but electricity generated with nuclear power."

Diary note by Chris Memminger said, "I am proud of my ancestor Christopher Gustavius Memminger of South Carolina, who was Secretary of the Treasury in the Davis Administration. He and those around him did such a good job at keeping the Confederate dollar strong and taking every advantage of the benefits of strong cotton exports in exchange for military equipment, steam engines and so forth. So much was accomplished in only those first ten months, as Professor Davis will be explaining further tomorrow. International trade will be the focus of my essay. Today was a good day. Goodnight."

Diary note by Marie Saint Martin said, "Tomorrow we will learn further how Secretary Judah Benjamin and my ancestor, Jules Saint Martin, were so, so important in the successful defense of Confederate Independence, perhaps mostly because of their superb management of the Confederate Secret Service. Operating throughout the Northern States during 1861 and 1862, Confederate Secret Service agents helped undercut the Republican arguments urging war against the Confederacy, and helped bolster opposition Democrat Party candidates in State and local

---

[45] In international law it is understood that breaking an armistice by one party is an act of war and the party breaking it is properly accused of starting the conflict.

[46] The Navy action at Fort Pickens is truthful history.

elections and in elections for the Federal House and Senate. And they really confused the North about what was going on in the South, to make the North believe that the South could not or would not defend itself militarily. Passive Resistance was exploited to its fullest. . . . . Oh, yes, I talked with the musicians in our team and we agreed to get together tomorrow afternoon. Looking forward to that!"

Part 1, Chapter 5, Day 4 – Confederates Decline to Fire on Fort Sumter and Intensify Propaganda and Military Preparations – Class Lecture, Thursday, June 9, 2011

Professor Davis continued with his lectures as soon as the twelve were seated and ready to listen.

News that the complete fleet of Federal warships had peacefully entered Charleston Harbor arrived in Washington City on April 13. To those seeking war, this result seemed devastating. Lincoln was in shock! The coveted "first shot" allegation was not his to exploit. Instead he faced a political contest between Davis Administration operatives (former Democrats) and Lincoln Administration operatives (now Republicans) -- and he already sensed that the Davis Administration was far more coy and manipulative than he and fellow Republicans had ever imagined. Republicans had been the masters of political demagoguery and deception. William Seward's maximum seemed to have always been: "Never tell the truth when a well-crafted lie will better serve our purpose." Confederates had always based their political arguments on the Constitution, on law, on individual liberty, on honor and honesty. Something had changed. But Lincoln had never met the Lafitte's.

## The Spring of 1861: A Time of Political Maneuvering, North and South

Lincoln sensed that, with no fireworks at Charleston, and already suffering from effective "peace" propaganda dispensed by the Confederate Secret Service, he had insufficient justification to call up militia from the Republican states -- too few would participate with any eagerness or commit to facing death on the battlefield -- and messages from several Republican governors, especially governor Edwin Morgan of New York, confirmed the public's timidity, particularly concerning the people in New York City and the surrounding metropolitan area. And the Republican governors of Ohio (Dennison), Indiana (Morton) and Illinois (Yates) expressed concerns that many people of the southern half of each of their States were of the Southern culture and would strongly oppose an aggressive military invasion unless, the United States was previously attacked by Confederate military. The United States Army had only 1,080 officers and not quite 15,000 troops -- a force that small could not even prevent secession in Maryland and Kentucky. If tied down in Maryland and Kentucky, no troops would be available to prevent secession in Virginia or Missouri, or invade states further south. What would Lincoln do with the troops in Fort Sumter and Fort Pickens? Those forces were too small to safely venture much beyond the city limits without being captured and rendered ineffective. He knew that he had to call up state militia to build an army of sufficient size to do more than prevent secession in Maryland and collect tariffs in a few seaports. Was he now moving toward a cat and mouse game -- jailing Maryland political leaders and chasing down incoming merchant vessels to force payment of import taxes? There was 1,900 thousand miles of shoreline along the Confederate coast. Lincoln had not the navy to patrol it all.

President Lincoln held a Cabinet meeting of April 15, 1861, to discuss how best to respond to the peaceful reinforcement of Fort Sumter and the "peace" propaganda campaign coming out of the Confederacy. It was becoming more readily known across the Republican states of the north that the people of the seven seceded states only wanted to be left alone. The rather "fantastic" false demagoguery of the 1860 campaign, in which Republicans portrayed the "slaveocracy" of the south as ruffians and villains intent on bringing slavery into the northern States, always a farfetched and illogical argument, but scary none the less, was losing its edge. Lincoln's allegation that lawless elements within the Seceded States had somehow executed an internal revolution was becoming a hard sell, more so in the face of the Confederate's "peace" propaganda campaign. The excitement was dying down. Editorials were appearing again, recommending that the seven wayward sisters be allowed to leave in peace. The Cabinet seemed to be in disarray. Secretary of State William Seward, of New York, reminded everyone that he had consistently argued that the Navy campaign against Fort Sumter and Fort Pickens had been a horrible idea from the start. Postmaster General Montgomery Blair, of Maryland, who had advocated the Navy mission and facilitated it through is wife's brother-in-law, seemed to be at a loss for words when asked, "What should we do now?" Treasury Secretary Salmon Chase, of Ohio, seemed focused on collecting taxes on imports when ships arrived at Charleston, but Navy Secretary Gideon Welles, of Connecticut, reminded the group that he would be unable to prevent incoming vessels from seeking another Confederate seaport elsewhere. Secretary of War Simon Cameron argued that many of the men and officers in the United States Army were reluctant to venture as small bands into the South Carolina and Florida countryside, realizing they would be outnumbered and liable to be captured and thrown in stockades far from the view of comrades. The other two, Bates of Missouri and Smith of Indiana, seemed to want to skirt militant talk. And it would be a long time before Lincoln's Cabinet would be able to agree upon a pro-active plan for dealing with the Seceded States. The three Confederate Commissioners had returned to Washington City again and were always eager to talk. Would any member of Lincoln's Cabinet dare to interact with any of the three?

With his Cabinet undecided, President Lincoln consulted again with Orville Browning of Illinois over his frustration concerning his failure to incite the "first shot." A long-time political friend from Illinois, Browning had written before the inauguration:

> "In any conflict . . . between the [Federal] Government and the seceding States, it is very important that the [Secessionists] shall be [perceived as] the aggressors, and that they be kept constantly and palpable [allegedly] in the wrong. The first attempt . . . to furnish supplies or reinforcements to Sumter will induce [a military response] by South Carolina, and then the [Federal] Government will stand justified, before the entire [Federation], in repelling that aggression, and retaking the forts."

But the Confederates were not behaving as Browning had imagined they would.

Meanwhile, on May 3, in London, Lord John Russell, British Foreign Minister, received the Confederate commissioners to Great Britain, William L. Yancey of Alabama, A. Dudley Mann, a Virginian and former United States career diplomat, and Pierre A. Rost, of Louisiana. (After receiving instructions on March 16, Yancey, Mann and Rost had traveled to Charleston and boarded a ship to England, departing on March 24). Although the meeting at this point was "informal," Russell seemed to understand that, by allowing Federals to reinforce Fort Sumter, Confederates were demonstrating a great reluctance to give President Lincoln his coveted "first shot," while gaining for themselves valuable time to build a military. He deemed the strategy a good political move in that it gave Republican Party politicians -- new to political power and with corresponding impetuous instincts -- time to consult cooler heads. He intended to consult with others in his government and, when appropriate, arrange a second meeting. In short, the diplomatic contact had been cemented. Soon thereafter, Rost, who had been born and educated in France and had helpful contacts there, left London for Paris, for that had been his final diplomatic destination from the start.

### The Seven States Negro Emancipation Conference

On Monday, May 13, 1861 the Seven States Negro Emancipation Conference convened in Montgomery. The Conference, essentially a committee made up of 21 men, three appointed by the governor of each Confederate State, were gathering to develop recommendations for a schedule, procedure and regulation for emancipating the enslaved negro population of each seceded State -- a slow-paced program lasting many years, it was presumed, recognizing that, although coordination would be advantageous, the actual decisions would be made independently by each State, for the Confederate Constitution prevented the central government from ruling on anything concerning emancipation. As Confederate Attorney General, Judah Benjamin was sitting in as a consultant, but he had no official authority. The 21 men appointed by the governors were all White men. But each governor also appointed one free person of color from his state, thereby making up a seven-man Advisory Panel of successful men who were of significant African ancestry. [47]

The immediate purpose of the Emancipation Conference was to dispense propaganda designed to encourage the Republican States of the North to let the South go its own way. But, this propaganda objective was hidden from the newspapermen who attended the opening part of the Conference.

The opening of the Conference, complete with introductions and statements of purpose, was attended by 14 newspapermen, 7 from seceded States, 3 from Democrat-controlled adjacent states and 4 from Republican-controlled states. And newspaper coverage was highly desired, for a program for eventual Negro Emancipation within the Confederate States was seen as a valuable propaganda tool, quite useful in impeding the Lincoln Administration's ability to gain the "high moral ground" as it sought to rally the people of the Republican states to support a call for state militia to reinforce Federal troops in a massive invasion of seceded sister states.

Although Judah Benjamin had no official capacity at the Conference, he did address the Delegates during the first hour, and those remarks were widely printed in newspapers across North America. A bit of his talk is presented below:

"Delegates, allow me to first address the seven free persons of color in attendance here today, each appointed by the governor of his state and asked to participate as an advisory panel. Gentlemen of the Advisory Panel, your contribution to the success of our efforts should be very important. So please pay close attention, discuss ideas among yourselves and with the three delegates from your respective States. President Davis and I want to encourage each State to think about a schedule and procedure for emancipation within its borders. And regarding our urgent need to defend this Confederacy's right to independence, we seek your help, the help of other free persons of color, and the help of persons of color still under ownership. Again, President Davis and I thank you for your help and advice.

"Now addressing the twenty-one Delegates, I congratulate you on taking the initiative in beginning a long and thoughtful process of coordinating the eventual emancipation of the bonded Negroes in your respective states. To be sure, you will be motivated to embrace a program that is most beneficial to each category of your Negro population. You will consider the husband and his wife. You will consider the young children and their nurturing. You will consider the faithful older persons and not leave them wanting. You will consider the young men and women -- many in the prime of young adulthood and eager and able to strike out on their own. You will remember that a relationship of bondage, between the owner and the slave, places well-understood

---

[47] In truthful history there was never a seven States Negro Emancipation Conference. In our alternate history, a conference is held as a propaganda event, aimed at confusing the North and reducing anger in Great Britain toward slave holders in the Confederacy. A bit latter you will see how the press is invited to the opening part of the conference, then asked to leave. After they leave, taking their stories to Democrat newspapers in the North and to Europe, delegates to the Conference talk about ensuring that the process is for propaganda purposes and emancipation is to be gradual and carefully managed. This Conference is a significant propaganda tool and served to slow the efforts of the Lincoln Administration to win support for a war.

obligations upon the shoulders of both -- the owner is responsible for the welfare of the slave and, in the case of the woman, for the welfare of her children -- the slave is responsible for being productive and cooperative to the best of his or her ability. And a responsible owner is sensitive to the desire of most bonded women to remain with her chosen husband. But, when children reach the productive age of, say 16 years, opportunities naturally arise for these young men and women to leave their parents and move on to a new life elsewhere when and if the owner sees wisdom in such a move, for the owner may, simply stated, have no remaining useful work for the maturing child and needs to ensure that, wherever that useful work can be found, a transfer to another owner might well be best for all concerned. Yet these decisions can be difficult, for so often, especially on rural farms, owner families and slave families have played together as children, and worked side-by-side as youths and young men and women. In short, many are close friends.

"As of our 1860 census, the Negro population in the seven Confederate states totaled 2,349,063 persons of which 36,811 were not slaves, but free and independent people of color. The corresponding population in the states to the north of our boundary totaled 2,090,450, of which 213,976 lived as free individuals in states that permitted slavery and 238,315 lived as free individuals in states further north, which are now controlled by the Republican Party. From the start of the importation of Negroes from Africa and the Caribbean, to its conclusion 53 years ago, only about 300,000 enslaved Africans were shipped into seaports along the shores of what is now the Confederate States of America. Yet, in our seven states we enjoy a Colored population that has expanded on the order of 800 percent, which constitutes evidence of, for the most part, good treatment with regard to bearable workloads, plus adequate food, shelter and medical care.

"Yet, many Negroes today naturally wish to join the ranks of their free and independent brothers and sisters. Furthermore, many owners of Negroes, especially those on very large and mature farms and plantations, are facing greater and greater problems in finding useful work to justify retention of the entire laboring group, especially in the future when advancing science, engineering and industrialization enables farm productivity improvements through new and exciting machinery and labor saving equipment, such as Cyrus McCormick's reaper. So, future economic concerns point to reductions in the work force on many farms, but some owners are reluctant to see some of their Negroes depart and face an unknown future under the ownership of another individual, perhaps hundreds of miles distant. Furthermore, the Republican states, for the most part, permit immigrants from Europe to freely come into their midst and settle there, but not the Negro. Enforced by its state constitution, Illinois, the home state of President Lincoln, prohibits immigration by a free person of color. [48] And movement by free and independent negroes within the states that do permit slavery can be a trying affair, for a counterfeit-proof method of issuing documents giving evidence of free status is badly wanting of improvement. So, I earnestly ask that you give some attention to the issue of improving our documentation of a person of color's free and independent status, including adoption of the photographic methods that are just now becoming available, for it is imperative that our free and independent people of color not be enslaved by criminals who circumvent our slavery laws.

"You will be looking toward drafting an emancipation schedule that will, perhaps, over a period of several decades, complete the emancipation of your entire population of slaves in your respective state. But you must show more urgency to advance emancipation

---

[48] Prohibition of Free People of Color moving into Illinois is truthful history.

than has Abraham Lincoln. For example, in a speech delivered at Charleston, Illinois, in debate with Senator Stephen Douglas, not quite three years ago, on September 18, 1858, before a crowd of 12,000, Lincoln said he envisioned a schedule for eliminating slavery that would exceed one hundred years. My, God, gentlemen, 100 years exceeds four generations. As Christian people, surely, we can do better than that.

I quote briefly from Lincoln's 1858 speech:

'I do not mean that when [opposition to slavery] takes a turn toward ultimate extension it will be in a day, nor in a year, nor in two years. I do not suppose that in the most peaceful way ultimate extinction would occur in less than one hundred years at least; but that it will occur in the best way for both races, in God's own good time, I have no doubt.' [49]

"So Mr. Lincoln envisioned that 100 years would be needed to complete a peaceful transition to a society where all Negroes would be free and independent. For God's sake, fellow Confederates, we can do better than that!

"Within the framework of an overall program for each of your states, you will undoubtedly be envisioning plans that foresee making free and independent even the last remaining slaves in far less time than one hundred years. And I leave those discussions to you, where they rightly belong. But let me make two recommendations for your consideration. First, if you find a way to begin a token emancipation process, on a very small scale to be sure, but in sufficient numbers to demonstrate the South's feelings of good will toward our loyal Negro population, then consider pursuing such a modest goal very soon, even this summer. Perhaps 2,000 of the most capable could be enrolled in a provisional program within weeks. Second, where the Confederate Government can be helpful over the next few weeks in providing security and transportation in support of a modest beginning of a token emancipation program, please ask us to consider participating. And give proper thought to where these newly-emancipated recruits would be relocated: consider four possibilities where they might settle:

1. Perhaps they would settle within the state where they presently live; or,
2. Perhaps settle in a sister state in the Confederacy; or,
3. Perhaps migrate to a state to the north of our boundary which also permits slavery; or,
4. Perhaps migrate even further north to a state, now controlled by the Republican Party, where a few free people of color presently live and where problems of reliable emancipation documentation would be a minimal concern."

At this point Judah Benjamin had concluded his presentation. This first phase of the Seven States Negro Emancipation Conference, which had been open to newspapermen and observers, was over. It had consumed just over one hour. The 21 Delegates, the Advisory Panel of free People of Color, and Judah Benjamin thanked the observers and newspapermen and announced they would, at that time, begin their closed door meeting, and would announce at some later time when a press release was forthcoming. Several days were envisioned for the discussions, as Delegates anticipated needs to periodically communicate with governors and other leaders in their respective States.

When the closed door meeting began, Judah Benjamin presented further guidance, which, for our purposes is best condensed into the following concepts:

---

[49] The quote and date of Lincoln's speech is truthful history.

- All recognized that slaves in the Confederate States were of widely different ability and that, in many hearts, considerable White blood flowed, meaning they were not a pure race, but a racial mix of varying proportions. Almost all living slaves had been born in a Southern state, for the African immigrant was now seldom seen. All attending the Conference recognized that many slaves were skilled at agriculture and animal husbandry; many were raising fine, moral families; many were leaders on the farms where they lived, including acting as foremen over others; many were exceptionally skilled at a trade, such as blacksmithing or bookkeeping.

- The care of children of slaves had to be carefully considered. Many slaves were old and deserved the light work assignments and care given by those who had owned them for many decades. But most importantly, all recognized that each individual was a unique person whose future path from slavery to independent living needed to be designed to best suit everyone with whom he or she was involved.

- The Conference realized that limiting emancipation to only slaves who would volunteer to migrate into a Northern state would sharply shrink the field of candidates. The South was their home, and migrating into a Northern state might result in harsh treatment, hardship and even death. There were real risks. But the immediate need was for heroes to step forward and help the Confederate Secret Service induce fear in the North that a Federal conquest of the Confederacy would likely result in hundreds of thousands of free people of color migrating into their state to become their neighbors.

- Although there was sincere interest in developing thinking regarding future emancipation, the propaganda usefulness of a token start was of paramount immediate interest, because impeding the Lincoln Administration's effort to win state militia support for a large military invasion of the Confederacy was imperative. That was the reason Confederates did not force Federals out of Fort Sumter and that was the reason they believed, through propaganda emerging from this Conference and other targeted messaging, they could secure further high moral ground.

- Therefore, Benjamin advised, "this Conference needs to advocate an emancipation plan that our States can embrace, which is very gradual and not absolute, which can be modified as the years pass by, which makes good common sense and which will be useful in winning support abroad, especially among the honest and good people in Great Britain, and in the Republican-controlled States to the north."

- "The Davis Administration does not envision compensated emancipation by which tax payers pay owners to make their slaves free and independent. So the plan emerging from this Conference must be considerate of the investment of the owner as well as the welfare and aspirations of the slave, thereby striking a balance whereby both interests are somewhat balanced."

- "The Davis Administration believes an immediate and public message should emerge from this Conference. Should not this Conference suggest a specific program for the immediate emancipation of, say 400 carefully selected and willing Negro families, totaling 2,000 individuals who will accept emancipation within a few weeks and embark on journeys to the Republican-controlled states to the North? That needs honest discussion."

- "Please understand me – we all know that the newly emancipated free people of color of which we speak will prefer to remain in the Confederate States and thereby avoid migration into the Republican States. But we need for the North to learn to worry, seriously worry, that forcing seceded states back under Federal control will result in Negro migration into their communities."

- "Consider a partnership whereby owners voluntarily emancipate the individuals and the Confederate Government handles transportation, financing and brief training to make the relocation program a success. Should not that be the bargain to be struck in the next few weeks, for time is of the essence?"

- "Another path to emancipation is being discussed among military men: emancipation in exchange for military service. You should consider a second emancipation program where men of color are accepted in State militia as trained fighting men. They would be spread out among the militia units and represent a small percentage of troop strength. If slaves, they would gain freedom after honorable service under battlefield conditions, for we greatly worry that all we are attempting to do peacefully will fail, and we will eventually face a military invasion."

- At this point Benjamin became quite specific about emancipation in exchange for migration north into Republican states: "You may have a better idea, but President Davis suggests 400 individuals from South Carolina be asked to accept emancipation in exchange for relocation to Massachusetts; 400 from Georgia be asked in exchange for relocation to New York State; 400 from Alabama be asked in exchange for relocation to Pennsylvania; 400 from Mississippi be asked in exchange for relocation to Ohio, and 400 individuals from Louisiana be asked in exchange for relocation to Illinois. This would total 2,000 individuals. By the way, the best estimate of the number of runaway slaves that have passed through the so-called 'underground railroad' on their way to Canada is approximately 2,000 individuals. So, we are asking the Republican states to the north to, this time, allow our emancipated people of color to live among their people and forego pushing them north to Canada. If the people of those states accept Negro emigrants, we believe they will enjoy the benefits of a multi-racial society -- and we encourage that. We believe you will have no problem getting enough owners to contribute the 400 agreeable families we suggest. President Davis will offer, from his Mississippi cotton farm, two very qualified families totaling 10 individuals, and he expresses confidence those will accept the proposal. We expect many more owners will strike such bargains with very qualified slaves."

- "Our emphasis on the propaganda purposes of our emancipation program must remain secret, and from time to time you will have to deny it."

The Seven States Negro Emancipation Conference concluded on Thursday, May 23, ten days after it had begun. The recommendations of the Davis Administration, as relayed by Attorney General Judah Benjamin were found worthy and became the backbone of the policy recommended to the respective States. A press release that Thursday afternoon was received by numerous newspapermen and forwarded to newspapers all across North America and to important cities in Europe. Because it was a sensational story, it received prominent publicity. It seemed to be a worthwhile propaganda tool, affording the new Confederate Government significant elevation toward higher moral ground.

Mr. Lincoln, less than three years earlier, had suggested that complete peaceful emancipation of all Negroes would require more than one hundred years — you heard me right — 100 years. The Seven States Negro Emancipation Conference recommended, as a general but not concrete guide, 50 percent emancipated by 19 years (1880), 90 percent by 29 years (1890) and 100 percent by 39 years (1900). And the Conference stressed marriage, keeping families together and keeping children with their mothers through age 16. The Conference recommended a work-for-emancipation apprenticeship program whereby young men and women who worked for owners from age 16 to age 23, a period of 7 years, if married, would have earned the right to request to become free and independent themselves and also any young children belonging to the couple. If not yet married, the age advanced to 25 years, resulting in a 9 year program (the status of young children belonging to an unmarried female at the 9-year stage was not clearly defined). The objective was to strike a balance between allowing the owner to receive the monetary value of at least seven years of work while also ensuring that the newly freed person of color was well trained and capable of successful independent living.

The delegates from five of the seven States also recommended that a limited number of adult Colored men be inducted into their respective State Militia. These men could be either free or slave. If slave, the owner was, of course, involved in the process. A slave who successfully supported his fellow militia men in peace and in war was promised emancipation by the thirty-sixth month of his service as would his wife and children. A free Colored man could also designate his wife and children to be emancipated by the thirty-sixth month should any be slaves. Colored men in the militia were to be armed and trained fighters, integrated into militia units in such a way that they were evenly distributed among the ranks. No Colored man could become an officer. Colored men were to be a small minority, representing not more than seven percent of troops (it was suggested that Louisiana allow up to ten percent). The Conference realized that White people would object to militia units made up entirely of Colored Men – to ensure proper behavior Colored men should be a small minority in the unit to which each man was assigned.

## The Confederate Secret Service Infiltrates the Northern Mind

While the various Confederate States considered how to deal with the recommendations of the Seven States Negro Emancipation Conference, rapid progress was made in recruiting the 400 families (2,000 individuals) needed for the first emancipation phase – a propaganda action -- and their relocation into the Republican states to the north. Within two weeks, secretly and without press coverage, by June 6, over one hundred newly-emancipated families from Louisiana, Mississippi, and Alabama were aboard steamboats moving north up the Mississippi and Tennessee rivers to Illinois and into the Ohio River and on to Ohio and Pennsylvania, and scores more were aboard steamships moving north up the Atlantic coast from Charleston and Savannah toward Massachusetts and New York. Agents in the Confederate Secret Service helped the groups move safely into new locations where they could settle down. Of European ancestry, each agent helped groups stay away from unnecessary public view and had handy papers showing the people in the groups were slaves being escorted into Canada or some other deception. The object was to get the groups settled within the targeted State before the commotion began. The typical family was a husband and wife and three children. The typical group was two families. The typical racial composition of recruits was nearly pure African ancestry, for it was considered helpful if the Negroes moving north were clearly African in appearance. However, a group leader was, on occasion, a man of mixed race with a noticeable European component in his ancestry. The agent brought money to allow each group to purchase a horse and wagon and some tools, and to buy food for two months. They brought clothing and blankets with them. But the summer weather was most helpful. These volunteers were brave people. They were moving into hostile regions in defiance of laws that excluded free people of African ancestry from taking up residence. They were pretending to be just passing through as persons bonded to an owner as long as that deception worked. Of course, they had been emancipated in exchange for volunteering for this Secret Service assignment, but that was their secret. As the weeks and months went by, some would suffer harsh treatment. Some would be robbed of everything they owned. Some women would be raped and some men would be killed, but the losses would not be nearly as bad as some had feared. In confronting these obstacles, the recruits showed immense courage, of which numerous monuments existing today throughout the participating States now testify. The Secret Service agents and the brief training the newly emancipated received before boarding the steamboats and steamships, and additionally while aboard, had been very helpful. Their presence in the North sparked controversies in many places and, after two or three months, news of such events became worrisome to many citizens of the Northern States. They were debating the question: "If we force the Confederates back under the Federal Government, will that not open the way for a million Blacks to come north and settle in our communities? If we just let the Confederates go, can we not easily exclude Blacks from our States?" [50]

The Confederate Secret Service, under the able leadership of Attorney General Judah Benjamin with the full support of President Davis and members of his Cabinet, grew over the summer of 1861 into a large and influential organization with agents working assignments all across the Democrat-controlled States to the north and, most importantly, the Republican-controlled States beyond. By the end of the summer the roster of agents out in the field and on the move who were working full time at their craft exceeded 1,000, and those who had lived and worked in their communities in the North for many years and were supporting the cause on a part-time basis, gathering information and disseminating propaganda, could never be counted, but surely exceeded 5,000. Many of these agents were women. And many of these agents and their supporting contacts were of full or partial African ancestry, which was most helpful since Republicans, by their nature, never suspected Negroes of being capable of working as secret agents, and many of these agents were from Louisiana with easy access to steamboat travel as far north as Wisconsin and as far east at Pennsylvania. Many spoke French or broken French which afforded important cover in communications, especially in written communication further confused by being put down in code. Substantial rewards were promised to Colored agents. If slave, they would be emancipated, along with family members. If free, they would be given money to enable the purchase of land or to improve their living standards.

The work of Secret Service agents and their contacts was particularly influential with Democrat political activists, with people living in the North who had relatives in the South, and with newspapermen looking for a good story. Through these channels, the State Republican parties stretching from Pennsylvania westward lost considerable influence and the peace movement grew strength. From time to time during the summer of 1861, the Lincoln Administration and cooperative Republican governors thought they were close to justifying a large call-up of State militia, only to shy away and wait for a better excuse, for the threat of another massive wave of State secessions loomed large.

Since February 1861, the Virginia Secession Convention had remained at the ready to vote on a three-day notice. The Maryland legislature, only on temporary recess, had a Secession bill out of committee and on the floor with defined districts for each Delegate (matched the Maryland House of Representatives districts) and in many of these districts, voters had selected their Delegates through local election processes. Kentucky, under the guidance of Democrat Governor Beriah Magoffin, was pursuing the same strategy as Maryland, but was further along in selecting Delegates. By August, Governor Magoffin believed he could orchestrate Kentucky Secession through the Convention process in 10 days and through a final vote by the people 10 days later. Except for Louisville, sentiment for secession seemed to have strong support in Kentucky if amplified by a military attack on a seceded State. The Governor of Missouri, Democrat Claiborne Jackson, was eager to advance secession and viewed the only obstacle in his way to be the large German immigrant population that had arrived in St. Louis during the 1850's. The fledgling Missouri Republican Party (although only of significance in St. Louis) had been unusually effective in organizing the Germans of that city into a paramilitary force which had cowed many long-time residents, most of those being of the Southern culture. But agents in the Confederate

---

[50] In truthful history free Blacks were excluded from settling in most northern States. They were excluded by State laws, and State constitutions. As a result, the presence of the volunteers in our alternate history was designed to challenge those laws for propaganda purposes, and to make citizens in the North eager to let Confederates go in peace in exchange for the racial purity they sought within their State.

Secret Service, selected for their skill in speaking German, were making good progress in breaking up the political union between Republican leaders and German leaders, ensuring that Confederate peace propaganda was effectively delivered in the city. In North Carolina, Tennessee and Arkansas, secession conventions had previously met and adjourned. But, the governors of all three States had called special summer sessions of their state legislatures to authorize each of those secession conventions to reconvene in the event the Lincoln Administration called for a military attack on sister States to the South. Democrat North Carolina Governor John Ellis was authorized to convene his state's convention, as were Democrat Tennessee Governor Isham Harris and Democrat Arkansas Governor Henry Rector. So the threat of imminent secession of Virginia, Kentucky, Missouri, North Carolina, Tennessee and Arkansas weighed heavily on the minds of Republican leaders in the Lincoln Administration. Of the eight Democrat-controlled states, only Maryland and little Delaware looked doubtful for secession if provoked. [51]

A major aspect of the Confederate peace propaganda was assurance that the Mississippi and Tennessee rivers would be open for steamboat traffic between the Confederacy and the United States. And as every week came and went it was more obvious to people along the Mississippi, Tennessee, Ohio and Missouri rivers that steamboat travel was unimpeded. [52] News in this regard was most influential in St. Louis, Evansville, Louisville, Cincinnati and Wheeling. Furthermore, the Confederate Government had set up steamboat checkpoints near the Mississippi-Tennessee state boundary to quickly inspect cargo and write up cargo manifests to be forwarded to Montgomery and to Washington City. Similar checkpoints were set up where railroads crossed the border. The Lincoln Administration was invited to also man import-export stations at these checkpoints, but throughout the summer, President Lincoln persisted in his fabrication that the Confederate Government did not exist. So the forwarded cargo manifests were only filed away in Washington City. In Montgomery, to support the Confederate peace propaganda program, they were totaled up and issued as press releases to newspapers both north and south. The Confederacy did not charge any tax on goods moving south through these river and railroad checkpoints, and the delay for inspection only took about one hour on average.

## Confederate Defensive Preparations — James Eads, John Ericsson and Cornelius DeLamater

Considerable progress was made during the summer in strengthening the capability of the Confederate States to defend against military attack. We first examine the efforts to strengthen defense against gunboat attacks from the north.

With the help of Pierre Lafitte, James Buchanan Eads [53] of Missouri was recruited in early May to contribute his remarkable ability toward the best Confederate defenses on the Mississippi and Tennessee rivers and to design and oversee construction of Confederate iron-clad gunboats of the most advanced designs.

---

[51] The history of the threats of secession by Virginia, Kentucky, Missouri, North Carolina, Tennessee and Arkansas rather accurately reflects truthful history, as does the lesser likelihood of secession by Delaware and Maryland.

[52] In truthful history, prior to Lincoln's proclamation of war, free navigation of the Mississippi River was assured by the Davis Administration and ignored by Republicans.

[53] Born in 1820 in Lawrenceburg, Indiana, on the banks of the Ohio River, just west of Cincinnati, Ohio, Eads had moved west with his parents to St. Louis, Missouri, where he grew up and remained. He was a self-trained engineer who had become wealthy salvaging boats that had sunk along the Mississippi River. He invented a diving bell with which he walked the river bottom, setting up rigging for salvage recoveries. And he knew the river better than even the best steamboat pilots, and river knowledge was a valuable skill indeed, as many wrecks had occurred over the past 40 years, since the beginning of steamboat transport.

Eads, operating under a contract with the Confederate Government, relocated his operations to Commerce, Mississippi and to Baton Rouge, Louisiana. From his St. Louis facility and other smaller facilities in Missouri he brought south his salvage boats and his equipment and tooling. Commerce was a small river town 45 miles south of Memphis, and Baton Rouge was a thriving city with considerable manufacturing capability. Furthermore, his knowledge of older steamboats available for sale and steam engines and other critical equipment was very useful in the direction of a sizable purchase program along the upper Mississippi River and the Ohio River. [54]

But James Eads did not have to work alone in pursuit of the river-defense goals of the Confederacy, for he had the help of John Ericsson. Ericsson was a Swedish-American inventor and noted mechanical and marine engineer. [55] Recruited in 1939 by Captain Robert Stockton of the United States Navy, Ericsson moved to New York City to design a steam-powered warship for the United States navy that utilized his twin screw propeller technology and other improvements. He was 36 years old. Three years later, the navy sloop he designed, *USS Princeton*, was launched. The *Princeton* was a technical success, winning a speed trial in 1843, beating the paddle-wheel steamer, *SS Great Western* -- then considered the fastest steamer afloat. However, the celebration was cut short when one of the two big guns on the *USS Princeton* exploded during a test firing demonstration -- a most unfortunate event since aboard the ship at the time was President John Tyler, Secretary of State Abel P. Upshur and Secretary of the Navy Thomas Gilmer. Although President Tyler escaped injury, the gun barrel explosion killed Upshur, Gilmer and six navy men. Captain Stockton blamed the failure of the gun on engineer Ericsson and made every attempt to avoid personal responsibility. But the facts of the matter pointed the finger at Stockton, for the main gun, still intact, had been designed by Ericsson with iron bands to re-enforce the barrel. A second gun, the one that exploded, had been designed by Captain Stockton. It was Stockton's gun that was inadequate. Although the gun's explosion was unrelated to the ship upon which it was mounted, the United States Navy declined to pursue construction of more warships driven by screw propellers. And, clever at Navy politics, Stockton's career advanced. [56] Meanwhile, John Ericsson's career declined. [57]

But John Ericsson remained in New York and continued to work closely with a successful industrialist, Cornelius DeLamater -- a relationship that advanced Ericsson's practical knowledge concerning all aspects of foundry operations and metal fabrication. By 1857, DeLamater Iron

---

[54] In truthful history, the Lincoln Administration successfully won over Eads to design and build iron-clad gunboats for the Federal invasion down the Tennessee and Mississippi rivers, and these Eads gunboats -- of superior design and rapidly manufactured by his company -- contributed greatly to Federal victories in that theater of war.

[55] Born in 1803 in Sweden, John Ericsson had, as a young man, developed impressive skills in surveying and mechanical design. In 1826, at age 23, he had moved to England where he excelled in naval design -- especially the screw propeller, which was to emerge as the replacement for the large paddle wheel. He had also become expert at steam engine applications and iron-clad battleship design.

[56] You have been reading truthful history. Captain Stockton's navy career continued upward. He rose in rank to Commodore and played a leading role in the conquest of the Mexican state, Alta Californio, which became the American state of California, of which he was military governor in 1846-1847. He was elected to the United States Senate as a Democrat from his home state of New Jersey in 1851, but resigned in 1853 to pursue a private career.

[57] The American navy distanced itself from Ericsson and designs based on the screw propeller -- an emotional and illogical decision since the explosion had nothing to do with the warship's propulsion. Meanwhile, Ericsson looked elsewhere for applications for his advanced naval technology. In 1854 he presented Napoleon III of France with drawings of an iron-clad armored battle ship with a dome-shaped gun tower. Although the French government "praised the work," it declined to build Ericsson's battle ship.

Works was a very large operation, proficient at all aspects of iron fabrication, with hundreds of skilled employees. [58]

At the same time that Pierre Lafitte was recruiting James Eads in St. Louis, two other agents in the Confederate Secret Service were in New York City recruiting naval engineer John Ericsson to work alongside Eads and were seeking to transform Cornelius DeLamater's iron works into a dedicated production facility to work full time secretly filling orders for the Confederacy. Ericsson was easily won over to the cause of the Confederate States, for he was still smarting over how he had been mistreated by Captain John Stockton of the United States Navy, and how it seemed so unfair that Stockton's career had advanced to great heights while his had been "brutally suppressed." Ericsson accepted a generous salary to leave New York and work with James Eads.

It took the Confederate agents a bit longer to win the cooperation of Cornelius DeLamater. He and wife Ruth, married for 17 years, had five daughters and one son. His focus had been on family and advancing metals technology, using his business skills and mechanical engineering skills to advantage. DeLamater was a good man. In hopes of winning his cooperation, the agents explained:

- The seceded States just wanted to be independent, but zealots in the Republican Party were maneuvering to launch a war to prevent it

- The stronger the Confederate defenses, the more likely would be a peaceful separation.

- The Confederate Government would present to both DeLamater and Ericsson opportunities to advance the technologies at which both are so proficient, unleashing their skills for the whole world to see.

Persuaded, DeLamater accepted handsome fees for entering into a secret cost-plus contract with the Confederate Government to supply future orders for a variety of items in sufficient volume to fully occupy his facility and its work force. A deal was struck and DeLamater began expediting the completion of orders on the books and clearing the slate for anticipated orders from the Confederacy. A secret book of accounts was set up so that men working on Confederate orders were unaware of the true customer. In a sidebar agreement, DeLamater agreed to let the Confederate agents recruit ten percent of his workforce, along with their tools, for jobs within the Confederacy, replacing them with a like number from the Confederacy in need of training in metals technology. A turnover every two months was thought about right. Yes, bringing skilled men into expanding Confederate metal working facilities was just as important as bringing in finished goods. Many of the items manufactured for the Confederacy were components for machining tools, shipped separately, but when assembled in the South, the finished assembly was ready for use in production of firearms, steam engines, etc. Most notable were hand presses designed for resizing brass casings from spent bullets, for it was very important that the brass casings be retained and recycled in the field.

---

[58] Born in 1821 near the Hudson River, half-way between New York City and Albany, Cornelius DeLamater had moved to New York City with his parents at age 3. He began work at age 16 in a small iron foundry in the city that was named Phoenix Iron Works -- "little more than a blacksmith shop" -- learning the business from the ground up. Soon after John Ericsson had arrived in New York City in 1839, he became friends with DeLamater and looked to Phoenix Iron Works to produce most everything he designed. At age 20, DeLamater and his cousin Peter Hogg bought the business, changed the name and continued expanding it. Then, four years later, in 1857, Hogg retired and the business became DeLamater Iron Works. This history of DeLamater and his New York City iron works is truthful.

At the same time, Ericsson packed into two bags his clothes and into four crates his engineering resource papers, calculations, designs and notes of all kinds and set out to board a steamer headed to New Orleans. He would be along-side James Eads by early June, and by late-June, the two experts would have a completed design for the Confederate River Defender Gunboat: a swift iron-clad gunboat suitable for chasing down and sinking any iron-clad gunboat the Federals might build and bring downriver. The focus would be on compact size, high speed, a low profile, shallow draft, good stability to ensure gunnery accuracy, and two rifled cannon with armor-piercing projectiles and good maneuverability. This revolutionary riverboat would be a shallow-draft, tri-hull design capable of superior pursuit and pin-point firing precision. Eads stayed close at hand directing construction, but Ericsson traveled to Baton Rouge, Montgomery, Savannah and elsewhere as needed to facilitate procurement of parts. When built, the resulting Eads-Ericsson craft would be a sight to behold. [59]

During the summer Eads, taking advantage of his diving bell technology, identified sites on the Mississippi River where snags could be moved into place to concentrate river traffic to narrow passages below which Confederate mines could be laid. A Confederate agent remarked, "Since James Eads is clearly the most skillful man in North America when it comes to removing snags from the river and salvaging wrecks sunk in the river, surely he will be the best at planting snags and mines in the river to sink boats coming down the river." Mines were built at armories in the Confederacy and shipped to Eads to be ready for deployment in the river bed if an invasion force threatened. [60] These mines were designed to be anchored to the river bottom, rest just below the water surface and explode when struck by a steamboat.

The coal torpedo and was also a significant weapon in the hands of Secret Service agents. These weapons were bombs designed to be inadvertently tossed into the fire under steamboat boilers. In one torpedo design, gunpowder and a fuse were built into iron castings made to look like a lump of black coal. The coal torpedo was particularly resistant to deterioration in rainy weather. The torpedoes were taken north to safe houses where Confederate agents could get to them when needed and toss them onto coal piles to be taken by crew onto steamboats. Eventually there would be a huge blast, the boiler would burst and the steamboat would quickly sink.

---

[59] The Confederate River Defender Gunboat was made of three hulls connected at the top but looking like three large canoes when viewed from below the water. By this method, the design ensured a stable platform for accurate firing and a fast speed. The starboard hull held one forward-facing cannon as did the leeward hull. The propulsion system was an Ericsson design, powered by one steam engine in the center hull, which drove a twin-drive-train gear box with two power takeoffs. The gear box contained two drive trains, each with a manual clutch, a forward gear and a reverse gear and a power takeoff shaft which sloped slightly into the water and drove the attached propeller. Stated another way the craft had one steam engine, one twin-drive-train gear box and two propellers, one between the center hull and the starboard hull, and one between the center hull and the leeward hull. The smokestack presented a very small target for the enemy —it was only 3 feet tall and contained a steam-driven fan to provide a forced draft at the firebox (a manual hand crank got the fire started and, once a head of steam was attained, the fan's steam turbine drove the fan). The deck on top was flat and iron-clad at critical points to deflect incoming artillery projectiles, especially from out in front of the craft, for it would normally be in chase mode. The craft had a draft of 3 feet and a height above the water line of 7 feet. The overall width was 20 feet and the overall length was 60 feet. The guns were aimed by steering the craft directly toward the enemy using a captain's cross-hair sight. With two guns in operation, a round could be fired every 45 seconds. The gunboat was designed to work very well during one-on-one engagements with the enemy, but it could find itself in dire straits if forced to fight off a pack of several enemy gunboats. But that was to be avoided and the fast speed of the gunboat, and its ability to turn around "on a dime" and rapidly flee to safety would prove very effective at the task to which it would be assigned. A favorite attack tactic would be to let the enemy pass by while hiding along the riverbank, then pursue and attack while chasing the enemy downriver, hopefully an enemy in a state of panic.

[60] The mine was activated when a man in a rowboat pulled the pin connected by a rope to a float. It would then explode when hit. When no longer needed, the mine could be raised to the surface by pulling a second rope and be defused. Sights on the river bank permitted locating every mine by triangulation.

While Eads and his men pursued advance their work, and while Secret Service agents pursued their goals, the Confederate Army was working to set up artillery to repulse invaders coming downriver. Guns were coming in from purchases made in Europe, and some from islands in the Caribbean were purchased cheaply and brought in for overhaul.

### The Summer of 1861, Confederate Strategic Plans Advance while, to the North, Democrats and Secret Service agents Agitate for Peace and Republicans Flounder.

During the summer of 1861 Confederate agents traveled widely in the manufacturing regions of the northern States, recruiting skilled workmen to take good paying jobs in the South and purchasing metal-working equipment to equip southern shops. Target industries were weapons manufacturing and steam engine manufacturing. Further west, agents sought used steamboats suitable for renovation and purchased them when they could. These were loaded with important equipment and supplies and towed downstream to mooring sites near Commerce and Baton Rouge.

Furthermore, by mid-summer, it was apparent to the Republican Leadership in Washington City that they could not be confident of achieving a majority vote in the Federal House or the Federal Senate in favor of a military invasion of the seceded States. The Confederate propaganda campaign had achieved great success within four neighboring States -- Virginia, North Carolina, Tennessee and Arkansas – success in each State at building a majority consensus to bring all resources to bear on building a well-armed State militia and in establishing a State Constitutional Convention empowered to proclaim secession at a moment's notice. Further north, in Delaware, Maryland, Kentucky and Missouri, public opinion was firmly against approval in Congress of military action against the seceded states. These eight States, represented in Washington City by 16 Senators and 57 Representatives, were firmly opposed to military action. Maybe Representative Francis Blair, Jr. in Missouri would vote for military action without provocation, but hardly anyone else. Provocation was the issue at hand. Without some sort of military attack upon Federals by at least a few Confederates, public opinion **against** going to war was gaining strength, month by month.

Agitation in most northern States over the summertime arrival of a few families of newly emancipated Negroes added to the problems besetting Republicans -- it was harder to demonize southern States people over slavery when northern States were in an uproar over the arrival of a few families of newly emancipated negroes -- it was harder to counter Peace Democrats who explained that Negroes would be barred from coming north if they lived in a separate country, a recognized Confederate country. The Abolitionists' higher moral authority was beginning to crumble as passions focused on Exclusionism and Deportationism.

In the Federal Senate Republicans had started out in March with 29 Republicans versus 24 Democrats and one (1) American Party fellow from Maryland. But, Republican Senator Ed Baker of Oregon had died in an accident and the Oregon Governor, himself a Democrat and opposed to going to war, had appointed a peace Democrat to fill the seat. [61]

That dropped the Republican strength to 28, only 2 more than required to win the "war" vote. But, several Republican Senators -- representing states where citizens were becoming more and more opposed to war -- were publicly advocating against military invasion. Most notable of this group was Martin Wilkerson of Minnesota and Preston King of New York.

---

[61] Senator Ed Baker's death is a deviation from true history. He did die, but in battle, and battle had not yet begun.

The situation in the Federal House, from the perspective of the Lincoln Administration, was even more troubling. The House was made up of 108 Republicans, 71 Democrats and 27 fence sitters, called "Unionists", "Unconditional Unionists", "Conditional Unionists", or members of the American Party, or whatever. These "27 third party" people were neither officially Democrats nor Republicans, but they were, with few exceptions, opposed to going to war without a provocation -- an armed attack of some sort by Confederates against Federals. So Republicans had a caucus of 108 in a House of 206 seats. That meant they needed 103 votes to win a "go to war" vote in the House. But the prospects of losing the support of at least 12 Republicans without provocation was deemed likely and the prospects of gaining the support of even one Democrat was remote at best. Only a few, if any votes from the 27 "third party" Representatives could be counted on. Vote counts by Republican leaders pointed to defections of as many as 7 of their own from New York, as many as 6 from Pennsylvania, as many as 6 from Ohio, and as many as 3 each from Indiana, Illinois, and Wisconsin. [62]

So, by mid-summer, when Republican leaders estimated their strength in a Senate vote to "go to war" and a House vote to "go to war," they continued to postpone any thought of calling for a Special Session of Congress — postpone the call in hopes that somehow, given more time, they could illicit the coveted "first shot" from some undisciplined Confederates.

### The Lincoln Paternity Scandal Weakens Support for President Lincoln

Also, by mid-summer, the Confederate Secret Service had constructed a rather complete story about Abraham Lincoln's paternity. His mother was Nancy Hanks of North Carolina – everyone agreed on that. But his father was probably not Nancy's husband, Thomas Lincoln of Kentucky. Secret Service agents had considerable testimony from witnesses in western North Carolina and eastern Kentucky supporting the argument that the President's father was Abraham Enloe of the mountains of western North Carolina, who lived in a valley south of the Great Smokey Mountains. Agents obtained evidence that contradicted Lincoln's "Thomas is my father " claim as he had written it in the Bible record he had worked up with his step-mother, Sarah Bush Johnston Lincoln, during a visit to her home a year or two after Thomas Lincoln had died. That would be about 1852 or 1853, about the time Abe sensed new political opportunities may be opening up. Furthermore, Confederate agents aimed to shame Abe for not attending claimed father Tom Lincoln's funeral in 1851. Lincoln's contrived Bible record smelled like a cover-up, and Abe's former law partner, Billy Herndon, was tricked into suggesting the same by a clever agent who approached him during May. Agents had consulted a small group of informed and important people in Kentucky who supported the claim that Abe was two years old at the time of the marriage – stating that Thomas Lincoln was his step-father, not his real father. So in the legal lingo of the time, Abraham Lincoln was a bastard. The true story of the President's birth and time as a little boy was thus:

> Nancy Hanks a young unmarried girl, born in Virginia and living in far western North Carolina while working as a servant for the well-to-do and large family of Abraham Enloe, became pregnant by Mr. Enloe. Nancy gave birth to a baby she name Abraham, after his true father. Mr. Enloe sent her away to a place near Bostic, North Carolina, where she gave birth. Within two years Mr. Enloe arranged for a young fellow, Thomas Lincoln, to accept Nancy for a wife, and the little boy, too, if he would take them to eastern Kentucky and care for them -- giving him a going-away present, as well. Therefore, when Tom and Nancy

---

[62] The vote estimates in the Senate and House are truthful tabulations of Republican strength except for Senator Baker. And in truthful history President Lincoln believed accomplishing his "first shot" political strategy was essential.

married in eastern Kentucky, there was this little 2-year-old boy in attendance name Abraham. So the President was about 4 years older than he claimed to be. [63]

## The Crisis Accelerates Toward a Showdown in the Federal Congress: September, October and November of 1861

With the Republican Party severely weaken by the propaganda campaign of the Confederate Secret Service and the continuing non-threatening posture of Confederates -- including going along with paying a few tariffs at Fort Sumter and unimpeded navigation of the Mississippi River -- Republicans were struggling to commandeer the votes needed to win support in the Federal House and Senate for a declaration of war. Once declared, it would be necessary to subjugate Democrat-controlled States that might not have seceded, but be uncooperative, such as would be the likely response in Delaware and Maryland, and maybe Kentucky, and maybe Missouri. After military action in the remaining Democrat States was accomplished, then, and only then, the Federal military could proceed south upon an invasion of the Seceded States and conquer their respective governments and the united Confederate military that would be supporting them.

Space in this work does not permit reporting on the political threats, intrigues and deal-making that surrounded the politics in the Northern States during September, October and November of 1861. Suffice it to say, the efforts were persistent and emotions swung back and forth. And those emotions frequently surged, here and there, as newly emancipated Negro families arrived and sparked Exclusionist anger. And politics worked against the war-hawks in the Republican Party as regularly-scheduled 1861 October-November local and State elections were voted upon and Democrats, more often than not, regained offices previously lost to the Republican advance that had begun in force in 1856 and become so dominant by late 1860.

That said, we now advance to the opening of the Federal House and Senate at the regular scheduled session on December 2, 1861.

### Thursday Evening Selected Diary Postings

Diary note by Carlos Cespedes said, "The five guests are now firm for the overnight sailing trip this weekend. Andrew Houston has good blue water sailing experience and I have named him first mate. Chris Memminger's family has all of those great thoroughbred race horses; so I asked him to join us in hopes he might someday return the favor and invite me to visit his stables and practice tracks. Three girls are joining us three fellows: Emma Lunalilo is so great on the water, I just had to ask her. Marie Saint Martin is such great fun, so I gave her the nod. Conchita Rezanov rounds out the crew. Andrew Houston insisted that I include her and, since he is first mate, I felt I could not refuse. I think Andrew has an eye for Conchita. Why not? She is gorgeous!"

Diary note by Andrew Houston said, "Will be going sailing with Carlos off the coast of Cuba Saturday. Honored to be asked. Will be six of us altogether. I will be the only crew with sailing experience, so Carlos wants me to be his First Mate. His family has a nice sailboat. Very worthy for overnight ocean sailing. He knows the waters and the boat very well and has handled it in stormy seas. Feel good about that. But will have to be on our toes, we will be responsible for

---

[63] In truthful history there is a real likelihood that President Lincoln's father was not his mother's husband. It is likely that he was four years older than claimed, and that the real father was Abraham Enloe of western North Carolina as related here in *The CSA Trilogy*. For documentation several sources are suggested, should you wish to inquire further -- The Bostic Lincoln Center Museum (Bostic, NC); *The Genesis of Lincoln*, by James Harrison Cathey (1899); *Lincoln*, by David Herbert Donald (Pulitzer Prize winner and the Charles Warren Professor Emeritus of American History and American Civilization at Harvard University, published in 1995); *Lincoln's Herndon*, by David Herbert Donald (1948); *The Eugenics of Lincoln*, by James Caswell Coggins (1940).

three women and one man who have never done this. Conchita is among the girls. To be honest, dear diary, it is the beautiful Conchita on that sailboat that excites me the most."

Diary note by Conchita Rezanov said, "Going to be flying to Cuba with Carlos and four others Saturday morning. Family company has its own jet. Goodness. Is there that much money in sugar cane? Hope to find out. . . . . Concerning this morning's lecture, I am reflecting on a parallel in strategies. The original seven Confederate States refused to ignite a war by firing on Fort Sumter. From that point the strategy was Passive Resistance. My family's Russian America refused to reveal that huge gold deposit in Nome, allowing our region of North America to win independence at a cheap price that we could afford to pay. Deception is often key to success in political maneuvers and often preferable to war."

# Part 1, Chapter 6, Day 5 – After Debate the US Congress Chooses War – Virginia, North Carolina, Tennessee and Arkansas Secede and Federal Preparations for War Intensify – Class Lecture, Friday, June 10, 2011

Professor Davis continued with his lectures as soon as the twelve essayists for the Sewanee Project were seated and ready to listen.

## December 1861: Federal Congress Convenes

The Federal Congress in Washington City did not begin deliberations until the customary first Monday in December, this being December 2, 1861, for President Lincoln and Republican leaders had failed to secure agreement during the Spring, Summer or Fall on calling a Special Session. The Lincoln Administration, the Republican Governors and the Republican leadership in the House and Senate, had been too unsure that, without a provocative "incident," they could get a majority "go to war" vote during a Special Session, so none had been called. Hopes that a few Confederates would be provoked into armed conflict had never materialized, quite to the amazement of Republican leaders.

At the opening of the December secession, the House elected Galusha Grow, Republican of Pennsylvania, as Speaker. The following history about that election of Speaker explains the difficulties Republicans faced in rallying Democrats go to war:

> Although the Republican majority assured a Republican would become Speaker, a "so-called" Republican from St. Louis, Missouri had been given unusual attention. His name was Frank Blair, his brother was Montgomery Blair of Maryland, Postmaster General in the Lincoln Administration, and the father of the two brothers was Francis Blair of Maryland — a newspaperman and historically a king-maker in the politics of Washington City, going all the way back to the days of Andrew Jackson. You see, the senior Blair saw a great political future for his sons if they became prominent Republicans with roots in Southern States, a very rare breed indeed. Some Republicans saw in Blair a propaganda tool with which they could entice Democrats to cooperate with their militant goals.

But Representative Thaddeus Stevens of Pennsylvania had wanted no "pretend Republican" as Speaker -- he wanted a "true Republican." He nominated Galusha Grow. Schuyler Colfax of Indiana was also nominated. After a few ballots, Grow was elected. And, as a thank you, Speaker Grow named Thaddeus Stevens as Chairman of the powerful House Ways and Means Committee, a post from which he would exert almost dictatorial power over the workings of the Federal House. [64]

## President Lincoln Asks Congress for Funding and Troops for an Invasion of the Confederacy

The following day Abe Lincoln delivered a written Message to Congress, which was read by the Clerk to a joint assembly of the House and Senate. In his message, Lincoln argued several points of Constitutional law, each designed to twist the truth to support his request for 400,000 men and $4,000,000 for a military invasion of the seceded States.

Regarding the legality of State Secession, Lincoln's Message cast off as "ingenious sophism" the crucial constitutional legal debate over whether the crisis was one of "secession" or

---

[64] This history of the Blair's, Colfax, Grow and Stevens is truthful with respect to the men but Grow's election as Speaker of the House and Stevens' appointment as Chairman of the Ways and Means Committee took place in the Special session of Congress called by President Lincoln for July 4, 1861. They remained in those positions for several years.

"rebellion." He alleged, "The sophism itself is, that any State may, consistently with the United States Constitution, and therefore, lawfully and peacefully, withdraw from the United States Federal Government without the consent of the Federal Government or of any other State. The little disguise that the supposed right is to be exercised only for just cause, themselves to be the sole judge of its justice, is too thin to merit any notice." So it was with this condescending subterfuge that Lincoln brushed aside the most important issue before the State governments and the Federal Government -- namely, the constitutional and legal arguments permitting and/or disallowing State secession.

And to underscore his "sophism" argument, Lincoln alleged that "no one of our States, except Texas, ever was sovereign." This was a blatant lie, clearly contrary to the Treaty of Paris where Great Britain had granted independence to each of the former thirteen colonies, each named individually, without mention of any sort of government over any of them. The reality had been that the thirteen Sovereign States, subsequently following their individual independences, had gathered together had and formed a "Continental Congress," later a "Confederation Congress" and afterward a "Federal Government" -- in all cases delegating to each sequential new general government only those powers not retained by the States or by the people, which were many, indeed.

And, finally, it must be reported that Lincoln totally ignored the sections of the Federal Constitution that prohibited the Federal Government or a State from taking military action against a State.

Had Lincoln sought a ruling or an opinion from the United States Supreme Court regarding State secession? Of course not! From the first day in office, the Administration's policy had been to ignore the Supreme Court as if it did not exist. Lincoln had the United States Army. The Justices only had papers. [65]

Regarding the support for secession among the citizens of a seceded State, Lincoln's Message alleged that, "It may well be questioned whether there is today, a majority of the legally qualified voters of any State, except for perhaps South Carolina, in favor of leaving the United States. There is much reason to believe that voting men who favor remaining in the United States are the majority in many, if not in every other one, of the so-called Seceded States. The contrary has not been demonstrated in any one of them." Of course Lincoln did not intend to suggest that Congress ought to investigate the level of support for secession then existing in the Seceded States. He wanted the question left dangling, for the truth of the issue was that support for secession had not declined from the days of the initial, fully adequate, votes. [66]

Regarding the lack of military conflict between April and the present month of December, Lincoln's Message submitted that, "The leaders over this so-called secession, what is more properly termed rebellion, and so-called Peace Democrats of the North, are clever like the copperhead snake." [67] He went on to explain that the copperhead will hide in the brush, in the wood-pile, even in the grass, seemingly peaceful and of no threat. But anger it too much, come too close to it, and it will strike at you with deadly force. It is still hiding there, for we are not yet too close. But our restraint has persisted far longer than it ought to have. We cannot allow this copperhead snake to give birth to more of its kind, moving ever closer to destroying this

---

[65] Lincoln's insistence on ignoring the Supreme Court is truth history.

[66] These Lincoln quotes of Lincoln's Message to Congress are truthful history, but had occurred in the July 1861 Special Secession.

[67] In truthful history Republicans called Peace Democrats "Copperheads." However Lincoln made no mention of "Copperheads" in his message to Congress in July or December 1861.

government, the government of the United States of America, the greatest government the world has ever known. For far too long we have delayed a decision to deal firmly with the copperhead. That is why, today, I am humbly asking you for the authority and the means of properly dealing with this rebellion crisis.

So President Lincoln asked the Federal House and Senate to approve a bill that called for a military build-up to a 400,000-man army, manned primarily by State militiamen, to be funded by $4,000,000, a huge sum in those days, which would require creative financing. He also asked for $1,000,000 and 1,000 men to fund and operate a stronger navy. He asked the Federal House and Senate to confirm in him the power to, as Commander-in-Chief, use whatever military action deemed necessary to secure the return of the seceded States to their "proper place" under the Federal Government, will all rights restored, subject to Congressional review. He appealed to the Democrat-controlled States to remain loyal to the Federal Government, to avoid being swept up into the secession fallacy, and thereby avoid facing the hard hand of the Federal military. For, he sternly warned, "The power of which I am asking from you, Representatives and Senators, shall be exercised to the fullest extent necessary to ensure loyalty among existing States and to return to the fold those which have already seceded." To Democrat-controlled Delaware, Maryland, Virginia, North Carolina, Kentucky, Tennessee, Missouri and Arkansas, Lincoln warned, with the strongest of words:

> "My friends of these Southern States, let us remain cooperative brethren who have in the past, can today, and will surely in the days of our joint glorious future, settle our differences, as they occasionally arise, with the just rule of law and the fair debate of our respective representatives."

The next day, Thaddeus Stevens of Pennsylvania, Chairman of the House Ways and Means Committee, organized his committeemen and began the process of drafting a bill to give President Lincoln the military force and legal authority he sought for an invasion of the seceded States and to exercise control over non-cooperative States, organizations, newspapers and individuals. Stevens had decided to put all issues under his committee, thereby avoiding going through the three House committees that would normally be responsible for drafting the bills envisioned: the Military Affairs and Militia Committee, the Naval Affairs Committee and the Judiciary Committee. Similar Bills were being drafted in three Senate Committees: the Senate Military Affairs and Militia Committee, under Chairman Henry Wilson of Massachusetts; the Senate Naval Affairs Committee, under Chairman John Hales of New Hampshire, and the Senate Judiciary Committee, under Lyman Trumbull of Illinois.

## Confederates Intensify their Propaganda Campaign in the North, Prepare for More Secessions

Meanwhile, telegraph lines to Montgomery, to the State capitals of every Confederate State, and to the State capitals of Virginia, North Carolina, Kentucky, Tennessee, Missouri and Arkansas, were busy relaying messages that were steadily coming down from Washington City in order to keep Democrat leaders across the South fully informed about the situation in the Federal House and Senate. As it turned out, a Democrat on each of the four committees named above had agreed to feed news of committee activity to a Confederate contact each night. The telegraph messages were nightly converted to code in Washington City and decoded at Montgomery and at each state capital. Coding and decoding was the responsibility of the Confederate Secret Service, which had agents posted at all necessary locations.

Meanwhile, the Governors of the six States most likely to secede — Virginia, North Carolina, Kentucky, Tennessee, Missouri and Arkansas — quietly called each State's respective standing secession convention to assemble within a few days to be on hand at each capital for the purpose of acquiring news and pondering response to anticipated threats. Publicity about the reconvening of these secession conventions was downplayed, but people in the know realized that each of the above-mentioned States had machinery in place to declare state secession within hours of hearing news of a vote in the Federal House and Senate to authorize, man and fund a military invasion of the Seceded states. For the most part, news out of Washington City was interpreted in Montgomery and then relayed by telegraph to the six participating State capitals -- Judah Benjamin and his Secret Service people being primarily responsible for that task. In each State most likely to secede, militiamen were put on alert status and plans were made to seize Federal facilities and arms within moments following secession. Of particular importance were the plans to take over United States military facilities in Virginia, including the Norfolk Navy facility and the armory at Harper's Ferry.

Information was flowing south, as just mentioned, but also flowing north. The Confederacy increased its propaganda messaging to newspapers and influential people in the northern States, especially the metropolitan region in south-east New York State, in certain parts of Pennsylvania where Democrats still had influence, and in southern Ohio, southern Indiana and southern Illinois. Intensified propaganda hammered six key messages. The propaganda:

1. Proved that major allegations in Abe Lincoln's Message to Congress were historically false;

2. Pointed to the peaceful behavior of the people within the Confederacy;

3. Alleged that Republicans planned to round up and deport all Negroes living in the United States (those not seceded), thereby creating an all-white society north of the Confederate States, and declared that a forced deportation plan of that magnitude to be extremely cruel and a violation of the teachings of Jesus Christ;

4. Pointed out that the Confederacy had already begun laying plans for gradual emancipation and in-state jobs for Negroes -- a far kinder and more economical plan -- to begin after normal diplomatic relations were established between Washington City and Montgomery;

5. Promised to continue tax-free freight passage up the Mississippi and Tennessee rivers and cooperation in collecting Federal import taxes at all Confederate border check-points;

6. Warned that, historically, the people of the Southern States, living in a vast region that was extremely difficult to occupy by military force, had been victorious in all military conflicts encountered in settling the land from the Atlantic out to Texas and would inflict a heavy death toll upon any military or naval attack from the north, accompanied by great weeping by the parents, widows and children of the Federal dead. [68]

In spite of the Confederate propaganda campaign in key areas of the Republican North, militant bills moved forward through the Federal House and Senate. On December 10 Thad Stevens presented his committee's bill to the House floor. It was in three parts — army/militia, navy and judicial. This set the stage for a raging debate between Republicans and Democrats, much of it covered by newspapers in the northern States. Democrats offered amendments, some of which stuck.

On the face of it, there seemed no way for the House to win passage. There were 206 members in the House, meaning 104 votes were needed to pass a bill. Republicans numbered 108, but several were clearly against military invasion. Reluctance to vote with the leadership was

---

[68] In truthful history the military death toll among Federals, from 1861 to 1865, would far exceed that of Confederates.

particularly strong in south-east New York State, and parts of Pennsylvania, southern Ohio, southern Indiana and southern Illinois.

Over on the Senate side, the bills from the three committees were all introduced on December 12. Immediately afterward, all three were read on the floor, a motion was made and carried that they be combined into one omnibus bill and debated and voted upon as one item. As in the House, debate raged on in the Senate, complete with extensive newspaper coverage in the Northern states.

News continued to flow rapidly by telegraph to Montgomery and the capitals of each Southern State, coded messages no longer being needed.

## The Federal Congress Authorizes an Invasion of the Confederacy

As Christmas loomed ahead on the calendar, pressure increased to cut off submission of amendments and further debate. It was late Friday, December 20 when the Senate finally passed its omnibus militant authorization bill. The Senate vote was 28 for and 26 against. The House continued through 3 pm Saturday before it passed its militant authorization bill, which had been spearheaded by Thaddeus Stevens. The House vote was 104 to 102. Clearly, at both sides of the Capitol, several Republican politicians had chosen to avoid being recorded as casting a yea vote if their participation was not essential to passage. Members of a Conference Committee were named immediately after the votes were cast and that group began its deliberations on Monday morning, December 23. A compromise version of the militant authorization bill was agreed upon on at 11:30 on the morning of Tuesday, December 24. By 4 in the afternoon, Representatives and Senators were in their seats and votes were called for in each chamber. The final bill was approved by almost the same small margin as before. But the compromise bill had to be drawn up into an official document for President Lincoln's signature. That was completed on the day after Christmas. In a small ceremony in the White House, with major Republican leaders in the House and Senate at his side, Lincoln signed the bill. It was called the Act to Recover Seceded States by Military Force If Necessary. Final amendments had sharpened the language to avoid the term Rebel or Rebellion. Democrats claimed a small victory in defining the title of the bill and a more significant victory in trimming the size of the military force a little from that requested by Lincoln.

The final bill authorized a military force of 350,000 men, that being a combination of regular army personnel and militiamen operating under the direction of regular army commanders. The final bill authorized an increase of 800 men for the navy. Funds authorized amounted to $3,500,000 for the army and militia and $800,000 for the navy. These funds were to be utilized over fourteen months -- from January 1, 1862 to February 28, 1863. States pondering secession were assured that they and their people would be treated with utmost consideration and respect if participants remained loyal to the Federal Government, even if militia from their region were allowed to not participate in the Federal military action against sister states and, or, seceded states. It was only demanded of states remaining loyal that it was imperative that they allow unobstructed passage and encampment of Federal troops and supportive militia throughout their boundaries, with full access to local supplies, all of which were to be paid for immediately. However, when disloyalty or obstruction was encountered by individuals or groups within states that were officially loyal, Federal forces and Federal courts were authorized to deal with such renegades as harshly as needed to abate such activities. The judicial portion of the final bill directed the Executive to use normal state and Federal courts in all loyal states and to limit martial law. But martial law was appropriate in states that had seceded or where resistance was on such a large scale that its courts were overwhelmed in dealing with the violence. The Executive was directed to permit a free and open dialog in states which remained officially loyal, guaranteeing freedom of speech and publication for all newspapers, pamphleteers, public speakers, etc.

Freedom of religious thought was guaranteed. Destruction of private or public property by Federal forces or supportive militia within loyal states was to be avoided wherever possible, and where it did occur, was to be compensated from a $500,000 fund created in the bill to dispense such monies. Persons of African ancestry were to be excluded from Federal forces and supportive militia, including laborers, and those that were slaves were to remain under their lawful owners, including those who tried to run away to a Northern state where slavery was prohibited. Seceded states were warned that resistance to occupation by Federal forces and supportive militia would be dealt with harshly according to the rules of nations at war. Even so, the people in seceded states, who offered no resistance to Federal forces or supportive militia were assured that their private property would not be intentionally destroyed, although, in the heat of battle and troop movements, destruction of private property and civilian life was often unavoidable, and there would be no compensation for such destruction. Surrendering troops of seceded states were to be confined in prisoner of war camps until loyalty and peaceful behavior was achieved throughout the seceded states. Most importantly, the bill encouraged seceded states to reconsider their defiant attitudes at the outset, and avoid bloodshed by laying down their arms and returning to their homes. Persons that offered no resistance and gave evidence of returning to peaceful civilian life would not be molested or retained in prisoner of war camps. The bill assured the nation that the object of the military campaign was to secure loyalty in the seceded states and, although the national debate over how to deal with slavery had seriously divided Republicans and Democrats and prompted some to resort to secession, it was not, repeat not, the object of this military campaign to interfere in any way with the laws and practice of slavery in any state where it is presently allowed. [69]

The time for the signing of the bill could not have been worse for the Lincoln Administration. Many men in the Federal army and navy were on leave for Christmas and New Years and the militiamen in the northern states were likewise scattered and not easily organized for action.

Across the North, news of the Declaration of War against the Seceded States was met with protests in regions in many locations, especially where the Republican Party was not in control. The Confederate Secret Service and the Department of Confederate Communication had been very effective in sowing the seeds of discontent within the North. The population realized they were under no threat of attack and that Confederates only wanted to be left alone. They saw no purpose in a crusade for emancipation, or in risking life to win a rich man's war to force the South to pay Federal taxes on imported goods. Two days after news of war arrived, the New York *World*, the major Democrat paper in the city and in the North, published a cartoon captioned "Lying Lincoln and Papa," which portrayed two very tall, thin men of similar appearance: on the left Abraham Lincoln in his exceptionally tall hat with a hint of the White House behind him; on the right the older Abraham Enloe with white beard and a hint of tall mountains behind him. [70] There was a riot in Democrat-dominated New York City against going to war and more than 40 Colored People were chased, harassed, and beaten, three of them suffering death (some protestors blamed Colored People for causing secession and war). The Confederate Secret Service and the Confederate Department of Communication had made important progress in building resistance in the North for a war against the South. Often citizens would protest against State militia as they

---

[69] In truthful history, the Republican campaign to conquer the Seceded States began with assurances that there was to be no interference in the institution of slavery anywhere.

[70] In truthful history the *New York World* was produced and published in New York City from 1860 to 1876 by Manton Marble. It was the major Democrat newspaper in the North. Thereafter ownership changed twice before the paper was acquired in 1883 by Joseph Pulitzer, the famous founder of the Pulitzer Prize for excellence in journalism.

gathered to drill, parade or get into railroad cars headed south. There was shouting, and spitting, thrown rocks and eggs during such events. [71] Public support for the war during January and February 1862 was strongest in the Northeast, but even there a religious segment of the population strongly argued against it. Such opposition to the war would be telling when Federal troops were advancing through the Confederate States, first facing little resistance, then, very suddenly finding themselves isolated from the North and in a fight for their lives. Many Federal soldiers, untested in war and feeling no obligation to risk death on the battlefield, looked for the first opportunity to find shelter and then surrender.

Not so in the Southern states.

### More Southern States Secede and Execute Plans to Defend Themselves

As soon as the preliminary House and Senate military bills had passed, that being by Saturday, December 21, news of the event and the essential content of the language of those bills arrived in Montgomery and the capitals of all of the Southern states. Democrat Governors in Virginia, North Carolina, Kentucky, Tennessee, Missouri and Arkansas quietly instructed the standing secession conventions to meet and begin deliberations on the proper response for each. By the day that President Lincoln signed the "Act to Recover Seceded States by Military Force If Necessary", that being Thursday, December 26, the Virginia Secession Convention had declared its state to be seceded. This was all that was needed to authorize the Virginia State militia to overwhelm the thin force at Harper's Ferry and begin the process of loading arms and arms manufacturing machinery on railroad cars and wagons for transport south toward the heart of the state. The Virginians were so swift with their work that over 90 percent of the useful arms, ammunition and equipment was headed south within 48 hours. Likewise at the navy facility at Norfolk, Virginia militiamen and skilled seamen had taken control of the facility to an extent necessary to prevent retreating Federal navy personnel from destroying much of what was left behind. Furthermore, about twenty percent of the Federal navy men then stationed at Norfolk refused to retreat, resigned on the spot, and joined in support of the Virginians. Those resignations were further evidence of the effectiveness of the Confederate propaganda campaign. [72]

The North Carolina Secession Convention declared its State to be seceded on Friday, December 27. The following day, December 28, secession conventions in Tennessee and Arkansas declared their States seceded. In these regions, as well, militiamen were successful in taking control of Federal armories and military facilities within their boundaries.

After stormy debate, the Missouri Secession Convention voted to secede on Thursday, January 2. But unlike elsewhere among the seceded states, Missouri was entering into something approaching a civil war within its boundaries. In St. Louis, the large population of German immigrants was generally opposed to secession, although operatives of the Confederate Secret Service had persuaded about one fourth of that population to forego opposing their State

---

[71] In truthful history, in July 1863, in response to the widespread Federal draft of immigrants, a horrific riot and race war erupted in Democrat-dominated New York City and lasted four days. The *New York Tribune* would estimate that the violence resulted in 350 deaths (mostly peaceful blacks), 650 injuries, and $1,500,000 in property damage.

[72] In truthful history, Federals set fires that destroyed most of the arms and machinery at Harper's Ferry and set fire to much of the naval ships and equipment at Norfolk.

government. Federals successfully defended their armory in St. Louis and within a few days moved to Illinois all military supplies within the facility. [73]

Secession in Kentucky would never be fully achieved. The Kentucky Secession Convention remained in session through January 31 without reaching a decision to secede, but it did insist on a neutrality for its state, and demanded that Federal forces moving against Tennessee stay clear of Kentucky land except for three defined in-state corridors: 1) the railroad from Louisville to Nashville, 2) the Cumberland River, and, 3) the Tennessee River. Kentuckians were tied so firmly to the Ohio River and so many Kentucky relatives lived in southern Ohio, southern Indiana and southern Illinois that leaving the United States was too difficult for too many. [74]

At Charleston and Pensacola, Federals possessed staging areas from which they could mount major offensives toward midstate farms, but multiple military advances southward from the north would be chosen by the Lincoln Administration as the preferred line of attack. So militaries at Charleston and Pensacola were ordered to stand firm, collect import taxes, but not advance.

## The Confederate Plan to Appear Non-Threatening

The Jefferson Davis Administration had discouraged secession in Maryland and Delaware for two reasons. First, every effort was being made to make the Confederate States appear in the North to be a non-threatening country. Peaceful co-existence and friendly cooperation was the image to be projected, and this was stressed in the propaganda campaign, which was proving more effective by the day. Second, because Delaware was only three counties, a pip-squeak of a state, it was of no use to the Confederacy and, logically speaking, did not merit two Senators anyway. Third, Maryland needed to remain in the United States to give free access from the North to the capital, Washington City. Maryland was a strangely shaped State, too. Baltimore was surely important, but the eastern shore was remote and the narrow strip of western Maryland, squeezed between Virginia and Pennsylvania, was an awkward administration. The population was quite mixed, and only the region around Baltimore and the Eastern Shore held a population that matched well culturally with the people of the Southern States.

In fact, there was already talk in Montgomery about keeping Confederate troops well south of Washington City, providing a buffer zone that would not be defended. This was considered another tactic to appear non-threatening. But there was one more idea behind it. A defensive plan called "Envelopment" was gaining traction in military defense discussions. The Davis Administration was adopting a military tactic focused on capturing large Federal armies in hopes Confederates could negotiate peace and permanent boundaries in exchange for releasing tens of thousands of captured Federals. The "Envelopment" strategy might succeed if Confederates were to be facing multiple Federal armies advancing southward simultaneously, on the same time schedule. Under this joint invasion threat, Confederates could pretend weakness as they retreated southward while working to cut off supplies from the Federal rear and disrupting communications between invading armies and Washington City. And this Confederate retreat and appearance of weakness could be coordinated among the defending armies so as to tighten the "Envelopment" noose around each opposing army at about the same time, forcing surrender of most of the men in each invading army, all within a short span of only a few days, mostly before the Lincoln Administration realized what had happened.

---

[73] In truthful history, Missouri struggled but did not secede. All arms in the Federal armory at St. Louis were removed to Illinois. Missourians suffered a civil war within their State.

[74] This account of Kentucky follows truthful history except defined corridors for military advance did not exist. In truth many Kentuckians went south to Tennessee and joined the Confederate military.

Although classical military strategists viewed the Confederate's "Envelopment" plan very difficult to accomplish, there was little reasonable alternative -- prospects for victory in a protracted, several-years-long war looked worse. You see, strategists in Montgomery believed that fighting, retreating, fighting, retreating, again and again would only draw out the conflict, promote escalation, on and on, season after season, until the more populous North overwhelmed the South with its much greater resources in manpower and weaponry. Quick, decisive military movements, aimed at taking captive and imprisoning large groups of Federals – the "Envelopment" plan -- was thought the best way to force Republicans to sue for peaceful acceptance of State Secession.

## Men of Color Are Recruited into State Militia

You will recall encouragement at the Seven States Emancipation Conference to induct Negro men into the militia of the various Confederate States. By September, 1861 this idea was being rapidly accepted, first this State, then that State, and the idea snowballed. Those inducted were fighting men, armed and trained. The rule requiring that they be evenly dispersed among the militia units, always only as a small minority, seemed to assure the White population that it need not worry about a Nat Turner style rebellion surfacing. Some who volunteered were free Colored men who simply wanted to show their patriotism. Others were free Colored men who planned to stay in their unit through thick and thin with expectation of gaining emancipation for a wife, and/or children who remained bonded. But more than half were owned as slaves and had struck an agreement with their owner to volunteer to serve with the owner's knowledge that success would result in emancipation for the volunteer and in many cases for his wife and children, but additional family emancipations varied depending on the State and on other factors. Often a volunteer Colored man was a close friend of a White volunteer – for example the farmer's son and one of his slaves of about the same age. But it was strictly forbidden that the Colored volunteer behave as a servant to the White man. In fact, in a few instances, where servant-master behavior was discovered, the White man was discharged, but the Colored man was retained under the presumption that he had been a victim of abuse. The presence of Colored men in Confederate State militia units was known to Republicans when Congress voted for a military invasion. And some historians believe the presence of Black Militiamen caused some Congressmen and Senators to worry they were again losing the high moral ground. For example, visions of White militiamen of Massachusetts fighting against and killing Virginia militiamen in a crusade to emancipate Black slaves in Virginia made far less sense when some of the Virginia militiamen were Blacks. Massachusetts Abolitionists were struggling to win there case for a holy crusade against evil Southerners.

## January through April 1862: the Federal Military Buildup and Confederate Preparations

From the beginning of January, the Lincoln Administration began a massive military buildup aimed at conquering each of the seceded states. The Administration had vowed to not recognize the existence of the Confederate Government in Montgomery, but, instead, recognize what had been the state government of each seceded state and, by conquering the capital of each seceded state, force each seceded government to repudiate secession, dissolved itself, and demand that its officials pledge allegiance to the government of the United States -- that completed, a new "Reconstructed" government for each state would be created under Federal oversight. The capitals were expected to surrender to Federal forces in the following sequence: Richmond, Nashville, Baton Rouge, Raleigh, Jackson, Columbia, Little Rock, Milledgeville (Georgia), Montgomery, Tallahassee and Austin.

A State-by-State conquest strategy had evolved from contentious debate among members of President Lincoln's Cabinet, certain leading Republican governors, and certain Senators and

Representatives. Some warned that it would be better to carefully probe Confederate defenses before committing to a massive coordinated invasion by Federal armies that was aimed at all of the state capitals. But others, fearing Confederate defenders would just shift about to concentrate on one invasion force, then another, advocated a simultaneous attack on all fronts to prevent Confederates from shifting about and concentrating forces. Lincoln made the final decision: it would be a coordinated simultaneous attack aimed at all state capitals. Why not just aim to conquer the Confederate capital in Montgomery? Well, Lincoln decided against that, asserting:

> "Since I will not recognize the so called Confederate States of America as a valid government, I will not force it to surrender and hand over control of each seceded state. Therefore, I firmly argue that the object of our simultaneous attack should be the conquest of and submission of the capital of each seceded state. If we simply go after the Confederate Government it will retreat from Montgomery when threatened and transform itself into a ghost on the run. We will not go chasing a ghost pretending to be a government that does not legally exist." Furthermore, Lincoln declared, "each Federal army is to be assigned the mission of progressing along its designated path from capital to capital until every capital on its assigned list has been conquered and has submitted to Federal rule."

Although state capitals could pretend to become mobile to escape subjugation, mobility was much easier for the Confederate capital at Montgomery. The Montgomery capital was newly established and Confederates stressed State Sovereignty over National Sovereignty. Republicans figured they could capture one state capital after another and steamroll toward victory, giving no special priority to far-off Montgomery, Alabama.

The missions, as agreed to and endorsed by Lincoln, were to be achieved by five major military divisions:

1. The mission of the Federal's Virginia and Carolinas Division was to force the surrender of three state capitals and the surrender of the corresponding state governments of Virginia, North Carolina and South Carolina.

2. The mission of the Federal's Tennessee and Georgia Division was to force the surrender of two state capitals and the surrender of the corresponding state governments of Tennessee and Georgia.

3. The mission of the Federal's Alabama and Florida Division was to force the surrender of two state capitals and the surrender of the corresponding state governments of Alabama and Florida.

4. The mission of the Federal's Mississippi River Division was to force the surrender of two state capitals and the surrender of the corresponding state governments of Louisiana and Mississippi.

5. The mission of the Federal's Missouri, Arkansas and Texas Division was to subdue the Missouri secessionists and their pro-secession government by occupying the state capital of Jefferson City, and then proceed south to force the surrender of two state capitals and the surrender of the corresponding state governments of Arkansas and Texas.

A very small percentage of Federal soldiers and cavalry were from the Democrat States of Delaware, Maryland, Kentucky and Missouri. Furthermore, in Ohio, Indiana and Illinois, the rural southern counties contributed few volunteers, for, in those three States, the northern Ohio River Valley, stretching up to the headwaters of tributary rivers and streams, had been mostly settled by people of the Southern Culture and they wanted no part in a war against kinfolk. When looking at the origin of troops gathering to invade the Confederate States, historians would remark how clearly the battles were between fighting men of the Northern Culture and fighting men of the Southern Culture. [75]

Notwithstanding Lincoln's refusal to recognize or negotiate with the Confederate Government, everyone knew that the great prize would be given to whichever division conquered the Confederate capital at Montgomery, Alabama -- the seat of power for the Confederate States of America. And a sense of a competitive race was hard to avoid, for the division to first conquer Montgomery would surely win the greatest glory. Thus, the urge to move rapidly toward objectives, in hopes of winning the big race, so to speak, was to contribute to reckless overreaching by Federal commanders and to facilitate Confederate efforts to lure the Federals into traps where tens of thousands could be forced to surrender. Although, the Tennessee and Florida Division ought to first reach Montgomery, if its progress were to be delayed, the glory of that accomplishment could be grasped by the Tennessee and Georgia Division, following its conquest of Milledgeville; by the Mississippi River Division, following its conquest of Jackson, or by the Virginia and Carolinas Division, following its conquest of Columbia. On the other hand, if the Navy could follow up its success at New Orleans with a successful attack at Mobile, enough troops might be brought to that landing site to mount a successful attack on Montgomery. Most likely, two or more of these Divisions might join forces outside of Montgomery at the same time to create a huge unstoppable force and to share in the glory.

## By this Time Confederate Defensive Capability, a Guarded Secret, was Greatly Improved

Fortunately for the Confederacy, the Lincoln Administration was unaware of the Confederate strategy of "Retreat, Envelopment and Capture" and of improvements gained in gunboat technology, repeating firearm and metallic cartridge technology, and in an expanded cavalry and enhanced troop mobility. There were rumors in the North of Confederate weapons advancements, but Republican leaders refused to believe them, thinking it to be one more example of Confederate propaganda. We only have space to present an overview of the status of these advancements as of April, 1862, the month that Confederates anticipated they would soon be facing the invasion of the Federal divisions.

### Confederate Progress Concerning Enhanced Gunboat Technology

Unlike the weakening Northern resolve to support a war of invasion, determination in the South for a patriotic and hard-fighting defense was continuing to gain strength. In parallel with the Department of Confederate Communication's campaign to weaken Northern resolve to fight a war of invasion, was its campaign to strengthen Southern resolve to defend mightily against an invasion should it come. And Southern resolve to mightily defend was encouraged by knowledge of Confederate advances in weaponry.

The program of gunboat design and construction overseen by James Eads and John Ericsson was highly successful. By mid-April 1862, ten Confederate River Defender Gunboats had been produced in construction yards at Commerce, Mississippi and Baton Rouge, Louisiana. Toward that goal Caleb Huse had found ready success in purchasing steam engines in England, Scotland and Europe, many arriving before March 1862, in ample time for installation in nearly-completed boats. He also acquired rifled artillery guns of high muzzle velocity and penetration capability for mounting on Eads' gunboats. The Confederate gunboats (see earlier footnote for design details) would prove very effective in crippling invading Federal gunboats advancing down the Mississippi River. With the help of the stores of hundreds of coal torpedoes and

---

[75] In truthful history the battles were primarily between fighting men of the Northern Culture and fighting men of the Southern Culture.

firewood torpedoes positioned along the Mississippi River and dispensed by the Confederate Secret Service, and with the help of James Eads' river snags and river mines, the Federal advance down the Mississippi would hopefully be halted not far downstream from Memphis, and halted not far upstream from New Orleans.

## Confederate Progress Concerning Repeating Firearms and Metallic Cartridges

Caleb Huse, acting as a purchasing agent for the Confederate Government had been especially successful in support of Josiah Gorgas' efforts to bring in large quantities of repeating rifles and introduce metallic cartridge technology. Huse and his team had acquired much of this improved technology weaponry from the United States, Great Britain, Belgium, the German States and France. Cotton was paying for it all, with credit liberally extended. Some of the acquisitions from Caleb Huse's team are presented in the following paragraphs.

Invented by Dr. Jean Alexander LeMat, of New Orleans, repeating short-range LeMat 9-shot pistols were produced in large quantities for use by Confederate cavalrymen. This unusual weapon, utilizing a 9-shot revolving cylinder for bullets, was capable of firing solid bullets out of the rifled pistol barrel or one round of "buckshot" out of an adjacent larger bore "sawed-off-shotgun" barrel. [76] By mid-April 1862, Confederates had received and distributed 15,000 LeMat 9-shot pistols, enough for every tenth cavalryman and many army officers.

Another important multi-shot pistol acquired in large numbers was the 1861 Confederate revolver pistol, which was produced under a Caleb Huse contract in Belgium. This revolver-style six-shot pistol was based on the design of Casimir Lefaucheux, a French gunsmith – a designed upgraded to use an improved brass cartridge, pioneered by Benjamin Houllier. [77] By mid-April 1862 Confederates had received and distributed 25,000 Lefaucheux-design six-shot pistols, enough for every seventh cavalryman and most officers.

Confederates also applied revolving cylinder technology in the design of five-shot rifles. History would prove that the Confederate 1861 revolver rifle was, in its day, the most advanced rifle in existence. A large order for parts needed to assemble the rifle had been placed by Caleb Huse and filled by factories in Belgium, France and England. This rifle was capable of firing five rounds at a one and a half minute reload cycle. In five minutes, the time it would take an attacking army, on the run, to cover one-half mile, the Confederate rifle could deliver 15 well-aimed defensive rounds per man. By mid-April 1862, the five Confederate divisions had on hand 60,000 Confederate 1861 revolving rifles, enough to give a 5-shot rifle to every third soldier in a unit, and they would be distributed in that manner.

This multi-shot rifle and the two multi-shot pistols mentioned above used cartridges, each made of a brass shell into which was inserted a copper-encapsulated compression cap, black powder and the lead bullet. By mid-April 1862, Confederates had obtained and distributed 5,000,000 brass-style cartridges designed to fit the revolving weapons, enough for 50 shots from each corresponding weapon. This represented a lot of new-technology firepower, but Confederates were cautioned to use bullets carefully to maximize kills and minimize wasted

---

[76] Either paper cartridges or brass cartridges could be used in the LeMat pistol. A cavalryman could fire this weapon at the rate of 9 rounds per minute, adding great firepower to a cavalry charge. By May 1862, 15,000 of these specialized 9-shot pistols were in the hands of Confederate cavalrymen. About half of the LeMat pistols were produced in France under a Caleb Huse contract, the remaining being produced in the **Conf**ederate States with imported machine tools. By the way, Dr. LeMat was a cousin to Confederate General P. G. T. Beauregard.

[77] This revolver-style, six-shot pistol was used by Confederate cavalrymen and also by ground troops when a backup sidearm was needed in close-range combat. By April 1862, 25,000 of these state-of-the-art pistols were in use by Confederate troops.

ammo. But empty brass shells were to be kept where possible and used in field reloading presses to make new bullets. [78] [79]

## Confederate Progress Concerning Field Artillery

Confederates had also made impressive progress in improving field artillery. Confederate artillery batteries had gained key firepower through additions of three innovative acquisitions, all made possible by the months gained during the first 14 months of Lincoln's presidency.

The Confederate horse-drawn 12-pounder Smoothbore Field Gun resembled the "Napoleon," a smoothbore gun-howitzer often cast of bronze, sometimes of iron. By mid-April 1862, Confederate divisions had on hand 500 of these guns, some obtained from Federal arsenals

---

[78] The Confederate brass cartridge contained a copper-encapsulated compression cap, only slightly smaller in diameter than the shell, followed by black powder, then the lead bullet (cylindrical at the base, tapered in the middle and pointed at the top). The assembled cartridge was then gently compressed under a calibrated spring and then the top of the shell was crimped around the tapered part of the bullet to complete the job. Assembly was possible at armament factories and in the field -- Confederates were required to collect in spent shell bags their spent shells so they could be reloaded at field cartridge reloading wagons which accompanied the divisions.

[79] The 1861 Confederate 5-shot repeating rifle consisted of 10 parts, made to exacting tolerances at various factories. Ten percent of production was selected randomly and secretly assembled at two locations in Europe to verify tolerances. The remaining parts, labeled as machine parts, etc., were shipped loose to the Confederate States to be assembled and test-fired at the receiving end. The parts were:
1. The rifle barrel, rifled and lapped at the back end.
2. The rear stock, made of wood.
3. The barrel grip, made of wood.
4. The cylinder, bored through to receive five brass cartridges, then lapped at both faces to exacting tolerances.
5. The hammer and spring.
6. The trigger and spring (a very light, predictable pull on this trigger).
7. The cylinder pin, which held the cylinder in position and around which it rotated.
8. The cylinder ratchet lever, at the side used to quickly rotate the cylinder to the next bullet.
9. The cylinder compression screw, push plate and lever assembly, of three parts the screw, push plate and lever, to be cranked down just before firing in order to close the gap between the lapped cylinder face and the lapped barrel back face to a near-zero clearance, thereby producing a near-perfect gas seal. This solved the grave problem of gas blowback into the shooter's face that had prevented the success of the Colt revolving rifle of 1855 design.
10. The component housing, a metal casting to which was attached the barrel, the cylinder, the trigger and spring, the hammer and spring, the ratchet, the cylinder push plate and compression screw with lever, and of course, the wooded grip and stock.

The Confederate 1861 revolving rifle could fire five rounds in the following manner:
1. Take rifle off shoulder and prepare to advance cylinder, 2 seconds
2. Advance cylinder to next bullet, 2 seconds.
3. Compress cylinder, 2 seconds.
4. Pull back hammer, 2 seconds.
5. Raise to shoulder and take aim, 4 seconds.
6. Fire, 1 second.
   - Total time for a firing cycle, 13 seconds.
   - Rounds fired in one minute, between 4 and 5.

The rifle could be reloaded with five new rounds in the following manner:
1. Time to eject spent brass casings into recycle pouch, 6 seconds.
2. Time to insert five new brass cartridges, 10 seconds.
   - Total time for reloading, 16 seconds.

in seceded States, some from State militia companies, but most from France, purchased as used artillery and renovated in Confederate shops. [80]

The Confederate Pack-Transport 12-pounder Smoothbore Light Gun was much like the model 1841 "Mountain Howitzer" used in the war against Mexico. The barrel and carriage could be quickly separated and loaded upon two stout mules, one set up to carry the 220-pound gun, the other set up to carry the 280-pound carriage (consisting of the axle, two wheels, and the tongue). By April 1862, Confederate divisions had on hand 100 of these mule-transportable smoothbore guns. Some had been taken from Federal arsenals in seceded States; others had been produced in Mexico, England and France.[81]

## Confederate Progress Concerning Enhanced Troop Mobility

First, Confederate military strategists wanted horses, lots of horses, both for cavalry and for pulling wagons and artillery batteries -- the higher the percentage of fighting men who had access to horses, the better. Mules were also sought. The population of mules and asses in the Southern States (below the Maryland-Kentucky-Missouri northern boundary) totaled about 800,000, compared to only 330,000 above that boundary, so there was no way to quickly boost the mule population. On the other hand the corresponding horse population north of the boundary was 4.4 million, compared to only 1.7 million to the South. So Confederates looked to the North for added horsepower and lots of it. To that end, the Confederate Secret Service and patriotic men and organizations had been purchasing horses from beyond the Confederacy. Kentucky is worth mentioning. A horse provisioning network there, operating for Confederate interests and with Confederate money, had been scouring southern Ohio, southern Indiana and southern Illinois, buying all good animals available and bringing them into Kentucky. From there they were delivered south, some by steamboat, some by the Louisville and Nashville Railroad and some, actually most, by young Confederate men riding and leading groups of twenty or more animals along roads and trails into the Confederacy where they were placed on good pasture where found, ready to incorporate into Confederate military divisions. Horses were also procured from Pennsylvania. There was an axiom in play here -- a good horse obtained from the North diminishes the future mobility of the Federal army. By November 1861, on the order of 100,000 good horses had been brought south into the Southern States, below the Maryland-Kentucky-Missouri northern boundary, easily sufficient to double the fraction of Confederates fighting as cavalry to just under one-third of fighting men.

Second, many horse-drawn wagons had been procured from tradesmen to meet specific needs. In addition to caissons and wagons for artillery support and general-purpose freight wagons, there were cook wagons, covered ambulances and cartridge wagons, the most advance units being equipped with the tools and hand presses necessary to resize and reload spent brass shells. Another essential item was the horse-drawn forge wagon, a blacksmith forge on wheels.

---

[80] The Confederate horse-drawn 12-pounder Smoothbore Field Gun used a 2.5-pound charge of black powder and a 12-pound spherical solid shot for knocking down defensive breastworks at a distance of up to 1,600 yards (5 degree discharge angle), or an explosive shell of the same size to kill and wound enemy troops at long distances, or a canister of grape shot intended to spread out many iron balls like a shot-gun charge and kill and wound enemy troops at short distances. The gun and carriage weighed 2,500 pounds and, with ammunition limber attached, required a team of six horses for transport along roads or fields.

[81] The Confederate Pack-Transport 12-pounder Smoothbore Light Gun was cast of bronze, used a charge of 0.5 pounds of black powder and could fire explosive shells, spherical case and canister, but not the heavier solid 12-pound solid cannon ball. It was capable of delivering an explosive ordinance against enemy troops at a distance of up to 1,000 yards (5 degree discharge angle), and was very effective at short distances when firing at enemy troops with canister shot. The advantage of this gun was the ability to secretly transport it through woods and over trails and to surprise the enemy by firing upon him from camouflaged, concealed positions.

These were built in large numbers. But the most innovative horse-drawn item was the cavalry travois, and this clever device would prove very effective in carrying out rapid troop movements to and from battlefield positions, these being essential maneuvers to enable the capture of sizable armies. [82]

## Federals Plan Five Major Coordinated Attacks for Early May, 1862

By the first of May, 1862, the Lincoln Administration had managed to recruit and organize the five major military divisions needed for the coordinated invasion of the Confederate States. Made up of state militia and Federal troops, the five Federal divisions had been strengthened to the following manpower levels, each organized under its division commander:

1. The Federal's Virginia and Carolina Division, gathered near Washington City, consisted of 130,000 men, of which 17,000 were cavalry -- Irving McDowell of Ohio, commanding.

2. The Federal's Tennessee and Georgia Division, gathered at Franklin, Kentucky, consisted of 70,000 men, of which 9,000 were cavalry -- William Rosecrans of Ohio, commanding.

3. The Federal's Alabama and Florida Division, gathered near Murray, Kentucky, consisted of 70,000 men, of which 9,000 were cavalry -- Ulysses Grant of Ohio and Missouri, commanding.

4. The Federal's Mississippi River Division, gathered near Cairo and Mound City, Illinois, along with four armored gunboats, just finished at Rock Island, consisted of 40,000 men, of which 5,000 were cavalry -- Don Carlos Buell of Ohio, commanding.

5. The organization of the Federal's Missouri, Arkansas and Texas Division had been slowed by the fighting in Missouri between the State militia and anti-secessionists. But, by the end of April, the State militia had been driven to the southern region of the state and the capital at Jefferson City was firmly in the control of anti-secessionists and their Federal backers. So, the Missouri, Arkansas and Texas Division, consisting of 40,000 men, of which 5,000 were cavalry, was prepared to move south to push resistance out of the state and then proceed into Arkansas, then Texas -- John Fremont, with family ties to Missouri, commanding.

## Prepared to Meet the Federal Attacks Were Five Confederate Divisions, Trained for Tactical Retreat, Envelopment and Capture

By the time that the five Federal divisions were in place just north of the Confederate boundaries, five Confederate divisions were positioned to entrap them at some strategic region

---

[82] The cavalry travois employed the concept of using the cavalryman's horse to rapidly relocate four armed foot soldiers in addition to the rider. To facilitate this ability, each cavalry horse was dressed out with straps across the chest and just below the saddle which did not interfere with normal cavalry functions, but to which could be quickly attached, on the left and on the right, the forward ends of the travois tow-poles. The travois tow-poles consisted of two saplings about twelve feet long that ran from the attachment at the horse, which was cushioned for comfort, to the ground behind. Two cross-poles ran from side to side, the lowest about a foot above the ground, the highest about three feet above the ground. In addition, a center pole ran from the forward cross-pole to the aft cross-pole to the ground. Two brace-poles were also incorporated, positioned in an "X" pattern to maintain the necessary travois shape. A three-inch-by-twelve-inch skid plate was carved and strapped to the bottom of each pole where it scooted along the ground. All seven poles were light and slightly flexible saplings of selected wood types allowing for toughness during use. A travois could be constructed in the field using a hatchet and knife to cut down and prepare the poles and strips of leather for binding. When needed, four foot soldiers could gather behind a cavalryman, tie a travois to the horse, sling their rifles across their backs, hop onto the bottom cross pole, hold onto the forward cross pole and be rapidly repositioned. Progress across open ground and roads was good. When encountering rough terrain, fences or small streams, the four riders could hop off in a second and run behind the horse, carrying the travois until the situation improved sufficiently to permit renewed riding. This maneuver was practiced often enough to make it effective and wagons containing fifty travois were part of an army's supply train.

along their path of advancement toward their respective State capitals objectives. The five Confederate divisions are now described, as of mid-April, 1862.

1. Positioned to entrap the Federal's Virginia and Carolinas division was a division of 80,000 Confederates, which included 25,000 cavalry -- Division 1, Robert E. Lee of Virginia, commanding. [83] The strategy was to permit Federal advancement southward into Virginia along a route from Washington City toward Richmond, with entrapment and forced surrender of the bulk of the Federal forces planned before reaching the capital. In support would be irregular forces known as the Virginia State Rangers, such as the "Moccasin Rangers" led by Captain George Downs. They would be particularly effective at harassing and confusing the untested advancing Federal soldiers and their commanders. [84]

2. Positioned to entrap the Federal's Tennessee and Georgia division was a division of 60,000 Confederates, which included 20,000 cavalry -- Division 2, Braxton Bragg of North Carolina, commanding. The strategy was to permit Federals to occupy the Tennessee capital, Nashville because it was too close to Kentucky to be defended. Afterward, the strategy was to retreat before advancing Federals hoping to entrap them near Tullahoma. As in Virginia, Irregular State Rangers would be involved in enabling the entrapment.

3. Positioned to entrap the Federal's Alabama and Florida division was a division of 55,000 Confederates, which included 18,000 cavalry -- Division 3, Sidney Johnston of Kentucky and Texas, commanding. The strategy was to allow Federals to advance along the Tennessee River, through western Tennessee, because in that region surrender could not be forced; then to make a stand at Pittsburg Landing and there inflict significant damage to the troops and their supplies, forcing them eastward of their planned line of advance toward Corinth, Mississippi. Eventual capture was anticipated in northeast Mississippi or northwest Alabama, in the hill country south of the Tennessee River. Here irregular State Rangers would be engaged to ensure success.

4. Positioned to entrap the Federal's Mississippi River division somewhere along its descent down the Mississippi River was a division of 30,000 Confederates, 10,000 of them cavalry, plus a fleet of Confederate River Defender Gunboats designed by Eads and Ericsson and built by Eads' workforce in Mississippi -- Division 4, Pierre Beauregard of Louisiana, commanding. Success in entrapping Federals descending the Mississippi River was dependent on preventing the capture of New Orleans, a task relegated to the Confederate Navy, Confederate artillery, and teams of Confederate mine-laying experts.

5. Positioned to entrap the Federal's Missouri, Arkansas and Texas division was a division of 35,000 Confederates, 12,000 of them cavalry -- Division 5, Sterling Price of Missouri, commanding. Capture was anticipated about half way between the Arkansas border and the capital city of Little Rock. Irregular State Rangers in Missouri and Arkansas would harass and confuse advancing Federals.

Since all but the Federal's Virginia and Carolinas Division were well west of Washington City, the Lincoln Administration had placed Henry Halleck over the four divisions that would be moving south through Kentucky and Missouri. So, Halleck, a seasoned military administrator, coordinated the efforts of Rosecrans, Grant, Buell and Fremont. But he was to remain rather far from the front lines, keep abreast of the situations by messengers and telegraph and take no part in battlefield decisions. Aware of this Confederate Secret Service agents were active at intercepting

---

[83] In truthful history, Robert E. Lee had not, at the beginning of the Federal invasion of the Confederacy, achieved a rank high enough to merit the command described in our alternate history. But history does show he deserved to take high command.

[84] In truthful history, nine 75-man companies of the Virginia State Rangers were authorized by the Virginia General Assembly in March 1862. Captain George Downs led one company, known as the "Moccasin Rangers."

messages going to Halleck and substituting misleading messages suggesting that the four advancing armies were proceeding as planned.

The Davis Administration organized its defensive command in a similar way. In Virginia and the Carolinas, Robert E. Lee was given full authority to direct all operations. But west of the mountains, where the greatest fighting was anticipated, overall coordination of the Confederate divisions was needed. That job was handed to Joe Johnston of Virginia, who, from a considerable distance beyond battlefield actions, and with good telegraph and express messenger support, stood ready to coordinate the efforts of Bragg, Sidney Johnston, Beauregard, and Price. The Confederate Secret Service, under Attorney General Judah Benjamin was responsible for maintaining telegraph communications to every state capital and gathering, analyzing and disseminating intelligence concerning troop strength, location and direction of movement. Furthermore, the Confederate Secret Service had developed a network of agents who spied on Federal activities, cut telegraph lines useful to Federals, repaired telegraph lines useful to Confederates, and distributed torpedoes.

### Friday Evening Selected Diary Postings

Diary note by Chris Memminger said, "All set for trip to Cuba for overnight sailing adventure. Our airplane landed at the airport late afternoon today, just before sunset. Although a jet, it is capable of landing on short runways, like here at Sewanee. That capability fits our sugar company needs well. Plan to be flying away to Cuba at 8:00 am in the morning. Will have light breakfast in flight.

"The music get together this afternoon was great. I even hit a few licks of Guantanamera to give the group a feel for Cuban music. It was appreciated. Think that Allan Ross and I will play well together. He plays country and western well enough on his guitar. In fact, everyone in the group contributes. Professor Davis? That man can play that banjo."

Diary note by Professor Davis said, "I did not give much consideration to musical ability when choosing the members of the Sewanee Project. But we were lucky to be blessed with musicians: five of the twelve can contribute in pleasing ways. Good time this afternoon finding out how we can mesh as a group."

Diary note by Allen Ross said, "Hope the sailing group has fun and that all goes as planned for them this weekend. I gave Carlos six frozen bison steaks for the on-board meals Saturday night. He says the sailboat has an above deck charcoal grill. Those steaks ought to taste real good. Music get-together this afternoon encourages me to believe we five can really make music together. I cannot match Carlos on Guantanamera, but we can play together in country style. Liked Amanda's play on the piano. She can just about play by ear, but finds sheet music helpful. Marie is compiling a list of songs and will be downloading music for all of us so it will be available the next time we get together."

## Part 1, Chapter 7, Days 6 and 7 -- The First Weekend and Six Go Sailing -- Saturday and Sunday, June 11 and 12, 2011

Six of the twelve Sewanee Project Participants spent the weekend on a sailing trip out of Mantanzas, Cuba. The story of that trip fills the pages devoted to Saturday and Sunday, June 11 and 12, 2011. The host is Carlos Cespedes, skipper. The guests are participants Andrew Houston of South Texas, first mate, Emma Lunalilo of Hawaii, second mate, and crew Conchita Rezanov of Russian America and South California, Marie Saint Martin of New Orleans and Chris Memminger of South Carolina. We begin the story at the Sewanee Airport.

The Carlos Cespedes sailing party left the airport at 8 am Saturday, June 11, bound for Mantanzas, Cuba. All six were excited in anticipation of the overnight sailing trip that Carlos promised. They would be aboard the family 50-foot sailing yacht, *Independence*, named for the July 4, 1870 independence of Cuba from Spanish rule, led by great-great-great-grandfather Carlos de Céspedes.

Getting to Mantanzas looked to be just as exciting. The Wright Executive Six, a six-passenger jet, was fast, sleek and comfortable, owned by the Cespedes family sugar company.

The jet landed at the Mantanzas airport at 10 am. By one that afternoon the yacht was provisioned and skipper, mates and crew were furnished with a fine lunch at the marina café. By 1:30 they were departing the harbor under partly cloudy skies and moderate winds – good sailing weather. Carlos was skipper (some call it "captain"). Andrew Houston had previous experience crewing on ocean sailing yachts, so Carlos logically named him "first mate." Emma Lunalilo was second mate based on her significant ocean sailing experience and her expert swimming and surf board experience off Hawaii beaches. The other three were new to ocean sailing (otherwise known as "blue water sailing"). So they were "crew." Conchita Rezanov was athletic and a whiz on the tennis court, but not a sailor. Marie Saint Martin was considered the boat entertainer based on her singing experience. Andrew Houston has brought along is guitar to accompany her. Chris Memminger was the typical passenger – no experience at sailing, an average swimmer in pools and lakes, and quite comfortable on dry land with his thoroughbred horses. Good crew and passenger mix. Should be fun.

Under diesel power the beautiful sloop-rigged sailboat left the harbor as crew looked back at the receding landscape. Once fully clear of land, Carlos turned the bow into the wind and crew began raising the sails, which were luffing as they rose. First the 1,200 square foot mainsail unfurled from the roller boom as the head of the sail traveled up to the top of the 70-foot mast. Then crew unfurled the jib sail that was rolled up on the spool that ran from the bow to a few feet short of the top of the mast. Carlos gave directions on how to set the main sheet (landlubbers call it a rope), which held the boom in position to enable the mainsail to best catch the wind, and the jib sheet, which held the jib sail in position to best catch the wind. That accomplished, Carlos cut off the engine and moved the wheel back to the right, setting the rudder to aim the sailboat toward the desired course.

Carlos set a course out of Mantanzas harbor due north so the crew could not complain that he was just a coast-line sailor. No, Carlos was a fine navigator, had all the charts and navigation aids, including radar and GPS, and was just fine on blue water north of Cuba, anywhere between Florida and South Texas.

The brisk 20 knot wind out of the west filled the sails and the sleek craft eagerly surged forward. "The wind is quite brisk," Carlos said. "Leave about two feet of sail rolled up on both main and jib. Do not extend it all out." Carlos gave first mate Andrew some instructions on trimming the two sails (winching in the main sheet and jib sheet just the right amount) to shape both sails to best advantage. That done, the crew found comfortable positions aboard the craft and settled in to enjoy the beautiful afternoon. It was exhilarating! The sailboat was heeled over quite a bit and crew was encouraged to mostly sit on the upwind side of the boat (the port side) so their weight would slightly serve to hold the boat a little more upright. Chris said he felt a bit seasick, so Emma gave him some ginger cookies and encouraged him to keep his mind off his queasiness and just look at the horizon. That seemed to help. The seas were choppy, but not rough. Four to five foot seas. Some waves breaking at the top. Just exhilarating. The waves were being pushed by the wind out of the west and the boat was sailing north, so, as each wave rested upon the port bow, the craft tilted further toward starboard and crew seated along the port side rose a foot or so, then fell about the same amount, then up again and down again, on and on. But the ginger cookies and Chris's focus on the horizon was allowing him to get by.

Carlos told everybody that time at the helm would be rotated every three hours. He would man it until 4 pm. Andrew would man it then until 7 pm. Emma would take it until 10 pm. Then Carlos would be on again from 10pm until 1am. Then Andrew would go at it again. Ocean traffic was not particularly busy, but all crew was encouraged to call out any vessel it spotted so the helmsman would be sure to know.

Soon after Andrew took the helm, Marie called out, "Get your Spanish guitar, Carlos, and let us have some music." With Marie's strong New Orleans-bred voice and the skipper's fine Cuban-bred guitar strumming, the sailors soon burst into song. Far out in the ocean, with no one else within sight, the six enjoyed being far away from the crowd and lost in themselves. "Michael, row your boat ashore" got the whole group singing along. When Carlos led off with a Cuban standard, Marie got the hang of it and away they went. Helmsman and crew joined in upon the singing of what is undeniably the most famous Confederate church hymn: "Say Brothers." You will find this one to be familiar:

"Say brothers will you meet us; say brothers will you meet us; say brothers will you meet us; on Canaan's happy shore." Then came the refrain: "Glory, glory, hal-le-lu-jah; glory, glory, hal-le-lu-jah, glory, glory, hal-le-lu-jah, for ever, ever, more." Perhaps the most heartily sung song was "I wish I was in Dixie's Land."

The singing lasted a full hour until someone asked about setting out some drinks. Oops!

Skipper Carlos replied. Folks my voice is giving out a bit and I believe drinks are in order. However, as skipper I must say that, while we are under sail, out in the ocean, no one is allowed to have any beer or alcohol. That is my rule. Mixing drinking alcohol and sailing is too dangerous. Sorry. Groans were recalled as having been heard, but they were brief. Conchita and Emma went down below and prepared drinks for everyone: fresh lemonade, Coca-Cola's, and iced tea, plus some more ginger cookies for Chris, who was barely controlling his sea sickness.

At 7 pm Andrew turned the helm over to Emma. Time to prepare supper while daylight is available. Conchita and Marie descended into the galley area below and got the supper provisions out of the refrigerator. "Wow!," came the exclamation from the galley. "We have bison steaks for tonight. Where did they come from?"

Carlos confessed in little secret. "Well, mates and crew, as you know, Allen Ross's family has a huge herd of bison on the hoof back in Sequoyah. In fact, he is serving bison steaks to the other six of our group in Sewanee tonight. He wanted us to have some, so he packed six on ice and I snuck them on the airplane and into the provisions for us to have for our supper. Nice, don't you think?" All agreed. Along with the bison steaks, the sailors would be having Cuban sweet potatoes; lettuce, cucumber and tomato salad; Cuban melons; and, for desert, peach cobbler with vanilla ice cream. Carlos had already started baking the sweet potatoes, so they would be ready just a soon as the steaks were done. After showing Conchita and Marie how to work the galley appliances, Carlos returned topside, announcing, "My galley work is done, it's topside for me."

Chris volunteered, "I will go down and help the girls." The rather large galley grill could handle three steaks at a time, so everything would be ready in about 30 minutes. The oven would be warming the cobbler as it cooled off. Conchita launched into cutting up the salad and filling up six salad bowls. Those would be passed topside as they became ready. But trouble was a-brewing even before that. Chris, bounded up the stairs to top-side and exclaimed. "Oh, I am bad sea-sick. No way I can endure down below with these rolling seas."

Carlos agreed. "You had better stay topside all through the night. We will make a place for you on the bench right there on the starboard side."

Supper was eaten while the sun descended, and was about over when it flicked out of sight along the western horizon, the sailors feeling fortunate to be blessed with a break in the clouds at that very important moment. During supper, Carlos gave Emma a short break from the helm to allow her to enjoy the meal. As the sun went out of sight, Robert asked Conchita and Marie how they had learned to be such good cooks.

Marie, replied, "We did not do all that much. The sweet potatoes were so easy, cutting up the salad was not hard at all, just as long as you braced yourself in the galley too avoid cutting yourself. It is a-rolling down there. Do you think, playing tennis has helped my balance?"

Carlos replied, "Doubt it. You are just naturally good at whatever you do." Marie blushed and let it drop.

Conchita added, "We are Confederate girls, you know, and, by and large, Confederate girls learn from their mothers that the way to a man's heart is through his stomach. So, learning to cook good Southern food is part of our family upbringing."

Marie challenged, "Well, I will make one comment about that. "The girls in New Orleans often grow up to become the best cooks of all. None across the Confederacy can please their man better than a girl from southern Louisiana."

Carlos finished off the patter with this observation: "Come on, you all. None of us is married and to my knowledge none are even close to becoming engaged. So this talk seems a bit premature all around." Then Carlos turned on the night lights (lights on the sailboat must be muted so the helmsman and look-outs can preserve their night vision) and he and Andrew descended into the galley to clean up the dishes.

At 9:30 pm Carlos figured it was time to turn the sailboat back toward home, giving instructions to maintain a southerly course at 189 degrees on the compass. He helped Emma turn the boat back toward Mantanzas. The wind was gusting up to 25 knots. So he cranked the roller reefing boom to wind down another three feet of mainsail and rolled up a corresponding amount of jib sail. Sailors call this reefing the sails.

Carlos helped Chris set up a row of cushions on the port topside bench and provided a sheet for him. Chris would be sleeping topside in hopes he would not be seasick. Andrew was topside, too, ready to take the helm from Emma at 10:00 pm. Andrew and Chris would be the only ones top-side from 10:00 pm to 1:00 am. There would be no moon until 3:00 am and clouds would be blocking starlight. Carlos had warned Emma and Andrew about the importance of scanning the horizon every five minutes and maintaining good night vision.

Carlos went below and helped everyone prepare their sleeping bunks and made sure the night ventilation was good. He then retired to his bunk, read for a bit in his bunk and fell asleep about 10:30 pm.

Thirty-nine minutes past midnight Carlos was startled by Andrew screaming at the helm:

"Shit!! Man overboard!! All hands on deck!! Shit!!

Before he could exclaim the third "Shit" Carlos was bounding up the stairs and Emma was close behind.

Chris had fallen overboard. No time now to explain how it happened. It was quite dark out there. No moon expected for three more hours. It was cloudy and rain had begun to fall. Lightning and thunder was blowing in rapidly from the west.

"Where is he now," Carlos shouted. "What course were you on?" "190 degrees as instructed, sir." "Give me the helm and point and keep pointing. Do not blink. Keep that arm extended toward Chris so I will know." "This boat is coming about to 10 degrees, heading north on the course we have come from." Carlos was turning the boat around to back track toward the man overboard, a practiced maneuver. But this was a sailboat and the boom, mainsheet and jibsheet had to be reset in the squalling wind and rough seas. By this time, Marie and Conchita were at the winches manning that chore, carefully listening to instructions from Carlos.

With Andrew's help, Emma had spotted Chris with help from a lightning strike and was keeping a steady eye on that course. She had already fastened on one life jacket when she asked, "Was he wearing a life jacket?" Andrew, without turning away from this lookout task replied, "No, he had been trying to sleep on the port-side bench there when he jumped up and rushed to the side of the boat to vomit. So sea-sick. A big wave and gust of wind healed the boat suddenly and he fell overboard. I tossed a life ring in his direction as soon as I could grab it." Lighting flashed again. Emma announced, "I just saw him." There was a splash off the port side. Emma was diving into the ocean. She had buckled a second, larger life jacket on top of the first, grabbed a water-proof flashlight and dove into the ocean life-saving style, without losing sight of the cloud pattern that defined the direction she would swim as she progressed toward Chris.

Now Emma was an exceptionally strong swimmer and used to those huge surfing waves along the Hawaiian coast. But, a second man overboard was not recommended procedure in circumstances such as these. But she sensed a terrible crisis at hand. The storm coming in from the west was now churning the ocean and she had learned from conversation that Chris was only an average swimmer. He was in grave danger of losing his life.

It took time to turn around the sailboat. The sails hung up briefly during the coming about maneuver. It was so dark. The lightning flashes were the only means now of glimpsing Chris among the rolling seas, and then only if the flash coincided with Chris being atop the crest of a wave. If he was down in the trough when the flash occurred, he was not seen. Same for Emma, as she swam head erect, eyes staring ahead. "Shout, Chris. Shout as loud as you can so I can hear were you are. I am swimming to you. Chris. Shout to me." Then she heard a shout. "Emma." "Here." "Emma." "Here." Although Chris was doing his best to be heard, he was gasping while trying to stay above water and the wind and rain was making a lot of noise.

Maintaining the desired course was difficult in the high wind and maneuvering toward Chris for pick-up would be difficult. Carlos shouted, "Roll in both sails, I've turned on the engine." Conchita and Marie did as directed, and soon both sails were all rolled up.

Now in normal "man overboard" sailboat maneuvers, it is very unlikely that a swimmer would reach the victim before the sailboat could be brought about and return for a pick-up. Not so this night. Difficulty in seeing the victim in the darkness and among the surging waves greatly complicated this rescue. And ocean swimmers of Emma's caliber were seldom aboard a sailboat. Of course Emma was wrong to dive in without permission from her skipper. But Emma had a mind of her own on this occasion. And away she had gone. She was off swimming back to the north while Carlos was only halfway through maneuvering the sailboat around to a northerly course.

"Emma." "Here." Those shouts were key to Chris' survival and he was doing his best to keep his throat clear for shouting.

Back on the sailboat, a grave mistake was made. At one flash of lightning, Andrew spotted something floating in the water at a distance that matched where Chris ought to be, but twenty degrees toward the east. He had not seen Chris for about 3 minutes, and figured that object was him. Not good. Andrew would be guiding the sailboat toward some floating debris. If that did not match the direction toward Emma's flashlight, the skipper's priority had to go to Chris, who had no life jacket.

Emma's swimming upon the rolling seas topped by white-caps and foam was a thing of beauty and efficiency. Fortunately the two life vests fit snuggly and did not impair progress as much as would be expected. Stroke after stroke, head high, hoping to catch sight of Chris atop a wave crest, Emma progressed toward the sound she faintly heard.

"Emma." "Over here."

Emma knew something was wrong when she observed that Carlos was on a course about 20 degrees divergent from the direction she was swimming. The sailboat, being faster, even passed her well off to the right. But she doggedly continued her powerful strokes, feet kicking and arms stroking down through the water.

"Emma."

She knew she was getting close. Then a lighting strike revealed a struggling swimmer.

"I've got you, Chris." "Do not fight me." "I have two life jackets." "One for you and one for me." "I am getting yours ready now." "Here it is." "Let us put this on." "Good boy." "I will buckle you up." "Snug and comfy."

"There." "Let me hear you cough." "Swallowed a lot of water?" "We deal with that back at the boat."

"I have a flashlight." "Carlos will see it and come to us." "Something must have thrown him off course." "But he will return."

"Emma." "Thanks to God you came." "I was about to drown."

Chris and Emma embraced among the rolling seas as she signaled Carlos with the flashlight. Before long Chris broke down in tears and uncontrollable sobs. He had faced death and survived -- an experience that would alter this young man's outlook on life forevermore.

Five minutes later, Carlos brought the sailboat alongside Emma and Chris. A ladder was lowered and Chris, then Emma climbed aboard. Then Chris just lay down in front of the helm and started to cry again. Emma understood. She went below for blankets and asked Conchita to make hot coffee and hot tea. Chris was to get one or both, along with the remaining ginger cookies. When they were ready she sat down beside Chris and helped him regain his composure. He had chosen the hot coffee. Emma said she preferred the hot tea and would like a sandwich to go with it. You see, that girl had been doing some hearty swimming and it was time to recharge her batteries.

"Conchita, make more hot coffee, but make it real weak. Chris needs to dilute the salt water he swallowed among his struggles. He needs to be doing some serious peeing." "I've have some more hot tea, as well."

By dawn, the storm had passed and the winds had substantially subsided to a comfortable 15 knots, still out of the west. Breakfast was good. Blueberry pancakes with butter and a mixed topping of fresh fig compote and pure maple syrup. Melon to boot.

The sailing party was back in Mantanzas harbor by noon. Carlos had supplemented the sailing with some diesel engine motoring to ensure that the diminishing winds did not make them late.

There was lunch at the marina and swimming in the club pool. Seems like the sailors were a bit salty. They claimed that they were now "blue water sailors." None disputed it. Then showers and dressing for the plane ride back to Sewanee.

The sailors would arrive in the Sewanee airport at 7:00 pm. Whow! Would they have stories to tell.

During the plane ride back to Sewanee, Andrew Houston and Conchita Rezanov sat across the aisle chatting and talking about all sorts of stuff, including tennis, of course. It was obvious to others that Andrew really, really liked Conchita. Without a doubt they would be seeing more of each other.

The next row of seats was taken by Carlos Cespedes and Marie Saint Martin. They were becoming fast friends. He was quite the charmer when strumming along on his guitar and she had a wonderful singing voice and wide range of musical interests. They would be seeing more of each other as well.

The back seating on the airplane stretched from window to window because no aisle was needed behind it. On that sat Chris Memminger and Emma Lunalilo. They chatted for a while, but Chris was still visibly shaken by the night's ordeal at sea. He was emotionally and physical wiped out. They laid back their seat and felt needed sleep coming on. Before long, Chris was asleep with his head on Emma's bosom, as she cradled him with both seats laid back. She was OK and he was OK. Everyone understood.

Now as the writer telling you this true story, I feel the need to explain. Chris was not a sissy. He had been working with horses since he was just a young pup. He had broken young horses. He had raced horses on flat tracks and over steeple chase jumps. On land, Chris was a tough as most any man. But on the ocean, among those waves, gasping for air in pitch black darkness. That experience had brought this tough guy to his knees.

## Sunday Evening Selected Diary Postings

Chris Memminger's and Emma Lunalilo's diary notes for Sunday are considered confidential. We do not wish to pry.

All the others on the Cuba trip wrote about the sailing and how thankful each was that Chris and Emma were OK.

Diary note by Carlos Cespedes said, "As skipper, I would never have permitted Emma to go into the water in hopes of rescuing Chris. In all of my sailing training, that was a definite "No, No". But I am so thankful she did it. Considering the gale-force winds; the pitch black darkness; and our error in mistaking debris for Chris when we got a glimpse during that lightning strike, I fear we would have lost Chris to the sea. I do not know how I would have ever forgiven myself. Thank God for Emma.

Diary note by Andrew Houston said, "When the man overboard crisis hit, I was the only person top-side except for Chris. The wind out of the west must have been gusting to 30 knots, so it kept the boat heeled over on the port side. One could practically reach the water when a wind gust struck the sail. Chris was bunked on the port side bench when he sensed he was about to throw up. Damn it! Chris was so damn careful to not vomit on the side of the boat that he leaned too far out over the water. That was just when the worst wind gust struck the sail. Chris simply fell head first into the water. I saw it, but it all happened so fast. All I could do was grab a life ring and toss it into the water while shouting that dreaded cry: "Man Overboard."

Diary note by Conchita Rezanov said, "Like the rest, when I heard Andrew shout, "Man Overboard," I raced up the gangway to topside and helped in every way I could. Following Carlos's directions, working the lines and winches to get the sails down so we could better maneuver by the engine. Straining to see Chris or Emma in the darkness or hear a shout among the roar of the wind and waves. At the same time I was praying for Chris and Emma. It is a miracle that we all got back to the harbor safely. Yet, I do believe I will go sailing again. Up until that horrible crisis, I know that I deeply loved it. Oh, yes. Andrew and I are going to play tennis first chance. I think he is a very good tennis player, but I might have to go easy on him so as not to hurt his feelings. Men are so sensitive about getting beat by a woman. I like him, too. It will be fun. I sense he likes me in a romantic way. That's OK with me."

Diary note by Marie Saint Martin said, "I know Chris was deeply shaken over the Man Overboard crisis. Up until that time, I was having a great time and felt safe even though the wind was howling and the waves were pretty high. Carlos had a way of assuring everyone that we would be fine, that the sailboat was capable of far worst weather and he had sailed it is such conditions. I was enjoying the adventure. I like Carlos. We really had fun yesterday afternoon when he played the guitar and we all sang. We are definitely going to do more of that. Perhaps I should take the lead in getting a music group started. Our group could include Carlos and Allen Ross on guitars and Amanda Washington on piano. We can include Tina Sharp. She plays the French horn very well, I am assured, so I am confident that she can sing as well. Might even lasso Professor Davis to join us with his banjo. I aim to look into it Monday afternoon."

Diary note by Professor Davis said, "Just learned that the overnight sailing trip off of Cuba almost ended in disaster. Chris Memminger was so sea sick that, while trying to throw up over the side of the boat, he fell overboard at the moment that a gust of wind and a big wave hit the opposite side. Was pitch black dark, a gale had come in from the west and he almost drowned. Emma grabbed an extra life vest and flashlight and dove into the ocean and swam . . ."

"Thank God Chris is OK. Emma is some kind of surfer woman. I had no idea she was capable of doing that, or that she would be willing to risk her own life like that. She is our heroine for sure."

## Part 1, Chapter 8, Day 8 – Having Finished Subjugating Maryland, Kentucky and Missouri, Federals Launch Coordinated Attack against Confederate States – Class Lecture, Monday, June 13, 2011

It was hard on Monday morning for the Sewanee Project team to settle down and focus on Confederate history. Professor Davis had prepared a fine lecture about the military contest, clearly to be a highlight of the four weeks together at Sewanee. It took a little over fifteen minutes to settle down and began to listen. Professor Davis began as we listen in.

### President Lincoln Issues the Attack Order, Targeted for May 5, 1862

On May 1, 1862, the Lincoln Administration issued orders to all five divisions to launch their respective attack strategies simultaneously, on the morning of Monday, May 5. The Confederate Secret Service intercepted the May 1 telegraph, decoded it, and alerted all five Confederate division commanders. The grand Confederate strategy of "Envelopment and Capture" was about to be attempted on five fronts. But first, the Federal divisions had to be allowed to advance with only token resistance, to build an overly-confident attitude and to lure them away from their lines of supply and into terrain that facilitated envelopment and forced surrender.

### May through Early June, 1862 — Tactical Retreat, Envelopment, Capture, and Imprisonment

The success of the 1862 Confederate military campaign, termed "Tactical Retreat, Envelopment and Capture," would become the focus of study by students of military strategy all over the world, even to this day. The history of the successful Defense of State Secession in North America would be as well known in military schools and textbooks in Russia, or France, or Germany or Japan, as it would be at West Point and Confederate military schools. And the essence of our 1861-1862 history is well known -- to varying degrees of thoroughness, to be sure -- by Confederates living today. So, only a few pages of this book need to be devoted to the story -- an overview will do nicely -- allowing the reader to devote more time to understanding "Why" the Confederacy is the "Greatest Country on Earth."

### Federal Virginia and Carolina Division Advances Southward (May 5 to May 25)

As previously mentioned, the mission of the Federal's Virginia and Carolinas Division was to occupy Richmond and force surrender of the Virginia State Government; then proceed to Raleigh and force the surrender of the North Carolina State Government; then proceed to Columbia and force surrender of the South Carolina State Government. Made up of militia and volunteers from the northeastern states, this division had gathered near Washington City and departed on May 5 on its march south to first conquer Richmond. This division consisted of 130,000 men, of which 17,000 were cavalry. Irving McDowell of Ohio was commanding.

Positioned to entrap this Federal division was Confederate Division 1, consisting of 80,000 Confederates, which included 25,000 cavalry. Nine companies of irregular Virginia State Rangers were in assigned positions to harass and confuse the Federal advance. Robert E. Lee of Virginia was commanding. The Confederate strategy was "Tactical Retreat, Envelopment and Capture" somewhere west of Richmond.

History shows that, from the start of the Federal advance on May 5, McDowell's Virginia and Carolinas Division appeared to Federals to be relatively unopposed as it advanced southward from Washington City toward its destination of Richmond, encountering -- as it appeared to advancing soldiers, cavalry and commanders -- only token resistance from Confederates.

Federals found it much easier than expected to get through Fredericksburg. Confidence grew at they proceeded further south toward Richmond.

But the resistance anticipated by the Federals to be at their front, materialized instead at their rear as, after eight days of the Federal's southward march, Confederate cavalry and irregular State Rangers began attacking supply lines, capturing horses, wagons and supplies, along with the troops responsible for those functions. Yet, the raids on the supply train were so swift and unnoticed, often during the night, that the general alarm was not fully sounded.

But when the Federal army reached the Pamunkey River, near Cedar Fork, the Confederates appeared in great numbers, causing the Federals to veer westward toward a perceived attacking position west of the capital city. Yet the big fight did not occur, for telegraph messages from Montgomery were advising Robert Lee to delay Envelopment a few days so that Washington City would not become alarmed by a Virginia defeat before defeats west of the mountains could be consummated. Must continue to make the Lincoln Administration believe that the invasion was going well.

By the night of May 17, the Federals were encamped on the east side of the James River. By that point, Confederates had completed their capture of the wagon trains and outlying Federal cavalry. And, over the past several days, Confederate cavalry had swept into the Federal army, at spots when opportunities arose, and seized many of the Federals' artillery pieces. Virginia State Rangers, such as Captain George Downs' company, and North Carolina Rangers had been particularly helpful in these captures of supply trains and artillery units. Lee's army was now ready to attack the Federal foot soldiers. It was there, with the James to the Federal rear, that Confederates would surround the Federal army and make a fierce attack with the full force of Lee's army and cavalry, employing the enhanced firepower of repeating weapons and many field artillery pieces.

An hour before dawn, the following morning, Confederates mounted a general attack from the east, the south and the north while cavalry and dismounted riflemen prevented retreat across the river to the west. Within three hours, all remaining Federal artillery was disabled. As darkness begin to set in that evening, May 18, 70,000 Federal troops and remaining cavalry, the fit and the wounded, laid down their arms and surrendered. The remainder of the 130,000 invasion force was dead (17,000), had been captured among the wagon trains (12,000) or managed to get away and flee back north (31,000). Most effective in forcing the surrender were the troops under Thomas Jackson. Most effective in directing the operation was the direction provided by the commander, Robert E. Lee. Within three weeks, by June 9, the 70,000 captives would be in 14 prisoner-of-war camps hastily established in the Piedmont region of North Carolina, between Greensboro and Charlotte, carefully dispersed to facilitate food supply, to minimize disease, to maintain a degree of secrecy, and to impede a mass rescue. The Lincoln Administration received news of the defeat on Wednesday, May 27, but the status of the 70,000 missing and their whereabouts was unclear.

<u>Federal Tennessee and Georgia Division Advances Southward (May 5 to May 25)</u>

As previously mentioned, the mission of the Tennessee and Georgia Division was to conquer Nashville, force the surrender of the Tennessee State Government, proceed southeastward, skirting Chattanooga, turn south into Georgia skirt Atlanta and force the surrender of the Georgia State Government at Milledgeville. While honoring Kentucky neutrality, an invasion force had gathered in southern Indiana, not far north of Louisville in preparation for moving down the Louisville and Nashville railroad to Franklin, Kentucky, the last sizable town along the railroad before crossing into Tennessee. By late April this division had fully arrived at Franklin and was making ready to move south into Tennessee to capture and occupy the capital city of Nashville. The Tennessee and Georgia Division consisted of 70,000 men, of which 9,000 were cavalry. William Rosecrans, of Ohio, was commanding.

Positioned to entrap the Federal's Tennessee and Georgia division was a division of 60,000 Confederates, which included 20,000 cavalry -- Division 2, Braxton Bragg of North Carolina, commanding. Because Nashville was so close to Kentucky and so easily attacked by Federal gunboats on the Cumberland River, the Confederate strategy was to permit Federals to occupy the Tennessee capital, feign surrender of the Tennessee State Government, then to allow Federals to venture southeastward along the railroad through Murfreesboro, then allow further advancement toward the southeast, but thereafter springing the trap to force surrender in the vicinity of Tullahoma.

History shows that, from the start of its advance on May 5, the Federal Tennessee and Georgia Division was allowed to advance southward toward its destination of Nashville, encountering, as it appeared to the soldiers, cavalry and commanders, only token resistance from Confederates. The march from the Kentucky State line to Nashville was only 40 miles and it was covered in four to six days, the first arriving on May 9. Although most of the city and state government officials and employees had evacuated, a few spokesmen remained to give the Federal commanders confidence that political reconstruction of the Tennessee State Government would not present unusual difficulties. A Federal detachment of 5,000 troops, of which 1,000 was cavalry, remained in the vicinity of Nashville throughout the month of May, while political agents from the Lincoln Administration obtained pledges to rescind State Secession and decreed that all men who resisted Federal occupation of Tennessee were denied the right to vote for the remainder of their lives.

Meanwhile, on May 13, Andrew Johnson -- the only senator of a seceded state to have remained in Washington after secession and now an enthusiastic supporter of the Lincoln Administration -- departed Washington City for Nashville, expecting to be sworn in as the Provisional Military Governor of the Reconstructed State of Tennessee. [85]

Also on Tuesday, May 13, the bulk of the Federal Tennessee and Georgia Division moved out of Nashville toward the southeast, aiming to occupy Murfreesboro, 30 miles distant, which had been the original capital of the state. Again, only token resistance was presented by Braxton Bragg's Confederate Division 2 on the march to Murfreesboro, because entrapment further down the line of march -- against the Cumberland Plateau in the vicinity of The Barrens, west of Tullahoma -- would be more certain than among the open farmland surrounding Murfreesboro, or even against the Highland Rim, which surrounded the lowland country of Middle Tennessee. Federals arrived in Murfreesboro on Friday morning, May 16, and occupied the town without resistance. Only a token representative of the local government was present, and this small group pledged its loyalty to the reconstructed government in Nashville.

On Sunday, May 18, the Federal Tennessee and Georgia Division moved out, continuing its southeasterly march toward Chattanooga, never veering far from the track of the Nashville and Chattanooga Railroad, which ran in a southeast direction, rising through Bell Buckle Gap onto the Highland Rim and on to Wartrace. From Wartrace it continued southeast, crossed the Duck River and arrived at Tullahoma, where it joined another railroad line that ran northeast to McMinnville. The Federals reached the vicinity of Wartrace by Thursday morning, a distance of 20 miles. After

---

[85] In truthful history, Nashville fell easily to Federal occupation and Tennessee Senator Andrew Johnson accepted President Lincoln's offer to become Provisional Governor. Later Andrew Johnson would be nominated as the Republican's 1864 vice-president candidate. In truthful history, after President Lincoln was killed by Maryland actor John Wilkes Booth, Andrew Johnson took the reigns as President and played a significant role in the political reconstruction of the conquered Confederate States.

the Federals left Wartrace, Bragg's Confederates and Tennessee Rangers began springing the trap, for the resistance anticipated by the Federals to be at their front, materialized instead from their rear, across the Highland Rim as Confederate cavalry began attacking supply lines, capturing horses, wagons and supplies, along with the troops responsible for those functions. Again, the raids on the supply train were so swift and unnoticed, often during the night, that the general alarm was not fully sounded. By the time the bulk of the invasion force reached a point midway between Wartrace and Tullahoma, on Friday, May 23, Confederate forces began turning the invaders toward their left, due east toward The Barrens and Savage Gulf. Surrenders were gained in stages, first this regiment and then that regiment, the troops on foot being the first to give up. By the time the remnant of Federals were driven into Savage Gulf, surrounded by imposing ridges of the Cumberland Plateau – high ground occupied by Confederate cavalry and artillery -- they were whipped. It was Sunday, May 25th.

After five days of fighting and retreat, of the 65,000 Federals who left out from Nashville, 11,000 had been killed, 30,000 had surrendered, a number of these wounded, and 24,000 had managed to escape the trap, most of them finding their way back to Nashville or to Kentucky. Of the 30,000 that had surrendered, 4,000 were cavalry. There were 3,000 wounded among the captives. The 30,000 captives were taken to 10 prisoner-of-war camps hastily set up at remote locations east of the Cumberland Plateau's eastern ridge and west of the Tennessee River, spread out between Lewis Chapel and Grand View. Within two weeks, by June 9, the captives were in their respective POW camps. The Lincoln Administration learned of the defeat on Tuesday, May 27, but the status and whereabouts of the 30,000 missing Federal troops was in a state of confusion.

<u>Federal Alabama and Florida Division Advances Southward (May 5 to May 26)</u>

As previously mentioned, the mission of the Federal's Alabama and Florida Division was to invade western Tennessee, heading due south along the course of the northward-flowing Tennessee River, proceeding to the Mississippi State line; then turn east into Alabama and then southeast through that State to occupy Burmingham, then move on to Montgomery and force the surrender of the Alabama State Government – and also force the surrender of Confederate Government officials that might have remained. Toward this objective, an invasion force had gathered in the vicinity of Metropolis, Illinois, which was just north-east of where the Tennessee River flows into the Ohio at Paducah, Kentucky, and not far east of where the Cumberland River flows into the Ohio. In groups, this invasion force had moved up the Tennessee River to a staging area west of Murray, in southwest Kentucky, some riding horses, some walking and some coming up-river by steamboats. They were preparing to invade Tennessee along a path paralleling the Tennessee River, where a fleet of gun-boats and steamboats would support the advance into southern Tennessee, as far as the Mississippi border. Since further support by gun-boats and steamboats would be arrested by the rapids at Muscle Shoals, the invasion force planned to proceed overland to Grand Junction, at Corinth Mississippi where existing railroads could be seized to transport the army east into northern Alabama. From there it would advance through northern Alabama and proceed south to force surrender at Montgomery. The final goal was to force surrender at Tallahassee, Florida. The Alabama and Florida Division, commanded by Ulysses Grant, of Ohio and Missouri, consisted of 70,000 men, of which 9,000 were cavalry.

Positioned to entrap the Federal's Alabama and Florida division was a division of 55,000 Confederates, which included 18,000 cavalry and State Rangers from western Tennessee, northern Mississippi and northern Alabama. This was Division 3, which was commanded by the able Albert Sidney Johnston of Kentucky and Texas. The strategy was to allow Federals to advance southward, up the Tennessee River, through western Tennessee, because in that region surrender could not be forced. Then, after Federals left the protection of their gunboats and steamboats at Pittsburg Landing, to make a fierce and rapid attack from the northwest about midway between

Pittsburg Landing and Corinth, Mississippi, to incite panic and force retreat toward the southeast, in hopes of effecting surrender and capture in northeast Mississippi or northwest Alabama, in the hill country south of the Tennessee River.

History shows that, from the start of the Federal's advance on May 5, the Alabama and Florida Division suffered extreme losses to its fleet of gunboats and steamboats as they steamed upstream against the heavy spring flow of the Tennessee River. For the most part, Federals did not understand what was happening. Disasters occurred often: suddenly, without warning, a boiler would explode, killing many of those aboard (if a gunboat, few of the crew survived). History reveals that the carnage was the result of torpedoes sneaked into the fuel supply and mines planted in the riverbed, many with associated river snags that encouraged pilots to steer free of a snag, but right over a mine. [86]

Unlike the river vessels, the cavalry, supply wagons and marching troops suffered little resistance as they progressed southward, never very far from the river. When, on May 19, the Federal division arrived at Pittsburg Landing, the jumping off point for Corinth, the different units -- those on boats that succeeded in getting upstream, foot soldiers, cavalry and supply trains -- were, to their surprise able to join up without harassment. The 66,000 Federals who succeeded in getting through Tennessee, of which 8,500 were cavalry, consumed May 20 and 21 getting organized for the march into Mississippi to attack Corinth and the railroad junction between the Memphis and Charleston Railroad and the Mobile and Ohio Railroad, located 10 miles distant to the south-southwest.

The Federals were confident and eager to be the first to reach Montgomery. The sense of a competition between the five Federal invasion forces was stronger than ever, especially a passion for the top commanders.

The Federals departed Pittsburg Landing during the morning of May 22, a Thursday. By mid-afternoon all units were on the road toward Corinth. It was then that the Confederate attack struck from the northwest. A massive attack in which 18,000 cavalry hit the Federal lines like a hammer, disrupting order and prompting many to retreat toward the southeast. Confederate foot soldiers joined in the push, along with mobile field artillery, such as the 12-pounder smooth bore guns carried by two mules. Both the Confederate travois and conventional wagons were used when helpful in bringing troops rapidly forward by a few miles here and there to maintain pressure on the retreating Federals, not allowing time for them to organize into defensive lines or erect protective breastworks. Some Federals succeeded in escaping back to Pittsburg Landing, but over half were driven across Yellow Creek into a rugged wilderness area south of the Tennessee River town of Hamburg, Tennessee. One would think the retreating Federals would make for Hamburg, in search of Federal gunboat and steamboat protection, although over half of those vessels had been destroyed, but Confederate cavalry and State Rangers prevented many from turning north toward the river. It was at Yellow Creek that the Federals were forced to surrender. During the panic, over 10,000 Confederates had raced around the retreating Federals to the south, along the Memphis and Charleston Railroad, crossed over the headwaters of Yellow Creek and then turned north along the east side of the creek to establish a stout defensive line that prevented the harried Federals from retreating further. Panicked just west of Yellow Creek,

---

[86] Successes against Federal boats coming up the Tennessee River were the work of Confederate Secret Service agents, working in the field, placing torpedoes and mines, produced with technical support from James Eads and Confederate munitions experts and fabricated by teams located in various shops. Operating from well concealed hideouts dug into the river banks here and there, were small teams of mine operators who made sure all was in readiness; they often released mines just when a Federal craft arrived, using concealed control wires that ran from the hideout, under the water and to the mine release pin. In truthful history, Confederates used coal torpedoes to trick Federals into mistakenly shoveling one into the firebox of the steam engine.

Federals were surrendering like dominoes, one unit after the other. This took place during the day of May 26, a Monday.

The final haul of captives totaled 35,000, of which 4,000 were cavalry. Approximately 3,000 captives were wounded. The Federal dead totaled 5,000. Within two weeks, by June 9, the captives would be distributed into 12 prisoner-of-war camps located in the remote northern Alabama hills, between Burleson and Peach Grove. The Lincoln Administration received word of this disaster on Thursday, May 29.

Future historians are often puzzled over why Washington City was unable to understand that its five Invading Armies were not in serious trouble. Well, part of the deception that blinded Washington City and the top Federal military command was the stream of messages passed along surreptitiously by the Confederate Secret Service, which assured that this army and that army was proceeding along its designated invasion path without difficulty.

## Federal Mississippi River Division Advances Southward (May 5 until Stalled)

The mission of the Mississippi River Division was to gain control of the navigation of the Mississippi River from the Ohio to the Gulf of Mexico, and to force surrender of the Louisiana State Government at Baton Rouge and the Mississippi State Government at Jackson. Toward this object, construction of iron-clad gun-boats had begun in haste at Rock Island, Illinois, to be used in descending southward down the Mississippi River. Also Navy warships and transports were upgraded in New York with improved armaments, in some cases with more powerful steam engines, and organized into an invasion force to enter the mouth of the Mississippi River and advance upstream to New Orleans and then force the government surrender at Baton Rouge. From the New Orleans-Baton Rouge staging area, armies would then be dispatched to force surrender of the Mississippi State Government at Jackson. The Federal's Mississippi River Division had gathered near Cairo and Mound City, Illinois. It was led by 4 armored gunboats, just finished at Rock Island and it consisted of 40,000 men, of which 5,000 were cavalry. Don Carlos Buell of Ohio was commanding.

Positioned to entrap this Federal division somewhere along its descent down the Mississippi River was a division of 30,000 Confederates, 10,000 of them cavalry, plus a fleet of 5 Confederate River Defender Gunboats designed by Eads and Ericsson and built by Eads' workforce in Mississippi. This was Confederate Division 4, commanded by Pierre Beauregard of Louisiana.

Success in preventing Federal navigation of the Mississippi River depended also on preventing the capture of New Orleans and Baton Rouge, a task relegated to powerful Confederate artillery, to three Confederate River Defender Gunboats, to a few Confederate Navy warships, and to teams of Confederate mine-laying experts.

Except for Federal cavalry, which proceeded south on horseback, the foot soldiers and supplies for the Mississippi River Division had been advanced southward from its staging base at Cairo, Illinois in shifts during April, as units and steamboats were available. By early May the division was set up just north of Tennessee and ready to invade further down the Mississippi River. As with the other four Federal divisions, the Mississippi River Division, departed into the Confederate portion of the Mississippi River, as directed from Washington City, on May 5. Federal cavalry did not experience difficulty until it arrived at the Chickasaw Bluffs, located north of Memphis in southwest Tennessee. But from the start at Island Number 10, just south of the Tennessee-Kentucky line, Federal vessels suffered considerable losses from explosions, the cause of which was at the time baffling. Defenses at Island Number 10 were significant, but designed to allow Confederates to escape down-river when needed to avoid capture. And at other points along the river, the emphasis was on getting coal torpedoes onto the invading boats and steering them above mines of the James Eads design. But the most important Confederate weapon was the Confederate River Defender Gunboat. Often, after a group of steamboats and/or gunboats passed by the hiding place of a CRDG, it entered the river and gave chase from behind, quickly catching up to within the range of its two guns, then firing. Within four rounds, the enemy vessel was normally stricken and put out of service or on its way to the bottom. No Federal gunboats ever reached the Mississippi State line. The torpedoes, slipped onboard by Confederate Secret Service agents, most of them African Americans, were very effective in disabling or sinking southbound steamboats.

### Federal Navy Advances Northward up Mississippi River (May 5 until Stalled at New Orleans)

Meanwhile, far to the south, a sizable fleet of the Federal Navy entered the mouth of the Mississippi at the Gulf of Mexico, but experienced difficulty in proceeding upstream to New Orleans. The three CRDG vessels and crew were generally effective in fighting off or sinking Federal craft coming upstream, but the most helpful deterrent were the snags and Confederate mines placed in the river. The fleet began its advance up the Mississippi on May 5, as directed by the Lincoln Administration, and it looked like, for several weeks, that it would never reach New Orleans. But, eventually about half of the fleet survived to approach the city. The Confederate Government in Montgomery decided to save the city from a bombardment from what remained of the Federal fleet and ordered the city to surrender. The surrender became official on May 26. But the fleet, weakened by the ordeal of getting upstream from the Gulf, stayed at the City, too weak to challenge the Confederate defenses at the capital city of Baton Rouge without support by Federal troops and cavalry. But Federal troops far to the north were experiencing great difficulties above Memphis, at the Chickasaw Bluffs. Fighting persisted between Federals and Confederates for a full week, but an Envelopment and Capture opportunity never occurred. Confederates had to settle for forcing the Federals to retreat north back into the northwest corner of Tennessee, where they would await reinforcements. By early June, it was apparent to the Lincoln Administration that gaining control of the Mississippi River south of Tennessee and north of New Orleans would take many more months of gunboat construction and a far larger concentration of troops and cavalry.

### Federal Missouri, Arkansas and Texas Division Advances Southward (May 5 to May 21)

As already mentioned, the organization of the Federal's Missouri, Arkansas and Texas Division -- commanded by John Fremont -- had been slowed by the fighting in Missouri between the State militia and anti-secessionists. But, by the end of April, the State militia had been driven to the southern region of the state and the capital at Jefferson City was firmly in the control of anti-secessionists and their Federal backers. So, the Missouri, Arkansas and Texas Division, consisting of 40,000 men, of which 5,000 were cavalry, was now prepared to move south through southern Missouri, pushing resistance out of the state, then proceed into Arkansas, force surrender of the State Government at Little Rock, then proceed into Texas and force surrender of the far-away State Government at Austin. John Fremont, with family ties to Missouri, was commanding.

Positioned to entrap the Federal's Missouri, Arkansas and Texas division was a division of 35,000 Confederates, 12,000 of them cavalry. This was Confederate Division 5, commanded by Sterling Price of Missouri. Envelopment was anticipated about half way between the Arkansas border and the capital city of Little Rock.

As ordered by the Lincoln Administration, on May 5 the Federal force departed Rolla, Missouri, located on the Gascouade River, and headed south toward Cedar Bluff. Resistance from Confederates and/or from Missouri Secessionists was minor, and only a few supplies and horses were lost to raiders, and the units remained intact. Progress on to Gainesville, Missouri was also relatively unimpeded. The raids on outliers intensified a bit when the division crossed over into Arkansas and crossed the White River at North Fork, but progress continued in spite of raids by State Rangers and the confusion they caused. By May 15 the division was at Kinderhook on the Little Red River. Three days later the division was at Lewisburg on the Arkansas River. A day was consumed crossing the Arkansas. And, although the objective, the capital city of Little Rock, was but 40 miles downstream, resistance had thus far been manageable, losses being confined to 500 troops and about one seventh of the supplies. The division departed the Arkansas River on the morning of May 20 toward Perryville, Arkansas, about 10 miles to the south. It was then that all hell broke loose. Confederate troops appeared on the east flank and on the west flank and cavalry closed in behind the back of the Federal division. In response, the division quickened its pace toward Perryville. But at Perryville, it encountered dug-in Confederate troops, arranged in an arc. The Federals closed ranks, seeking protection from each other, making the damage of the Confederate artillery even more deadly. Confederate cavalry attacked nearly all who attempted escape. By sundown, the Federals sensed that they were surrounded. Mutinous declarations permeated the night. When dawn broke the following day, Wednesday, May 21, white flags began appearing and Federal deserters begin crossing over to the Confederate lines, hands raised in abject surrender. By 2 o'clock in the afternoon John Fremont -- the proud, cocky "Pathfinder" -- the husband of the politically influential Jessie Benton Fremont -- the largely incompetent commander of the Federal's Missouri, Arkansas and Texas Division -- and the former 1856 candidate for President for the Republican Party of the northern States -- sought to negotiate. Sterling Price, commander of the Confederate Division 5, and the dejected Fremont met in a tent erected between the lines and struck a deal. If the Federals would lay down their arms, and submit to a lottery, then, Federals could bury their dead at a gravesite within their lines, all of the wounded would be allowed to retreat back to Missouri and all of the healthy would be subject to a 50/50 lottery -- heads you are a captive to be escorted to a prisoner-of-war camp somewhere in Texas -- tails you may high-tail it back to Illinois or points beyond under Confederate cavalry escort, never to ever again take up arms against the Confederate States of America, Missouri of any State that seeks to secede. Fremont had no choice. His men preferred to take their chances in a coin toss than be certain of imprisonment.

So within an hour, lines for surrender were formed up and Confederate officers began listing each surrendered individual in the "book of life." An entry was made for each Federal -- name, age, home town and state, next of kin, where born, citizenship, if an immigrant the year of arrival, healthy-sick-or wounded and where, if healthy, was the toss, Heads or Tails. All was completed and movement north and south began at 9 in the morning of Saturday, May 24. In graves lay 4,000 dead Federals. Headed north under Confederate escort were 4,000 surrendered wounded Federals and 15,750 healthy Federals who had come up "tails." Headed for Texas under Confederate escort were 15,750 healthy Federals who had come up "heads." By June 7, they would be dispersed in 7 prisoner-of-war camps stretching from Jacksboro to Quitman. The Confederates would terminate the escort at Licking, Missouri, giving rise to the ditty composed by a notable captive:

> "On the way down to Perryville, Ol' Fremont led us through Licking.
> But when we got to Perryville, Fremont's fair boys took a Licking.
> For the lucky ones returning, he made us revisit Licking."

The Lincoln Administration received news of the disaster at Perryville, Arkansas on May 28.

## Over a Four-Week Span, The Lincoln Administration and the North Receives Repeating and Devastating News

News of the failures of the five coordinated invasions of the Confederacy hit the Lincoln Administration in repeated blasts. The arrival dates of each devastating military report, in chronological sequence, were as follows:

- Virginia and Carolinas Division defeat: May 27. [87]
- Missouri, Arkansas and Texas Division defeat: May 28.
- Alabama and Florida Division defeat: May 29.
- Mississippi River Division and New Orleans stalemate: early June.
- Tennessee and Georgia Division defeat: May 27.

The count of Federals imprisoned in Confederate prisoner-of-war camps totaled 150,000. Federal battlefield deaths totaled a little over 40,000. Confederates had captured huge quantities of modern firearms, ammunition and artillery, horses, wagons -- so much an army needed to wage war. The Federal army was decimated, with no hope of rebuilding a new invasion force prior to the November 1862 elections, which meant that Republican candidates had no way to offer encouragement to their electorate. Confederate propaganda -- effectively distributed by the Secret Service -- was persuading many in the northern States to advocate, "Let Them Go in Peace." The height of the election season -- July, August and September -- was on the horizon. Several states actually voted in October and those would surely go Democratic. Recognition of the Confederate States of America as a sovereign among the nations of the world was clearly anticipated, with Great Britain and France likely to lead the way. Abolitionists had, through their campaign against the Southern States, built political support in Bleeding Kansas and empowered the rise of the new Republican Party in the Northern States, but could it at this late hour somehow resurrect renewed enthusiasm for conquering the seceded States? Or would the Abolitionists' plea against slavery be recast as a plea to rid their region of people of African ancestry -- a plea for racial cleansing -- a plea to drive Colored people out of the northern States and into the Confederate States? The Lincoln Administration had decided to throw all of its military might against an untested Confederate army without first testing the strength of their adversary. If it had worked, all the seceded States would have been forced to rescind secession, State by State, and bow to Federal might. But the untested Federal troops sent south simultaneously on paths of invasion -- having no passion derived by a need to defend family and home -- having no passion derived from a cause worth fighting for -- having no passion derived from desperate battle experience -- having not yet seen the elephant -- did panic when the elephant was seen, failed to match their foe and soon surrendered in large numbers. [88]

## Monday Evening Selected Diary Postings

All diaries commented on the weekend's near-disaster sailing trip, but we need not put those comments here. Those selected below present other thoughts.

Diary note by Amanda Washington said, "Benedict Juárez is such a nice man. At 27 years he is about the oldest of our group. Has already built a small house he calls his "bachelor pad.""

---

[87] It was with remarkable coordination that Confederates had been able to steer Federals along an extended path to the James River, west of Richmond, and consume valuable time in order to delay the envelopment two extra weeks so as not to alarm the Lincoln Administration prematurely.

[88] The importance of testing an enemy's military strength before committing all of your forces is often found in human history. An example is the First Battle of Bull Run (Manassas) at the outset of the truthful history of the War Between the States, in which Federals turned and fled in panic when Confederate's started to gain the upper hand.

Seems to be so handy with tools and making most anything. A philosophy major with remarkable hands-on building skills. Only one I have ever known. Don't see that where I am from. Had supper together. He spoke again of the Monterrey Way – 'If it can be made, we can make it best.' He probably has more to teach our group than any other person, including me. . . . . Loved today's lecture. One important reason that our Defense of Independence was so successful was the cooperation and bravery of brave Colored people, who helped the Secret Service by carrying out tasks, like delivering messages and propaganda and mines and torpedoes. They succeeded because Federals were blind to the idea that a person of African ancestry could be supportive of the Confederate cause. And the vast majority was faithful to their slave-holding families, allowing the men-folk to leave home for military service. That too, the Republican mind did not think possible."

Diary note by Robert Lee said, "Supper with the heroine herself. None other than Emma Lunalilo, surfer and ocean swimmer extraordinaire. She told me about the man overboard rescue . . . . My thoughts about Emma as a person: impressive; self-confident; compassionate, intelligent, perhaps a future governor of her state of Hawaii. I came away most impressed. Would I go out with a surf board on those huge waves? No way. I had much rather write about events and people that to be central in the story. Have a short story already in my mind. Perhaps I should call it. 'Man Overboard: Crisis and Heroic Rescue'."

Diary note by Conchita Rezanov said, "Andrew Houston is a big, tall Texan. Also 23 years old. Says he is an accomplished tennis player – played on the Hughes-Sharp tennis team. I just now checked their record on the internet – not so good. But I need a fast workout and men are normally stronger players. So we will be on the court for an hour before supper tomorrow. A tall handsome dude. I like him -- will consider this 'a date'. But can a petroleum engineer lighten up and not be overly serious?"

Diary note by Andrew Houston said, "Finally got my turn for the supper date with the beautiful Conchita Rezanov. I am smitten. Have a date to meet at the tennis court tomorrow at 5:15 pm. People know me as a very good tennis player: big serve, firm and well-placed ground strokes, sharp volleys at net, quick about the court. But, if I lose, it will be the most beautiful loss of my 23 years. . . ."

## Part 1, Chapter 9, Day 9 – Confederate Military and Political Strategy Succeeds, Resulting in Montreal Negotiations Over the Boundary and Relocation of Colored People – Class Lecture Tuesday, June 14, 2011

This morning, the twelve members of the Sewanee Project were ready to settle down and listen to Professor Davis present the history of the negotiations, boundary settlement and relocation of Colored people southward into the Confederate States. This is an important aspect of Confederate history and can be confusing to some. So all were eager to hear Professor Davis explain it in his words.

### Great Britain and France Recognize the Confederate States of America

Great Britain and France would soon grant recognition to the Confederate Government in Montgomery. William L. Yancey of Alabama, the Confederate Ambassador to London had, over the past 12 months, developed a good working relationship with Lord John Russell, the British Foreign Minister, and it was becoming apparent in London that the States joined together in the Confederate States of America had successfully and jointly defended their respective secessions and their honor, and were deserving of recognition by the world's leading powers. Furthermore, Confederate propaganda concerning future emancipation of bonded African Americans had encouraged the British and the French to view the emerging country more favorably than at first. The critical meeting between Yancey and Russell took place on Monday, June 16. Russell had already received reliable reports from the British embassy in Washington City, so the details of the situation submitted by Yancey's just-arrived documents were readily accepted as factual. And a sense of trust and respect was solidifying. It was clear that secession had been defended successfully and any remaining Republican Party hopes for surviving the October and November 1862 elections, and afterward mobilizing a new, better equipped, and larger Federal invasion force were quite remote at best. Meanwhile, in Paris, Pierre A. Rost, the Confederate Ambassador to the French Government had conferred over the past 12 months with leaders in the government of Emperor Louis Napoleon III and developed a warm relationship -- what could be termed a "wait and see" but friendly relationship. Well, by mid-June the waiting was over and the seeing was at hand. From Washington City a message from Henri Mercier, the French Minister to the United States, had been recently received, laying out the case for recognition and strongly recommending immediate action toward that goal. So, between June 17th and June 20th, diplomatic conversations between France and Great Britain concluded with a decision to recommend official approval of joint recognition. In London, Parliament concurred. In Paris, French authorities concurred. And the joint decision to formally recognize the government of the Confederate States of America was announced on June 26. The news reached Washington City and Montgomery on July 4th in time to contribute to the celebration of the Independence of the original thirteen colonies, a victory won on battlefields in the Carolinas and Virginia 81 years earlier.

### August through November, 1862 — The Decline of Republican Party Power

In the United States the election season began in earnest in early August. At stake was control of the Federal House and Senate and elections in numerous States, counties, towns and cities. All seats in the Federal House were up for election. One-third of the seats in the Federal Senate were up for election. The Democratic Party was re-energized.

### The Stephen Douglas Peace Plan

Senator Stephen Douglas of Illinois, who, four years previously, had won the 1858 Illinois Senate election contest, which featured the famous seven Douglas-Lincoln debates, was considered the leading northern States Democrat when it came to formulating a unified

Democratic Party peace plan. [89] And being the leader that he was, Douglas contrived a peace plan, discussed particulars with other leading Democrats, and all agreed to keep the plan secret until it had been discussed with President Lincoln. The Douglas Peace Plan stipulated:

1. Formally recognize the Confederate States of America and its States as a free and independent country.

2. Enforce an immediate cease fire.

3. As temporary measures, withdraw Federal troops to positions north of the Confederate boundary with three exceptions: 1) troops to remain in Nashville to enforce the Reconstructed Tennessee State Government, Andrew Johnson, Military Governor; 2) Troops and navy support to remain at Fort Sumter and Fort Pickens, and 3) a modest navy presence to remain at New Orleans.

4. The 150,000 prisoners-of-war captives held by Confederates are to be cared for humanely and allowed to communicate by mail with family.

5. Great Britain and France are to serve as moderators to facilitate a negotiated settlement of issues that divide the northern and southern States with particular emphasis on: 1) Transfer a strip of land in northern Virginia to Maryland to aid in preserving the capital at Washington City; 2) In general, establish a boundary from the Atlantic to the Pacific that facilitates control of immigration and cross-border tariff collection; 3) Transfer to Confederate control, the land west of Arkansas that has been settled by Cherokee and the other four "Civilized Tribes," 4) Cede a sizable strip of arid western land between Texas and southern California to give the Confederacy a Pacific seaport.

6. Restore open navigation of the Mississippi River with Federal import duties collected at Cairo, Illinois and/or New Orleans.

7. Satisfy the demand of the vast majority of White people of the Republican States that Colored People be excluded from their region. Since the Republican Party was launched in 1854, its primary political demand had been to exclude slaves from all National Territory and future states. Now, with a failed military invasion campaign and 150,000 northern troops imprisoned, the passion for Exclusionism in the Republican states -- for an all-White society -- had risen into a deafening roar. That vast political majority demanded relocation of all slaves and free Colored people who lived on land that would remain in the United States following the boundary settlement. They demanded that even the 238,315 free Colored people who presently lived among them in the Republican States be relocated elsewhere.

7a. Accordingly, the Douglas Peace Plan called for resettlement somewhere in the Confederacy of all slaves living on land that would remain in the United States following establishing the boundary. New owners in the Confederacy must purchase resettled slaves, but commit to making them the first in line for emancipation after the promised Confederate Emancipation Program is launched. The money paid to purchase the Negro slaves would go half to the owner forced to sell and half to a Federal compensation program to aid families of soldiers killed under fire during the 1862 invasion.

7b. Each State remaining in the United States would decide on the disposition of its free Colored population. As for Illinois, Douglas advocated issuing modest

---

[89] Senator Stephen A. Douglas of Illinois, the recognized leader of the Democratic Party in the Northern States during the 1850s and up to the start of the Lincoln Administration, in truthful history, died on June 1, 1861 of throat cancer. But in our alternate history of that time, the throat cancer that would debilitate Douglas during the last month of his life, would not take hold of him until five years later. In this alternate history he remains vigorous with impressive leadership ability for five more years, not passing away until June 1, 1866.

travel grants to all Illinois Colored people and ensuring that they be safely relocated to a sister State in the Confederacy, Liberia, Haiti, Central America or wherever -- the receiving country or State being responsible for the welfare of those received.

8. At the time of implementation of the agreement, the Confederacy was to hand over the 150,000 captives at border locations convenient to the home State of each man.

## The Amazing Douglas-Lincoln Meeting at Soldier's Home

Considering the arguments presented by both Douglas and Lincoln during the famous 1858 debates, few expressed much surprise that the Douglas plan was heavily weighted toward a program of Exclusion, of racial cleansing. When completed in rather short order, the United States would have no noticeable population of Colored people. Although Whites and Negroes might live in harmony in the Confederate States, the issue of race would never again become a divisive political weapon in the North – in the United States. But Douglas had to persuade fellow Democrats and gain some traction with Lincoln himself.

Most notable of the meetings and discussion among political leaders was the August 4 meeting between Douglas and Lincoln, held at the Soldiers' Home, near Washington City, a favorite get-away for Abe and Mary Lincoln during the hot August weather. [90]

I am able to present the meeting of Judge Douglas and the President as it took place on Monday, August 4, 1862, complete with the conversational dialog. This detail of history would not become known publicly until after the death of Judge Douglas, when son Stephen Douglas, Jr. would discover a written report of the discussion his father had written up the day following the meeting with Lincoln, afterward tucking the pages into a hidden drawer in his desk. Here we have a great opportunity to live history as if we were there.

Senator Stephen Douglas, known as Judge Douglas for many years due to a brief stint as a judge in Illinois, walked up to the entrance of the Soldiers' Home, and, after giving evidence regarding his identity to a guard, advanced and knocked on the door. Answering at the door was Captain Derickson, who was of a small detachment of Pennsylvania troops, known at the Bucktail Brigade. Douglas introduced himself: "I am Senator Stephen Douglas of Illinois. Have known the President since before he was married and, although I have no appointment, I anticipate that he will allow me to visit with him a bit to discuss some important political matters. Would you be good enough to notify him that Judge Douglas has come to the Soldiers' Home in hopes of seeing him today?"

Captain Derickson replied, "Please take a seat in the front room while I inquire about the President's availability."

After about 10 minutes, Derickson returned and said, "The President and the First Lady are presently occupied in a spiritual gathering, but he hopes to be able to break away within the hour, and wishes that, if you have time to wait, that you are made comfortable." [91]

Sure enough, about 45 minutes later, the door opened and the tall, lanky President entered the front room, extended his hand and exclaimed, "Judge Douglas, I am glad you are here today.

---

[90] Many of the reflections presented in the conversation between Douglas and Lincoln are based on true history, including past quotes by both men. All quotations based on historical fact during this meeting are provided to you in italics so that you are aware of that.

[91] Fact: true history records that Mary Lincoln engaged many times with mediums in an effort to reach out to Willie's spirit and that Abe was present at these séances on a few occasions. Willie was Abe and Mary's deceased son, who had died six months previously of "bilious fever," probably being typhoid fever, at age 11, in February 1862.

America is in a pickle of a predicament and, to the extent that you might help us out of this mess, I look forward to learning about your ideas, your advice. Let us go into that room over there where we can talk in private."

The short stocky Douglas replied, "Thank you for seeing me today. I was telling your bodyguard that we have known each other since before you were married. I know the loss of your son Willie must still be hard to bear. It's not yet quite six months since you lost that dear eleven-year-old boy. So hard. When I arrived, Captain Derickson told me that, at the time I arrived, you and Mary were involved in a spiritual gathering. How is she doing; does she receive comfort through the church?"

Lincoln answered, "Well . . ." then pausing a while, continued, "Well, because you have known Mary as long as I have, and can perhaps understand, I will confess that she has been consulting mediums, what some folks call the occult, holding séances in search of a connection to poor Willie's spirit. She is still in one of these sessions as we speak. Most of the séances she has arranged have taken place without me, but I have been dragged into a few, including the one this morning."

"Does Mary believe she has connected with the spirit of son Willie?"

"She tells me that she thinks she has, but the connection has been fleeting and only made her more determined to keep trying. She seems to be happier when she senses a spiritual contact with poor Willie, even a fleeting contact. If it restores some happiness in her outlook, then I figure it may be productive."

Tell me, Mr. President, when you join in one of Mary's séances, how does it affect you?

"Frankly, Judge Douglas, I feel the whole weight of the world is pressing down on my shoulders. This morning I even asked the medium to help me connect with some source of divine guidance capable of giving me direction in the office to which I have been elected. Believe me when I tell you in confidence, if I may, some days I wish you had been elected President instead of me. If you, as the leading Democrat of the northern States, held this office, the southern States would not have left us and I would have not felt the necessity to go to war to force them back in. Oh, what a mess we have on our hands now, my friend. Why has God dealt us this horrible hand of cards?"

"You are right about secession. With a Democrat in the White House, South Carolina and the other southern States would still be a part of the United States. But, concerning the hand that God has dealt us, I was always of the opinion that you were a religious skeptic and only quoted the Bible in speeches for political effect. I vividly remember your 'House Divided' speech four years ago. Tell me if you will, are you now a Christian, Abe?"

Abe cautiously replied, "Again, my answer is given in confidence: Mary and her preacher say that I am outside the church and I suppose, by the teachings of the Bible, I must be. I am spiritual Judge Douglas, but in a different way. But, enough of this 'spirit talk'. How can you help the United States? Tell me about your thinking."

At that point Judge Douglas leaned forward and began introductory comments that would set the stage for his plan for extricating the United States from the grip of the failed military invasion of the Confederate States.

"Mr. President, the mid-term elections are only weeks away and I am certain that Democrats will win control of the House and be very competitive in the Senate, perhaps in control. The nation is demanding an end to the military invasion of the Confederacy and the return of the 150,000 prisoners of war. We have only enough combat ready troops and weaponry to assemble one invasion force of sufficient strength and commitment to conquer, perchance, even Richmond, the State capital nearest to your greatest political strength and our greatest industrial and financial strength. For over three weeks, recognition of the Confederacy by London and Paris has been widely known. Politics in a democracy being what it is, Mr. President, the people are earnestly speaking and it seems to me you have no alternative but to negotiate a peace settlement with the Davis Administration in Montgomery. They have never sought to conquer us, as you know in your heart, in spite of your political posturing. They only want secession to be recognized so they can proceed in building a separate country, a country which, in time, ought to be our best friend."

Judge Douglas paused, hoping to glean a sense of how Abe was going to react. Then the President said, "Are you about to propose that we two tired old politicians bury the hatchet and work together to bring about the settlement you envision?"

"Yes, Mr. President, I suppose that I am."

"Then tell me where you would draw the boundary, how you would handle navigation of the Mississippi River, how you would secure the border and collect the tariffs and, most importantly, what you would do with the Negroes."

"Well, Mr. President, irrespective of the political struggles in Kentucky and Missouri, first your administration must declare a cease-fire and recognize what is obvious to everyone -- that the Confederate States of America exists as a legitimate government of the eleven seceded States. We must drop the political rhetoric, the silly notion, that we are fighting rebels who seek to destroy us. We must accept the truth of the fact that we are fighting secessionists who just want to live separately and peacefully apart. That means you establish diplomatic relations with Montgomery, even if on an informal basis. Abe, we have to begin to talk to one another."

"If your Democrats support recognition, I believe I can agree to it. What then."

"And tell me Judge Douglas, what about our troops in Nashville, who have secured the Reconstructed Tennessee State Government, which is pledged to rescind secession? Do we have to give that up? Kentucky might hang in the balance."

"Not yet, not at first, Mr. President. For the time being, as negotiations play out, we keep troops in Nashville and we sustain the government we set up under Military Governor Andrew Johnson. We also keep our Navy forces at New Orleans, Fort Pickens and Fort Sumter in Charleston harbor. But all of our forces act under a cease fire, ordered not to fire unless fired upon."

"But, Judge Douglas, the Confederates have us on the run, what prevents them from attacking our meager outposts at Nashville, New Orleans or measly Fort Sumter. God, knows, I wish I had never heard of that pile of rocks in the center of Charleston harbor."

"Mr. President, please doubt not my loyalty to our country when I tell you that I have contacts with the Confederate Secret Service, led by Judah Benjamin, and they assure me that the government in Montgomery can sustain a peaceful cease-fire if, but only if, that government is recognized as legitimate and diplomats are exchanged for the purpose of beginning the search for a settlement."

"What about London and Paris, Judge Douglas, if we accept their oversight in the negotiations, will they oversee them in a fair manner?"

"Again, Mr. President, rest assured that my efforts have been honorable when I tell you that, over the past three weeks, I have been in conversations with Henri Mercier, the French minister, and he assures me that, if asked to do so, London and Paris will jointly oversee negotiations and will do so fairly."

"Where?"

"He suggests Montreal."

"So, Judge Douglas, where do you foresee drawing the boundary lines? Confederate Virginia is just across the Potomac River. I can see it from southern windows in the White House. Must we move the United States capital to Philadelphia or . . . , you name it?"

"Mr. President, reliable sources have told me that Montgomery and Virginians are willing to barter a land trade to give Washington City a buffer zone to its south. I am told that even the victorious Confederate General Robert E. Lee would be willing to give up his estate -- Arlington, on the south side of the river, also within your view from the White House -- if a good overall land trade was agreed to on both sides. In exchange for a comfortable swath of northern Virginia and the return of our imprisoned troops, the Confederacy seeks western land that connects it to southern California and the Pacific Ocean. That is mostly dessert, they will argue, not worth much to us, but considerable to them. So they give us what is dear to us, and we give them what is dear to them."

"What about Kentucky and Missouri, do your sources give a clue to what would happen there?"

"I have heard it proposed that elections by county might be held in Kentucky and Missouri, for the purpose of guiding negotiators in splitting those two States. We might, in the long run, lose southern Kentucky and southern Missouri to more secession demands, but retain the south side of the Ohio River and St. Louis and all of the Missouri River. We have a shot of gaining western Virginia along the Ohio. By recognizing the right of State secession, the consequence of recognizing the Confederacy, we keep alive secession political struggles in Kentucky and Missouri. It might be best to divide those States for the sake of unity within our country. Nip the southern Kentucky and southern Missouri secession blight in the bud. Our people want peace, Mr. President -- an end to the struggle between the Southern culture and the Northern culture. A boundary line that gives southern Kentucky and southern Missouri to the Confederate States will go a long way toward defusing future demands for State Secession,"

"My goodness! You present the struggle as one between the 'Southern culture and the Northern culture.' What about the 'slave power?' I thought we were fighting the 'slave power.' Now you say we are fighting the 'Southern culture.' Explain that for me, Judge."

"Mr. President, we have both been exposed to the Southern culture through our marriages. Your wife Mary was born and raised in Kentucky. Well, I was 34 years old and in Congress when I married Martha Martin of North Carolina. You may recall that I met Martha through her cousin, Congressman David Reid of North Carolina, who occupied the seat next to mine in the House chamber. Romance blossomed and we married. We had two boys, Stephen, Jr. and Robert. The following year Martha's father died and she inherited a 2,500-acre cotton farm in Mississippi, along with more than 100 slaves. That was 14 years ago, in 1848. I managed the farm mostly from afar, but made periodic visits. I also traveled the Southern States on campaign trips. As a Democrat, I have enjoyed close relationships with many political leaders from the Southern States. So, taken all together, Mr. President, I have acquired a rather detailed understanding of the Southern culture. Being born and raised in Vermont and upstate New York, I have also acquired a rather detailed understanding of the Northern culture. There are differences, and the reasons for them go way back to the first settlers to arrive here from Europe -- differences between settlers at

Jamestown, Virginia, and settlers at Massachusetts Bay and New England. [92]   As you know, Martha has been dead a long time; died of complications during the birth of our daughter, who also died a month later. That was a sad, sad time in my life. Six years of happy marriage, then she was gone. Yet it helps me understand the hurt you and Mary feel over the loss of Willie. By the way, for some time the Mississippi farm has been in a trust for the boys, and I have no control over it at all. It's best that way. Senator Douglas owning slaves is bad for politics in Illinois. Yes, for a man living in Chicago and Washington City, I understand both cultures rather well. [93] But, Mr. President, with all due respect, sir, I fear that your understanding is a bit wanting."

"A bit wanting, you say?"

"Frankly, Mr. President, you have never traveled in the Southern States to a meaningful degree. And I don't want to sound harsh or threatening, but I owe it to you to give you the full story so you will know what you are up against, in total, not just in part. Although you were born in the South, your youth was spent in Kentucky and Indiana. Now, I perhaps should not mention this, but some knowledgeable Kentuckians question your paternity as you wrote in the Bible record you worked up with your step-mother, Sarah Bush Johnston Lincoln, during that visit to her home a year or two after Thomas Lincoln died. You are aware of how agitators against this war have called you "Lying Lincoln" and claimed that your true father was a North Carolinian named Abraham Enloe. I know that hurts, but let me assure you I have had no part in such bastardy name-calling. I trust your word – that Thomas Lincoln was your true father. But trust in this regard is hard. Your Bible entry was made in 1852 or 1853, about the time you sensed new political opportunities may be opening up for you. Although you decided to forgo attending your claimed father Tom Lincoln's funeral in 1851, you made a special trip to visit your step-mother for the apparent purpose of establishing your birth date in that newly purchased Bible. That smells like a cover-up, my friend. And your former law partner, Billy Herndon, suspects it as well. A small group of informed and important people in Kentucky attest to that being the truth of it. Thomas Lincoln was your step-father, not your real father. So in the present legal lingo, you are a bastard, if you will pardon my language. Does the true story of your parentage go like this, as I understand it from reliable sources?

"Nancy Hanks, born in Virginia and living in North Carolina, while working as an unmarried servant in far western North Carolina, became pregnant by a well-to-do married man with wife and family, by the name of Abraham Enloe. Nancy gave birth to you at a place well east of Enloe's place, but he arranged for a young fellow, Thomas Lincoln, to accept her for a wife, and the little boy, too, if he would take them to eastern Kentucky and care for them. Gave him a going-away present, as well, as I hear it. Therefore, when Tom and Nancy married in eastern Kentucky, there was this little 2-year-old boy in attendance, who was you, my friend. So you are about 4 years older than you say you are and your father is not Thomas Lincoln.

"Mr. President, I would not use this information to tarnish your image because that is not the way I conduct my political affairs. But there are people who would use it if they saw no other way to gain your political cooperation. Enough said about this, Mr. President. Allow me to say we both should take this issue off the table and commit to saying nothing more about it. I just

---

[92] Students and writers of truthful history have long recognized the existence of two cultures, one prominent in the North and the other prominent in the South.

[93] Stephen Douglas' biographical sketch of himself is truthful history.

wanted you to know what I have been hearing and that it is coming from reliable and capable sources." [94]

"Judge Douglas, I know not of these so-called reliable sources, but let me assure you that my father was Thomas Lincoln and the birth date I wrote in the Bible of which you refer is the truth. My mother always said I was large for my age, even when I was little, and that is the sum total of it. If you have nothing more constructive to say, let me suggest that this interview is over."

"Regarding your father, Mr. President, I have nothing more to say, and rather regret that I mentioned the subject. It just slipped out as I was beginning to discuss your perception of the Southern culture. Pardon me for that impropriety. I will speak of it no further. But I do have more to say concerning the grave issues before the country, and assure you my further comments will not be unpleasant or threatening."

"Very well, Judge Douglas, you clever fox, tell me what I do not understand about the Southern culture."

"Mr. President, the short of it is that you have had little exposure to the Southern culture. You've made a few visits to Mary's relatives in Kentucky. As a very young adult, you made two flatboat trips down the Mississippi River. Those do not afford a fellow an understanding of a people and their culture. Your political friends in the Republican Party, frankly sir, share your relative ignorance on the subject. When it comes to understanding the people your Massachusetts Abolitionist friends so passionately despise, I must tell you those know-it-alls are the most ignorant of them all. For that reason, it is advisable that you seek out and strongly consider the advice of folks who do understand the Southern culture. Such understanding is necessary to make sense of what ought to be done with our divided nation and our Negroes during this time of unprecedented crisis."

"So, Douglas, I suppose you want to teach me about the Southern culture and the Negroes. Fire away. Your elaborate preamble now completed, please deliver the meat of your message. Are you now going to tell me about the Negroes?"

"Mr. President, the Southern culture is a by-racial culture, made up of White people and Colored people. The races are accustomed to living together in communities and often on the same farms and plantations. It is a successful culture that began in Virginia, was mostly responsible for winning independence from Great Britain, and has subsequently expanded across the Ohio River Valley, to Missouri and to the Republic of Texas, now the State of Texas. In the South one sees a broad spectrum of personal relationships. On occasion a Negro slave is abused, to be sure. But so often, one finds friendships between Whites and Negroes who live in the same communities and even on the same farms and plantations. They often grow up together, play together, work together, hunt together, and go to church together. In a nutshell, that is the Southern culture. So different from Massachusetts or land along the Great Lakes."

"To further explore our relative understandings of the Southern culture, Mr. President, let us review your speech before the Illinois Republican Convention at Springfield on June 17, 1858,

---

[94] In truthful history there is compelling, though inconclusive, evidence that Abe Lincoln's father was not his mother's husband, Thomas Lincoln. Abe Lincoln was likely four years older than he reported and born out of wedlock. The belated family Bible entry is truthful history. If not Thomas Lincoln, the most likely father was Abraham Enloe of western North Carolina.

4 years ago, when you were launching your campaign to take my Senate seat. There you proclaimed:

> *"A house divided against itself cannot stand. I believe this government cannot endure, permanently half slave and half free. I do not expect the Union to be dissolved — I do not expect the house to fall — but I do expect it will cease to be divided. It will become all one thing, or all the other. Either the opponents of slavery will arrest the further spread of it, and place it where the public mind shall rest in the belief that it is in the course of ultimate extinction; or its advocates will put it forward, till it shall become alike lawful in all the States, old as well as new — in the North as well as the South." [95]*

"You see, Mr. President, that speech was essentially non-sense. Why? Because it was not based on an understanding of the Southern culture. The people of the Southern States have never intended to enslave people living in the Northern States, such as Illinois -- have never intended to move with slaves into Illinois and take up residence. There was no threat of enslaving people in the North. End of story! You proclaimed that a house divided against itself cannot stand, but that you did not expected it to fall. Mr. President, if it cannot stand, it must fall. In fact, just weeks before you became President, it fell."

Lincoln replied, "That's what I said in Springfield and soon afterward I maneuvered you into allowing me to join you in seven debates, scattered across the State. The Douglas-Lincoln debates. I suppose you want to quote something I said there as well. Do you?"

"Might as well, Mr. President, quote you, and quote me as well. By recalling quotations from the two of us during those seven debates, I believe we can gain a measure of understanding regarding what we ought to do with the Negro today."

"At the debate in Ottawa, Mr. President, you submitted:

> *"I have no purpose, directly or indirectly, to interfere with slavery in the States where it exists. . . . I have no purpose to introduce political and social equality between the White and Negro races. There is a physical difference between the two, which, in my judgment, will probably forever forbid their living together upon the footing of perfect equality; and inasmuch as it becomes a necessity that there must be a difference, I, as well as, Douglas, am in favor of the race to which I belong having the superior position." [96]*

"Mr. President, in those remarks you confirmed the attitudes of voters all across the North. The people of the Northern States do not want Negroes living in their communities. For God's sake, the Illinois State Constitution forbids a person with only the slightest drop of Negro blood from taking up residence within our borders. [97] We can divide into three categories the attitudes of Northern people toward people of full or partial Negro blood. The vast majority belong in a category I call "Exclusionists." These people want to exclude Negroes and Colored people from their State. Others belong to a category I call "Deportationists." They want to round up Negroes and "colonize" them in Africa, Central America, South America, or somewhere else. Many influential people like this idea. But there is a third category, to which very, very few people belong. That is the category I call the true "Abolitionists." A true Abolitionist wants to help slaves become free, even purchasing them and training them to be self-sufficient, one would

---

[95] This is the exact wording, as presented in italics, of Lincoln's speech in Springfield on June 17, 1858.

[96] This quotation in italics is the exact wording of Mr. Lincoln's remarks at the debate in Ottawa, August 21, 1858.

[97] The prohibition against any person appearing to have even a small fraction of African ancestry taking residence in Illinois was in the State constitution, was enforced, and is truthful history.

presume. But to this category very, very few belong. Mr. President, I am sure that, in your heart, you recognize that almost everybody who calls himself an Abolitionist merely wants to meddle in someone else's business, not help the Negro."

At this point President Lincoln countered: "You have been quoting me, Judge Douglas. At our 1858 Illinois debates you were the Senator from Illinois, a leader in the Democratic Party in the Senate and standing for re-election by our state legislature. As a Republican, I was opposing you. Quote for me something you said at some point during those seven debates that might help us sort through the mess we find ourselves in today. Quote from that debate again, if you can."

"Mr. President I do believe I can do that. It was at Alton, the last debate on October 14, that I warned you before a crowd of 5,000 the following truth:

"I said, our founders had agreed to form a government over thirteen States, uniting them *together, as they stood divided into free and slaves States, and to guarantee forever to each State the right to do as it pleased on the slavery question. Having thus made the government, and conferred this right upon each State forever, I assert that this government can exist as they made it, divided into free and slave States, if any one State chooses to retain slavery. Mr. Lincoln says that he looks forward to a time when slavery shall be abolished everywhere. I look forward to a time when each State shall be allowed to do as it pleases. If it chooses to keep slavery forever, it is not my business, but its own; if it chooses to abolish slavery, it is its own business, not mine. I care more for the great principle of self-government, the right of the people to rule, than I do for all the Negroes in Christendom. I would not endanger the perpetuity of the Union. I would not blot out the great inalienable rights of the White man for all the Negroes that ever existed. Hence, I say let us maintain this Government on the Principles that our fathers made it, recognizing the right of each State to keep slavery as long as its people determine, or to abolish it when they please'.*" [98]

"You make a valid point, Judge Douglas. But that water is over the dam. All but four Southern States seceded. The Union is broken. We cannot remake the history of it. But we must do all we can to prevent further secessions. So, Judge Douglas, what should we do now?"

"Mr. President. You are right. We must avoid further secessions. We must not let future fusses over Negroes ever again divide our citizens. We agree that the people of the Northern States do not want Negroes for neighbors. That is the fact we face. They want them to remain in a Southern State where they are accustomed to living, or be "colonized" elsewhere. That's what the so-called Underground Railroad was all about -- keeping runaway slaves moving north until they left the United States and self-colonized in Canada. And that should be our goal in a negotiated settlement with Montgomery. We should tell Confederate ministers that, 'Together we will draw a boundary between our governments, but it must be agreed that all Negroes north of that boundary must be resettled to somewhere south of it, and that no Negroes can ever cross northward-bound over the boundary to live among our people, in our country.' You said it yourself in Springfield in 1858. 'A house divided against itself cannot stand.' Our house is the Northern States and it will stand for hundreds of years if we remove the divisive issue of Negroes and Whites living in the same communities."

"If we act as statesmen instead of politicians and negotiate a reasonable settlement, we can cast off the Confederate States and reconstruct the remaining United States into the greatest nation of peace and prosperity and opportunity that ever existed for White people."

---

[98] The portion in italics is the exact wording of Douglas' remarks at Alton on October 14, 1858.

"So, Judge Douglas, in your judgment, a plan as you have described, will return the 150,000 soldiers presently held captive in Confederate prisons. When do the people in Illinois regain access to commercial river transportation to the port at New Orleans?"

"As you know, Mr. President, after the secession of Mississippi and Louisiana, the river was open to free trade and Federal tariffs were being collected at the Mississippi-Tennessee border, but that capability was terminated by Montgomery in December, on the same day you signed the bill authorizing military force against the South. I anticipate the river being opened to commercial traffic very soon after signing a cease fire agreement."

"In your judgment Douglas, will our Federal Government have the legal authority to free slaves living on land that remains in the United States, or will authority to free them and define emancipation details and procedures reside in the individual States?"

"That issue will only concern Delaware, Maryland, Kentucky and Missouri. We can count on little Delaware to cooperate. The southern boundary of Maryland will substantially expand, if my thinking prevails, when it receives some of northern and western Virginia and that prize will encourage the cooperation of that government. Kentucky and Missouri may well divide, smaller southern portions going to the Confederacy, expanding Tennessee and Arkansas. Those people have a big job in sorting all of that out. We ought to leave the emancipation details to the people of the Southern culture who best understand the issues involved. So, in short, our Southern States -- Delaware, Maryland, Kentucky and Missouri -- must define emancipation details and deportation procedures pertaining to the Negroes residing within their borders."

"What about the free Negroes, Douglas, will the Federal Government have authority to exclude them from our nation, to forcibly colonize those who do not leave willingly?"

"Mr. President, let me assure you that free Colored people will depart swiftly as White people will make it known that such people are not welcome to remain in their communities. Most will resettle in the Confederacy, with some going to Canada and some by sea to wherever. I can only hope that Canadians do not try to block migration into their country, but we cannot be sure. I do believe the Confederacy will accept all free Colored people who migrate south, and I assure you they will remain free, they will find the Southern culture an attractive destination."

"Douglas, I have devoted much time and political capital toward colonization of Negroes. I rather firmly believe that Confederates will refuse to accept any more Negroes. They have more now than they need, for Heaven's sake."

"Mr. President, do not be so sure of that. I know the people of the South much better than you know them. If we negotiate in good faith, Confederates will accept our Negroes, slave and free, and give them good homes. Those who are now free will remain free and those who are still slaves will have opportunities to learn to be self-sufficient and to gain freedom in a reasonable length of time. We just have to negotiate this plan, which gets rid of our Negroes, and, at the same time, gives Abolitionists in our Republican States the rights to boast that they freed the slaves."

"I remain doubtful of Confederate acceptance, Douglas. The Federal Government may yet have to arrange for and pay for deportation to Africa, Central America or South America. Congress recently appropriated one million dollars to pay for a colonization program and that is already available. Thad Stevens pushed a $500,000 colonization bill through the House, and you managed to expand the funding to $1,000,000 in the Senate. [99] That will give us a good start."

"Don't be too hasty, Abe. Give Confederates a chance to accept our Colored people."

"You are probably dreaming, Judge Douglas. My government ought to begin immediately with the resettlement program, starting with the Negroes living in Washington City who are being emancipated now -- that is, those not taken to Maryland at the last minute and sold. Immediately after the cease fire agreement, we ought to be able to free up ocean transport to begin the movement of these people."

Lincoln then said, "I have already supported colonization in Haiti and some want to establish a Negro colony in Central America at a place they call Chiriqui. In addition to our standing colonization destination of Liberia, my administration has, during the past few months, collected invitations to receive colonists at St. Croix, Surinam, Guiana, British Honduras, New Granada and Ecuador, and more invitations are expected. How many, in your opinion, Douglas, would we need to send off?" [100]

Douglas replied, "That depends of Confederate acceptance or rejection. There at about 240,000 free Colored people living in our Northern States. Half may migrate willingly, but we may need to apply pressure to see the remainder off. There are about 550,000 Negroes living in Delaware, Maryland, Kentucky, Missouri and here in the District of Columbia. [101] Many will probably be living in regions that will be taken by the Confederacy and their status would not change. Many will be relocated within their respective States to land that is taken into the Confederacy and their status would not change either. Overall, we may need to resettle by law one quarter of that population. That presents a resettlement burden of about 250,000 individuals. But let us hope Confederates will accept these people."

"Douglas, I am still anticipating colonization. That may require more than $1,000,000, but our military will probably shoulder much of the cost, providing soldiers to help gather individuals to seaports and get them boarded, plus Navy transports to take them to their respective destinations. We can do what we need to do."

"Well, Douglas, you've presented and argued for an impressive a list of suggestions, quite a plan, I must say. Are you through, or is there more?"

"Mr. President, this seems like a good place to conclude my remarks. How can I be of further help?"

"Douglas, I believe the issue now sits in my lap, and, unlike you, I remain doubtful of Confederate willingness to accept more Negroes. But, I have called a Cabinet meeting for day after tomorrow, on Wednesday, August 6. I will place your plan before them for discussion. If they see merit in it and if Democrats and Republicans in our country can bury the hatchet and agree on a plan that saves us from further unnecessary divisive political agitation, while, at the

---

[99] In truthful history, on July 16, 1862, the Federal House and Senate approved a bill, subsequently signed by President Lincoln, which appropriated $500,000 to finance deportation (colonization) of African Americans -- money that would be spent for that purpose. This truthful history preceded the fictional Soldier's Home meeting by over two weeks. In truthful history Senator Douglas was dead of throat cancer. Here, in our story, Douglas is alive and remains as the leading Democrat in the Senate. He is reminding Lincoln that he had succeeded in doubling deportation funding to $1,000,000.

[100] In truthful history the Lincoln Administration actively deported Negroes to land set aside in Haiti and engaged in negotiations to allow deportations to foreign lands elsewhere. Relocating Negroes to Africa (Liberia) was a long-standing American program supported by so called Abolitionists.

[101] Truthful population figures from the 1860 Federal census.

same time, resettling the Negroes living in the North and bringing back our captured troops, then it seems to be in our best interest to draw an intelligent boundary between the secessionists and ourselves, a boundary that preserves our capital where it is and gives us the best land on both sides of the Ohio River Valley."

"Thank you, Mr. President. Then I will take my leave."

With that, Senator Stephen Douglas departed the room, walked to the front door of the Soldiers' Home, said goodbye to Captain Derickson, and departed. Moments later, Abe Lincoln walked over to the room where he and Mary had been in séance with the medium, wondering if contact had been made with dear Willie's spirit — the results of which are lost to history.

But what is not lost to history is the determination in the Republican States to forcefully implement ethnic cleansing within their respective regions and in portions of Democratic States that would remain under the Federal Government. And history would prove that Colored people, free and slave alike, who migrated south into the Confederate States would be so, so glad to have been welcomed there and given the opportunity for success in their lives, the lives of their children, the lives of their grandchildren, and their descendants yet unborn.

## Selected Tuesday Evening Diary Postings

Diary note by Tina Sharp said, "Robert E. Lee IV and I shared a table at supper tonight. One would think that, being descended from the great Confederate General, this man would be too proud to care about me and what I am doing. But he really seemed to care and I found the time together enjoyable. He wanted to know about my career as a nuclear engineer and about the Comanche Peak Nuclear Station renovations. Perhaps it is the aspiring writer's mind set: always wanting to know about other people and their cares. Always gathering information for the next story, the next book. Very handsome and easy to like. Knows far more history than I do. If he resembles his ancestor, General Lee, then I can understand why the first Robert was so effective at building a team and leading his men. . . . . After supper we musicians gathered in the faculty lounge to play and sing together for almost two hours. This group is fun and capable of putting on a show. Amazing! Look forward to the next get together."

Diary note by Robert Lee said, "Giving up much of Virginia's territory in its north and west was hard for my beloved State, the mother State of our former country, the United States. My ancestor Robert E. Lee, after such brilliant leadership in the Defense of Virginia and Richmond, lost his beloved home along the Potomac River across from Washington City. As you know, Virginia had given the Federal Government control over what became Kentucky and far more than that, for the Mother of States had held title to that vast expanse of territory extending far to the northwest, out to Chicago and beyond. What became Ohio, Indiana and Illinois was territory that belonged to Virginia during colonial days and at the conclusion of the American Revolution. [102] But, it seems that Virginians were continuing the tradition of Nation Building, agreeing to give up valuable settled and developed land in exchange for a far greater western expanse of arid land awaiting settlement and development. All Confederates should be appreciative of Virginia."

Diary note by Marie Saint Martin said, "Just got back from playing together with our musicians. After supper we played in the faculty lounge for a couple of hours. Was great fun. I had gathered up some music off the internet, and this was especially helpful to Amanda on the piano. This group seems capable of putting on a respectable performance by the weekend of the

---

[102] It is truthful history that Great Britain acknowledged that Virginia held title to vast land stretching out to the northwest. It is also truthful history that Virginia gave the right to manage the settlement of that land to the American government soon afterward. This, among other facts of American history justifies recognition of Virginia as the "Mother State" that gave birth to much of the United States.

Confederate Celebration. Tina Sharp, although a French horn player, improvises harmony and sings it well. I have always sung lead, and relied on others to harmonize. Great fit, us two girls."

**Part 1, Chapter 10, Day 10 – Negotiations at Montreal Result in a Boundary Line from the Atlantic (in Northern Virginia) to the Pacific (in Southern California) and Resettlement of all Colored People North of that Boundary– Class Lecture, Wednesday, June 15, 2011**

### President Lincoln and His Cabinet Debate Alternatives

Two days later, as planned, on August 6, President Lincoln sat down with his Cabinet, all of them Republicans, in search for a way out of the military crisis. Present was Secretary of State William Seward of New York, Secretary of War Simon Cameron of Pennsylvania, Secretary of the Navy, Gideon Welles of Connecticut, Secretary of the Treasury Salmon Chase of Ohio, Attorney General Edward Bates of Missouri, Postmaster General Montgomery Blair of Maryland, and Secretary of the Interior Caleb Smith of Indiana.

The meeting began at 1:00 in the afternoon. By 2:00, the thoughts of various Cabinet members had been offered and briefly discussed. It was about that time that Lincoln presented, in some detail, the plan he had received from Senator Stephen Douglas, widely recognized as the leader of the Democratic Party, alleging that the plan was mostly his own thinking, but that Judge Douglas had suggested an item or two. From that point forward, the discussion centered on what we know to have been the Douglas plan. Blair of Maryland was enthusiastic about a boundary that gave his State a swath of northern Virginia, including land belonging to Robert E. Lee. And others saw merit in a boundary that avoided the embarrassment of relocating the capital. Bates of Missouri quickly endorsed moving all Negroes out of States north of the boundary line, emphasizing:

> "Clearly, going back to the War against Mexico, our history proves that the major divisive factor in our country is the issue of Negroes living among us, whether slave or free. If Negroes are moved south of the boundary, this agitation will be gone and happiness will return. I personally know several families on large farms, with fifty or more slaves each, who would love to reduce their work force, but see no way to do it. This gives them an out. The future of the southern States is a growing Negro population destined to become a burden on Southern society. We do not want that to happen to us. Have it happen to them! Let us relocate ours now, while we can. That, gentlemen, will be our victory and the secessionist's loss."

Caleb Smith of Indiana, offering his viewpoint as the Secretary of the Interior, agreed that, with slight exceptions, the desert region west of Texas was of little value to the United States:

> "Concerning New Mexico Territory, we might keep the territory capital at Santa Fe, but to the west there is nothing but desert and canyon country. Concerning the State of California, if we retain Monterey and everything north of there, we are only giving the secessionists the southern California desert. It seems to me that the Gadsden Purchase of that strip of Mexican land, now in southern New Mexico Territory, was money wasted in 1853 by the Franklin Pierce Administration, wasted for a railroad never built. Good riddance, I say. Desert land from Texas to the Pacific in exchange for good land east of the Rocky Mountains and removal of our Negroes would be a good trade, if carefully negotiated."

Secretary of State William Seward submitted that, given a chance, he was confident he could strike a hard bargain in negotiations, and viewed the relocation of the Negroes to be essential to any acceptable plan. Secretary of War Simon Cameron expressed his great concern for Federal troops held in Confederate prisons and argued that the sooner they are brought home, the more lives would be saved.

Secretary of the Navy Gideon Wells promised that navy warships and transports could be fitted to move thousands of Negroes to Central America, South America and/or Africa, and that the colonization program could be carried out economically if it was begun very soon, while seamen remained enlisted and ships remained in a seaworthy condition.

Salmon Chase also stressed a rapid resolution to the crisis, submitting that every week of delay would cost the Treasury several million dollars.

The Cabinet resumed their discussions the following day, August 7. At the point in time when Abe Lincoln thought he had the votes, he proposed the following question:

"Resolved:

1. "That the United States Government, for the purposes of securing a negotiated settlement, does recognize that eleven States have seceded and fought with some success to militarily defend said secession; and does recognize that the Confederate States Government is the proper agency to negotiate on behalf of said seceded States; and does recommend a cease fire on both sides; and does recommend that the United States Government appeal to diplomats in Great Britain and France to jointly manage negotiations toward goals of:

2. Drawing a logical boundary between the two parties;

3. Arranging for Negroes living north of the boundary to be resettled into regions south of the boundary or elsewhere;

4. Arranging for all prisoners of war to be freed and returned to their home States;

5. Ensuring free navigation of the Mississippi River;

6. Ensuring collection of standing tariffs on all listed goods moving across said border;

7. Arranging that said border be secured, to the extent possible, from illicit cross-border movement of persons, animals and goods, including Negroes."

The Cabinet voted. The resolution passed. At a press conference that afternoon, President Lincoln presented the approved resolution to newspapermen and political leaders. Announcing that Senator Stephen Douglas had given his support moments earlier, the President encouraged speedy review of the Resolution in the House and Senate -- both just now returning from a two-week temporary recess, which had allowed members to visit their home States and districts for consultations with constituencies.

## The Montreal Treaty Negotiations

Events were moving rapidly, to say the least. Within a few days, the Confederate Government in Montgomery voted to approve the resolution as a suitable framework for immediate negotiations. Likewise, under the leadership of Senator Stephen Douglas, the House and Senate approved resolutions of endorsement. Both Great Britain and France agreed to jointly facilitate the negotiations at Montreal. And that they did. All parties understood the urgency of the issue. On Monday, September 1, 1862, the parties gathered and negotiations began. History knows the full story. But space has only been set aside in this book for a presentation of the results, so the reader must look elsewhere for stories of the gives and takes and the individuals involved.

By the way, Confederate negotiators arranged for the Federal Government to purchase Arlington plantation, the ancestral home of General Robert E. Lee's wife, Mary Custis Lee. The Lee's were obviously sad over the loss of Arlington House and Arlington plantation, especially Mary and the children, but emotions gave way to reason. The family realized it no longer wanted to live directly across the Potomac River from Washington City, with that magnificent view of the capital, now controlled by the Republican Party, which had waged war against the South. The family owned plantations further south in Virginia, such as the 4,000 acre White House plantation and the 3,500 acre Romancoke plantation. There and elsewhere the family's future surely lay. Mary had a good cry, but reason returned. The price paid for Arlington House and the surrounding 1,100 acres was just. Soon afterward, the Federals would transform Arlington plantation into a huge military cemetery, and, over the next few years, many Federal soldiers who died in the invasion of the Confederacy would be exhumed, transported to Arlington and reburied there. The Lee family's acceptance of the transfer of valuable northern Virginia land in exchange for vastly more far-western arid land was trumpeted as an example of Confederate patriotism, and many other land owners in the transferred portion of Virginia accepted the boundary settlement as a reasonable division of the two countries. [103]

We now advance to presenting the settlement itself.

## The Negotiated Boundary

The agreed boundary was defined thusly: "Beginning on the Atlantic shore at the northern boundary of Virginia (near 38 degrees 0 minutes latitude) follow the existing boundary to the Chesapeake Bay, then across the Bay to the mouth of the Rappahannock River, then follow the stream in a northwest direction until reaching 78 degrees 0 minutes longitude, then proceed north on that line until reaching 39 degrees 0 minutes latitude, then west on that line until reaching 81 degrees 0 minutes longitude, then south on that line until reaching 38 degrees 0 minutes latitude, then west on that line until reaching 84 degrees 0 minutes longitude, then south on that line until reaching 37 degrees 30 minutes latitude, then west on that line until reaching 85 degrees 0 minutes longitude, then south on that line until reaching 37 degrees 0 minutes latitude, then west on that line until reaching the Mississippi River, then upstream until reaching 38 degrees 0 minutes latitude, then west on that line until reaching the existing boundary separating Missouri and Kansas, then south on that boundary until reaching 37 degrees 0 minutes latitude (the southern Kansas boundary), then west on that line until reaching the eastern California State boundary, then southeast along that boundary until reaching 36 degrees 0 minutes latitude, then west on that line until reaching the Pacific Ocean.

The negotiated boundary was to be a guide, not a rigid routing of the boundary. Refinement of the boundary, during surveying, allowed a deviation of up to one-quarter mile to avoid unnecessarily dividing a group of related buildings or a small town. And the line could be moved up to 5 miles from the negotiated route to get around major obstructions in the terrain that prohibited practical road building. This flexibility was permitted for a period of five years following the settlement, after which the boundary was fixed. A boundary road and secure fence was a firm demand of United States negotiators who insisted that every effort be made to prevent Negroes from entering their country and to prevent smugglers from bringing goods north without paying the Federal tariff. [104]

---

[103] In truthful history Arlington, the ancestral home of Mary Custis Lee, is the national military cemetery on the south side of the Potomac River. Mary (Mary Anna Randolph Custis) was the daughter of George Washington Parke Custis, the grandson of Martha Washington and the adopted son of President George Washington.

[104] The boundary road and fence was to be completed in five years' time, which was comprised of a graded roadbed, 45 feet wide, sloped from the center toward the outside for drainage of water. Along the center-line of this road, which matched the exact boundary, was to be constructed a strong ten-foot high fence. Both sides of this graded roadbed were to be cleared for easy visibility to a distance of fifty feet from the fence. Locked gates were to be provided every 10 to 20 miles. A gate would be unlocked by Federal revenue and border control agents when permitting and monitoring import/export trade and passage of individuals.

The location of the following landmarks helps in visualizing the routing of the boundary:

• In Virginia, that portion of Fredericksburg on the south side of the Rappahannock River remained in the CSA, but a large amount of northern Virginia was transferred to Maryland and the USA, including Alexandria, Manassas, Reston, Winchester, Morgantown, Clarksburg, Wheeling, Parkersburg, Charleston and Huntington.

• Southeastern Kentucky below Mount Sterling was transferred to Virginia and all of extreme southern Kentucky west of London was transferred to Tennessee, including Mount Sterling, Hazard, London, Somerset, Middlesboro, Corbin, Monticello, Glasgow, Bowling Green, Hopkinsville, Murray and Mayfield.

• The southern third of Missouri was transferred to Arkansas and the CSA, including Rolla, Carbondale, Malden, Poplar Bluff, Springfield, Nevada and Joplin.

• Native American lands west of Missouri and Arkansas, south of Kansas and Colorado, north of Texas and east of New Mexico Territory was designated as being within the CSA and to be reserved as a Territory for Native Americans and their descendants. This large area would become the Confederate State of Sequoyah, but the treaty did not address that issue. The so-called "panhandle" in the west of that Native American territory was immediately transferred to Texas.

• Most of New Mexico Territory was transferred to the CSA. From it, two new Confederate States would be created, but the treaty did not address that issue. The eastern half, including Santa Fe, Albuquerque and Las Cruces, would become the Confederate State of New Mexico and the western half, including Flagstaff, Phoenix, Tucson, Las Vegas and the Grand Canyon would become the Confederate State of Arizona, but the treaty did not address that issue.

• A major portion of California, essentially the arid far-south, was transferred to the Confederate States, including Bakersfield, Santa Maria, Santa Barbara, Los Angeles, Palm Springs and San Diego. This Confederate State would be known as South California, but the treaty did not address that issue. Federal negotiators did not realized that, in the future, with expanded technology and electric power, Colorado River water could be impounded and distributed to enable development of this arid desert land. So they greatly underestimated the value of the land they were relinquishing in the trade.

On Friday, September 19, 1862, the Montreal Treaty was signed by negotiators for the United States and the Confederate States as well as the ministers representing Great Britain and France. It was sent immediately to Washington City and Montgomery with expectations of quick ratification by both governments. The United States Senate and the Confederate State Senate were both already in session, awaiting receipt of the treaty. One week later, on Friday, September 26, the treaty was ratified by the Confederacy, and three days later, likewise by the United States.

### The British and French Joint Boundary Monitoring Commission

Neither the South nor the North fully trusted the other side to honor the treaty just signed. Confederates had witnessed too many broken treaties with Native American nations to fully trust the Great White Father in Washington to honor a treaty. Republicans in the North did not fully trust Confederates to collect import taxes on goods moving north across the negotiated boundary. Some even feared escaped slaves and colored people might migrate north across the boundary. Monitoring the flow of goods coming up the Mississippi River looked to be enforceable, but, the land boundary was thousands of miles long, and smuggling was a real danger to the collection of Federal import taxes. So both sides agreed to the proposal that a joint British-French team of boundary monitoring officials would help ensure honest law enforcement along the boundary. It was to be clearly marked with a fence line, and both sides of it were to be cleared for horse-drawn wagons to ride alongside, except for rough terrain, where a path for a man riding a horse would be provided. Furthermore, a telegraph line was to be run along the fence line from the Atlantic to the Pacific, with many stations along the way to ensure speedy and reliable communications involving Confederate Boundary officials, United States Boundary officials and British-French Monitoring officials. The cost of the services of the British-French Monitoring officials was to be shared equally by the Confederate States and the United States. Since the boundary matched the northern edge of eight Southern states, the British-French Monitoring team was to consist of fifty officials: five for each state boundary section, five for Davis and five for Washington City. Of course, these fifty officials were not capable of riding the boundary and manning the designated boundary crossings and import duty stations. That was not their role. Their role was to judge the behavior of the two treaty signees and cry foul when dishonesty was discovered. This program would work well as the decades would roll by. In the year 1912 the Confederate States and the United States would agree to discontinue the British-French Monitoring program. It had worked well for 50 years, but no longer was thought to be necessary.

## The War Between the States Was Over

In accordance with the treaty provisions, all captured Federal soldiers were soon moving north under Confederate guard in convoys, to be turned over, at various points along the boundary, with documentation and one man at a time, to receiving United States Army officials. Within five weeks' time, all men had been thusly processed and the resulting documentation of the process seemed acceptable to both sides.

## The Resettlement of Negroes

Also, in accordance with the treaty provisions, Federal soldiers, working north of the boundary, gathered up all Colored people, even including those with barely noticeable African ancestry, and began the processing of each. However, history of events in Maryland, northern Virginia, northern Kentucky and northern Missouri shows that about one-third of the bonded Negroes living north of the boundary at the time of the cease-fire, had, over the previous few weeks, been sold by their owners to other persons living south of the boundary as private transactions. Those sales obviously reduced the number of bonded Negroes that Federals had to process and relocate in accordance with the terms of the treaty.

Federal soldiers brought Negroes to processing stations where officials first attempted to group together all members of the same family and extended family. Even friends were grouped together for processing, for such groupings were very important to the future welfare of all, especially the children and the elderly.

For each person perceived to be independent (not a slave to someone else) detailed paperwork was prepared to document each individual's status, past work experience, family relations and friends, and all were assigned to cohesive groupings. Groups were escorted under Federal guard in convoys, to be turned over, at various points along the boundary, to receiving Confederate immigration officials, who reviewed the documentation of each person, further inquired about family ties, work skills and religious affiliation, confirmed acceptability of each grouping or modified it, and then coordinated each group's further migration to a State and county where they were to initially reside, with a letter of introduction for the county court house where their settlement was to be coordinated to ensure, although free, these people would be successful in their new environment.

Federal officials interviewed each bonded Negro and, if available, his or her owner, and prepared documentation regarding former owner (name and address), past work experience and family relations and friends. Speedy freedom was promised to all, but indenture for three years was thought a wise move for many to ensure they were successful as independent persons. All were assigned to cohesive groupings and also moved to the border to be delivered over to Confederate immigration officials. Because these individuals had no experience living independent lives, Confederate officials paid particular attention to each person's apparent ability to succeed without going through a transition period. Inquiry was made regarding religious affiliation, if any. Most did need to experience a transition period because of immaturity, dependent children or dependent parents, or lack of competitive skills. For those needing to experience a transition period, border officials sought to place groups in States and counties where coordinating officials were standing by to place them in transitional three-year indenture contracts. Accordingly, with interviews and documentation completed, groups were escorted by Confederate guides, selected from among former soldiers, to their selected destination and there turned over to the local indenture coordinators. This program of transitional indenturing would prove a great success, with almost ninety percent of adult individuals deemed suitable for independent living at the end of their three-year's service. The remainder entered into a second three-year contract. At the end of that period, everyone was, by law, declared independent. Success of the program is proven by the very small number of immigrant Colored people requiring subsequent State welfare support after six years of indenture. Colored children without support from family or friends were turned over to a welfare organization which arranged for foster care. The sick or lame were also treated with appropriate care through church-affiliated groups. [105]

Although during the meeting at the Soldier's Home Senator Stephen Douglas recommended to President Lincoln that a sizable portion of the Negro population in the North ought to be "colonized" overseas, that need never developed. The Confederacy was clearly the choice destination of Negroes living north of the new boundary. It was never necessary for the United States Government to "colonize" Negroes in Haiti, Africa, South America or anywhere. A few went to Canada, and a smattering went overseas, but the vast, vast majority accepted the Confederate proposal for resettlement in the South. By far the most common destination was to Texas, New Mexico Territory and South California.

We are now arriving at the final events that need to be reported concerning the Confederate's defense of independence.

## Final Events Concerning the Defense of Independence

The final events suitable for reporting here can be presented in a punch list of statements:

- The counties along the northern boundary of the Confederacy were reorganized by respective State legislatures to stand alone or merge with neighbors.

- Elections of the fall of 1862 were held as scheduled, and a new census was taken in 1863, to be effective in organizing districts for elections scheduled for the fall of 1864.

- The Confederate Constitution remained unaltered over the subsequent few years, and was judged to apply to the western regions of New Mexico Territory and South California.

---

[105] It will be hard for many readers to understand how successfully Colored people transitioned from slavery to independent living under the training and guidance of former slave owners, and oversight by Confederate officials. But, our alternate history is far different from truthful history. In truthful history, the South was devastated; the economy was destroyed, jobs were few, food was scarce for several years and sickness was so prevalent among Colored people that an estimated 200,000 died as a result of diseases spurred by the War and the Political Reconstruction that followed. Furthermore, the enormous disruption of Negro family groupings fed immoral and criminal behavior. In our alternate history, a far more moral and successful Colored population is sustained going forward through future generations.

Having concluded his presentation on the successful defense of State Secession and the negotiated boundary treaty and the resettlement of Colored people, Professor Davis invited all twelve essayists to a celebration party he had arranged immediately following supper:

"Everyone, you are invited to join me for a celebration party beginning an hour before supper. I have arranged for supper to be delayed one hour, we will all have the normal free time allotment this afternoon. We have much to celebrate! So, with that said, please join me and my wife near where we normally have supper. This treat is on me. You all are going to be magnificent when presenting your essays before the television cameras on our sesquicentennial celebration on July 4. So let us celebrate the first phase of our country's success this evening."

Marie Saint Martin replied: "I have an idea – let's bring our instruments and play a couple of relevant songs during the celebration party. We have worked up two that would be fitting. There is a piano there for Amanda. Allen, will you bring your guitar? With Professor Davis's banjo in hand, we can do it."

Professor Davis agreed: "I will bring my banjo. It is a done deal. Fifteen minute limit. Judith suggests we dress up in the Southern tradition. Coats and ties for men, dresses for ladies."

## Independence Celebration Party

Professor Davis's celebration party was splendid. Joe and Judith Davis were a handsome couple to be sure. Andrew Houston and Robert Lee seemed to be competing for time with the beautiful Conchita Rezanov. Chris Memminger seemed to be forever thanking Emma Lunalilo for saving his life, while Skipper Carlos Cespedes seemed to have accepted Emma's decision to dive into the stormy and dark ocean with flashlight and life jacket in a desperate swim toward the shouts from help. Isaiah Montgomery and Amanda Washington, both looking fine, seemed to be enjoying sharing conversation. Allen Ross, dressed in fine western gear, was questioning Robert Lee about the trip to Big Bone cave planned for the coming weekend. Marie Saint Martin, dressed in fine New Orleans style, and Tina Sharp, dressed like -- how do I say: like a nuclear engineer? – were discussing the upcoming singing while Judith looked on. Then Judith turned to Tina and said, "Why don't we get together tomorrow night and play some French horn duets. Will be fun." Tina replied, "Sure. I know I will learn something from you. My endurance will be suffering from lack of play. You know, the lip loses its stamina and flexibility through inaction." Benedict Juárez and Professor Davis were discussing agricultural management and how to maintain harmony among the shareholders, when Marie interrupted and announced, "Time for music, you all."

With that, the musicians among those attending gathered around the piano and made ready to perform. Seated at the piano, Amanda keyed notes to help Professor Davis tune his banjo and to help Allen and Carlos tune their guitars. Tina and Marie took a sip of water to clear their voices. The six were ready. To the others, Amanda said, "You all will know these two songs, so please join in."

"As you all know, we Confederates love to sing 'Dixie,' but with revised words that change the perspective to a Southern viewpoint: change it from a person up north looking at us "away down south" to we "here at home" looking at ourselves. As you know, the 'Dixie" we love goes this way:

"We're . . .
Proud to be in the land of cotton.
Old times here are not forgotten.
Gon'a Pray.  Come what may.
Gon'a stay, in Dixie Land.

"In Dixie Land where I was born.
Early on one frosty morn.
Gon'a pray.  Come what may.
Gon'a stay, in Dixie Land.

"I'm so glad that I'm in Dixie.
Hooray!  Hooray!
In Dixie Land I'll take my stand
To live and die in Dixie.
Hooray!  Hooray!
We Love, Love, Love . . . our Dixie!"

Thanks for joining in.  Now let us close with our Confederate States Anthem, our beloved, 'Diversity' song [106].

"We are one.
We are free.
We are the Great
Diversity

"From Carolina's sandy beach,
Westward to the Pacific shore,
From Artic ice beyond our reach,
To warm Gulf waters we adore.

"We are one.
We are free.
We are the Great
Diversity. . . . ."

The brief party hosted by Joe and Judith Davis was good fun.  And it represented another step toward bringing the twelve essayists together as a united group focused on doing their very best to understand "Why the Confederate States are the Greatest Country on Earth" and to prepare to explain the "Why" of it before a vast television audience as the sesquicentennial celebration would be drawing to a close in 19 days.

## Wednesday Evening Selected Diary Postings

---

[106] You will read much about "diversity" in *The CSA Trilogy*.  Although in truthful history, in the year 2011, the word "diversity" means many different things to many different people -- in our alternate history of the Confederate States of America its meaning is more narrow and is understood as a feature of Confederate society to be celebrated.  In the CSA, "diversity" speaks of the range of racial and ethnic ancestries of the Confederate people. Confederates do not all look alike and their talents and abilities vary broadly.  But they are Confederates, true and true. They speak the common English language.  Immigrants who have arrived since 1865, most of them from Europe, had learned and continue to learn English and blend into Confederate society.  So "diversity" to a Confederate does not mean diverse cultural behaviors, does not mean that Muslims can disrupt the Christian social norm, does not mean that racial and/or ethnic gangs can get away with bad behavior, does not mean that political agitators can desecrate the monuments erected to honor long-ago Confederates.  Stated in a positive way, the diverse peoples within our States have subordinated their former cultures to become compatible with the Southern culture and the governments within the various States and the Confederate Government at Davis.

Diary note by Isaiah Montgomery said, "Benedict Juárez and I shared supper tonight. Most interesting fellow. He is of almost pure Native American ancestry. Real proud of the manufacturing powerhouse in his State of Costa Este. Monterrey is the main city and he lives there. Has a Ph.D. in philosophy and a bachelor's degree in history and came across as a great conversationalist. So interested in my Mississippi farming background and how my African American ancestors carved out a farming cooperative for ourselves. Was interesting to compare our backgrounds, experiences and interests. I like him a lot and expect we will become pals over the next three weeks -- not because we are alike, but because, although we are so unalike, we both are so interested in other people. . . . . Today's lecture was on the Boundary Treaty and Resettlement of Negroes. I was reminded that quite a few of the people who today live in and work in Mound Bayou Corporate Plantation are descended from Negroes who resettled in that part of Mississippi from north of the Boundary Line. And they hold stock in our corporation like I do. Although a minority of the population when they arrived in our area from up North, their contributions were greatly appreciated. Many had arrived with more education than their new neighbors and took pride in teaching others.

"There is a relevant story passed down by my Montgomery ancestors, two slaves owned by President Jefferson Davis and his older brother Joseph. They say that President Davis, upon accepting the position of Provisional President, anticipated leading the Confederate States as an honorable and truthful political leader, and as an experienced and successful military leader. That was his background and that was consistent with his character. But that attitude experienced helpful change when, on the day of his inauguration, President Davis met Jean Lafitte, the old, but reformed, former pirate made famous by Andrew Jackson at the Battle of New Orleans. With Judah Benjamin's help, Jean opened Mr. Davis's eyes to the value of a strong Confederate Secret Service and the artful, widespread and persistent application of clever propaganda aimed at the Northern States and the political attitudes of the people within each. And many Southern Negroes, accepting assignments as Secret Service Agents, went North, carrying messages, dispensing propaganda and warning people that a Federal conquest of the Confederate States would result in hordes of Blacks migrating North to become their neighbors. The message: let the South live in peace, nationalize your practice of prohibiting immigration by Blacks, and keep your States even more pure in the skin color of its dominant people. At Mound Bayou we honor these Negro Secret Service Agents every July fourth. Have a monument to them at Mound Bayou, too. It is a lovely monument."

Diary note by Allan Ross said, "I am so proud of my Cherokee ancestors and how they supported the Confederate States and won for themselves and our other four neighboring civilized tribes the independence available to us through the Confederate Nation/State of Sequoyah. I firmly believe that, if Confederates would have failed to win their independence, we Native Americans would have suffered great abuse and would forevermore be treated as a sub-class in North America. [107] We can certainly look to our north, to the United States, and clearly see Native Americans suffering in so-called Reservations: poor, forced to live on the worst possible land, with restricted opportunities, and dependent on Federal subsidies." At the party, Robert Lee and I talked about a caving trip he wants to make this coming weekend. Calls it Big Bone cave. Says lots of salt peter vats constructed during the War of 1812 and the War Between the States are still present in the cave because the cave has remained exceptionally dry over the past 150 years. I have never been caving. Will give it a try."

Diary note by Marie Saint Martin said, "We played pretty well at the party this evening. Will do better as we practice more. Will add more songs to our play list. Judith complemented

---

[107] Truthful history supports the prediction presented in Allan Ross's diary entry.

us. That goes a long way. As I prepare for bed, I am thinking of the heroic men of Louisiana that were so effective in defending our independence. A special thank you bedtime prayer goes to my ancestor Jules Saint Martin, who was so effective at helping the Confederate Secret Service under the overall direction of Judah Benjamin, Confederate Attorney General. Without our very effective Secret Service during 1861 and 1862, it remains doubtful that our Confederate ancestors would have successfully defended our independence against the large and well-armed, but untested, army gathered up by the Lincoln Administration and cooperative Republican governors of the Northern states."

Diary note by Chris Memminger said, "My great, great, great grandfather, Christopher Gustavus Memminger of South Carolina, President Davis's Secretary of the Treasury, has passed down through descendants this important message: A major reason that the Confederate States succeeded in acquiring the best in military weaponry during 1861 and the first months of 1862 was because Confederates enjoyed a strong positive balance of trade and a strong Confederate dollar. And I believe that Secretary Memminger had a lot to do with that success. I toasted him tonight at the party to a rousing response from others, especially Professor Davis, who shouted. 'Bravos to Secretary Memminger'!"

Diary note by Robert Lee said: "You heard a lot in Confederate military history about my great-great-great-grandfather General Robert Edward Lee. He did a fine job leading the Confederate Division charged with defending the advancing Federal army as it progressed southward through Virginia, aimed at capturing Virginia's capital, Richmond, and then proceeding further south toward State capitals in North Carolina and South Carolina. He embraced the Confederate strategy of Retreat, Envelope and Capture, and, to an extent, his was the most difficult to accomplish. His great challenge was to deceive the advancing Federal army into a sense of confidence, contentment and patience, and delay springing the trap for many days. If General Lee had too soon Enveloped and Captured the opposing Federal army, the Lincoln Administration would have signaled the other Federal divisions to close ranks, maintain a path of retreat and respect the fighting spirit of the Confederates. Lincoln would have warned that Confederate retreats were not from weakness, but designed to draw Federals into a trap in which they could capture most of the weaponry and most of the Federal soldiers, still green untested troops, in one bold stroke. I am proud of General Lee and proud to carry his name. I like to think Conchita would be proud of the Lee name, too.

"Oh well, going caving this coming weekend. To Big Bone cave. Have permission from the land owner to enter the cave, which is normally locked up to protect the bats. Allen Ross will join me. I have received word from a Nashville caving friend of a crawlway recently discovered. We will go equipped with knee pads and dust masks, and prepared to do one hell of a lot of crawling. Will return Saturday night, probably totally exhausted. But there is hope that we will enter into a cave passage never before seen by humans or at least never seen since those long-ago salt peter mining days. "

Diary note by Andrew Houston said, "Played doubles with Marie against Conchita and Professor Davis. We lost. I was easy on my serves to Professor Davis in the early going, but picked up the pace in the last set, hitting volleys at him and in efforts to pass him. Conchita covered three fourths of the court, allowing Professor Davis to just stand his ground and use his quick hands to return volleys at Marie. It got vicious. Did not seem fair. Of course we lost. Oh, well. Great party tonight. My ancestor Sam Houston did not favor Texas secession, but was outvoted on the matter. He lived to see its successful defense. I just wish he could see the Confederate States today and observe our great diversity and our great success – to hear people say that the Confederate States are the greatest country on Earth. Time for night night."

Diary note by Amanda Lynn Washington said, "My ancestor, Booker T. Washington, of Virginia would be proud of the success today of the Confederate States of America. He played no role in the Defense of Secession, but he sure was a leader in the education of Colored people in the following decade. Makes me laugh – just thinking about how those holier-than-thou Northern Puritans thought they had won a great benefit for the United States by forcing the Confederates to accept their deportations of people of African descent to south of the negotiated boundary. Ha! Serves them right! We taught them a thing or two! But will their descendants ever come to realize the value to society of a diverse population?"

Diary note by Professor Davis said, "I played doubles tennis this afternoon with Conchita, Andrew and Marie. We were a bit rushed, because we had to quit in time to shower and dress before the celebration party. Was fun in spite of the fact that Conchita's ability on the court is far beyond any of us. Her closest competitor is Andrew Houston. Has a very good game, has the genetic male advantage, and has played singles with Conchita since arriving in Sewanee. Hear she let him win one of the matches they have played so as to not overly bruise his ego. They seem to be great friends. I had an easy time of it, for my partner was Conchita. Andrew and Marie were partners across the net from us. Had some trouble with Andrew's powerful serve, but played well enough for a seniors player. Was fun and needed the exercise. We won. Will do this again." As we prepare for bed, Judith tells me that the party was very successful. She believes it was a great way to bring the twelve essayists closer together and will pay great dividends over the coming two and a half weeks.

## The Close to Part One, *The CSA Trilogy*

Dear reader: Congratulations! You have completed Part One of *The CSA Trilogy*. Part Two and Part Three continue the story. The Sewanee project continues. Professor Davis will next be telling the twelve essayists the history of the French Intervention in Mexico, the consequential secession of the provinces of northern Mexico, their successful fight for independence, and the region's transformation into six States within the Confederacy. There will be more: the story of Cuba, Russian America and Hawaii. Beyond that, you will experience the amazing CSA history, including the War against Imperialist Japan, going forward to the 2011 celebration. Professor Davis hopes to see you auditing his remaining classes. More weekend adventures await you as well.

# The CSA Trilogy

An Alternate History/Historical Novel about Our Vast and Beautiful Confederate States of America

A Happy Story in Three Parts of What Might Have Been

1861 to 2011

## The CSA Trilogy, Part 2 -- How the Confederate States Expanded to Include the State of Cuba, Six States Out of Northern Mexico, the State of Russian America, and the State of Hawaii -- An Alternate History – 1862 to 1877

### Foreword

Thanks for your interest in this alternate history and its associated novel overlay, which is presented as a trilogy covering 150 years of the Confederate States of America, from its formation in early 1861, to the celebration of the sesquicentennial of what is widely considered to be "the Greatest Country on Earth." The three parts of this *Trilogy* match the three major stories of the Confederate States. This is Part 2. We assume that you have already read Part 1 of this trilogy.

**Part Two.** With the Confederate States now established and unchallenged, we proceed to Part Two. Here our alternate history follows to a remarkable extent truthful history of the 1860's and early 1870's. What makes our alternate history for Mexico, Russian America, Hawaii and Cuba possible is the presence of the Confederate States. It is really amazing to understand how the successful defense of the Confederate States quickly snow-balled into successful independence movements in Cuba, the northern region of Mexico, Russian America (known at Alaska in truthful history) and the Hawaiian Islands. With Confederate help and encouragement, these successful independence movements resulted in the addition of nine more States within the Confederacy – the State of Cuba, six States out of Northern Mexico, the State of Russian America and the State of Hawaii. These rapid events, to a great extent consistent with truthful history of those regions in those times, will thrill the reader. All of this takes place between 1863 and 1877.

You already know that this is a happy story, so much happier that the truthful history of the conquest of the Seceded States -- a four-year military nightmare that resulted in the death of approximately one million people, about half from the United States and about half from the Confederate States.

And you have been invited to ask, "Did this calamity have to happen?" Actually, the answer is "No". Alternate futures are always possible in human events. Looking back from our vantage point today, we realize that a change in certain historic circumstances could have often dramatically changed the course of human history, and, moving forward, even to redefining the world as we know it today.

You already know that most of this trilogy reads like an alternate history, but parts do read like a novel. We hope you continue to enjoy the experiences and interpersonal relationships developed during the character's four weeks at the University of the South, in Sewanee, Tennessee. You have already experienced the weekend adventure where six were engaged in an overnight sailing adventure off the coast of Cuba. Now you will be experiencing the adventure of two exploring an old historic cave west of Sewanee.

# Part 2, Chapter 1, Day 11 – Chaos During the French Intervention Allows Northern Mexico to Win Secession from the Central Government in Mexico City and become Six Confederate States – Class Lecture, Thursday, June 16, 2011

You learned in Part One that our twelve essayists are in a classroom setting during the morning, Monday through Friday, listening to Professor Davis present a segment of Confederate history that will help them develop their answer to the question "Why are the Confederate States the greatest country on Earth?" We are here again in that classroom on Thursday morning. You are listening in. Professor Davis begins.

In the several years following the peace settlement between the United States and the Confederate States, the former remained relative stable in size and configuration, but, to the contrary, the latter, the Confederate States of America, entered into a dramatic era of expansion -- expansion in several directions. And, in every case, the expansions were predicated on strict State Sovereignty concerning all political bodies involved. We will review these historical events one at a time – first Mexican State Secession, then Russian America, then Cuba and, finally, Hawaii.

## Overview of Mexican State Secession and Reconfiguration

Inspired by the successful secession of numerous States in the southern part of the United States, important Mexican political leaders, most importantly Benito Juárez, led a movement that resulted in the successful secession of numerous States in the northern half of Mexico. The story of why and how this secession movement arose and succeeded will be related a bit later in this chapter, but first it is appropriate to define the resulting expansion.

The Treaty of Saltillo, signed on May 5, 1866, hammered out the boundary between the part of Mexico controlled by the French Intervention, versus the seceded states to the north -- defined in terms of longitude and latitude to facilitate the construction of a secure fence separating the two nations[108]. Thus, the boundary, measuring 685 miles in length, could be readily defined in a single sentence:

"Beginning at the Gulf of Mexico, the boundary follows the latitude of 21 degrees and 30 minutes until it arrives at the longitude of 100 degrees; from that point proceeding south until it arrives at the latitude of 20 degrees; from that point proceeding west until it arrives at the Pacific Ocean; thereby ensuring that both Baja California and Baja California Sur are placed in the northern nation."

North of the boundary, the following 15 states and territories became part of the Seceded Mexican States:

| Original State/Territory | Area, sq. miles | Population | Reconfigured State |
|---|---|---|---|
| Baja California | 56,126 | 28,535 | Costa Noroeste |
| Sonora | 69,249 | 133,668 | Costa Noroeste |
| Chihuahua | 95,540 | 198,184 | Costa Noroeste |
| Coahuila | 58,531 | 170,242 | Costa Este |
| Nuevo Leon | 24,771 | 198,145 | Costa Este |
| Tamaulipas | 30,984 | 132,696 | Costa Este |
| Sinaloa | 22,500 | 179,460 | Central Norte |
| Durango | 47,613 | 225,015 | Central Norte |

---

[108] The May 5, 1866 Treaty of Saltillo is our alternate history.

| | | | |
|---|---|---|---|
| Zacatecas | 29,067 | 280,537 | Central Norte |
| San Luis Potosi 9/10ths | 21,244 | 317,720 | Costa del Sur |
| Nayarit | 10,756 | 90,713 | Costa Sudoeste |
| Aguascalientes | 2,168 | 61,764 | Costa Sudoeste |
| Jalisco 2/3rds | 20,229 | 459,519 | Costa Sudoeste |
| Guanajuato 9/10ths | 10,635 | 581,082 | Central del Sur |
| Queretaro 1/3rd | 1,506 | 46,159 | Central del Sur |
| Total Reassigned to North | 500,919 | 3,103,439[109] | |
| Total for Original Mexico | 757,368 | 8,209,368 | |
| Percent Reassigned to North | 66.1 | 37.8 | |

So, this new country, made up of seceded Mexican states and territories, contained 66 percent of the land, much of it quite arid and sparsely populated, and 38 percent of the population that had been originally within Mexico. In 1870, to facilitate a reasonable merger into the Confederate States of America, the 15 seceded Mexican states and territories were consolidated into six (6) sovereign States. These were named and organized as follows:

| New States | Area, Sq. Mi. | Population | Original States/Territories |
|---|---|---|---|
| Costa Noroeste | 220,915 | 360,387 | B. California, Sonora, Chihuahua |
| Central Norte | 99,180 | 685,012 | Sinaloa, Durango, Zacatecas |
| Costa Este | 114,286 | 501,083 | Coahuila, Nuevo Leon, Tamaulipas |
| Costa del Sur | 21,244 | 317,720 | San Luis Potosi (9/10) |
| Costa Sudoeste | 33,153 | 611,996 | Jalisco (2/3), Nayarit, Aquascalientes |
| Central del Sur | 12,141 | 627,241 | Guanajuato (9/10), Queretaro (1/3) |
| **Total** | **500,919** | **3,103,439** | |

The above is the outcome. We now turn the clock back a few centuries to present the history of Mexico. Why devote pages to that history? Because only then can you understand that it was from the ashes of Spanish America's horrific history that six great Confederate States arose. To keep this history at a reasonable number of pages, parts of the history are abridged to speed your reading.

## The Spanish Conquistadores and the Conquest of Central America and Beyond

In 1492 Christopher Columbus "sailed the ocean blue," discovered a few Caribbean islands, and launched the great wave of European colonization of the American continents that would be led by the people of Spain, their government and their Catholic church, with lesser involvement by the Portuguese. What had spurred forward this zeal for exploration? Why had the torch -- formally carried by others, including the Vikings -- passed over to Spain? The answer is found in analysis of the Spanish experience over the previous 700 years. [110]

You see, the people of Spain had for seven centuries suffered invasion and widespread occupation by Islamist militants, beginning in 711, and peaking under the powerful Umayyad Caliphate (929-1031). Finally, in 1492, the last region of Islamic control, the Emirate of Granada, would be retaken by Catholic forces under the leadership of Queen Isabella of Castile and her husband Ferdinand II of Aragon. So, for seven centuries prior to the year of the first voyage of

---

[109] These population numbers represent the actual 1900 census for the truthful Mexican States divided by 1.65. An earlier census was never taken in truthful history.

[110] The following history of the Spanish and Natives in what would become Mexico is truthful history as we best understand it today.

Christopher Columbus, the Spanish people would have suffered Islamic domination and Islamic-Christian conflict.

This writer, among others, believes this seven-century-plus encounter with militant Islamists had perceptibly transformed the character of a large percentage of male Spanish men -- transformed them through both environmental interactions and through evolutionary genetic interactions -- not everyone, to be sure, but many -- enough to tilt the bell curve defining the range of character traits among individuals toward a generally fervent, crusading, intolerant, militant, religious spirit. This was the nature of the men who left their women behind and ventured east across the Atlantic as Spanish conquistadores. [111]

Aided by favorable and predictable westward-flowing trade winds off of northern Africa, a distance not all that far from Spain and Portugal, the challenge was being met to discover what lay to the west of the vast Atlantic Ocean. Once land was found, a safe return was possible by slowly sailing north until reaching the eastward-flowing trade winds off the coast of North America, which returned the explorers to the Spanish coast. Once begun, exploration and conquest proceeded rapidly.

By 1511 the Spanish were at Cuba. By 1514 Cuba was mostly occupied. By 1517 Cuba, under the rule of Spanish governor Diego Velásquez, was completely subdued and already decimated by disease. Small westward probes along the continental coast were already underway. Then, in February 1519, the amazing band of 500 Spanish soldiers and adventurers, under the leadership of Hernando Cortés, who was supposedly to be subservient to governor Velásquez, set out from Cuba to conquer what was to become known as Mexico.

These 500 men set out in 11 ships, complete with 16 horses, 10 brass guns (cannons) and four light field artillery pieces known as falconets. The human population of the land which they aimed to conquer -- to become New Spain, then the Republic of Mexico -- is not known with any degree of accuracy, but a widely accepted estimate is 25,000,000. Before describing the invasion by Cortés's little brigade, it is appropriate to describe this land and its people.

Historian Henry Bamford Parkes described the people as follows: [112]

The natives "were divided into a large number of different tribes who spoke different languages and were politically independent of each other. In the [arid] north, the population was small and lived mostly in a state of savagery." In the rather fertile south, "there was a dense population who lived by agriculture, and among them were tribes who had developed civilized institutions," which were -- in areas where they existed -- crude, cruel and controlled by a priest-hood that held power over their superstitious subjects through mysticism, temple building, frequent human sacrifice and magical deceptions.

"In spite of their linguistic and political differences, the [native] people of Mexico sprang from the same racial stock and had similar physical and mental characteristics. They had brownish complexions, broad cheek-bones, straight black hair on their heads, and little hair on their bodies. By temperament they were patient rather than aggressive, given to a stoical endurance rather than to conflict. In their intercourse with each other, cheerfulness and good humor was the dominating note, and courtesy became a ritual . . . . Never having developed any strong sense of personal individuality, they rated human life

---

[111] Islamist militants mentioned in this history of many centuries ago should not be confused with the Islamist terrorists active today in several regions of the world, but their intolerance of people not bound to their Muslim faith was, nevertheless, extreme and harsh.

[112] Although this report is troubling to read, it follows truthful history as we best know it today. *A History of Mexico*, by Henry Bamford Parkes, 1938, pages 3-9.

cheaply. For them the individual counted for little, and the welfare of the tribe was everything. . . . With a bias toward the concrete, they were uninterested in the abstractions of metaphysics, and had little of that capacity for seeing the general in the particular which leads to scientific discovery; but they excelled in the visual arts. Their inability to apprehend abstractions was discernible also in their forms of government; for though they had little sense of individuality, they had not acquired a political or social consciousness like that of the European nations. Their loyalty was not to the abstractions of society and the state, but to the neighbors and kinsfolk who comprised their tribe and to the chieftains who embodied it."

In areas with sufficient rainfall, in the central and southern sections, "they lived chiefly on maize, which was planted in hillocks with pointed sticks; when the maize was ripe the women ground it into flour and molded the flour-dough into tamales or beat it into flat tortillas, which were cooked over charcoal fires. They also cultivated frijoles and certain other fruits and vegetables, and seasoned their food with chilies. They drank chocolate, while, from the sap of the maguey plant, they made an intoxicating liquor known as pulque. Fish and certain animals and birds, such as turkeys and quail, were eaten as delicacies, but their diet was mainly vegetarian. For clothing they used textiles made from cotton or from maguey fibers. They lived, for the most part, in huts made of wood or adobe and thatched with maguey. Horses, cows, sheep, and pigs were unknown. They had no beasts of burden, so that all labor was performed by human beings. They had never invented the wheel or the plough. Although they had begun to use copper, tin, and lead, and to make ornaments out of gold and silver, they had never discovered iron."

"Never having developed a system of phonetic writing, [they] had no written literature . . . and for music they had few string or wind instruments. But in pottery and textiles, in the carving of wood and stone, and in the manufacturing of gold and jade ornaments, their best creations were, in their own kind, the equals of any produced in the other hemisphere."

"They worshipped a number of different gods, representing the welfare of the tribe or the powers of nature, who were symbolized by half-human, half-animal figures. They built temples to these gods on the flat tops of pyramidal mounds. The priests wore robes of black or red and crowns of feathers, and never cut or combed their hair. They guided the activities of the tribe, ascertaining the will of the gods by rites of divination. They maintained schools where children were instructed in singing and dancing and religious rituals, and preserved historical and astronomical knowledge."

"The practice of human sacrifice was universal. The victim who was offered to one of the gods was led up the steps of the pyramid into the temple, where a group of priests seized him and tore out his heart. The wooden image of the god was them smeared with blood, while the corpse was rolled to the foot of the pyramid. It was believed that the gods fed on human blood and that their strength would decay if they were not provided with victims. Since these victims were regarded as embodiments of the deity, portions of their bodies [were] ritualistically eaten after the sacrifice; and since they were promised especial honors in the next world, they did not always accept their fate with any great reluctance; some of them seem, on the contrary, to have welcomed it as an honor. For the most part, however, especially among those tribes who practiced human sacrifice most frequently, the victims were slaves or prisoners of war, who were kept in cages and carefully fattened before they were immolated. . . . But religious celebrations, in spite of the odor of blood which pervaded the temples and clung to the long hair of the priests, were more often [than not] occasions of rejoicing."

"Closely associated with the priests were the [chiefs], who led the tribes in war and whose powers occasionally became almost monarchial. Among the more advanced tribes a class of secular nobility was also beginning to emerge, some of whom owned slaves."

But in the tropical swamps and jungles from Yucatan to Chiapas to Guatemala and westward into neighboring highlands, gone was the great Mayan civilization, which seemed to have begun in the fourth century and for unknown reasons perished in the ninth century. Yet, a remnant had returned, and the Maya language was still being spoken in sections.

At the time of the Spanish arrival, the Aztecs were in control of central Mexico, headquartered in a magnificent and large city named Tenochtitlán, a city built upon what was once islands in a shallow lake named Texoco, whose ruins are beneath present-day Mexico City. The Aztecs had risen to power by conquering the Nahua tribes known as the Chichimecas, who had come down from the mountains to the north of the central valley and conquered the Toltecs. Other notable civilizations had flourished in several regions of this land, in valleys walled off by protective mountain ranges: to the southeast Cholula had been impressive; far to the south in Oaxaca the Zapotec civilization still flourished.

Cortéz's Conquistadores first reached the continent by the northern coast of the Yucatán peninsula, there discovering a native tribe and a Spaniard who had shipwrecked seven years earlier and escaped being sacrificed to the Maya gods, a fate suffered by his fellow sailors. Through this contact, Cortés acquired a translator who spoke the Maya language, and the ability to start learning about the land and the tribes he aimed to conquer and how he could persuade a tribe here or there to provide guides and warriors to assist in the conquest of disliked neighbors -- and to help discover where was the gold and silver, for, at the outset, taking the natives' gold and silver was more important than taking their land. [113]

Cortés's Conquistadores returned to their ships and sailed south-eastwardly along the coast to Tabasco. Here the natives set upon them in large numbers, but "the Spaniards had the advantages of firearms, of steel swords, and of coats of mail; but it was their horses that finally gave them the victory. It became evident during the battle that the natives, who had never seen horses before, regarded them as supernatural creatures and supposed the horse and rider were all one animal." Defeated, the native chiefs "submitted and brought presents," Cortés preached them a sermon, Father Olmedo celebrated Mass for them and pronounced them vassals of the Spanish King. The natives reciprocated by presenting the Conquistadores with 20 virgins, which were distributed among the victorious Spanish men. This began the process by which Spanish men, far more often than not, fathered children with native women, sometimes typical native women, sometimes esteemed daughters of chiefs. At first these children would be half-breeds, called creoles. But, when the boys grew up, they would take native wives and those children would be quarter-breeds, and on down the line to eight-breeds, as so forth. Since Spanish women came to Mexico in numbers far, far less than Spanish men, pure-breed Spanish daughters born in Mexico represented a very small percentage of the population that possessed significant Spanish ancestry.

Departing Tabasco, the Conquistadores sailed westward along the coast to San Juan de Uloa, near the present harbor town of Vera Cruz. Here Cortés encountered Aztec emissaries who had already heard of his explorations and greatly feared the consequence. The ruler over the Aztecs, Moctezuma, was located in his palace in the splendid city named Tenochtitlán (presently buried beneath Mexico City). His emissaries sought to persuade the invaders to depart. They brought gifts and Cortés demonstrated the power of his guns and his horses. More beautiful gifts arrived: notably "two great disks, as large as cartwheels, which were made of solid gold and

---

[113] The history of the Spanish Conquistadores is truthful history, although disturbing to read.

silver and which symbolized the sun and the moon . . . ten bales of cotton . . . many gold birds and animals . . . and a [returned] Spanish helmet filled with gold dust." Mistake: thusly Montezuma "advertised" the great wealth he possessed. Cortés now knew where to get the gold. He decided to settle down at the coast and seek alliances with Aztec enemies to facilitate the conquest of Moctezuma's world. He renounced his presumed subordination to Diego Velásquez, the governor of Cuba. He then ordained a town, named it Vera Cruz, and proclaimed himself and his Conquistadores to be citizens of said town, an allegedly Spanish town, and declared that valuables taken from the natives anywhere and everywhere in the future would be divided, one-fifth for the King of Spain, one-fifth for the expedition leader, Cortés, and the remainder to be divided among the Conquistadores.

From here Cortés and his Conquistadores proceeded to subjugate Cempoala, of the Totonac tribe, leaving there an altar to the Virgin Mary before returning to their ships at Vera Cruz. Boldly, he ordered his Spanish ships burnt to prevent retreat and headed with 400 Conquistadores, 200 Totonac porters, 40 Totonac nobles and the native girls on his westward march, up through the 10,000 foot pass beneath the snow-capped peak of Mount Orizaba, across a stretch of desert and into "fertile valleys, thickly planted with corn and magueys", arriving finally at Tlaxcalan, a city protected by a huge nine-foot-high masonry wall stretching across the valley, from mountain to mountain. Impressed, the Tlaxcalans decided to ally with the White men for the purposes of defeating their arch enemy, the Aztecs.

Now Cortés had an army of considerable size. In addition to his 400 Conquistadores and the girls, valuable as interpreters, he now had 6,000 Tlaxcalan warriors "as an escort." The military objective was Cholula, a city to the south, located in a "valley filled with cornfields and watered by innumerable canals," the "sacred city of [the ancient feathered serpent god] Quetzalcoatl, with its great pyramid and its four hundred temples -- a place of pilgrimage for all the tribes of the plateau." It was a gruesome encounter: Two thousand Cholula men were slaughtered, "the temple was burned and a great cross was erected atop the shrine to the god Quetzalcoatl, dominating the scene of the massacre as a symbol of the might of Spain."

With the subjugation of Cholula and the mastery of the important god, Quetzalcoatl, now complete, Cortés -- with his 400 Conquistadores, the Tlaxcalan allies, and translation assistance from the girls -- was in command of the situation. Not so Moctezuma -- severely cowed by reports of Cortés's "mastery" of the god Quetzalcoatl, Moctezuma, extremely superstitious, was feeling defeated even without a fight. So he dispatched Aztec guides from his palace to escort the Conquistadores to the Valley of Mexico (called Anáhuac by the natives) and to the main Aztec city Tenochtitlán. Cortés was now ready to go forward. "From Cholula the Spaniards climbed the pass below the smoking cone of Popocatépetl and descended through pine forests and maguey fields" into what would become known as The Valley of Mexico. "As they came down into the valley and saw, spread out before them, the shimmering waters of the lakes and the white houses of innumerable towns, they could scarcely believe their eyes. . . . They passed along the shores of Chalco and of Xochimilco . . . and came to Ixtapalapán, a city of white stone houses with delicately carved woodwork of cedar, filled with orchards and rose gardens and fish ponds; here Cuitlahuac, the brother of Moctezuma, gave them entertainment for the night." Looking out from this location they saw an amazing sight: "a concrete causeway ran westwards and then northwards across Lake Texcoco, and at the end of the causeway, five miles away but clearly outlined in the bright air, was the city of Tenochtitlán, with its 100,000 inhabitants and magnificent pyramids, temples and buildings.

At dawn the next day Cortés, on horseback, rode forward onto the causeway toward Tenochtitlán, with the fully-armed Conquistadores, the Tlaxcalan allies and the girls following. "At the entrance to the city were two parallel files of Aztec nobles and between them, carried on a litter surmounted by a canopy of featherwork fringed with jewels, was Moctezuma." After exchanging greetings through interpreters, they proceeded into the city and were given lodging in the "palace of Axayacatl, on the west side of the temple enclosure." Moctezuma seemed to consider his surrender complete, explaining that he "would accept the king of Spain as his master and provide Cortés with all that he might ask for." But Cortés did not trust Moctezuma, the Aztec people, or his own men to remain peaceful -- any incident could ignite war. So, a few days later, Cortés told Moctezuma that he was to be a Spanish prisoner, confined by the Conquistadores at the palace of Axayacatl. Moctezuma consented and explained to witnesses that he had agreed to the arrangement. But fifteen Aztecs were soon accused of instigating the capture and were consequently "burnt alive" in front of the room where Moctezuma was confined. "Afterwards Cortés embraced his prisoner, declaring that he loved him as a brother and that Moctezuma should govern not only Tenochtitlán, but other kingdoms which Cortés would conquer for him." Moctezuma agreed and he "continued to act as chieftain while living in the Spaniards' headquarters and was willing to do whatever Cortés demanded."

How could the Spanish have so easily conquered Central America? Historian Henry Bamford Parkes explains: "The Indian lack of individualism and habits of obedience, which gave them strength as long as they had good leaders, now made Spanish control so much the easier." This was especially true of the compliant nature of natives living in towns and cities in populous, fertile regions, complete with demanding gods and blood-soaked temples where frequent human sacrifices kept individualism in check. You see, after a spate of sacrificial killings, the people remaining alive celebrated because they had once more escaped the priest's knife, and again wished not to offend the murderers. This characterized the central and southern region of Mexico. But, to the north, including all of the area that would be included in the Seceded Mexican States, this habit of obedience to authority was far less pronounced. In that arid region the natives were normally on the move and expressing the independent character typical of Native Americans living in what would become the United States and the Confederate States.

Now, Cortés told Moctezuma that the Spanish king needed gold and lots of it. Conquistadores spread out searching for gold and gold mines. "The wealth was brought to Cortés, and after he had set apart a fifth for the king and a fifth for himself, the remainder was divided among the Conquistadores."

Space in this history has been allowed for coverage of the conquest of Mexico by Hernando Cortéz and his band of Conquistadores so that you, the reader, can experience some early history of Central America in sufficient detail to appreciate the character of the Spanish men and of the native people. For a contrast we remember that, in settling North America, and land that became the United States and the Confederate States, European men, primarily English speaking, brought with them women and even children, and European-Native mixed race descendants were not particularly significant in populating the early United States. But in Central America, the Spanish men seldom brought with them women, resulting in a population where people of European ancestry were predominantly of mixed race. This resulted in a nation fraught with problems of a poor economy, disruptive racial divisions, stark three-tier class divisions and dysfunctional concepts about what constitutes good government -- some attitudes anchored in strong-man tribal loyalties, some attitudes anchored in competitive struggles among ruling elites, some attitudes anchored in religious mysticism and priestly control over society -- these conflicts most times being resolved by civil wars and dictatorship -- these conflicts seldom resolved by employing multi-class democratic ideals.

Following the conquest and subjugation of central Mexico, the Spanish turned south in a campaign to conquer southern Mexico and to proceed on into Guatemala and Honduras, subjugating those regions by 1525. By 1526, with great difficulty, Yucatán was subjugated, for "nowhere in all America was resistance to Spanish conquest more obstinate." In 1531 Spaniards, under Francisco Pizarro, turned to the Pacific coast of South America, conquering the capable Inca Empire and there, "gathering loot which dwarfed the glory of Tenochtitlán and treating his victims with a cynical brutality of which Cortés would have been incapable."

But even by 1535, except for the Pacific coast northward to half-way up what would become the seceded Mexican state of Sinaloa, and the Gulf coast up to the northern boundary of the state of Vera Cruz, "the mountains to the north of Mexico City and the lands beyond "were still unconquered and unexplored." This vast region, much of it arid, mostly sparsely populated with independent-minded natives, would be explored over the subsequent generations.

Francisco Vásquez de Coronado, with 300 men, 1,000 horses and droves of cattle, sheep and pigs, joined by an army of Native allies, ventured north in February 1540 from the Pacific-coast town of Compostella of what would become the state of Nayarit. They eventually reached the upper Rio Grande valley in the present-day Confederate State of New Mexico, then ventured further north into the prairies of present day Kansas, finding no gold and retreating back to central Mexico, and leaving behind their horses and cattle -- these animals later serving to provide ponies for the plains natives of North America and the Mexican states of Chihuahua and Durango, and long-horn cattle for Texas and the Plains. The Spanish hold over New Mexico and Santa Fe "was always weak. . . . In 1680 the Indians rebelled and massacred the Spaniards or drove them southwards; and they were not reconquered until 1694. The mountainous region of the state of Zacatecas proved very difficult to conquer, in spite of its great potential wealth in silver mines. But the bulk of the area of what would become the Seceded Mexican States was under Spanish control by 1550, with particular attention to the rich silver mines, such as the Veta Madre lode of Guanajuato. Furthermore, Guanajuato was also the center of some of the most fertile farming land in Mexico. By 1548 there was a steady flow of silver out of Mexico. Querétaro, not far north of Mexico City, "was conquered by Otomi chieftains, who had adopted Spanish names and the Spanish religion and who were rewarded with Spanish titles." The far-northern Mexican territories/states of Lower California, Sonora, Chihuahua and Coahuila were slowly occupied by Spanish influence, the arid areas holding cattle ranches and the few valleys supporting agriculture. In this region, an independent attitude was particularly prevalent. Catholic Friars played a major role in pacifying the natives of Mexico and teaching them civilized living. They were especially effective in this regard in the northern part of Mexico, which would become the Seceded Mexican States.

## New Spain

In the year 1800 Spain ruled over a large portion of North, Central and South America, but in a manner that would prove to be untenable, for she had always ruled for the object of enriching Spain --think gold and silver -- with little regard for building a sustainable colony in the New World. The Spanish domain in Central and North America was especially vast. At this time "the Viceroy of his Most Catholic Majesty, residing at Mexico City, ruled supreme over a great part of the entire continent of Central and North America, from Guatemala to Vancouver's Island and from Florida to San Francisco." Much of this vast land would be taken by the United States, through a combination of purchases and war prizes:

- In 1803 Napoleon "sold his plunder — known by the general name of 'Louisiana,' for a pitiful sum, to the United States."

- In 1819 Ferdinand VII sold to the United States the Peninsula of Florida and the adjacent districts to the west. Furthermore, that sale acknowledged that Spain was giving up it rights to the far northwest, north of California, which became the States of Oregon, Washington and Idaho, even including Vancouver's Island.

Why did prosperity and good government so elude New Spain?

- Nothing that could be produced in the mother country was allowed to be grown in New Spain, including grapes and olive trees, and high import tariffs protected favored goods exported from the Mother country.

- No man could hold a government office in New Spain who had not been born in the Mother Country; this policy was not, in theory, racial, for pure-blooded Whites born in New Spain, were excluded from the privilege of office.

- Import-export trade -- and Spanish control thereof -- was restricted to two ports and only two ports: Vera Cruz on the Gulf and Acapulco on the Pacific.

- Education in New Spain was limited to non-existent. "No book could be introduced into New Spain without the sanction of the Inquisition."

- Travel into and out of New Spain was severely restricted: Few Mexicans were permitted to travel abroad or to visit Spain and a license to enter New Spain was tightly controlled from Madrid.

- New Spain was ruled as a Church-State Colony and the Ecclesiastical Power of the Catholic Church "was uncompromising" and complete.

Yet, "the Viceroys kept things quiet in the Colony, and they remitted silver to Madrid" ($14,000,000 in silver in 1809, for example). "No more was asked of them. The people were, of course, kept down; but they had no desire to rise."

Kept down, that is, until Miguel Hidalgo inspired 50,000 to rise up and take over the important and rich town of Guanajuato, in the state of the same name, a future Seceded Mexican State. But on Christmas Eve, 1813, this rebellion was defeated by Spanish troops under Agustin de Yturbide. But Agustin de Yturbide was an ambitious man. When a minor revolt surfaced in the southern province of Guerrero, Yturbide, instead of directing his men to defeat the enemy, struck a bargain with their leader, also named Guerrero, to join forces. In this manner "he persuaded both his own troops and those of the enemy to acknowledge him as the leader of a new combined insurrection." Over a period of months, Yturbide gathered support for his revolution throughout New Spain; then he and his revolutionaries marched on Mexico City, arrested the Spanish Viceroy, Apodaca, in his palace and ordered that he leave New Spain. Yturbide then proclaimed that he would become Emperor of the Republic of Mexico.

Victory over Spain was achieved. In October 1821 the last Spanish army left the mainland of New Spain. A Junta speedily convened and Yturbide, supported by the Army and by the Clergy, was elected Emperor of Mexico under the title Agustín I, and receive his crown on July 21, 1822. We now look at the nature of the people and the political struggles within this new independent Mexico.

With the ouster of Spanish rule, Mexico was an independent nation, "but the task of liquidating the institutions bequeathed by the Spanish Government and of creating a Mexican nationality was only beginning." The next 45 years "was to be a period of anarchy, revolution, and civil war" involving conflicts concerning all meaningful issues facing the new country and its extraordinarily diverse population. The Spanish had begun a racial caste hierarchy from the beginning. Struggles between the classes defined by this caste structure would be central to fomenting conflict throughout the period following independence. The names of the classes in this caste hierarchy need to be carefully defined.

The Peninsulares were people of pure Spanish ancestry who had been born in Spain (being a pure-blooded Spaniard born in the Western Hemisphere did not count). During the Colonial period, the Spanish Government had restricted every government office of any importance to a

Spanish man born in Spain, to ensure the gold and silver kept coming to Spain. Almost all Peninsulares left Mexico upon independence, "taking their money with them." This totally depleted the ranks of experienced government officials and drained significant money from the economy. Peninsulares were also in control of important offices in the Catholic Church, although some Friars had not been born in the mother country.

The Criollos were people of pure or near-enough-pure Spanish ancestry who had been born in Mexico. Since Mexico had been conquered by Spanish men and few Spanish women had ventured forth to Mexico, most sons and daughters born in the land with Spanish ancestry were born to Amerindian concubines, or wives, of Spanish men. If a daughter grew up and had a daughter by a Spanish man, that daughter would be three-fourths Spanish. If that daughter grew up and had a son by a Spanish man, that boy, upon reaching adult-hood, if he looked like and talked like a Spanish man, would be considered a Criollo (seven eights Spanish). The Criollos were better educated and far more capable and prosperous than the lower classes, and, accordingly, were eager to replace the departed Peninsulares as governmental and economic leaders. Yet, this class was a small percentage of the population and there was difficulty in reconciling democratic ideals with Criollo supremacy.

The Mestizos were people whose ancestry was a racial mixture of Spanish and Amerindian. They generally spoke the Spanish language and had adopted the Spanish culture to a clearly noticeable degree. The Mestizos were the largest class in Mexico at the time because disease had decimated the pure-blooded native Amerindian population, which had plummeted from an estimated 25,000,000 just prior to the Spanish conquest to between 3,000,000 and 4,000,000 at the time of Mexican independence. The Mestizos were handicapped in two ways: they had been denied educational opportunities and, on average, their cognitive ability was slightly below that of people of pure Spanish ancestry. [114] Because of these two handicaps this group, diverse within itself, to be sure, struggled to win the recognition that a democratic society normally grants to its majority population. [115]

The Amerindians, already mentioned, were the lowest class in the Mexican caste system and numerically they were a minority.

Two long-dominant Mexican institutions would conspire together to maintain control over the new Mexican government -- those institutions being the army and the Catholic clergy. [116] The army was far larger than necessary for a peaceful society and officers were eager for promotion

---

[114] The following numbers on average cognitive ability of these two racial groups help to quantify the difference: the mean I. Q. for the pure-blood Amerindian was probably about 85 and the mean I. Q. for the pure-blood European was probably about 100.

[115] As in athletic ability and musical ability, cognitive ability varies considerably among individuals in the same family, among individuals in the same community and among individuals of the various races of mankind. These differences can be estimated by studies conducted over the past 100 years. To learn more about the numbers presented in this paragraph, reading *Understanding Creation and Evolution* by Howard Ray White, 2018, is recommended.

[116] The army maintained its own system of courts, designed to try only its own people. The Catholic Church maintained its own judicial system, which tried every issue that might involve its clergy, no matter its nature. So, "as long as the generals and the clergy remained independent of civil authority, Mexico was in a state of anarchy." Unlike the army, which was far larger than necessary, the clergy was shrinking and "many of the missions and the churches in the Amerindian villages had been almost abandoned. Only half a dozen monks occupied some of the great Franciscan and Dominican monasteries, spending the revenues from the haciendas attached to them. The convents of nuns had become asylums for aristocratic ladies; into many of them only girls from wealthy families were admitted; the nuns lived at their ease, each with her personal servants. . . . The clergy would not only keep their revenues and their privileges; they would also fight freedom of opinion, secular education, anything which might undermine the power which ignorance and superstition had given them over the masses."

and increased pay. And the army collaborated with the Catholic clergy, which had been a major church-state institution for many, many decades -- for two centuries. During the colonial period, 12,000 Catholic churches had been built, many of them finely decorated. The Catholic clergy were accustomed to being supported by the taxpayers and maintaining control over the vast lands and properties that the organization had accumulated over the past 200 years -- property that was always free of taxation. These "two institutions, in particular, made democracy impossible."

But the greatest obstacle to government stability was bankruptcy. In 1821 the silver mines, having been flooded, produced very little. [117]

Three political factions vied for political power:

• One faction of the Criollos organized politically as Conservatives. This Criollo faction wanted to prevent attainment of democracy because being a small minority they would lose long-held privileges and wealth enjoyed by all Criollos and the army and the clergy.

• The other Criollo faction organized politically as Moderados. This group was made up of lawyers and intellectuals who hoped to create in Mexico a parliamentary democracy modeled after the United States or Great Britain. The Moderado idealism was mightily opposed by the army and the clergy.

• The Mestizos represented the great majority of the population and stood to gain the most from a move toward democracy. "Led by a group of liberal intellectuals, the Puros, they were the champions of social revolution; they demanded the abolition of clerical and military non-civil courts, the confiscation of clerical property, and the destruction of caste distinctions." They were considered the "Liberals."

The strength of the Conservatives lay in the City of Mexico and in the central provinces, where Spanish rule had been most firmly established. Liberalism prevailed in the mountains of the South and in the northern territories -- Zacatecas and Durango and San Luis Potosi -- where property was more evenly divided, with fewer haciendas and a larger number of rancheros, and where the Amerindian tribes were more militant." This geographic divide in power base framed the political struggle as between a central government in Mexico City (with the provinces relegated to no more than large counties), versus a decentralize government structure where the provinces were far more sovereign and the central government in Mexico City was theoretically limited to issues of a national nature: international trade, tariffs and foreign affairs. The Mestizos were attracted to decentralization and were adopting a pattern of local chiefs not unlike the Amerindians were accustomed to following. Historian Henry Bamford Parkes explained it this way: "The conflict between conservatism and liberalism became a conflict between centralism and federalism."

Augustin de Yturbide's rule as "Emperor" did not last long. Three years after the Spanish withdrawal, in 1824, the Moderados took control of the government and attempted to create a true federalist republic with important State rights. They organized Mexico into nineteen states and four territories. They adopted a Federal Constitution and Federal Congress and permitted states to elect governors and legislators. Similarities to the government organization of the United States were evident, except that only Catholicism was allowed and trial was by judge, not by jury. Guadalupe Victoria was elected President. But this leap into democracy and State Rights was too

---

[117] Between 1821 and the year of Mexican State Secession, "the annual revenue of the government averaged ten and a half million pesos," but "its expenditures averaged seventeen and a half million pesos," leaving a deficit of 67 percent of revenue. This huge and unpredictable deficit pushed the government to "mortgage itself to foreign bankers and industrialists."

fast for a country fraught with class struggle. Two loans, each exceeding three million pounds sterling, plus lesser infusions of capital from Germany and France would soon become an unmanageable burden.

Meanwhile, as the last Spanish armies had left Mexico in 1821, some Americans, encouraged by Mexico's independence from Spain, sought to immigrate westward to Mexican land, north of the Rio Grande River, which would become Texas. A notable leader of these immigrants was Stephen Austin. To be sure, these immigrants were sworn to be good Mexican citizens, foreswearing their allegiance to the American State which they had left behind. But trouble soon arose. Because so many came from Tennessee and other Southern States, authorities in far-off Mexico City became alarmed. They moved to enforce the Catholic restriction and to outlaw bringing into Texas any African slaves. But the greatest concern was the number of immigrants. This land was very sparsely settled at the time of Mexican independence from Spain and the influx of former Americans was transforming the land north of the Rio Grande into an American society. In 1830 the Mexican government, now under President Vicente Guerrero, as a result of a military coup de grace, decreed that no more immigrants from the United States were allowed and that customs duties were to be collected at the Louisiana border. But these rules were unenforceable in vast Texas.

When Antonio López de Santa Anna gained power by another military coup de grace in January 1833, the new government moved to quell a growing independence movement in Texas. In December 1835 a Mexican army under General Cos attacked San Antonio but the Texans (both recent immigrants and Mexican Texans) drove the Mexican army back across the Rio Grande. In response, Santa Anna took command of a Mexican army and laid siege on the Alamo at San Antonio and overcame the Texans trapped inside, killing all to the last man. This slaughter infuriated Texans and under the leadership of immigrant Sam Houston of Tennessee, Santa Anna's army was defeated at San Jacinto and Santa Anna was captured and forced to guarantee the independence of Texas. So Mexico lost control of its land north of the Rio Grande River.

Texans proclaimed the Republic of Texas an independent nation, on October 22, 1836, with Sam Houston as its first president. Although the Mexican government in Mexico City refused to officially recognize Texas independence, it was powerless to do anything about retaking its lost territory. The Republic of Texas would flourish for ten years as an independent nation. During those same years the Mexican government at Mexico City was in turmoil. Santa Anna was in power and out of power as political winds shifted about. [118]

Ten years later, on February 16, 1846, the Republic of Texas would merge with the United States with the promise that it would enter as one State, but would be able to divide itself into as

---

[118] Although a French fleet had appeared off Vera Cruz, demanding payment of claims valued at 600,000 pesos, Santa Anna led the Mexicans in repulsing the attack, negotiating a promise to make the debt good, but losing one leg to a cannon ball. This episode restored his reputation and re-ignited his political career. Yet the Conservatives kept Carlos Maria de Bustamante in office for another four years. A military coup de grace in 1841 resulted in Santa Anna taking control of the Mexican government where he assumed dictatorial powers, but a year later, to escape the wrath of intensifying opposition, turned over power to his vice-president Nicolás Bravo and retreated to his hacienda, Manga de Clavo, near Vera Cruz. "Bravo nominated a Junta of Notables, which in 1843 produced another new constitution under which the president was to be virtually a dictator. Santa Anna was then elected President." Santa Anna then set out to collect taxes in earnest -- "by enacting forced loans from the Catholic Church, by increasing import duties twenty percent, and by selling mining concessions to the English, he raised revenue twice as large as his predecessor's." A year later, in 1844, a portion of the army, under General Paredes, revolted; and when Santa Anna marched against him, a popular insurrection in the City of Mexico restored Gómez Pedraza and the Moderados to power. Mild but honest, General José Joaquin Herrera became president. Defeated by Paredes, Santa Anna fled into the mountains of Vera Cruz. He would be captured and "allowed to retire to Havana, Cuba." Herrera remained in office for a year. In January 1846 Paredes marched on the City of Mexico while Herrara fled.

many as five States when population growth in Texas merited it. In early 1846 there was also trouble from the north. [119]

In 1846, with Texas now an American State and Mexican land farther west indefensible, Democrat President James K. Polk, of Tennessee, and his fellow Democrats apparently decided to create a military incident to serve as an excuse to go to war against their southwestern neighbors for the purpose of acquiring all the land west of Texas, out to the Pacific Ocean. United States troops under Zachary Taylor of Kentucky stationed themselves near the Rio Grande River to demonstrate that the land north of the Rio Grande River was part of Texas. The military incident occurred on April 25, 1846, when a small portion of Taylor's troops were attacked at the Rio Grande River, Mexican President Paredes having refused to acknowledge that to be the proper southern Texas boundary. On May 13, 1846, the United States Congress declared war on Mexico.

Americans living north of the Ohio River and all across the southern States were enthusiastic about going to war against Mexico; less so Americans living in the northeastern States, but those people were not really needed for a successful pursuit of the war's aim -- to take away from Mexico all the land west of Texas. Volunteers came forth rapidly and within a few months an American army under Zachary Taylor, overcoming substantial resistance, had advanced south into Mexico, taking Matamoros, Monterey and Saltillo, and American troops under Stephen Kearney had easily occupied Santé Fe and Las Vegas. Along the Pacific, without facing significant resistance, settlers in Oregon had ventured south and occupied the upper Sacramento Valley, and the American Navy had occupied Monterey, San Francisco, Sonoma and Los Angeles. The Mexican Government was powerless to defend its claim to the sparsely-settled land between Texas and the Pacific Ocean.

Meanwhile the Mexican Government was in turmoil. In August 1846, Paredes was deposed and Gómez Farias and the Liberals were returned to power, reestablishing the Mexican Constitution of 1824, which defined a decentralized federal structure. But, in hopes of winning the military struggle against the United States, the Liberal dominated Congress gathered and named Santa Anna as acting president and demoted Farias to vice-president. Santa Anna, adept at working both sides of the fence, had managed to return from exile and make himself available to lead the Mexican armies. [120]

At the same time, with a federal government structure established in August 1846, two states, Michoacán and Oaxaca, acquired Liberal state administrations. The governor of the state of Michoacán was Melcho Ocampo, a scholar and a scientist . . . who was devoting himself to the limitation of ecclesiastical power and to the scientific improvement of agriculture. . . . In the state of Oaxaca a pure-blooded Zapotec Indian, Benito Juárez, was governor. Of Benito Juárez, much will soon be said. But we must now return to the story of the war.

---

[119] In truthful history, the Republic of Texas is the only land to enter the United States as a former nation, by way of a merger of sovereign countries, with the exception of the original thirteen colonies, which had 1), proclaimed independence, 2), defended the same and 3), won recognition by Great Britain as each being sovereign States with recognized boundaries. A substantial part of the Republic of Texas, northwest and west, was transferred to the United States (to become western territory up to part of future Utah) in exchange for money claimed to be owed to creditors. But one can argue that the land for money swap was demanded by the United State to prevent the new State of Texas from being as large in land as had been the Republic of Texas.

[120] By January 1847 Santa Anna had collected an army of 25,000, which he financed partly by wholesale confiscations and partly out of his own pocket. He confronted the American army near Saltillo, near a hacienda named Buena Vista, where he held a three to one advantage in manpower. But the Mexicans, unable to withstand the American's artillery or fighting skill, retreated back towards Mexico City. After arriving at Mexico City Santa Anna agreed to retire as acting President, to depose vice-President Farias and name General Anaya as acting president.

Santa Anna departed with his army to face a second invasion attack by the American army, under Winfield Scott, which was arriving by sea to the port of Vera Cruz. [121] By August Scott was advancing with his army toward Mexico City. Unlike elsewhere, the fight for Mexico City was intense, but, on September 13, 1847, the Americans entered the city and accepted its surrender.

Again the political complexion of Mexico changed. The Moderados gained a majority in Congress at the expense of the Liberals, and they were determined to make peace. "Peña y Peña, the chief justice in the Supreme Court, assumed the presidency, established a government in Querétaro, and opened negotiations. . . . Santa Anna, deposed from the presidency, fled into the mountains." The American negotiators were General Winfield Scott and Nicholas Trist, an American State Department clerk. The Mexicans had little choice in the matter. Mexico was forced to agree that they had no claim to Texas and was forced to sell to the United States the land west of Texas, stretching out to the Pacific. The compensation was $15,000,000 dollars plus cancellation of unpaid claims. "On March 10, 1848, the Treaty of Guadalupe Hidalgo was ratified by the United States Senate. By the end of July all American troops were departed from Mexican soil.

Following the war and the loss of the vast, but sparsely settled, territories west of Texas, Mexico enjoyed a period of relative peace -- "a singular absence of revolutions." The Moderados remained in power and, in June 1848 restored Herrera to the presidency. Two years later, in the first peaceful transfer of power since independence, Mariano Arista was elected to succeed Herrera. The money received from the United States helped Herrera and Arista to satisfy the many demands on the treasury from the military, from government employees and from lenders. The political relationship between the central government in Mexico City and the various State governments shifted power to the latter, in accordance with the constitutional assurance of a federal structure.

## Benito Juárez

We now go back two years to discuss two liberal governors. The governor of the state of Michoacán was Melcho Ocampo, "a scholar and a scientist . . . who was devoting himself to the limitation of ecclesiastical power and to the scientific improvement of agriculture." The governor of the state of Oaxaca was Benito Juárez, a pure-blooded Zapotec Indian. A brief biography of Juárez is appropriate:

> "Born in an Indian village in the mountains, unable even to speak Spanish until the age of twelve, Juárez had come to the city of Oaxaca as a household servant, had been given an education by a philanthropic Criollo, who had intended him to become a priest, and had finally graduated from the institute, opened a law office, and married the daughter of his first employer. Silent and reserved, without the intellectual brilliance and learning of Ocampo, Juárez was earning a reputation for administrative honesty and efficiency and for the democratic simplicity of his manners. Inheriting a bankrupt administration, he [would leave] office with 50,000 pesos in the state treasury." [122]

---

[121] The Americans easily defeated the Mexicans at the seaport and advanced to healthier upland country. Santa Anna and his Mexican army attempted to block further American advance toward Mexico City by staging a defensive line at Cerro Gordo, where the road wound up the mountain. But "the Mexican army was cut to pieces" and the survivors fled back toward Mexico City. For several months Scott waited at Puebla, free of harassment.

[122] *A history of Mexico*, by Henry Bamford Parkes, third edition, 1960, pages 223-224. Most of the quoted segments that present truthful history of Mexico are also taken from Parkes's 1960 third edition. There are many such quotes and they are not referenced by footnotes as is the biographical sketch of Juárez.

With both Ocampo and with Juárez, evidence of successful state governmental independence was being exercised and influencing the struggle between advocates for continuing a centralistic Mexican government structure and advocates for transforming Mexican government toward the federal structure that was so successful in Texas and the United States.

But the administrations of liberal de-centralists José Jaoquin Herrera and Mariano Arista did not last. Arista was overthrown in January 1853 in a military coup d'état led by the Criollo conservative centralists. This faction placed Antonio López de Santa Anna in power, empowering him to act as a dictator for one year. Since the new government was a centralized power, "liberal governors," such as Ocampo and Juárez, "were removed by troops." Furthermore, "newspapers, which failed to sing the praises of the clergy and the dictator, ceased to exist." A rapidly growing colony of [Mexican] exiles gathered at New Orleans, where Ocampo found work as a potter and Benito Juárez supported himself and his family by rolling cigarettes."

In Mexico City, factions competed for power within the Santa Anna administration. The army was especially influential. It "increased to 90,000 men, and Spanish and Prussian officers were imported to discipline it. A revolution against the Santa Anna administration gained momentum in March 1854 when state rights advocates Juan Alvarez and Ignacio Comonfort published the Plan of Ayutla, calling for a temporary dictatorship by the chief of revolutionary forces, followed by the election of a convention which would draft a new constitution. [123]

Recognizing the futility of resistance, Santa Anna, who consistently maintained his path of retreat, "slipped out of Mexico City and published his abdication upon reaching Perote. The people of Mexico City at once declared for the Plan of Ayutla; cheered for Álvarez and Comonfort, looted the houses of Santa Anna's wealthy supporters, and made a bonfire of Santa Anna's coaches." At Santa Cruz, in August 1855, he boarded a ship and retreated to his hacienda in Venezuela. Santa Anna would never return to a leadership position in Mexico.

In accordance with the Plan of Ayutla, Juan Álvarez, despite his lack of education and his Amerindian and Negro descent, was declared president by a junta. He then proceeded to organize a government at Cuernavaca, which included Benito Juárez as Minister of Justice, and then relocated it to Mexico City to cement national authority. A few days later Minister of Justice Benito Juárez "began the attack on the [conservative centralists] by decreeing the abolition of the clerical and military courts, which had long exempted Catholic Church officials and clerks and long exempted army officers from being subjected to civilian courts and related judicial oversight. Juárez's quick decree, known as the Juárez Law, immediately stirred up opposition within army and Church ranks and provided fodder for political conflict.

Under pressure, Álvarez transferred the presidency to Ignacio Comonfort, a Criollo of a devout Catholic family, who aspired for a "peaceful and harmonious Mexico" achieved by "winning the consent of the reactionaries to a program of reform." But that was not to be.

In June 1856, Comonfort's treasury secretary, Miguel Lerdo de Tejada, proclaimed what was to be known as the Lerdo Law:

> All the estates directly owned by the Catholic Church or by corporations were to be sold, the proceeds, after deduction of a heavy government sales tax, going to the Church.

---

[123] This revolt would probably have succeeded if Santa Anna had not been able to raise $10,000,000 from the United States by his sale of Mesilla Valley and additional lands along the north-western Mexico border, termed the Gadsden Purchase. He raised additional money by enslaving and selling Yacatecan Indians to Cuban plantation owners for 25 pesos a head. These sales gave Santa Anna sufficient funds to pay the salaries of men in the Mexican military and government. Yet, the Plan of Ayutla remained a rallying cry for the opposition through early 1855. The rebellion became irresistible.

Commonly held public land associated with towns and with Amerindian villages were to be sold, denying access for grazing or gardens.

It turned out that "the persons who benefited by the Lerdo law were mainly foreigners, such as newly arrived British, French and German men, easily acquiring important Mexican land and clerical haciendas. This would enable such new-comers to quickly achieve "a powerful position in Mexican society."

A revolt rose up soon afterward, but was successfully put down by March 1857, partly, one would presume, by hopes tied to a new Constitutional Convention, controlled by Moderados, who had been at work on a new Mexican Constitution, completing it one month earlier. Elections under the new Constitution were soon afterward held, resulting in Ignacio Comonfort being elected again as President and Benito Juárez being elected President of the Supreme Court, which put him in the position of succeeding Comonfort if the office of President became vacant.

The ever-present struggle "between Church and State was more than Comonfort could endure." He believed "The people of Mexico wanted their religious services," and he could not bring himself to stand in their way. "In the autumn of 1857, when the new Congress met, Comonfort asked for a suspension of the guarantees of civil liberty and for a revision of the entire 1857 constitution." In December, Félix Zuloaga, "once a cashier in a gambling house and now General in command at Tacubaya," led a revolt against Comonfort, Juárez and Lerdo, "took possession of the City of Mexico, dissolved Congress, and arrested Juárez," and forced Comonfort to accept his Plan of Tacubaya. The Catholic Church wanted more: it also wanted the repeal of the Juárez Law and the Lerdo Law. Conservatives declared Zuloaga to be President and the Juárez Law, the Lerdo Law and others repealed.

Meanwhile, Benito Juárez, President of the Supreme Court, escaped to Querétaro, where a faction of seventy Congressmen reassembled and declared him President because President Comonfort had broken his pledge to support the 1857 Constitution. No longer considered President, Comonfort fled to the United States. But "Querétaro was impossible to defend." So Juárez and his government retreated to Vera Cruz, which was loyal to his rule. "For nearly three years President Juárez was destined to remain in Vera Cruz, while the clericals held the City of Mexico; and the country was plunged into the bitterest of its civil wars," which lasted from early 1858 to early 1861.

During this three-year era of civil war, while Benito Juárez remained at Vera Cruz sustaining the Liberal government of which he believed himself to be President, rivals competed for control of Mexico City. "Through 1858 the conservatives were winning victories." But the Catholic Church had lost confidence in President Zuloaga and the clerical faction made Miguel Miramón President. Miramón's army assaulted Vera Cruz in an attempt to destroy the Juárez government but his men failed to penetrate its defenses. Juárez retaliated by proclaiming the confiscation of all ecclesiastical property except the actual church buildings. [124]

---

[124] Juárez, in July 1859, announced that "all ecclesiastical property except the actual church buildings were to be confiscated without compensation. . . . Whereever the liberal armies penetrated, churches were stripped and gutted. . . . They seized the sacred relics and images in the churches and piled them on bonfires." Uncooperative priests and monks were shot. By these assaults Juárez supporters "taught the Mexican people that one could lay hands on the clergy without being smitten with the wrath from Heaven."

Miramón's army attempted again to penetrate the defenses at Vera Cruz, but failed. Finally, his army suffered an important defeat in August 1860 at Silao, where supporters of Juárez, led by González Ortega and others, captured 2,000 prisoners. [125]

But Miramón's clerical Conservatives were rapidly losing the civil war. In October 1860 Liberals forces under González Ortega "took Guadalajara, and the following month took Calderón." By this time Liberal forces were converging on Mexico City from several directions. On December 22, at San Miguel Calpulalpan "the last of the Conservative army was cut to pieces" and the Liberals won their final victory. "On January 1, 1861, González Ortega, at the head of a 25,000 man army, rode into the capital of the Republic." President Benito Juárez arrived from Vera Cruz ten days later. "Mexico was, for the first time, under the rule of a civilian." But the country was bankrupt and in many ways wasted.

Benito Juárez was re-elected President in March 1861 and González Ortega was elected Chief Justice of the Supreme Court, meaning he was first in line to succeed to the office of President. [126]

In July 1861, Juárez "decreed suspension for two years of all payments on foreign debts."

To the north, the United States was split and distracted by State Secession. Seeing this as an opportunity for conquest, Napoleon III of France figured he could expand his empire.

## Napoleon III, Maximilian and the French Intervention

Meanwhile, in Europe, Napoleon III of France talked the British and the Spanish into joining him in dispatching warships to Vera Cruz to pressure Mexico to pay up on its foreign debt. "General Prim at the head of a Spanish army arrived at Vera Cruz in December, and was joined by the English and French detachments in January 1862." Before long it became apparent that the French were insisting on "12,000,000 pesos in cash in compensation for injuries allegedly suffered by French citizens, and recognition in full" of the 15,000,000 pesos in Jecker bonds. Realizing that such demands were impossible, and that such bullying left no opportunity to recovered more legitimate investments, the British and Spanish forces departed in April, reducing the conflict to one between Napoleon III and Benito Juárez. With the United States distracted in its State Secession conflict, Napoleon III figured he needed a deceptive scheme in which Mexican people would "invite" a prince of royal European blood to accept the title of King of Mexico.

But the initial French force of 7,500 men was insufficient to overcome the Juárez government. At Puebla, "on May 5, 1862 (Cinco de Mayo), the French army, with the loss of more than a thousand men, was flung back to Orizaba and the coast." It appeared that the Juárez government was stronger than anticipated. [127]

---

[125] In that same month, a Liberal army under Porfirio Diaz captured the city of Oaxaca. Another Liberal army, under Manuel Doblado, captured a silver train belonging to a British mining company that was worth more than a million pesos. Miramón was involved in equally criminal monetary shenanigans: "he took 700,000 pesos, which had been set aside for the British bondholders, from the house of the British legation in Mexico City, and made a bargain with a Swiss banker and mine-owner, Jecker, swapping 750,000 pesos for 15,000,000 in Mexican bonds. The Jecker bond scandal would surface again.

[126] Juárez faced great difficulties, for the members of Congress quarreled and little was being done to build a government. Some demanded Juárez's resignation. And Leonardo Márquez's guerrilleros were still about, killing. There was no money and seemingly no way to raise revenues.

[127] Up to this point, the history of the French Intervention is truthful history. Beyond this point in time, truthful history blends with our alternate history as a result of the Treaty of Montreal, signed in 1862 between the CSA and the USA.

But Napoleon had other issues to also ponder. By September 26, 1862, the Confederate States and the United States had both approved the Montreal Treaty, recognizing State Secession and formalizing an adjusted boundary between the two countries. With peace returning to lands north of Mexico, was it prudent for Napoleon to withdraw? He and his advisers pondered the question and the decision fell on the side of maintaining face and believing that neither the Confederate States of America nor the United States of America wanted to engage France alone. So, Napoleon decided to proceed to greatly reinforce his troops at Vera Cruz. The intervention force was quadrupled to 30,000 men. The new French commander was General Forey.

This assault by this huge French force led by the determined Forey, was more than the Mexican Government could withstand. On March 16, 1863, Puebla was placed under siege. On May 16, after two month's under siege, without ammunition or food, the Mexican army, under González Ortega, surrendered. The French marched the surrendered army to Vera Cruz and shipped officers to France, but two key officers, Ortega and Porfirio Diaz, managed to escape. Meanwhile, on May 31, unable to defend Mexico City, President Benito Juárez and his government retreated northeastward to the city of San Luis Potosí. A week later, on June 10, the French, under Forey, entered and occupied Mexico City. "What survived of the Mexican Clerical-Conservative Party was gathered into an assembly of notables; and the assembly promptly offered the crown to Prince Maximilian of Austria."

The French army expanded its control of central Mexico, forcing the Juárez government to retreat steadily north toward the border with the Confederate State of Texas. He relocated from San Luis Potosí to Saltillo, to Monterey. "By March of 1864 the Juárez government "controlled only the far north; Comonfort was killed in battle and the other Liberal generals began to take refuge" in the Confederate States. In the South, "Liberal leader Juan Álvarez, now 74 years old, was still master of Guerrero and Porfirio Díaz controlled Oaxaca. But the French held most of the cities; and everywhere they court-martialed or terrorized Liberal sympathizers and organized rigged elections to endorse an invitation that Archduke Maximilian become King of Mexico." This is a strange tale. Just who was this royal-blooded European, this Maximilian?

Archduke Maximilian was the younger brother of the Hapsburg Emperor of Austria. Thirty-two years old and for seven years married to his second cousin, Princess Charlotte of Belgium, daughter of Leopold I, King of the Belgians, Maximilian was extremely well educated, tall and handsome, and had excelled in the Austrian navy, small as it was. It seems that Maximilian, being the younger brother, had little prospects for rising to become King somewhere in Europe, so that made him available for the assignment to Mexico.

Brief mention of the background of French Emperor Napoleon III is appropriate.

The famous Napoleon I, who had led France in the conquest of much of Europe before being deposed himself, was Napoleon III's uncle. In 1848, during the time of the Second Republic of France, Napoleon III had been elected President by popular vote. He took the title "Prince-President." Soon thereafter, a 1851 coup d'état by factions opposed to republican government seized control, but did not replace Napoleon III as the head of government. Instead leaders of the new government proclaimed a Second French Empire and named Napoleon III as Emperor. That was the situation at the time of the French intervention in Mexico.

Maximilian, deceived into believing the people of Mexico supported his rule, accepted the offer of the Mexican crown. "By the Convention of Miramar, Napoleon III promised that French troops should remain in Mexico until the end of 1867." That gave Maximilian about three years to secure power on his own accord. But the Convention also stipulated that Mexico pay back the 270,000,000 francs that the French had already spent, plus 1,000 Francs per year per French soldier going forward, plus all the debts due as of 1861 to England, Spain and France, including the so-called Jecker bonds. To bankroll Maximilian's first three years, banker's loaned about 55,000,000 francs. All of this additional debt figured to triple the Mexican foreign indebtedness in one stroke of the pen. [128]

Maximilian and wife Charlotte arrived in Mexico City in April 1864 where he was proclaimed Emperor of Mexico. He quickly witnessed ample evidence that he was not welcomed by the people and that the Juárez government was still a force with which to contend. But the French army remained intent on subduing political opposition and expanding its control, and assurances of its success were offered.

Meanwhile, President Benito Juárez only controlled the far north and had resorted to maintaining a mobile government in a horse-drawn carriage. This was the state of affairs when the first meeting took place between President Juárez and three Commissioners representing Confederate President Jefferson Davis. [129]

The meeting took place on Monday, September 16, 1864 at an obscure farmhouse just outside of Paso del Norte in the Mexican State of Chihuahua, just across the Rio Grande River from El Paso, Texas. By the way Paso del Norte is now named Ciudad Juárez. The meeting focused on discussions of Mexican State Secession and secret, but decisive, Confederate support of an independence movement among the northern States of French-occupied Mexico. The Confederate Commissioners, dressed as ordinary Mexicans and arriving on horseback and riding in wagons to avoid suspicion, assured Juárez that their government could provide weapons, intelligence, administrative guidance and financing to help secure independence from the central government at Mexico City, and that secrecy concerning the proposed cooperative effort would aid in achieving eventual success. Furthermore, the Confederate Commissioners assured Juárez that if Seceded Mexican States consolidated to sizes and populations consistent with those in the Confederate States of America, that each consolidated State would be a candidate for merger with the Confederate States in the manner similar to the way the Republic of Texas had merged into the United States 18 years previously. By way of explanation, the Delegates estimated that, before the passage of many years, the State of Texas was destined to divide itself into four States: North Texas, East Texas, West Texas and South Texas. They said it seemed possible that northern Mexico could be consolidated into five or six future Confederate States and merged into the Confederacy accordingly. Only by separation from the perpetual, tumultuous, and authoritative central power in Mexico City, could Mexicans of the northern region gain hope for peace, religious freedom, rational taxation, independence and prosperity. Slavery? That was an issue for each State to control. The Commissioners told Juárez that, based on Mexican history, they assumed that the seceded Mexican State constitutions would not permit an individual to own another person and that it would be guaranteed that each State would be empowered to, itself, decide the matter.

---

[128] Only 55,000,000 franks were left of a 114,000,000-franc financing deal after retention of one-third as a banker's discount and another one-fourth in banker's future interest. Furthermore Napoleon III made sure that his people controlled the purse strings by ensuring the French had control over the army and army paymaster, and over the Mexican customs offices and over the Mexican treasury office. Soon after his arrival, Maximilian would discover that he was "virtually powerless. Both purse and sword was controlled by the French." Although the financial and political situation in Mexico had been horrendous for decades if not centuries, as reported herein in the previous pages, the future portended to be far more desperate.

[129] At this point, for the first time, we deviate from true Mexican history.

## Confederate Aid to the Juárez Government in Retreat

The Confederate Commissioners extended their support to fifteen northern Mexican governments should they secede. But it would be necessary for each to individually choose secession and be prepared to defend that decision. It seemed obvious that the seceded Mexican States would need to coordinate their actions and organize jointly to effectively defend secession. Of utmost importance was the role to be played by President Benito Juárez. Question: was he to surrender his office of President in exile of the whole of Mexico and assume the leadership of the seceded Mexican States, or was he to continue to maintain his existing office in exile and continue to give encouragement to all the bands of Mexicans who were still fighting, mostly as guerillas, in a desperate attempt to overthrow the intervention by the French and Emperor Maximilian? To help Juárez answer that question, the Confederate Commissioners submitted rather tough, definitive language. Their position was essentially this:

> "The Confederate Government has no interest in helping overthrow the French intervention all across Mexico because it anticipates that subsequent political factions centered in Mexico City would continue to fight, year after year, coup d'état after coup d'état, for control and would continue to drive the nation deeper and deeper into debt, bankruptcy and chaos. For that reason the Confederacy has no interest in being a partner to sustaining a Mexican government where all power is held in Mexico City. If the Juárez government insists on continuing to fight for all Mexicans, north, central and south, then it must pursue that course alone. On the other hand, if it is willing to restate its mission to facilitating the secession and independence of the States and territories of northern Mexico, then the Confederacy is confident that goal can be achieved within a year or two. And the Confederate leaders believe a merger with the Confederate States of America, peace, freedom and prosperity is a likely final outcome."

The Confederate Commissioners then became quite specific. They told President Juárez that 15 named Mexican States and territories would be supported in the event of secession, but that any State south of the list would not be supported and, in those regions secession was discouraged, for they were too easily trapped in the web of a centralist Mexican government.[130]

Three weeks later, on Monday, October 10, 1864, a second meeting took place at the farmhouse just outside of Paso de Norte. Benito Juárez reported that he was prepared to state his position regarding taking leadership over a Mexican State secession movement. From the size and nature of the Mexican delegation assembled around the farmhouse, it was evident that he had given it great thought and had contacted men from across the north. There were approximately fifty men present, all arriving in secrecy, from all across the northern regions of Mexico. President Juárez told the Confederate Commissioners:

> "I was born in 1806 to a poor Zapotec Indian family in the small village of San Pablo Guelatao, in a mountainous region of the State of Oaxaca, a southern Mexican State. No Spanish blood, no European blood flows through my veins. I lost my parents at a young age but found help and guidance in the city of Oaxaca, where I learned the Spanish language and obtained an education sufficient for me to succeed as a young lawyer. I eventually became Judge and Governor of the State of Oaxaca. I later became Minister of Justice and Religion in the national administration of President Alvarez. But, when Comonfort replaced Alvarez as President, I was forced to retire to Oaxaca. And power

---

[130] The fifteen included the entirety of nine (Baja California; Sonora; Chihuahua; Coahuila; Nuevo Leon; Tamaulipas; Sinaloa; Durango; and; Zacatecas), and portions or maybe all of six (San Luis Potosi (perhaps not all of it); Nayarit (probably all of it); Aguascalientes (probably all of it); Jalisco (perhaps not all of it); Guanajuato (probably most of it); and Queretaro (possibly less than half of it).

struggles continued in Mexico City as you well know. Eventually, I was elevated to President of the Republic of Mexico, but was not able to administer the office from Mexico City very long because of more power struggles, followed by the French Intervention. And here we are today considering secession by the northern States. Yes, together here today asking an Indian to lead a secession struggle contemplated by the States of northern Mexico — an Indian of the once proud and once influential Zapotec race located in what is now southern Mexico. I am a man from lands that lie in southern Mexico. Furthermore, loyal Mexicans still look to me as the President of what is left of our national government, our lawful government over all of Mexico, a government in flight. Yet, you believe I am the man best suited to lead the secession of the northern States? Why is that so? Help me to understand."

Judah Benjamin, seated among the Confederate Commissioners, rose and submitted an answer anchored in reason and experience.

"President Juárez, sometimes a people cannot be effectively led by one of their own, cannot effectively be led by one who has risen up through the ranks so to speak. Why? Because conflicts and jealousies consume the energies of the candidate peer leaders who would be normally considered for the top position. This is such a time. The people of the northern Mexican States need a leader who is above the competition normally encountered among present leaders of northern Mexico, a leader who can unite everyone, a leader who has proven a capability for doing so. You might wish to lead your native State of Oaxaca in secession, but success of such a venture is impossible. You might wish to overthrow the French intervention and Emperor Maximilian and lead a recaptured nation of Mexico from the government center at Mexico City, but we cannot help you to do that. If you choose to lead a State secession movement in northern Mexico, we can help you make it successful and the people of northern Mexico and your personal family will forever love you for it."

The answer was translated into Spanish. The Mexicans in attendance, all gathered about the farmhouse, paused in their response, but only for a minute. Then a low chant began in the back and became louder, then thunderous: "Juárez! Juárez! Juárez! Juárez! . . ."

About five minutes later, Benito Juárez slowly rose from his chair, stood before his table covered with its papers and looked across the field of people, many of them probably just as capable of being the leader of Mexican State Secession as he. The chant continued: "Benito! Benito! Benito! Benito! . . ."

The President of Mexico, in exile, then pronounced:

"I have made my decision for my family and for the people and families of all of northern Mexico. Our northern States shall secede and I shall lead the effort if you will have me. Stated another way, after the northern States have announced their respective secessions, as the President of Mexico in exile, I shall recognize the secessions and wish each seceded State the greatest of success. I will then dissolve my Mexican government in exile and work toward the success of the secessions and toward an eventual partnership with the Confederate States of America."

This was followed by celebration and excitement. After about fifteen minutes, the Confederate Commissioners suggested to President Juárez that he assemble an executive committee to meet inside the farmhouse with the Confederate Commissioners and their aids for the purpose of drafting a plan of action and deciding on important matters.

In the executive meeting held in the farmhouse that day, deeply held emotions struggled for expression and resolution. Benito Juárez turned to General Richard Taylor, recalled that his father Zachery had led the American invasion of northern Mexico only ten years previously, [131] and inquired, "How can the people of northern Mexico trust men who were so recently our enemies?" Richard Taylor gathered his thoughts and carefully and passionately answered. Benito was satisfied.

Then Richard Taylor turned to John Rogers, also among the supporting delegation and said:

"We have with us today, here in support of our Commissioners, John Rogers, a great leader of the Cherokee Nation, which recently supported the Confederate cause, defending against the Federal invasion. Confederate President Jefferson Davis and many in high office in the Confederate Government are hoping to one day see a Native American State established west of Arkansas and north of Texas. It will be a fine country reserved for Native Americans who will enjoy the freedoms that result from local government. Let John Rogers explain more about the bonds of friendship between the people of the Confederacy and their Indian friends."

John Rogers began by explaining that his mother was half Cherokee and his father was full Cherokee, so he was three-fourths Indian blood. He explained further.

President Benito Juárez thanked John Rogers and acknowledged that it was important for the Indian people of his country to hear encouragement from Indians living in the Confederacy, for all over the Americas, north and south, the Indian has greatly suffered and, although our logical minds reason that Europeans had no way of preventing the deadly diseases that have decimated our populations, we need to join together in nurturing our broken spirits and together find a hopeful path forward.

Then Juárez enquired about financial help:

"My friends, Mexico is bankrupt, a thousand times bankrupt. If the northern states successfully secede how do we get out from under the foreign debt that seems so impossible to ever pay?"

Confederate Secretary Memminger then rose to speak:

"Mr. President, I am Christopher Memminger, Secretary of the Treasury in the Jefferson Davis Administration. President Davis and I have discussed Mexican debt in great detail. So my remarks will be consistent with his views. My state is South Carolina, obviously a long way from here, a long way from Texas. The financial condition of the Confederate States of America is sound. We have a strong export business and a good credit rating among banking interests in Europe. This puts us in a position where we can be helpful. Regarding obligations after the secession of the northern Mexican States, we first recommend the following:

1. The French debt being accumulated by the French military in Mexico should be fully renounced as invalid in all Mexican states.
2. The debt of the so-called Jecker bonds should be fully renounced as fraudulent.
3. The debt claimed by Spain should be renounced on the basis that she has already taken from New Spain and from Mexico far more than she deserved to get. No more should be paid by the seceded northern states.

---

[131] The history of Richard Taylor's father -- General Zachery Taylor and later US President Zachary Taylor -- is truthful.

4.    The debt claimed by Great Britain should be acknowledged as legitimate and it should be prorated between the Mexican central government and the seceded northern states.  We suggest that one-fifth of the British debt should be accepted by the seceded states and we are in a position to advance a loan that will enable the seceded states to satisfy that debt on a time-table suitable to London.

Benito Juárez replied that he agreed with the Confederate analysis, that it basically matched his view of the matter and that the indicated loan would be most useful.  He submitted that, because finance was not his expertise, he would consult later with experts whom he trusted.  He added, "in general, I anticipate agreement."

At this point, General Taylor presented a plan to secretly provide Confederate military advisers and weaponry for the cause of defending secession of the northern Mexican states.  He recommended that each seceded state organize a state militia, that each militia be armed, but dispersed in the manner of a guerrilla defensive strategy.  The Confederacy will be sending ten Spanish-speaking men to Mexico City to serve as spies for our cause and to influence Maximilian and to dispense deceptive propaganda.

Taylor promised field artillery and munitions for each seceded state. Delivery would be made across the northern border with the Confederacy and along the coastline of the Gulf of Mexico and the Gulf of California.  He promised approximately 200 military advisers, mostly drawn from Texas.  He promised to quickly install effective telegraph communications. [132]

Finally, he recommended that the Juárez Government remain totally mobile, basically a government operated from a stage coach drawn by four horses, as had been the case recently -- that it be always on the move and that decoys and deceptive maneuvers be employed to sustain secrecy.  "If this plan is adopted," he said in conclusion, "I feel certain of success."

Secretary Memminger then submitted guidance from President Davis.

President Davis has recommended that each state call an assembly "for the announced purpose of passing a resolution of support of, and submission to, the rule of Emperor Maximilian, and to pray for his good health and long life."  And each assembly should go through the motions of doing just that.  But, when French authorities and their supporters were not present, a majority should secretly reconvene and pass an ordinance of state secession, the date for its public announcement to be coordinated by President Juárez.  Then, after all northern states are prepared for the secession announcement and when the militia in each state is armed and in readiness, the announcement of state secession should be broadcast and the military defense will begin.  Before long, Memminger predicted, the government of Emperor Maximilian will be scrambling to hold onto central and southern Mexico, leaving northern Mexico unmolested to go its own way.  Anyway, Emperor Napoleon III has only committed to keep French troops in Mexico through the end of 1867.  That is not much time to subdue the whole of the country.

As guidance regarding language to justify state secession, Memminger suggested an outline of a typical ordinance of State Secession.  He assured President Juárez that decisions regarding all

---

[132] A telegraph line between Montgomery and El Paso would be in operation within 10 days, and from El Paso to San Diego in 20 days, from El Paso to Brownsville in 30 days.  Operating to and from the El Paso communication hub, and to and from telegraph stations just inside the Confederate border, he recommended a relay of messengers on horseback.

of the matters presented by the Confederate delegation were for him and his people to make. The Confederate advice was purely suggestions to be adopted, modified, discarded, whatever. [133]

At this point the discussions drew to a close and the Confederate delegation withdrew back into Texas by several routes, all in disguise. The general population was totally unaware of the momentous events that had been taking place right under their noses.

## Mexican State Secession

Afterward, operating from the horse-drawing carriage, the Juárez government held discussions with political leaders across northern Mexico, meeting important leaders in every northern state, while not revealing the magnitude of the movement in sister states. Juárez was unable to visit each state personally, for time did not permit it. But his deputies held meetings in states that Juárez missed. Juárez personally visited four states/territories along the Confederate border (Chihuahua, Coahuila, Nuevo Leon and Tamaulpas) and then moved south to visit San Luis Potosi, Guanajuato, eastern Jalisco and Zacatecas. Each state was asked to decide for itself regarding a vote to secede. During November, assemblies were called in each secession-minded state for the announced purpose of formally acquiescing to the supremacy of the Maximilian government, but secretly for the purpose for instigating secession. During December 1864, these meetings occurred and the resulting public announcements predicting pledges of allegiance to the supremacy of the Maximilian government were widely publicized, aided, of course by the clandestine efforts of the Confederate spies and secret Juárez agents in Mexico City. But the secessionist factions, in the know, in each assembly, met separately and prepared secession documents that all signed.

By early January 1865, the Juárez government was ready to spring the trap. Secession documents were in place in twelve of the fifteen states encouraged to secede. It had been necessary to depose four of the governors who had refused to cooperate, but that had taken place quietly and had not raised much suspicion. Juárez believed the other three states would come along once the day arrived for secession to be announced, and when, on the following day, he would recognize the twelve secessions and dissolve his government with pledges to work for the defense of secession. Juárez notified the seceding states that they should each target Monday, January 16, 1865 to individually announce their state seceded.

And that they did. On January 16, twelve states individually announced their secessions and three more would be seceding over the next two weeks. But certain portions of San Luis Potosi, Guanajuato, Queretaro and Jalisco seemed reluctant to go along and a division of those four states was held likely. Divisions of that nature did not disturb the Juárez government or the sister seceded states, for a new national boundary, more easily surveyed and defended, was

---

[133] "Whereas, the Mexican state of _____ has in place state, local and town governments, and, Whereas, the central government in Mexico City has usurped powers not delegated to it by the 1824 Mexican Constitution, and, Whereas, the central government in Mexico City has been unable to repulse the invaders from France, and Whereas, bankruptcy of the Mexican people, this state and the central government in Mexico City is impossible to reconcile, yet grows worse, and, Whereas, the lives, welfare and happiness of the people of this state are grossly impaired by miss-rule and militant terrorism from Mexico City, and, Whereas, civilized people all over the world agree that a government receives its power by the consent of the governed, We the people of the state of _____ do hereby secede from the central Mexican government in Mexico City, from the French Intervention, from the rule of Emperor Maximilian, and rulers and governments that might in turn succeed him, Thereby, Elevating _____ to the position of a free and independent state, with sovereignty sufficient to join together with other such seceded Mexican states, to seek mergers with the Confederate States of America, to secure our safety and to advance our freedom and prosperity. . . . This Ordinance of State Secession, having been approved by a majority in attendance in the convention called to evaluate such important matters, is validated by we the undersigned, who witnessed and endorsed this event on the day of _____, in the month of _____ in the year of _____."

deemed likely in the final negotiated agreement, and viewed as more desirable for the Confederate States government. [134]

On February 1, the seceded Mexican states joined in a Compact of Military Cooperation, and elected Benito Juárez to be its President. This "Compact," not a government in the normal sense, was charged with coordinating military defense and negotiating with foreign powers (French and Confederate) and remaining Mexican states on behalf of the seceded states.

Soon, news arrived in Mexico City of the secession of twelve, then fifteen northern states, supported by rumors that the seceded states were in consultation with the Confederate States of America for merger into that government. Maximillian and French forces were simply stunned! Everywhere there was great confusion. And, in states to the south and east of Mexico City -- such as guerrilla-infested Guerrero and Michoacán, Porfirio Díaz's Oaxaca, and Puebla and Vera Cruz, the major seaports of the country -- pronouncements and agitation for independence from French rule magnified concerns that the Maximilian government was faced with war on three fronts, not just the north, but the east and south as well. Soon, French forces discovered that militia of the Seceded States had been greatly reinforced by Mexican volunteers and by Confederate arms, smuggled in right under their noses, complete with a significant number of Confederate military advisers, mixed among the units. Within three weeks Marshall Bazaine, commander of French forces, faced with suppressing resistance movements in all directions, made a secret decision to position his troops to the east and south of Mexico City, with emphasis on Puebla and Vera Cruz to maintain a retreat route to France -- this resulting in little opposition to the success of secession of the eleven states north of seceded Querétaro, southern San Luis Potosí, Guanajuato, and Jalisco. In fact, with the Confederate navy positioned along the coastline of the seceded states, the northern-most states were able to send much of their militia south to aid defense of the border seceded states.

You will recall that, by Napoleon's Convention of Miramar, he had promised French military support to Maximilian through the end of 1867, but not beyond. In return, Maximilian was to have completed paying back the huge debt the French alleged to be owed them. The end of 1867 was only 23 months into the future, little time for suppressing renewed revolts in all directions, and scant chance of significant progress toward payment of the alleged debt. By early April 1865, Marshal Bazaine was telling Maximilian that re-conquest of the seceded Mexican states was hopeless and government efforts ought to be focused on getting as much wealth as could be accumulated out to Vera Cruz for shipment to France.

It is now appropriate to relate the very important role played in the history of Mexico by Profirio Diaz, of Oaxaca -- a lawyer, skilled politician and excellent military leader -- who had been imprisoned by the French at Puebla, in the Convent of Santa Catarina, during most of February and March, 1865. [135] With the help of accomplices, he had escaped on March 20, made his way to the state of Oaxaca and begun raising a guerrilla force. Diaz was a man of two persuasions. As a resident of and leader in Oaxaca, he favored the idea of limited power at Mexico City -- from this viewpoint, he and Benito Juárez shared a similar philosophy of limited

---

[134] On January 16, the following states and territories individually announced their secessions: Baja California, Sonora, Chihuahua, Coahuila, Nuevo Leon, Tamaulipas, Sinaloa, Durango, Zacatecas, San Luis Potosi (perhaps not all of it), Nayarit (probably all of it), Guanajuato (probably most of it). The Juárez government expected secession decisions would soon follow in the following three states: Queretaro (possibly less than half of it), Jalisco (perhaps not all of it), Aguascalientes (probably all of it).

[135] In true history, since being captured in February 1865, Porfirio Diaz, a liberal leader of Oaxaca, skilled as a politician and military leader, was imprisoned in Puebla, first at the Convent of Santa Catarina, then at the Convent of Compañía. He escaped from the latter on September 20, 1865. In our alternate history, Porfirio Diaz escapes from the former in March, 1865.

republican government. But, from the viewpoint of his personal ambitions, which were large indeed, Diaz favored a dominant government at Mexico City, if he could personally control it as Dictator or Emperor. So, faced with the secession of the northern Mexican states, Diaz made a crucial decision: he would break with Juárez and fight for his state of Oaxaca and the other central and southern Mexican states in a renewed military campaign to drive out the French and reestablish a Mexican government in Mexico City that was independent of influence by France or the Confederate States. So, in rallying men to his cause, Diaz denounced both the French and the Confederates. Armed with that philosophy and skilled as a political and military leader, Diaz began raising an army capable of driving out the French and taking over Mexico City. But the campaign would take considerable time.

By July 1865, militia of the seceded states were in control of the border of that portion of Mexico that Compact of Military Cooperation President Benito Juárez wanted included in the Seceded States, this area including that northern portion of the state of Vera Cruz that lay east of San Luis Potosí. At this point, through agents in contact with Marshal Bazaine, Juárez managed to negotiate a cease fire between militia and French-controlled forces, to be enforced along a boundary then occupied by his militia. With the cease fire in place, negotiations soon begin in New Orleans, Louisiana on terms for French recognition of the independence of the Seceded States. Principles present at the negotiations were, for the Secessionists, Sebastián Lerdo de Tejada, and for the French Interventionists, Alphonse Dubois de Saligny. For the Confederate moderators, President Jefferson Davis named three notable Catholics: General P. G. T. Beauregard, Bishop Patrick Lynch, and Secretary Stephen Mallory. Eventual acceptance by the French of the independence of the Seceded Mexican States seemed a forgone conclusion. [136]

Negotiations centered on the exact boundary of remaining Mexico and the money paid by the seceded states to French debt holders. Lerdo de Tejada held out for inclusion of land to the south of the seaport city of Tampico, which was at the southern tip of the state of Tamaulipas, very close to the northern boundary with the Mexican state of Vera Cruz. The agreed boundary began in the east at 22 degrees and 30 minutes latitude, proceeded west to 100 degrees longitude, south to 20 degrees latitude, and west to the Pacific. [137]

The boundary agreed upon, much time was then devoted to negotiations about money, because getting as much money as possible was the major aim of the French, who were approaching the negotiations as a lost cause with respect to reviving their control over Mexico (the French Intervention). You will recall that Confederates had advised Juárez that it supported the view that no alleged French debt should be considered an obligation of the Seceded States,

---

[136] General P. G. T. Beauregard had been in command at Charleston, Bishop Patrick Lynch of Charleston, had been Confederate Ambassador to the Papal States during the defense of the Confederacy, and Confederate Navy Secretary, Stephen Mallory, had kept abreast of developments along the coastline of the Seceded Mexican States. Sebastián Lerdo de Tejada, the truest friend and companion of Benito Juárez, a Criollo of pure Mexican-born Spanish blood, was born in central Vera Cruz state and was a prominent Liberal in the governments of Comonfort and Juárez. French diplomat Alphonse Duboise de Saligny knew America well, having been involved in the initial days of the French intervention, having been involved as a diplomat in Washington, D. C. and having been involved in earlier matters concerning the Republic of Texas. General Beauregard was the primary individual on the Confederate moderator team, while Lynch and Mallory were free to come and go periodically as needed.

[137] Lerdo de Tejada won acceptance of a southern boundary in the East of 22 degrees, 30 minutes, which took from northern Vera Cruz state, the towns of Panuco and El Higo as well as the northern half of Isla Juan Ramirez and half of adjacent Laugna de Tamiahua. But extending that boundary westward was only acceptable to the longitude of 100 degrees, at Rio Verde. Just below Rio Verde, the agreed boundary ran south along the 100 degree longitude until reaching latitude 20 degrees. This placed the important city of Queretaro within Seceded States, while leaving considerable land north and northeast of Mexico City within the remaining country. Falling north of the 20 degree boundary and within the Seceded States as it progressed westward toward the Pacific, was Acambao, Pajacuarán, Laguna de Chapala and the important Pacific seaport of Puerto Vallarta.

178

that one-fifth of the English debt, in fairness, should be considered a Seceded State obligation, and, perhaps one-fifth of the Spanish debt, as well. Of course, the French negotiators were determined to extract money to pay off some of the French debt. [138] Finally, to seal the deal and get the French out of the way, Confederates agree to finance payment to them of $3,300,000. With that agreed to, the remaining task was to deliver the money. That was arranged. [139]

With the French in possession of the $3,300,000 in silver, the Treaty of Saltillo was signed on May 5, 1866.

Now free to concentrate all of its force on central and southern Mexico, the French maintained considerable control, especially over Mexico City, Puebla, Vera Cruz and the intervening land. Yet, under the leadership of Porfirio Diaz, the resistors remained a constant threat. In the meantime, the French gathered all portable wealth they could find, moving it to Vera Cruz for shipment to France. A full year passed while the Mexican resistance slowly gained ground against the stubborn French. By May 1876, it was evident that the French were losing ground to Diaz's Mexicans. But the going was slow, for arms for Diaz's men were primitive and scarce, far less formative that the arms that had quickly empowered the secessionists to the north. On the other hand, the French were packing up to leave Central America and evacuation was in the air. In October 1867, Diaz's army was able to take control of Puebla and Mexico City, and, there, he pronounced a new Mexican government while Maximilian fled toward Vera Cruz. French evacuation of Vera Cruz was already underway. During October and November, evacuations included many French troops, many Intervention supporters, and most of the wealth confiscated by the French army. By December, the French were totally gone – Maximilian, too. [140]

## The French Withdrawal

Back in Europe, Napoleon III's days of rule over France would soon be drawing to a close. In less than three years, with Prussia under Otto von Bismarck rising to what would become the dominant power in Europe, the French would finally face an overwhelming adversary. The Franco-Prussian War would erupt in August 1870 and French forces would be soundly defeated. Napoleon III, in the field with his army, would be captured. Marshal Bazaine would assume command of French forces, but to no avail. The French would lose valuable territory and prisoner Napoleon III, his wife Eugenie and their son would be exiled in England. The Second French Empire would be over. The German states would be united under the German Empire, with Prussian King Wilhelm I at the head. Germany would take most of Alsace and part of Lorraine. The French Empire would become much weaker, never again ruled by a monarch. These developments in Europe would become instigating factors in the launch of World War I.

---

[138] The English debt amounted to $85,000,000 in American dollars. The Spanish debt amounted to $17,000,000. And the French so-called debt was $30,000,000 and growing, depending on whose numbers one looked at. The Confederates had already agreed to finance the payment of one-fifth of the English debt, that being $17,000,000. One-fifth of the Spanish debt was a debatable matter. Here, the Confederates eventually agreed to finance one seventh. That amounted to $2,400,000. The French debt amounted to Convention debt of $300,000, Jecker bonds of $15,000,000 and Claims of $12,000,000 plus all sort of nonsense about paying for the French Intervention, which was alleged to escalate the total a great deal. Finally, to seal the deal and get the French out of the way, Confederates agree to finance payment of all the $300,000 Convention debt and one-fourth of the French claims.

[139] The French were to be paid in full in silver. A loan was agreed to and the silver was delivered at the Gulf seaport of Tampico, Tamaulipas state. Much of it was freshly mined Mexican silver, some was donated or loaned by patriots. About one-third was supplied on loan by Confederate banks. The payments toward loans accepted as due to England and Spain was refinanced on a schedule to be paid in full by the governments of the seceded states, after consolidation into 5 or 6 states, the first payment due in 3 years, the balance due in the twelfth year.

[140] In truthful history Archduke Maximilian, the Emperor of Mexico, according to the French Intervention, was captured by Benito Juárez's forces, tried and executed on June 19, 1867.

In Mexico, Profirio Diaz would gain more and more power, becoming a virtual dictator within two years following the evacuation by the French. He would hold dictatorial power until forced to flee as a result of the Mexican Revolution of 1911. [141] Diaz would rule over what remained of Mexico for 35 years. Four years later, he would die in Paris at the age of 74 years. The rest of the history of that truncated and troubled nation is beyond the scope of this book.

With Benito Juárez serving as moderator over negotiations among the Seceded and Independent Mexican States and parts thereof, governments were combined and boundaries were drawn which condensed the number down to the six States that are familiar to us today:

- Costa Noroeste
- Costa Este
- Central Norte
- Costa del Sur
- Costa Sudoeste
- Central del Sur

These six States would be merged into the Confederate States of America in 1870, the year of the Great Confederate Expansion.

### Thursday Evening Selected Diary Postings

Diary note by Chris Memminger said, "Supper shared talking with Allen Ross. Thanked him for the bison steaks we sailors enjoyed off the coast of Cuba and apologized that I was not fully able to enjoy mine Saturday evening. I told him that it tasted great at the time, but that I was far too seasick to hold it down. Told him that I tried the vomit trick over the side of the sailboat and got tossed into the ocean in the process. Allen asked, 'Did Emma really save your life? Was the situation that desperate?' I answered yes, 'it was that desperate and without Emma's rescue I truly believe I would not be here sharing a meal with you.' Allen asked me if Robert Lee had said anything about going caving this coming weekend. I said, 'no' -- anyway, I have had plenty of adventure for a long, long time. Allen said that Robert had mentioned a cave trip and had a cave picked out. Called it 'Big Bone Cave.' Allen told me he was going to do it."

Diary note from Benedict Juárez said, "Shared supper table tonight with Conchita Rezanov. Since Professor Davis lectured on Mexican history today and will present Russian America tomorrow, history was on our minds. I told her stories about the Mexican Secession, my ancestor, President Benito Juárez, and statehood for our six Seceded States. She told me stories about Russian America during colonial days, her ancestor Nikolai Rezanov and Confederate support for independence and subsequent statehood. Both are such powerful dramas! I told her that today I have felt like I was the center of attention. Everyone said they were so grateful and impressed over what President Juárez was able to accomplish with such meager resources -- and against the powerful French Intervention and those turncoat Mexicans, especially those near Mexico City, who had chosen to switch rather than fight. They said no Native of the American continents had accomplished so much in human history as had my ancestor. Wow! It is hard for me to be humble and avoid the "big-head." But I must do that. Conchita will be next for adoration. Professor Davis will be lecturing on Russian America tomorrow. Makes me shiver! It was so

---

[141] In truthful history, Profirio Diaz took control as President of Mexico in November 1877, held power until 1880, took power again in 1884 and held it until overthrown in the 1911 Mexican Revolution – that being a span of 30 years.

darn cold in the far north during Russia's colonization of what became Russian America -- hard to imagine that humans would be willing to live in such miserable weather. Yet, it was the long-ago ice age that enabled humans to cross over from Asia to North America, walking on foot. My ancestors walked further south, to what has become the Confederate States, and others proceeded further -- as far as the tip of South America. Just shows you the toughness of our ancestral Natives of the American continents. Tomorrow, Conchita will be the focus of everyone's attention. I will enjoy the rest from all the attention."

Diary note from Conchita Rezanov said, "Supper with Benedict Juárez tonight. What perfect timing! He thrilled me with stories about his ancestor, President Benito Juárez, and the Mexican States Secession. Said he had been the center of attention all day. Said all that attention would switch to me in the morning. Goodness! Although my great-great-grandfather Nikolai Rezanov was very important in the history of Russian America, I will continue to assert that, when seeking to boil the story down to the most important man of all, that man has to be the incredible Aleksandr Baranov. I'm excited about tomorrow. Need to try to get some sleep."

Diary note by Marie Saint Martin said, "Had supper with Second Mate Andrew Houston. Oh, that man overboard crisis was so scary. Andrew told me again how Chris tried to avoid messing up the boat when he leaned over too far to vomit. He was so sea-sick, poor fellow. But I assured Andrew that it was not his fault that Chris fell overboard. Yet, Andrew said that it was his fault that he mistook debris for Chris when that flash of lightning gave us a view out ahead. He had been wrong to encourage Carlos to change course about 20 degrees. If Emma had not been swimming out to Chris with a life jacket and flash light, Andrew submitted that his spotting error might have cost both of them their lives. . . . I changed the subject. Said come to the music session I have arranged for tomorrow after supper. We both need an emotional rest from the events of last weekend. Nice and peaceful. He said that he and Conchita had a tennis date tomorrow, but they will be all ears after supper. He is a nice man. I get the feeling that he really likes Conchita. I understand. She is gorgeous."

Diary note by Allen Ross said, "Told Robert Lee that I would join him on the caving trip Saturday morning. He seemed pleased and gave me a long list of what to wear and bring along. He had most of it, or knew where to get it: various lights, helmet, water bottles, small back-pack, gloves. But I will come dressed in my work boots, blue jeans, and long-sleeve shirt. Says the temperature in the cave will be about 58 degrees. We will see lots of bats resting there prior to leaving for their summer night insect feedings. Says the cave was used years ago to leach salt peter from the guano-rich cave dirt to make gun powder. Lots of wood vats remain intact because the cave is too dry for them to rot away. At the time of long-ago saltpeter leaching days, water was brought to the vats from outside through 'pipes' made by boring out small tree trunks. There is even a kind of railroad over the vats that helped bring fresh cave dirt to the vats and to take away spent cave dirt. Need to see that stuff."

## Part 2, Chapter 2, Day 12 – The Heroic Story of Russian America and How It Became a Confederate State – Class Lecture, Friday, June 17, 2011

Perhaps no story in *The CSA Trilogy* is more thrilling than the history of Russian America. Yet, not nearly enough space is available to tell it completely in this book. All twelve were soon seated and anticipating listening to Professor Davis tell the Russian America story and probably jealous that Conchita probably already knew the history just as well as their instructor, and more of it than time would permit today. We now listen in as Professor Davis begins.

By way of introduction, allow me to quote from the opening paragraph of *Russian America, the Great Alaskan Venture, 1741-1867*, by Hector Chevigny, published in 1965. This definitive history of the subject begins thusly, and cannot be improved upon:

> "For speed, vigor, and daring, nothing in the history of the White race surpasses the feat of the Russian frontiersmen who, beginning in 1579, conquered Siberia. They numbered no more than a few thousand. They had no charts, no foreknowledge of what lay ahead, no instruments to guide them other than their own senses. Yet, within sixty years (by 1640) they had that huge expanse in hand to its Pacific shore. They reached also for Manchuria and Mongolia. Possessed apparently by a passion for distance, they went on expanding the Russian empire for 250 years. Although unschooled in ocean navigation, after learning in 1741 how far America lay from Asia, they set out for it, doing so in vessels in which today only madmen would venture on those northern waters. . . . In the whole vast country of northwestern North America, there they made peace with the natives, engaged with them in a cooperative and lucrative fur trade, and brought many into shared settlements. Almost all were men, and many consequently took native women as wives and raised families together. They built "some forty posts scattered as far as the Yukon." [142]

The story of how Russia made her claim on the far northwest corner of North America begins with Czar Peter the Great, "a giant of a man," measuring six feet eight inches tall, who was passionate about science and exploration. He built Russia's first navy, consisting of 800 ships and 30,000 sailors. And it was on his death-bed in early 1725 that Peter the Great instructed Vitus Bering, a Dane in the Russian navy, to lead men across Siberia with tools and iron, then build ships on the Pacific coast, then sail eastward across the North Pacific and explore the northern reaches of the North American coast that was known to exist, but had not yet been seen by a European. By right of discovery, Russia would lay claim to the lands explored. His widow Catherine I would continue Royal support for the Bering expedition.

Bering began his expedition at Irkutsk, located where the Angara River flows northward out of Lake Baykal into the Yenisey River, through Siberia and into the Arctic Ocean. You may have heard of Lake Baykal, the well-known, huge and deep freshwater lake just north of Mongolia. From Irkutsk the expedition progressed eastward on Lake Baykal, then crossed over land for a short distance to enter the Lena River Valley, which ran northwestward for a distance of 1,500 miles to the Russian outpost of Yakutsk. Then the hard part began. They had to proceed due west for 700 miles, across the formidable Stanovoy Mountains, climbing 5,000 feet to cross over passes before arriving at the Russian coastal outpost named Okhotsk, located on the coast of the Okhotsk Sea, which gave ready access to the upper north Pacific Ocean. Bering and is men reached Okhotsk in the fall of 1727. From Okhotsk the explorers sailed across the Okhotsk Sea and set up a shipyard on the east coast of the Kamchatka Peninsula, the most eastward part of

---

[142] Much of the history that is further presented within quotations is taken from of *Russian America, the Great Alaskan Venture, 1741-1867*, by Hector Chevigny, published in 1965. In our alternate history, the population of Russians in Russian America will be growing considerably larger than the 1,000 of truthful history.

Asia. Just south of Okhotsk lay vast China, which, by the Treaty of Nerchinsk, blocked Russian use of the much easier route to the east coast along the Shilka River, and then the Amur River, which today forms the southern boundary of Russian Manchuria. [143] That then-forbidden southern route to the Pacific would have avoided both the Stanovoy Mountains and the Sikhotealin Mountains as its waters directly flow into the southern tip of the Okhotsk Sea. So Bering and his crew had taken the far more difficult route to faithfully obey the rules of the Treaty of Nerchinsk, which had been signed 38 years earlier, in 1689, on behalf of Emperor Kangxi of China and Czar Peter I of Russia.

Unfortunately, this first attempt by Bering to discover the northwest tip of North America was quite disappointing. A "little packet boat named the Saint Gabriel" was constructed and sailed northward to verify that Asia did not cross over to America, and that was all. Bering returned to Saint Petersburg in 1730 and reported his findings.

Eventually a larger expedition was launched with Bering again at the head, involving 900 people, including scientists. After a repeat of the arduous journey down the Lena River and across the Stanovoy and Sikhotealin Mountains and across the Okhotsk Sea to the eastern shore of the Kamchatka Peninsula, two boats were constructed: the *Saint Peter* and the *Saint Paul.* Then, in June 1741, they set out across the Pacific for America; Vitus Bering as captain of the *Saint Peter* and Aleksei Chirikov of the *Saint Paul.* Before long the fog and weather caused the two ships to lose sight of each other, so Bering and Chirikov each had to go it alone. Bering managed to eventually reach the east coast of North America, viewing the awesome Saint Elias mountain range, east of present-day Anchorage. But Bering did not tarry long on his newly-discovered coast. He soon ordered the men to head home. Scurvy was already taking a toll. His ship, the *Saint Peter,* broke up in a storm at an island 110 miles east of the Kamchatka Peninsula. There Vitus Bering died in early December, 1741, apparently of scurvy. His second in command, Captain Sven Waxell, of Sweden, took over. Stranded on the island, "Survivors got through the winter by subsisting on the seals and the other abundant wildlife, including many otters. Next year, 1742, their strength restored, they built a boat from the wreckage of the ship, and, looking like the wild beasts whose skins they wore, they made it to Petropavlovsk, the base built by Bering on Kamchatka Peninsula." Waxell wrote a comprehensive record of the voyage including important charts. [144]

Aleksei Chirikov had fared much better aboard the *Saint Paul.* He and his crew had discovered much of the chain of the Aleutian Islands stretching off to the east, and, most importantly, had discovered the abundant sea otter, blue fox and fur seal, harvesting a huge number of pelts and arriving back at Kamchatka far earlier. Russia could claim the far northwest corner of North America based on the right of discovery, but the land seemed far too harsh and far away to merit further expenditure of Russian money and commitment by the Russian navy. So, for 39 years the exploration of the Aleutian Island chain and the harvesting of furs was the work of assorted teams of independent Russian and Siberian individuals, often joining with Aleut hunters, but without any overall leadership.

---

[143] The Treaty of Nerchinsk, the first between China and a European power, was signed in September 1689. "It was to determine much of the history of the Far East for the next 150 years and to affect North America as well. The vastly important Amur River was given to China forever and Russians were forbidden access to it.

[144] The account of Swedish Captain Sven Waxell (1701-1762) is truthful history and he deserves much credit for his skill and diligence in recording the voyage and charting the islands and routes travelled. His sketch of a native kayaker was the first illustration of a Russian America native, and his sketch of the soon-to-be extinct Steller sea cow is the only illustration existing today.

In 1781, dependence on independent Russian and Siberian individuals changed with the formation of the Golikov-Shelikhov Company, led by 34-year-old Grigorii Shelikhov and his wife Nataliia. [145] Their expedition set out across the Okhotsk Sea toward the Pacific in August of 1783. Amazingly, Shelikhov had launch this project in only two years, including recruiting 200 men, and moving the cattle and the supplies eastward across rugged terrain and building three ships: two galiots and a sloop. Nataliia and her husband were on the larger galiot, which had been named *Three Saints*. The second galiot was named the *Saint Michael Archangel*. The sloop was named the *Saint Simeon*. The eastward voyage along the Aleutian chain of islands was fraught with difficulties. But by July 1784, the Shelikhov's, with two of the ships, finally reached 100-mile-long Kodiak Island, located south of the present city of Anchorage. Remarkably, Grigorii Shelikhov made peace with the Kodiac natives and there built the first settlement on western North America north of the tiny presidio of San Francisco, which Spaniards had founded eight years earlier. The Kodiak Island settlement, a little village named Three Saints Bay, consisted of "seven or eight individual dwellings, a set of bunkhouses, a commissary, a counting-house, barns, storage buildings, a smithy, a carpentry shop, and a ropewalk." The Shelikhov's returned to Okhotsk, then made the long journey to their home at Irkutsk, near Lake Baykal, arriving in early 1787.

Beginning in the summer of 1791, Aleksandr Baranov began serving the Golikov-Shelikhov Company as its Chief Manager in America. Although 44 years old upon his arrival that year at Kodiak, and at the time suffering from serious pneumonia, Baranov would become the most important individual in the history of the colony. Of lowly birth, Baranov was a self-made man of recognized ability. In younger years he had learned German and educated himself reading scientific books. Impressed with Baranov's drive and knowledge, Shelikhov had given him a five-year employment contract to manage the American affairs of the Golikov-Shelikhov Company. In return, Baranov received ten shares in the Company and sufficient funds to pay his debts and provide for his wife and daughter, who lived in western Russia, in the town of Kargopol. As had many of the men, Baranov, although still married, as a peace-keeping gesture, took for himself a native girl to be his wife. He named her Anna. She was the daughter of the chief of the Kenitze, who lived in the vicinity of what the explorer Cook had named William Sound. "Although not yet a full-grown woman, she was darkly beautiful of eye, features and carriage."

In 1793 a Golikov-Shelikhov Company ship arrived with supplies and materials essential to building a new ship, including tar, rigging and iron, and in September 1794 the Baranov-built ship was launched. The Russian population on Kodiak Island had grown considerably, for Shelikhov had send 150 more company employees, and ten Russian Orthodox clergymen headed by the Archimandrite Iosaf. Among the ten was Juvenaly. [146]

Sadly, in the summer of 1795 Grigorii Shelikhov, age 48, died at Irkutsk of an apparent heart attack. But two sons-in-law would continue the Shelikhov family's efforts to develop Russian America: Nikolai Petrovich Rezanov had married Anna Shelikhova in October 1794, and Mikhail Buldakov had married the older daughter a few years earlier. The Rezanov and Buldakov names will pepper our future history. In the year following Grigorii's death, 1796, Russian Empress Catherine the Great died, leaving the throne to her son Paul, to be known as "Mad Paul," for the

---

[145] In English translations, different methods of spelling Russian names are encountered. I have chosen the spellings you will see from time to time in this work. With respect to Nataliia, I am using the double-"i".

[146] In truthful history Juvenaly would be murdered two years later by mainland natives and later proclaimed a saint by the Russian Orthodox Church. His feast day is celebrated on July 2 and he is also commemorated with all the saints of Alaska (September 24) and with the first martyrs of the American land (December 12). Our alternate history does not have space to cover such details, but a footnote concerning this event seemed appropriate.

man was not mentally stable, so it seemed. Under these conditions, Nataliia Shelikhov, now a widow, journeyed to Saint Petersburg and attempted to establish a monopoly trading company that included Ivan Golikov and her son-in-law Nikolai Rezanov. The Shelikhov-Golikov proposal was rejected. But a new organization was subsequently configured, named the Russian-American Company. Nikolai Rezanov convinced Czar Paul to sign the Russian American Company charter on July 8, 1799. He and Mikhail Buldakov would play major leadership roles in this new enterprise. The charter established a monopoly on trade in the far northwest of North America, giving those operating in the region one year to either become members of the Company or leave the territory. The charter made Aleksandr Baranov the Chief Manager of Russian America.

By the way, two years earlier, in 1797, Baranov's native wife Anna had given birth to a strong and healthy son, whom they named Antipatr, "after the saint on whose day he was born." At the time Baranov was 50 years old.

By 1799, Baranov's domain, now under the Russian American Company, was already extensive: stretching from Yakutat northward to Bristol Bay, complete with nine posts, including Kodiak, which had 40 buildings. In that year Baranov decided on a major expansion to the south to expand his domain far to the east of Kodiak Island, to the coastal island of Sitka. Sitka was in the heartland of the Tlingits, a remarkable native people. So, forgoing hunting during the summer of 1799, Baranov led a force of 100 Russians, 700 Aleuts and 300 mainlanders to Sitka to build there a formidable fortress surrounded by outbuildings, all protected by a stockade. The resulting fortress was "made of timbers two feet thick and measuring 70 by 50 feet at the base, with an upper story jutting out two feet farther. High watchtowers stood at two corners." But the effort would be a complete disaster -- in June of the following year Tlingits would reduce the fort to "a mass of ashes surrounded by severed heads impaled on stakes." Only 23 would escape death: 18 Aleut women, 2 Aleut men and 3 Russian men.

But, Baranov would succeed in retaking Sitka Island and building a Company headquarters town there to be named New Archangel. Sitka Sound provided an excellent harbor.

Had it not been for foreign friends, the Russians at Sitka would have starved. The sloop *Ermak*, "which had been built for the retaking of Sitka," was dispatched to Hawaii to procure food. Would she survive the voyage? She not only survived the voyage, she "returned laden with pigs, taro, bananas, yams, and coconuts, none of which King Kamehameha would take payment. He was, he had said, "glad to help brother monarch Baranov in his time of need." Furthermore, from the New England region of North America came the brig *Peacock* with promised tools and workmen and the brig *O'Cain* with more guns, greatly needed to ward off attacks on the Sitka settlement by resurgent Tlingits. By August 1805, New Archangel would be rather formidable, with 20 guns mounted on fortifications on the high ground facing the fine harbor of Sitka Sound, below which, near the shore, were situated new "cabins, bunk-houses, a commissary, and other structures, including a barn for a few cows."

Meanwhile, Nataliia Shelikov's son-in-law, Nikolai Rezanov, had boarded, at Kamchatka, the Company brig, the *Maria*, and was already headed for the Aleutian Islands and Russian America. Upon arriving at Kodiak Island, Rezanov, saddened to find no significant schools for the natives, resolved to store in a shed for future use the considerable library of books he had brought along. In August 1803, Rezanov proceeded on to New Archangel on Sitka Sound, where he found 400 Aleuts and Russians and had reason to appreciate the progress Baranov had made at the new Company headquarters town.

# Map of Russian America during Colonial Days

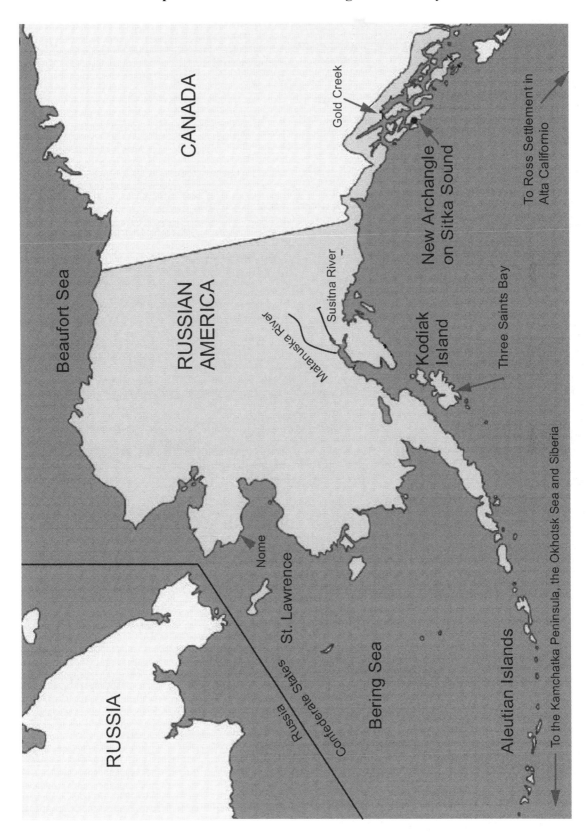

Shortly after Rezanov's arrival, Baranov attempted to resign and enter into retirement. Horrified at the thought of it, Rezanov persuaded the capable Baranov to reconsider and stay in command, promising enlarged powers, including "entire freedom of judgment in his commercial relations with foreigners," credit at European banks, a future "medical staff and a hospital, pensions for the faithful," and the "advancement of education for both sexes." Now content to remain in command, Baranov would outline plans for future expansion of Russian America. The focus would be to the south: a base at the Columbia River, recently explored by Americans Lewis and Clark, and another base a little north of the Spanish settlement of San Francisco. There Baranov would be seeking to establish farms. Furthermore, Baranov planned to exercise with Hawaiian King Kamehameha, his new power to negotiate "relations with foreigners."

But the winter of 1805-1806 was unusually harsh. "Unremitting gales lashed the coast," a Company ship "went down with all hands," and half of a baidarka fleet perished. The Tlingits returned to warfare, overrunning the ten-year-old settlement of Yakutat, killing everyone save ten, who were enslaved. The unrelenting gales prevented a voyage to Hawaii for fresh food, resulting in a scurvy epidemic at winter's close.

As soon as the weather broke in February 1806, Nikolai Rezanov set out to explore the Columbia River, taking the *Juno*, a large, well-armed schooner purchased at a "large price" from an American the previous fall. But the *Juno* crew, somewhat incapacitated by scurvy, seemed unable to bring the large ship over the bar at the mouth of the Columbia River, resulting in a decision to proceed, instead, further south to San Francisco to meet the Spaniards who were there maintaining their most northern outpost.

The March 1806 San Francisco visit by Nikolai Rezanov and the *Juno* would greatly help the Russian America Company's future efforts to feed its people. Rezanov had spotted a river valley north of San Francisco that could support future company farms, and his request for Spanish permission for Company employees to live there and develop farmland was granted. The produce would be shipped to Russian America and the farm workers would be Company employees and any Natives willing to help. The Russian farming site would be known as Ross Settlement. Located in what would become California's Sonoma County and Mendocino County, it was within a valley alongside the Slavianka River. The major coastal features were Rumiantsev Bay and Ross Cove. A stockade and fortified Company headquarters would be built high above Ross Cove. Here the Company would operate a major agricultural and pelt gathering enterprise for many years. The name Ross Settlement would be given to emphasize the Company's political connection with Imperial Russia, which was called "Rossiia." [147]

But the March 1806 visit of Nikolai Rezanov and the *Juno* at San Francisco was even more enjoyable because of a developing noble love affair. Rezanov, 42, tall and handsome, especially when decked out in his most splendid clothes, accented with fine furs and diamonds, swept "off her feet" the daughter of the fellow in charge of the San Francisco station. An unusually beautiful girl of fifteen years, Nikolai charmed her completely, playing his violin and telling stories about glorious Saint Petersburg. Within the brief six-week span of the visit, the teenager announced that she would marry no man but Nikolai Rezanov and that she would remain faithful to that pledge until he returned to fetch her. Her name was Maria Concepción Arguello and, fortunately for the Russians, her father was in charge at the time, because the two superior officials happened to be away on a visit to Monterey. An immediate marriage was not possible, for it required that Concepción change her faith to Russia Orthodox and seek approval of the Vatican and the King of

[147] The story of Ross Settlement is true history. But it did not expand as much as would be presented in future pages of *The CSA Triology*, and the population would never rise to the extent we will be describing. In truthful history Americans could rename the river the Russian River and rename the bay Bodega Bay.

Spain. But her father blessed the future marriage, Rezanov was delighted over the girl, and the betrothal was considered all but finalized. Meanwhile, fresh fruits repaired the scurvy damage among the crew. Trade commenced. The cargo in *Juno's* hold was unloaded and the space was filled with urgently needed food. The *Juno* was back in New Archangel by June, unloading the valuable stores of foodstuffs, supplementing the supply delivered in the meantime by Joseph O'Cain's American ship.

By early 1809, all needed permissions would be in place for a lawful and honorable marriage between Rezanov and Concepción. [148] So the future husband, having completed updating business arrangements with officials of the Russian American Company, left Saint Petersburg for the east. By June he was aboard the Company ship, *Neva*, as it departed Kamchatka. By August he was at Sitka Sound. There, Rezanov saw considerable expansion as he toured this new Company headquarters settlement, which Baranov had named "New Archangel." At the top of the knoll was the completed home of the Chief Manager and the administrative offices of the Russian-American Company, "an impressive two-story structure built of great square-hewn timbers." This and a parade ground were within an enclosure "crowned with a kremlin" in characteristic Russian style. Within the building, to be called "Baranov's Castle," was impressive furniture and a piano, all imported from Europe. But more importantly, "there were a banquet hall and a library, which was hung with good paintings and lined with 1,200 books in many languages."

By now New Archangel was a busy seaport. "Some fifty ships a year now visited the north Pacific, and rare was the vessel not in need of some repair after a long voyage. New Archangel had the only facilities north of Hawaii." And Baranov was in control of operations. Each year he contracted with two or three shipmasters to poach otter off the California coast using large crews of "Aleuts and their gear," gear that was essential. "Baranov loved his role as host to New Archangle's visitors. . . . He proudly showed off his castle and tendered banquets in a style that would become legendary." New Archangel had even assembled an orchestra of sorts. Years earlier Baranov had composed a "patriotic hymn" for his colony, titled, "The Spirit of Russian Hunters," generally known as "Baranov's Song."

### Nikolai Rezanov and Maria Concepción Argüello

In August 1809, Nikolai Rezanov left New Archangel for San Francisco to marry Maria Concepción Argüello. The wedding took place on August 24, 1809. The father, José Darío Argüello, 56, gave the bride away. Brothers Luis Antonio Argüello, 24, and Santiago Argüello served as groomsmen.

---

[148] We now deviate from truthful history, for in real history Nikolai Rezanov and Maria Concepción Argüello would never marry. He would die nine months after departing San Francisco. The wedding of the gallant high-ranking Russian official and the beautiful Spanish girl was not to be, for the winter of 1806-1807 would take its toll. Nikolai Rezanov would fall ill during his overland trip from Irkutsk to Saint Petersburg. Sick and exhausted, he would fall from his horse while blindly pressing westward toward his far-away destination, passing away in early March 1806. Baranov would not learn of Rezanov's death until 1807. For perhaps two years Concepción would dutifully wait for her betrothed return before news arrived of his demise. Yet she would never love again, never marry. At the age of 60, in 1851, after Alta Californio would be taken by the United States, she would enter the new Dominican Convent the sisters would establish there.

So, from this point forward the account of Nikolai Rezanov and Concepción Argüello represents a fictional, although realistic, historical novel. Unless noted on future pages, our account otherwise remains truthful to actual history.

The mother, Maria Ygnacia Moraga de Argüello was most pleased. She could not have been prouder of the rising stature of the Argüello family, already quite impressive for life on the frontier of New Spain. [149]

The newly married couple arrived at New Archangel during the late fall and there experienced the winter of 1809-1810. Maria Concepcíon Argüello de la Rezanova, nicknamed Concha as a child, was a spirited and naturally adventurous young woman of 18 to 19 years. She wintered over well, seeming to readily acclimate to the cold, damp weather and the limited foods of Russian America.

The Rezanov's left New Archangel in the spring of 1810, stopping a few times for inspections of Kodiak and the Aleutians. Nikolai wanted Concha to experience the real Russia, complete with a westward overland journey across the vast expanse of the Russian Empire, and the adventurous Concha was eager to give it a try. The couple arrived at the coastal port of Okhotsk in June and then journeyed across the formidable Stanovoi Mountains and up the Lena River to Irkutsk, arriving at that major trading town in September. It would appear that Concha had the endurance of the family of her husband's first wife, Anna Shelikhova Rezanova. Nikolai had told his bride all about the Shelikhov family, about his first wife, Anna, about his late father-in-law, the amazing businessman, Grigoriii Shelikhov, and his equally amazing mother-in-law, Nataliia Shelikhova.

True to her pledge, Concha readily endured the journey and the couple arrived in marvelous Saint Petersburg in late February 1811. Over succeeding months, Nikolai would have important business at the headquarters of the Russian American Company. They would find the building that housed the Company and the furnishings to be most impressive, and the officers of the Company to be prominent Russians. But none of the officials had ever seen the Russian America of which they were responsible for managing. Consequently, the Rezanov's presence in Saint Petersburg was to be most important. At Saint Petersburg, Nikolai and Concha visited his former mother-in-law Nataliia Shelikhova and his former (deceased) wife's sister Audotia and her husband Mikhail Buldakov. "Handsome and urbane," Buldakov, had been Chairman of the Board of the Russian American Company since 1800.

Upon arriving in Saint Petersburg, Concha suspected that she was with child and, at the first family gathering, discussed it with Nataliia, with whom she instantly bonded. [150] Almost immediately, she would tell Nataliia that, if the suspected baby was a girl, she would be named Nataliia. Soon, the pregnancy was a certainty, and a girl would be born and the given name would be as promised. Another baby would bless the Saint Petersburg home of Nicolai and Concha in 1813. It would be a boy. The given name would be Jose, to honor the mother's father, Jose Argüello, commander of the Spanish mission town of San Francisco.

Meanwhile expansionist goals for Russian America were fading fast. Ambitions to expand Russian America to the Columbia River had never been realistic, considering the small population of Russians present in the colony. The expedition of Lewis and Clark, sponsored by

---

[149] In truthful history, the Argüello family played a major role in the history of Alta Californio, both in the past and in the future, as viewed from the date of our present story line. Father José Daríko Argüello had been the founder of Los Angeles and was presently Presidio of San Francisco. Brother Luis Antonio Argüello would be Chief Manager of Alta California from 1822 to 1825. Brother Santiago Argüello would be Commandant of the Presidio of San Diego and also mayor of Pueblo de San Diego. Santiago's daughter and Concepcion's niece, Maria Luisa Argüello, would marry Agustín V. Zamorano, who would be provisional Chief Manager of Alta Californio from 1832 to 1833.

[150] Nataliia Rezanova, in truthful history died in 1810 in Saint Petersburg. In our story she lives three years longer, until 1814.

President Thomas Jefferson of Virginia, would soon open the way for pioneering Americans to emigrate westward across the plains and mountains in covered wagons to settle the fertile land they would call Oregon Territory. In 1811, the "rich and powerful" John Jacob Astor established a northwest colony named Astoria and was organizing a major fur trading operation. Since the Spanish were making no progress in expanding settlement northward along the Pacific and since Baranov's Russians simply had not the population to expand southward, it was becoming increasing apparent that the Americans and, possibly the British, were going to expand westward to occupy the vast, sparsely settled region between Russian America and San Francisco.

But the war between Great Britain and the United States, called the War of 1812, brought new energy to Chief Manager Baranov and the people of Russian America. Maritime shipping was at a standstill, and some fine vessels were for sale at cheap prices, allowing the Company "to acquire a first-rate merchant fleet." Baranov "had seven vessels capable of high seas voyaging by the close of 1813, and four for coastal navigation. More were to be acquired before the end of the War of 1812. With no delay, Baranov put each of his new masters and ships to work, sending them to the Philippines, Indonesia, Hawaii, and Californio."

Just before the close of that remarkable year, in November 1814, the Russian frigate *Surorov* arrived at New Archangel with Nikolai and Concha Rezanov and their new daughter, Nataliia, and son Jose. This was the first Company ship to arrive in Russian America in four years because Napoleon had forced Russia to devote all resources to driving off the French invaders. And the *Surorov*, recently purchased from the defeated French, was working for the Company, further adding to its fleet. Also aboard the *Surorov* was surgeon Dr. Egor Schaeffer, a German.

Dr. Egor Schaeffer and Alexsandr Baranov would soon become important in the history of Hawaii. That story will be told in the subsequent chapter, The Story of Hawaii. Here, in the Story of Russian America, it is only appropriate to mention that, in January 1815, a Russian American Company ship, the *Bering*, after taking a large load of supplies at the Hawaiian island of Oahu, encountered a violent storm, was driven ashore, and wrecked at Waimea, Kauai Island. Most of the supplies were dragged on shore and stored under the control of the King of Kauai Island, Kaumualii. Baranov wanted to recover those shipwrecked supplies and Nikolai Rezanov was planning to remain at New Archangel anyway and was glad to assume responsibilities during his absence. So, in May 1815, Baranov and Schaeffer boarded a ship for Hawaii. Baranov would arrange for the recovery of the stored supplies at Kauai Island and be back in New Archangel by July 1816. His year in Hawaii would initiate a strong bond of friendship between the Monarchy and the Russian people. Furthermore, Dr. Schaeffer would contribute to the science of Hawaiian agriculture. [151]

In November, 1816, with Baranov now returned, and after two years overseeing Russian America, Nikolai Rezanov, Concha and the two children departed New Archangel for Saint Petersburg. This trip would be totally by sailing vessel, far less arduous than the 1810-1811 overland trip by three-horse sleigh. They reached the Russian capital in late March 1817. Two years into the future, in July 1819, the charter empowering the Russian American Company would expire if not renewed. And important Russian navy officers and certain jealous Russian bureaucrats would be scheming to prevent renewal, hoping to gain political power over the colony that Russian merchants had built. [152]

---

[151] The story of the shipwreck and Dr. Schaeffer's departure to recover the supplies is truthful history. However Baranov did not go with Schaeffer, and, as you know, Rezanov was dead by this time.

[152] The struggle between the Company and Russian Navy is consistent with truthful history.

In Saint Petersburg, the Russian American Company was of considerable importance. By 1817 it "had become the foremost factor in the fur trade of the world, [now] surpassing the far older Hudson's Bay Company, its only comparable rival. Rezanov, as the only member of the Board of Directors to have firsthand experience in Russian America, would be essential to winning an extension of the charter on reasonable terms. The head of the organization was handsome, urbane Mikhail Buldakov, who had successively been re-elected chairman of the board ever since 1800." You will recall that Buldakov was married to the daughter of the late Grigoriii Shelikhov and his wife Nataliia. Of course the Saint Petersburg family reunion of the Rezanov's, the Buldakov's and Nataliia, now quite advance in her years, was a wonderful event.
[153]

While the Rezanov's remained in Saint Petersburg, the Company frigate *Suvorov* arrived in New Archangel in July 1817. Aboard the vessel was Semyon Ivanovich Yanovskiii, second in command and "a handsome and pleasant officer, who was liked by all classes, had an excellent mind, was widely read, and was exceptionally honest and straightforward. His future in the service looked bright." He took an immediate romantic interest in fifteen-year-old Irina Baranova, the daughter of Aleksandr Baranov and his Kenaitze wife, whom Baranov had accepted in 1792 and afterward named Anna.

You will recall that two children had been born to Alexsandr and Anna: Antipatr, now twenty years old, and Irina, 15. Both children had received significant education. Antipatr longed to enter the Naval Academy, but a sponsor had not yet come forward. Irina "was a ravishing little beauty, dark-eyed, dark-haired, and fine-featured." Yanovskiii was seemingly enthralled over

---

[153] In truthful history, with Rezanov dead and no member of the Board able to provide first-hand, on-site testimony regarding the truthful progress of the Russian colony and the character of the management of Chief Manager Aleksandr Baranov, certain enterprising Russian navy officials were successful in convincing the Crown to delay its decision on extending the charter for the Russian American Company while navy officials conducted an investigation of the management of the colony and the conduct of its Chief Manager. So the charter was extended only a few years, until 1821, to provide just enough time for the investigation and the writing of the Navy's report. The leader of the navy's effort to take control over Russian America was Captain Vasilii Golovin, "a man singularly devoted to advancing the Navy, one of its best speakers and writers, a master of invective, and no respecter of merchants in general," an officer who "knew the colony, having visited it twice, each time gathering detrimental information. . . . Golovin's harshest words were for Baranov, whom he declared to be in need of investigation for criminal wrongdoing." Furthermore, Golovin obtained approval to personally conduct the investigation and "write the report."

In truthful history, at the meeting of the Company Board, with accusing navy men present, Chairman Buldakov struggled to salvage what he could of merchant control over the future of Russian America. Furthermore, he believed the more serious of the allegations against Baranov were false, although he had never been to the colony or met Chief Manager Baranov. Buldakov knew that Baranov considered him "a close personal friend," and that Baranov totally trusted him. He was aware that Baranov had named him to be "co-guardian of his children in his will."

To salvage some remnant of control, the Board agreed to name Captain-Lieutenant Leonitii Hagemeister to replace Baranov as Chief Manager of Russian America. Hagemeister had visited the colony eight years previously, and at that time had insulted King Kamehameha of Hawaii, undoing the goodwill that had been cultivated by Baranov. "By virtue of his war record," Hagemeister "stood high in the estimation of his colleagues, though why so poor a diplomat should have done so is a mystery." Perhaps Golovin had advanced Hagemeister's name because he had found in him an officer who was totally deceived into believing that all of his charges against Baranov were true. Golovin needed a zealot to crusade against the besieged Chief Manager.

The history of the Navy's successful campaign to discredit Chief Manager Baranov and seize control over the management of Russian America does not occur in this historical novel because the presence of Nikolai Rezanov defeats Golovin's campaign. So Hagemeister is not named Chief Manager and Baranov is continuing to hold that office until the end of the present charter, scheduled for July 1819. Our story returns to New Archangel and the arrival of the Company frigate *Suvorov*, returning from Saint Petersburg.

Irina's play at the piano, her spirit and her dark beauty. Semyon Ivanovich Yanovskiii and Irina Baranova were married in New Archangel on January 26, 1818, Hagemeister having approved it for the Navy and the father of the bride eagerly blessing the union: [154]

"The little church in the old ship was packed as Father Sokolov married the couple, who then left on a wedding trip, which, for Yanovskiii, was also to be an inspection tour of the colony," because Baranov was planning to recommend that his son-in-law take over as Chief Manager as soon as it could be blessed by the Company Board.

Meanwhile, back in Saint Petersburg, the Rezanov's were ensuring that the Company was positioned to win a renewed charter and to expand its mission in the colony, while recognizing that its territory would never be expanded. The shape and size of Russian America was fixed.

Yanovskiii and Irina had returned to New Archangel from the honeymoon and inspection trip to Kodiak and beyond, and the fine reception received was a great boost to their spirits. During the spring and summer of 1818, Aleksandr Baranov trained his new son-in-law to take over as Chief Manager, for he was looking forward to retirement. Months earlier, soon after the wedding, Baranov had forwarded a request to Saint Petersburg that his retirement be granted and that Chairman Buldakov and the Company Board approve Yanovskiii as his successor. Approval arrived on the *Kutuzov* in late October 1818. Aboard the *Kutuzov* was Vasilii Golovnin, arriving to make inspections. Seeking to display goodwill toward Baranov, Golovnin appointed Antipatr Baranov to the Russian Naval Academy, to begin the young man's education on the warship normally commanded by Golovnin himself. Of this appointment of his son, Aleksandr could not have been more proud.

Aleksandr Baranov had accomplished much during the twenty-seven years he had overseen Russian America. He wanted to retire in Hawaii, but played along with Golovnin's scheme to take him to Saint Petersburg, figuring he would jump ship when stopping in Hawaii to get supplies. On November 27, 1818, Baranov was aboard, the *Kutuzov*, bound for Saint Petersburg with Leontii Hagemeister at the helm. The *Kutuzov* entered the harbor of Lahaina, Maui in the Hawaiian Islands on the incoming late morning tide in late December. Aboard in an aft cabin with Aleksandr Baranov was his trusted friend Richard. Hagemeister had promised Vasilii Golovnin that he would bypass Hawaii while in-route to Saint Petersburg in order to prevent Baranov from leaving the ship and perhaps remaining on shore, but he felt he had an excuse to pull into the harbor for fresh fruits and vegetables to ensure the health of the crew.

So he had done it; come in on the morning tide and kept considerable distance from the waterfront. But, he sternly announced that no one was to leave the ship. As expected, the natives were eager to sell fresh fruits and vegetables directly out of their canoes and several beautiful bare-chested native girls were with them, all too eager to entertain the crewmen with dancing and swimming in the water below, and thereby improving sales and prices paid. Baranov, pretending to be ill, remained in the cabin for most of the day. Fortunately, Hagemeister was rather distracted, spending all afternoon and into the evening in his cabin with the two girls he had invited to come aboard.

---

[154] In truthful history the marriage took place as reported here. But Hagemeister, using the authority given him by Golonov, after the wedding, announced that Baranov was being removed as Chief Manager and that Yanovskiii was taking his place. He planned to send Baranov back to Russia, hoping for an early demise. Hagemeister figured that he would use Yanovskiii to briefly win a measure of good will among the Russian American population, then depose him after the Navy gained full control over the colony through the renewed charter. But in our story, Baranov remains Chief Manager while he is training his new son-in-law to take the reins in the near future, as soon as it could be approved by the Company Board and then, after all was in place, he hoped to retire in Hawaii.

Soon after dark set in, Richard opened a cabin window overlooking the sea and let down a rope ladder secured by a slip knot. In the water below was a small canoe that had come alongside the *Kutuzov* unnoticed, alerted to be there by a note Richard had passed to a fruit seller during the day. Baranov slipped out the window, down the ladder and into the canoe. Richard followed, releasing the slip knot after reaching the canoe and gathering up the rope ladder. The Hawaiian put a blanket over his two passengers, tossed some straw on top and slowly paddled away. The log would conclude, "Baranov and Richard, drown. Lost at sea."

Dr. Egor Schaeffer, Father Herman and King Kamehameha were all glad to see Aleksandr Baranov and Baranov expressed the same sentiment, having doubted he would ever get back to Hawaii. The leader of Hawaii and the former leader of Russian America, both legends in their own time, discussed many things. [155]

Meanwhile, in Saint Petersburg, the Rezanov's and the Buldakov's and the Board awaited a decision to extend the Company's charter for another twenty years. The antagonist, Vasilii Golovnin, at New Archangel hoping to find evidence to incriminate former Chief Manager Baranov, had found nothing. Accountant Kirill Khlebnikov discovered that, in fact, Baranov had been generous almost beyond belief. So, when Golovnin reached Saint Petersburg in late 1819, his report simply said:

"After a thorough investigation of the accounts of the Russian American Company during the oversight of Aleksandr Baranov, and after further analysis of other aspects of the late Chief Manager's leadership, we find no basis for criticism of his management."

The charter renewal was signed in June, 1819 to be in effect until July 1839. The new charter expanded the mission of the Russian American Company in several ways.

- A Russian whaling industry would be developed and made equal in importance to the fur trade.

- The natural resources of Russian America would be discovered and exploited in a systematic and persistence manner.

- The Company's agricultural base north of San Francisco, Ross Settlement, would be expanded.

- Under Company guidance, up to 50 Russian families, including women and children could be recruited to come to Russian America as colonists.

- The requirement that Company employees return to Russia after fifteen years of service was relaxed if adolescent children were dependent on them.

---

[155] In truthful history Alexsandr Baranov did not disembark from the *Kutuzov* at Hawaii. In truth, Hagemeister made sure that the *Kutuzov* bypassed Hawaii. King Kamehameha had died while the ship continued on into the South Pacific. In truth, as previously mentioned, Dr. Schaeffer had not remained in Hawaii to help Hawaiian's improve their agriculture. "After ten storming weeks, with a stop only at Manila, Java was reached, and, in early March, the *Kutuzov* entered the harbor of Batavia." Mysteriously, it remained at Batavia for five weeks, "leisurely dickering with officials of the Dutch East India Company, either indifferent to the effect on Baranov or hopeful of hastening his death." Baranov's biographer would write:

"The climate of Batavia is known to be trying to any European, especially the advanced in years. It was worse for a man accustomed to the life Baranov had lived. He was running a fever when the *Kutuzov* put to sea again. Four days later he was dead. The date was April 12, 1819, according to the official announcement later made by the Company. His body was committed to the Indian Ocean."

- The Board appointed Semyon Yanovskiii to remain at his post of Chief Manager.[156]

Regarding the southern boundary of Russian America, the Crown in Saint Petersburg did not press the issue. In 1824 it signed a treaty with the Americans agreeing to the old boundary, and in 1825 signed a similar treaty with the British. The Russian Navy, supposedly seeking the glory of expanding the Russian Empire, achieved nothing but an embarrassment.[157] Progress in advancing Russian America was admirable during the oversight of Chief Manager Yanovskiii. Furthermore, Ross Settlement continued to expand up the Slavianka River Valley even though all settlers were essentially employees of the Russian American Company.[158]

Meanwhile, far to the south, the invitation to Moses Austin to bring Americans to the New Spain frontier north of the Rio Grande (Texas) was viewed as an encouraging opportunity that might be made available to permanent Russians settlers who could emigrate to Ross Settlement north of San Francisco. If Austin could strike a deal for Americans to settle on Spanish land north of the Rio Grande, Russians ought to win a similar deal for Russians to settle on Spanish land north of San Francisco. If so, permanent settlers could come and supplement the rotating Company employees presented engaged in farming there. A summary of developments follow:

You will recall that the Mexican people won their independence from Spain in October 1821 when the last of the Spanish military left the mainland. At Mexico City, Stephen Austin persuaded the junta instituyente to approve a grant similar to the one given to his father, Moses, and to qualify himself to be an empresario, which empowered him to manage the selling of and settlement of 67,000 acres of Texas land and to arrange for the emigration of 200 families, a bit later expanded to 300 families. By 1825 Austin had brought the first 300 families into Texas.

Meanwhile, Nikolai Rezanov and family arrived in New Archangel in April 1825. There were now one daughter, Natalia, age 12, and two sons, Jose, age 11, and Luis Antonio, age 9. The Yanovskiii children, all born at New Archangel, were son Alexsandr, age 5, born in 1820, daughter Anna, age 3, born in 1822, and son Antipatr, a newborn infant at the time of the Rezanov's arrival.

It was fortunate that Nikolai Rezanov had arrived in April 1825 because the new Mexican government had been agreeable to English-speaking immigration from the north-east into Texas.

---

[156] In truthful history, the Russian Navy would be empowered to dominate rule over Russian America by virtue of the new charter signed a bit later in September 1821. Captain Vasilii Golovin would be placed on the State Council. Captain Matvei Muraviev of the Navy would replace Chief Manager Yanovskiii who would return "to Russia with his exotic wife Irina," because, in the Navy's view, his marriage would be "seen as an undesirable link with the past." Foreigners would be excluded from the waters of Russian America, and the Russian Navy would enforce it. Navy men would bring wives and children to New Archangel and those families would "live as well as they could according to the ways of upper-class Saint Petersburg." Emigration by Russian families would be tightly restricted to avoid disrupting control over the serf population of Mother Russia. In reality, procedures for land distribution in Russian America were not considered.

[157] In truthful history Lieutenant Semyon Ivanovich Yanovskii was Chief Manager from October 1818 to September 1820.

[158] The truthful history of Russian America, from 1820 to 1830 was one of stagnation, for the Navy was only interested in advancing its internal interests, and the Chief Managers it arranged to be appointed, Navy Captain Matvei Muraviev (1820-1825) and Ivan Chistiakov (1825-1830), did nothing beneficial for the colony. Without Yanovskiii, as presented in our alternate story, the economy stagnated, the natives and part-bloods lost influence, and there was no expansion in the Russian population in the colony. But otherwise, the account above resembled the true history.

Therefore, time was ripe to seek agreement for a much larger settlement of Russian-speaking colonists into the Slavianka River Valley north of San Francisco. The Rezanov's set sail to negotiate a settlement deal.

Nikolai Rezanov and Concha arrived in San Francisco, called Yerba Buena, in May 1825. They were eager to visit the Argüello family. Concha's brother was there, holding the office of Chief Manager of Alta Californio, along with his wife Maria, and the family gathering was wonderful. Nikolai submitted his proposal to expand the colonization of the Slavianka River Valley. He promised to ensure that these Russian families would remain and take personal claims of land, would be dutiful subjects under Mexican Californio authority, and be valuable additions to the population of the state. Concha implored her brother to embrace her husband's proposal to admit Russian-speaking long-term immigrants. Luis was sold. The arguments presented by Nikolai and Concha were too logical to resist. Yes, those Russian-speaking immigrants, freed from being simply employees of the Company, would be worthy additions to the Alta Californio population, especially in the region north of San Francisco, where the threat of American encroachment from Oregon Territory would be of greatest concern. Luis agreed to write a letter of acceptance.

A few days later the Rezanov's departed by their sailing vessel for San Diego, where Concha intended to visit her other brother, Santiago Argüello, who was commandent of the Presidio of San Diego. It took little persuasion to gain Santiago's endorsement. Yet, he also drafted a letter listing justifications for the project. Now it was time to sail further south and go overland to Guadalajara to visit Concha's aging father, José Darío Argüello.

Concha was greatly relieved to find her father alive, although in declining health. Her mother, Maria Ygnacia Moraga de la Argüello, was in better health, and so very excited to see her daughter and son-in-law, for she had never expected to again lay eyes on them.

The Rezanov's departed Guadalajara for Mexico City well-armed with letters of support and at an opportune time in Mexican history, for the central government was, in 1825, limited in power by the new Mexican Federal Constitution and the individual states were sovereign over most matters. Even Alta Californio was being given great latitude in making policy. And President Francisco de Victoria was at that time resolutely committed to abiding by constitutional limits to federal power. The Rezanov's also met with Vicente Guerrero and won his support. The Rezanov's left the capital with President Victoria's signed letter of acceptance of the Slavianka River Valley settlement plan. [159]

By early August 1825, the Rezanov's were at the Pacific coast boarding a British ship bound for Hawaii where they would spend two weeks in September enjoying time with Alexsandr Baranov, Dr. Igor Schaeffer, Father Herman and Kingdom leaders, including the successor to the late King Kamehameha, who had died soon after Baranov and Richard had arrived five years previously. Upon the Rezanov's arrival, it was quite evident that Baranov and Father Herman had made great progress in advancing ties between Hawaii and Russian America – ties so helpful to these two maritime resources for the vast mid-to-north Pacific. And Nikolai and Concha knew their time in Hawaii over those two weeks had added to the friendships that Baranov and Father

---

[159] In truthful history, the lease on the region around Ross Settlement was never expanded. Throughout the history of this agricultural settlement, only Company employees would be permitted to farm the land along the Russian River. It would forever be closed to Russian-speaking settlers who wished to remain past the employment deadline. In truthful history, nothing similar to the agreement to allow immigrants into Mexican Texas ever took place north of San Francisco.

Herman had nurtured. Nikolai would have much to report about Hawaii and Ross Settlement when he and Concha arrived in St. Petersburg.

Nikolai and Concha arrived in Saint Petersburg in time to celebrate Christmas with Mikhail Buldakov and his wife and children. You will recall that Rezanov's first wife was the late Anna Shelikhov, sister to Buldakov's wife. It was wonderful to be together again, but Nataliia Shelikhova was dearly missed. She had passed away in 1818.

The Board of the Russian American Company convened on January 9, 1826. Chairman Mikhail Buldakov called the meeting to order, and thanked Nikolai Rezanov for completing yet another trip into the field on behalf of the Board, including visits and examinations of conditions at several posts in Russian America, at Ross Settlement and at San Francisco. And he thanked him and Concha for their efforts to arrange for better relations with the government of Alta Californio, the central Mexican government at Mexico City and with influential leaders in Hawaii. But most of all, Chairman Buldakov thanked Concha for her unwavering support of her husband's career and her eagerness to be at his side, with the children, always at the ready to be personally helpful in advancing the interests of her husband and of the Company. He added, "Few women in Russian history have done more in support of a husband as has the Spanish lady who has joined us today to grace this Board Room with her well-known charm: the beautiful, capable and influential Maria Concepción Argüello de la Rezanova."

Nikolai Rezanov presented his report of the past year-and-half of travel through Russian America and beyond; his findings; his observations; his discussions; what he saw as problems needing further work. He described what he saw as opportunities for further expansion of Company activities; of the performance of Chief Manager Semyon Yanovskii's administration; of employee morale, and of the status of relations with the Hudson Bay Company, with American neighbors, with the Mexican governments and with the influential people in Hawaii.

The Board members were easily sold on the settlement plan. The vote was overwhelmingly in favor of approval. Now, the job was to sell influential Russian nobles to relax and not object to the departure from the homeland of a very small portion of the Russian serf population. When millions were working as serfs, how would 50 families be missed? That was the argument. And it was persuasive. The Company Charter, active from 1821 to 1829, was amended to permit introduction of 50 families each year into the area of Ross Settlement. Many were expected to come from an estate with a population of serfs beyond that needed.

But a new man was in charge of the Russian Government. Czar Alexander I had died a few weeks earlier, unexpectedly, on the first day of December, 1825, "worn out at age forty-eight." His brother Nicholas, 29, assumed the Crown. The creed of Nicholas I came to be expressed by the three words: "Orthodoxy, Autocracy, Nationalism." There would be no doubt but that Czar Nicholas would decide the matter, and that would be it. In fact Nicholas I would reign for 30 years, until his death in 1855.

Fortunately, Nikolai Rezanov and Chairman Buldakov were equal to the task. In the end the Crown gave its blessings. But rumor has it that Concha managed to attend a gathering which included the Czar's wife and so charmed her with tales of the Rezanov's travels across Russia, throughout Russian America and down through Mexico that Nicholas had no choice but to approve the charter in order to find happiness in his bedroom.

Company chairman Mikhail Buldakov passed away in 1828, after serving in that capacity for over twenty years. This occurred shortly before the expiration of the second charter. The Board elected Nikolai Rezanov to the post of Chairman, thereby retaining the Shelikhov influence. Nikolai would find it necessary to remain in Saint Petersburg most of the time. Chief Manager Semyon Yanovskiii, who, you will recall, was Baranov's son-in-law by virtue of his marriage to the lovely part-blood Irina, would be replaced by a "distinguished explorer and scientist," a man of Estonian German birth, the impressive Baron Ferdinand von Wrangell. Rezanov figured he needed to be at New Archangel to ensure a smooth transition. Therefore, he left Concha and the younger children -- Nataliia, now 16, and Luis Antonio, now 13 -- at Saint Petersburg and, taking the older son, 15-year-old Jose, along, he began the overland trip across vast Russia to the Pacific coast. Along the way he anticipated meeting up with Ferdinand von Wrangell. What a marvelous trip was in store for young Jose! Wrangell was to hold the office of Chief Manager for five years, from 1830 to 1835.

Nikolai Rezanov arrived at New Archangel in July 1829 and there conferred with Manager Chief Semyon Yanovskiii and Ferdinand von Wrangell, who was to take over as Chief Manager, by year-end. Actually, Rezanov had caught up with Ferdinand von Wrangell at Okhotsk and they had sailed across the Okhotsk Sea and the Pacific Ocean together. So the two leaders came to know each other well. In this "small, testy man, red of beard and hair, an Estonian German by birth," Rezanov was again face-to-face with one of Russia's greatest adventurers, explorers, scientists, geographers, and seamen -- an unbelievably rugged individual. And Nikolai had son Jose alongside in all of the transition meetings.

Meanwhile, there were 150 independent Russian families at Ross Settlement already working new farms. In charge as Colonial Administrator at the present time of 1829 was Pavel Ivanovich Shelikhov, who was no relation to the Shelikhov's who had been so important in Company history. Pavel had been in charge at Ross since 1824 and was scheduled to move on. Who should replace him? Wrangell turned to Semyon Yanovskiii and said, "If you and Irina and the children would accept relocation to Ross Settlement so that you could administer this important arm of Company operations, I would be most honored and gratified." Wrangell could rest easy that he had the best man in charge of Ross Settlement and that he could focus on exploring inland Russian America, finding agricultural land and new mineral and animal resources, and figuring out how to exploit them. He remarked to Rezanov, "I hear that some natives have found copper and find it useful. Perhaps we can discover workable deposits of copper, silver and gold. Yes, finding gold would be nice."

Jose had pleaded with his father to be allowed to stay behind and work with Ferdinand von Wrangell. He would soon be 17 years old and was confident of his future, if given a chance. As fate would have it, Nikolai, now 66 years old, would never again journey to Russian America. But his experience and judgment at the helm as Chairman of the Board would continue for 7 more years, until 1837.

With the possible exception of Alexsandr Baranov, Ferdinand von Wrangell would be the most successful Chief Manager ever to hold office at New Archangel. [160] Early on, Wrangell was studying where he could launch a successful agricultural settlement within Russian America. It did not take him long to figure it out. He found it in the valley of the Susitna River and the branch valley of the Matanuska River. The soil, laid down by glaciers during the last ice age, was easy to work, reasonably level and fertile, and the surrounding mountains offered shelter from winds. Wrangell sent word to Dr. Schaeffer in Hawaii to gather up seeds of barley, oats and other grains and seed potatoes, and agricultural reference books, and board the next Company ship departing

---

[160] The history of Baron Ferdinand von Wrangell is truthful with regard to his former accomplishments and his arrival in 1829 and taking the office of Chief Manager in June 1830, but his accomplishments, although remarkable in truthful history, would not be as great with regard to advancing agriculture and resource exploration and development as is being presented in this alternate history. His term as Chief Manager concluded in October 1835. As previously mentioned, for several pages Dr. Schaeffer's work is not factual history, for he had left Hawaii in disgrace many years earlier.

for New Archangel to begin reassignment to develop agriculture in the Susitna-Matanuska Valleys. Accordingly, Schaeffer was at his new assignment by early June of 1830.

Slowly, but surely, under Wrangell's direction, the Russian American Company developed a whaling fleet in competition with that of the American whalers. Ships designed for that purpose were built in Company shipyards, the design being less rugged and less expensive since Company ships did not have to sail the long passage from the northeastern United States around treacherous South America to the northern Pacific as did the American ships. In each trip, Aleuts in their small boats teamed with their companion whaling ship to harpoon a huge animal and help bring it alongside the mother ship for transport back to the coastal ports, where the blubber was cut off, fires were built and the oil was rendered. By being so close to the whaling seas and having remarkable working relationships with the natives, the Russians held clear competitive advantages over the Americans.

The prospecting teams of 1831 discovered evidence of gold, particularly at the headwaters of a creek, which they named Gold Creek. There the prospecting team brought back gold nuggets "as large as peas and beans." Other evidence of gold was found, but nothing as promising as at the headwaters of Gold Creek. [161] The prospecting teams of 1832 and 1833 were less successful. The prospecting teams of 1834 and 1835 went north up the Susitna River, passing the Alaska Mountain Range to their west and entering central Russian America which was relatively free of mountains and where the great Tanana, Kantishna and Yukon rivers sustained wide valleys. Evidence of gold was found in the Yukon River. Jose Rezanov, now a grown man, went prospecting with a team in 1834 and in 1835.

Concerning agriculture, it was soon apparent that potatoes would grow well in the Sisitna Valley, especially if the most cold-tolerant variety could be found in the Andes Mountains, the homeland of that plant. Consequently, in 1833, Chief Manager Wrangell sent Dr. Egor Schaeffer to the South American Andes to find and bring back candidate potato plants. He brought plants that produced small black potatoes which did very well and served as cross-pollination stock to improve the cold tolerance of the Russian American potato.

Every year since 1830, independent Russia families had been coming to Ross Settlement to claim land in the Slavianka River Valley, clear a portion of it, and begin farming and stock-raising. By the summer of 1835, 347 independent families were settled in Russian America and at Ross Settlement.

The year 1835 was the last year of Ferdinand von Wrangell's tenure as Chief Manager of Russian America, for it was thought that his expertise and experience was needed in Saint Petersburg as a member of the Company Board. So he departed for that city and was replaced by Ivan Kupreyanov, who was accompanied by his wife Yuliya Ivanova. Jose Rezanov, now 22 years old, was appointed assistant administrator reporting to Chief Manager Kupreyanov. [162]

---

[161] Fifty years after the 1830 date of our alternate history, in 1880, Chief Kowee, a Tlingit, reported that gold nuggets could be found along Gold Creek, and it was little effort for prospector Joe Juneau and his sidekick to work upstream to find the source at Snow Slide Gulch, at the creek's headwater. This launched the gold rush that gave birth to the town of Juneau, which was named for Joe Juneau. Americans would relocate the capital of Alaska Territory from Sitka to Juneau in 1906.

[162] Ivan Kupreyanov, in truthful history, was in charge of Russian America from 1835 to 1840 and his wife Yuliya was with him and did start the school. He did build the impressive residence, library and museum, which Americans would improperly name "Baranov's Castle." Reference to progress in agriculture, Russian whaling, geology, prospecting, and gold panning is not truthful history for the years 1835 to 1840. Of course Jose Rezanov is not a historically truthful person.

Semyon Yanovskiii and wife Irina continued to represent the Company at the agricultural endeavors at Susitna and Matanuska river Valleys, and the new black potato variety brought in from the high country of the Andes was showing good promise.

In 1840 Chief Manager Ivan Kupreyanov was replaced by Arvid Adol Etholén. He would hold the office of Chief Manager to 1845. [163] The major event in Etholén administration was the growing emigration of Americans into the Willamette Valley of what would become Oregon Territory. Covered wagons, departing Independence, Missouri and following the Oregon Trail, began arriving in the fertile far-west valley in 1841 bringing in families of settlers. At this time the region called Oregon was jointly administered by the British and the American governments. It would be 5 years before those two governments would agree to establish the 49th parallel as the lasting boundary between British America and the United States. Soon Oregon farms emerged. Where was the crop surplus to be sold? Well, the best prices would be found just up the Pacific coast in Russian America. In response to developing Oregon agriculture, Chief Manager Etholén decided to recall Company employees at Ross Settlement, bringing them north to Russian America while leaving the independent farmers to carry on with their farms. By 1843 all that would remain of Company employees would be a Company agent and one assistant, and their job was to coordinate markets for the farm products of the approximately 300 independent Russian-speaking families that remained in the Slavianka River Valley.

In early 1842 Chief Manager Ivan Kupreyanov dispatched Alexsandr Yanovskiii to be its agent at Ross Settlement to coordinate with the remaining independent Russian settlers. As you recall, Alexsandr Yanovskiii, age 22, was the son of Irina Baranova and the late Semyon Yanovskiii. Semyon had died in 1838, leaving Irina, now 39, so she accompanied her son to Ross Settlement as did his sister Anna, age 20, and not yet married, and his younger brother Antipatr, age 17. Their living quarters were in the Company fortress, which some called Fort Ross.

Meanwhile, in Saint Petersburg, Chairman Ferdinand von Wrangell and the Company Board were negotiating with Tsar Nicholas to win approval for another twenty-year extension of the second charter. The effort was reasonably successful and the third charter was signed on schedule in 1841 to be in effect for the subsequent twenty years, until 1861. So this would be the charter in effect at the time of State Secession and the formation of the Confederate States of America.

And the role of the Russian Orthodox Church was expanded in Russian America, for the Synod voted to make Russian America a separate diocese, and Tsar Nicholas was persuaded to name Father Ioann Veniaminov to be its Bishop. To expand support of the new Russian America diocese, rules in the Company Charter controlling the conduct of Orthodox priests and missionaries were liberalized to ensure that conversion had to be voluntary, without coercion, and that Natives and part bloods could be inducted into the clergy, and that native languages could be used in the conduct of the Liturgy. In 1848 the colonial clergy, then numbering about fifty, would assemble at New Archangel for the dedication of the little Cathedral of Saint Michael.

In 1845, Mikhail Tebenkov replaced Arvid Adolf Etholén as Chief Manager. Etholén would hold the office until 1850. [164]

The biggest event in North America during the administration of Mikhail Tebenkov was the United States' war against Mexico, which changed the political map of a vast region of the

---

[163] The story of Arvid Adolf Etholén is truthful history. He was Chief Manager from May 1840 to July 1845.

[164] The story of Vice Admiral Mikhail Tebenkov is truthful history. He was Company Chief Manager from July 1845 to October 1850. But our alternate history presents much less influence by the Russian Navy and much more influence by Russian settlers during these five years.

continent south of Oregon Territory and west of the new State of Texas. The Oregon boundary had been settled at the 48th parallel, so the British seemed secure against American aggression. But what about Russian America? If the Americans heard about large gold deposits in Russian America, Tebenkov must have realized, "Nothing would have stopped them from venturing north and taking over that outpost of the Russian Empire." This is why gold sites were secret and prospecting was discouraged.

All that remained of the Russian culture in Alta Californio were the farming families in the Slavianka River Valley in the region that been the Company's Ross Settlement. And among the independents remaining were the Pomo natives who had chosen to work and live alongside the Russian-speakers and to sometimes intermarry.

Then came the United States war against Mexico, launched from the Texas border in May 1846. American invasion of Alta Californio soon followed at a quick pace, for that was much of the prize sought in this war. The Californio Mexicans in the lower Sacramento Valley and San Francisco and points south were easily overwhelmed by the American forces led by navy commanders John Sloat and Robert Stockton, and army commander Stephen Kearney. The American navy was easily taking the seaports along the coast of Alta Californio. Americans were in control of the Sacramento Valley by June 1846 without much loss of life, for the Mexican opposition was inconsequential. On July 23, 1846, Commander John Stockton gave John Fremont the rank of Major and set him on a course to gather up, in the upper Sacramento Valley, a force of 428 Americans composed of his survey crew and illegal immigrants from Oregon Territory who had joined those already arrived.[165]

It was John Fremont's gang of fighting men, primarily illegal American immigrants, which confronted the Russian-speaking farmers in the Slavianka River Valley in August 1846. The farmland and grazing land that had been developed by the independent Russian-speaking settlers along the Slavianka River Valley began, as the crow flies, about 20 miles east of where the river discharged into the Pacific Ocean and stretched up the valley for 30 miles toward the north, the first third being farmland and the remainder being grazing land and some vineyards and orchards. About 190 Russian-speaking families lived and worked this agricultural region and their contact with Russian America and the Company Chief Manager was through the designated agent, Alexsandr Yanovskiii, now 26 years old, who held his office at the old Company stockade, called Fort Ross, and oversaw a shipping office in a small building at Bodega Bay, a little over 20 miles to the south of the Fort. With Alexsandr Yanovskiii was his family, consisting of his mother, Irina Baranova, his sister Anna, 24, and his brother Antipatr, 21. Since arriving with her brother on his new assignment in 1842, Anna had married Fedor Ivanov, 26, son of independent Russian farmer Andrei Ivanov and his part-blood wife Vera. Anna now lived in the mid-section of the farming valley on farmland that had been developed by the Ivanov family.

Upon arriving at the northern-most farms, Fremont and his force of Americans saw a mixed people, some who looked like Europeans, some who look like Natives, and some who looked like mixtures of the two races. To them the scene was puzzling. These strange people seemed to be prosperous and to be living in a well-developed agricultural region. Strange, indeed! The invaders looked upon what they saw with covetous eyes. That herd should be mine; that house, that field, that orchard, that barn.

Soon after Fremont's advance, Fedor Ivanov, the husband of Anna Yanovskiii, had encountered the first wave of retreating settlers while the couple had been on horseback minding their herd of cattle, which were grazing along the river. Feeling immense responsibility for the

---

[165] The story of John Fremont is truthful history.

welfare of the settlers, the young couple felt obligated to remain at the rear of the retreating settlers to ensure none were left behind. It was while Anna was checking a barn for people and useful horses that her attackers rushed forward. They were three of Fremont's men who had gotten a bit ahead of the pack. Entranced by Anna's unusual beauty, derived from the mix of handsome Russian and exotic Native blood, the first invader grabbed the young woman, ripped off her dress and threw her upon the hay. Another grabbed her while the first stripped off his clothes and made ready to be the first to rape the restrained woman. Anna's cries for help were not at first heard by Fedor, who was checking out a house across the river. But hiding in the loft of the barn were two Natives who normally worked alongside the family that owned the farm. One Native grabbed an axe, the other a pitch-fork, and together they leaped down upon the rapist and his assistant, quickly dispatching both. Then, before the third could get to his rifle, they tackled that man, swiftly cut his throat and stabbed him in the back. Within two minutes all three were dead. As it turned out, the rape had just begun and Anna would suffer no physical damage, although the emotions of the event would forever frame her loving attitudes toward her native brothers and her hateful attitudes toward the United States people.

All of the Russians were inside the Fort by nightfall of the second day of the invasion crisis except for the pickets guarding the approaches and the workers gathering in water and food. To that end, five were killing and dressing five beeves to stockpile some meat. For a day, it seems that the invaders lost track of the Russians. But on the morning of the fourth day, about 200 invaders appeared and took their measure of the situation. On the fifth day their leader, John Fremont, appeared. On the morning of the sixth day, Fremont and Yanovskiii agreed to parley, the latter bringing along an interpreter who lived among the settlers. While the two sparred over the issue of Manifest Destiny versus the settler's rights to property, life and happiness, the Chief Manager of the Russian American Company, Mikhail Tebenkov arrived off Fort Ross Cove in a Company ship flying the Company flag.

Now, Mikhail Tebenkov was no lightweight in the affairs of the Russian Empire. An 1821 graduate of the Russian Naval Academy, for 25 years he had been a noted officer of impressive accomplishments; presently he was Chief Manager of Russian America and a Director on the Company Board; his career would elevate him to Vice Admiral of the Imperial Russian Navy. His job was to protect the lives and welfare of Russian citizens wherever they may be. He understood international law and that the government of the United States did not want to create an international crisis over the mistreatment and the terrorizing of a mere 190 pioneering Russian families living along a remote valley in Alta Californio. Tebenkov fired off three cannon to get the American's attention.

When John Fremont heard the artillery fire, he stopped the parley to investigate. Yanovskiii explained the situation and asked that the captain of the Company ship be allowed peaceful access to join in the parley. Fremont agreed. By nightfall it was agreed that the Russian settlers could stay or leave: if they left they would be compensated for the productive farms they would be abandoning; if they stayed, they would be allowed to become American citizens and would be encouraged to learn the English language. It was decided that the settlers should vote and the decision would be by the majority of the heads of the families. But if the vote called for staying, all would stay; if the vote called for leaving as refugees, all would leave. The vote was to leave. Each head of family gave account of acres under cultivation, number of cattle and horses, size of house and barns, number and age of fruit and nut trees, vineyard dimensions if any, and acres of pasture, and this was recorded as two identical lists. Fremont signed both for the United States and Tebenkov signed both for the Russian Empire. Each had his signed list. That was the end of it.

But where would the refugees go. In was September 1846 and winter would soon arrive in Russian America. What about the Hawaiian Islands? Alexsandr Baranov had gone there. Father Herman, too. An Orthodox mission had been operating on the big island for 24 years. Although slowly expanding, it was well established. They would go to the big island of Hawaii! Company Chief Manager Tebenkov agreed.

Six ships arrived at Hawaii, the big island, with 188 Russian refuge families in late October and early November, 1846. Tebenkov had been right. The Hawaiian government did accept the refugees and instructed all to stay together on the big island under the oversight of the Russian mission.

But the company agent, Alexsandr Yanovskiii, did not journey to Hawaii. He, his brother Antipatr, his mother Irina Baranova, and his sister Anna and her husband Fedor Ivanov returned to New Archangel. There, they were to play important roles in the future history of Russian America.

Chief Manager Tebenkov advanced the money owed to each head of household. Seventeen months later, the United States Government reimbursed the Russian American Company in full. But Anna Yanovskiii Ivanov would forever harbor an intense hatred toward Americans and their so-called "Manifest Destiny." That hatred, also felt throughout the Baranov and Rezanov families, would play a significant role in the future history of Russian America.

Back in Saint Petersburg, the danger from the American's so-called "Manifest Destiny" prompted Tsar Nicolas I to intensify the navy presence in Russian America and to ensure adequate defenses, in spite of the fact that the high cost of the defensive stance threatened to eventually surpass the financial gains the Company was bringing to the Crown and other stockholders.

In October 1850, Navy Captain Nikolay Yakovlevich Rozenberg (1807-1857) replaced Chief Manager Mikhail Tebenkov. In March 1853, Aleksandr Ilich Rudakov (1817-1875) took charge of the office of Chief Manager, but held it only one year, until April 1854. But the next man to hold the office would stay for five years. He was Captain Stepan Vasiliyevich Voyevodsky (1805-1884). A career Russian naval officer, an 1822 graduate of the Russian Naval Academy, an experienced seaman with 31 years of navy experience, Voyevodsky would serve as Chief Manager of the Russian American Company for five years, until June 1857. [166]

The February 1855 death of Tsar Nicholas I greatly impacted the future course of events in Russian America. His son Aleksandr II took the throne on March 2, 1855 at the age of 36 years. The new Tsar was well educated, handsome, fit and of a persuasion to liberalize rule over the Russian people. But first he had to contend with the Crimean War, which, since October 1853 pitted the Orthodox Christian Russian Empire against the Sunni Islamic Ottoman Empire over allowing Christians the right to practice their religion in the Holy Land. In this, the first of modern wars, Russia was seriously humiliated. And the new Tsar and his influential brother, Grand Duke Konstantin Nikolaevich, set out immediately afterward to move Russia forward, to modernize it, on several fronts. [167] The navy must be modernized: that would be a focus of the capable Konstantin. And it was quite obvious that the Russian navy had bigger problems to deal with than protecting the far-eastern territory of the Russian America Company. Across the vast Russian Empire, agrarian domination over society and government policy must be broken to make way for industrialization. And there was no better place for Russia to experiment with

---

[166] The three Chief Managers mentioned above, Rozenberg, Rudakov and Voyevodsky, were in office as indicated according to truthful history, except the last, Voyevodsky, held office two years longer, to 1859.

[167] The story of the Crimean War is truthful history.

freeing the serfs than to expand their immigration to Russian America. For sure more settlers would be needed if Russian America was to be defended against the Manifest-Destiny-minded Americans, already bursting with expansionist passions fueled by the discovery of gold in California.

The first order of business was to amend the Company charter of 1840 to expand the immigration of independent Russian settlers. The Russian America census taken in 1853, near the close of Rosenberg management, reported a total of 5,650 independent Russian settlers (including 3,400 pure-blooded children), 4,000 independent part-blood settlers, and 800 pure-blooded employees of the Company. Many were occupied with farming in the Susitna River Valley, but others were involved in prospecting, fur trapping, fishing and salt and smoke curing of the catch, whaling, construction, shipbuilding, the crafts, etc. [168]

The second order of business was to move administration of Russian America from a senior Navy official to a capable civilian leader who was born and raised in the colony. There were not many men of sufficient ability from which to choose, but fortunately there were two, Jose Rezanov and Aleksandr Yanovskiii, and von Wrangell knew both of them.

You will recall that Jose Rezanov had been only 17 years old when, with his father Nikolai's reluctant permission, he had been allowed to remain in New Archangel to gain an education at the feet of the learned von Wrangell, just installed as Company Chief Manager. During those five years, he had learned much and his mentor had been impressed. When von Wrangell's term as Chief Manager ended in 1835, Jose Rezanov had remained in the colony to assist the new Chief Manager, Ivan Antonovich Kupreianov, joining Company prospecting parties, working alongside Dr. Egor Schaeffer in his agricultural endeavors, and assisting Kupreianov in administrative matters. In 1839, at the age of 26, Jose married the lovely Maria Koroliov, 20-year-old daughter of Rodion Koroliov, a settler from eastern Russia who had come over in 1823, and a Tlingit woman called Katerina. By the time that the new Chief Manager, Arvid Adolf Etholén, took office, in 1840, Jose was 27 years old, newlywed and had, with a partner, begun a private business pursuit involving the curing of fresh salmon, by drying, salting and/or smoking, and then packing in tightly-constructed wood barrels for export. But he would have to rely entirely on his business partner for several years, because Etholén proposed that Jose and Maria accompany him to Russia so the newly-weds could visit Jose's sister Nataliia and his brother Luis Antonio, where they lived in Saint Petersburg. Furthermore, Arvid promised that Jose would be employed as a clerk at the Company headquarters and, through experiences there and elsewhere in Europe, gain important knowledge and contacts needed to further his career when he returned to Russian America.

Jose and Maria reached the capital city in 1841. Of course, the time the newly-weds spent with Nataliia and Luis Antonio was wonderful. All were in good health. Nataliia was married with two bright and energetic children. Luis, also a newlywed, was full of excitement. By and by, Jose settled down into his new job as a clerk at the Company headquarters and had frequent

---

[168] In truthful history the immigration of independent Russian settlers was so minor that the maximum population of Russians of pure blood in the Territory blood never exceeded 850, and those were almost all Company employees. In truthful history Ferdinand von Wrangell temporarily left Navy service to be Chairman of the Board of the Russian American Company from 1849 to 1854. Leaving the Company, he returned to the Navy to be Chief Director of the Hydrographical Department; then in 1855, Chief Assistant to the High Admiral, Grand Duke Konstantine; then in 1858, Member of the Counsel of the Empire; then, in 1859, Admiral and General Aide-de-camp to the Tsar, Alexander II. Recognizing the vast potential of Russian American resources, von Wrangell would be the most powerful voice in opposition to the sale of the territory to the United States Government. Yet, he was never successful in promoting settlement by a sizable number of independent Russian families.

occasion to interact with Board Member von Wrangell. They talked about exporting fish, especially salmon, to Asian markets, directly or by way of Hawaii. Von Wrangell recommended that Jose investigate the new canning technology, which ought to be superior to the salt-curing process for preserving fish in wooden barrels..

In May 1846, Jose Rezanov and wife Maria and their two sons, Nikolai and Rodion, left Saint Petersburg for New Archangel by crossing Asia to Okhotsk, and then sailing along the Aleutian Islands to Kodiak and to Sitka Sound. By August they were at New Archangel. Jose was glad to discover that the salmon salt-curing and smoke-curing and packing business was doing well.

In 1851, with canning technology finally becoming economical, Company President Wrangell obtained Board approval to start a salmon cannery at Sitka using licensed Evans and Taylor technology, fabrication machinery and tin-coated iron sheets, all supplied from the eastern United States. [169] Pressure sterilizers were also purchased to ensure the proper temperatures were attained. Jose Rezanov's salmon processing company supplied the canning factory with ice, fresh salmon and workers. The Russian American Company's Sitka salmon cannery began operation in the spring of 1854. Records for 1856 show that 48 metric tons of salmon was salt cured, smoke cured, or canned and shipped out from Russian America, about half going to Hawaii for trans-shipment to China, the remainder going to east Russia.

During this time, there was also a rather secret prospecting story to cover. When Chief Manager Rosenberg was replaced by Aleksandr Rudakov in March of 1853, Aleksandr Yanovskiii, age 32, resigned from the Russian America Company to fully engage in his prospecting and mining interests. He formed a small company in partnership with his brother Antipatr, 27, who also resigned. The brothers named their entrepreneurial venture "The Baranov Mining Company," to honor their grandfather and gain immediate name recognition. By 1857, Baranov Mining had five prospecting teams in the field, and one 14-man gold mining site in operation. But the potential wealth of this mining site was a closely guarded secret.

But this was an era that would be transitioning from Navy oversight to settler oversite. Chief Manager Stepan Voyevodsky, the last of the appointed Navy men, finished his term in May 1859. Jose Rezanov was the choice to take the helm and launch a new era in the development of Russian America. From now on, Russian America would be led by men who had grown up in the colony. [170] [171]

---

[169] Alan Taylor and Henry Evans, Jr. of the eastern United States were truthfully pioneers in the development of canning technology as reported in this alternate history, but the Russian American Company never constructed a salmon cannery.

[170] In truthful history, high ranking Navy officers continued to Manage Russian America from the office in New Archangel. Following Captain Stepan Voyevodsky as Chief Manager were Captain Johan Hampus Furugelm, serving from June 1859 to December 1863, and Prince Dimitrii Petrovich Maksutov, serving from December 1863 to October 1867.

[171] Johan Hampus Furugelm (1821-1909) was a Russian Navy man of noble Swedish birth, whose highest rank would be Vice-admiral. He would be in charge until December 1863, to the mid-point of the American War Between the States. With that war dragging on for years and years, the Russian Government thought it prudent to continue assigning top navy officers to oversee Russian America. Rear Admiral Dmitry Petrovich Maksutov, who had been Assistant to Furugelm since 1859, held the office for the remaining four years, until October 1867. He, too, was trained in the Russian Naval Academy, graduating in 1847. He served in the Black Sea fleet during the Crimean War. He came to Russian America in 1859 to be an assistant to Chief Manager Furugelm. Maksutov would remain in office until he was directed to sell all fixed company assets and relocate to Russia all Company employees desiring to leave, in order to make way for the new owners, represented by the United States Army and Navy under the command of Jefferson C. Davis, United States Military Commander of Alaska (no relation to the President of the Confederate States of America). Before retirement Maksutov would rise to the Navy rank of Counter-Admiral.

And Russian America would be better off without Navy rule. [172]

Big news? In 1858 China relinquished its control over the important Amur River, being unable to defend it against Russian steam-powered river boats and overall expansion pressures from Europeans and Americans. No longer would Russians have to cross imposing mountains in traveling eastward to the Pacific.

The great opportunities now available in far-east Asia caused Russian leaders to think in terms of prioritizing the country's utilization of military and economic resources. It was impossible to take advantage of all available regions for expansion. Although the Russian Empire had accomplished much, some leaders were becoming concerned that the vast region of the world now under Russian control could not be effectively defended. Choices needed to be made, they argued. Priorities needed to be established. Should Russia almost abandon Russian America to ensure adequate capacity to defend the Empire's major presence on the Pacific? The Treaty of Aigun of 1858 would document China's cession of all land north of the Amur River. But more was to be given up. Two years later, by the Treaty of Beijing of 1860, the Qing rulers of China ceded to the Russians the large Pacific island of Sakhalin, the Straight of Tartay and the Pacific coast south of the Amur River, from the mouth of the Ussuri River all the way to the northern border of Korea. At the southern end of that cession, at the fine harbor located there, Russia would construct the ice-free seaport of Vladivostok, which would become, for the foreseeable future, the home of the Russian Pacific Fleet. Now, that was a lot of responsibility suddenly heaped upon the Russian Navy.

Under this threat to possibly sell Russian America, Ferdinand von Wrangell had declined an 1854 appointment to be Chief Director of the Navy's Hydrographical Department. [173] Now, six years later, the wisdom in that decision was ever more apparent when, in 1861, eleven southern States proclaimed secession and Republicans moved toward military conquest of the Seceded States. This display of reckless military aggression in North America worried leaders in Russian America, in Canada and in Mexico. How would this new war affect those three regions? Could the Russian Crown afford to defend Russian America? Would it be wiser to just sell it?

The Company Chief Manager at New Archangel was also the Chief Manager of the colony, so Jose Rezanov was to wear two hats. To lighten his workload he was to have under him an assistant Chief Manager and a Peoples Council of 21 representatives from around the colony. He was to appoint the Councilmen and to rely on them for advice and communications in and out of New Archangel.

Defend or sell? At this point the Crown wanted to keep Russian America and defend it if it must. And that seemed to be working at the time. As reorganized, Russian America was rather successful during the course of the War Between the States and the negotiated settlement at Montreal. But, in spite of the return of peace in North America, a powerful faction within the Government in Saint Petersburg, led by the Tsar's brother, Konstantin, believed Russia ought to

---

[172] Our alternate history decides that these final two Navy-career Company Chief Managers were not selected because Tsar Aleksandr II and Konstantin agreed that it was time for the Navy to pull back from oversight to make way for greater influence by the community of settlers, thereby allowing Russian America to transition from, 1), a monopolistic trading company territory dominated by Navy officers, to, 2), a Russian colony headed by a Chief Manager with expanded immigration and a more diverse economy. Konstantin believed Russian America was too great a drain on Navy resources and, if not made self-sustaining, ought to be sold. Aleksandr II believed expanded settlement in Russian America could contribute in his new efforts to gradually free Russia's serfs in the homeland, who had for so long been bound to the land.

[173] In truthful history, von Wrangle resigned and took the Hydrographical job.

sell the colony. According to reports reaching Saint Petersburg, the flow of promised gold from mining operations was disappointing, in spite of efforts of a sizable number of independent prospectors and miners. The fur trade was very depressed. Whale oil production was flat at best. Salmon canning was going well, but competition from new Columbia River canneries was severe. Unlike the early days of settlement, many recent settlers were typically arriving in the spring, but giving up in the fall and returning to Russia to avoid the upcoming harsh winter. Feeding the immigrant settlers, now numbering 12,000, was no great problem, but, all in all, the powers that be in Saint Petersburg were disappointed in the results. So, a faction advocated selling the colony.

The sell faction, led by the Tsar's brother, Konstantine, understood that a sell of Russian America had to be negotiated in secrecy and, when consummated, sprung like a trap upon the settlers and Company employees living there so as to avoid prematurely creating panic and disturbing the peace and profitability of the region. So, they reasoned, feed the settlers some pabulum in the form of a renewed charter while arranging to sell the place out from under them. Advocates faced two formidable opponents to any sell plan. The Russian Foreign Minister, Prince Aleksandr Gorchakov strongly opposed selling. Company President Frederick von Wrangell was emotionally and rationally bound to sustain the colony as it was now organized, with responsibilities now shared between settlers and Company men.

But the Russian Minister to the United States, Edouard de Stoeckl, who had married Eliza Howard, a prominent American lady of Massachusetts, saw matters differently than did the Czar. Soon after the Treaty of Montreal, he decided to explore a purchase deal with the Abraham Lincoln Administration. Toward that goal he met with Secretary of State William Seward of New York, and also with the Chairman of the Senate Foreign Relations Committee, Charles Sumner of Massachusetts. Well, the War Between the States had destroyed the popularity of the Republican Party in the northern States, and President Lincoln, William Seward and Charles Sumner had minimal influence. Treasury Secretary Salmon Chase of Ohio had no money to spare, having lost the tariff revenue from imports at former southern States seaports. [174] Seventeen years ago, the people of the northeastern States had generally opposed the War against Mexico, which had been fought to expand the southern part of the country out to the Pacific. Without question, they did not want the obligations of overseeing and protecting Russian America which did not even geographically join with the northwestern territories of the country. That was the end of it and Stoeckl abandoned the idea.

But the Tsar's brother and the Admiral-General of the Russian Fleet, Grand Duke Kotantine, was not to be denied. In March 1863 he persuaded Vice Admiral Mikhail Tebenkov to secretly go to the Confederate States of America, and encourage the Jefferson Davis Administration to purchase Russian America. He knew his history. He knew that, since the early days of Colonial America, it had been Southern families, of the Southern culture, who had primarily pioneered westward expansion. For the most part, Southern families had been the Nation Builders of North America. So, with ample charts and records stuffed in a large sea chest, and without telling fellow Board members what he was up to, Tebenkov set out for the Confederate States accompanied by an interpreter.

On May 21, 1863, Secretary of the Confederate Navy, Stephen Mallory met Russian Agent Vice Admiral Mikhail Tebenkov at the Montgomery train station and the two got to know each other that evening over dinner. Mallory was full of questions about Russian America, the

---

[174] In truthful history, prior to the secession of Southern states in 1860-61, seventy percent of the revenue financing the United States Federal Government had been derived from tariffs on goods imported into Southern States seaports, from Delaware to Texas. The loss of that revenue was, in truthful history, a major reason the Lincoln Administration had gone to war to conquer the Confederate States.

Company and the value of the furs, the fishing, the whaling and the mining. Where Mallory had questions, Tebenkov had answers. He had a sea chest full of answers. The next day President Davis was invited to participate in discussions. Toward the end of the meeting Tebenkov proposed that the Confederate States purchase Russian America.

President Davis's first response to the suggestion of purchase was this:

"Under the leadership of President Thomas Jefferson of Virginia, the former United States did purchase Louisiana Colony from France in 1803 and, later, did pay Mexico for its sparsely settled northern lands to ensure a favorable treaty settling its 1846-1848 war against them, but our Confederate States are strictly a union of sovereign States and it would be more fitting for Russian America to become an independent State, as had the Republic of Texas, and, following that, merge into the Confederacy by treaty. That was the path taken by the people of Texas. So, does the question not revolve around granting independence to Russian America? Perhaps the money you seek in compensation could be acquired as part of an independence settlement."

Secretary Mallory added:

"You can readily understand that the marine shipping capacity of the Russian American Company would be most helpful in continuing the economy and well-being of an independent Russian-speaking State."

Secretary Memminger then added:

"The Confederate Treasury should be able to back a financial settlement in support of creating an independent Republic of Russian America."

No more space is available in our book for reporting on this set of historic meetings at Montgomery, which historians would call the Russia-Montgomery Conference. But you now have a flavor of what transpired. Considerable credit for the warm display of cooperation and friendship goes to that sea chest of charts and documents that Agent Tebenkov brought along and his great knowledge of his subject, too often a rarity in salesmen, and also in diplomats that one encounters in the history of mankind. It was agreed that everything said at the meeting was said in secrecy to be discussed in America with no one else, except for Senator William Gwin who now represented Confederate California in the Confederate Senate.

You will recall that, since mid-1859 and the beginning of Jose Rezanov's term as Chief Manager of the Russian America Company, a Peoples Council of 21 representatives had been created to represent the interests of the settlers who were not Company employees. At the time of the historic Montgomery meeting, Aleksandr Yanovskii was Chief of the People's Council, which represented the people of the colony under the oversight of Chief Manager Jose Rezanov. You will also recall that Antipatr Yanovskiii owned a company involved in supplying fish to the Russian America Company's salmon cannery. Well, the Yanovskiii brothers, Aleksandr and Antipatr, decided to secretly form a committee to begin a secession movement, a group they referred to as the "Independence Committee." From Confederate Senator William Gwin they obtained a copy of the American Declaration of Independence, the original constitution of the Republic of Texas, the Texas State Constitution and the Confederate States Constitution as reference documents. Most important, the secret "Independence Committee" knew something that was unknown to Chief Manager Rezanov and to Saint Petersburg: there were large, easily recovered deposits of gold at the western extent of the colony, near a village called Nome. Given time, a few hundred independence seeking Russian American men and women could collect enough gold to purchase Russian America for themselves and their people.

Let us now catch up on Antipatr Baranov, 67, the son of the late Aleksandr Baranov and his Native wife. We now bring the story of Antipatr Baranov up to the present time of this history. You will recall that, at the age of 22, Antipatr had left Russian America with Vasilii Golovinin in 1818 to begin a career in the Russian Navy.

Antipatr Baranov remained aboard Vasilii Golovnin's ships until 1821, when the commander became assistant Director of the Russian Naval Academy. It was at that time that Antipatr became a student at the Academy and specialized in legal issues. Before long, Antipatr acquired a good understanding of law and reasonably good facility with the English language, having spent two years studying in England while on the Navy payroll. Retiring from the Navy in 1840, Antipatr took a job at the Russian America Company headquarters in Saint Petersburg as a law clerk. In 1851, he transferred to the New Archangel office. He retired in 1861, at the age of 65 years. Antipatr Baranov would be instrumental in translating and interpreting the Declarations and Constitutions supplied by Senator Gwin. And he would be an important contributor to the writing of the Declaration of Independence and the Provisional Constitution of the Republic of Russian America.

The Declaration was signed on Thursday, November 19, 1863. [175] Prominent signers were Aleksandr Yanovskiii, Antipatr Yanovskiii, Antipatr Baranov, Irina Baranova, Nikolai Rezanov, Rodion Rezanov, Fedor Ivanov and Jose Rezanov, the last also being the Chief Manager.

At this point the Declaration was secret, known only to the signers. The Independence Committee named four people to carry the Declaration to Saint Petersburg to present it to Tsar Alexander II and his government. The agents were Antipatr Baranov, son the man Saint Petersburg leaders recognized to have been the most important founder of the Russian America culture; Fedor Ivanov and his wife Anna Yanovskiii Ivanova, the young couple you recall having endured the invasion of Alta Californio by Americans under John Fremont; and Luis Antonia Rezanov, the Chief Manager's brother. The four secret agents discussed matters again with Confederate Senator William Gwin before departing New Archangel on Monday, November 23 for the new Russian port at the mouth of the Amur River in Manchuria. From there they travelled up the Amur on a steam-powered river boat for 1,750 miles until reaching Chita on the Shilka River, where they disembarked to take horse-drawn conveyance, mostly on winter-time sleighs, the remainder of the way to Saint Petersburg. The four secret agents arrived in the capital city two months after departing Russian America, on Tuesday, January 26, 1864.

On Friday, Antipatr Baranov managed to speak to the Russian Foreign Minister, Aleksandr Gorchakov, telling him that he had an important message from leaders in Russian America concerning the potential sale of the colony to a foreign power. Gorchakov suggested they meet later that day for a stroll in the park. This took place. Baranov told him that many important leaders in the colony were offering to reorganize the colony into an independent nation capable of ruling itself and of returning to the Russian Empire monetary compensation equivalent to what could be achieved through a sale, if the Crown would concur and agree to reasonable payment terms. By way of encouragement, Baranov submitted that their independence plan allowed the Russian culture to survive and continue in North America; allowed the Russian American Company to remain engaged in business there; allowed the Russian Orthodox Church to remain and continue serving the needs of the people; allowed the Crown to receive value equivalent to a land sale to a foreign power; gave the Russian Empire the opportunity to terminate its obligations

---

[175] In truthful history, on Thursday November 19, 1863, United States President Abraham Lincoln spoke a few words at the Federal's dedication of its military cemetary located near Gettysburg, Pennsylvania.

to supply and defend the colony, thereby enabling it to redirect those resources to the Amur River Valley and the Manchurian Pacific region, recently acquired; and, finally, allowed Tsar Alexsandr II to give independence to his North American colony, without war and killing, something the British and Spanish monarchies had failed to do in conflicts concerning their respective colonies. Baranov then concluded, stating: "In the years to come, long after the Crown is passed on and both you and I have gone to our reward, the people of Russia, the people of the world, will look on the history of this decision and praise your government for it. Granting independence is the honorable decision."

Well, for three days the Admiral-General of the Russian Fleet, Grand Duke Konstantine had been aware of Antipatr Baranov's arrival in Saint Petersburg and suspected involvement with an Independence Movement. So he had set a spy on Baranov's tail to observe. When the walk in the park with Foreign Minister Gorchakov was observed, Konstantine resolved to have Baranov thrown in jail while he investigated further.

When Antipatr Baranov failed to return that day, Luis Antonia Rezanov, told Fedor and Anna Ivanov to lay low and protect the Declaration of Independence documents while he sought to meet with Company President Frederick von Wrangell. Two days later Luis succeeded in meeting with von Wrangell and explaining Antipatr Baranov's mysterious disappearance. During the conversation it became apparent that von Wrangell knew a great deal about efforts in Saint Petersburg to sell Russian America, and that no one else in the Company or on the Board knew about it. The next day von Wrangell managed to get with Foreign Minister Aleksandr Gorchakov and to bring Luis Rezanov along. Now that was a tumultuous meeting! "Disappeared, I was just with Baranov walking in the park three days ago. Wonderful old man, such a great career was his, you know. And a half-blood, too." Well, within three days Baranov was found in jail and released, while Grand Duke Konstantine struggled to extricate himself from the debacle. This fuss became known to Tsar Aleksandr himself. He called in Gorchakov and Konstantine to explain what the fuss was all about. This resulted in the Tsar's decision to call before him the following day: his Foreign Minister, Aleksandr Gorchakov; his Admiral-General of the Russian Fleet, Grand Duke Konstantine; Vice Admiral Mikhail Tebenkov; Company President Frederick von Wrangell and the Chief Manager's brother Luis Antonia Rezanov, who was asked to bring along pertinent documents. With these five men and the pertinent documents before him, the Tsar gained a good understanding of the situation at New Archangel, at the Confederate States Capital of Montgomery, at Company headquarters in St. Petersburg, in his Foreign Office, and in his Navy. After three hours of debate he asked if anyone could justify selling the colony to a foreign power, given the opportunity to gain the same objectives and more through a transition to an Independent Russian America. Of the few replies offered, all were feeble and unconvincing. The Tsar then pronounced the meeting concluded and asked Foreign Minister Gorchakov to seek out the Confederate States Minister to the Russian Empire and invite him to an audience with the Crown.

The Confederate States Minister to the Russian Empire was Thomas Watts, 45, of Alabama, who had held the Confederate Cabinet office of Attorney General before becoming the Confederate Minister to Russia in anticipation of helping the independence movement.

Confederate Minister Thomas Watts, Independence Agent Antipatr Baranov and Foreign Minister Aleksandr Gorchakov met with Tsar Aleksandr at the appointed time. Baranov presented the Declaration of Independence with all of the signatures. The Tsar asked, "Is my Chief Manager of Russian America, Jose Rezanov, a party to this demand for independence? My God, he could be hung for treason!" Baranov replied, "Yes, he has signed, while faithfully carrying out the duties of the Chief Manager's office. At that time, on that very day, he signed his letter of resignation and asked me to bring it to you, to hand it to you at the same time that I delivered the Declaration of Independence. Here is Chief Manager Rezanov's letter of resignation. He is now considered resigned." Tsar Aleksandr asked, "How much money can the government of an Independent Republic gather up as payment and how will you be able to do that?" Baranov replied, "We feel confident, that by a vigorous effort at mining our natural resources, we can gather up as much as two million in Confederate dollars each year. Would your Honor be satisfied with an overall payment of eight million dollars?" The meeting continued for several hours. At the end, Confederate Minister Thomas Watts pledged that he had been informed that his government would guarantee a payment in five years of up to eight million dollars.

The Tsar asked, "Mr. Baranov, your father, although small of stature, was a giant among the men who led the development of our distant colony. To him we all owe a great deal. But I cannot grant independence through you or the Independence Committee you represent, I can only grant independence to an established government. Can you provide evidence of that?" Baranov replied, "While my friends and I were traveling west across the Pacific and Asia, leaders of our Independence Movement were drafting a Constitution of the Republic of Russian America. It was taken by ship to Los Angeles and by pony express to Texas. From there the text of it was transmitted by telegraph to Montgomery, to New York, to London and to Saint Petersburg, where it was delivered to the Confederate Embassy. I now have it and submit to you that it is as fine and fair a construction for a modern government that has been created by man. With your permission, your honor, allow me to give this copy to your Foreign Minister for his evaluation. We of the Independence Movement pray that the Crown will find our proposed government worthy of representing the people of what we hope will be your former colony. We will soon have names associated with the offices authorized by our provisional Constitution."

So Aleksandr had the facts before him and saw clearly that the honorable decision was to grant independence and rely on the Confederate States to make sure the experiment was successful, at least successful to the extent that the Russian Empire would receive its money. As Antipatr Baranov turned to leave, the Tsar asked, "And just where are the settlers going to find all that gold?" The reply: "They have found some, but will have to find much more. Yet, they remain confident. Russian America is a really, really vast land." Foreign Minister Gorchakov remained behind for a bit. The Tsar exclaimed, "Have I just agreed to give away for a mere eight million dollars a colony worth many times more, a land plentiful in gold? Repeatedly, I have been told by Company officials that very little gold has been found since that strike at Gold Creek." Gorchakov replied, "Mostly, plentiful in ice, permafrost and snow, your honor. But the essence of the issue is that we cannot defend the colony against future "Manifest Destiny" zealots. We desperately need to divert Russian military resources away from that colony and to the greater needs in the Amur Valley and the Manchurian Pacific coast. If a lot of gold is discovered in Russian America, men from the United States will invade and take it for themselves. We cannot defend against that." The Tsar concluded, "In that reasoning, my friend, you are right. Our priority must be in Asia. But I want all of the eight million dollars this year. Tell Confederate Minister Thomas Watts that we will grant independence to Russian America if the Confederate Government will pay us $8,000,000 in gold within six months. President Davis can bargain with the independence leaders of Russian America to be reimbursed on whatever terms his government will accept. But St. Petersburg wants the gold very soon, within six months."

Thomas Watts cabled Montgomery that very day. President Davis and his Cabinet deliberated. The big question was "where is all that gold?" The Cabinet wanted to know that the gold would be readily gathered up, but realized that secrecy was needed to prevent a horde of prospectors racing north after it. Davis summoned Senator William Gwin, who represented Confederate California in the Confederate Senate, and asked him in secret, "Where will the Independence Committee of Russian America gather up $8,000,000 is gold?"

Gwin motioned to Davis to join him on a walk outside, away from everyone. Then he answered, "The gold is in a far northwestern region called Nome. Lots of gold. Easy to gather from stream beds. We only have to keep that location secret from the world at large until $8,000,000 worth is gathered up."

Davis had one more question. "Bill, what is Russian America worth to our Confederacy?"

The answer: "In the decades ahead, Mr. President, one hundred times that much."

The Cabinet agreed to an $8,000,000 loan to be paid in five years. It would only take four years to pay it off.

So, the decision was essentially made to grant independence to the colony of Russian America through the government of the people, for the people and by the people, as perceived within the construction of the provisional Constitution. There would be a President and Vice President, a House of 23 and a Senate of 11, and a hierarchy of courts ranging from magistrates to a supreme court. The President's Cabinet would consist of six positions: State, Treasury, Attorney General, Postmaster, National Guard, and Navy. The male electorate would be divided into three classes: of Pure European Blood, of Part Blood, and of Native Blood. Every male 21 years or older would be entitled to vote, in near-term elections, but at some future time it was planned that only tax-payers could vote in elections for the Senate. In the House 9 seats would be reserved for Pure Bloods, 7 for Part Bloods and 7 for Natives. In the Senate 5 seats would be reserved for Pure Bloods, 3 for Part Bloods and 3 for Natives.

Back in Russian America, the first election was held in mid-April 1864. In early May a joint session of the House and Senate elected Jose Rezanov to the office of President and, for Vice President, Timofei Kavanskii, a Part Blood from the colony's main agricultural region who was popular with the Natives. By the first of June 1864, President Rezanov had completed appointing his Cabinet and the Senate had confirmed them. The Secretary of State, Aleksandr Yanovskiii, had an important role to play. He appointed Antipatr Baranov to be the Minister to the Russian Empire, which was fortunate in that the elder Baranov had remained in Saint Petersburg.

The government of Tsar Aleksandr II granted independence to its colony of Russian America in August, 1864, and the ceremony commemorating the historic event took place at New Archangel on October 18, 1864. The Russian Flag came down and the Russian American Flag went up. A small delegation of Confederate officials witnessed the event. It would be their job to take gold worth $1,250,000 back to Montgomery, the first installment of the total of $8,000,000 owed. [176]

---

[176] In truthful history the United States purchased Russian America for $7,200,000, a deal arranged between Russian minister Edouard de Stoeckl and Secretary of State William Seward of New York, with a treaty signing on March 30, 1867. Senator Charles Sumner of Massachusetts, Chairman of the Senate Foreign Relations Committee, invented the name "Alaska," and it stuck. Many Americans opposed the deal, especially in the eastern States, and called it "Seward's Folly." Transfer of ownership from the Russian Empire to the United States took place at New Archangel when Major General Jefferson C. Davis (not to be confused with the Confederate President) arrived with 250 soldiers supported by two supply ships to take military control of the vast land. The harbor was already full of Company ships preparing to evacuate men and materials:

New Archangel "was already jammed with people, men, women, and children having come in from all parts of the colony with tons of baggage. There were the officials and their families, who, together with a number in the capital, were scheduled to leave directly Russian rule was over. The exodus would begin with the departure of the ship being readied for sailing to the Baltic. The town was filled with the sound of hammering and sawing as crates and boxes were made for the shipping of pianos, books, clothing, and other personal belongings."

Where did that gold come from? Well it came from the beaches and creeks in the far western coast of the new nation, in the vicinity of a place called Nome. The existence of this gold strike, known for over two years, was a secret, and the hundreds of miners engaged in the panning and recovery were mostly Natives, folks who could be trusted to keep quiet. A footnote is appropriate: the Russian American Company had for many years pursued a policy of keeping the location of gold deposits secret, discouraging gold rush fever in hopes of keeping its employees focused on the fur and whale oil business, and preventing California prospectors from getting a whiff of the prized yellow metal. [177]

In spite of its low population, the Republic of Russian America would later, in 1870, transform itself into a State to be merged into the Confederate States.

### Selected Friday Evening Selected Diary Postings

Diary note by Isaiah Montgomery said, "Supper with Amanda Washington. Of the twelve, only she and I have African ancestors, so we talked about how hard was the life of distant cousins who remain in our native continent. I asked her if she planned to ever visit West Africa or the Congo? She said, in fact that she was hoping to arrange it. Said school grants are available to fund trips to West Africa. She wants to apply for one at Virginia College for Negro Education -- I find that old-fashion name amusing. That is where she is working on her Ph. D. It's in Lynchburg, Virginia. Says the trip would be essential for research she needs for her Ph. D. thesis: 'A Comparative Study of the Reading Capabilities of Confederate and West African Negroes.' I can't believe it! She actually said that the grants included a companion to accompany her on the trip. Me. Me. Me." [178]

Diary note by Amanda Washington said, "I think I have found the perfect companion for the West Africa research trip I am planning – Isaiah Montgomery. Two years older at 27 years, Isaiah already has such depth of experience in managing Colored-owned agricultural operations along the Mississippi River, as part of Mound Bayou Corporate Plantation. I am a city girl. If I pair up with a Black corporate farmer when in West Africa, my research will be greatly improved -- gives the team far better balance. Furthermore, Isaiah is from a long line of cotton farmers. He is a man of the soil; farming is in his soul. But there is another reason to be excited about this idea. Isaiah is a rugged and handsome former football quarterback. There may be some romance

---

[177] The truthful history is very different and very sad. On October 18, 1867, the Russian representative, Captain Aleksei Peshchurov, and the American representative, Brigadier-General Lovell Rousseau, played out the ceremony. "To the beat of their drums, under the command of Peshchurov, the 90 sailors and the 180 soldiers from a Siberian regiment who made up the garrison of the town marched up to the . . . flagstaff flying the imperial emblem." From the ships came Rousseau and Davis with his 250 troops. The Russian flag was lowered and the American flag was raised. Cannon salutes followed. Davis was now in command and he immediately took over the barracks belonging to the Siberians. The Americans quickly renamed the capital town of New Archangel, for the name reminded them of the Russian people who had pioneered the land. Thereafter, it was to be called simply "Sitka."

Very little of the Russian culture remained. The most noticeable remnant of its past existence is what remained of the Russian Orthodox Church. The Russian church would send funds to Alaska for fifty more years, as part of a missionary organization established by Ioann Veniaminov, following his elevation to Metropolitan of Moscow. Church fathers in Alaska would maintain orphanages and seventeen schools. Even by 1887 the Russian Church spent more on schooling than the United States Government. But, by and large, the American military occupation of Alaska destroyed what had been a vibrant culture of three peoples, Russians, Part-Bloods and Natives, a diverse population that got along remarkably well.

[178] What Isaiah meant was "only she and I have African ancestors that we know to exist." None of the other ten essayists had any African ancestry of which they knew, but slight traces of ancestry from sub-Sahara Africa unknowingly exist in the DNA makeup of many people in the Confederacy today in situations where the extent is slight and not readily noticeable. The reader might want to consult *Understanding Creation and Evolution* by Howard Ray White, and *DNA USA: A Genetic Portrait of America* by Bryan Sykes.

here. But I do have trouble thinking of myself in future years living on a Mississippi cotton farm. Well, time for night-night."

Diary note by Emma Lunalilo said, "Had supper with Marie Saint Martin, one of the novice sailors. Boy, did we have a lot to talk about! . . . . She gushed over my heroics as so many have. But, diary, I need to tell you about this lovely 23-year-old lady. She is quite the singer. Has her own New Orleans-style jazz band back home, and she is so excited about getting a music group together here in Sewanee to liven up the place. She has created a music group from five among the Sewanee Project. Allen Ross and Carlos Cespedes are playing guitar and singing. Amanda Washington is playing piano and singing harmony. Professor Davis is playing banjo. Right after supper they got together in the faculty lounge and several others on our team just sat in chairs and listened. They hope to get together again Saturday morning. . . . . But what about Monday morning? Marie advised me to expect that the group's "great admiration" would fall on my shoulders on Monday because Professor Davis will lecture on Hawaii, Our Pacific State. She said that Conchita Rezanov was eager to hand the torch to me. Hawaii does not have a bigger than life hero similar to the Mexican States or Russian America. We Lunalilo's should be able to retain our humility."

Diary note by Allen Ross said, "I will be off caving with Robert Lee in the morning. Have gathered up a helmet, good boots, blue jeans and an old smallish back pack. Robert said he had everything else we would need. Big saltpeter cave about two counties away. We will use my pick-up truck. . . . Had supper tonight with Tina Sharp, the nuclear engineer. She said she loved my gift of bison steaks last Saturday. We are quite different. My career points toward managing a vast bison ranch and directing the crew under me. Her career points toward managing some phase of a complex nuclear power plant and directing engineers and technical people under her. I will be concerned with weather (like drought and blizzards), keeping stout bison fences in repair, breeding choices, harvesting the meat and getting it to market at good prices. Her career points to concerns with some important phase of nuclear reactor operation, maintenance, safe shutdown capabilities and designs relating to those issues. She is part of a very large team, many highly educated and proficient at complex technical issues. And decisions are based on inputs from many others. By comparison, I almost work alone and make decisions alone -- my team will never exceed 20 men, almost all Native American fellows. I am just a glorified cowboy who tends big burley bison instead of more easily managed beef cattle. But she liked my bison steaks. She will have more before we wrap up this adventure on the evening of our 150th Anniversary. But for me, it is off to Big Bone Cave in the morning."

# Part 2, Chapter 3, Days 13 and 14 – The Second Weekend and a Caving Trip - - Saturday and Sunday, June 18 and 19, 2011

## Big Bone Cave, Saturday, June 18

Robert Lee packed the caving gear into Allen Ross's pickup truck and the pair of cave explorers were off to Big Bone Cave by 7: 30 Saturday morning. Just down the road at Monteagle, the cavers discussed the coming trip over a full breakfast of country ham biscuits, eggs, grits, orange juice and coffee. Cavers need a full course breakfast.

Alan asked, "So, Robert, where is this Big Bone Cave?"

"It's in Van Buren County, an hour and a half drive. We go down off the Cumberland Plateau from here, taking the expressway northwest, in the direction of Nashville, until we reach Manchester. Then we leave the expressway, heading northeast to McMinnville. We'll pass through a very small town called Bone Cave. The cave is under Bone Cave Mountain, a little further to the northeast, off Bone Cave Mountain Road."

"If most everything nearby is called Bone Cave seems like every inch of it will be fully explored and mapped by now. Lots of cavers must have been there by now,"

"Well, Alan, the story of Bone Cave is rather long. Lots of men were in the cave during the War of 1812 and during the first few years of our Confederacy. They were there digging up the dirt, hauling it to wooden vats, pouring water over it, collecting the nitrate-rich liquor below the vat, hauling that outside to cast iron pots and boiling the liquor to concentrate it and recover the nitrate to make gun powder. They called the recovered nitrate, "saltpeter." Miners worked inside the cave by torch light. It was a highly developed operation back then. As long as the main cave passages provided plenty of nitrate-rich dirt, no need to explore deeper. Anyway, torches burn out and leave you in the dark. Dark is bad. A caver lost in the dark in a big cave might die before he is found. But today we will take with us a variety of dependable lights."

"Why is the dirt in Bone Cave exceptionally rich in nitrates?"

"Bats, millions of them over thousands of years. But bats do not use the cave now. Too dry for them. But the dropping from long ago, when the cave was not so dry remains. All those bat droppings became guano and guano is rich in nitrates. The cave is very dry because surface water does not seep down into the Monteagle limestone from which it has been carved. We will be wearing dust masks like folks wear to ward off dust when sanding or spray painting."

"It must have been hard mining and leaching the soil during 1812 through 1814 and during 1861 and 1862 to recover saltpeter. When did miners get access to better lights than pine torches?"

"Allen, you are about to be impressed, for I know the answer to that bit of historical detail. When water is dripped onto calcium carbide, acetylene gas is released, which, as you probably have observed, burns with a bright flame. In 1892, Thomas Wilson invented a commercial method for producing calcium carbide. In 1902, Frederick Baldwin invented the miner's carbide lamp, compact enough for a miner to comfortably wear on his helmet so the light pointed wherever he looked. So, miners in 1862 had to wait 40 years to get a carbide lamp. That technology was a major boost to the underground mining industry. Today we use electric lights powered by lithium batteries. Don't weigh much, so we can carry along a large backup supply of them."

"What's the story behind the 'big bone'?"

"Well, Alan, during the saltpeter leaching activity in support of the War of 1812, a fellow discovered the bones of a giant ground sloth in the cave, preserved by the dry conditions. It was taken to the Academy of Natural Sciences in Philadelphia. Even today, it represents the only known specimen of a giant ground sloth with a complete pelvis. Turn right here, that road will take us to McMinnville."

"How big is this cave?"

"Really do not know, Allen. It's been closed off to caver's since 1919, and there is a story about that. Big Bone Mountain has been owned by the Barlow family for 200 years of so, since settlers first crossed the Cumberland Plateau into Middle Tennessee. They gave permission to recover saltpeter during the War of 1812 and during the defense of the Confederate States because then access to more economical nitrate sources was closed off and demand was urgent. After about 1870, recovering saltpeter from the cave was too labor-intensive to be economical, so the Barlow's told folks to keep out of the cave. Anyway, it was a Barlow that had discovered the "big bone" and he did not want other people going into the cave and messing around with the history of the place. Later, another Barlow worked on an archeological dig in the entrance area of the cave to recover Native American artifacts and to record how they had lived some 5,000 years ago. So that Barlow decided to keep folks out who might disturb the archeological site. To enforce that decision, they build a ten-foot masonry wall across the cave entrance."

"But that wall did not keep Susie Barlow out of the cave one day when she was determined to keep away from an abusive sweetheart. Lover-boy had threatened her with bodily harm if she did not submit to his advances. Determined to escape, Susie grabbed some food, water, clothing, matches, three torches and a 10-foot ladder and snuck off to the cave. No one knew what she was doing. She used the ladder to get her stuff and herself over the wall, then pulled the ladder up to the other side and began to hide out there. But lover-boy, spotting some tracks leading toward the cave, suspected she might be hiding there. He got a ladder and came after her the next day. Susie heard him coming and ran deeper into the cave with her matches and torches. He followed her, but could not reach her. She got deeper and deeper into the cave, into it for about a half mile or so. Lover-boy got scared and left. He not only left the cave, he left Van Buren County never to return. Tragedy struck. Susie's torches gave out and she became stranded in the pitch black darkness of the cave. She was lost. She must have crawled around here and there for a few days. She eventually died of thirst. It was two months later that the Barlow's found their dear Susie. From that point forward they declared the cave haunted. No one could go in unless on real important business. To keep folks out, the wall was extended to the roof of the cave entrance except for a five by ten foot opening to let the bats in and out. That opening was covered with cast iron bars spaced ten inches apart. Only bats could go through it. Of course there was a padlocked steel door placed in the wall so that the Barlow's could give access when they wanted to. They are going to let us through that door this morning."

"Barley Barlow and I were roommates while I worked toward my Master's degree at the Calhoun School of Government Studies in Athens, Georgia. He told me about the haunted "Big Bone Cave" on the family property and I told him about my many adventures exploring caves in Alabama and Tennessee. He said that, as a special friend, he would ask the family to give me permission to enter the cave to explore the farthest reaches of the passages. That, Alan, is what we are going to do today."

"Do you have a plan to search out a particular section?"

Yes, Alan, I have a plan based on a tip I recently received from a friend. Will tell you about that later. We are now leaving McMinnville; turn right ahead."

We next visit these eager cavers at the Barlow farmhouse.

The elder Mr. Barlow opens the door and says, "You must be the cavers that Barley asked me to let into the cave. Said to tell you he is sorry that he had to be away from home this weekend. You young fellows are mighty lucky to get this chance to explore the Big Bone, few are allowed in, you know."

Robert expressed his thanks and his disappointment at missing a chance to see Barley. Then Mr. Barlow climbed into his truck and led the cavers to the end of the dirt road, within a hundred yards of the cave entrance. Robert and Alan grabbed their caving gear, Mr. Barlow grabbed the key to the lock on the cave entrance gate and all three walked up the hill. At the entrance, Mr. Barlow unlocked the steel gate and said, "Fellows, I am going to lock it again and pass you the key. No need for you to knock on the door and give it back. Just put it under that rock outside the cave, over there and I will pick it up in a couple of days. Enjoy your adventure. So long." And Mr. Barlow drove away.

Robert and Alan put on their heavy caving shirts and gloves, adjusted their backpacks, put on their helmets, hid the key just inside the cave, turned on the lights on their helmets, continued into the cave, and slowly adjusted their eyesight. Within less than 100 yards, Alan exclaimed, "Look at those wooden vats full of cave dirt. They are still here in good condition. It's like we are transported in time back 150 years." Robert replied, "Just like photos I have seen. The preservation is amazing." Further on Robert pointed upward and said, "Look at those wooden rails supported by beams wedged between the two walls. Those were for the dirt transport carts. Diggers further in the cave filled carts with fresh dirt and pushed them onto that railroad and towed them forward to dump the contents into one of these leaching vats." Alan added, "Good engineering. And the rails are still here. . . . There is one of the carts to our left." Robert pointed to wooden poles suspended between the pair of rails. "See those poles, long and straight, one connected to the other, end to end. The poles are bored out the full length to create pipes that are connected end-to-end to carry water to the leaching vats. Much of that is still here after 150 years, too." One end is tapered on the outside and the other is tapered on the inside so the poles can be connected end to end to create a long continuous pipeline. A plug could be removed every so often to dump water into a selected vat, in dripping fashion I presume. Then, all that was left to do was to gather the nitrate-rich water into buckets at the bottom of the vat and haul them outside to the boiling pots to concentrate the saltpeter." [179]

After taking some photos and further inspecting the saltpeter works in the cave passages, the cavers proceeded further to explore further into the cave. Alan asked, "When we were passing through Manchester you mention a plan you had for exploring a certain part of this cave. What is that plan, friend? Where are you taking me today?"

OK, Alan, it is time. We are well equipped with dust masks, gloves and knee pads. Alan we are going to be doing a lot of crawling on our hands and knees. Here is a sketch I received from my caving friend who lives in Nashville, name of Chuck Smith. He and a caving buddy had received permission to explore the cave about 8 months ago. They were in a small dead end branch passage room in the cave, about a quarter mile in from the entrance when they started digging out some rocks. When they detected a flow of fresh air they suspected a continuation and dug more and more. In about an hour they had opened the passage enough to squeeze through. It opened up as they progressed, but only sufficient to crawl on hands and knees. Well they crawled and crawled and crawled. After two hours they came to a little wider place and there decided to turn around and head back out. No dust mask; worn out gloves, no knee pads. In fact their knees

---

[179] The description of Big Bone Cave and the Saltpeter works is truthful history. The writer has been there and can vouch for it.

were getting raw. Had enough. Might come back another day. While crawling they could tell that no one had ever crawled through that passage. It was virgin cave."

"Virgin cave?"

We cavers call a cave passage "virgin" when it is apparent that no human has ever preceded us. A human cannot move through a dry, dusty cave without leaving a trace of having done so."

"Alan, are you a good crawler?"

"Mom and Dad said I was a demon at crawling before I learned to walk."

"You look lean and fit. I figure you to be a good crawler. Let's use this diagram to find the place that Chuck discovered last year."

And that is what Robert and Alan did. They found the opening into a small crawlway passage and arranged their equipment for the anticipated long day's crawl. They lightened up their packs, leaving one behind, while taking only the essentials: a half-gallon of water, four extra batteries for head lamps and four chocolate bars. We pick up the conversation an hour into the crawling.

Robert asks, "How you doing back there Alan?"

"Still back here, just behind you. Have we reached the point where Chuck turned around?"

"Not yet. Time for a ten minute break some water and half a chocolate bar each"

We again pick up the conversation one hour later:

Robert exclaims, "Hey. Here it where Chuck and friend turned around. Beyond this bit of wider space is virgin cave. We are about to become the first humans to enter the continuing passage."

"More crawling I presume?"

"We take another break before proceeding. Knees OK?"

"Knees OK. The pads fit well."

After a total of three hours of crawling, the passage changed dramatically. Cavers Robert and Alan were able to walk in a crouched style. Two hundred feet further they could walk upright. Not much further Robert announced an amazing discovery:

"Alan, we are no longer in virgin cave. This passage must be ten feet wide and twenty feet high. Humans have walked through here before. Several of them. Carrying torches. But look, the foot prints are covered with a light dusting of soot. The people who came through here last preceded the smoking condition prevalent during the salt peter mining work of 1861 through 1863. We sure as Hell know that these folks had not crawled through the passage we have come through. And we sure as Hell know that this soot had not travelled through that long, long crawlway either. Alan, I believe we have entered into another cave system that folks long ago accessed through a different entrance, an entrance from the outside long since covered up to hide it from view."

Cavers Robert and Alan then proceeded to explore the "new cave" they had discovered in hopes of finding evidence of what they suspected had to be a covered up "new entrance" from the outside. The "new cave" passages branched off in several directions making the features more interesting than the Big Bone cavethey had left when they had begun the big crawl. Yet smoke from the 1860's had deposited a thin but perceptible soot color all over the dusty, dry dirt floor covering the foot prints that had been laid down one hundred and fifty years earlier, or perhaps even before that time. And everywhere they stepped, they created a new footprint which so disturbed the soot layer that it disappeared, revealing the red-brown dusty dirt as before. "This is neat," Alan said, "we can follow our tracks back to where we have come just like walking on new-fallen snow."

And on the explorers walked. Before long, Alan mentioned to Robert, "Your headlamp seems to be getting dimmer. Time to change the battery?" Robert replied, "We have several in the backpack you are carrying for us. I'll get a little more use on this battery and then we will sit down, take a rest break, have some water and chocolate, and do a battery change.

They had explored their discovery for a full hour when they arrived at place within the maze of passages where some maneuvering was required. The floor had risen perhaps fifteen feet, bringing them much closer to the roof of the passage. To the left was an opening in the floor that fell away into a narrow tight canyon, a deeper place, too narrow to climb down into. Above was the passage roof. They were back in crawl mode, but, looking out ahead as far as Alan's head lamp showed, the passage seemed to enlarge again. So the cavers were again on their hands and knees.

That is when tragedy struck. It was so stupid, too. How could cavers be so stupid?

Robert had taken off the backpack containing all the water and batteries in preparation for the crawl maneuver around the narrow canyon that dropped down from the floor and below the passage roof. In making that simple maneuver, Alan lost his grip on the backpack and cried out as he saw it fall into the narrow tight canyon. He reached after it, thrusting his arm and head after it, but it had fallen away too fast.

Cavers come prepared to handle two disasters without difficulty, perhaps not as often three. Losing the pack was the first disaster. The second immediately followed: In lunging down head first into the narrow tight canyon after the pack, Alan's head lamp crashed against the wall and broke free of his helmet, falling into the canyon, chasing the pack to well beyond reach. Everything critical to their survival was in that pack: all the spare batteries, all the flashlights, and all the water. Everything had been placed in the pack to make the long crawl more comfortable. No spare batteries or small flashlights had been stuffed into pants pockets upon reaching the walking passages as would have been normal caving practice. Too excited about the discovery to think about distributing those critical resources. "Shit."

Were Robert and Alan about to face that dreaded third disaster? After repeated exclamations of "Shit" and similar curses over "stupidity". The two sat down to plan for their retreat from the cave. The key was to reach the crawlway before Robert's head lamp gave out.

They proceeded immediately to retrace their steps. But Alan was prone to stumble in the dim light from Robert's lamp and progress became necessarily cautious. They had backtracked through some branches in the passage maze causing them to miss the most direct route a couple of times. Dimmer still the light. Eventually it went out. Total pitch black darkness surrounded the cavers.

Robert tried to take the blame for the disaster, telling Alan, "It's all my fault. I should have made sure that we distributed our supplies when we resumed walking. I always carry spare lights in my pockets. Headlamps can break and packs can be lost. I should have known better. Just got caught up in the excitement of the discovery." Then Robert proposed a plan.

"Alan, I left a note with the second pack at the entrance to the crawlway. When we are missed, a rescue party will be organized and come searching for us. When they find the note, they will enter the crawlway and keep on coming until they find us. This is Saturday, mid-afternoon. We will not be missed until Monday morning at breakfast. The rescue party will be organized later in the morning and enter the cave Monday mid-day at the earliest. It may take them four hours to find that pack, then another three to get to us. So we are looking at 55 hours or so to survive here in the cold dark cave. Let us bed down in a comfortable spot in the dirt floor and lie close together to preserve body heat and conserve body fluids. Get some shut-eye and pray for the best. Make sure your long sleeve shirt is buttoned up tight and your clothing is as warm as you can make it. Then we lie down together." And that is what they did. That is where we leave this story as of now.

## Sunday Evening Selected Diary Postings

Diary note by Professor Davis said, "Tonight I was told that no one has seen Robert Lee or Allen Ross this evening. That's odd. They went caving Saturday morning and should have been back, Saturday night or today at the latest. But they are grown men and Robert is experienced at caving. Must assume it will turn out OK. But if they are not at breakfast Monday, I am going into rescue mode. I hope I can sleep."

Diary note by Tina Sharp said, "Real worried that no one has seen Robert or Allen today. I just check Allen's room. No answer when I knock. Marie is worried, too."

Diary note by Conchita Rezanov said, "I checked with Andrew and others. No one seems to have seen Robert or Allen today. Thought they would be back for Sunday supper or not long after that. Will have to send experienced men after them if they are not back by breakfast. Are they still down in that cave? Goodness. I just said a prayer for them. God be with them tonight."

## Part 2, Chapter 4, Day 15 – The Story of Hawaii and How It became a Confederate State – Class Lecture, Monday, June 20, 2011

### Rescue

Robert Lee and Alan Ross, the desperate, chilled cavers, still lay close together sharing warmth, deep in Big Bone Cave, in a dark passage not traveled by humans for the previous one hundred fifty years.

Meanwhile, back topside in Sewanee, Professor Davis and ten of the twelve gathered for breakfast. Two were missing. After about ten minutes, Davis remarked, "Does anyone know where Robert and Alan are?" Several responses suggested there might be a serious problem. "They went cave exploring Saturday morning." "They took Alan's truck." "Have not seen either since then." "Has anybody seen the truck?" "Caving might be exhausting, perhaps they overslept." "I heard talk of Big Bone Cave."

Professor Davis rose from his chair and said, "I have heard enough. I am leaving right here on this breakfast table the notes I intended to use this morning for the lecture on Hawaii. Emma, I am asking you to take over for me and lead this morning's history class. I want two among you to accompany me now. We are going to see about Robert and Alan right away. Volunteers? Several hands went up. "Conchita, Isaiah, let's go." And off they went.

Professor Davis quickly handed out two assignments: "Isaiah, go to Robert's room and Alan's room and knock on the door real loud. If you get no answer, search for Alan's truck. Then wait for Conchita. Conchita, go over there to the administration building and hand them this note asking for keys to Robert's room and Alan's room and bring them to Isaiah so that, if they are not in their rooms, you all can unlock the doors and search for clues. I will be making telephone calls and getting my truck ready for the three of us to head off. They had mentioned Big Bone Cave, is that right?"

The telephone rang at Cumberland Caverns and Roy Wilson answered. "Roy, this is Joe Davis up at Sewanee. There may be a caving accident. Only know that two of my young people went caving at Big Bone Cave Saturday morning and have not returned as expected by this morning. Can you help?"

Roy replied, "Sorry to hear that Joe, hope the wife and kids are well. OK. This is what I will do first. I will call the Barlow farmhouse and see what they know. They do not allow anyone into that cave without permission and it is seldom that permissions are ever given. The entrance is fenced off and they hold the key to the gate. Will call you back soon. Keep at the ready."

Fortunately, Mr. Barlow was at the farmhouse telephone when it rang and told Roy that he would hop in his truck and look into the situation at the cave entrance.

Fifteen minutes later Joe's cell phone rang. "Joe, this is Roy. Mr. Barlow confirmed that he had let two cavers through the cave entrance door Saturday morning and he just now discovered that their truck was still near the cave, the access door remained locked, and the key was not under the rock just outside the entrance as instructed. Mr. Barlow is sure those two have been in the cave since Saturday morning. He was almost sobbing when he told me, "Roy, this seems terrible. It seems like a rerun of the tragedy that befell our dear Susie so many years ago. Please send help. I am going to get the spare key."

With that Joe and Roy devised a plan. Roy would call hearty, experience cavers Roy knew in Nashville and ask for volunteers to grab their equipment and head for the Nashville airport. Joe said he would call the appropriate people to arrange for two helicopters to fly the rescue team from the airport to a grassy pasture on the Barlow farm. He also notified the Van Buren County sheriff's department. Then he rounded up Conchita and Isaiah and headed down off the Cumberland Plateau toward Manchester, McMinnville and the Barlow farm.

"What did you all see in Robert's and Alan's rooms?" Conchita replied, "We brought their diaries. It mentions the cave trip, but gives no clues beyond what we already know." The three were at the Barlow farmhouse about 80 minutes later. Roy Wilson and a caving friend, being closer, had been able to get there faster. They had been looking around in the cave for about twenty minutes.

Twenty-five minutes later, two helicopters arrived with four of those hardy experienced cavers from the Nashville Grotto of the National Speleological Society. These four soon disappeared into the darkness of the cave, carrying along some hot chocolate and blankets provided by Mr. Barlow and his wife.

"What can we do, asked Conchita?" Professor Davis made the decision. "We three will remain topside preparing whatever might be useful. Let's prepare more food and drink and bring it to the entrance. After over 48 hours, if we are lucky, we will find them lost in the cave, stranded without any light and suffering from cold, thirst and hunger. They will need to be revived from that before they will be able to come out on their own. It may not require simple walking. The journey may be rather arduous. We do not know."

Conchita lamented, "Oh, I hope it will be no worse; that neither have fallen, broken bones or worse. Professor Davis, I really like Robert Lee and I want to tell him that. So badly do I want to tell him that!"

Meanwhile, deep in the cave, about an hour later, one of the rescue team who had arrived by helicopter discovered the pack left by Robert and Alan at the entrance to the long, long crawlway. They were so thankful that a pack was left behind, for no rescuer would have thought it would be in such an obscure crawlway that the cavers had ventured. But most important, Robert's note was found on the pack:

"Saturday, June 18, 2011. Robert Lee and Alan Ross entered this crawlway passage at noon intending to find the end of it."

This was the spot! Roy chose three of the fittest and youngest of the rescue team, got out knee pads and dust masks, and made sure each had two backup lights, extra batteries, a police whistle, and lots of water. Then he devised for each a drag-behind pack stuffed with blankets, chocolate bars, hot coffee, and soup, the latter having just arrived through the efforts of Joe, Conchita and Isaiah. Very soon, the three were off on a long crawl in search of whatever turned up.

Two hours passed. Roy and his assistant manned the post at the beginning of the crawlway. Having heard no news from within, a caver had long ago walked back to the cave entrance to tell the news of the note and the plan forward. Conchita, almost in tears, exclaimed, "Thank God, Thank God, a note!" She asked, "I am no use here. Can I go into the cave to where the note was found and wait there? I have boots and suitable clothes. Just need a helmet and lights." She got the affirmative nod, got the provisions, plus more coffee in a thermos, and followed the messenger caver back the half-mile trek to the site of the note.

Conchita did not know it, but about the time she arrived at the entrance to the crawlway, the three hardy rescue cavers heard a cry, seemingly in response to the blowing of the police whistle.

"Help!" "Over Here!" Those cries were faint, but reassuring. The fresh footprints in the soot tainted dusty cave dirt gave a hint at where to go, but bothersome passage choices abounded, and the "Help" cry weeded out most. About fifteen minutes later they converged on Robert and Alan, lying on the cave floor embracing each other to conserve body heat.

"Thank God!" moaned Robert. But Alan was too far gone to talk – speechless and shivering from the accumulation of cold and lack of food and water. "I am not so bad off," Robert said. "But Alan is in desperate need of help – water; food; blankets; rubdown, everything you have."

And the rescue team proceeded accordingly. Two picked up Alan and placed him in the middle of a blanket. They took off his boots, added additional socks to his feet and got into the blanket beside him as if he was the hot dog and they were the bun. With the blanket wrapped around the three of them, the rescuers began the rubdown while the third fed Alan hot coffee through a straw and placed small bits of chocolate into his mouth. Special attention was given to wrapping the blanket around his head.

While Alan was receiving this extreme revival therapy, Robert managed to sit up, on a blanket, and wrap it around his body. The third rescuer took off Robert's boots, gave him some coffee and chocolate and commenced to apply a rubdown, concentrating on the legs and feet, where cold becomes most acute during times of hyperthermia, saying, "Don't bother to tell us how you lost your lights. That can come later. For now, just realize that both of you are going to be OK, and focus on regaining your strength. Take the nourishment. It's a long crawl out of here and we are going to stay with you as long as it takes to revive you so that both of you can make the journey out to the start of that long crawlway."

After an hour of attention by the three rescuers, one headed back through the crawlway to notify the rest and to prepare to assist in the return crawl. When finished the long crawl and reported the news, another Nashville caver replaced him and began the crawl back to the rescue site, dragging along more hot coffee, hot soup, cookies, and stuff. He also carried a note from Conchita, addressed to Robert. It said:

"Hey, big guy, resurrect that resourcefulness and ruggedness that has been handed down to you from your great-great-grandfather, General Lee, and get your butt out of this cave. We have a date to go dancing and I aim to keep it. With deepest affection. Conchita Rezanov."

By the time the new rescuer arrived, Alan seemed to be ready to attempt the crawl. So, after more hot coffee and hot soup, the long crawl was begun: a rescuer, Alan, a rescuer, Robert, and a rescuer. Alan was to set the pace and the one in front and the one behind him was to assist as needed.

It went well. In three and a half hours, the five emerged at the end of the crawlway.

Both cavers got big hugs from Conchita, but it was obvious that her hugging of Robert was especially prolonged. Now folks, Robert was actually quite a sight to behold -- course beard, matted red hair, and a dirty face covered with smudges, soot and red cave dirt. His clothing was quite a mess and the smell would have normally been repulsive. Yet Conchita hugged a long time and kissed him on the cheek repeatedly. She was so relieved to see him -- unable to control the emotions.

A county rescue squad had brought in litter carriers anticipating a need to carry the two cavers out to the ambulances waiting at the entrance. But Robert and Alan waved them off. It felt so good to be upright walking again after that long crawl and that old masculine pride was kicking in. Beautiful Conchita was right there to be impressed, and neither worn-out caver was about to give in to litter carriers as long as they could walk out.

It was 9:00 at night when the cavers emerged out of the cave to the cheers of the watchful. The moon was rising and twilight was subsiding. They piled into the two trucks, Joe Davis driving his and Isaiah Montgomery driving Alan's. All were back at Sewanee by 10:30. A late supper with the other eight was shared at the cafeteria (All the caving bunch -- Robert, Alan, Professor Davis, Isaiah and Conchita -- took quick showers, donned fresh clothes and joined the celebrators in record time.) There was a lot to be thankful for.

It seemed that no one noticed that Andrew Houston seemed jealous of Conchita's obvious affection for Robert. Andrew was attracted to the beautiful and athletic tennis playing Conchita, more so after the tennis matches they had fitted into the Sewanee schedule. And that sailing trip off Cuba had further enhanced the bond he felt toward Conchita. Allan was surely thankful to see Robert and Alan back safely, but troubled over Conchita's apparent affection for Robert. Perhaps her affection was a fickle thing -- toward one fellow for a bit, then toward another, and on and on. "Tennis," Andrew thought -- "First chance, we must again play tennis."

"My goodness," one would exclaim to a person nearby, "on our first weekend the crisis was a man overboard sailing off Cuba. On our second weekend, two are lost in Big Bone Cave. What is next? Are we prone to disasters by some unknown fate?" A consensus seemed to emerge -- no more risky adventures.

At 11:30 Professor Davis rose and held high a glass containing the last sip of his Jack Daniels sour mash whiskey. "It is time for bed everyone. No diary notes tonight. But, before falling asleep, do give a prayer of thanks to God Almighty. Tomorrow's schedule is delayed one hour. See you all at breakfast at 8:30 sharp."

Although Professor Davis and two Sewanee Team essayists were elsewhere all day, the necessity of continuing the lecture series has persisted. So, now, dear readers, before we leave this day, Monday, June 20, 2011, we must backtrack and attend the lecture on Hawaiian Independence that Emma Lunalilo had presented during the morning using the notes that Professor Davis had handed over to her at breakfast. The Hawaiian Independence lecture follows:

## European Involvement in Hawaiian History

The history of the Hawaiian Islands is the story of the struggles of the Hawaiian people and their Kings and Chiefs; struggles to survive horrific disease epidemics introduced by sailors out of the east; struggles to sustain their population and to remain relevant in their rapidly changing world. It is the story of competition between missionary groups for dominant influence over the population regarding spiritual, economic and political matters, for, more and more, the influence and ambitions of so-called missionaries seemed to be unrestrained. The story of the Hawaiian Islands concerns struggles between the competing national interests of the Pacific naval powers: the United States, Great Britain and France, and later the Russian Empire. [180] It is the story of the competition for trading rights and favorable tariff status. It concerns Hawaii seeking recognition by powerful foreign governments and assurances that the natives and the land would not be swallowed up by foreign aggressors. It is the story of men of the European race scheming and competing to acquire the good agricultural land, especially the land suitable for sugar plantations and sources of water for their irrigation. It is the story of educated men of the European race maneuvering into influential government offices -- ministers, judges, cabinet officers -- all supposedly acting as servants of the Hawaiian King, but steadily scheming and, acting together, becoming more important than their superior. It is the story of a rapidly diversifying Hawaiian Islands population: while the native population declined from disease, the mixed blood

---

[180] In truthful history, the Russian Empire was inconsequential in Hawaiian history..

population and the non-Hawaiian population rapidly grew, especially among the agricultural workers imported from China, Japan, Portugal and the Seceded Mexican States. [181]

It all began in January of 1778 when two sailing ships of the renowned world explorer Captain James Cook of the British navy came upon the Hawaiian Islands chain while sailing north from the Society Islands toward the northwest coast of North America. Cook named the islands the Sandwich Islands, in honor of the Earl of Sandwich, then first lord of the admiralty. These mid-Pacific islands -- Kauai (the oldest and most western), Oahu, Molokai, Lanai, Maui and Hawaii (the newest, by far the largest and the most eastern) -- were destined to become the most valuable land and harbor in the Pacific Ocean due to their central, yet remote, location. At this time, four different chiefs ruled over their respective domains within the chain of islands, and wars among them were common. Yet the populations were healthy and relatively disease-free, comfortable in their mild and care-free environment, having been isolated from other human populations for a period of perhaps 1,000 years. No metal ores were available and the people experienced a comfortable stone-age existence. Individuals and classes were regulated by traditions and the kapu system, with deference to many gods and magic.

Meanwhile, far to the east, the British were struggling to re-establish control over the thirteen North American colonies, which had joined together and proclaimed their independence.

Many years after the discovery of the Hawaiian Islands by Captain James Cook, a chief on the big island of Hawaii began a military campaign to conquer the islands beyond his control and thereby place the entire chain under his rule. Aided by firearms acquired from foreigners, Chief Kamehameha waged war until, by 1795 at age 36, he had conquered all but the furthest away island of Kauai, separated from the others by a wide and often-turbulent sea.

Nine years later in 1804, ships of the Russian American Company began visiting the Hawaiian Islands in search of food for its settlements in Russian America. Kamehameha welcomed the Russians and, when opportunities arose, gladly traded food for the otter pelts offered in exchange. King Kamehameha sent word to the Chief Manager of the Russian American Company, Aleksandr Baranov, that he would "gladly load a ship every year with swine, salt, sweet potatoes, and other articles of food, if the Russians would pay with sea-otter skins at a fair price." But the Russians were often short of sailing vessels suitable for the journey and only occasionally sought Hawaiian food, often skipping a year or two, while they instead strove to set up their agricultural base at Ross Settlement in Spanish Alto Californio, just north of San Francisco.

But, in January 1815, a Russian American Company ship, the *Bering*, after taking on a large load of supplies at Oahu, encountered a violent storm, was driven ashore, and wrecked at Waimea, Kauai Island. At this time, Kauai, the farthest west and most remote island, was under the control of King Kaumualii, who, five years earlier, had given up a degree of his independence and acknowledged that he was a suzerain of Kamehameha and obligated to pay annual tribute. The captain of the *Bering*, Captain Bennett, an American working for the Company, "gave the wrecked ship to King Kaumualii in return for assistance in saving the cargo. Leaving the cargo in care of the Kauai king, Captain Bennett returned at the first opportunity to New Archangel, headquarters of the Russian American Company, with the news of the disaster. [182]

---

[181] In truthful history, the power over political and economic matters in Hawaii remained in the hands of no more than 2,000 people who were of European blood and their mixed-blood offspring.

[182] The story of the wreck of the *Bering* is truthful history.

By this time, the Russian American Company "had become the foremost factor in the fur trade of the world, [now] surpassing the far older Hudson's Bay Company, its only comparable rival."

As mentioned briefly in the chapter on Russian America, Chief Manager Aleksandr Baranov was eager to recover the supplies from the shipwreck at Kauai and also to see the wonderful mid-Pacific islands for himself and to meet and cement a bond of friendship with King Kamehameha. Fortunately, Nikolai and Concha Rezanov were at New Archangel and able to handle oversight of the Company's affairs while Baranov journeyed to Hawaii to meet with Kamehameha and negotiate the recovery of shipwrecked supplies. And, as you will recall from the chapter on Russian America, Baranov was taking along Dr. Egor Schaeffer, a man unusually talented and learned in natural science, botany and medicine. In May 1815, four months after the shipwreck had occurred, Baranov and Schaeffer departed New Archangel on a Company ship bound for the Hawaiian Islands. [183]

By July, Baranov and Schaeffer were at Kailua on the coast of the big Island, Hawaii, where King Kamehameha was residing. The meeting was most fruitful. Baranov charmed Kamehameha and Kamehameha charmed Baranov. Simultaneously Dr. Schaeffer impressed the King with his medical skills, successfully aiding in the recovery of three sick members of highly regarded nearby families. Dr. Schaeffer asked for and received permission to explore the botany and minerals on the island of Hawaii. But Baranov advised: "Search as you like for samples of plants, little creatures and minerals, but make sure you are attentive to opportunities for advancing the agricultural potential of the land, and when sick are encountered, help where you can." Schaeffer agreed and left on his exploration journey, which would take considerable time, for the environment of the 4,030 square mile "Big Island" was quite diverse, including coastal lands, plains and very high volcanos, three cold and one active, as well as regions that were damp, regions that were dry and all those in between.

Meanwhile, Baranov sought to cement bonds of friendship between himself and the King; between the Russian people and the Hawaiian people, and to enhance the success of trading between Russian America and the Islands. Expecting a cooperative attitude at Kauai, the King gave Baranov a signed "order requiring Kaumualii to deliver to him the cargo of the *Bering* or to pay him for it." It would be up to Baranov to enforce the order. Meanwhile, while Dr. Schaeffer explored the island as a scientist, Baranov, as an honored guest of the king, got to know the people of the Islands and their leaders. Time was available, for Company ships were not expected to arrive to recover the supplies at Kauai until the spring of the following year. That was not a problem, because Nikolai Rezanov would be expected to oversee Company matters from New Archangel.

Of major significance during this these nine months would be progress in establishing the foundation of an Orthodox Church mission in the Hawaiian Islands. Fortunately, King Kamehameha felt the need for a Russian presence in the Islands to counterbalance the growing influence of the British and the Americans, and perhaps the French and Spanish. The more he dealt with multiple nations populated by the advanced civilizations of the European race, the more secure he believed would be the continued independence of the Hawaiian people -- let them compete among themselves for influence, the King reasoned, while we ensure that no one becomes dominant. And he wisely saw that the religious institutions of these various European peoples would be a window through which he and other islanders could come to understand and take advantage of the superior advancement of these foreign people.

---

[183] In truthful history Dr. Egor Schaeffer went to Hawaii alone while Alexsandr Baranov remained at New Archangel and in truthful history Nikolai Rezanov was dead and Concha was unmarried.

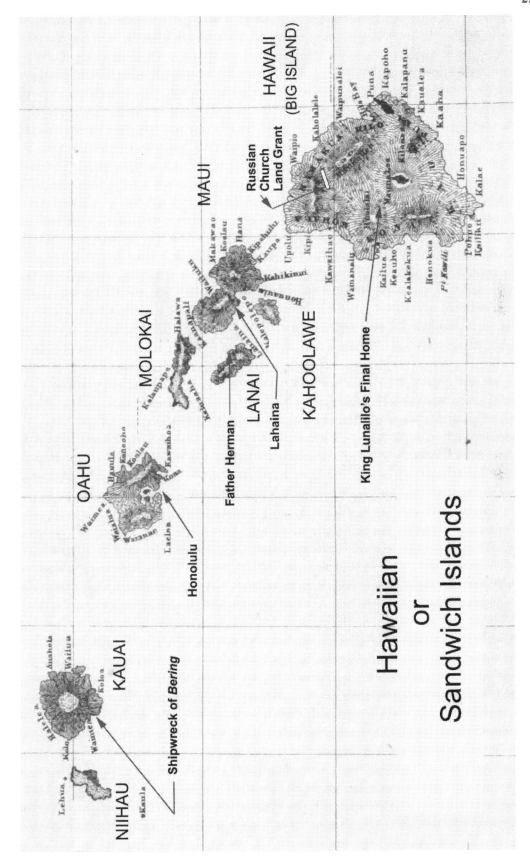

Hawaiian
or
Sandwich Islands

NIIHAU

KAUAI

Shipwreck of *Bering*

Lehua

Anahola
Wailua
Koloa
Waimea
Kaula

OAHU

Honolulu

Waimea
Waialua
Kaneohe
Koolau
Waianae
Laeloa
Kawaihoa

MOLOKAI

Kalaupapa

Halawa
Pukoo

Father Herman

LANAI

Lahaina

KAHOOLAWE

Lanai City
Kaumalapau

Kahoolawe

MAUI

Makawao
Koolau
Hana
Kapahulu
Kaupo
Kahikinui
Upolu
Kipa

King Lunalilo's Final Home

Russian
Church
Land Grant

HAWAII
(BIG ISLAND)

Kohala
Waipio
Kawaihae
Wamanalu
Kailua
Keauho
Kealakekua
Honokua
P't Kawili
Pohira
Kailiki

Waipunaalei
Hilo Bay
Puna
Ikapoho
Kalapanu
Khuelea
Kaaha
Honuapo
Kalae

HILO

MAUNA

So, after several in-depth conversations between Baranov and the King and his family and associates, concerning the God of the Russian people, Baranov agreed to write Nikolai Rezanov that there was a genuine need to establish an Orthodox mission in Hawaii and that a Russian mission would be welcomed. [184]

Aleksandr Baranov envisioned a mission led by Father Herman, Monk of the Russian Orthodox Church, who had come to Kodiak Island 21 years previously with the original group of eight Monks recruited from Russia's Valaam Monastery by Grigorii Shelikhov. Baranov and his family knew Father Herman well, and loved him for his efforts in educating his native wife Anna and their children regarding religious and secular subjects while he had been absent from New Archangel, away elsewhere. In addition to the Bible, Herman had taught practical subjects, such as mathematics, carpentry, agriculture and animal husbandry. For about five years he had resided on Spruce Island, leaving the nearby Kodiak Island mission to Father Joasaph. At the advanced age of 59 years, Father Herman was struggling to survive and care for orphans and give religious and secular instruction to them and the few natives on the little island, where he had "built a small chapel, school and guest house, while food for himself and the orphans was produced from his own experimental garden." [185] Believing that this wonderful and truly devoted monk deserved a broader reach for his evangelism and, on a more practical note, that he deserved the personal comfort of living in the Hawaiian Islands, Baranov penned a letter to Nikolai Rezanov recommending that Father Herman lead the mission to Hawaii.

On December 15 1815, Father Herman arrived in the Hawaiian Islands with two English translators, a sea-chest of his books and papers, a sea-chest of church sacramental items, and four Natives from the Kodiak region. Aleksandr Baranov was pleased and Father Herman was elated, almost believing that he had been "miraculously transported to a Heavenly Paradise." Those were the first words out of his mouth upon greeting Baranov, but both men took it as a joke. Dr. Egor Schaeffer was on-hand for the greeting as well. He had already searched for a good site for the Orthodox Mission:

> The site needed to be readily accessible to the King's government but not exposed to aggressive foreign adventurers. The northeastern side of Lanai Island looked like the place. It was located only 15 miles down-wind (west) from the whaling seaport of Lahaina, Maui, and there was also discussion in King Kamehameha's government of, within a few years, relocating the capital of the seat of government from the big island of Hawaii to bustling Lahaina. The southwestern coast of Lanai was very dry because of Mount Lanaihale, but adequate rainfall occurs on the eastern coast, and streams come down the mountainside. No attractive harbor site existed, ensuring that Lanai Island would not become an object of foreign shipping interests.

So Father Herman and his assistants settled on the island of Lanai, on the windward, northwest coast, downstream from Maunalei Valley. The population had declined over the past generation, but farmers and fishermen still inhabited portions of the fertile north coast and the valley of Maunalei. Hawaiians called the place Keomuku. Father Herman named his mission Doroga Domoy, which means "Homeward Bound."

Mission Doroga Domoy was up and running when three Company ships from New Archangel arrived at Lahaina, Maui in April 1816 to take Aleksandr Baranov aboard and then recover the shipwrecked supplies at Kauai Island. Baranov held a farewell meeting with the king, his family and several of his chiefs, and with Father Herman and Dr. Schaeffer, to ensure that he

---

[184] In truthful history, the Russian Orthodox Church never had significant influence in Hawaii.

[185] The story of Father Herman in Russian America is truthful history.

was leaving with the Russian interests and friendships intact. Since Schaeffer had already filled several sea chests with samples, measurements and written notes, Baranov encouraged the scientist to move about the islands and help with the advancement of agricultural opportunities, including at the mission on Lanai Island. The stop over at Kauai Island by the three Company ships was successful. Baranov and the recovered supplies were back at New Archangel by July, ready to take aboard pelts for western trade. [186]

During his year-long absence from New Archangel, Aleksandr Baranov had accomplished more than recovery of the supplies from the shipwrecked *Bering*. He had advanced relations between Russians and Hawaiians and established the first Orthodox mission at the Islands. [187] [188] [189]

Our story now advances to 1818, and Aleksandr Baranov's return to Hawaii aboard the *Kutuzov* and his secret escape during the night. You will recall reading in the previous chapter how Chief Manager of the Russian American Company, Aleksandr Baranov managed to return to Hawaii two years later. That account is repeated here to improve the transition:

> The *Kutuzov*, with Hagemeister at the helm and Baranov on board, entered the harbor of Lahaina, Maui on the incoming morning tide in late December 1818. Aboard in an aft cabin were Aleksandr Baranov and his trusted friend Richard. Soon after dark set in, Richard opened a cabin window overlooking the sea and let down a rope ladder secured by a slip knot. In the water below was a small canoe that had come alongside the *Kutuzov* unnoticed, alerted to be there by a note Richard had passed to a fruit seller during the day. Baranov slipped out the window, down the ladder and into the canoe. Richard followed, releasing the slip knot after reaching the canoe and gathering up the rope ladder. The

---

[186] In truthful history, the cargo of the wrecked Bering was recovered, but Baranov was not present.

[187] The truthful history of Dr. Egor Schaeffer's time at the Hawaiian Islands is far different from that told here. Nikolai Rezanov was long dead and not available to relieve Aleksandr Baranov from his responsibilities at New Archangel. Therefore, Dr. Schaeffer traveled to the Islands alone to arrange for the release of the shipwreck supplies. He did conduct personal scientific explorations as reported herein, and did obtain the written order to take possession of the shipwreck supplies, but, upon going to Kauai Island, he deceived King Kaumualii into believing that the Russian Empire would support a revolt against the rule of King Kamehameha. Furthermore, in return he received permission to set up a sugar plantation in the valley of Hanaei and, during the spring, summer and fall of 1817 a substantial fort was built at Waimea and the Russian flag was raised over it. When Saint Petersburg learned about Schaeffer's scheming, the government denounced the idea and Schaeffer was forced to flee the Hawaiian Islands never to return again. King Kamehameha remained in control of all of the Hawaiian Islands.

[188] In truthful history Father Herman remained on Spruce Island, caring for orphans, teaching and cultivating his experimental garden until his death in 1837. In 1970 "the Holy Monk was glorified by the Orthodox Church of America, in impressive ceremonies at Kodiak, Alaska, and the Blessed Father Herman of Alaska entered the ranks of Saints who are interceding on behalf of American Orthodoxy."

[189] In truthful history, Mormons from Salt Lake City, Utah came to Hawaii on a supposedly evangelical mission in 1850. In 1854, responding to opposition by other missionary groups, the Mormons retreated to Lanai Island and there set up a commune named the "City of Joseph." But in 1858 the Mormons returned to Utah at the request of Brigham Young to help fight the Mormon War. But one Mormon returned: in 1861 Walter Murray Gibson returned and purchased considerable land on Lanai Island and started farming. Three years later the Mormon Church excommunicated Gibson because he was exploiting Church property for personal gain. That set the course for the conquest of Lanai Island. By 1870 Gibson owned most of the island. In 1922 James Dole bought the island and developed much of it into "the world's largest pineapple plantation," to become Dole Food Company. David Murdock purchased the island and other Dole operations in 1985. In 2012 Larry Ellison, after making billions with his Oracle Corporation, purchased the island. Ellison owns 98 percent of the land; the State of Hawaii owns the remaining 2 percent.

Hawaiian put a blanket over his two passengers, tossed some straw on top and slowly paddled away. The ship's log concluded, "Baranov and Richard, drown. Lost at sea." [190]

By evening, Baranov and Richard were with Dr. Egor Schaeffer who, as you will recall, had remained behind in the islands after Baranov's 1816 departure.

Dr. Egor Schaeffer, Father Herman and King Kamehameha were all glad to see Aleksandr Baranov and Baranov expressed the same sentiment, having doubted he would ever get back to Hawaii. The leader of Hawaii and the former leader of Russian America, both legends in their own time, discussed many things. Of course, Kamehameha said he was very grateful for the agricultural help and expertise of Dr. Egor Schaeffer, and seemed to be confident that the partnership would bear much fruit, more for the benefit of the Hawaiian people than for the foreigners present on the islands. And, perhaps more importantly, the king praised the work and teachings of Father Herman and relished telling the story of the two weeks he and his family had spent with the monk at Lanai Island.

Aleksandr Baranov enjoyed renewing friendships made in 1816, but, as the early months of 1819 progressed, worries mounted over a decline in the king's health. By late April it became evident that Kamehameha was dying. Dr. Schaeffer succeeded in making him more comfortable and it did seem that his ministrations were helping. But they were insufficient. By May 7 even the normally robust king knew the end was near. His thoughts turned to the gods of the Islands and the God of the foreigners. He had been most impressed over the God of Father Herman. Near the king's bedside, but not too near, waited Baranov, Schaeffer and Herman. Strained conversation turned to religion and God. Baranov assured his friend that God would be blessing him, his family and the Hawaiian people. But Kamehameha interrupted, asking, "Whose God? The God of the Americans, the God of the Russians, the God of the Pope who lived in Rome? Figuring out 'whose God' can be most puzzling!" But after brief thought, the dying King called the family and leadership to gather closer around his bed to listen to what he was about to say. He instructed his scribe to write down every word. Then, he gathered his strength and decreed:

"Let it be known, and let it be written, that on this day, I, Kamehameha, King of the Hawaiian Islands, do invite the Church of the Russian People to establish a mission in our midst, on the big island of Hawaii, and to receive a grant of 5,000 acres of good agricultural land to be used to support their mission, which shall include educating the Hawaiian people in fields of science, mathematics, agriculture, seamanship, language and government, but most of all in knowledge of the true god of man and what He expects of His people. So long as that Church is faithful to these goals, it shall remain in ownership of this grant of land, but not otherwise.

"And to give life to these projects, I ask that my friends, Father Herman, Aleksandr Baranov and Dr. Schaeffer, be consulted regarding communications with the leaders of the Russian Church and in making sure the grants of land are among the most productive available and that the missionaries are sufficient for our needs."

"And to provide a religious retreat for the missionaries of the Russian Orthodox Church and Hawaiian believers, an additional 5,000 acres of good agricultural land is to be given on the small island of Lanai." [191]

---

[190] In truthful history, the ship that Baranov was on did not stop in Hawaii enroute to Saint Petersburg and Baranov died of disease while the ship was under sail in the South Pacific.

[191] In truthful history, King Kamehameha died a few weeks earlier that reported herein and did not experience contact with Baranov. The decree granting two parcels of 5,000 acres each is our alternate history.

Shortly after the passing of Kamehameha, Dr. Schaeffer resigned from the Russian America Company and departed Hawaii for Europe, loaded with his specimens and scientific notes, intending to present his findings and publish an account of his observations. Upon his departure, Baranov suggested, "You will encounter Russians and Germans who might be interested in immigrating to the big island of Hawaii. We need more people here skilled in agriculture. Perhaps you can return soon with a group of settlers. I believe the new king will permit it if, say, no more than one hundred come."

Twelve months later, a missionary team of Puritans arrived at Kailua, Hawaii, on April 4, 1820, seeking permission to establish evangelical mission sites in the Hawaiian Islands. They had left Boston, Massachusetts five months previously on the brig *Thaddeus*, having endured a long and arduous voyage. The group consisted of "two ordained ministers, Rev. Hiram Bingham and Rev. Asa Thurston; a physician, Dr. Thomas Holman; two schoolmasters and catechists; a farmer, Daniel Chamberlain; their wives; and three Hawaiian youths who had been attending the Foreign Mission School at Cornwall, Connecticut. These seventeen persons constituted the original Hawaiian Puritan church, whose membership would be greatly increased by later additions. Accompanying them on the voyage to Hawaii were five children of the Chamberlain family and a young Hawaiian chief, George P. Kaumualii, son of the king of Kauai. This prince had been a sailor in the American navy and later a student at the Foreign Mission School, where he made an excellent record as a student, but gave no very satisfactory evidence of being a Christian. [192]

Nevertheless, some hopes were pinned to the Prince's return to Kauai in the company of the missionaries, which won for them the enduring friendship and support of the island's ruler, King Kaumualii. Upon arrival, the Puritans learned that King Kamehameha had died the previous year and that the new authority at the capital of the Hawaiian Islands was his son Liholiho. They also learned that Father Herman had established a mission of the Russian Orthodox Church at the small island of Lanai almost five years earlier and that King Kamehameha, just before death, had proclaimed that a site would be set aside on the big island of Hawaii for a far more extensive Orthodox mission.

Over the past four years, King Liholiho and other chief's and princes of the islands had spent significant time, at least six weeks in total, on Lanai gaining an understanding of the Christian religion as proclaimed by Father Herman. So the King and his associates now questioned Rev. Hiram Bingham and Rev. Asa Thurston about Puritan teachings as they attempted to understand the difference in Puritan teachings and Father Herman's teachings. Discussions continued for four days, for Liholiho was most inquisitive. He quickly sensed that these Puritans were very stern, controlling and demanding. So, adopting a cautious attitude, the king decided to reserve the big island of Hawaii for the Russian Orthodox mission while giving permission to the Puritans to establish missions on only the two most distant islands, at Honolulu, Oahu and at Waimea, Kauai. Two years later, in 1822, Rev. William Ellis, an Englishman, who had worked in Tahiti and learned that language, which was similar to Hawaiian, gave assistance to the Puritans, helping them to learn to preach in and write in the Hawaiian language.

The missionaries from the Russian Orthodox Church that King Kamehameha had requested just before his death in 1819 arrived at the big island of Hawaii in early June 1821. Nikolai Rezanov had been instrumental in their recruitment and had provided transportation on Company vessels. The group consisted of four monks from the Valaam Monastery near Saint Petersburg, two priests from the theological seminary at Irkutsk in the western region of Russian Siberia and six supportive farm families from the Irkutsk region, including 22 children. Upon their arrival,

---

[192] The story of the first arrival of missionaries from the northeastern United States is truthful history.

Father Herman greeted them warmly, eager to pass the torch to the new and far younger arrivals. King Kamehameha II (Liholiho) welcomed the Russian mission and honored his father's promise of 5,000 acres of select agricultural land on the big island to be a gift to the Orthodox mission as long as it was faithful to its missionary charge. The selected 5,000 acres began near Waimea and proceeded east-north-eastward toward Honolaa, measured out as 1 mile wide by 8 miles long. It represented only 0.2 percent of the area of the island, but did comprise some of the very best farmland. This stretch of land received between 30 and 80 inches of rain in normal years, depending on the location along the 8 mile extent of the farm, thereby affording opportunities to engage in a variety of agricultural and husbandry efforts. Furthermore, it was along the major trail between the west coast and the east coast of the island, affording many opportunities for interaction with the native population and visitors to the island. The missionaries only occupied as much of the land grant as they could utilize, but more would arrive in the years to come and all of the acreage would eventually be utilized effectively in support of the mission. Father Herman remained on Lanai Island. [193]

Dr. Egor Schaeffer arrived at Lahaina, Hawaii in December 1822 with a group of 47 Germans aspiring to flee their homeland and settle in the Hawaiian Islands. Among Germans he had found considerable sentiment to flee Germany and Europe for America or elsewhere. And, in Schaeffer, such people found a leader. King Kamehameha II was welcoming. He agreed to allow the Germans to settle on the big island on lands that could be leased but not purchased. Marriage with native women was permitted. They agreed to study the Hawaiian language and strive to integrate into the island society. Between 1822 and 1828 approximately 2,200 Germans would immigrate to the big island. In a like manner approximately 1,200 Russians would come. So, unlike the smaller islands of the chain, such as Oahu, Maui and Kauai, the big island was evolving into a German and Russian settlement, far outstripping the English speaking residents on the other islands. [194]

During these years King Kamehameha II and Queen Kamamalu journeyed to Great Britain in hopes of forging good diplomatic relations between the two nations. But the trip ended in tragedy. The royal couple died in London, in July 1824 of measles. And they had failed to gain a promise from King George IV that the British Navy would intercede on behalf of the Hawaiian people if a foreign nation, such as the United States, France or Russia, attempted to take possession of the mid-Pacific island nation. On May 6, 1825, George Anson, titled Lord Byron, arrived at Honolulu on a British ship, the 46-gun frigate *Blonde*, with the bodies of King Kamehameha II and Queen Kamamalu. During their absence, the islands had been ruled by a regent, Kaahumanu, the wife of the late Kamehameha I, known in the islands as the kuhina-nui. Kaahumanu, enjoying her power and domineering in its exercise, would rule until her step-son

---

[193] King Kamehameha, nearing death in 1819, had no encounter with Russians that year; the promise of 5,000 acres for a Russian mission is not truthful history. When Puritans arrived in the Islands in April 1820, they were allowed to establish a mission on the big island as well as Kauai and Honolulu. No Russian Orthodox mission was ever established on the big island of Hawaii. Today, the 250,000 acre John Palmer Parker Ranch and Farm contains the 5,000 acres our story gave to the Russian mission. John Palmer Parker, of Massachusetts, jumped ship while in Hawaii around 1809 and maneuvered into a close relationship with King Kamehameha about the same time he married Chieftess Kipikane, perhaps a granddaughter of the king, but certainly a woman of royal blood. The couple's sons married Hawaiians and through those connections and subsequent descendants the family managed to acquire the best agricultural land on the big island of Hawaii, amounting to 10 percent of its total land area.

[194] In truthful history Dr. Schaeffer left the Hawaiian Islands in June 1817 and returned to western Russia and to Germany. In 1821 he organized a group of 47 Germans aspiring to flee their homeland and escorted them to Brazil. Between 1824 and 1828 he is credited for bringing 5,000 Germans to Brazil where they settled in rural colonies. They eventually formed the core of the first foreign units in the Brazilian Army. Settling there himself, he died in Brazil in 1836.

Kauikeaouli, 12, would become 21 years old and take the title Kamehameha III. Under these trying conditions, the teenage Kauikeaouli had become rebellious. [195]

By the age of 20 years, Kauikeaouli had tired of his rebellious behavior and sought to flee the female domination exerted by his step-mother and the holier-than-thou social domination of the Puritan missionaries. Where best to go for counsel than to quiet and peaceful Lanai Island, a short 15-mile ocean canoe paddle from Lahaina, Maui. Where best to go than to Father Herman's mission. Unlike the citified Massachusetts Puritans, Father Herman had long endured the hardships of the Aleutian Islands. The Puritans, eager for land and political influence, talked one way and acted another. Father Herman "walked the talk," seeming in every way sincere and dedicated to the service of his God. Kauikeaouli's father, King Kamehameha, I, had invited Father Herman to relocated to the Islands and had found comfort and guidance at his feet, at least he had claimed to have -- that being before the Puritans had arrived. Kauikeaouli wanted real man-to-man talk not lectures from his step-mother and her friends. So the young king and three friends, all young Hawaiian men his age, set out from Lahaina for Lanai on a beautiful morning in April 1834. The outrigger canoe was fast and they were strong. Within two hours they were pulling the sleek craft up onto the beach.

At Lanai there were no female temptresses lurking about seeking influence with the king, no rum or intoxicating drinks, no carousing crowds or Honolulu bars. In this environment Kauikeaouli absorbed education and wisdom from the aged Russian monk and the small group of assistants at the mission. He found solid ground, a rock so to speak, upon which he could absorb wisdom and intelligently and caringly lead his people. He began to understand Christ, sin and forgiveness, human history, and the ways of people of the European race in peace and in war. He improved his knowledge of scientific issues and where to get answers to questions that would arise in the future. He better understood the need to be wary of political manipulators and schemers intending to deceive, and how to recognize such behavior when it confronted him. He and his friends remained with Father Herman for 21 days and nights. They would return several times during the remaining course of the year.

Early in 1835 Kauikeaouli asserted his authority as king, became Kamehameha III, reaffirmed his step-mother as kuhina-nui and recognized the authority of the Council of Chiefs. So from that point forward the government of the Islands was shared between the king, the kuhina-nui and the Council. Kamehameha III retained for himself authority over the larger issues and let his step-mother deal with day-to-day governmental matters.

That was the political situation when, in December 1838, Father Ioann Veniaminov visited Hawaii on a trip from New Archangel to St. Petersburg. He remained on the big island for a full week, ministering to the Orthodox mission and interacting with Kamehameha III. This visit was very influential in strengthening the bonds between the mission and Orthodox Church leadership at New Archangel and at Saint Petersburg. [196]

A few months later, King Kamehameha III and the kuhina-nui, guided by the Council of Chiefs, proclaimed the Hawaiian Declaration of Rights of 1839. That was followed a few months later with approval of the Hawaiian Constitution of 1840. [197]

Clearly, with guidance from Europeans, the government of the Hawaiian Islands was progressing toward the rule of law, guaranteed individual rights, and reasonable relationships

---

[195] The story of Kamehameha II and his wife and their death in Great Britain is truthful history.

[196] In truthful history, Father Ioann Veniaminov was a great leader of the Russian Orthodox Church, both in Russian America and in Russia, eventually rising to the supreme position of Metropolitan of Moscow.

[197] The Hawaiian Constitution of 1840 is truthful history.

between natives and immigrants.   Puritans from the United States were becoming very influentially in Hawaiian politics and commerce by this time, and that influence was central to the wording of the new constitution.

The Constitution of 1840 gathered the islands into four political divisions, with a governor over each.  The central government was divided into three branches; Executive, Legislative and Judicial.  At the head was the king and the kuhina-nui, "who together wielded the supreme executive authority."  Legislative power was held by two houses, "the representative body," composed of people elected by the citizens," and the "council of chiefs, which included the king and kuhina-nui."  The Supreme Court was "composed of the king, the kuhina-nui and four other judges appointed by the legislative "representative body."  So the king and the kuhina-nui were wired into each of the three branches of government, but were only supreme in one, the executive, and no one individual held firm power in any branch.

By this time, much of the Hawaiian government was administrated by men of full or partial Western European ancestry.  Six men of Western European ancestry were key figures in administering the Hawaiian government and ensuring that their friends were successful in their endeavors.  Much should be said about the unusual influence of such men.  But available space requires the story be truncated.  Five of these men were of the Northeastern United States:

- Dr. Gerrit Judd (1803-1873), a physician born in New York State, who had married New Yorker Laura Fish and soon afterward sailed to the Hawaiian Islands as part of the third Puritan missionary group to be sent out.  In 1842 he resigned from missionary service, took over the government Office of the Treasurer where he was the "most conspicuous and influential member" of the executive department of the Hawaiian government. [198]

- Rev. William Richards (1793-1847) of Massachusetts arrived in the islands as a Puritan missionary in 1823 at the age of 30 with wife Clarissa.  He resigned in 1838 to draft the Hawaiian Declaration of Rights (1839) and the Constitution of the Kingdom of Hawaii (1840).  Afterward he escorted Prince Timothy Haalilo on a foreign diplomatic mission, served on the Privy Council, the House of Nobles and as Minister of Public Instruction. [199]

- John Ricord (1813-1861), a lawyer born in New Jersey, arrived in Hawaii in 1844, soon afterward swearing allegiance to King Kamehameha III and taking the government

---

[198] One of the most notable administrators was Dr. Gerrit Judd (1803-1873).  Judd was born in New York State and there received an education as a physician.  In 1827 he married New Yorker Laura Fish and soon afterward sailed to the Hawaiian Islands as part of the third Puritan missionary group to be sent out.  Assigned to the Puritan mission at Honolulu, he had ready access to influential people.  In 1842 Judd resigned from missionary service to take over the government Office of the Treasurer.  Dr. Judd "was for a dozen years the most conspicuous and influential member" of the executive department of the Hawaiian government, not leaving until 1854, to retire to his 622 acre farm (the family would eventually expand the farm to 4,000 acres).  Others welding important executive and judicial power included Rev. William Richards, John Ricord, William L. Lee, Rev. Lorrin Andrews, David Malo and John Ii.

[199] Rev. William Richards (1793-1847) of Massachusetts, educated at Williams College and Andover Seminary, arrived in the islands as a Puritan missionary in 1823 at the age of 30 with wife Clarissa.  He resigned from missionary service in 1838 at the age of 45 to work for King Kamehameha III, drafting the Hawaiian Declaration of Rights (1839) and the Constitution of the Kingdom of Hawaii (1840).  In 1842 and 1843 he and Hawaiian Prince Timothy Haalilio jointly represented the King as Special Envoys charged with securing from Great Britain and the United States recognition that Hawaii was an independent nation.  Upon his return he was a member of the king's Privy Council and a member of the upper legislative body, the House of Nobles.  In 1846 he became the kingdom's first Minister of Public Instruction.  He died the following year.  Afterward family members resided in Massachusetts, thereby playing no further role in the evolution of the kingdom.

post as Attorney General and Registrar of Conveyances and accepting appointment to the Privy Council. [200]

- William Little Lee (1821-1857), born in New York, was a Harvard-trained lawyer who arrived in Hawaii in 1846, soon gaining appointment as Chief Justice of the Supreme Court. He was elected to the House of Representatives and was Hawaii's ambassador to the United States. [201]

- Rev. Lorrin Andrews (1795-1868), born in Connecticut, arrived with his wife in Hawaii in 1828 as a missionary and soon specialized in learning the Hawaiian language, translating and printing books and, in 1836, starting the first Hawaiian newspaper, *Ka Lama Hawaii.* Although not legally trained, he was appointed Judge of Foreign Cases, Associate Supreme Court, and Judge over Divorce and Probate. [202]

- Robert Crichton Wyllie (1798-1865), born in Scotland, was a physician and businessman who arrived in Hawaii in 1844 as acting British Consul. Soon King Kamehameha III named Wyllie his Minister of Foreign Affairs and his Secretary of War, and appointed him to a legislative seat in the House of Nobles. [203]

---

[200] John Ricord (1813-1861) was born in New Jersey into a prominent family, studied law in his uncle's office and was admitted to the bar in Buffalo, New York in 1833. As a lawyer he spent time in Texas, Oregon and then Hawaii, arriving in the islands in 1844. The following month he swore allegiance to King Kamehameha III and accepted appointment as the kingdom's first Attorney General and Registrar of Conveyances. The following year the king appointed him to the Privy Council. He was a founding member of a board to review land titles. Ricord was very influential for a few critical years in the kingdom, but resigned his offices and left the islands 1847, never to return.

[201] William Little Lee (1821-1857) was born in New York, graduated from Norwich University, then Harvard Law School. After a brief stint practicing law in New York he planned to migrate to Oregon Territory by sailing ship. But the ship experienced damage while passing around Cape Horn and detoured to Hawaii for repairs in October 1846. John Ricord, mentioned above, convinced Lee to remain in Hawaii, that making the newcomer only the second formally trained western lawyer to engage in legal work there. After Ricord left the following year, as mentioned above, Lee took over as the principal legal authority at the service of King Kamehameha III. The following year he became Chief Justice of the newly established Supreme Court. He was elected to the House of Representatives in 1851 and helped draft the 1852 Constitution of the Kingdom of Hawaii. As Chancellor, Lee represented Hawaii at Washington, D. C., charged with seeking improved treaty relations through the Franklin Pierce Administration, but was not successful. He died in Hawaii in 1857 at the age of 36, and his widow Catherine returned to New York, continuing to receive some income from her late husband's interest in a Hawaiian sugar plantation.

[202] Rev. Lorrin Andrews (1795-1868) was born in Connecticut, graduated from Jefferson College and attended Princeton Theological Seminary. Deciding to become a missionary, he and wife Mary arrived in Hawaii in 1828. His main work as a missionary was in learning the Hawaiian language, translating and printing. He printed the first Hawaiian newspaper, Ka Lama Hawaii starting in 1836. Students that he educated worked with him on translations and printing to build the first library of books in the native language. He left missionary work in 1842 to concentrate on writing and printing and in service to the kingdom. Although not legally trained, he was appointed Judge of Foreign Cases including appellate jurisdiction. In 1852 he was appointed Associate Justice to the new Supreme Court, and, in 1854, Judge over Divorce and Probate. He resigned from court work in 1855 and resumed translating and publishing. His eyesight eventually failed and he died in 1868.

[203] Robert Crichton Wyllie (1798-1865) was born in Scotland and earned a medical diploma at the University of Glasgow. In 1842 he left England for Mexico to investigate troubled financial investments, and then looked in Alta Californio for opportunities before settling in Hawaii in 1844, briefly acting as British Consul. Impressed and seeking to counter excessive American influence, King Kamehameha III, within days, named Wyllie his Minister of Foreign Affairs and his Secretary of War, and appointed him to a legislative seat in the House of Nobles. So, by March 1845, Scotsman Wylie was thrust into three powerful positions. While remaining in the king's service, he bought a coffee plantation on Kauai, but the land was too low and wet, so he converted it to sugar cane. In 1850 he was a founding member of the Royal Hawaiian Agricultural Society. He ensured Hawaii was officially neutral in the War Between the States. Introducing a British look in appearances, he insisted on formal European-style uniforms for royalty and cabinet officers. He remained in the office of Foreign Minister until his death in 1865, having served in that capacity for twenty years. His nephew inherited the sugar mill but committed suicide upon discovering it was deeply in debt. Wyllie is buried in the Royal Mausoleum of Hawaii, which had just been completed at the time.

In February 1845, King Kamehameha III relocated his residence from Lahaina, Maui to a newly-built palace in Honolulu, Oahu. In celebration, "a soiree in the manner of European royalty was held at the palace, when the king received the diplomatic and consular corps, the officers of the U. S. frigate *Brandywine*, and the principal foreign residents in what was evidently the most brilliant reception ever witnessed in Honolulu up to that time." In May the legislature opened in Honolulu as "a new royal standard was unfurled and greeted by a salute from the guns of the fort and the British frigate *Talbot*. The next day the legislature was occupied listening to the reports of Minister of the Interior Judd, Minister of Foreign Relations Wyllie and Attorney General Ricord." Land was being transferred to so-called naturalized foreigners. To the Hawaiian people evidence abounded that their nation was being taken over, acre by acre, office by office, by foreigners and Part Bloods born to foreign men and Hawaiian wives. These events led to "an extensive protest movement against the introduction of foreigners into the government and the body politic, and against the giving of land to foreigners." [204]

As you had previously read in the Story of Russian America, 188 Russian refuge families departed in 1846 from the Slavianka River Valley and Ross Settlement for the Hawaiian Islands, fleeing John Fremont's gang of fighting men, a sideshow in the American invasion of Mexican Alta Californio. Four ships arrived at Kailua, on the big island of Hawaii, in late October and early November, 1846. Russian American Mikhail Tebenkov had been right. The Hawaiian government did accept the refugees and instructed all to stay together on the big island under the oversight of the Russian mission. Apparently, the distrusting feelings that natives harbored against foreign influence did not seem to apply to these Russian refugee families. King Kamehameha III permitted the refugee families to settle in and around the 5,000 acre farmland allocated for the Russian Orthodox mission near Waimea, Hawaii. These Russian refugees looked like friends who would join with them, the natives, in opposing the subjugation of Hawaii when, or if, the United States sought to take their island home like they had just taken the homes of the Mexicans in Alto Californio and elsewhere.

The year 1850 marked the beginning of extensive ownership, in fee simple, of the best land in the islands. On July 10, 1850 a new law gave "aliens resident in the Hawaiian Islands the right to acquire and hold land in fee simple and to dispose of the same to any person resident in the kingdom whether subject or alien." Passing land down to children through inheritance was thereby assured. And the cost of land was rather economical. By this act, the change in the land ownership situation was complete. Over the next decade to 1860 nearly all of the government-held land was sold and much land held by natives slipped into the hands of aggressive foreign buyers. The argument had been that foreigners, adept at developing agricultural land and making it productive, would be hiring natives to do the work and would boost the overall economy of the islands, particularly considering the growing market for products to the East, in California.

Although families from the northeastern United States seemed to dominate political and commercial activities on most of the islands, over on the big island of Hawaii, Russian and German families were making lasting friendships with native Hawaiians, whose distrust of power-grabbing and fortune-seeking Americans was steadily growing.

## Kamehameha IV

Kamehameha III died December 15, 1854, leaving no living son. "His nephew and heir, Prince Alexander Liholiho was immediately proclaimed king under the title of Kamehameha IV," and was inaugurated on January 11, 1855, taking an "oath to maintain the Constitution of 1852."

---

[204] The story of Kamehameha III and the dominance of American and English influence is truthful history. But the story of time with Russian Americans and their influence on the King is our alternate history.

He would celebrate his 21st birthday a month later. A grandson of Kamehameha I, he was well educated in Hawaiian and English; had visited England with his elder brother Lot, and was prejudiced in favor of English influence over America influence. He had already served on the Privy Council for three years. Two years after taking the throne, he married Emalani Naea Rooke, who was of one-fourth British ancestry, her grandfather on her mother's side being John Young, a British-born military advisor to Kamehameha I. [205]

Greatly concerned over the rising political and economic influence of Americans living in the islands, Kamehameha IV sought a counterbalance through a reciprocity treaty with the United States government that would serve to reduce tariffs, stabilize the relationship between the two nations and validate the government of the Kingdom of the Hawaiian Islands. But that effort was not successful. On the other hand he and Queen Emalani were successful in improving health care for the Hawaiian natives, resulting in the construction of The Queen's Medical Center in Honolulu and expanded health-care education. Their only son, Prince Albert, died in 1862 at the age of four years. [206]

## Kamehameha V

Lot Kamehameha became King of the Hawaiian Islands on November 30, 1863, taking the title, King Kamehameha V. He would reign nine years. At age 18 years, Lot had travelled with his younger brother Alexander Liholiho, 15, to America, England and France under the guidance of Dr. Gerrit Judd. He had served in the Privy Council from age 21 to 24 and in the House of Nobles from that point until assuming the throne.

The initial Cabinet was "Robert C. Wyllie, a Scotsman, for foreign affairs; Charles de Varigny, a Frenchman, for finance; C. G. Hopkins, an Englishman, for the interior; and C. C. Harris, an American, for attorney general." The major event in the reign of Kamehameha V was his issuance by executive edict of a new Constitution to replace the 1852 version, which had been in effect for twelve years, which his Cabinet had prepared, which called for imposing stringent limitations on potential voters. Qualified as in the 1852 version were all males born before 1840 -- 24 years old during the first year of the Constitution, advancing thereafter. But for younger males to qualify, they had to, at a minimum, be able to read and write and possess real estate valued at $150, or hold a property lease valued at $25 per year, or have annual income of $75. As the years would advance, this requirement would reduce the voting power of native Hawaiians and increase the voting power of the naturalized foreigners. In spite of the highhanded way in which the new Constitution was put through, it would remain in effect throughout the reign of Kamehameha V. This new Constitution also expanded the power of the king, for it freed the executive from the control of the Privy Council and it abolished the office of the Kuhina Nui. As a consequence, the influence of the foreign-born Cabinet expanded.

During the reign of Kamehameha V, considerable progress was experienced in agricultural development of the islands, particularly at the big island of Hawaii and the island of Lanai, where Father Herman had originally established his small Orthodox mission. In the smaller island a thriving pineapple operation was begun. By 1872 a thousand acres were producing pineapples and a cannery was processing the fruit for export. The pineapple cannery on Lanai had been

---

[205] Emalani had been adopted "under the Hawaiian tradition of hanai" by her childless maternal aunt, Grace Young Rooke, and husband Dr. Thomas Rooke, a physician who had been born, raised and educated in England. Politically influential, Dr. Rooke was a member of the lower house of the legislature at the time of the marriage. Kamehameha IV would reign until his death at the age of 29 on November 30, 1863, the cause of death being reported as chronic asthma. He suffered from the disease throughout his reign and may have actually been the victim of tuberculosis.

[206] The story of Kamehameha IV is truthful history.

established by a subsidiary of the Russian American Company, adapting its salmon canning technology and importing British tin-coated sheet steel. But the cannery was operating as a separate Hawaiian business in the control of a group of Russian and German residents of the islands. The arrangement was splendid. Native Hawaiians cultivated the pineapple, sold their fruit to the cannery, which processed it and sold the result to the Asian and American markets. [207]

Also on the big island of Hawaii, experts and entrepreneurs from South Carolina and Texas pioneered the raising of cotton and its processing into fabric. Experienced growers of sugar cane had come from Louisiana to the big island and favorable spots elsewhere in the islands to begin the cultivation of sugar cane and its refining. Hawaiian sugar was being exported to Asia. Certain zones on the big island of Hawaii could be adapted to the growing of wheat, and that was helpful in diversifying the agricultural base. Entrepreneurs from Texas and the former seceded Mexican States were leaders in the raising of cattle for milk, meat and hides. But cotton was not the only source of fiber. Wool was being produced by a small clan of Irishmen who had brought in sheep, by 1872, numbering 1,000 head.

As a rule of thumb, the big island of Hawaii and small Lanai were enjoying strong agricultural economies, whereas the mid-sized islands of Oahu and Maui were more reliant on commerce and trade. Russians, Germans, Confederates and Mexicans were leading the economy on Hawaii and Lanai and Americans, dominated by a merchant and political core, seemed to be in control on Oahu and Maui. The labor resources were different, too. On Hawaii and Lanai, imported labor, where required, was mostly Mexican. On Oahu and Maui imported labor was mostly Japanese and Chinese. The differences were quite obvious, as if two cultures persisted. Those differences seemed familiar to the Confederates on the Big Island, Hawaii, who likened it to the differences that had given rise to political sectionalism in America during the 1850's, which had precipitated State Secession and a War Between the States.

Kamehameha V died at age 42 years on December 11, 1872. William Charles Lunalilo would succeed him. [208]

## King Lunalilo and the Republic of the Hawaiian Islands

Upon the death of Kamehameha V, two candidates for King were active in seeking election by the legislature. In addition to William Charles Lunalilo, David Kalakaua sought the honor. Both had similar genealogical ties to the House of Kamehameha, but their agendas for ruling the islands differed greatly. Lunalilo had more liberal attitudes about giving more political power to the Hawaiian people than did Kalakaua, the former promising to amend the Constitution to give the people a greater voice in the government and to replace most foreigners in the government with native officials, and insisting that the Hawaiian people, not the legislature, elect the next king. The people were enthusiastic for Lunalilo. The foreigners and business community favored Kalakaua.

A popular referendum vote for King was held on January 1, 1873 and Lunalilo won by an overwhelming majority. The following week, the legislature unanimously voted Lunalilo king. Because Lunalilo's popularity was so great, and because he became king through a democratic process, he would become known as the "The People's King."

---

[207] In truthful history, as of 1870, the former Mormon missionary, Walter Murray Gibson, owned Lanai Island. In 1922, James Dole bought the island and created the world's largest pineapple plantation.

[208] The story of Kamehameha V is truthful history with the exception of portions concerning Russians and Germans and agricultural exports from their efforts.

A grandnephew of Kamehameha I and a second cousin to King Kamehameha IV and King Kamehameha V, William Charles Lunalilo was not of the house of Kamehameha. He had been declared eligible to someday become King by a declaration of King Kamehameha III and was subsequently educated in the Royal School where he learned to speak English and fairly well mastered English literature. As a child and teenager he held title to a vast amount of government land by right of inheritance. He loved music and wrote Hawaii's first national anthem, which was Hawaii's version of "God Save the King."

King Lunalilo was charismatic and popular among the Hawaiian natives, but, was already suffering from excessive drinking of alcohol and a lung infection, which was degenerating into consumption (tuberculosis). Perhaps he hoped the alcohol would help control his lung disability.

King Lunalilo would subsequently transform the kingdom into a republic, a pivotal event in the history of the islands. We will now acquire an understanding of how that happened.

Seven days after the death of Kamehameha V, Lunalilo proclaimed:

> Whereas, it is desirable that the wishes of the Hawaiian people be consulted as to a successor to the Throne, therefore, notwithstanding that according to the law of inheritance, I am the rightful heir to the Throne, in order to preserve peace, harmony and good order, I desire to submit the decision of my claim to the voice of the people.

"The new sovereign was inaugurated amid a magnificent ceremony on the following day at Kawaiahao Church. At once, King Lunalilo fulfilled his election promise by submitting several proposed amendments to the constitution, the most important being one to do away with the property qualification for voters. Thirty amendments were passed by the special legislative session of 1873, and referred for final action to the regular session of 1874." [209]

Within three months of the inauguration, it was apparent to people close to King Lunalilo that his lung infection, his consumption, was getting far worse and immediate medical attention and regimented isolation, rest and exceptionally healthy nourishment were called for. Honolulu was definitely not the place for such care. Disease often spread around the harbor town and political passions cast doubt on the sincerity of certain "so-called" doctors. But at the big island of Hawaii, at the Russian Orthodox mission up in the high country of that island, were excellent sites for isolation from disease agents and for extended rest and healthful nourishment, and there was a German doctor on the island who many considered to be the best available. Seeking to expand his nutrition and disease studies Dr. Benjamin Malamed had come, with his microscope, stethoscope and other tools of the medical profession to join the German and Russian settlements on the big island two years earlier, in 1872. [210]

So, a house was constructed on the Big Island, Hawaii, for the King's full-time use. While King Lunalilo rested at the specially constructed house the high country above Kona in the saddle

---

[209] The story of Lunalilo's election as King is truthful history except his public proclamation is paraphrased.

[210] A German of excellent medical training, Benjamin Malamed, age 31 years, had studied in Germany, alongside Robert Koch, often interacting with pioneering professors of medicine, such as Friedrich Henle (early advocate of the germ theory of disease), Karl Hasse (he published in 1846 "An anatomical description of the diseases of the organs of circulation and respiration), Rudolf Virchow (the "father of modern pathology" who discovered that "the origins of cells was the division of pre-existing cells"), and Wilhelm Ebstein (a pioneer in the study of human nutrition). However, his presence in Hawaii is not truthful history.

between the dormant volcanic peaks of Hualalai and Mauna Loa, he accepted the treatment overseen by Dr. Malamed, and the governance of the Hawaiian Islands continued to function. [211]

Named to the King's Cabinet were Charles Bishop, Minister of Foreign Affairs; Edwin Hall, Minister of the Interior; Robert Stirling, Minister of Finance, and Francis Judd, Attorney General. Judd was an American and Bishop and Hall were descended from New England missionaries. Stirling was a Scotsman. Also named to Lunalilo's Cabinet was Emalani Naea Rooke, Minister of Public Health. She would play a major role in maintaining productive relationships between factions in the Hawaiian government. [212]

From his rest home in the high country of Hawaii, with the assistance of Queen Emalani's travels to and from, King Lunalilo was able to win support in the 1874 legislature for the liberal changes to the constitution which he had sought from the beginning of his reign. Now the Hawaiian people were able to hold their own, politically, against the influence of the foreign factions in Honolulu.

Through the year 1874 King Lunalilo managed to retain sufficient health to fulfill his role as leader of his people. His lung infection, called "consumption" was not getting better, but it was not getting worse. The diet was helpful as was sunshine and excellent air. The alcohol vapor treatments were no burden, actually rather enjoyable, and may have helped. But in March 1875 there was a serious medical scare. [213] Lunalilo lay on his right side for two weeks in hopes the perforation in his right lung would seal itself off. It worked. The crisis passed. But it was an historic warning.

From this point forward Lunalilo and Emalani began serious consideration of a plan to transform the Hawaiian government, from a kingdom with a king, a legislature, and a court, into a republic with a president, a legislature, and a court. It was obvious that the Hawaiian people were suffering from premature death and declining population. A government dependent on transferring power from king to son to grandson was not viable. A revised constitution would

---

[211] Upon examination of the king at Wiamea, Hawaii, Dr. Malamed found overall weakness and pale coloration indicating poor overall health, found shortness of breath, and heard through his stethoscope considerable difficulty in the lungs, especially the right lung. These were all symptoms of consumption, a debilitating disease for which no cure was known. But he held to emerging theories that treatment should consist of three actions: 1) regimented, worry-free, prolonged rest in an area where the air was rather dry, clean and pleasant, 2) exceptionally healthful nutrition rich in fruits and vegetables, with a modest amount of meat and fat and very clean water, and 3) twice-daily supervised inhalation of vapors of alcohol to cleanse the lungs accompanied with gentle coughing to clear the lungs. In late March this program of care was undertaken in a newly constructed and simple house in the high country above Kona, in the saddle between the dormant volcanic peaks of Hualalai and Mauna Loa.

[212] Emalani Naea Rooke, age 37, of Kamehameha family lineage (through the brother of Kamehameha I), was the daughter of High Chief George Naea and High Chieftess Fanny Kekelaikalani Young; had been adopted by her maternal aunt and husband, Englishman Dr. Thomas C. B. Rooke of Honolulu; had been educated at the Royal School where she became fluent in Hawaiian and English and developed expert horsemanship. In spite of the fact that she was not a pure-blooded Hawaiian, she had married King Alexander Liholiho Kamehameha (Kamehameha IV) at age 20, taking the title of Queen Emalani. She gave birth to a male child two years later, but the child died at age two and her husband, the king, died the following year. Queen Emma had been celebrated for her efforts to improve the health care of the Hawaiian people, most notably for her sponsorship of the Queen's Hospital in Honolulu, established in 1859. So, she was a logical choice for the new Cabinet office of Minister of Public Health, and her expert horsemanship readily qualified her to travel frequently between King Lunalilo's rest cottage, situated high above Kona, Hawaii, and the main commercial and government center of Honolulu, Oahu. The story of Emalani Naea Rooke is truthful history except she was not appointed Minister of Health under King Lunalilo.

[213] The right lung perforated and collapsed within the king's chest. Dr. Malamed resorted to a simple surgical procedure: he cut a small incision between two right ribs and inserted a small glass tube to release the air trapped from around the collapsed lung. He then took a rubber hose and connected one end to the glass tube and the other he inserted into a jug of rum. The rum sealed off incoming air and gave evidence of emerging bubbles of escaping air.

give the native Hawaiian people the power to elect a native to be their president in spite of opposition from powerful foreigners in Honolulu. So be it. Let them elect a president to serve for a term of designated years, then elect another. When all was legally arranged, Lunalilo would abdicate and give power to Hawaii's first president.

Emalani trusted the foreign minister from the Confederate States of America, Jose Luis Argüello. Jose Argüello was of Spanish descent, of Confederate South California and a nephew of Concha Argüello Rezanova, whom you will recall from the chapter on Russian America. Emalani invited Jose Argüello to come and meet with King Lunalilo at his rest cottage in the high country of the big island, an invitation rarely offered due to the perceived need for isolation for medical reasons. Argüello explained the difference in the culture of the United States people and of the Confederate States people and the advantages of a federation in which individual states reserved for themselves the bulk of governmental power. He further warned that these mid-Pacific islands would eventually be conquered in an invasion by a foreign power, such as the United States, or by a political coup d'état hatched by foreigners in Honolulu. He advised a transformation from a kingdom to a republic and adoption of a political structure that would allow, at some future date, a merger into the Confederate States in a manner similar to the merger that brought in the Seceded Mexican States, Cuba and Russian America. He suggested that the king invite two experts to come to the big island of Hawaii to consult: one from Texas and one from a former seceded Mexican state that had joined the Confederacy in the Great Confederate Expansion. Regarding the issue of personal ownership of slaves, he assured Emalani and Lunalilo that such matters were totally controlled by state governments. "Do not be concerned about it." Not long afterward, representatives from the Confederate states of South Texas and Central Del Sur came to consult with Emalani and Lunalilo, helping the Hawaiian leaders to move forward with confidence toward a transformation into a republic. From the Confederate State of Russian America, Timofei Kavanskii came to the big island and conferred with Emalani and Lunalilo. You may recall that Timofei Kavanskii was a Part Blood from Russian America's agricultural region and that he had held the office of Vice President during the Republic's first term, beginning in 1864. Emalani and Lunalilo were particularly interested in the details of Russian America's transformation from a Company-managed colony, to an independent republic, and then to statehood. The Russian Orthodox Church and the Mission had been on the big island of Hawaii for many years and both King and Queen expressed their deepest respect for the honesty and dedication of the Russian people associated with Orthodoxy.

King Lunalilo called a special session of the legislature to convene at the big island of Hawaii in March 1876. For this gathering, two meeting halls, temporary housing and a kitchen had been erected near the king's rest home, a joint construction project of the island's Russians, Germans and Hawaiians. Because of the revised constitution of 1874, both legislative houses were dominated by native Hawaiians. Emalani and Lunalilo presented their draft of a constitution for the Republic of Hawaii and recommended that both houses of the legislature engage in debate aimed at granting approval. Lunalilo explained that his extremely poor health was itself a demonstration of the obvious fact that susceptibility to disease and premature death -- prevalent among the Hawaiian people since the arrival of Europeans -- required that leadership of the islands by birthright was fraught with difficulty, probably doomed to failure. It was imperative that the king be replaced by an elected president who served only a limited number of years. Lunalilo promised that he would abdicate as soon as the new constitution was approved. That would pave the way for elections in accordance with a Constitution of the Republic of Hawaii. Regarding the makeup of the upper house of the legislature, he encouraged debate, but the lower house ought to be open to all Hawaiians without regard to race. The electorate must consist of all males and females who are citizens, without regard to race, of age 18 or more. One asked, "Why so young; why the women, too?" Lunalilo replied, "The life expectancy of the Hawaiian people is short. Hawaiians have always looked to their women for leadership and the men are often leaving our islands on adventure, many dying while away from home. We need all Hawaiians to participate in voting."

The legislature approved a constitution much like that submitted to them. The logic of arguments by Emalani and Lunalilo was too convincing to seriously refute. But this constitution had to also be approved by a re-elected legislature before it was considered the law of the land. Four months later elections were held for a new legislature, organized as before with the same seats, but containing newly elected representatives. This re-elected body also approved the new constitution. King Lunalilo signed the document on August 15, 1876. He then submitted his letter of abdication to become effective when the kingdom transformed into the republic on January 1, 1877. Elections were scheduled for November 15. This gave Hawaiians three months to select their new governmental leaders.

Three candidates were in the running for president. David Kalahaua declared for the office. He was previously mentioned as a candidate for king in the January 1873 contest, which had resulted in the election of Lunalilo. So in Kalahaua's candidacy the people were able to vote for a man who would have probably become king if the new constitution had not transformed the kingdom into a federation. Kalahaua was favored by the American faction and strongly endorsed by John Owen Dominis, since 1864 the governor of Oahu. [214]    From the island of Maui, John Makini Kapena announced his candidacy. [215]    The third serious candidate for president was Samuel Kipi, of the big island of Hawaii. Born at Hilo, Kipi, 51, had been Land Appraiser for the big island for three years and was serving in the House of Representatives. He was appointed Governor of the island of Hawaii in 1874. Kipi, the oldest of the candidates was favored by Pure Bloods, especially because he had been born and raised on the big island, away from the influence of the foreign factions in Honolulu. In general, pure blooded Hawaiian voters thought favorably of the foreign settlers of Russian and German extraction on the big island; it was the Americans on other islands that gave pause for worry. With those foreigners about, a political coup d'état had always seemed to be just around the corner.

## President Samuel Kipi

Samuel Kipi won the election for president. On January 1, 1877, with the newly elected legislature in attendance, King Lunalilo presented his abdication and Samuel Kipi was sworn into office. The Kingdom of Hawaii was history. [216]    The Republic of Hawaii was the future.

---

[214] Born in New York, John Owen Dominis had come to the islands with his parents as a child and had risen to power as the result of his marriage in 1862 to Liliuokalani, daughter of a royal high chief couple of the house of Kalakaua. As governor of the island of Oahu, site of Honolulu, and being married to Liliuokalani, Dominis favored Kalahaua for obvious reasons.

[215] John Makini Kapena had recently become the circuit judge for Oahu and seemed well connected with influential people, partly because of his 1863 marriage to a pure blood Hawaiian, Emma Malo, daughter of a notable Christian minister and historian, David Malo.

[216] King Lunalilo died one year after taking office. The legislature elected David Kalakaua to be the new king. Because Kalakaua and many of the legislators did not favor the many amendments to the constitution that had been advocated by the deceased Lunalilo and provisionally approved by the 1873 legislature, only one change was given final approval by the 1874 legislature: providing universal suffrage to all men age 21 or more. Kalakaua would be king until his death in 1891. He would be succeeded by Liliuokalani, the Hawaiian lady mentioned previously as the wife of John Dominis. She would be known as Queen Liliuokalani. During her reign, in 1893 she would be compelled to abdicate by an internal coup d'état forced on the islands by Americans. With American warships about, the kingdom of Hawaii was defenseless. The coup d'état that perpetually seemed "just around the corner" finally showed its ugly head in 1893. It seems surprising that the easily foreseen event had taken so long to materialize.

In spite of Dr. Malamed's efforts, the last Hawaiian king, William Charles Lunalilo, passed away on February 3, 1978, a year after transforming the Kingdom into a Republic. He was survived by his wife, Miriam Auhea Kekauluohi Lunalilo and a 19-year-old son, Charles Lunalilo (the ancestor of Sewanee Project essayist Emma Cathrine Lunalilo). [217]

## Monday Evening Selected Diary Postings

Diary note by Professor Davis said, "Back in Sewanee at 10:30 tonight. What a day! But, thank God everybody is OK. Nobody, I mean nobody, is going to engage in any more adventures before we conclude the Sewanee Project and present those twelve essays on the televised sesquicentennial celebration on Monday, July 4. Two weeks to go and we need no more "excitement." This coming weekend, I will take Amanda Washington, Tina Sharp, Benedict Juárez and Isaiah Montgomery on an overnight hiking trip along the beautiful Cumberland Plateau along the Fiery Gizzard Trail. They deserve a weekend get-away, too. Done that trip several times. Might sound "fiery," but it is easy hiking. I will be there to make sure no one gets crazy. Two sensible young men. Two sensible young women and little ol' me. No problem! I can handle it! . . . . . Good time with musicians this weekend. We are going to perform during the July 4 celebration festivities. Selected our music for that event this weekend. Everyone was present except Allen, who, we now realize was without light deep in Big Bone Cave. Now we know that Allen will be fine and his guitar will blend well with all that we will do. . . . . . I told everybody that breakfast is delayed one hour in the morning."

Diary note by Emma Lunalilo said, "What a day!! Professor Davis asked me to tell the story of Hawaii this morning. I hope I did a good job. Professor Davis's lecture notes were well organized, and that was helpful. At lunch everybody expressed genuine admiration for the Hawaiian people and all the difficulties they had suffered from European diseases, rambunctious sailors and Puritan deceit. Even so, Hawaiians managed to retain their independence, transition to democracy, and secure an agreement with the Confederate States that enabled Hawaiian statehood. That said, with whom did the supper schedule pair me with? Chris Memminger! He could not stop hugging me and thanking me for swimming to him with a life vest and flashlight. I do not know what possessed me to do that – pitch black dark, rough seas, strong winds, sailboat struggling to come about. What I did was not the result of logical thinking. It was just wildly impulsive. But the impulse resulted in success. Cannot fault it for that. What a day! Need to take it easy tomorrow."

Diary note by Robert Lee said, "Got back to Sewanee at 10:30 tonight. Thank God. In reality, Big Bone Cave is a rather safe cave. That we got into trouble is unheard of. But that was a very long crawlway, by far the longest I have ever struggled through. And, well, diary, when you got no light all you can do is pray for rescue. Thank God for those who understood the problem and figured out where we had gone. Roy Wilson and his caving buddies from Nashville were terrific. What on earth can I do to properly thank them?

Diary note by Allen Ross said, "What an ordeal. Back here a bit after 10 pm. Clumsy me! How could I have lost our pack down that hole in the cave floor? That long, long crawlway had led us to a large cave passage where no man had been for over 100 years. We wanted to see more of it, but safety required we repack our stuff and began heading back. That is when we lost our

---

[217] In truthful history, King Lunalilo never married: twice he sought to marry Victoria Kamamalu, but her brothers twice refused to allow it. The marriage to Miriam Auhea Kekauluohi is our alternate history as is the birth of son Charles. King Lunalilo did try to regain his health by moving to Kailua-Kona on the big island. But the effort was a failure. He returned to his private residence in Honolulu a few months later, where he died on February 3, 1874.

242

pack down that hole in the floor. Darkness came upon us soon afterward. Goodness we were only getting our lights organized for the long crawl back. How can we ever repay Roy Wilson and those Nashville caving heroes who figured out which passage we had taken and had come to our rescue."

Diary note by Tina Sharp said, "I really like Allen Ross. Was so worried all day. We are so different, but we really hit it off when together. Rugged bisonboy with a heart of gold. That Native American characteristic, I suppose. I am so glad he is finally back in Sewanee safe and sound. Would not be able to sleep tonight otherwise."

# Part 2, Chapter 5, Day 16 – The Story of How the Spanish Colony of Cuba Won Independence and became a Confederate State – Class Lecture, Tuesday, June 21, 2011

The 12 gathered Tuesday morning to hear Professor Davis present the history of Cuba's fight for independence from Spain. All were glad to be returning to the normal classroom environment. No caving crisis. Professor Davis again at the front of the room. Today, everyone will be gushing over the heroic story of Cuban independence over Spain, statehood for Cuba, and the leadership of Carlos' great-great-great-grandfather, Carlos Manuel Céspedes. Much to look forward today, this morning!

## How Cuba Became a Confederate State

Without a doubt, the independence of New Spain (Mexico) had inspired Cubans to likewise seek to govern themselves. But the Spanish Government persistently enforced its power over this, the most important island in the Caribbean Sea (south coast) and Gulf of Mexico (north coast) -- important because of Cuba's huge production of cane sugar, by far its most valuable export crop. In the late 1860's Cuba was supplying one-fourth of the world production of cane sugar, and Spanish taxes on that industry were large. Cuba's population was counted in 1862, yielding a total of 1,396,470 persons in total. Of these, 232,433 were free persons of African ancestry, about 390,000 were slaves and about 60,000 were Chinese contract laborers. Of the 713,000 Whites, those born in Cuba numbered about 656,000 and those born in Spain about 57,000. The island measures 745 miles long by 19-to-119 miles wide. But, before taking focus on Cuba, we travel east across the Atlantic Ocean to understand the political chaos in Spain during the years following Mexican independence.

In Spain, King Ferdinand VII had taken power in 1813, after the successful ousting of the French under Napoleon Bonaparte. Ferdinand VII retained the throne for 20 years, until his death in 1833. At that point, his little daughter, Isabella II, age three years, assumed the Spanish throne. Of course, an office of Regency was necessary to act on behalf of the three-year-old "Queen." For the first seven years, the office of Regency was held by the little girl's mother, Maria Christina, who had been the child of King Francis I, the Bourbon King of Sicily, and his fourth wife, whose name is irrelevant.

Isabella II became Queen in her own right in 1843 upon reaching the age of 13 years. Her first task was to marry, and that was arranged on October 10, 1846, when Spain's Moderado Party made her marry her double-first cousin, Francisco de Asis de Borbon, then 24 years old and holding the title, Duke of Cadiz. Isabella would directly reign from 1843 to 1868, but not with effective control over the Spanish government. Her reign was a period of "palace intrigues, back-stairs and antechamber influences, barracks conspiracies, and military pronunciamentos to further the ends of three competing political parties: Moderados, Progressives and Los Liberales de la Unión. [218]

Meanwhile, across the Atlantic in eastern Cuba, unrest had been building strength for several years. The Spanish-born, representing 8 percent of the population, were appropriating over 90 percent of the island's wealth and the Cuban-born of Spanish descent, called Creole, still had no political rights. In May 1865, Cuban Creole elites placed four demands upon the government of Spain: tariff reform, Cuban representation in the Cortes Generales (the Spanish parliament), judicial equality with Spanish-born, and full enforcement of the ban importing slaves. Spain did not relent. The oppression continued. Discontent was particularly felt by the

---

[218] The story of Isabella II is truthful history.

farmers in Eastern Cuba, the more rugged and remote section of the 745-mile long island. That is where Francisco Vicente Aguilera and Carlos Manuel de Céspedes lived.

By the summer of 1866, these two influential men, both owners and operators of sugar plantations, had been anticipating the next new political upheaval in the government of Spain, to the east, across the Atlantic. So, they were discussing how to prepare to launch a revolution against Spanish control over Cuba when the time was right. Vicente Aguilera was considered the wealthiest plantation owner in Oriente, the eastern-most province of Cuba. Carlos Manuel de Céspedes was a Cuban farmer, an operator of a sizable sugar plantation, and a lawyer of considerable means in Eastern Cuba. These two were far from the political and mercantile hub of Havanah (written as Havana in English), which lay in the far-western quarter of the island.

Freedom-seeking men like Francisco Vicente Aguilera and Carlos Manuel de Céspedes had not been pondering revolution alone. Confederate political and military leaders had been supportive of a Cuban revolution ever since the Treaty of Saltillo, signed on May 5, 1866, giving independence from Mexican and French rule to the secessionists of northern Mexico, led by Benito Juárez. And the isolation of Cuba's Oriente province from the power center at Havanah facilitated natural cooperation between Confederate advocates and that region's independence-minded leaders. [219]

We now introduce the Confederates. The decision to offer advice and support to Cuban revolutionaries was triggered by a meeting between Carlos Manuel de Céspedes and Confederate Secretary of State Judah Benjamin when both had, by chance, been together in New Orleans in November 1866. That meeting became the basis for an enabling decision by the Confederate administration of President Jefferson Davis.

In December 1866, President Davis agreed that his Secretary of State, Judah Benjamin, should draw up a plan for assistance to potential future Cuban revolucionarios. Accordingly, Benjamin gathered a secret team under the title of the "Cuban Independence Committee" to plan a strategy for assistance. Among members of the secret Committee were Stephen Mallory of South Carolina, former Confederate Navy Secretary in the Davis Administration; Pierre Lafitte, of Confederate Secret Service fame; Josiah Gorgas, former Chief of the Confederate Ordinance Bureau; Raphael Semmes of Maryland, the famous commander of the raider, *CSS Alabama*, Robert Garlick Hill Kean, a Virginian and, since March 1862, Head of the Confederate Bureau of War, a division within the War Department, and Lieutenant General Nathan Bedford Forrest, the famous Confederate cavalry officer. Early meetings had persuaded the Committee that the fall of the government of Queen Isabella II would probably occur within a year or two, meaning that the next few months represented a rare opportunity to give assistance to what ought to be a successful revolution designed to liberate Cuba from Spanish control.

Accordingly, a delegation of three, consisting of General Forrest, Pierre Lafitte and Robert Kean, was given instructions and dispatched to Oriente Province to make secret contact with potential revolutionary leaders. They arrived at the seaport town of Manzanillo in February 1867 and proceeded in disguise to Bayamo where they were welcomed by Francisco Vicente Aguilera and Carlos Manuel de Céspedes at the latter's nearby sugar plantation, La Demajagua. In the course of one week, plans were laid to support a revolution. Céspedes, who had spent several

---

[219] In truthful history the United States had, several times, sought to purchase Cuba or enforce the Monroe Doctrine by demanding withdrawal of Spanish control. Democrat President Polk considered paying up to $100,000,000 for Cuba. Democrat President Pierce had advocated purchase or Monroe Doctrine enforcement. Democrat President Buchanan had supported paying up to $30,000,000 for Cuba. But Northern States politicians opposed every effort and nothing materialized. After the War Between the States the dominant Republican Party had no interest in helping the Cubans.

years in Spain and knew Spanish politics well, had confirmed that he believed the reign of Isabella II would soon fall, and that the opportune time for a revolt would be immediately afterward, while the mother country was in political confusion. So the Cuban Revolution should be launched soon after receiving word of the fall of the Isabella Government. All agreed to the timing.

Pierre Lafitte advised the Cubans to form and expand a secret society of revolutionary cells that were positioned throughout the island, with particular interest in planting cells near coastal fishing villages, where arms could be easily supplied and revolucionarios could be brought in and taken out. He added, "Since Cuba is over 700 miles long with many harbors, it will be important to take control rapidly before the new government in Spain realizes the extent of the revolution and gathers up and dispatches a fleet of warships and transports with reinforcements. Revolucionarios ought to be in total control of the island within 8 months of the launch of the revolution, 12 months at the most. Merely advancing a front by land over 700 miles may proceed too slowly, so it is important that the uprising becomes widespread all the way to the western end, and that railroads be seized to facilitate revolucionario troop movements. Militia and propaganda groups planted in the western half of the island facilitate rapid westward advancement when the time comes."

Nathan Bedford Forrest concurred, "Yes, the government replacing the deposed Isabella would probably be in firm control within a year, so the Cuban Revolution must be swift if it is to be successful. Speed of advancement will be enhanced by a fleet of coastal boats and a trained cavalry, complete with field artillery. So, preparation should include the acquisition of horses and coastal boats. Field artillery is too hard to keep hidden, so it should be quickly supplied from Confederate ports upon notice of the launch of the Revolution."

Francisco Vicente Aguilera submitted, "We can organize secret revolutionary groups across the island and designate horses and riders, but we need arms of all types, especially the most modern available rifles and pistols. All of those resources can be dispersed and hidden on the island. But how can we obtain arms. We may have only a year, perhaps two, to make that happen."

At this point Robert Kean entered into the discussion. "The Confederate Government can supply the arms and munitions you will need. It can extend credit to a legally-organized Cuban Revolutionary Committee, backed by commitments to provide sugar in payment, ten percent within a year and the balance within four years of the success of the Revolution. If the Revolution fails and the Committee is killed or dispersed, the balance will be forgiven."

Nathan Bedford Forrest added, "You will need more than good timing, dispersed revolutionary groups and horses, boats and arms, and seizure of railroads. You will also need military training. Let me suggest that a camp be set up in Alabama, north of Mobile, for the training of military leaders of the future revolution. Farmers make good soldiers and leaders of troops, but only after trained in important military skills. Cubans trained in Alabama can return and become the leaders who train their companies of troops. The Confederate Government will set up the secret camp and make it available to arriving Cubans. We can also help with training in railroad skills, including operation, upkeep of railroad tracks, locomotives, steam engines and rolling stock. I will probably be in charge of the camp and I assure you it will be most helpful to your success. Who should we Confederates look to as the primary leader of the future revolution?"

Francisco Vicente Aguilera, a leader in his own right and the owner of the largest sugar plantation in the province, answered: "The most capable man to lead our revolution is without a doubt Carlos Manuel de Céspedes. As you have seen, he runs a model sugar plantation, he is skilled in law, he knows Madrid and Spain from personal travels and he is of the prime age of 47 years. You, Carlos will be our leader." The other Cubans agreed and Carlos accepted the challenge of leadership.

Nathan Bedford Forest then provided the assurance Céspedes and fellow revolucionarios needed. "When the Cuban Revolution subdues significant resistance fully across the island, including in the capital city of Havanah, and then proclaims Cuban Independence, the Confederate Government will recognize that Independence and warn the Spanish Government that Confederates will not tolerate a Spanish attempt to re-conquer the island by military means. If necessary, we will overlook isolated pockets of Spanish resistance, but you must take Havanah. By this proclamation, you will receive direct Confederate military support when and if needed. Prior to that time, covert support can be expected, but our people cannot allow themselves to be bogged down in a protracted guerilla war."

"What about slavery," Céspedes then asked?

Pierre Lafitte answered, "That is a question to be answered by the new Cuban Government."

Céspedes replied, "I anticipate that my slaves will be qualified, eager for freedom and ready to support the revolution upon our launch, whenever the opportunity comes."

Between the days of this planning conference and the launch of the Cuban Revolution in October 1868 much preparation would be accomplished. Over 100 military leaders would be trained at Nathan Bedford Forrest's camp north of Mobile, especially in cavalry tactics and needed skills to commandeer and use railroads. Confederates would deliver weaponry, including a sampling of modern repeating rifles and revolver pistols, which would be dispersed and hidden away. Secret revolutionary cells would be organized, even into the western provinces. Coastal boats useful for advancing revolucionarios would be identified and kept at the ready, including the 13 modest but fast steamboats that would be "sold" to various sugar plantations under the guise of work boats. Over 300 horses would be imported for future cavalry use. Revolutionary committees would be established at the terminus of every major western railroad. A fast printing press and ample supplies of paper and ink would be set up and be at Céspedes's disposal -- at the ready to dispense propaganda.

And that was how the Confederate Government arranged to secretly support the, then future, Cuban Revolution.

In July 1867, Vicente Aguilera founded the "Revolutionary Committee of Bayamo." This secret conspiracy rapidly spread to Oriente's larger towns, especially to Manzanillo, where Carlos Manuel de Céspedes became engaged. At his sugar plantation, Céspedes called his slaves together and invited them to support the then-secret revolution in exchange for emancipation. They agreed, others were encouraged as well. In the far eastern quarter of the island, many, both free and slave, were just waiting for the signal to revolt. [220]

In September 1868 the anticipated Spanish revolution blossomed. Called the "Glorious Revolution," it was launched when Admiral Juan Bautista Topete mutinied in Cadiz. Soon afterward, General Juan Prim and General Francisco Serrano announced support for the Spanish revolution. The Queen fled to Paris to eventual exile after her Moderado generals made an ineffective defensive stand that was easily crushed by Generals Serrano and Prim at the Battle of Alcolea. This revolt would establish the First Spanish Republic. Two years later, on November

---

[220] The story of the Revolutionary Committee of Bayamo and Céspedes involvement is truthful history.

15, 1870, the ruling Cortes would elect Amadeo I, second son of Victor Emmanuel II of Italy, to serve as King of Spain. [221]

It was during this chaos of Spain's "Glorious Revolution" that Carlos Manuel de Céspedes launched a revolt in Cuba, acting quickly upon news of the flight of Queen Isabella II to Paris. We now turn our attention back to Cuba and the Grito de Yara of October 10, 1868.

### Carlos Manuel de Céspedes and the Grito de Yara

When news of Queen Isabella's flight to Paris arrived in Cuba, Céspedes and like-minded men quickly stepped forward, proclaiming the Cuban Revolution. The heart of the announcement was the Grito de Yara, written by Céspedes and presented on October 10, 1868 at Yara, a small town in eastern Cuba located halfway between the cities of Bayamo and Manzanillo. [222]  In English "Grito" means "He shouted." The Grito said:

"In rebelling against Spanish tyranny, we want the world to know the reasons for our action.

"Spain governs us with blood and iron; she imposes on us levies and taxes as she pleases; she has deprived us of political, civil, and religious freedoms; we are subjected to martial law in times of peace; without due process, and in defiance of Spanish law, we are arrested, exiled and even executed.  We are prohibited free assembly, and if allowed to assemble, it is only under the watchful eyes of government agents and military officers; and if anyone clamors for a remedy to these abuses, or for any of the many other evils, Spain declares them a traitor. . . ."

For the remaining text of the Grito de Yara inquire on the internet.

Before moving forward into the story of the Cuban Revolution, let us ask why had the Spanish government in Madrid been so determined to retain the Spanish colony of Cuba?  The answer lies in the richness of Cuba and its key location in the Caribbean Sea, on its south coast, and Gulf of Mexico on its north coast. In the 15-year span from 1853 to 1868, Cubans had built 784 miles of railroad lines operated by 21 railroad companies -- on a per-capita basis the greatest concentration of railroads on earth.  These railroads had been built from within the island to the coast to ship coffee and refined cane sugar from inland plantations (farms) to the coastal ports of Havanah, Matanzas, Cárdenas, Isabela, Nuevitas and Gibara on the north coast and Batabanó, Cienfuegos, Casilda, Tunas de Zara, Santiago de Cuba and Caimanera on the south coast. Exports of cane sugar and, to a less extent, coffee, made Cuba a valuable Spanish asset and the market accessibility provided by the new railroads was rapidly increasing the volume of Cuban exports.  Although inland-to-coast railroads were in abundance on the island, an interconnecting east-west railroad line was just beginning to emerge.

The revolt launched by Céspedes was not the only opposition to rule from the new government in Madrid, Spain, which had recently deposed Queen Isabella II, who you will recall had first held title through a Regent at age 3, then as herself since age 13.  Soon after Céspedes' Grito de Yara, Captáin-General Francisco Lersundi, commander of Spanish forces in Cuba, proclaimed that, although Queen Isabella II had fled into exile in Paris, he supported her out-of-power Spanish government and refused to recognize the authority of the new government in Madrid. But he was no friend of Céspedes' revolucionarios; he was just as hostile to the rebellion in Cuba as to the revolution in Spain.  Lersundi's stand was attractive to Cubans who had been

---

[221] The story of the "Glorious Revolution" in Spain is truthful history.

[222] The history of the October 10, 1868 "Grito" at Yara is truthful in every way.

born in Spain, these being the upper class in Cuban society. Furthermore, Lersundi needed Spanish-born Cubans to reinforce his military, for the 22,000 regular Spanish soldiers stationed in Cuba were unreliable, "consumed and devoured by various diseases inherent to the climate." So, immediately following the Grito de Yara, during November and December 1868, Lersundi managed to recruit many military volunteers from among Spanish-born Cubans. These he organized into a state militia, calling them "voluntarios," and to these men he paid wages from special taxes levied on merchants, landowners and slave traders. [223]

But Captáin-General Lersundi, in spite of brutal military tactics, failed to subdue the revolucionarios in their eastern stronghold. So, in response to the failure of Lersundi's militancy, the Spanish government ousted him and dispatched a more peaceful man to Cuba, Capitán-General Domingo Dulce y Garay, in hopes of gaining a negotiated settlement.

## Capitán-General Dulce

Capitán-General Dulce arrived at Havanah in January 1869, three months after the Grito de Yara. But, even though Lersundi had left, more than 20,000 voluntario militiamen remained, determined to thwart efforts by Dulce to negotiate a peaceful settlement with the revolucionarios. So, handicapped by the unofficial but stubborn and powerful opposition by the voluntarios, Dulce was unsuccessful at winning cooperation through negotiation and governmental reforms. Anarchy seemed close at hand. [224]

The voluntarios faced another powerful organization in Cuba, centered in Havanah. It was the Casino Español, the Spanish Club. Made up of the most influential Spanish-born residents of Cuba -- many being successful owners of sugar plantations, most being of wealth and influence -- the Casino Español was in a way as influential as it would be if it was a truly constitutional legislature. [225] Its members were opposed to the extremely high taxes and fees imposed by the Spanish Government in Madrid, but, with greater vigor, they opposed any political movement that gave power to the Cuban born Creoles or opened a pathway for emancipation of Cuban slaves, believed essential to profitable production of cane sugar.

And cane sugar production was big business in Cuba, for the western portion of the island by itself was suppling one fifth of the world's supply of cane sugar. The President of the Havanah Casino Español was Don Julian de Zulueta, owner of four plantations – España, Alava, Billaya and Havannah – complete with interconnecting railroads, and each worth $1,500,000. [226]

Another powerful owner of expansive sugar plantations was Don Juan Poey, the son of a Frenchman and a Cuban lady, and considered a Cuban born Creole. Sixty-nine years old and exceptionally well educated, Poey enjoyed great influence and drew upon his unmatched

---

[223] The story of Captáin-General Francisco Lersundi is truthful history.

[224] The story of Capitán-General Dulce is truthful history.

[225] The story of the Casino Español is truthful history.

[226] Zulueta also owned other enterprises, including mercantile, industrial and commercial ventures, not to mention his frequent acquisition of additional sugar cane farmland and sugar cane processing facilities. Born poor to a laboring family in the Basque region of Spain, he arrived at Cuba, "without a farthing, without education," but, through hard work and natural leadership ability, had advanced to become the richest and most powerful man on the island. Zulueta had much invested in maintaining the status quo. But he was nimble and able to forge new alliances if convinced that Spanish born dominance was about to be overthrown.

experience and contacts. You will find the footnotes below concerning Don Juan Poey interesting. [227] [228]

Since Confederates had become involved in the early stages of revolutionary planning and had provided critical secret, covert military support when needed, the revolution launched by Céspedes and his supporters on October 10, 1868 had advanced rapidly. [229]

On December 8, 1868 Céspedes commissioned Jose Valiente as the Revolutionary Government's representative to the Confederate States of America. The letter of instruction stated, "I have determined to direct to you this communication so that you will serve to represent us before that Government and make all possible efforts, as a good patriot, to obtain the protection of the Confederate Government and the recognition of our provisional Government." He further stated, "You are empowered to establish communications with other foreign nations that offer, if not to help us, at least to be neutral in our war against the oppressiveness and tyranny of Spain." Commissioner Valiente proceeded to set up office in New Orleans and seek widespread support for the Revolution throughout the Western Hemisphere. As you have previously read, the Confederate Government had long ago promised Céspedes that it would secretly support the Revolution. It had been supportive and would continue to be. [230]

---

[227] In truthful history, three years into the future, during the course of the Céspedes's Revolution, a particularly observant European visitor, Antonio Carlo Napoleone Gallenga, would gain a measure of Zulueta and Poey and set the following observations down in writing in his book, *The Pearl of the Antilles*, written in 1872 and published in 1873. He would write:

"Of the two men, Don Juan Poey evinces the greatest interest in the welfare of the Island, apart from its connection to Spain. He is a little slight man, about 70, with an intensely French countenance, beaming with something of the liveliness and intelligence of the late President of the French Republic. A man of extensive scientific acquirements, he converses most agreeably on almost all subjects. If Don Julian de Zulueta is by nature a rough sort of king, Poey seems intended for a very consummate statesman and diplomatist. In the opinion of all men Don Juan Poey is the one who best understands the real position of affairs in this country, and who has always the keenest insight into the intricacy of the grave questions which await a speedy solution. Zulueta rules by strength of will, but Poey leans to circumstances, which he acknowledges to be stronger than any man's will. Zulueta only asks how long it may still be possible to fight on; Poey considers how soon and with what good grace it may be advisable to give in."

[228] In truthful history, Céspedes's revolution would reach a stalemate in the summer of 1869, 9 months after the "Grito". In truth, the Spanish born and the voluntario militia would never fail to hold firm control over all of western Cuba and most of central Cuba, forcing the revolucionarios to resort to guerilla warfare in eastern Cuba and the eastern part of central Cuba. This was the situation when European visitor Antonio Carlo Napoleone Gallenga arrived in 1872 to study the Cuban situation, which resulted in his informative book, *The Pearl of the Antilles*. Antonio Gallenga (1810-1895) was born in Italy and educated there at the University of Parma. He was supportive of the 1830 French Revolution and for a while was a deputy to the Italian parliament. For twenty years, beginning in 1859, he was a correspondent for *The Times* of London, a highly regarded newspaper, and it was in that capacity that he visited Cuba during 1872.

[229] In truthful history this rebellion would be fought for ten years and be eventually crushed by Spanish forces.

[230] In truthful history, Jose Valiente was appointed as foreign Commissioner as stated. However the Confederate States did not exist. So, in truthful history, efforts to win outside support for the Revolution centered in New York City, home to many influential Cubans. In the late 1840s and 1850s Jose Luis Alfonso, Cristobal Madan and other emigres had urged the annexation of Cuba to the United States. But Northern States opposition to expanding the region in America where slaves were permitted to live prevented these Cubans' advocacy from gaining traction. Of course, after the War Between the States resulted in the conquest and political reconstruction of the former Confederate States, few Cubans trusted that they would be treated fairly if absorbed as an American state. Specifically, the several Cuban committees in New York City, the most notable being Valiente's Sociedad Republicana, disagreed on seeking an independent Cuban Republic versus seeking a state of Cuba within the United States. Failure to agree on this fundamental policy choice contributed to ineffectiveness at New York, and failure to obtain American help was a major reason for the eventual defeat of the Revolution in 1878, ten years after its inception.

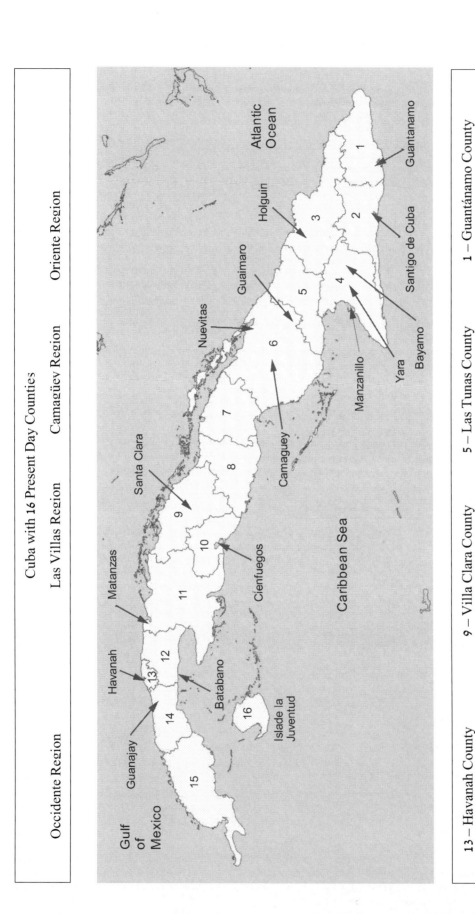

Cuba with 16 Present Day Counties

Occidente Region   Las Villas Region   Camagüev Region   Oriente Region

1 – Guantánamo County
2 – Santiago de Cuba county
3 – Holguin County
4 – Granma County

5 – Las Tunas County
6 – Camagüey County
7 – Ciego de Avila County
8 – Santi Spiritus County

9 – Villa Clara County
10 – Cienfuegos County
11 – Mataanzas County
12 – Mayabeque County

13 – Havanah County
14 – Artemisa County
15 – Pinar del Rio County
16 – Isla de la Juventud County

Footnote: In truthful history these 16 counties are the present-day 16 provinces of Cuba

Within 6 months of Céspedes' proclamation of independence, by April 1869, revolucionarios had gained control over much of eastern Cuba.

At this point, in early April 1869, at the town of Guáimaro, located in the newly defined province of Camagüey, revolutionary leaders -- military, economic and political -- gathered for the purpose of organizing a new and independent government structure for the whole island. Guáimaro had been taken by liberation troops in the early days of the revolution. This gathering of leaders, under the direction of Carlos de Céspedes, approved a constitution for the Republic of Cuba, which was approved by the Guaimaro Assembly on April 10. It divided the island into four provinces, from east to west named: Oriente, Camagüey, Las Villas and Occidente, each equally represented in the central government's legislative branch, the Representative's Chamber. Modeled after the Confederate Constitution, it called for a civil government divided into three branches: executive, legislative and judicial. The President had to be Cuban-born of 30 years or older in age. Holding the greatest power was the legislative branch, to be termed the House of Representatives, membership being divided equally among the four provinces, each electing two Representatives. The House was empowered to elect a President of Cuba, the General in Chief over the forces of the Liberating Army, the Secretaries and other officials and employees. It elected Carlos Manuel de Céspedes to the office of President of the "Republic in Arms" and elected General Manuel de Quesada as Commanding General of the Cuban Liberation Army. Quesada had served Benito Juárez as a general in the War against the French Intervention and the War of Mexican State Secession. Major General Ignacio Agramonte headed the Army of Camagüey Province. Major General Francisco V. Aguilera headed the Army of Oriente Province, and also served as Vice President under Céspedes. Major General Federico Cavada, who had also fought in the War of Mexican Secession, headed the Army of Las Villas Province. Regarding freedom for slaves of African ancestry, the Constitution was specific. It stated that all enslaved men voluntarily inducted into the Liberation Army and obedient to officers would be emancipated after the Revolution achieved success throughout the island. During the term of President Céspedes, the House would pass 24 laws, including the Law of Free Trade, the Law of Civil Marriage and the Law of Public Instruction. At the top of the third, judiciary branch of government was the Supreme Court of Justice. Below it were courts for civil and criminal judges. All males of 20 or more years, both White and Afro-Cuban were entitled to vote. Only slaves and Chinese contract workers were excluded. Elections would be held on September 25, 1869. [231] [232]

## Expanding Revolutionary Control into Central and Western Cuba

By April 1869, revolucionarios were recognized as in control of Oriente Province and the eastern region of Camagüey province. Before them to the west was more prosperous central Cuba, consisting of the western part of Camagüey province and, more importantly, the province of Las Villas, with its centrally located large town of Villa Clara, which featured a railroad connection to the southern seaport of Cienfuegos. Further westward, in the seat of power, Havanah, Céspedes' revolutionary propaganda campaign was peeling away support for Spanish rule, especially the support of people who desired freedom from Spanish rule but were too timid

---

[231] The above history of the April 1869 Constitution is truthful history. We now depart from truthful history in order to reveal important Confederate support. In our alternate history, we find that emancipation was further defined.

[232] In our alternate history, we take Gallenga's account as of 1872 and use that insight to construct a revised history for 1869 and 1870 which would have been the logical consequence of support by the Confederate States of America for Céspedes's revolution. Trust me when I say that the revised history you will be reading in the next few pages, empowered by support by the Confederate States of America, is a logical extension of what might well have occurred. You see, the course of history often turns on singular events such as the successful secession of the Confederate States.

to support it until success seemed likely. And the inevitability of success was the revolucionarios' key propaganda tool.

But Céspedes rightly viewed the standoff in Havanah between Captáin-General Dulce and Spanish-born Cubans as fertile ground upon which to build support for the revolution through artful use of propaganda. And the Republic of Cuba in Arms government and Constitution, established at Guáimaro in early April was the cornerstone of the revolutionary propaganda message. Céspedes' modern printing press, well equipped with paper and ink, was busy producing documents designed to incur a belief in the inevitable success of the revolution and the hopes for the improvements it promised to Cubans of all walks of life, free or slave, native-born or Spanish-born. A sophisticated propaganda distribution network spread bundles of pamphlets by boat, by horseback, by farm wagons and by inconspicuous Negroes as far away as the western extremity of the island. The propaganda effort soon dampened enthusiasm and support for the voluntario militia. That militia had peaked in manpower at 20,000, but declined to 7,000 and those who remained were losing their will to risk death in a fight. By May 1869, revolucionarios, in full control of Oriente province and most of Camagüey province, were planning an assault on the important province of Las Villas. Secret revolutionary cells were established in important locations in western Cuba. The main resistance to final triumph was centered in and around Havanah where the voluntario militia still held unchallenged power.

Céspedes' revolucionarios saw control of Cuba's railroad network (the westward half of the island, from Villa Clara and beyond) as key to taking control in Havanah. Centered in Havanah and totaling 1,000 miles in length, Cuba's railroads opened an easy and tolerably safe communication with Matanzas, Cardenas, and Sagua la Grande on the northern coast, with Villa Clara in the centre, and with Batabanò and Cienfuegos on the southern coast. From these major towns, branch railroads extended further. By June 1869, Cespedes' revolucionarios had important covert operatives in Matanzas, Cardenas, Sagua la Grande, Villa Clara, Cienfuegos, Batabanó and Guanajay. These revolutionary groups, operating in secret, had already collected arms supplied by Confederates and smuggled in by revolucionarios. They had spies among most groups of railroad workers and plans were being laid to commandeer the rails as Revolucionarios advanced westward toward their final goal, Havanah, where one swift, final assault would be launched. And they were busily trying to recruit a very important potential supporter -- none other than Don Juan Poey himself. Twenty-seven years ago, in 1842, the Caminos de Hierro de la Habana Company, backed by wealthy sugar planters and represented by Don Juan Poey, by far richest of them all, had purchased, from the financiers, the new railroad leading to and from Havanah. So Poey was well-connected and influential among railroad men.

During late April, Carlos Manuel de Céspedes had convinced Don Juan Poey to meet with him and other revolutionary leaders at Guáimaro, the Camagüey Province town where the Republic of Cuba in Arms had been proclaimed six weeks earlier. There, Poey became convinced that Céspedes' revolution was anchored in honorable independence from Spanish rule, that it promised an enlightened democratic government structure and a wise program of gradual emancipation. Furthermore, he saw solid evidence of important military support by the Confederate States of America. Soon afterward Céspedes travelled in secret to Poey's sugar plantation, Las Cañas, and there, the two men persuaded 19 owners of mid-island and western sugar plantations to join a secret revolutionary advisory group to be aligned with the revolucionarios. Thirteen of these men were Spanish-born members of the Casino Español and the rest were Cuba-born. This group took the secret name, Las Cañas Advisiorio. Their mission was to facilitate cooperation between revolucionarios and Spanish-born and Cuba-born men who desired for the revolution to succeed, but with a result that was beneficial to all Cubans. This group in particular looked forward to an alliance with the Confederate States of America that would lead to Cuba's admission as a State in a manner similar to the admission of the Spanish-speaking states which had successfully seceded from Mexico.

At this point in time, Capitán-General Domingo Dulce y Garay, the Spanish ruler over Cuba was being removed from command in disgrace. The commanders of the various battalions of voluntarios came to tell him that he would have to resign. Detained and transferred to a warship, Dulce sailed for Spain on June 5 – a humiliating and ignoble end to his brief service in Havanah. Lieutenant General Antonio Caballero de Rodas was soon crossing the Atlantic to take control. [233]

With revolucionarios in control of Oriente and Camagüey provinces, the next objective was to gain control of Las Villas, the west-central province. [234] This would prove difficult but achievable. Near the western boundary of Las Villas province was the eastern terminus of the existing east-west railroad line. This railroad terminal, at Macagua, was heavily defended, but its occupation was necessary. It was 40 miles north-northwest of the southern seaport of Cienfuegos, 50 miles southwest of the northern seaport of Isabela, 50 miles west of the central city of Santa Clara, 40 miles southeast of Cardenas, and 110 miles east of Havanah.

The fight to take control of Las Villas province was the hardest fought of the revolutionary campaign. Reinforced by rail, Spanish troops and voluntarios, well provisioned with ample weapons, field artillery and horses, put up a stiff fight. The battle raged for two months, but with every fight it seemed that the revolucionarios somehow advanced -- there were more of them. The Spanish troops felt they had nothing worthy to fight for, often retreating and hiding from exposing themselves. The voluntarios were of the upper class, many Spanish born, and their will to risk death was constantly shrinking. The important town of Villa Clara, located in the center of Las Villas province was surrendered on June 10, 1869. The important southern seaport town of Cienfluegos fell to the revolucionarios on June 21, the assault aided by important support from the Confederate Navy (it kept the Spanish fleet away, but did not shell coastal defenses). Now revolucionarios were able to receive arms and supplies at the seaport of Cienfluegos and ship them rapidly by railroad into the heart of the island at Villa Clara.

On June 28, 1869, Spanish Capitán-General Caballero de Rodas arrived at Havanah to take political and military control. He brought along 4,000 Spanish reinforcements and plans were underway to bring in 30 Spanish war ships by early the next year. [235] But would these reinforcements be too little too late? Rodas had no choice but to willingly submit to the Voluntarios, who demanded that their commanders act independently of Rodas' direction. Meanwhile, the Revolucionarios controlled the two easternmost provinces and were advancing westward across the third.

Following the conquest of Villa Clara and Cienfluegos, the subsequent coordinated attack on the western part of Las Villas province was impressive to behold. Operating often at night, locomotives and railroad cars were diverted east to behind Revolutionary lines, first to Macagua, then, as the Revolutionary line advanced westward, commandeered locomotives and cars were brought east of Colon, then east of Perico near the western boundary of Las Villas Province. The

---

[233] The departure of Capitán-General Domingo Dulce y Garay is truthful history.

[234] In truthful history the revolucionarios failed to control land any further west than the Spanish Júcaro-Morón defensive wall at the western boundary of the east-central province of Camagüey. From there to Macagua was 130 miles. So the farthest sustained Revolutionary advance restricted them to occupation (as guerillas), only 43 percent of the length of the island and far, far less than that much of the population.

[235] The arrival of Caballero de Rodas with 4,000 Spanish reinforcements is truthful history, as was the plan to follow with 30 Spanish war ships.

western province of Occidente was next. By this time, late July, many leaders in Cuban society were beginning to accept the inevitability of Revolutionary success. And Céspedes' effective Revolutionary propaganda campaign served to alleviate fears of a disastrous outcome among the wealthy and upper class people.

Employing night-time surprise attacks, Revolucionarios seized railroad assets along the line that led to the important seaport of Cárdenas, in the vicinity of Jovellanos and Palma. On August 20 a coordinated land and sea attack on Cárdenas resulted in a two-day victory. The Cardenas seaport, on the north coast, was thus secured and warships of the Confederate Navy prevented Spanish ships from entering the harbor. Capitán-General Caballero de Rodas, his reinforcements of 4,000 Spanish troops and the discouraged voluntarios were unable to stop the onslaught. Furthermore, as had been the case so often with newly arrived men from Spain, sickness greatly reduced the ranks of available healthy soldiers.

Next was the attack on the seaport of Matanzas, at the heart of Cuba's richest sugar producing area and the last northern seaport before reaching Havanah. More locomotives and rail cars were seized from the Matanzas rail system. Then, another coordinated land-sea attack yielded Matanzas to Rebel control on September 3. Again the Confederate Navy prevented Spanish ships from entering that harbor.

The final assault would be upon Havanah. This was a land assault from the west, from the south and from the east, plus a coordinated Confederate naval presence at the harbor entrance. But first we must look at the southern seaport of Batabanó. A major asset of the Spanish in Havanah was the railroad south to the seaport of Batabanó, which was connected to the capital by a direct railroad line. Voluntarios in Havanah viewed the railroad to Batabanó as their means of escape if all defensive efforts failed. But this was not to be available. While Spanish troops and Voluntarios concentrated to defend Havanah, Revolucionarios took control of the rail head at Guines and then San Felipe. Soon they were ready for a coordinated land and sea attack on Batabanó. It fell in 10 hours on September 17. Revolucionarios had recruited important supporters and supplied them with arms during the past 12 months, and when called forth in Western Cuba they came forward to re-inforce Revolucionarios from the east. To a great extend Batabanó fell from within.

## The Fall of Havanah and the República de Cuba

With Batabanó and San Felipe in Revolutionary hands and more locomotives and rail cars at the ready to advance artillery and troops, Céspedes' forces concentrated at three points for the final attack on Havanah. From the south troops gathered at San Felipe and began advancing north along its railroad toward Havanah. From the west, troops gathered at Guanajay and began advancing east along its railroad toward Havanah. From the east, Revolucionario cavalry commanded by General Forrest and heavily supported by Revolucionario troops advanced toward Havanah (there was no coastal railroad here; by the way). Forrest had decided to personally lead the main portion of the Revolucionario cavalry soon after the writing of the constitution. Students of history remember that seizing Havanah from the sea was extremely difficult, for the harbor's fortifications were formidable. But the fall of those fortifications was not necessary to achieve victory. The people of Havanah knew the Spanish cause was hopeless. The island would soon be in the hands of the Revolucionarios. So Havanah fell from the land attack while the harbor defensives stood as ineffective monuments to a powerful Spanish New World legacy of glorious days gone by. In Havanah, at the Plaza de Armas, Revolucionarios received the surrender of the Spanish Government. Céspedes signed for the Republic of Cuba. Capitán-General Caballero de Rodas signed for the Spanish monarchy. The surrender took place at noon on October 1, 1869, celebrated each year as "Cuban Independence Day."

The Provisional Government of the República de Cuba was established on October 15, 1869. This was merely an update to the organization of the Provisional Government established in April 1869 at Guaimaro -- the Republic of Cuba in Arms. A Cuban Federal Constitution was drafted, establishing a federal government of limited powers and recognizing four states within the island. A major aspect of the revised Constitution was the division of the legislative branch into a House and a Senate.

Elections were held in December 1869 to ratify the Constitution of the República de Cuba and Presidente Céspedes and members of the Legislatura de Cuba and other officials took office on January 1, 1870.

During March 1870, Cuban and Confederate officials negotiated a merger treaty that was to enable the República de Cuba to transform itself into a State and accept admission into the Confederate States of America. The Confederate Senate approved the treaty in April. In Havanah, delegates to the Convención Constituyente Cubana unanimously agreed to the merger and then drafted a State Constitution and government structure, which included dissolving former states and defining new counties.

In May 1870, Cuban men who were qualified to vote went to the polls and elected legislators and a governor. With only token opposition, Carlos Céspedes was elected to the office of Governor of the State of Cuba.

In Havanah, on July 4, 1870, in a ceremony held in the Plaza de Armas, the flag of the República de Cuba was lowered and the flag of the State of Cuba was raised. On the eastern side of the Plaza stood the Palacio de los Capitanes. It was in the Palacio that officials signed the documents accepting the State of Cuba into the Confederate States of America. In the center of the Plaza de Armas, a statue would be erected to honor Carlos Manuel de Céspedes – leader of the Cuban Revolution, President of the Republic of Cuba and first Governor of the State of Cuba. [236]

In accepting statehood in the Confederate States of America, Cubans were agreeing to support a language transition from Spanish to English. This need to support uniformity in language within the Confederacy had also been understood in the seceded Mexican states and in Russian America. It would take time. But a pledge was taken to teach English in all Cuban schools and to make proficiency in the language a requirement of a satisfactory education. Of course, today, Spanish is considered a secondary language and 97 percent of native Cubans normally converse in English. It is the language of government, business and public communications, including newspapers, radio and television.

### In Truthful History, Cuba Was to Suffer Persistently, Even to this Day

Tragic is the true history of the fight for Cuban independence that began at the eastern end of the island with Carlos Manuel de Céspedes's Grito de Yara on October 10, 1868. An abridgement follows.

- From October 1868 through 1873, 3,118 political prisoners were executed and 7,082 were taken prisoner whose fate is unknown. [237]

---

[236] By the way, speaking truthfully, the statue of Carlos Manuel de Céspedes in the center of the Plaza and the flag in the Palacio remain and are often viewed by today's tourists.

[237] These truthful facts are from *The Book of Blood: An Authentic Record of the Policy Adopted by Modern Spain to Put an End to the War for the Independence of Cuba* (October, 1868 to November 10, 1873), by Néstor Ponce de León.

- The rebellion lasted 10 years, until finally crushed in 1878.

- Throughout the 10-year conflict, Spanish forces far outnumbered the rebellion forces. Yet, insurgents remained contentious through mastery of guerrilla warfare even though Spain dispatched 174,948 troops across the Atlantic in an effort to defeat the rebellion. Of these Spanish troops, 8,112 died in battle and 91,112 died of disease, the worse killers being yellow fever, smallpox and cholera.

- During the ten-year conflict, the Spanish government in Madrid dispatched eleven supreme commanders to Cuba, one after the other, to take turns directing the fight against the Revolucionarios.

- Because of frequent regime changes in Spain, the Madrid government was unable until 1876 to devote full resources to stamping out the Cuban insurgency.

- The United States government in Washington took no significant interest in aiding the Liberation Army of Cuba.

- The Spanish authority signed a peace agreement, known as the Pact of Zanjón on February 10, 1878, but some fighting continued until May. Céspedes had been killed four years earlier, on February 27, 1874, by Spanish troops who refused to let him go into exile.

- Twenty-one years later, in 1895, a renewed fight for Cuban independence surfaced in the eastern part of the island. This time 80 percent of revolutionary forces were of African ancestry. But Revolucionarios were at the outskirts of Havanah in January 1896. Yet the Madrid government countered with General Valeriano Weyler, Marques de Tenerit and more troops. Weyler pushed the revolutionaries back, broadly imposing harsh treatment as the conflict continued through 1897 and into 1898. But this time Spain's fate would be different.

- On February 15, 1898, the battleship U.S. Maine, lying peacefully at anchor in Havana harbor, complete with 258 American sailors aboard, was demolished in a "gigantic explosion." The battleship quickly sank and all aboard died. History would show that the cause was an "internal coal fire in a bunker adjacent to the ships munitions magazine." But, at the time, Americans quickly took the event as justification to declare war on Spain. Not just war within the island of Cuba, but war against Spain worldwide. Americans wanted control over all of the remaining Spanish colonies: Cuba, Puerto Rico and The Philippines. So, rejecting Spain's offer to grant independence to Cuba, President William McKinley, Republican of Ohio, asked Congress to declare war on Spain. Complying, Congress declared war on Spain on April 25, 1898.

- The Spanish-American War progressed rapidly. Spain was totally overmatched. Its navy was demolished. Destroyed were the Spanish Pacific fleet at the Philippines and then its Atlantic fleet at Cuba. On the island of Cuba, in the famous charge up San Juan Hill by Theodore Roosevelt and troops termed the "Rough Riders," 3,000 Americans advanced against 1,000 Spanish troops and won the fight, but they suffered 223 killed and over 1,000 wounded, compared to Spanish loses of half that number. However, Spain was on its knees, its fleet destroyed, and the last of its colonial empire now hopelessly indefensible. Spain surrendered on July 17, 1898. The conquest of Spain's colonies – Cuba, Puerto Rico and The Philippines -- took less than 3 months.

- Now, it seems that the McKinley Administration and the Republican-controlled House and Senate did not want to annex Cuba as a territory to be under American rule. They did take over Puerto Rico and The Philippines, perhaps because those islands made useful bases for the American navy. Instead, they just put Cuba under 4 years of military rule, eventually allowing it to be an independent nation. It seems that the Republicans did not want to become involved with the large population of people of African ancestry that lived in Cuba. But the saga of Cuba was not over.

 • Fifty-five years later, on July 26, 1953, Fidel Castro, 26 years of age, launched a communist insurrection in eastern Cuba, first attacking weapons stores at Bayamo and Moncada to arm his men. Although captured and incarcerated for two years, Castro managed to sustain the insurrection he had started. By 1956 Castro was leading a more powerful insurrection, but by 1957 he was still only able to lead a guerrilla campaign. In 1958 the Cuban Communist Party rallied to Castro, naming him their leader. Cuban Dictator Fulgencio Batista was nearing defeat. On December 31, 1958, Batista departed Cuba on an airplane, never to return. His reign had lasted 25 years.

 • On January 2, 1959, from a balcony overlooking the elegant Parque Céspedes in Santiago de Cuba, in the far eastern region of the island, Fidel Castro made his first speech as the new dictator of Communist Cuba -- choosing to do so at region where Carlos Manuel de Céspedes had begun his campaign for Cuban independence 91 years earlier. [238] You see, Fidel Castro, the demagogue, seemed to be calling forth Céspedes's ghost in a strange attempt to justify a very different Cuba than had been proclaimed in the Grito de Yara on October 10, 1868. Instead of independence and freedom for the Cuban people, the lovely 745-long island was sinking into a communist dictatorship more oppressive than anything the heroic champion of Cuban independence could have imagined. As of the writing of this book, the Communist dictatorship of Cuba has lasted 59 years, and the oppression goes on.

## Tuesday Evening Selected Diary Postings

Carlos Cespedes Tuesday evening diary posting said, "On Thursday everybody gushed over Benedict Juárez and his ancestor, President Benito Juárez. On Friday everybody gushed over Conchita Rezanov and her Russian America heroes. On Monday everybody gushed over Emma Lunalilo and those good people who transformed those mid-Pacific islands into an independent democracy and then won statehood in the Confederacy. Today, everyone was gushing over the heroic story of Cuban independence over Spain, statehood for Cuba, and the leadership of my great-great-great-grandfather, Carlos Manuel Céspedes. I admit it. I felt honored and proud at the same time. What a story! What a story! But Robert Lee has a great story, too. Had supper with him tonight -- the great-great-great-grandson of General Lee. During our first three days Professor Davis helped us understand how President Davis, General Lee and many other great formative leaders of the eleven seceded States directed the successful defense of the Confederacy against invaders from the north. Nevertheless, at supper tonight, Robert insisted on praising Carlos Manuel Céspedes, perhaps a bit too much. I just turned it around and told him, 'You are mighty kind, but if I was forced to choose between these two great leaders, my ancestor or yours, I would choose General Lee.' We decided to let it go at that. But, diary, I am very, very proud on my Céspedes roots. Goodnight."

Diary note by Amanda Washington said, "The wonderful fact about our Confederate States is the way that our country was created by people of such diverse racial backgrounds. Of course it all started with people of the European race declaring secession and winning that independence. But African Americans in the seceded States were helpful then in the best way they could. And the Five Civilized Tribes supported the seceded States and won great benefits as a result. [239] Then Mexicans of mostly Native-American blood won independence from the Mexican provinces

---

[238] The writer visited Santiago de Cuba in 2017 and viewed "the elegant Parque Céspedes."

[239] In truthful history many in the Five Civilized Tribes supported the Confederate States, although some did not. The most famous Confederate was General Stan Watie of the Cherokee Nation.

north of Mexico City, then reorganized and joined the Confederacy. In Cuba, people of African ancestry were very important in helping in that fight for independence from Spain. Russian America was a great cooperative effort between people of Russian (European) ancestry and people of Native American ancestry. Hawaii completes the story with the great contribution of the Polynesian race. We are a diverse people and that will be a theme of the July 4th celebration."

Diary note by Marie Saint Martin said, "Congrats to Carlos on Cuban independence and the great leadership by his ancestor, President Céspedes. And congrats on his Spanish guitar playing. He will be a great contribution on July 4th when our music group will be performing."

# Part 2, Chapter 6, Day 17 – The Great Confederate Expansion, July 4, 1870 – and Final Expansion, July 4, 1877 -- Class Lecture, Wednesday, June 22, 2011

This Wednesday morning Professor Davis will present the second climax in our story, titled *The CSA Trilogy* – The Confederate expansions of 1870 and 1877. The twelve essayists are in their seats, clearly in a celebratory mood. We listen in as Professor Davis begins.

## Overview of the 1870 and 1877 Expansions

The following timeline presents key dates by which you may follow the Great Confederate Expansion of 1870.

<u>1862, September 29.</u> The Montreal Treaty is signed and ratified by the USA and the CSA, establishing boundaries and relocation of people of full or partial African ancestry who lived in what remained of the Unite States.

<u>1864, October 18.</u> Mother Russia grants independence to Russian America for payment of $8,000,000 in gold (advanced by the CSA, and repaid in gold that was gathered near Nome by citizens of the Republic of Russian America over the next four years).

<u>1866, May 5.</u> Treaty of Saltillo signed between the government of the Seceded States of northern Mexico and the French occupiers of Mexico. This established the Republic of North Mexico, whose independence is assured by the CSA.

<u>1870, March.</u> Cuba wins its independence and agrees to a merger treaty with the CSA.

<u>1870, July 4.</u> The day of the "Great Confederate Expansion. On that day the following takes place:

The State of Texas divides itself into four States: East Texas, South Texas, North Texas and West Texas.

The Territory of New Mexico becomes the State of New Mexico.

The Territory of South California becomes the State of South California.

By treaty between two nations, the Nation of Sequoyah becomes a State within the Confederate States of America.

By treaty between two nations, the Republic of Russian America becomes a State within the Confederate States of America.

By treaty between two nations, the former Seceded Mexican States, now reorganized as six States, are merged into the Confederate States of America, thereby adding six to the Confederate number.

By treaty between two nations, the Republic of Cuba becomes a State within the Confederate States of America.

That was the "Great Confederate Expansion." The flag now had 25 stars. But more expansion was yet to come. Seven years later, Confederates enjoyed their second "Concluding Expansion," the Expansion of 1877, growing the flag to 27 stars:

<u>January 1, 1877.</u> King Lunalilo abdicates this throne over the Hawaiian Islands, making way for the Republic of the Hawaiian Islands with Samuel Kipi as President.

<u>July 4, 1877.</u> The Confederacy celebrates its Concluding Expansion, adding Arizona and the Hawaiian Islands as states:

The Territory of Arizona becomes the State of Arizona.

By merger treaty, the Republic of the Hawaiian Islands becomes a State within the Confederate States of America.

## The Confederate Expansions by the Numbers

After the settlement of the boundary with the United States, the original 11 Confederate States were characterized by the following land area and population, as measured in 1870. Remember that the boundaries of Virginia, Tennessee, and Arkansas had changed as a result of the Montreal Treaty:

| State | Area, Sq. Mi. | Population (1870) |
|---|---|---|
| Virginia | 58,694 | 1,667,177 |
| North Carolina | 53,818 | 1,339,201 |
| South Carolina | 32,020 | 917,288 |
| Georgia | 59,425 | 1,480,136 |
| Florida | 65,755 | 244,072 |
| Tennessee | 50,226 | 1,699,002 |
| Alabama | 52,419 | 1,246,240 |
| Mississippi | 48,431 | 993,506 |
| Arkansas | 76,390 | 1,179,354 |
| Louisiana | 51,840 | 908,644 |
| Four Texas States | 275,570 | 1,023,224 |
| **Total** | **824,588** | **12,697,844** |

As mentioned before, it was in 1870 that the State of Texas was allowed to subdivide itself into four (4) States, thereby giving it eight (8) Senators instead of only two. As previously mentioned, this right to divide had been promised at the time of the merger agreement between the United States of America and the Republic of Texas. So, the Confederate States were, in 1870, honoring this promise. The State of Texas, comprised of 275,570 square miles and an 1870 population of 1,023,224, subdivided itself into East Texas, North Texas, South Texas and West Texas.

Furthermore, by the Montreal Treaty, Confederates controlled the following territories:

| Territory | Area, Sq. Mi. | Population |
|---|---|---|
| New Mexico | 121,589 | 101,061 |
| Arizona | 125,054 | 11,590 |
| South California | 68,752 | 224,100 |
| Sequoyah [240] | 62,909 | 181,067 |
| **Total** | **378,304** | **517,818** |

---

[240] In truthful history Sequoyah would be divided into Oklahoma Territory and Indian Territory. No census would be taken before 1900. The 1900 census revealed 398,331 in Oklahoma Territory (western part) and 392,060 in Indian Territory (eastern part) for a total of 790,391. In truthful history, Oklahoma Territory was taken from the relocated Five Civilized Tribes, leaving them less than half of the land they had been promised prior to removal from east of the Mississippi River. After the War Between the States, whites were encouraged to migrate into Oklahoma Territory in a great land rush. Upon Statehood in 1907, whites held the majority and ruled the State of Oklahoma, reducing the Native Americans to second class citizens. The estimated 1870 population of Sequoyah in our alternate history is 181,067, the result of immigration of Native Americans and friends of Native Americans into the region. There would be no 1900's "land rush" and Native Americans, many of them part blood, would remain in political control.

The Confederacy also added the population of the resettled African Americans. Since some had not yet settled in specific States, that population is not included in the numbers above.

**Population**

Resettled African Americans — 731,000

So, after adding the resettled African Americans from the Northern States, the sum of area and population for States and Territories of the Confederacy was:

| States and Territories | Area, Sq. Mi. | Population (1870) |
| --- | --- | --- |
| States and Territories [241] | 1,202,892 | 13,946,662 |

Now we look at the mergers into the Confederate States of the lands and peoples of the Seceded Mexican States. You will recall that the Treaty of Saltillo was signed on May 5, 1866 between numerous northern Mexican States, led by Benito Juárez, and the French Intervention, led by Maximilian. The resulting nation, The Republic of North Mexico, held 65 percent of the land of Mexico, much of it quite arid and sparsely populated, and 36 percent of the population of Mexico. In 1870, to facilitate a reasonable merger into the Confederate States of America, the seceded Mexican states had been consolidated into six (6) States.

| State | Area, Sq. Mi. | Population | Original Mexican State |
| --- | --- | --- | --- |
| Costa Noroeste | 220,915 | 360,387 | B. California, Sonora, Chihuahua |
| Central Norte | 99,180 | 685,012 | Sinaloa, Durango, Zacatecas |
| Costa Este | 114,286 | 501,083 | Coahuila, Nuevo Leon, Tamaulipas |
| Costa del Sur | 21,244 | 317,720 | San Luis Potosi (9/10), |
| Costa Sudoeste | 33,153 | 611,996 | Jalisco (2/3), Nayarit, Aquascalientes |
| Central del Sur | 12,141 | 627,241 | Guanajuato (9/10), Queretaro (1/3) |
| Total [242] | 500,919 | 3,103,439 | |

We now take into account the merger into the Confederacy of the Republic of Russian America. You will remember how, with the valuable support of the Confederacy, the people of Russian America won their independence from Mother Russia on October 18, 1864 and became the Republic of Russian America. For six years this new country had been successful. Population had expanded and industries had grown, such as fishing and canning. Much gold had been found, the $8,000,000 debt had been paid, and the currency was strong. So, from this firm foundation, the Republic of Russian America transformed itself into a State and merged into the Confederate States of America.

| State | Area, Sq. Mi. | Population |
| --- | --- | --- |
| Russian America | 663,300 | 60,000 |

The story of the successful Cuban Independence Movement was both heroic and inspiring. With important help from the Confederacy, Cuba's independence from Spanish rule was certified on October 1, 1869 at the Plaza de Armas, where Carlos Manuel de Céspedes signed for Cubans and Caballero de Rodas signed for the Spanish monarchy. The Republic of Cuba took over the reins of government and peace prevailed. Less than a year later, the Republic transformed itself into a State and merged into the Confederate States of America.

---

[241] The truthful 1870 population of the 11 Confederate States, plus West Virginia and what would become Oklahoma, was 9,992,309.

[242] These population numbers represent the actual 1900 census for the truthful Mexican States divided by 1.65. An earlier census was never taken in truthful history.

| State | Area, Sq. Mi. | Population |
|---|---|---|
| Cuba | 42,426 | 1,414,508 |

We now total the land area and population of the Confederate States of America following the great 1870 expansion. Note that the land area and the resulting natural resources had precisely doubled, from 1,202,892 to 2,405,792 square miles. The population had increased 33 percent, from 13.9 million to 18.5 million people.

| All CSA States | Area, Sq. Mi. | Population |
|---|---|---|
| Grand Total | 2,405,792 | 18,524,610 |

For a comparison, we observe that the land area and population of the United States for the year 1870 was as follows. [243]

| All USA States | Area, Sq. Mi. | Population |
|---|---|---|
| Grand Total | 2,000,638 | 24,708,843 |

So, in exchange for returning prisoners of war and accepting 731,000 Northerners of noticeable African ancestry, the Confederate States was able to negotiate land trades in Virginia, Kentucky and Missouri, take over governorship of the Indian Territory of the Five Civilized Tribes and extend its boundaries out to the Pacific. Thus established as a Confederacy of mostly sovereign States and recognized territories, Confederates were soon afterward successful in assisting Liberals in Mexico in achieving a Secession of the northern Mexican States; in helping the people of Cuba achieve independence from the Spanish monarchy, and in assisting the people of Russian America in their drive for independence. So, as of July 4, 1870, the Confederate States managed to have under its control twenty percent more land than was under the control of the United States of America at that time (2,405,792 versus 2,000,638 acres).

But one more expansion was to come: allowing the Republic of the Hawaiian Islands to transform itself into a State and merge into the Confederacy. Also, the Territory of Arizona was granted statehood. This final expansion, called the "Concluding Expansion," would take place seven years into the future, on July 4, 1877.

| State | Area, Sq. Mi. | Population |
|---|---|---|
| The CSA in 1870 | 2,405,792 | 18,524,610 |
| State of Hawaii [244] | 6,423 | 59,742 |
| CSA 1877 Total | 2,412,215 | 18,584,352 |

[243] The truthful United States 1870 population was 38,155,505, in spite of the fact that deaths due to four years of war had stricken approximately 1,000,000 Americans and Confederates. Adding these people back in increases the population to 39,155,505. However, in our alternate history we recognize that eagerness to come to the United States from Europe was not as prevalent due to the Montreal Treaty's consequent deflating effect on the economy of the Northern States. For that reason, in our alternate history, overall population growth is curbed by 2,000,000. The result is a United States 1870 population of 24,708,843 (38,155,505 + 1,000,000 − 13,946,662 − 500,000).

[244] The 1872 Hawaiian population per Ralph S. Kuykendall was, in truthful history, made up of 51,531 people of full or partial Hawaiian ancestry, 2,944 Caucasian immigrants, 2,038 Chinese immigrant workers, and 384 others for a total of 56,897. Our alternate history increases this number by 5 percent.

# A Map Illustrating the Consolidation of 16 Seceded Mexican States and Territories into 6 Confederate States

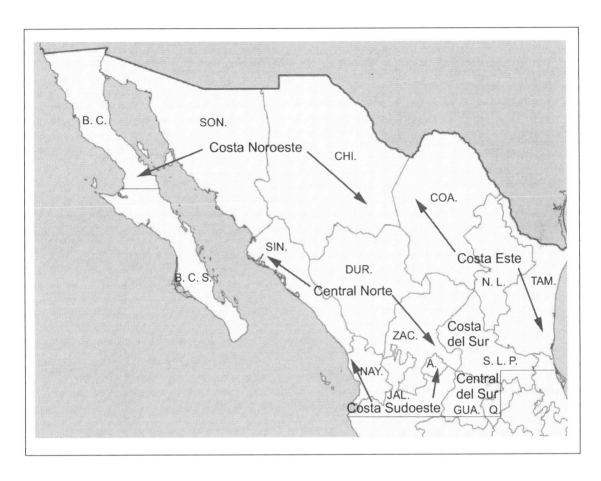

Note to Reader: To make this map more familiar to readers of *The CSA Trilogy*, the Mexican states are presented using modern day boundaries and there are no territories. Note that Baja California is divided into Baja California and Baja California Sur.

The 16 Mexican States are shown in abbreviated names. The notations are presented below:

| | | | |
|---|---|---|---|
| B. C. | Baja California | ZAC. | Zacatecas |
| B. C. S. | Baja California Sur | A. | Aquascalientes |
| SON. | Sonora | S. L. P. | San Luis Potosi |
| CHI. | Chihuahua | N. L. | Nuevo Leon |
| COA. | Coahuila | TAM. | Tamaulipas |
| SIN, | Sinaloa | GUA. | Guanajuato |
| DUR. | Durango | Q. | Queretaro |
| NAY. | Nayarit | | |
| JAL. | Jalisco | | |

## Celebrating Our Confederacy

The Concluding Expansion resulted in a country made up of, in a manner of speaking, 27 States of remarkable diversity in both geography and population. The Confederate Senate contained 54 seats and the Confederate House of Representatives contained five times as many seats -- 270 seats -- which were allocated based on the total population census of each State, updated each decade. Although individual States established voter qualifications, mostly similar to those reported in another chapter of this book, at the Confederate level of government, every citizen was figured into his or her share of Representatives in the Confederate House (immigrants and visitors that were not bona fide citizens did not add to the count). One note is obvious: of the 54 senators and 270 Representatives, the original Confederacy and the three territories it acquired between Texas and the Pacific was home to the political majority and original Confederates felt secure in that. Those 17 States were represented by 34 of the 54 Senate seats and about 75 percent of the Representative seats.

The celebration of the Concluding Confederate Expansion on July 4, 1877 was certainly magnificent, but the celebrations of the Great Confederate Expansion on July 4, 1870 was even more so, and that is the event most often revered. Enthusiasm ran high. The Confederate Flag of 1870 contained three bars -- two red, one white -- which people now argue represent the three races of man – Caucasian, Negroid and Asian (which included Native Americans). In a field of blue the flag contains 25 stars of equal size, each representing a Confederate State. The center, containing 3 stars, was surrounded by a circle of 7 more stars and that by a circle of 15 stars, giving a total of 25 equal-sized stars.

There were celebrations in all 25 State capitals, but the most moving was the celebration at Davis, which was widely attended and included an amazing program of parades, music and feasting (yes, there was plenty of barbeque, corn on the cob, vine-ripe tomatoes, watermelon and peach pies). The parades seemed endless, as companies of Confederate veterans joined with veteran militia from Cuba, the Seceded Mexican States and Sitka, Russian America.

In the summer of 1870 Davis was mostly drawings on paper -- visions on engineering and architectural plans. But key avenues had been laid out and graded, and the central park had been landscaped, complete with an elevated band shell, it's back resembling a 50 foot wide by 25 foot high by 25 foot deep sea shell -- one quarter of a sphere -- designed to project sound forward toward the audience that was to be positioned within a field 200 yards wide by 400 yards deep. This was to be the site of the celebration festivities, including the speeches and the musical performances.

The expansive program of music that day was extraordinary. Of course various marching bands were playing Dixie on almost every street corner, but not during the formal music presentations in the late afternoon and evening.

The most moving event of all was the mass choir assembled from dozens of African American churches that performed three songs that were so, so meaningful.

First, the massed choir sang "Say Brothers Will You Meet Us on Canaan's Happy Shore," composed by William Steffe of South Carolina in the early 1950's. A compelling and beautiful song of invitation, it had been and still is widely sung in Confederate States tent revival meetings, encouraging attendees to come forward, accept Christ and join the flock of believers. The chorus,

"Glory, glory, hallelujah!" was exceptionally moving and even more so when sung by an African American mass choir.[245]

Next, the massed choir sang "Amazing Grace," as arranged by William "Singing Billy" Walker of Spartanburg, South Carolina. [246] The result was spell-binding.

> "Amazing Grace, how sweet thou art
> That saved a wretch like me!
> I once was lost, but now am found,
> Was blind, but now I see.
>
> "'Twas grace that taught my heart to fear,
> And grace my fears relieved,
> How precious did that grace appear
> The hour I first believed. . . ."

Immediately following the mass choir performance, former President Jefferson Davis mounted the podium to address the huge crowd. Of course, in spite of the acoustic band shell behind him, many were too far away to hear his "sweet voice," but they were thrilled to see him, even from three hundred yards away and looked forward to reading the text of his speech in the morning newspaper. That speech is presented below:

> "Four score and fourteen years ago our fathers brought forth on this continent a new country, conceived in Liberty and dedicated to the proposition that all men are created equal.
>
> "This human right to liberty was successfully defended in a great War Between the States, testing whether any country so conceived and dedicated could long endure. Confederates met on five battle-fields in that war and won the day for Liberty and justice for all men of all races of mankind -- for ourselves, our children, our grandchildren, and beyond.
>
> "During the past decade of the 1860's, many brave men suffered in our battles for liberty – in Virginia, in Tennessee, in Alabama and Mississippi, in Arkansas. Beyond our original boundaries, many more brave men have also suffered in battles for liberty -- in the seceded Mexican States, in Cuba, and in Russian America – all of them giving their lives so that Liberty may, for the first time, be won for their families.
>
> "But, in a larger sense, we cannot properly dedicate, we cannot consecrate – we cannot hallow – the grounds where they died. The brave men, living and dead, who struggled there, have consecrated it far above our poor power to add or detract. The world will little note, nor long remember what we say here, but it can never forget what they did there. It is for us the living, rather, to be dedicated within this Confederacy to the unfinished work which they who fought have thus so nobly advanced. It is rather for us to be here dedicated to the great task remaining before us – that our diverse citizenry learn to be bound together by speaking to one another in the English language – that those

---

[245] In truthful history, the music and chorus of William Steffe's "Say Brothers" was transformed into the Northern State's abolitionist song, "John Brown's Body," and shortly afterward into their equally horrific military conquest song, "The Battle Hymn of the Republic," adapted from a poem by Julia Ward Howe of Boston.

[246] William "Singing Billy" Walker encouraged singing by church choirs using "shaped note" musical notation, and pioneered in the teaching of choral music to members of small-town Southern churches. His song books, including *Southern Harmony*, were widely used in the mid-1800's. He is most famous for adapting the melody of the traditional British song, "New Britain" to the popular poem by Anglican clergyman John Newton of England: "Amazing Grace." It is Singing Billy's version of "Amazing Grace" that is sung world-wide today.

remaining in bondage, already greatly reduced over the past decade, will, in an orderly and humane manner, be advanced to successful independent living and citizenship -- that our borders will be defended and immigration will be encouraged, but regulated – that State Sovereignty will be preserved within the goals of a limited central government, which is so essential to maintaining harmony among a people of such diverse heritage.

"In this way we shall take increased devotion to the cause of Liberty for which those brave men gave the last full measure of devotion – that we here highly resolve that those dead shall not have died in vain – that within this diverse country, under God, we shall sustain our birthright of Liberty – and that government of the people, by the people, for the people, shall not perish from the earth." [247]

At the conclusion of Jefferson Davis's speech, the mass choir again engaged in song, this time presenting the newly commissioned Sovereign States Anthem, newly composed and arranged for eight parts by one of Nashville's finest Baptist musicians. It was sung acapella (no accompanying musicians) with such purity of pitch and balance of parts that experts with ears highly trained in the art of music pronounced it the finest performance presented anywhere on this earth up to that time in human history. Sadly, the invention of audible recording technology, would await a few more years.

### Sovereign States Anthem

We are one [248]
We are free
We are the Great
Diversity

From Carolina's sandy beach,
Westward to the Pacific shore,
From Artic ice beyond our reach,
To warm Gulf waters we adore.

We are one
We are free
We are the Great
Diversity

Asia, Europe and Africa --
The roots of our family tree.
It was God's plan -- shout out hurrah --
That we could live in Harmony!

---

[247] The writer asks that you be understanding of his passion concerning the parody of President Lincoln's Gettysburg Address. Perhaps, by reading the above similar speech, given in a very different and fictional situation, you, the reader, might better understand the extent to which Lincoln's brief November 1863 speech (easily read on the internet) mischaracterized the political issues that produced and sustained, over the course of four bloody years, the War Between the States. Of course, in our alternate history President Lincoln had no opportunity to deliver an address to commemorate soldiers who died at Gettysburg, Pennsylvania. In our alternate history, in this historical novel, there was no fighting at Gettysburg.

[248] In almost every other country in the world, this type of music would be called the "National Anthem," but Confederates have to this day remained adamant that theirs is a country made up of States that remain "Sovereign" except for the limited powers assigned to the government at Davis as detailed in the Confederate Constitution. They call the CSA a "country," not a "nation."

We are one
We are free
We are the Great
Diversity

The Lord knows of our faithfulness
And leads us toward prosperity.
His love enables our toughness,
Honor and generosity.

Diverse, Diverse we are Diversity. [249]

## The British Brass Band Concert

The final event that evening was a marvelous brass band performance. Brass band music had become very popular in the British Isles during the 1850's and 1860's and Confederates loved the similarities to the military bands heard during the brief War Between the States. But the British brass band that the Confederates Celebration Committee had commissioned to cross the Atlantic and to present the final event of the evening truly amazed everyone. The core of the brass band was the Black Dyke Mills Brass Band from Queensbury, West Yorkshire, England. This core band was supplemented by additional musicians and instruments, yielding a then state-of-the-art outfit.[250] Situated on the band shell platform to project the music forward toward the audience, the result thrilled everyone, even those 250 yards away. The crowd was electrified as soon as the concert began with *I Wish I was in Dixie's Land*. Other memorable favorites of the Southern States included *The Bonnie Blue Flag, My Old Kentucky Home* and *Oh Shenandoah*. Texans loved *The Yellow Rose of Texas*.

---

[249] You will read much about "diversity" in *The CSA Trilogy*. Although in truthful history, in the year 2011, the word "diversity" means many different things to many different people -- in our alternate history of the Confederate States of America its meaning is more narrow and is understood as a feature of Confederate society to be celebrated. In the CSA, "diversity" speaks of the range of racial and ethnic ancestries of the Confederate people. Confederates do not all look alike and their talents and abilities vary broadly. But they are Confederates. They speak the common English language. Immigrants who have arrived since 1865, most of them from Europe, had learned and continue to learn English and blend into Confederate society. So "diversity" to a Confederate does not mean diverse cultural behaviors, does not mean that Muslims can disrupt the Christian social norm, does not mean that racial and/or ethnic gangs can get away with bad behavior, does not mean that political agitators can desecrate the monuments erected to honor long-ago Confederates. Stated in a positive way, the diverse peoples within our States have subordinated their former cultures to become compatible with the governments that exist within the various States, and with the Confederate Government at Davis.

[250] Englishman John Foster (1798-1879) -- owner of Black Dyke Mills, a very large woolen weaving mill in Queensbury -- loved to play the French horn and loved music. To further that interest he had, in 1855, created, from among his employees, the Black Dyke Mills Brass Band. In the course of 14 years, they had grown so much in musical excellence that they were considered to be among the best in Great Britain. So, in January 1870, his band was invited by the Celebration Committee to perform at Davis on July 4. As of this writing, the Black Dyke Brass Band still exists in Queensbury and is still considered one the best brass bands in the world. The British brass band that thrilled attendees at Davis on July 4, 1870 was made up of expert musicians performing with the following brass instruments: 1 soprano E-flat cornet; 9 B-flat cornets; 1 B-flat flugelhorn; 3 E-flat alto horns; 2 B-flat baritone horns; 2 B-flat tenor trombones; 1 C bass trombone (notated in bass clef); 2 B-flat euphoniums; 2 E-flat tubas (notated in treble clef), and 2 BB-flat tubas (notated in treble clef). Percussion would be added to the classical brass band in future years and percussionists normally make up part of today's brass bands in Great Britain and in the Confederate States. Find recordings of Black Dyke Band music on the internet.

Cubans jumped for joy at the playing of *The Bayamo Anthem* (El Himno de Bayamo) and *The Bayamo Song* (La Bayamesa). [251]

Citizens of the Seceded Mexican States clapped and waved upon hearing God and Liberty (*Dios y Libertad*), which had become the Mexican National Anthem in 1854, before the French Intervention and the secession of the northern Mexican States. Apparently, the people of the Seceded States felt that anthem was theirs to keep, so they cheered it wildly. [252]

The few Russian Americans who had been able to make the trip to Davis were thrilled and honored by the playing of the new arrangement for brass band of Modest Mussorgsky's previously never performed *A Night on Bald Mountain*. The story of how that came to be is worthy of a bit of digression:

It was not difficult to find appropriate music to celebrate statehood for Cuba and for the seceded Mexican States, but finding music to celebrate statehood for Russian America presented a distinct challenge. But Englishman John Foster, the owner of the Black Dyke Mills band, was up to the task. He traveled to Russia to consult with music composers and instructors at the Saint Petersburg Conservatory, and soon learned that Modest Mussorgsky (1839-1881) had written, two years earlier, a score containing some wild and wooly orchestral music that had not yet been performed. Foster liked the composition. It would sound as wild and foreboding as Russian America must be – sound like the challenge being met bravely by the heroic Russian American people who lived there. Mussorgsky agreed to license the rights to arrange the composition for brass band and Foster soon had a polished score for expert brass musicians. That is the story of how *A Night on Bald Mountain* came to be played by a brass band at Davis on July 4, 1870. It thrilled all that heard it, for they felt they had seen, in music, a picture of wild and wooly Russian America. [253]

The final brass band number was the Confederate Anthem, the anthem previously sung acapella by the choir. At this point, the members of the choir were dispersed among the audience to help in leading the singing. The Brass Band played an introduction and the dispersed choir began to sing, line after line, and the audience got into the act and joined in as best they could – especially when it came time to join in with:

We are one
We are free
We are the Great Diversity . . .

---

[251] In truthful history El Himno de Bayamo (The Bayamo Anthem) was written in 1868 by Perucho Figueredo, a participant in the Battle of Bayamo in 1868, in which the Cuban Revolutionaries defeated a portion of the Spanish army. A related song, La Bayamesa (The Bayamo Song) was first composed in 1851 by Revolutionary leader Carlos Manuel de Céspedes and compatriot José Fornaris.

[252] Dios y Libertad (God and Liberty) was written in 1854 by Francisco González Bocanegra (lyrics) and Jaime Nunó.

[253] At Saint Petersburg Foster sought advice from leading Conservatory pianist, composer and conductor Mily Balakirev (1837-1910) and other emerging Russian composers. Balakirev, visualizing in his mind's eye what wild, mountainous and frigid Russian America must look like, remembered the yet-to-be-performed work by a promising composer at the Conservatory by the name of Modest Mussorgsky (1839-1881). Mussorgsky had written a score containing some wild and wooly orchestral music two years earlier, but it had not yet been performed (truth be known, Balakirev did not like the work). Taking this suggestion from Balakirev, Foster met with Mussorgsky at his apartment near the Conservatory and there also got to know his roommate, Nikolai Rimsky-Korsakov. Foster liked the composition. It would sound as wild and foreboding as Russian America must be – sound like the challenge being met bravely by the heroic Russian American people who lived there. Mussorgsky agreed to license it for brass band and the three men set about copying the score and rearranging the music right there at the Conservatory. Five days later Foster was on a ship heading back to England with the draft of *A Night on Bald Mountain* for Brass Band. That is the story of how *A Night on Bald Mountain* came to be played by a brass band at Davis on July 4, 1870.

# The Subsequent Evolution of the Confederate Music Culture

Historians claim that the July 4, 1870 celebration of the Great Confederate Expansion marked the beginning of a distinct Confederate Music Culture. This is a good place to tell you about that.

Without a doubt the British Brass Band Movement was embraced by Confederates and many a town prided itself in building a band shell and founding its own brass band. Percussion was added to punctuate the rhythm and the beat. Brass bands would even compete in music contests in the Confederacy like they were in Great Britain. Of course this made for a vigorous market for brass band instruments (imported and those made in the CSA under British license). The more affluent homes had a piano and a cornet or other brass instrument. Apparently, the brass band was a good fit for the small town, rural culture of the Confederacy. During the years following the 1909 invention of electric sound amplification the brass band became less important as it became possible to amplify all types of music performances for the enjoyment of large audiences. Even so, the distinct sound of the brass band is still enjoyed to this day among many Confederates.

Other forms of Confederate music evolved from the early brass band era of the 1870's. Talented and creative brass musicians put aside sheet music and improvised a distinctly personal style of play, and gathered together and formed popular Jazz bands. To cornets and other brass instruments were added reeds, such as the clarinet and the saxophone. Percussion was extensively used. The focus of this movement was along the Mississippi River, from Memphis to New Orleans, and people of color were often considered the best Jazz musicians. In fact, Jazz music is an important Confederate gift to the world.

On the other hand, the roots of Confederate music precede the brass band and jazz. The roots go back to musical interaction between Whites and Colored people in the South in early colonial days. And it is this interplay between the two races and their two very different remembered origins that became the foundation of Southern music. To the Scots-Irish fiddle and other stringed instruments was added the banjo and the guitar. The banjo originated in West Africa as the "kora" and the "ngoni" -- both made from dried gourds, cut in half and covered with animal skin to create a resonance chamber, to which a stick was fastened, followed by strings (thin strips of animal hide) tensioned to proper tuning. Early banjoes were first made and played by Negroes in the Caribbean before the settlement of North America. From those islands, musicians and banjoes came to the Southern colonies. The guitar, with roots in Spain, made a similar trip into the Southern colonies. Upon this early musical history, much of what we know as Confederate music has been derived. Let us now shift our view to the British Isles.

Music from rural England, Scotland, Wales and Northern Ireland was the colonial foundation of much of what became Confederate music. Picking up the fiddle, guitar (from Spanish roots), banjo (from West African roots), dulcimer and string base, string bands presented what was called Mountain music, Folk music, and Country music. From that evolved variations such as Blue Grass Music and Western Swing Music. Going back to the roots of the Confederate experience in North America, it was this music, made up of stringed instruments and singers, that best and most consistently characterized Confederate music. When amplification became available for sound stages, musicians playing this distinctly Confederate music began performing for large crowds. Radio came along about the same time, followed by Television in the 1950's. Perhaps nothing is as distinctly Confederate as is Country music and its cousins. The capital of this entertainment industry is Nashville, Tennessee.

There was a parallel development in the rising popularity of Latin music in the Seceded Mexican states and in Cuba. Here, the brass band influence combined with Latin rhythms, stringed instruments and percussion to create the Mariachi band and other styles so popular in those far-south regions and within the original Confederate States as well. The capital of Mexican Mariachi is clearly the vibrant city of Guadalajara, situated in a broad and fertile upland valley where both agriculture and industry contribute to the region's economy. In the State of Cuba a parallel musical development has arisen and the center of this culture is at Havanah. So, here again, diversity within the Confederate States has nurtured music and entertainment cultures that look like a multi-colored, multi-patterned quilt draped across a major part of the globe.

Confederates remain to this day the most reverent Christian nation on Earth. And Christian music is a major part of our culture, ranging from gospel music, complete with its country and African roots, to favorite hymns, many having been written 200 years ago, and many accompanied by fine church organs. Tradition is important, but new music is always being written to expand the repertoire. Christian churches densely dot the Confederate landscape. Most popular are the Baptist, Methodist, and Presbyterian Churches of the original Confederate States and the Catholic churches of Cuba and the Seceded Mexican States. The Russian Orthodox Church is strong in Russian America and in Hawaii.

Confederates do not speak of their music as if it is one distinct style, for it ranges widely in musical styles. But, across that broad range of styles, the world hears what it recognizes to be "Confederate Music."

One cannot cover Confederate music without also telling the story of Confederate stage plays and motion pictures and television. As you know, the capital of the Confederate motion picture industry is at Hollywood, California, just north of Los Angeles. Other major centers for motion picture production are Guadalajara and Atlanta. And, people recognize that Confederate motion pictures are more popular around the world than productions from anywhere else -- more popular than motion pictures produced by British companies, by United States companies, or by companies from any other country. Why would that be so? Historians agree that the preeminence of Confederate motion pictures can be attributed to the following factors:

- The obvious racial diversity within the Confederacy is evident in actors of all racial backgrounds, encouraging viewers around the world to connect with certain individuals and to appreciate a successful multiracial society.

- The great diversity in geography in the Confederacy offers amazing scenic variety -- from verdant farms, to bustling cities -- from frozen Russian America to balmy Gulf and Caribbean beaches -- from broad plains to tall mountains -- from deserts to stunning Hawaiian landscapes.

- The diverse culture within the Confederacy encourages tremendous screenplay variety, giving broad appeal to diverse audiences.

- Confederate immigration policies have always attracted talent from around the world and that is evident in Hollywood. Just look at the most famous Jewish men of the industry during the golden age of the 1950's and 1960's -- amazing talent and business sense.

- Confederate moral standards have guided its motion picture industry toward common sense standards of decency – call it wholesomeness -- which, history shows, appeals to the core of the motion picture audiences (companies elsewhere are left to appeal to the fringes).

A similar story tells the history of the Confederate television industry, so it need not be repeated here.

At this point it is appropriate to close the chapter on the two Confederate Expansions. Confederates love to celebrate this event every Fourth of July. They are uniformly proud of their country and thankful that it has been as successful as history tells us that it has been.

## Another Celebration Party

At the close of his lecture, Professor Davis remarked, "Anybody game for another party before supper. Judith and I will again host. You see, our last party did not properly give reason for celebrations by Benedict Juárez, Conchita Rezanov, Carlos Cespedes or Emma Lunalilo. Now we can do that and enjoy celebrating the inclusion within our Confederate States of the State of Cuba, the six States from former northern Mexico, the State of Russian America and the State of Hawaii. We shall gather at the normal supper time, enjoy the party, engage in a toast or two, perhaps sing a song, and then go to supper an hour later than normal. Agreed? Comments?"

Marie Saint Martin: "Great idea. We must honor our additional states. Please, Carlos, bring your Spanish Guitar and help us all sing, 'Guantanamera,' that great Cuban patriotic song."

Carlos Cespedes: "Will do. I will print off copies for everyone, for all must join me in singing, especially singing the chorus. Are we dressing up again?"

Professor Davis: "Why not. That was fun last week. You all were so handsome and beautiful. Let us dress up again."

## Celebrating Our Greatly Expanded Boundaries and Diversity of Population

The guests of honor at Professor Davis's celebration party were Carlos Cespedes, Benedict Juárez, Conchita Rezanov and Emma Lunalilo. All four were dressed in meaningful ways.

Carlos's attire seemed like a flash-back to the days when Cubans were struggling to win independence from Spain. His was the attire of a well-dressed sugar planter of Spanish descent who felt generous toward his field workers, free and slave alike, but who might have been at the time engaged in important business dealings away from the farm. He looked smart, but not too much – boots, riding pants, white shirt, leather vest, kerchief, and a brimmed hat that fitted particularly well. He sported a bit of gold, but not very much. Pocket watch and chain. Dusty colors predominated.

Benedict's attire looked like it had been tailored after a photograph of his famous ancestor, President Benito Juárez. He was dressed in black pants, a white shirt with black bow tie, and black waist-length coat. He sported a white kerchief and a black hat of moderate brim. He portrayed a Mexican independence leader dressed to move about his realm in a covered wagon, always on the move to avoid capture, but every day dressed to command respect at a moment's notice when necessary. His shoes resembled ordinary field boots. Nothing fancy about them. But his garments were clean and freshly pressed, for he was "dressed to command respect".

Conchita's attire complemented her youth and tennis-sculpted athletic body. Yet there were elements of her attire that spoke to her ancestry and long-ago days in Russian America. Figuring out how to manage such a thing on a hot day in Tennessee's mid-summer must have been a challenge. Yet it was one that she amply met. Her knee-length yellow dress was accented by an unbuttoned vest made of thoroughly scrapped, soft seal skin, fur-side out, wearable on a warm day when unbuttoned. Upon her golden hair, which was combed straight down, was a small skull cap rimmed with a thin accent of fur from a polar bear, not warm, mind you, but truly a fitting accent accessory. Her shoes were made of moose hide and trimmed with a bit of fur around the ankle. Of course, she was a hit.

Emma's attire was fully fitting for a warm June day in Tennessee. And it displayed a totally Hawaiian look, complete with a strapless, flowered dress, perhaps suitable for dancing, that dropped to her ankles, brought tight around her waist with a blue sash. The flowers in her hair were Hawaiian accents none could ignore. Her sandals looked beach-ready. Her powerful broad shoulders, arms and hands confirmed she had long been a master of great ocean waves and rides upon the rolling surf. And none doubted that in every respect she was beautiful.

Professor Davis and Judith welcomed the four guests of honor with obvious delight, greeting each individually; then Joe turned toward the other eight, pointed toward the four guests of honor, and exclaimed, "Fellow Confederates have any of you ever seen a more glorious answer to the question: 'Why are the Confederate States the Greatest Country on Earth'?"

"Bravo! Splendid! Beautiful! So Handsome!

As the four stood side by side, as in a receiving line, the other eight moved forward to individually congratulate the honored guests.

But Chris broke ranks and rushed toward Emma, hugged her tightly, kissed both cheeks and exclaimed, "My heroine, you look amazing; I will never be able to thank you enough. How we all love Hawaii and its people of Polynesian descent! Carlos, standing alongside, turned toward Emma and added, "Emma, you have taught this skipper that occasions arise when one feels she must violate established rules for handling a crisis at sea. You ignored the rules and risked the loss of two lives in your quest to save one. Only a person of your skills and bravery could have succeeded. I have learned that the rules of the sea are written to guide normal people -- that those rules can be successfully violated by people of exceptional ability. God has blessed you, for sure."

Together, Andrew Houston and Allen Ross approached Benedict Juárez and expressed admiration for Confederates whose ancestry was significantly of the Native American race. Allen told Benedict, "We Cherokee and others of the Five Southern Tribes who live in the State of Sequoyah are especially fond of Confederates of Native blood beyond our state and feel a special bond exists between our peoples and peoples of the seceded Mexican states, who, like ourselves, are predominantly descended from Natives who arrived in the Americas over ten thousand years ago. My brother, none proves the benefits of diversity more than have our peoples." Benedict concurred, "You speak the truth! Our seceded Mexican states would have failed in gaining independence without the support of Texans and the special friendship that has existed between Sam Houston and the Cherokee people." We are the ones who will forever thank Confederates for helping us achieve our dream of independence from oppressive dictators operating out of Mexico City." Andrew Houston submitted another view: "Our Confederate ancestors would have failed in efforts to help were it not for the brilliant leadership and crafty strategy employed by President Juárez. Shall we not shake hands in agreement? Conchita, standing nearby added, "Hey fellows, add my hand in that shake. The Natives of Russian America also deserve credit for helping our colony achieve independence and become a Confederate state."

Marie Saint Martin came to Carlos Cespedes, gave him a hug and said, "Skipper, why don't we celebrate contributions made to our Confederate States by the Cuban people? No better way to celebrate than to sing "Guantanamera." Grab your Spanish guitar and lead us in the great Cuban patriotic song.

Soon, Carlos was ready and the essayists were before him holding the music sheets that he had handed out. Carlos explained, "This is a song about a peasant farm girl from Guantanamo, a province in Eastern Cuba. We will sing an English translation with the exception of the chorus, which is 'Guantanamera, Guajira Guantanamera." That translates to Guantanamo, Peasant Girl from Guantanamo."

Carlos played an introduction and then began to sing, soon joined by all the others:

Guantanemera,
Guajira Guantanamera.
Guantanemera,
Guajira Guantanamera.

I'm just a man who is trying
To do some good before dying;
To ask each man and his brother;
To bear no ill toward each other.
This life will never be hollow,
To those who listen and follow.

Guantanemera,
Guajira Guantanamera.
Guantanemera,
Guajira Guantanamera.

I write my rhymes with no learning,
And yet with truth they are burning;
But is the world waiting for them?
Or will they all just ignore them?
Have I a poet's illusion -
A dream to die in seclusion?

Guantanemera,
Guajira Guantanamera.
Guantanemera,
Guajira Guantanamera.

A little brook on a mountain,
The cooling spray of a fountain,
Arouse in me an emotion,
More than the vast boundless ocean,
For there's a wealth beyond measure
In little things that we treasure.

Guantanemera,
Guajira Guantanamera.
Guantanemera,
Guajira Guantanamera.

There was appreciative applause. Then Professor Davis handed out champagne glasses and Judith followed pouring for a bit of toasting. All glasses at the ready, Professor Davis raised his high and offered:

"I propose a toast to our four honored guests and the Confederate states they represent – 'May we always admire, respect and engage the diversity they represent'."

"Here, here!"

The evening was off to a good start.

To everyone, Judith said, "Let us celebrate with song this great Confederate expansion and the resulting growth in our diversity by gathering at the piano with Amanda and singing our country's anthem, 'Diversity'."

We are one.
We are free.
We are the Great Diversity . . . .

Cheers followed the singing.

As Amanda Washington rose from the piano bench, Isaiah Montgomery hugged her and said, "Beautiful. Love your playing. The celebration of diversity originated with people like us of African descent. They showed others how to celebrate with laughter, music, colorful clothing and dancing. It was our ancestors that first proved the benefits of a diverse society. After the Great Confederate Expansion, the benefits of diversity became far broader and even more apparent."

At this point, Allen Ross and Robert Lee came up to Professor Davis to again express a special thanks. Landing a playful punch on Robert's shoulder, Allen thanked Professor Davis for so quickly organizing their rescue at Big Bone cave. Robert and I are quite sorry for causing so much trouble, but have come to understand over the past couple of days how remarkably skillful you were to sense the problem so quickly and organize a rescue led by experienced cavers out of Nashville. You were great and we will be ever thankful. God knows, without light so deep in that cave, beyond where the long crawlway had opened into a walking passage, we could not even feel our way back to where we had left that long crawl with any certainty. Robert had advised, "Stay put, pray and hope for rescue." Events proved that was the right thing to do. Thank God there was a backpack at the entrance to the crawlway that served as a clue of where we had gone.

A bit later, Professor Davis Robert Lee, Emma Lunalilo and Tina Sharp were engaged in conversation. Tina said, "It's been a very rewarding experience for me so far, Professor Davis. As we advance to Confederate history that followed the Great Confederate Expansion, we will be discussing our country's remarkable growth in inventiveness, commerce and industry -- from the 1880's to 2010, a period of 130 years. That will include my ancestor's role in the big oil boom in Texas."

Professor Davis added, "It will." Turning to Emma, he said, "Also, Emma, we will discuss the attack by Imperialist Japan on your state of Hawaii, at Pearl Harbor, and how we Confederates joined with Nationalists in China and took the war to Japan. Victory by the Confederate-Chinese alliance resulted in pacifying Japan and redirecting its government toward democratic ideals."

Robert Lee then said, "During my political science studies, I focused with special interest on the political transition in China during those years: the conflicts between Nationalists and Communists, concerns over province rights versus national rights, and how we Confederates helped guide them to a government structure patterned after ours. We think of China as a country of similar people, but in reality, the ethnic diversity in China has challenged that country to rethink how to use diversity as a positive attribute of society. They understand that now, and have learned how to manage diversity for the benefit of all. Furthermore, our cooperative efforts with the Chinese Nationalists helped them defeat the Communists and create a great county, recognized world-wide as an example of how to succeed within a diversity society."

Tina Sharp then offered her expertise regarding nuclear power and the atomic bomb, saying, "It was in Tennessee and Georgia that Confederates developed the atomic bomb with essential help from key Jewish immigrants from Europe. The rapid pace of that development was amazing -- and so important to establishing the Confederate States as a leading military power. To save lives otherwise lost in a land invasion of Japan by Confederates and Chinese, we dropped one atomic bomb in a remote area to demonstrate its devastating power. Seeing that massive explosion, Imperialist Japan quickly surrendered and allowed Confederate and Chinese troops to peacefully occupy their island and reorganize their government. From that point, going forward, we have become a world leader in nuclear power. Sixty percent of Confederate electricity is generated by nuclear power and no Confederate nuclear power station has ever experienced a safety failure that has hurt citizens or forced an abandonment of a power plant."

And, dear readers, those and other aspects of 130 years of Confederate history will be presented in Part 3 of The CSA Trilogy. You will enjoy reading about quite a few inventors and industrial leaders who came to the Confederate States and played major roles in expanding and diversifying our economy. You will read about our remarkable population growth. After concluding all of that history, you will join in the Sesquicentennial celebration.

Finally, you will read the text of the 12 essays by the twelve Sewanee Project team members as presented before a vast television audience from the University of the South on July 4, 2011 -- each, from different perspectives, aimed at answering the principle question: "Why are the Confederate States the Greatest Country on Earth?" There is much to learn in Part 3. So please read on.

## Wednesday Evening Selected Diary Postings

Diary note by Andrew Houston said, "I was especially lucky to be scheduled for supper with Benedict Juárez tonight since this morning's lecture was on the Great Confederate Expansion. First and foremost among the added States were the Seceded Mexican States, reorganized into six states as requested -- an amazing story of which his great-great-great-grandfather played such a crucial role. Who would have thought that the August 1855 forced exile of dictator Antonio López de Santa Anna would, over the next two years, result in 1), the election of Benito Juárez as Minister of Justice and his "Juárez Law" that outlawed special clerical and military courts, 2) his election as President of the Supreme Court, 3) his elevation to President of all of Mexico after President Ignacio Comonfort resigned in late 1857. All of that in only two years! . . . . But the lawful Juárez government was soon on the run -- victim of violent conflict between Catholic privilege and liberal democracy. Into that turmoil Emperor Napoleon III injected his French Intervention, which began with the landing of 7,500 French troops onto Mexican soil in 1862, and his installation two years later at Mexico City of his obedient lackey, Archduke Maximilian. Since 1858, President Juárez's legitimate government had avoided Mexico City, leaving that political cock-fight to others. Eventually his government would only hold a narrow strip of land just south of my State of Texas – sustained by a thread as a mobile government in a horse-drawn carriage. But Maximilian had ruled from Mexico City for only a few months before the Confederate States secured their independence in the treaty of Montreal, enabling them to give important aid to Juárez. The outline of the plan to support Mexican State secession was hammered out between Juárez and Confederate Commissioners in September 1864. It worked! The northern half of Mexico seceded, Mexico City gave in, the French left, and a boundary line was established at the Treaty of Saltillo in May 1866. Free of control from Mexico City the Seceded Mexican States consolidated into six States and gained admission into the Confederate States of America. What a story. So inspiring to share it tonight with Benedict Juárez."

Diary note by Tina Sharp said, "Isaiah Montgomery and I are looking forward to the hiking trip with Professor Davis, Amanda Washington and Benedict Juárez. We ate supper together tonight. Will go to the Fiery Gizzard trailhead Saturday morning, hike with backpacks, overnight, proceed to the trail's end, and return Sunday afternoon. I need the exercise and the camaraderie ought to be great. I truly admire Professor Davis and love his history presentations. My education to become a nuclear engineer involved just enough history to get by. So this four-week immersion is just what I need. And I can learn so much from Amanda Washington and Isaiah Montgomery. Wonder if a romance will spring up between those two? Might happen! But would Isaiah ever leave the farm; would Amanda ever be happy as a farmer's wife? No telling. But most of all I have already learned so much from Benedict Juárez. He can do anything, and takes life so calmly as he does it. This overnight backpack trip is the main event for our third weekend. The first two were almost disasters. Surely not this one. What can happen to five backpackers on Fiery Gizzard trail? Have to ask how the trail got its name. Night-night."

Diary note by Carlos Cespedes said, "Lecture today on the Great Confederate Expansion. Great time for the people of Cuba. . . . On another subject, must note that we musicians, all of us, were together in the faculty lounge this afternoon rehearsing for the July 4th performance."

Diary note by Benedict Juárez said, "In a way today's lecture was the climax of the whole story of the Confederate States, because today we enjoyed the story of the Great Confederate Expansion. Long live the people of the seceded Mexican States. Amazing!"

Diary note by Conchita Rezanov said, "Today's lecture completed the building of the Confederate States, including Hawaii. Much of the reason for success in the Hawaiian Islands can be attributed to the Russian Orthodox Church and to the Russian Americans who settled on the Big Island."

# The CSA Trilogy

An Alternate History/Historical Novel about Our Vast and
Beautiful Confederate States of America

A Happy Story in Three Parts of What Might Have Been

1861 to 2011

## The CSA Trilogy, Part 3, How Confederates Retained their Cherished Principle of State Sovereignty and Respect for Population Diversity while Developing the World's Greatest Economy, An Alternate History – 1878 to 2011

### Foreword to Part 3

Thanks for your interest in this alternate history, presented as a trilogy, which covers 150 years of the Confederate States of America, from its formation in early 1861, to the celebration of the sesquicentennial of what has become the Greatest Country on Earth. The three parts of this trilogy match the three major stories of the Confederate States. We assume that you have already read the first and second part of this trilogy.

In Part 3 we witness the alternate history of how Confederates created a vibrant modern economy in the subsequent 134 years, to the sesquicentennial celebration of 2011. Most importantly, we learn the history of how Confederates encouraged immigration of men and families of remarkable talent, thereby facilitating a rapid industrial expansion, and how Confederates accomplished that remarkable achievement without losing the cherished principle of State Sovereignty (State Rights) and while encouraging respect for the country's very diverse population. Regulations over slavery remained the prerogative of each State, but that does not impede a rather rapid transition from slavery to independent living for families of African descent. Part 3 concludes with the heart-warming celebration of the Confederate Sesquicentennial at the University of the South in Tennessee.

You already understand that this trilogy is primarily an alternate history of 150 years of the Confederate States, and that the writer has overlaid a novel involving twelve individuals of remarkable ancestry who are studying these 150 years and preparing essays to explain "Why the Confederate States are the Greatest Country on Earth." In the closing chapter, these twelve will be reading their essays before you and a world-wide television audience on the evening of the Sesquicentennial Celebration. You will continue to follow our fictional characters – impressive and accomplished young people – through the third part of this trilogy.

You already know that this trilogy is a happy story, so much happier that the truthful history of the conquest of the Seceded States -- a four-year military nightmare that resulted in the death of approximately one million people, about half from the United States and about half from the Confederate States.

And you have been invited to ask, "Did this calamity have to happen?" Actually, the answer is "No". Alternate futures are always possible in human events. Looking back from our vantage point today, we realize that a change in certain historic circumstances could have often dramatically changed the course of human history, and, moving forward, even to redefining the world as we know it today.

You already know that most of this trilogy reads like an alternate history, but parts do read like a novel. We hope you continue to enjoy the experiences and interpersonal relationships developed among the twelve essayists and their professor during four weeks at the University of the South, Sewanee Tennessee. You have already experienced the weekend adventure where six were engaged in an overnight sailing adventure off the coast of Cuba. You have already experienced two exploring an old historic cave west of Sewanee. In Part 3 you will experience the adventure of five enjoying a weekend hiking overnight backpacking trip on the remote Fiery Gizzard trail east of Sewanee. Unlike the two previous week-end trips, this overnight hike will be pleasant, and afford a better understanding of the characters involved.

## Part 3, Chapter 1, Day 18 – Studies of Early Invention and Industrialization within the Confederate States – Class Lecture, Thursday, June 23, 2011

Today's presentation on studies of industrialization within the Confederate States will focus on the early years in which agrarian society enjoyed major steps toward becoming self-sufficient in the production of goods that had so often been imported or produced locally in craft workshops. Of course there is insufficient time to present a comprehensive history of this subject. So we will rely mostly on examples and spotlighting selected important industries -- especially examples of how remarkable individuals played major roles in advancing our country's industrialization in the critical early years.

With respect to industrialization – in iron smelting, metal working and machine tools, in building steam engines, locomotives and steam ships, in fabric and garment manufacture, and so forth -- and with respect to transportation – canals and railroads -- the Northern States were far advanced over the Southern States when, by early 1861, the Republican Party had taken control of the office of governor in every one of them and had finally taken control of the Federal Government. The South knew that advancing Confederate industrialization beyond the little then existing was the big challenge that lay ahead. It leaped into the task in many ways right away, with a focus on acquiring the means of production – steam engines, machine tools, metal working, etc. Although first efforts were directed at importing such equipment, almost in parallel the South sought out immigrants who were expert in science and engineering, in metal working from mining the ores to making the finished products, in textile manufacturing, railroad technology, etc.

Imports of essential equipment, for military and civilian use, had proceeded rapidly during 1861, taking advantage of the Lincoln Administration's inability to rally the North to go to war prior to Congress convening in December. Even during the war year of 1862, Confederates were remarkably successful in bringing essential equipment through the Federal blockade.

After the Treaty of Montreal, the Confederate effort to embrace industrialization took off with gusto. Great Britain was the Confederate's most important industrialization help-mate. We will look at several key industries one at a time.

### Ferrous Ore to Iron and Steel to Rail, Plate and Bar, then to Finished Products

Confederate sources of Ferrous Ore useful in iron smelting were available in the mountains of western Virginia southwest to the mountains of northern Alabama as well as in western Tennessee and eastern Texas. Coal deposits were plentiful in western Virginia southwest to northern Alabama, in western Arkansas and eastern Sequoyah and northern New Mexico. So it was natural that western Virginia, eastern Tennessee and northern Alabama became the focus of development of the Confederate Iron and Steel industry.

Confederate coal is of the common bituminous variety, which means it has too many impurities to be used directly in reducing iron ore to molten iron metal in a blast furnace. So it must first be purified in a coking oven or coking furnace to force out the impurities and produce coke, which is then transported to the site of the iron smelter. In early days, purifying coal to make coke took place in many, many small "beehive ovens," each about 12 feet in diameter at the base and closing in at the top at a height of about 8 feet. Coal was shoveled into the oven and ignited, but soon thereafter the supply of air was purposely reduced, reducing the burn rate and allowing the impurities in the coal to be driven out by intense heat. These coal impurities escaped into the atmosphere and, over time, severely damaged area vegetation and rendered the nearby region less than healthy. Confederates recognized this problem early on and replaced their multitude of "beehive ovens" with larger forced-air coking furnaces which recycled and incinerated the off-gas impurities, thereby releasing harmless carbon dioxide, water and slag to the environment. Using either process, the result was coke, almost pure carbon.

Confederate iron ore was mined and then transported to the blast furnaces where molten iron was to be obtained by firing a mixture of ore and coke. The chemistry was basic. The sought compound in iron ore is Ferric Oxide and Ferrous Oxide, both compounds of iron and oxygen. To obtain molten iron, the carbon in coke is combined with the oxygen in the ore, giving metallic iron and carbon dioxide. Molten iron can be cooled and processed into plates, bars and rails and can be further worked with hammers to give wrought iron. It can also be cast in molds to give cast iron of various shapes. But iron is generally inferior to steel.

During the 1860's steel-making technology was in its infancy. The process developed by Englishman Henry Bessemer had limited application. But by 1868 the steel-making process developed jointly by William and Friedrich Siemens in England and Emile and Pierre Martin in France was the needed breakthrough. Confederates leaped upon this new technology, licensed the Siemens-Martin technology, recruited immigrants skilled in its methodology, and pioneered in making the new Confederate steel industry the best in North America. From Great Britain, Confederates imported iron and steel processing equipment, including roller mills, extrusion dies, conveyors, steam-driven stamping machines and forging hammers, and so forth.

Next came a huge Confederate investment in machine tools, the tools, many rather large, that are required to convert iron and steel into machinery capable of making finished products -- such a steam engines; marine ships and river boats; locomotives and rail cars; steam shovels, cranes and mining equipment; textile machinery and sewing machines; farm plows, planters and harvesters; carriages and wagons; pumps, heat exchangers and vessels for cooking, refining oil and making chemicals; and the list grew as tools were designed to make products not previously conceived. Trade with Great Britain was vigorous. Confederate cotton went east; British tools came west.

## The Confederate Textile Industry

But British help was not limited to exporting machinery to the Confederacy and licensing the needed British technology. British help was, to an equal extent, provided through immigration of English and Scottish men who came to invest in Confederate industry and, in many cases, to start up industrial enterprises here and there across the vast Confederate landscape. Frequent was the partnership between an owner of one or more Confederate plantations, who provided capital and lucrative contacts, and the Scotsman or Englishman who provided some capital, but, most importantly, knowledge of the industry and where help was available across the Atlantic. Many from "over there" were enticed to immigrate and seek industrial opportunities upon reading one of the Confederate newspaper advertisements that frequented newspapers in Great Britain, Germany and France. The following is an example of a Confederate recruiting advertisement that was hard to resist:

> Textile skills needed. Immigrate to the Confederate States of America, where opportunity abounds. Northern Mississippi Cotton Growers Association seeks textile manufacturing experts and investors to join with its members in the design, procurement, construction and operation of a large cotton mill to process raw Mississippi cotton into finished, dyed and printed cloth. Vast supply of cotton is assured. Markets for finished cloth are assured. If you have the skills that our Association needs, please contact us and tell us about yourself, your experience and knowledge. Speaking English is an advantage, but is not essential. Investors should also reply. Assistance with expedited immigration and settlement of selected applicants is assured. Write to NMCGA at P. O. Box 175, Oxford, Mississippi, CSA, care of Wade Hampton, III.

The above is an example of "vertical expansion" in a Confederate industry, where the Southerners not only grew and picked the cotton – they also aimed to convert the fiber into finished cloth. Instead of exporting the cotton to another country (the United States or England) for conversion to cloth and then importing the cloth or ready-made clothing, Confederates were doing it all where the cotton was grown and picked. An 1860 economic statistic explains the reason for processing the cotton into cloth near the fields where it was grown. In the United States in the year before secession, 1860, cotton cloth factories, mostly in the northeast, spent $52,666,701 purchasing cotton; employed 114,955 people (mostly women and children in conditions often worse than experienced by Southern slaves); and sold the cloth for $107,337,783. Of course! Confederate cotton growers wanted to make the cloth in their own regions; avoid the transportation cost; avoid the New York City manufacturer's factoring expenses; avoid paying the tariff to ship the cloth away and the clothing back home, and give employment to 114,955 Confederates. As would be expected, by the early 1870's textile companies in Massachusetts and elsewhere in the northeastern United States protested loudly. They sought even higher tariffs on cloth and clothing exports to the Confederacy, but this increased the economic depression they were suffering, especially after Confederates retaliated by imposing a 15 percent export fee on cotton shipped to the United States (but not to Europe or Great Britain). One after one, northeastern textile factories shut down and laid off workers, reducing overall capacity to one half of what it had been in 1860. Idle textile equipment, including spinning machines and looms, were sold to Southern buyers who moved them to newly-constructed textile factories, spanning the South from North Carolina to Texas. In time Texas would be the Confederate's greatest producer of cotton. We now understand that the underlying motives behind the 1850's "Abolitionist" political agitation in its homeland of Massachusetts was primarily aimed at controlling cotton economics -- from, factoring, to planting and picking, to shipping, to processing into cloth and clothing, to selling back to the South. [254] But, in reality, that political movement only hastened the decline of the "New England Textile Monopoly."

## Confederate Agricultural Equipment Design and Manufacturing

Here is another example of a Confederate advertisement that visionary people in Great Britain and Europe had difficulty resisting:

Industrial metal working skills needed for new agricultural equipment manufacturing factory. Immigrate to the Confederate States of America, where opportunity abounds. Alabama Farm Equipment Corporation of Greater Selma seeks people with metal working skills capable of producing precision, interchangeable parts on an industrial basis. Here, at beautiful Selma, Alabama, we need precision iron and steel fabrication experts and investors to join us in the design, procurement, construction and operation of a factory to produce the most modern and innovative machinery for the Confederate agricultural industry, both horse/mule drawn and steam powered, as appropriate. Targeting efficient design and manufacture at minimal cost, we will be manufacturing saws, plows, planters, various harvesters, hay mowers, rakes and balers, stationary and field threshers, corn shellers and storage silos, as well as a complete line of hand tools.

Good supply of iron and steel is anticipated. Markets for finished products are assured. If you have the skills that our Corporation needs, please contact us and tell us about yourself, your experience and knowledge. Speaking English is an advantage, but is not essential. Investors should also reply. Assistance with expedited immigration and settlement of selected applicants is assured. Write to AFEC at P. O. Box 79, Selma, Alabama, CSA, care of.

---

[254] Generally speaking this motive of the New England Textile companies is truthful history.

The call for farm mechanization technology experts to come to the Confederacy was eagerly answered. Agricultural equipment manufacturing was already firmly founded in the North by 1860, so people across the Atlantic with that expertise and drive were naturally drawn to immigrate to the South where they could find less competition, enthusiastic employment, available business deals, and certain and expanding markets. A study of the United States machinery manufacturing economy in 1860, the year before secession, revealed that the cost of raw material was $19,444,533 and the value of finished product was $52,010,376. Furthermore, the industry employed 41,223 people. So it was natural for enterprising Southern farmers to pool available resources and start up farm machinery manufacturing factories to utilize the Confederate iron and steel becoming available, the available labor, and to give expression to the inventive mind of the Southern farmer. Anyway, southern soil and crops differed significantly from Northern soil and crops, so who could better design, test and make the farm equipment that worked best in the South than the Southerner himself?

## Confederate Leather Working Industries

Before the invention of plastics, leather was as essential to an economy as were metals, wood and fibers. So Confederates were quickly weaned from dependence on the established leather processing facilities near the great slaughter houses in the North, most notably, Chicago. Texas and lush pastures in the hills from Virginia to northern Alabama were feeding fine herds of beef and sheep for both meat and hides. Looking again at the leather, boot and shoe industry, we see how important was the Confederate movement toward establishing a much stronger presence within its borders. A study of the United States leather industry in 1860, the year before secession, revealed that the cost of raw material was $44,520,737 and the value of finished product was $67,306,452. Furthermore, the industry employed 22,679 people in cleaning and tanning the hides. A study of the United States boot and shoe manufacturing economy that same year revealed that the cost of raw material was $42,728,174 and the value of finished product was $91,889,298. Furthermore, that work employed 123,026 people. The South already enjoyed a share in both industries, but Confederates felt strongly that they wanted to process all available leather within their own borders. And, by 1875, essentially all of the leather needed in the Confederacy was processed internally, including final product conversion. Some beef was exported to Northern slaughter houses, primarily for the meat, and the leather resource went along for the ride. Again we see the importance of an industrial vertical integration, from Confederate beef and sheep to Confederate leather goods: boots, shoes, coats, belts, and machinery uses, such as drive belts and pump seals.

## Barbed Wire and the Revolution in Fencing Pasture

Perhaps the greatest revolution in animal husbandry and cattle ranching was the invention of barbed wire and the resulting low-cost manufacturing method of trapping sharp and short wire barbs within two twisted wires. It was not long before 1867 that Lucien Smith of Ohio discovered that cattle would not press against a fence containing sharp barbs, a trait that nature had discovered far back in time as thorn trees evolved that survival technique. Patents were filed but, because a large variety of barbs seemed to work, no person held a monopoly on design or fabrication method. So barbed wire quickly became a people's invention, a product no one person controlled. Confederate cattlemen, from Virginia to Texas and south into the seceded Mexican States seized upon the opportunity barbed wire gave to fence in the range and reduce the manpower required to manage herds of cattle and sheep. Fabrication of barbed wire required only a modest investment: wire extruder, barb inserter, wire twister and wire spooler. So, by the mid 1970's several dozen barbed wire manufacturing companies were fabricating and distributing barbed wire all across the Confederacy. Few innovations have been as important as barbed wire in the rapid expansion of cattle and sheep ranching across the vast, virgin lands of the Confederacy.

You have been learning about selected examples of important expanding Confederate industrial developments during the first years of our new country. Many more examples would be helpful, but our time is limited and we must call this subject done for today.

## Thursday Evening Selected Diary Postings

Diary note by Benedict Juárez said, "Got a pair of new shoes for this weekend's backpacking trip. Tina Sharp is excited about getting out on a trail. We all have been sitting too much in class and in the library. Am going to wear these new shoes all day tomorrow to make sure they are a good fit. Will be good to have Amanda Washington along. I want to learn more about her education experiences with minorities. Her ancestor, Booker T. Washington, pioneered hands-on education and teaching trade skills. I like a good balance in student teaching: learning and practicing knowledge gleaned from books, which involve one's mind; combined with learning and practicing trade skills, which involve one's hands."

Diary note by Allen Ross said, "We musicians had a practice session this afternoon on the patio outside the faculty lounge before supper. There was Professor Davis on banjo, Carlos Cespedes on Spanish guitar, Amanda Washington at piano, and me on western guitar. Marie St. Martin and Tina Sharp were our singers. Afterward, Marie and I were scheduled for supper together. Good timing. She has done so much to bring us together as a music group and to provide some leadership, including collecting music from the library and printing off a copy for each of us. Someone will say, 'We ought to sing such and such next time'. Marie will reply, 'I'll get that music for us'. But we are inclined to improvise as well, especially inventing our own variations on the instrumental parts."

Diary note by Tina Sharp said, "After supper I got together with Professor Davis's wife, Judith, and we played French horn duets together. She is so good -- first horn in the Nashville Symphony. Got some good suggestions that might improve my playing, too. . . . . Regarding today's lecture, being the only engineer on our team, perhaps more that the other eleven, I appreciated the early contributions to Confederate progress that we got from immigrant inventors and industrialists. To me it was a refresher course of my early scientific studies."

Diary note by Chris Memminger said, "Today's lecture reaffirmed my belief that we owe so, so much to those early immigrants into the Confederate States who contributed so much to our industrialization and advancement. Why did they choose to come here? They came because they saw opportunity, open markets for new products, a strong Confederate dollar, and a people who encouraged and helped in every way possible. They came because no one was here to compete with them in the pursuit of their goals."

# Part 3, Chapter 2, Day 19 – Study of Population Growth and Human Diversity in the Confederacy from Then to Now – Class Lecture, Friday, June 24, 2011

The story of Confederate population expansion is not just about the large families for which Confederate couples have been noted. It is not just about the welcoming immigration policies of the State governments within the Confederacy. It is more than that. The story's most noteworthy aspect is the quality of emigrants that have been encouraged to immigrate to the Confederate States. So, as we present this study of Confederate Population Growth, please pay particular attention to Confederate immigration policies over the past 150 years.

The population in the Confederate States was 18,584,352 persons at the time of the final expansion, 1870, plus the 1877 Hawaii addition. Before detailing the racial breakdown of this number, it is appropriate to reveal the definitions used for that purpose.

- A person is classified as of European ancestry if he or she is at least seven eighths of the European race.

- A person is classified as of African ancestry if he or she is at least one eight of the African race.

- A person is classified as of Native ancestry if he or she is at least one eight of the Native American race. Many people of the Seceded Mexican States are of this class and almost all of the people in Sequoyah are of this race.

- A person is classified as of Asian ancestry if he or she is at least on eight of the Asian race. Most of the people of Hawaii were of that race early on. The Polynesian people are classified as of the Asian race in this study.

People of mixed race who are not classified as of European ancestry, are placed in a race category based on the following priority ordering. If at least one eighth African, then the category is African; if not African, if at least one eighth Native, then the category is Native; if not African or Native, if at least one eighth Asian, then the category is Asian. By this method, it becomes possible to place individuals into one of four race categories. If, instead, all possible combinations of racial mixing were tallied separately, the analysis would become too complex for a study such as this. Just keep in mind that all possible combinations on racial ancestry are present among the Confederate population, those many variations are just too complex to itemize here.

Using the above four-part basis of categorization, the following is the racial breakout of the 18,584,352 people living in the Confederacy in 1870 (plus 1877 for Hawaiians). The percentages follow each category.

| | | |
|---|---|---|
| European | 9,403,683 | 50.6% |
| African | 5,556,721 | 29.9% |
| Native | 3,549,611 | 19.1% |
| Asian | 74,337 | 0.4% |
| Total | 18,584,352 | 100.0% |

As you can see, Confederates who were of the European Race (7/8ths or more of the race) were barely in the majority at this time, amounting to 50.6 percent. Confederates noticeably of the African race totaled almost 30 percent. Those of the Native race, who mostly lived in the Seceded Mexican States, totaled just over 19 percent. The Asian population was just shy of one half of one percent. Confederates, by and large, thought this racial diversity would be a fine basis from with to build the future Confederate States. But there were strong beliefs that immigration policy should favor expanding the European portion of the future population – but not just by allowing any Europeans into the Confederacy that showed up on a passenger ship arriving from Europe or the British Isles, or crossing the northern border from the United States. Confederates wanted to be more selective about who was invited into the new country.

So the concept of sponsoring immigrants gained great favor and became the norm throughout the States of the Confederacy. The Confederate embassies in the United States, the British Isles and Europe became clearing houses for prospective immigrants. First the Confederate Congress established an immigration quota for each decade. The quota for the 1870-1879 decade was set at six percent of the 1870 population (because Confederates of the Asian race were initially so few in number, Congress favored an eight to 9 percent quota of that race for each decade). This quota established the number of people of European ancestry who would be allowed to immigrate into the Confederate States during that decade. But each immigrant needed a sponsor and a destination to qualify to be placed on the approved list. Then, based on a system of priorities, the applicants received their immigration permits and sponsors were contacted to coordinate the arrivals.

What about the system of priorities? It went like this. People sought after for special skills were given high priorities. Skills helpful to building a stronger Confederate economy were the most sought. Strong family units were often given high priorities. A balance between immigrant females and immigrant males was persistently maintained. A strong Christian faith or Jewish faith was a plus on all applications because church groups and Jewish groups were often sponsoring immigrants to come to their communities. Ability to speak English was a plus and hopeful immigrants often worked at learning to speak at least a little English to gain advantage over others applying.

One might have thought that Confederates were compassionate and open to allowing people into their country who had been victims of wars, pestilence and racial and religious violence. But that was not the case. Confederates believed that an invitation to immigrate and become a Confederate was a precious gift not to be given away as a helping hand to downtrodden and suffering mankind. So charity seldom figured into the immigration process. Some might think that policy mean-spirited, but Confederates just believed it was common sense. They reasoned that it was impossible for them to save all of the people of the world from bad outcomes, that it was not their job to even try to do so. They considered themselves to be "Nation Builders." But figured it involved building their country, not everybody else's.

By 1890 the Confederate population had doubled to 36,559,697. Most of this was the growth at home due to the large family sizes notable for that three-decade period. Among all races, couples, on average, gave birth to enough children to see four grow up to be adults capable of raising families themselves. It is interesting to observe that the passion for large families was shared by all four Confederate racial groups, none differing much from the other. The racial makeup of the Confederacy had significantly changed over the past thirty years (1870-1890). Immigration had increased the portion of the population of European ancestry from 50.6 percent to 58.7 percent. And the skills immigrants brought with them benefited the country as had been hoped.

Moving forward one more generation, to 1920, we see a continuation of the population expansion pattern established by the previous generation. The Confederate population again doubled to 74,059,276. And the population of Confederates of European ancestry, previously 58.7 percent, rose to 62.6 percent. Families were large again, on average couples were seeing four children growing up to themselves raise families. By the way, improved health care was beginning to enable parents to give birth to fewer children than had their parents and grandparents and still enjoy seeing four children grow up to raise families of their own, a process that would continue up to this very day. This pattern continued for all Confederate racial groups. The Confederate Congress had continued to permit and encourage immigrants of European ancestry, having set an 1891 to 1920 target of 18 percent of the 1890 population base (36,559,697 times 0.18 = 7,075,073). The Asian target had been set at 25 percent.

The percent of the population of European ancestry climbed again as designed. Moving forward to the next generation, to 1950, we see the Confederate population again double to 150,989,289. But signs of slightly smaller family sizes were beginning to be seen on the horizon. Yet, the population figures again showed, on average over that 30-year span, couples saw four children grow to adulthood and be prepared to raise families themselves. The 18 percent target for immigrants of European ancestry had been continued by the Confederate Congress. The Asian immigrant target was continued at 25 percent. And immigrants of European and Asian ancestry were continuing to bring with them great skills useful in strengthening the economy and vitality of the country. In 1950, 66.3 percent of the Confederate population was of European ancestry.

Over the next generation, from 1950 to 1980, the passion for large families subsided a bit. Instead of four children per couple attaining adulthood, the average declined to three and a half. This slowed population growth. On the other hand Congress continued to encourage immigration for this 30-year period in the same amounts: immigrants of European ancestry in an amount equal to 18 percent of the 1950 total population and of Asian ancestry in an amount equal to 25 percent. The 1980 Confederate population was recorded as 248,791,404 and of that number 69.8 percent were of European ancestry. Immigration was becoming a bigger factor in Confederate population growth and in moving the racial makeup more rapidly toward European ancestry. The Asian population, only 67,913 in 1977, was now 1,344,331, equal to one half of one percent.

We now arrive at the most recent census numbers for the Confederate States of America -- the census of 2010. The trend toward reduced family size continued with this latest generation of Confederate couples. On average a couple saw three children grow up and become adults. This trend was consistent over all four racial groups. The 1980 Congress had continued the 18 percent and 25 percent immigration targets for this 30-year period, giving immigration a yet larger role in defining this generation's population growth story. The 2010 Confederate population came in at 328,164,836 and of that number the racial mix was as follows:

- Of European ancestry: 73.1 percent
- Of African ancestry: 16.0 percent
- Of Native ancestry: 10.2 percent
- Of Asian ancestry: 0.7 percent

The 2010 Confederate Congress modified the country's thinking of immigration policy for the first time in one hundred and fifty years. Invitations to emigrate to the Confederacy no longer limited qualified candidates to European or Asian ancestry with quotas defined for each. The country was quite populous in 2010, in fact, exceeding the population of the United States by 87 percent. So the immigration quota was reduced to 12 percent for the 30-year period from 2010 to 2040. This will amount to expectations of almost 40 million new immigrants over the next 30 years, on the average, 1.3 million arrivals each year. Expectations for family size are a continuation of three children per couple growing up to become adults. Although immigrants from Africa, India, South America, and Asia will not be prohibited or constrained because of their racial ancestry, Confederates will still be insisting on bringing in immigrants with skills valuable to expanding the economy and promoting Confederate society. Expectations are that, as long as the population is maintained at 70 percent European ancestry or higher, the diversity of the peoples of our country will continue to be a blessing to all.

The Confederate population density of 136 persons per square mile is still less than in India (953), Germany (593), or the Confederate Provinces of China (370), but more dense than the United States (88), Brazil (62) or Russia (21).

A quick note about our friends to the north: The United States population as of 2010 stood at 175,426,391 persons. Of these, 65,717,000 lived between the Atlantic and the Ohio River; 66,532,000 lived beyond the Ohio out to the Rocky Mountains, and 43,177,000 lived further beyond, out to the Pacific. Diversity in the United States is less pronounced than in the Confederacy. Around 85 percent of the people are of European ancestry, 8 percent of Asian ancestry and the remaining 7 percent have been a broad mix of people from the Indian subcontinent, from the Islamic nations of the Middle East and refugees from violence in Africa and South America. Confederates seldom leave to immigrate into the United States. Those few that do report that they are feeling unwelcomed.

It is time to call complete this session on Confederate population studies. For more information that interests you specifically, the Sewanee library has all the answers you might ask. Enjoy the afternoon.

## Friday Evening Selected Diary Postings

Diary note by Isaiah Montgomery said: "Got ready for tomorrow morning's backpacking trip. Should be a good time. Good group, too. Not too much adventure, thank goodness. I have never been out on the ocean on a sailboat at night in a storm and I have never been caving. But I do like backpacking, so this should be great. I was scheduled to have supper with Benedict Juarez. He is set to go backpacking. I guess the ladies will be OK. And Professor Davis is no spring chicken. Benedict and I agreed to shoulder the heavier packs and help everyone along as needed. I am carrying a backpacking saw and hatchet for getting firewood for Saturday night."

Diary note by Carlos Cespedes said: "Had supper with Tina Sharp. She is a very good singer, who can back up Marie St. Martin with well-chosen harmonies. She just sings harmony by ear. Looks like the music group will not be getting together this weekend. Half of the group will be off backpacking. All six of us will get together again Monday night. I wonder if Professor Davis will take his banjo on the backpacking trip? Will get together this weekend with Allen Ross and Marie St. Martin to work up a couple of trios. None of us are backpacking. Marie singing and Allen and I on guitar. That's a fine combination. We really do need to work up Guantamera. That song is like the Cuban national anthem, some say. Should we do it in authentic Spanish? Maybe."

Diary note by Professor Davis said, "Will set out on the hiking and overnight camping trip in the morning. Should be a fine time. Great weather forcast. No trouble."

Diary note by Benedict Juárez said, "Today's lecture was a presentation of the growth in Confederate population. Interesting. Had not reviewed that in many years. A continuing large birth rate, improved medical knowledge and care, and targeted immigration of contributing families has ensured that our country has remained prosperous and successful in many ways. If we had allowed large numbers of South Americans and Africans to come to the Confederacy as immigrants, the resulting imbalance of racial mix and ability would have been detrimental to the success of all Confederates. Our racial balance, I believe, has been ideal and remained ideal because, collectively, we wanted it that way. And I speak from the Native American heart."

Diary note by Amanda Washington said, "Looking forward to this weekend's hiking and overnight camping. I wonder if the others can keep up with me. Isaiah told me he would carry the heavy packs so we girls would not struggle. Ha! Amanda Washington has not struggled on a hiking trip since she became ten years old. Daddy is witness to that."

## Part 3, Chapter 3, Days 20 and 21 – The Third Weekend, a Pleasant Overnight Hike and Tent Camping – Saturday and Sunday, June 25-26, 2011

By now, none of the twelve Sewanee Project participants had any desire for adventure – not after that sailing trip and that caving trip. But an easy backpacking trip along the edge of the beautiful Cumberland Plateau could not possibly present any danger. Professor Davis, an avid backpacker and hiker himself, and quite fit for his age of 72 years, would lead a group of the four who had neither gone sailing or gone caving. They would backpack and camp overnight, sleeping in hammocks along the Fiery Gizzard Trail in Marion County in the South Cumberland State Park, and cooking over a campfire. The whole bit. The weather promised to be just fine. And the five would get to know each other much better. So after a hearty breakfast, the five threw their packs in the back of Professor Davis's pickup truck and off they drove toward the trailhead between Monteagle and Tracy City, about 20 minutes from Sewanee. Two friends of Professor Davis would be driving a car to the trail start end and repositioning the truck to the trail end later that day so it would be waiting on the five when they were ready to drive back to Sewanee on Sunday afternoon.

It was a good group:

Tina Sharp, being the serious-minder nuclear engineer, would keep Professor Davis engaged in conversation about science and history.

Amanda Washington, an academic city girl by nature, would enjoy time with the rugged Mississippi farmer, Isaiah Montgomery. Put another way, she would be feeling a need for down to earth conversation about down to earth matters and down to earth people who had historically gotten down to earth to plow, sow and harvest to make a living for themselves and their families.

In turn, farmer Isaiah Montgomery would find city girl Amanda interesting and would hope to spend much more time with her.

Benedict Juarez of one of the seceded Mexican States, was the fourth backpacker. One would think that he was just going along for the walk, but such thinking would be off the mark. He was really quite interested in all sorts of people, and he would find both Amanda and Isaiah to be fascinating studies of folks rather new to his observations, for he had never spent time in Mississippi or in Virginia.

The Fiery Gizzard Trail starts at the end of Fiery Gizzard Road up on the plateau and runs for 12.5 miles, starting at Grundy Forest and ending at Foster Falls. The Park Brochure says, "Hikers may observe nature, swim in Fiery Gizzard Creek, see spectacular rock formations, cascading streams, waterfalls, rocky gorges, panoramic overlooks and lush woodlands. The trail has been rated by Backpacker magazine as among the top 20 in the country and should not be missed." Well, our five backpackers were going to enjoy hiking it and cooking and overnighting around a fine campfire.

The backpackers were walking the trail very soon after locking up the truck. After an hour they came to Blue Hole Falls.

After another hour and a half they came to Sycamore Falls.

Thirty minutes after departing Sycamore Falls they descended into Fiery Gizzard Gorge. This would be the most strenuous of the distance to be hiked. But swimming in Fiery Gizzard Creek during the heat of the afternoon promised to make the effort worthwhile.

Tina Sharp asked Professor Davis, "How did Fiery Gizzard Trail get its name?" A teasing answer came back, "Well, it got its name from Fiery Gizzard Creek." Tina shrugged, "OK, smarty pants. Where did Fiery Gizzard Creek get its name?" Laughing, Professor Davis took a deep breath, as if to tell a long, learned story; then he said, "Well, Tina, nobody knows for sure."

Toward the end of the day's hike, the five backpackers would begin the ascent up the "rocky and strenuous" trail, by which they would climb out of Fiery Gizzard Gorge. After the assent, they would hike a bit farther to Raven's Point Overlook. The plan was to cook supper and bed down for the night just below Raven's Point Overlook.

Soon after filling the water bottles and beginning the assent out of the gorge containing Fiery Gizzard Creek, sounds emerged from the lips of determined Amanda Washington, set to the rhythm of the little red steam engine nursery rhyme: "I think I can. I think I can. I think I can . . . ." Benedict dropped back and said, "Amanda, give me that pack. I not only think you can. I know you can." The little steam engine, the load lightened, replied, "Thanks to friends, I know I can . . ."

"How long is this assent, Professor Davis?" The reply: "Done this at least a dozen times. But to tell the truth, it is remarkably difficult. Experienced hikers claim this assent is 'possibly one of the most rugged and difficult trails in Tennessee'." A groan was heard from the back, "Not good! Spent too much time behind a desk, too little time at this sort of thing." It was Tina Sharp.

Isaiah dropped, back, "No need to apologize. Those long hours behind the desk at Comanche Peak Nuclear Station were worthwhile. Give me that pack. You will be fine. Just relax your mind, breath steadily and from deep down, just like you told me you did when playing the French horn. Get into a rhythm and take it one step at a time, at a pace you can maintain. We are in no hurry. I can give you a hand over any rough spots that worry you. We do not want to see anyone fall down.

Professor Davis called back, "Time for our first break. We will take a 5 minute break every 15 minutes until we reach the top." And on they went.

The view from Raven's Point Overlook was spectacular with the sun now low enough in the western sky to cast the first shadows from the taller topography, giving outline to the terrain. Then it was back down a couple hundred yards to the spot chosen for the overnight camp.

Conversation around the camp cook-fire revealed a good bit about the interests and personalities of the backpackers – we look at those aspects of the weekend adventure that are most worthy of including in this story.

All four of the young backpackers assumed that the best campfire cook would be Professor Davis. So experienced at it, they assumed. But they were to find out that Tina Sharp was a crackerjack cook. Her mother, a high school home economics teacher, had taught her so much, and she had brought along a half-dozen seasonings including fresh herbs, select onions and bell peppers, to greatly enhance the meal. But the campfire did present a challenge. Where on the hot coals, how close, etc.? That's where Benedict Juarez applied his talents for imaginative construction. Before long he had put together a sort of oven from hot rocks and dirt. And he used to good affect the sheets of aluminum foil that Professor Davis had brought in his pack. This enabled Tina to present a flawless meal. Professor Davis just sat back and enjoyed watching the young people display their talents.

Soon, the group began to discuss the day's sights.

Amanda: "My favorite was swimming just below Sycamore Falls in Fiery Gizzard Creek. The falls were twelve feet high. It was lovely. And the pool below was so, so refreshing."

Tina: "My favorite, too. But wasn't Blue Hole Falls beautiful."

Benedict: "I can't believe it. That huge old hemlock tree was figured to be 500 years old."

Amanda: "Yeah. It was lovely down there along Fiery Gizzard Creek, but the climb back out was a hum dinger."

Tina: "Perhaps that's why it's named Fiery Gizzard. The climb out causes your gizzard to burn as in a fire."

Benedict: "Maybe. Hey. Where is my gizzard anyway? Do I have a gizzard?"

Isaiah: "That's a question for a farm boy. You all do not have gizzards, so the fire that might be in your belly is not a fiery gizzard. It might be a fiery stomach, but not a fiery gizzard. Birds have gizzards. There are three major organs in a bird's digestive system: the crop, the stomach and the gizzard -- the gizzard is the largest of the three. I enjoy eating fried chicken livers and fired chicken gizzards on occasion. Don't tell me that I am the only person here who has killed and dressed a chicken."

There was silence.

Professor Davis: "Lots of Southerners my age have eaten gizzards. But few among this young generation have, I fear."

That was the case. Only Isaiah had experienced the fried gizzard delicacy.

Tina: "Birds can fly, so ascending out of Fiery Gizzard Gorge would not set their gizzards on fire. What on earth suggested such a name for this creek and this gorge?"

Professor Davis: "Apparently, in the 1870's the Tennessee Coal and Railroad Company built a crude experimental blast furnace in the gorge to test if the local coal could produce good iron. Three days after the first firing the test results disappointed and the furnace structure collapsed. Oh, the outfit had named their blast furnace the "Fiery Gizzard." A name that crazy was bound to stick, I suppose."

Then Professor Davis began what would become the conversation theme for the evening: "You all represent the diversity that is characteristic of the Confederate States of America. Let us discuss personal experiences growing up as children and young adults. Tell each other about times when you felt put down because of racial or ethnic differences and how you coped with those discriminations. Tina, you and I are of the classic founding race of the Confederacy, the European race. Benedict, you are of the Native race that has occupied our continent for 10,000 years. Amanda and Isaiah, you are both mostly of the African race, descended from people who were captured by fellow Africans, sold into slavery and transported across the Atlantic to work farms in the American colonies, the early United States, Spanish Cuba and Spanish Mexico. So, who would like to start with a personal story?"

"I have given great thought to this issue, so perhaps it is fitting that I began." Amanda Washington continued, "Like most Confederates with African ancestry, I am of mixed race, approximately 50 percent African, 40 percent European and 10 percent Native. Seems to me that my great-great-grandfather, Booker T. Washington, understood the challenges facing Confederates of African ancestry quite well and understood how to successfully meet those challenges. He realized that each person is unique. Even brothers differ remarkably, and sisters differ remarkably as well. Yet people are similar within their group. Most likely, brothers or sisters are more alike than neighbors of the same racial makeup. People of the same race, taken as a group, are more similar than people of different races, viewed as groups. Somewhere in the middle are people of mixed race. Booker T. understood racial differences, what he called 'racial strengths and weaknesses', and pioneered an African American education philosophy that focused on building on strengths."

Isaiah, whose ancestry is 75 percent African and 25 percent European, added, "Yes, building on those strengths that are characteristic of racial ancestry is the key to personal satisfaction and happiness. Strive to do what you are good at -- simple as that. I observe that people of African Ancestry are very good at agricultural work: they tend to be strong, agile, adept at outdoors field work and easy-going in personality -- sorry Tina, we perceive you as being real serious; we respect and admire that; but if the world only contained real serious people what a mess it would be. At Mound Bayou along the Mississippi River, we build on African American strengths in field work and easy-going community happiness. Everyone at Mound Bayou is of African ancestry – it averages over 75 percent – and residents of our race do it all -- from the highest levels of management and finance to the lowest novice field hand and cook and bottle washer. And the music. You have to visit Mound Bayou on Saturday night to hear the singing and watch the dancing. But you will have to join in the revelry. Standing around and watching is frowned upon."

Tina Sharp looked up from her cooking and countered, "I'm not that serious, you all. I like music and I also like to sing and dance. I am a very good French horn player."

Isaiah replied, "That may be true, but the West Texas Youth Orchestra and the Atlanta Civic Orchestra play serious classical music, carefully written down by brilliant composers. At Mound Bayou, folks sing and play by memory, by ear, and sometimes make up variations as they go along. We have gathered up a book of songs. Go to the internet and look for 'Songs from Mound Bayou, Mississippi'. It's a great collection."

Tina countered, "I sometimes play my French horn in the same manner, Isaiah. In the Comanche Peak Brass Quintet, we improvise jazz and variations on folk songs and Negro Spirituals and stuff, without reading music. I like to think that diversity in music is a major characteristic of the Confederacy. It's evidence of the different ways we can express our concerns and our happiness, 'our sad times and our glad times'. You name it. The Confederacy is admired world-wide for the music -- the great variety of music -- that comes from our country. Although classical and symphonic music available in the Confederacy is very fine, it is no better than that produced in the United States or Europe. But, in almost every other style, Confederates lead the world. I'm a little serious. But that's just me."

Professor Davis asked, "Benedict Juarez, what do you have to say? Give us a Native perspective."

"Tina, it's OK to be 'a little serious'. In some ways I am, as well. But I am no musician. You all, this conversation is actually right down my alley and I am enjoying listening to what is being said. Being seven eights Native, I am close to being of pure racial ancestry. Recently completed my Ph. D. in Philosophy in Ciudad Juarez in the State of Central Norte. I might claim to be an expert in the subject we are discussing, but I do not believe anyone can truly master this subject. Yet I tried to master it during my doctoral studies and wrapped it up with my thesis, titled, 'Quantifying the Distribution of Human Talents, Strengths and Weaknesses within and between Races and Ethnic Groups'."

"Whoa!, Tina interrupted. "Professor Davis, you have set us up. Is that fair?" After the laughter subsided, Tina continued, "We three novices are discussing a subject that Benedict knows like the back of his hand!"

Professor Davis replied, "I know, Tina. I did that on purpose. You see, all five of us have a great opportunity to learn a lot about human nature just sitting around this campfire talking among ourselves."

"I'm glad you did," Tina replied, "And the surprise helps to enhance our senses and our desire to learn more. But for now, the campfire meal is ready and it's time to eat. Come and get it!"

The meal was quite good by campfire standards. Particularly the bison steaks that Alan has given and Benedict Juarez had toted along in his backpack in cold-pack bags, 7 pounds that he was glad to carry. The roasted peppers and onions enhanced the flavor (Benedict got some hot peppers, but others declined). "What's wrong with you all, Benedict teased, "tummy can't handle the Mexican hot peppers?" There was no answer, for others were heaping roasted potatoes and sliced apples onto their plates. Isaiah gave grace and the five dug in.

The meal over, conversation again turned to characteristics of racial and ethnic differences.

Benedict Juarez led off with a brief summary of his doctoral dissertation:

"Yeah, it was titled 'Quantifying the Distribution of Human Talents, Strengths and Weaknesses within and between Races and Ethnic Groups.' Tina, you would have liked the math and statistics in the work. To 'quantify' one must reduce concepts to numbers. To present a 'distribution' one resorts to statistical methods."

"Makes sense," Tina submitted, "I use math and statistics all the time in my work at Comanche Peak Nuclear Station."

Benedict continued, "To define 'Talents, Strengths and Weaknesses' one must employ the tools of the philosopher, tools I came to understand in my undergraduate and graduate work, for my degrees are in Philosophy. The difficult part is that related to the touchy issues of race and ethnicity."

"So how did you handle that?," Professor Davis asked.

"Carefully, very carefully," came back the answer. "But one cannot understand we human beings without addressing racial and ethnic characteristics. Yet, tactfulness does help. You see, it is apparent to me, and to you all as well, I hope, that God created the first human beings about 200,000 years ago in East Africa. This was a supernatural event, it was not normal evolution. It appears that God decided that human beings would share the genetic makeup of life that had evolved over millions of years on Earth up to that time, and it appears He employed gene sharing on purpose to make it easier for us to succeed in the varied environments here on earth, from very harsh environments to very pleasant ones. He did not create us as a strange creature like some science fiction 'Martian'. God gave us over 98 percent of the genetic code of our nearest animal relative. We were made to fit in here on Earth, but to be remarkably superior when organized into communities.

"Christians like me believe that God also gave us a soul that could achieve eternal life. The concept of a soul is based on faith alone.

"Now 200,000 years was not that long ago. Given five generations per century, that calculates to 10,000 generations. Over that span of human reproduction, our relatives spread all over the world, met different challenges of weather (hot to freezing, wet to dry); challenges of food supply (that varied a lot); challenges of fighting off predators (wolves, tigers, snakes, you name it); challenges of disease (all sorts); challenges of tribal warfare (lots of that), and so forth, and so on. And people became widely separated, preventing a remix of the divergent gene pool. So, over those 10,000 generations, differences emerged and were sustained among widely separated human populations, and the most dramatic differences we classify by defining three major races of mankind and many sub-categories of more minor racial differences. We have the original race, the African race, but within the African race are many more sub-categories than are found to exist among the other two races. Amanda and Isaiah, you are of substantial African ancestry, but may be of different subcategories of that broad, diversified race when looking back to where your African ancestors came from. In Asia, humans evolved into the Asian race. Eventually, some people of that race migrated to the American continents, creating here an Asian race sub-category, call Native American. I am seven eights of the Native American subcategory of the Asian race. In Europe humans evolved into the European race of which we all five of us share a bit of ancestry: one hundred percent shared by you two, Professor Davis and Tina Sharp; forty percent shared by you, Amanda; one-fourth shared by you Isaiah, and one-eight shared by me."

"The concept of supernatural creation of the first human beings is fairly well grounded in scientific evidence, but remains debatable. However, after the creation of the first man and woman, which we Christians call Adam and Eve, human evolution began to diversify within subsequent generations over the succeeding 10,000 generations. That's the word: 'Evolved.' We are the result of evolutionary processes before Adam and Eve (to ensure a small amount of initial genetic diversity) and the result of evolutionary processes after Adam and Eve -- but Adam and Eve themselves were God's creation. And here we are today, all over the world – a diverse population of 10 billion humans, all descended from God's Adam and God's Eve, all differing from one another due to human evolution."

At this point the discussion circled around faith in God, the human soul and everlasting life in Heaven. And I see no need to report to you that portion of the campfire talk. So we listen in again when the discussion returns to racial characteristics.

Amanda injected, "I believe that diversity within a human population is essential to prosperity and happiness. Today, a successful society must be exceptionally diverse, more so than ever before. Five hundred years ago humans were primarily living off the land in self-sustaining family groups. Today, advanced technology removes almost everyone from the land and self-sustaining family groups and places them in diverse occupations, and in various jobs throughout manufacturing, construction, transportation, wholesale, retail, government work, and so forth, and so on. People are happiest when they work and feel productive -- that is human nature. A person who is lazy and dependent on the care of others is inherently an unhappy person. And, this is the main point: people like to work at something that they are good at. Tina, you may be good at cooking, but you want more than to work as a cook in a fast food restaurant. Another person, perhaps a young person might be real happy at the cooking job. Another person might become a fine chef, make a career in the restaurant business and be happy at that. Isaiah, you are probably good at working as a field hand, but you have greater talents, and, to be happy, you need to be in a management position. Benedict, you are a rugged fellow who would make a fine construction worker -- a carpenter, mason, roofer, plumber, and so forth – but you have greater service to bring to your people. And as a teacher, it will be my goal to instill this attitude in my students. 'All work is honorable and can be a source of happiness. Just make the best of your talents, work hard to enhance them and fine a field of work that will bring you happiness'."

Benedict added further support to Amanda's argument:

"A family does not have to be wealthy to be happy. My research supports that fact. I found wealthy people who were unhappy – husband frustrated, wife overworked and kids getting into trouble because the parents were trying to do too much and were not at home when they needed to be. They had money and a nice home, but they were not happy.

"On the other hand, my research found many families that were happy in spite of the fact that they were not wealthy, just bringing in enough money to be comfortable and taking pride in doing a lot of things for themselves. Where the wife stayed at home, I often heard it said, 'I save our family more by staying home than I could make if I left home five days a week to work elsewhere.' These families did not have big houses, but they were often happy. That really impressed me."

"My mom often said the same thing," Tina added. "She did not work outside of the home, but she was terrific at saving money, providing a happy home and raising us kids. That freed Dad to work hard at his career and not to worry about the family. And Mom was happy. And we young'uns were happy. She was smart and capable of a fine career for herself, but a happy family made her happy. Around our house the watchword was always, "If Momma aren't happy, ain't nobody happy!""

Isaiah interjected a related and confirming thought. "You know, Tina, the school systems in the Confederate States teach teenagers self-reliance and homemaking/parenting/home maintenance skills to enable them to be self-sufficient in varied ways when they grow up and marry and become parents. We think learning that basic skill set is just as important as any other subject in middle school and high school. Not so up north in the United States. Up there courses in homemaking/parenting/home maintenance were long ago dropped to make room for other courses. And look at the result. Up there people experience far more broken families, children out of wedlock, drug dependency, single mothers on welfare and unhappiness. The crime rate is higher, too."

Amanda agreed. "We Confederates live in a society that is built on a solid rock -- the traditional family. Professor Davis, what has your reading and study over the decade revealed? Has any society in world history thrived over an extended period, say several centuries, after it abandoned firm support for the traditional family?"

"No, Amanda, no society in human history has thrived after abandoning reliance on the traditional family."

"I want to ask Benedict a question. Benedict, does your research indicate that, of the three major races, one is more faithful than another in reliance on the traditional family?"

"Not within the Confederacy. Building and maintaining the traditional family constitutes about eighty-five percent of the population in each race and racial mix. It seems like God made us that way and we in the Confederacy are smart enough to understand that."

Professor Davis turned to Isaiah and asked, "Tell me about your experiences in suffering racial discrimination. Isaiah, being of seven eights African ancestry, some know-it-alls would anticipate that you have suffered racial discrimination. Let us start with you. Any examples worthy of mention?"

"I am probably not a good example of African-Confederates who might be subject to racial discrimination. Since I went to the Mound Bayou High, essentially the whole class was of significant African ancestry. But when I went to college, I was thrown together with other races. There my situation was different from most. I felt sorry for the white boys, those of European ancestry, who failed to make the football team, or if they did, spent far more time on the bench than on the field. I played quarterback and had to remind myself to not get too uppity or cocky around campus. I was a good student, but not among the brightest. When it came to playing football, the best players played. There was no racial discrimination. There was no racial diversity at Mound Bayou. We suffered no racial discrimination. But ours is an unusual situation."

Amanda then engaged the subject. "Being one-half of African ancestry, and being thrown in with lots of people of European ancestry, I went through many situations where I might be subjected to racial discrimination. I understood that boys of European ancestry were not prone to ask me out on dates. That was understood. Confederates are diverse in their racial makeup, but most feel like they want a sweetheart and future spouse to be of their own race. It just seems to feel right. I am OK with that. I never hankered to go out on dates with boys of European ancestry even though I am forty percent of that racial background. When I eventually fall in love and desire to marry, I anticipate my man will have some African ancestry."

Benedict took his turn, reporting, "Although my ancestry is seven-eighths Native, people of European ancestry often think of me as being 'Hispanic' because I am of the Seceded Mexican States. But where I grew up, there were finer distinctions. People in my region recognized the differences between residents who were primarily of Native ancestry versus residents who were primarily of European ancestry. Language differences are now minor, mostly just a manner of speaking and some variation in accent. English is now predominant. Some Spanish words remain, but few speak only Spanish anymore, and it is not possible to use Spanish when addressing business issues or government issues. Some old families in our region who are of European ancestry still put on airs and behave a bit snooty, but they are a small minority and are mostly ignored. Because our government structures are strictly democratic, people like that do not hold power in government, and in business they would be shunned if they behaved too badly.

"I believe our school system has exerted the strongest influence on our people over the past six generations, since we joined the Confederate States. Remaining in the Spanish-speaking tradition would have been so natural, but every Seceded State was determined from the outset to transform its people into an English speaking society that could readily assimilate into the Confederate States to the north. At the outset, that goal was written into each State Constitution. Our people took the challenge seriously. Speaking English was a badge of honor and each generation became prouder of that badge and more determined to acquire it. When radio and then television arrived, we experienced a surge in our passion to learn to read and speak English, and used those technologies as the great teacher that they were. Today, the great teacher is computers and cell phones and tablets and internet access. It's all in English. It gives us all full time access to the whole world.

"That being said, even over the 27 years that I have been here on Earth, I have seen decline in discrimination against people of Native ancestry. Today, I consider it minor. Our people are respected because we are so good at working in construction, manufacturing, agriculture and other endeavors that are physical in nature. Most prefer to leave to others the office work, the mental gymnastics, the engineering and planning work, clerking and so forth. Most say, 'give is a physical job worth doing and we will amaze you with our proficiency, our stamina, our stick-to-it-ness, and we will be happy doing it'. And that work pays well enough, so these folk are comfortable and happy with their lives and their families. They so love children, your know. I'm talking big families averaging 4.3 children per couple."

Professor Davis then asked Tina for her input. "What about you, Tina, have you seen discrimination growing up, in school or in business?"

"People always speak of discrimination as actions against people who are not of European ancestry. When discrimination is aimed at my people, seems like it is referred to as 'reverse discrimination'. I can't say that I have suffered 'reverse discrimination'. If I had been a good athlete, I would have probably suffered it some, but that was not my bag."

The campfire discussion lasted until 10 pm. Then it was hit the sack.

Breakfast the following morning was simple. No cooking. Just sweet rolls, bison jerky, apple slices and coffee.

The hike out from the campsite just below Raven's Point Overlook amounted to 8 miles of relatively easy walking along the top of the Cumberland Plateau, that is, except for the 200 foot drop down into and out of Laurel Branch Gorge, complete with myriad rocks. It was about three in the afternoon when the backpackers reached Foster Falls -- another great place to cool off in the mid afternoon heat.

By 3:30 that afternoon, they were back in Professor Davis's pickup truck, which had been relocated by two friends. By 4:30 they were back at Sewanee. Fate had been dealt a blow. No crisis as in the sailing trip off Cuba. No crisis as in the caving venture at Big Bone Cave. Just some tired people that Sunday. On Monday and Tuesday, perhaps several sore muscles would deliver further reminders of the ups and downs of Fiery Gizzard Trail. But the lasting reminders of the weekend would be the binding friendships that adventuring together is capable of producing.

## Sunday Evening Selected Diary Postings

Diary note by Marie St. Martin said, "Had great fun this weekend doing trios with Allen Ross and Carlos Cespedes on guitar. To my great delight, Carlos taught us to really sing Guantanamera the way it ought to be sung. He wrote it out in Spanish and we sung it that way, too. Allen picked up on the chord progression while Carlos played lead guitar with lots of fancy licks. . . . . Reflecting on the tribulations of the sailing trip two weeks ago, Skipper Carlos and I agreed it was nice to be safely in Sewanee doing our music thing. Allen added, 'Sure as Hell beats being stuck deep in a long-forgotten cave passage without any light. Let's play another song and calm our minds'. Allen and Carlos can jam pretty well to not be professional musicians. I like the combination of Allen's western style with Carlos' Spanish style -- great sound. The five backpackers got back in time for supper. All said it was a great weekend. I asked Tina Sharp if the trail was really 'fiery.' She replied, 'Just a carry-over name from an old iron furnace'."

Dairy note by Andrew Houston said, "Played tennis with Conchita twice this weekend, singles both days. I think she let me win this afternoon. Felt sorry for me; my bruised masculinity, I suppose. She is so, so good. I have a good serve, but she is so agile on the court and anticipates so well. Her return of service is fantastic. If I come to net, which I am prone to do following a good first serve, she often returns a winning passing shot or a deft lob. I often just beat myself trying too hard, making unforced errors. And I find it hard to concentrate. Picture this: here stands Andrew Houston, single, unattached, looking across the tennis net at gorgeous Conchita. Fellows, whom among you would be thinking about winning a tennis game?"

Diary note by Professor Davis said, "Back from Fiery Gizzard trail. Went very well. Benedict and Isaiah carried the heavy loads and the ladies did fine. But the conversation was what most impressed me. I am supposed to be the professor, for goodness sake. But I felt like a student myself as I listened to the conversation around the camp fire last night. These young men and women are amazing."

Diary note by Conchita Rezanov said, "Andrew Houston asked me out tonight on a date. Went to nice steak restaurant that featured a little jazz band off to the side and lovely snapper with all the trimmings. Andrew must have made a special arrangement for the cozy dimly lit corner. He is quite the romantic, and oh so handsome to boot. I then began to understand why I had trouble staying on my game when we played tennis this afternoon. He won! Said I had allowed me to win out of pity. Not all that true. Watching him across the net, good looking, sweaty, and working so hard, I lost my concentration and made too many unforced errors. I want to spend more time with him. Tonight was a good beginning. Really enjoyed our date. Goodness, it is already 12:15 in the morning. Got to hit the sack."

# Part 3, Chapter 4, Day 22 – An Overview of Confederate History from 1870 to 1890 – Class Lecture, Monday, June 27, 2011

As the twelve Sewanee Project team members gathered Monday morning to listen to Professor Davis present an overview of Confederate history from 1870 to 1890, they were glad that all had experienced a satisfying weekend, free of crises. But how could Professor Davis cover such a huge topic in just one morning?

## Introduction

Because so much happened in Confederate history between 1870 and 1890 telling the full story is not practical. So I have decided to focus on the original eleven Confederate States and on helping you understand how the people of the Confederate States transformed their country from an agricultural society that included slavery to a far more diversified agricultural-industrial society free of "slavery obligations". Unless one realizes the extent of the owner's obligations toward his or her slaves, the term "slavery obligations" might seem strange. But, as the Confederate States industrialized and farm machinery replaced man and mule, the agricultural workforce dramatically declined. Eventually, the obligation to sustain a slave family from birth to death became financial nonsense. For this and many other reasons, slavery rapidly declined in the decades following the Montreal treaty boundary settlement. The transformation from an agricultural to an industrial economy was amazing and some readers will find the story hard to believe, especially readers in the United States who might puzzle over our history.

So, perhaps to help cynics understand how it happened, the stories in this chapter will focus on key people who did so much to advance our country from a position of world leadership only in agriculture to a position of world leadership in both agriculture and industrial technology. There is a theme to the story, a lesson to be learned. It is this: because Confederates emphasized recruiting immigrants capable of making outstanding contributions to their country, many did come, and great inventions were discovered, and great new industries emerged. The contributions of exceptionally talented immigrants were, so, so important to the rapid scientific and industrial advancements during the early decades of our Confederate States. Therefore, much of my presentation this morning will focus on key people who came to our country and blessed it immensely.

## Confederate Agriculture, Corporate Farms and Emancipation

Prior to the creation of the Confederate States of America, the economy of the Southern States was overwhelmingly based on agriculture. And economic studies prove that in no region of North America were farms more productive on an output per worker basis than in the South during the 1850s, especially the large farms that were called "Plantations." For a reason not unlike that of the textile manufacturing industry of the northeastern United States region, the greater efficiency per worker was the result of the more intensive utilization of the labor force. In northern textile factories, management made sure the work of the employees was organized to maximize efficiency and productivity. In Southern cotton, sugar, rice and tobacco plantations, management likewise made sure the work of slaves and their overseers was organized to maximize efficiency and productivity. Studies show that, comparing Southern farms to Northern farms, which were smaller operations, productivity per worker for those in the South (free and slave combined) exceeded productivity per worker in the North by roughly 35 percent. Did the slave and free farm workers in the South work longer hours? No, the Southern slave and free workers had more free time. Were the slaves worked to death by being driven to the breaking point? No, the slave enjoyed raising families and living about as long as the free (note comparative population expansion statistics). Evidence shows that the advantage for the large Southern farm was in the organization of the work and the intelligence applied to the administration and productivity of the place, from conditioning the soil to harvesting the crop and sending it to market. Like the industrial factory of the North, the agricultural "factory" of the South benefitted from improved productivity over the older home-craft, "cottage" industries of prior centuries.

As a result, as the years prior to 1860 evolved into subsequent decades, it naturally flowed that leaders in the past agricultural industry, which had been mostly based on slave labor, would become leaders in the future agricultural industry, which would be based on corporate farms and the labor of independent people. And this transition from privately held Southern plantations to Southern corporate farms moved in concert with programs to train and make independent the men and women who were slaves at the beginning of the Confederate States of America, as well as their children. [255]

In each decade, from 1861 going forward, corporate farms grew in number and land area. By 1870, 24 percent of former slaves were independent and those over 16 were employed except for the mothers at home tending to the children. This movement away from slavery interdependence steadily grew. By 1880, 90 percent had transitioned to independence. It seemed that only the elderly were hanging back, benefiting from the "retirement benefits" awarded by many long-time masters or their children. The last Confederate slave was "Uncle Horace", 103, of Mississippi, who passed away in 1913.

There is insufficient space in *The CSA Trilogy* to tell the story in detail, but by reading a speech given by Booker T. Washington before the Cotton States and International exposition in Atlanta, Georgia on September 18, 1883, one gets the spirit of cooperation that was so important to the success of our country of such amazing diversity. By this time, free people of color were a major population in the Confederate States and Booker T. Washington was encouraging their employment for the benefit of all Confederate people. And his advocacy had long been rather broadly embraced, for recruitment of immigrants was seldom aimed at gaining agricultural workers, or laborers in factories. Immigrants being recruited had more advanced skills. The text of Washington's historic speech follows, slightly abridged: [256]

"Mr. President and Gentlemen of the Board of Directors and Citizens:

"One-third of the population of the South is of the Negro race. No enterprise seeking the material, civil, or moral welfare of this section can disregard this element of our population and reach the highest success. I but convey to you, Mr. President and Directors, the sentiment of the masses of my race when I say that in no way have the value and manhood of the American Negro been more fittingly and generously recognized than by the managers of this magnificent Exposition at every stage of its progress. It is a recognition that will do more to cement the friendship of the two races than any occurrence since the dawn of our freedom...

"A ship lost at sea for many days suddenly sighted a friendly vessel. From the mast of the unfortunate vessel was seen a signal, "Water, water; we die of thirst!" The answer from

---

[255] In truthful history, by 1865, Southern farms and plantations were bankrupt or nearly so, the labor force was scattered, disrupted, confused and pulled away from former relationships of mutual dependence. Many Confederate soldiers were dead. And in many places the land was abandoned to irrecoverable topsoil erosion. This prevented the happy outcome presented in our alternate history -- the story of a transition "from plantations to corporate farms" and a transition "from a prideful slave work ethic and sense of 'family' to being trained for independence and motivated to embrace a prideful work ethic as a valued employee on a corporate farm."

[256] Booker T. Washington's speech was given by him as shown here on September 18 at Atlanta at the Cotton States and International Exposition on the indicated date, but 12 years later, in 1895. Because out alternate history allowed for more rapid progress for free people of color, the event is presented as having taken place in 1883.

the friendly vessel at once came back, "Cast down your bucket where you are." A second time the signal, "Water, water; send us water!" ran up from the distressed vessel, and was answered, "Cast down your bucket where you are." And a third and fourth signal for water was answered, "Cast down your bucket where you are." The captain of the distressed vessel, at last heeding the injunction, cast down his bucket, and it came up full of fresh, sparkling water from the mouth of the Amazon River. To those of my race who depend on bettering their condition in a foreign land or who underestimate the importance of cultivating friendly relations with the Southern white man, who is their next-door neighbor, I would say: "Cast down your bucket where you are"— cast it down in making friends in every manly way of the people of all races by whom we are surrounded.

"Cast it down in agriculture, mechanics, in commerce, in domestic service, and in the professions. And in this connection it is well to bear in mind that whatever other sins the South may be called to bear, when it comes to business, pure and simple, it is in the South that the Negro is given a man's chance in the commercial world, and in nothing is this Exposition more eloquent than in emphasizing this chance. Our greatest danger is that in the great leap from slavery to freedom we may overlook the fact that the masses of us are to live by the productions of our hands, and fail to keep in mind that we shall prosper in proportion as we learn to dignify and glorify common labor, and put brains and skill into the common occupations of life; shall prosper in proportion as we learn to draw the line between the superficial and the substantial, the ornamental gewgaws of life and the useful. No race can prosper 'till it learns that there is as much dignity in tilling a field as in writing a poem. It is at the bottom of life we must begin, and not at the top. Nor should we permit our grievances to overshadow our opportunities.

"To those of the White race who look to the incoming of those of foreign birth and strange tongue and habits for the prosperity of the South, were I permitted I would repeat what I say to my own race, "Cast down your bucket where you are." Cast it down among the eight millions of Negroes whose habits you know, whose fidelity and love you have tested in days when to have proved treacherous meant the ruin of your firesides. Cast down your bucket among these people who have, without strikes and labor wars, tilled your fields, cleared your forests, built your railroads and cities, and brought forth treasures from the bowels of the earth, and helped make possible this magnificent representation of the progress of the South. Casting down your bucket among my people, helping and encouraging them as you are doing on these grounds, and to education of head, hand, and heart, you will find that they will buy your surplus land, make blossom the waste places in your fields, and run your factories. While doing this, you can be sure in the future, as in the past, that you and your families will be surrounded by the most patient, faithful, law-abiding, and unresentful people that the world has seen. As we have proved our loyalty to you in the past, in nursing your children, watching by the sick-bed of your mothers and fathers, and often following them with tear-dimmed eyes to their graves, so in the future, in our humble way, we shall stand by you with a devotion that no foreigner can approach, ready to lay down our lives, if need be, in defense of yours, interlacing our industrial, commercial, civil, and religious life with yours in a way that shall make the interests of both races one. In all things that are purely social we can be as separate as the fingers, yet one as the hand in all things essential to mutual progress.

"There is no defense or security for any of us except in the highest intelligence and development of all. If anywhere there are efforts tending to curtail the fullest growth of the Negro, let these efforts be turned into stimulating, encouraging, and making him the most useful and intelligent citizen. . . ."

Much of the smoothness of transitions from slavery to independent living is to be credited to the growth of corporate industry. Of course, corporate farms were excellent at facilitating transitions to independence. But corporations involved in non-agricultural industry and commerce were just as helpful. The construction industry was great at transitioning men from slavery to independence. The textile industry -- both in fabric making and in garment making -- was great at facilitating transitions for men and women alike. So was the food processing industry, which hired men and women who had been slaves. And the list goes on and on. The Confederacy steadily expanded from 1), a predominantly agricultural industry in which machinery was steadily replacing workers, to 2), many diverse industries. In lockstep, plantation children, small farmers and former slaves found their way from the farm to more gainful employment elsewhere in the country's industrial mix.

If we fast-forward to today, we see that Confederate farms and large privately owned farms are the most productive in the world, animal husbandry included. Confederates provide enough food to feed all citizens and to export far more than that to other nations. The foodstuffs output of the original Confederate States, of Sequoyah and the western States out to South California, of Cuba, the former Mexican States, and Hawaii are amazing. Add that to the seafood from Russian America, the Atlantic, the Pacific and the Gulf. Add to that the seafood from fish farming. The total is enormous -- a testament to the amazing productivity of a diverse society where individual strengths and resources are routinely organized in a way that benefits all.

## Confederate Marine, River and Rail Transportation Expansion

It is often said that the transportation network within the Confederate States is a primary reason for the country's remarkable success. Although Confederate marine, river and rail transportation made great strides up to the year 1890, expansion has obviously been continuing up to this day. But, we can look at the early strides in expanding these modes of transportation up to 1890 and then look ahead a bit to progress over further decades of growth. First we look at seaports and shipbuilding.

Before State Secession, the Southern States were America's major exporting region. So, during the 1870's and 1880's great effort was expended on constructing and maintaining excellent seaport harbors and docks. Harbors were dredged further to accommodate larger ships and more rugged docks were constructed as needs dictated. Freight handling at seaport docks was steadily streamlined and accelerated. Railroads were built down to and across major docks. Powerful rail-mounted, steam-powered cranes sped up loading and unloading. Outgoing freight was palletized before arriving at the dock to facilitate rapid loading onto ships and similar procedures were encouraged for foreign seaports to improve loading cargo to be delivered to Confederate seaports. Looking beyond 1890, we see that Confederates would utilize diesel powered trucks fork-trucks and cranes to bring goods to ship-side and take goods away. More recently, Confederates would introduce the 40-foot sea-land stackable steel container and pioneer in building cargo ships that carried stackable containerized cargo on top of the ship's deck. But the advances, observed through today, began with important advances up to 1890.

Early on, emphasis was placed on developing a Confederate ship-building industry. Shipwrights from Great Britain and the northeastern United States were recruited, as were mechanics and craftsmen. New enterprises blossomed and extensive ship-building yards were established in Norfolk, Virginia; Charleston, South Carolina; Mobile, Alabama; Baton Rouge, Louisiana; Houston, Texas; San Diego, South California and Tampico, Costa Este.

We now turn to inland waterways. Although the success of railroads was making it difficult to justify new canal projects, one important project was underway by the late 1870's because it enabled water transportation between the Tennessee River and the Gulf of Mexico without going north to the Ohio River. This was the Tennessee-Tombigbee Canal, which permitted river traffic to travel from the Tennessee River, entering at a point near our capital Davis, to the Tombigbee River, exiting into the Gulf of Mexico near Demopolis, Alabama. Furthermore, when completed in 1883, it gave the Confederate capital at Davis direct waterway transport to and from the Gulf of Mexico. Even today, waterways remain the cheapest method of shipping bulk cargo such as coal, oil, stone, and mined ores.

We now turn to railroads and locomotives. After the boundaries were defined in the Montreal Peace Settlement, the Confederacy was a large country, and it grew much larger within a decade. So, accelerated railroad construction was quickly encouraged by the various States. Private railroad companies, often startups, accepted the challenge. And, in the various States, Governor's Multistate Railroad Commissions coordinated the planning of the routes and the package of incentives to facilitate land acquisition and encourage startups. Early on, the concept of a country-wide railroad network gained favor. Set aside was the idea or promoting railroads from A to B because business interests in A and B wanted interconnecting railway service. Instead plans were drawn and endorsed for a country-wide railway network that benefitted all because it promised to be efficient, rapid and comprehensive. First a study of the future optimum railroad gage indicated that, because locomotives would become much more powerful and trains much longer, it would be prudent to widen the Confederate Standard Track Gage of 5 feet to 6 feet.[257] The express railroad network would be built to this wider gage and the gage of existing railroads could be widened in time with revamped roadbeds and new crossties. At the core of the express network were two major triple-track, east-west, express trunk lines, built to allow simultaneous, around-the-clock traffic in both directions with minimal delays (the triple track allowed a fast train to pass a slow train and provided a third track to allow one to be out of service for maintenance). The southern east-west express trunk line was planned from Savannah, Georgia to Baton Rouge, Louisiana to Houston, South Texas to Guadalajara, Costa Sudoeste. The northern east-west express trunk line was planned from Norfolk, Virginia to Atlanta, Georgia to Memphis, Tennessee, to Dallas, North Texas, to San Diego, South California. Running north to south were seven express branch lines, also triple-tracked. The most eastward was the Atlantic Line, which ran from Richmond, Virginia to Miami, Florida, staying sufficiently inland to avoid excessive bridging of waterways. To the west of that was the Valley Line, which ran from Lexington, Virginia to Knoxville, Tennessee to Atlanta, Georgia to Mobile, Alabama. To the west of that was the East Mississippi Line, which ran from Nashville, Tennessee to Jackson, Mississippi to New Orleans, Louisiana. To the west of that was the West Mississippi Line, which ran from Little Rock Arkansas, to Port Arthur, South Texas. To the west of that was the East Gulf Line, which ran from Oklahoma City to Dallas to Texas City (Galveston), East Texas. To the west of that was the West Gulf Line, which ran from Lubbock, Texas to Guanuaxuato, Central del Sur. To the west of that was the East Pacific Line, which ran from Phoenix, Arizona to Guadalajara, Costa Sudoeste. Finally, the plan for the West Pacific Line called for it to run from Los Angeles, South California to Puerto Vallarta, Costa Sudoeste. By 1890 much of this railroad network was built. Ten years later, this planned network of triple-track express railroads would be finished. Furthermore, many single-or-double-track feeder railroads would be

---

[257] At this time standard gage in the northern States was 4 feet 6-1/2 inches and in the southern States most gages were 5 feet 0 inches. In our alternative history, the Confederacy, in a far-sighted move, decided to build its future express rail network on a 6-foot gage, while expanding the 5-foot spans of existing roads as locomotives and rail-cars were scrapped or modified. In truthful history the United States remained on its 4 foot 6-1/2 inch gage and forced the Southern States to narrow its gage to match. The wider Confederate rail gage enables faster, taller and safer rail transport on tracks built to tighter curves, and adapts better to modern 8-foot wide sea-land containerization standards.

constructed to connect to the express network, such as the Richmond to Charlotte to Atlanta to New Orleans interconnecting line.

## The Father of Confederate Chemical Technology -- Wilhelm von Hofmann

Chemical science would become critical to the expansion of Confederate industrialization in many fields: fabric chemicals and dyes; crop fertilizers and soil conditioners; medicine; refining of mined ores; refining of petroleum for fuels and lubricants; food preservation; leather tanning; explosives; paints and finishes; improved rubber, and inventing many new synthetic materials. But chemical technology in both the United States and the Confederate States was far behind the world leader – Germany -- and its forerunner, the various Germanic States. Europeans were trying to catch up, including Great Britain. But Germans were at least one generation ahead of everybody else. It made no sense to try to build Confederate expertise in chemical technology from within. Instead, bringing important teaching and researching chemists from across the Atlantic was clearly indicated. So, an effort to recruit scientists was launched in early 1863, soon after the Treaty of Montreal had been signed the previous September.

The University of Nashville was soon a leader in this recruiting effort. Middle Tennessee and University leaders placed their hopes on recruiting chemist Wilhelm von Hofmann from Great Britain. Those hopes heighten upon receiving encouraging news from the Confederate minister to Great Britain, James Mason. The story of how this all came about for the benefit of Confederate chemical science and engineering is worthy of two pages.

The stark contrast between German chemical advances and American backwardness is hard to exaggerate. Without a doubt, the greatest leader in chemical teaching and laboratory procedures was Justus von Liebig, who trained hundreds at the University of Giessen, Grand Duchy of Hesse. [258] He is known as the founder of modern agricultural chemistry and inventor of nitrogen-based artificial fertilizer, and as the pioneer in precision chemical laboratory methods. But perhaps his most important contribution was in teaching these methods and this knowledge to hundreds of students. Among them was August Wilhelm von Hofmann. We now turn to our story about him.

August Wilhelm von Hofmann (1818-1892) was a leader in chemical technology in both the German States and in Great Britain. Born in Giessen, Grand Duchy of Hesse, he studied organic chemistry in the city of his birth and received his Ph.D. in 1841 under von Liebig's direction. Two years later he became one of Liebig's assistants. Two years after that, in 1845, he was recruited by Prince Albert and others close to Queen Victoria to take the position of Director of a new institution: the Royal College of Chemistry, located in London. This institution was to focus on "practical chemistry" and it would have strong support from Prince Albert, the husband of Queen Victoria and father of her nine children, he being known officially as "Albert, Prince Consort." The Royal College of Chemistry under Hofmann's leadership was very successful in training students in chemistry, enjoying strong support from Prince Albert and other British industrial and educational leaders who recognized the importance of the program. But when Albert died in December 14, 1861 (note that this was the same month as South Carolina's secession), the College lost a key supporter and advocate, and, in the aftermath, the British government and the country's industry lost interest in science and technology education. So, the Royal College of Chemistry fell on hard times. It's Director, and most important professor, August Wilhelm Hofmann, felt the loss deeply, for he had considered Prince Albert a dear friend and key supporter. Of the loss he wrote:

---

[258] Until 1871 Hesse was an independent nation ruled by the Grand Duchy; afterward part of the German Reich. He held a post as professor at Giessen from 1824 to 1852; after that taking a less stressful post as a researcher and professor at the Ludwig Maximilian University of Munich.

Albert's "early kindness exercised so powerful an influence upon the destinies of my existence. Year by year, do I feel more deeply the debt of gratitude which I owe to him." [259]

It was during the December holiday period of 1863 that the Confederate Minister to Great Britain, James Mason, invited August Wilhelm von Hofmann to dine and discuss a new opportunity in the Confederate States. Communications from the University of Nashville had convinced Mason that Middle Tennessee, the former home region of U. S. Presidents Andrew Jackson and James K. Polk, was fully engaged in providing strong financial backing to a major Department of Chemistry and Engineering at the University of Nashville. Applying his impressive skills at entertaining and persuasion, Mason made it hard for Hofmann to refuse the invitation -- "At least visit Tennessee and see what they wish to offer you." And that is what Hofmann did. In fact the whole family left London together, disembarked at Charleston and traveled by train to Nashville. They were hooked. Professor Bushrod Johnson was especially effective in selling the offer. So, we now tell the story of the University of Nashville and Professor Bushrod Johnson.

Professor Johnson, better known as General Bushrod Johnson, had been an important military leader in the War Between the States, but his greatest talent and expertise was in education, mathematics and chemistry. Born in eastern Ohio across from Virginia (now part of Maryland) and raised as a Quaker, he had graduated from the United States Military Academy in 1840, and led troops in the Seminole War in Florida and in the War against Mexico. Resigning the military in 1847 he had moved directly into teaching, taking the post of professor of natural philosophy and chemistry at the Western Military Institute, after that professor of mathematics and engineering at the University of Nashville. He served in the Confederate military during the War, rising to the rank of General. By the fall of 1863 he was back at the University of Nashville resuming his old teaching post. [260]

Hofmann's wife and family were charmed by the many friendly receptions at Middle Tennessee homes, typically surrounded by farm fields covered by limestone-sweetened black dirt (not the red clay further south). He saw these fields as great locations to apply improved nitrogen-based fertilizers. And visitors from northern Mississippi were doubly excited about applying Hofmann's aniline dyes to fabrics made in cotton mills they were planning. Furthermore, family members were greatly impressed by the Southern hospitality that surrounded them. English was not a big problem for the Hofmann's. Much of that had been mastered in London. So August Wilhelm von Hofmann accepted the offer and left soon for London to pack up many crates of laboratory equipment, books, manuscripts, notes and supplies, plus the family personal possessions. By August 1864, the University of Nashville was starting up its Department of Chemistry and Chemical Engineering -- the Chemistry department to research and the Engineering department to work out practical applications derived from the new knowledge. [261]

Hofmann would be very influential in advancing agricultural and chemical science, but always with one eye on practical applications and urging widespread training of students and

[259] This history of Justus von Liebig, August Wilhelm von Hofmann and Prince Albert is truthful up to this point. We now change the story to our alternate history.

[260] In truthful history Bushrod Johnson's birthplace was in eastern Ohio, across from what became northern West Virginia. He arrived at the University of Nashville in 1866, not in 1863 as told in our alternate history, a move made possible by the early ending of the military conflict.

[261] By the way, the author graduated from Vanderbilt University in 1960 with a degree in chemical engineering. In truthful history, the University of Nashville fell on hard times during the War Between the States and the Political Reconstruction that followed. It was rescued by Commodore Cornelius Vanderbilt (1794-1877) of New York City, a brilliant, self-made entrepreneur who became one of the richest people in United States history.

farmers.  He was often visiting Tuskegee Institute in Tuskegee, Alabama to coordinate his work with that of its application-oriented professors -- especially Tuskegee's founder Booker T. Washington and its most influential botanist, George Washington Carver.  Hofmann presented chemical ways of fixing nitrogen to soils using products from the growing fertilizer manufacturing industry.  To that Carver added, "but only after using legumes such as sweet potatoes, peanuts and cowpeas in a crop rotation program.  And, man, oh man, aren't those sweet potatoes and peanuts good to eat."  Hofmann and Carver "fed" on each other and respected each other in the highest way.  And even today, it is hard to say which man was the most effective at improving agriculture in the Confederate States, especially among the red clay soil regions.  The answer has to be --- together Carver and Hofmann were far more influential than either could have been alone.  A brief biography of George Washington Carver is appropriate.

Born in 1865 in northern Arkansas, in the Confederate States, George Washington Carver, while a young boy, suffered the loss of his mother, an African American servant bonded to Moses Carver and wife Susan.  The Carver's raised the little boy out of a sense of duty and helped him get a good education.  He loved plants and growing things, and that led him into the field of botany.  At the age of 19 years he was completing his bachelor's study in botany at American Baptist College[262] in Nashville, one of the finest Black colleges in the Confederate States, and within walking distance to the University of Nashville where Professor Hofmann was often helpful and where the best library could be accessed on special permission.  Two years later he had completed his master's degree.  At that time, in 1896, at the age of 21, Carver took a job at Tuskegee Institute as the head of its Agriculture Department.  He would be most recognized for his advocacy of rotating cotton fields between cotton and legumes such as sweet potatoes and peanuts.  Carver would work as a professor at Tuskegee for 47 years, not passing away until 1943 at the age of 78. [263]

We will soon return to the story of the University of Nashville.  But let us look into the history of the Statue of Liberty, a gift to the Confederate States by the people of France.

## The Iconic Statue of Liberty in Charleston Harbor

The Statue of Liberty rests on a high pedestal that rises from the central courtyard of Fort Sumter in Charleston Harbor. [264]  It was donated by the French people as a tribute to the persistence with which the Confederate people sustained the republican ideals of the original United States as they confronted the necessity of State Secession and heroically defended the principles of Individual Liberty and State Sovereignty.  The Statue had been proposed in 1870 by French law professor and prominent political leader Édouard René de Laboulaye.  French sculptor Frederic Auguste Bartholdi was to design the statue.  Gustave Eiffel, of Eiffel Tower fame, was to build the statue.  The inner structure was to be of iron and steel.  The exterior "skin" was to be of copper sheet.  It was to be huge: a robed female figure representing *Libertas*, the Roman goddess, who was to be holding forward a torch and presenting a tablet evoking the law and recording three

---

[262] In truthful history George Washington Carver received his general education in Kansas and botany education at Iowa State Agricultural College.  American Baptist College in Nashville was founded much later, in 1924.  The first Negro college in Nashville was Fisk College founded in 1866 with support from the Church of Christ and Clinton B. Fisk of New York State, who had led the Republican political reconstruction of Tennessee.

[263] The story of George Washington Carver is truthful history except that his birthplace remained in Missouri, never being moved into Arkansas by the Montreal Treaty.  He did accept the position at Tuskegee in the year named, where he pioneered in advocacy of cotton field crop rotation, using sweet potatoes and peanuts to add nitrogen to the soil and to raise healthful foods.

[264] In truthful history the French-donated Statue of Liberty was erected in New York Harbor.  In our alternate history, the people of the United States failed to raise sufficient funds to build the statue's foundation and the French preferred to donate the statue to the Confederate States anyway.

dates: July 4, 1776, honoring the original American Declaration of Independence; September 19, 1862, honoring the treaty signing at Montreal: and July 4, 1870, honoring the Great Confederate Expansion. The Confederates were asked to finance and build the pedestal upon which the stature was to be mounted. The French were to finance and build the statute in France; disassemble it and transport it to Charleston, and then reassemble it. It was to be very large, towering 151 feet above the pedestal, which was to rise well above the fortifications of Fort Sumter. The project had proceeded as planned. The Confederates had been especially eager to finance and build the pedestal. In fact it was ready about 13 months before the French arrived with the statue. Ever since its erection, immigrants arriving at Charleston are first greeted by the Statue of Liberty and seem always to be thrilled by the sight of it towering so high and so eager to welcome those who have succeeded at immigrating to the Confederate States, the land of Individual Liberty and State Sovereignty. The statue was dedicated on October 28, 1882.[265]

## Thomas Edison and the Birth of Confederate Technological Leadership

It is hard to present a discussion of the technological advances in the Confederacy between 1870 and 1929 without talking about Thomas Edison. So a brief biography seems appropriate.

Thomas Edison was the son of Canadian Samuel Ogden Edison, Jr. and wife Nancy Matthews Elliott, born in central New York State. Grandfather Samuel, Sr. had fought on the British side in the War of 1812. And father Samuel, Jr. had fought on the losing side in Canada's Mackenzie Rebellion of 1837. So, to escape retribution, the father left Canada to resettle his family in northern Ohio, just below the Great Lakes. It was there, on February 11, 1847, that Thomas Edison was born, the couple's seventh and last child. The family later moved a little farther west to east Michigan where Thomas grew up and received home schooling from his mother. A bout of scarlet fever during childhood greatly impaired his hearing, prompting him to take up training as a telegraph operator for Western Union. At age 19, in 1866, he was transferred to the telegraph office in Louisville, Kentucky. It was there, a year later, that fate changed history.

Edison was working the night shift at the Associated Press bureau news wire when trouble arose for this young man, who was full of curiosity, exceptionally intelligent and creative. He loved to read and to experiment over scientific questions that interested him, and electricity especially intrigued him. So he was often preparing a lead-acid battery to provide electricity for experiments he might conduct during the night when the telegraph keys might be silent for a spell. It was on one of these nights that he accidently spilled sulfuric acid onto the floor. He did not mop it up quickly enough, for some ran down through the floor boards onto his boss's desk immediately below. The next morning Thomas Edison was fired. The boss held no sympathy for the young experimenter.

As it turned out Professor Bushrod Johnson of Tennessee was in the telegraph office that morning arranging for a wire to be sent to Professor Wilhelm Hofmann at the University of Nashville. We pick up on the conversation at that moment:

> Johnson exclaimed, "Goodness, sir! What did this young man do to earn such a tongue lashing and be preemptively discharged?"

---

[265] This history is truthful with regard to the three Frenchmen mentioned: Bartholdi, Eiffel and Laboulaye and the design of the statue. However, we represent our alternate history with regard to the site where the statue was erected and the eagerness with which it was received in North America. In truthful history, when proposed by the French to be erected in New York harbor, Americans were slow to contribute money for the pedestal. The project was near death when publisher Joseph Pulitzer, a prominent Democrat (and, by the way, a friend of Varina Davis), launched a drive for contributions in his newspaper, the *New York World*. The statue was completed much later, being dedicated by Democrat President Grover Cleveland on October 28, 1886.

Boss replied, "He is always experimenting and getting into mischief.  Spilled acid on my desk last night.  He is out of here." [266]

Johnson: "Send this wire to Chancellor Lindsley at the University of Nashville.  I am leaving Louisville for Nashville on the mid-day train and expect to be met at the station.  A fine chemist will be coming along.  What is that young man's name?"

Boss: "Thomas Edison.  He's bad hard of hearing.  Made it extra hard on me."

Professor Johnson then turned around and quickly departed the telegraph office to catch up with young Edison.  Moments later he spoke loudly and directly at the young man:

Johnson inquired: "Thomas Edison!  If you have no better offers, allow me to invite you to come to the University of Nashville for discussions about your future.  I will pay your way.  We leave soon from the Louisville and Nashville Rail Station.  If you want to come, get your things and meet me at the Station right away."

Edison replied: "Sir, I have no better offers.  Nashville intrigues me.  I will be at the Station in 45 minutes."

And that is the beginning of one of the most important events in the history of Confederate technology. [267]

Thomas Edison arrived at the Louisville and Nashville Railroad station as promised.  Professor Johnson purchased tickets for himself, for the young chemist recruit, recently from the Royal College of Chemistry in London, and for Edison.   At the boundary between the United States and the Confederate States, the train pulled over to the southbound track siding for inspection by Confederated Customs, Visas and Immigration agents.  An inspector entered the rail car and announced: "All Confederate citizens remain seated.  All others please rise."  Edison and the recruited chemist stood and awaited instructions.  When the inspector reached their seats Professor Johnson showed his Confederate passport and handed over two visa applications that he had prepared during the trip south (By 1870 no Confederate citizen could leave the Confederate States without obtaining a modern CSA passport bearing a photo of his face and detailed description of race, date of birth, birth state, weight, height, occupation, etc.  Failure to comply made re-entry awkward.  Johnson told the inspector, "This is John White, a fine chemist, and Thomas Edison, a gifted investigator of electrical phenomena.  I am sponsoring both for a visit to Tennessee, to the University of Nashville, for up to three months from today.  I vouch for them and expect you will find these visa application papers to be in order."  After looking over the visa application papers, the inspector took one copy of each and instructed, "Young men, within ten days you must go with Professor Johnson to the visa office in Nashville and obtain official visas containing your photographs and statistical data.  Do you understand me?"  The replies were "Yes, sir."  And that was a typical procedure for controlling the flow of people in and out of the

---

[266] The Thomas Edison biography is truthful up to being fired because of the acid spill at Louisville.  Our alternate history begins with Bushrod Johnson's entrance.  In truthful history he would move to New Jersey through the generosity of a fellow telegrapher, Franklin Leonard Pope, and from there engage in an amazing career: inventing the carbon microphone; a long-life light bulb; electric power distribution technology; fluoroscope X-ray imagining; stock market ticker; motion picture camera and projector; and improved rollers and crushers for ore mining.  In all, Edison's name was given to 1,093 U. S. patents.  His only under-achievement was too long advocating Direct Current power distribution in the face of George Westinghouse's advances in Alternating Current power distribution.  His name is associated with the following companies: Commonwealth Edison, Consolidated Edison, Edison International, Detroit Edison, Edison Ore-Mining Company, Edison Portland Cement Company, and Southern California Edison.  Events following the day the acid dripped onto the boss's desk at Louisville are our alternate history.

[267] The story of General Bushrod Johnson is truthful history except he was not at the telegraph office and did not persuade Thomas Edison to come to Nashville.

Confederate States. The fence along the Kentucky-Tennessee border was basically complete and smuggling and illegal immigration had become difficult by this time. It would become much more difficult in the years ahead.

Professor Hofmann and his servant met the train at the Nashville station and all went together to quarters at the University. The young chemist that Professor Johnson had recruited was quite excited to meet the famous Professor Hofmann, suggesting to young Edison a sense that these people and this place was perhaps special indeed. During the next few days Johnson took Edison around the campus, introducing him to others that would interest him and most notably to General Edmund Kirby Smith, who had just taken the position of President of the Atlantic and Pacific Telegraph Company. That sealed the deal. Edison got an offer he could not refuse: 1) access to the University for selected classes and to the electrical laboratory; 2) a part-time job offer as a telegraph operator at A and P, and 3) a chance to work with A and P Telegraph technical people on budding technology about which they were experimenting. It would be from this small start that Thomas Edison would embrace the Confederate States, make pioneering technological advances, and build huge companies.[268]

## Cyrus McCormick and the Mechanization of Confederate Agriculture

Another major contributor to Confederate industrialization was the McCormick family. The McCormick's were Virginians who relocated to Chicago to be close to the agricultural flatlands of the Midwest, where they could engage better markets. It is now appropriate to tell about this family and what compelled them to immigrate to the Confederate States.

Cyrus McCormick (1809-1884) was born and raised on the family farm in the Shenandoah Valley of Virginia. Eldest of eight children, he was the son of inventor Robert McCormick, Jr. and Mary Ann "Polly" Hall. Inspired by designs Robert had seen of a horse-pushed reaper developed by Patrick Bell in Scotland, he developed a horse-drawn reaper, first demonstrated in 1831, and obtained a patent in 1834. His draft animals did not trample the wheat moving forward because the machine was cutting off to one side. McCormick produced and sold 86 during the years 1842 through 1844 all built on the farm by his sons and a skillful slave, Jo Anderson. McCormick obtained a second patent on reaper improvements in 1845. The following year, he died at the age of 66 years. A year later, sons Cyrus, 38, and Leander, 26, left the Shenandoah Valley for Chicago, intending to establish a reaper manufacturing and sales business there.

Chicago was a fine reaper manufacturing location. Good transportation and good access to the rapidly expanding wheat fields of the mid-west, where the soil was deep and black and relatively stone-free. Brother William joined them in Chicago two years later at the age of 34 years.

Business was good, but there were patent infringement problems and lawsuits, most notably the 1855 high profile lawsuit: McCormick Company, plaintiff versus John Henry Manny's company, defendant. It was originally scheduled for Chicago, but was relocated to the court in Cincinnati. Big-name lawyers were involved:

- For McCormick: Reverdy Johnson, Democrat of Maryland and Edward Dickerson, expert patent attorney of New York.

- For Manny: George Harding of Pennsylvania, Edwin Stanton, Republican of Ohio and Abraham Lincoln, Republican of Illinois.

---

[268] The story of General Edmund Kirby Smith and the Atlantic and Pacific Telegraph Company is truthful. A major Confederate General in the War, he served as President of A & P from 1866 to 1868.

Manny's lawyers won the case, the opinion being written by Judge John McLean, Republican of Ohio. The McCormick brothers, of the Virginia culture and Democrats to the core, fumed and fussed over the judgement, but remained in Chicago producing reapers and shipping them widely. The next year, 1856, McCormick Company produced and sold and delivered 4,000 reapers. Business remained at that pace until they lost patent protection in 1861. During the War Between the States, Cyrus McCormick was an outspoken critic of the Lincoln Administration and suffered for it in the hostile Chicago political environment. But they persevered and continued selling their reapers. They could ignore the political and hateful attacks of the 1860's, but not the Great Chicago Fire of 1871. The McCormick factory burned down. That was the decisive blow: The McCormick's were relocating everything to the Confederate States. [269]

Leander McCormick took the lead in finding the new Confederate site and relocating. Immigration papers and paperwork were no problem. The McCormick's and key staff and machinist and sales/repair people were easily welcomed into the Confederate States, and many chose that option. In the spring of 1873 McCormick Brothers Harvesting Machine Company began production in a new factory just outside of Birmingham, Alabama. Raw materials were plentiful and rail transportation was good in all directions. Labor was readily available. And the Tuskegee Institute set up special training courses on its campus, 130 miles to the south, and also at the McCormick plant site. As the years went by, new agricultural machinery was invented and history would show that no company did more to mechanize agriculture than did McCormick Brothers Harvesting Machinery Company, now known as International Harvester Corporation, with offices and factories worldwide.

For the next decade McCormick Brothers expanded production of reapers and added many more horse-drawn agricultural machines -- field preparation, planting, cultivating and harvesting products -- to their catalog and distribution network. By the 1880's no Confederate State was without some McCormick products. But the era of agricultural machines pulled across fields by horses, mules or other draft animals was coming to a close. First steam-engine-powered machines were introduced. Awkwardly heavy for field work, these would soon be replaced by machines powered by gasoline engines. And that development brings us to the story of Henry Ford.

So, tomorrow, my class lecture will begin with the story of Henry Ford.

## Monday Evening Selected Diary Postings

Diary note by Emma Lunalilo said: "Had supper with Robert Lee tonight. The schedule had us paired at a table for "getting to know you conversation," as Professor Davis persists in calling it. I like Robert well enough. A bit serious for me, perhaps, but the world needs all personalities. Of course this rugged fellow from Alabama does love his horses and outdoor adventures. Including exploring caves!! We are all glad that dangerous adventure is history. I doubt I would make a good cave explorer and I doubt Robert would make a good big-wave surf board rider. And believe me, diary, those waves in Hawaii are really big, hard to imagine for an Alabama fellow who likes to surf fish along the Alabama beaches. The Gulf is like a lake. Robert really knows how to engage in conversation, to really get to know a person in just one hour -- a talent he says he is nurturing to help him become a better writer. That's what he really wants to

---

[269] The McCormick story is truthful history up to this point. In truth, the McCormick's rebuilt the factory in Chicago following the fire and continued on, expanding markets. Cyrus suffered poor health and brother Leander took the reins, changing the name in 1879 from "Cyrus H. McCormick and Brothers," to "McCormick Harvesting Machine Company." Since 1902 the business has been known as "International Harvester Cooperation." Cyrus McCormick died at home in 1884 and is buried in Chicago. A stature to Cyrus McCormick dominates the Green at Washington and Lee University in Lexington, Virginia.

become – a writer. . . . .    Now I sense that Robert has taken a real liking to Conchita Rezanov. And he is upset that Andrew Houston, the big and suave tennis player, is monopolizing time with the Conchita beauty.  He asked me all about her and her likes and dislikes.  I tried to assure him that Conchita does not want to get serious about anyone right now, that she and Andrew are just having fun enjoying their common interests. . . . . .    All that said, I had to ask him about Carlos Cespedes.  Robert said he thought Carlos a great guy, but had not been with him a lot socially. Did not go sailing with him and is not in the music group that Marie Saint Martin has organized. But he said he and Carlos were together often in the library comparing notes and tossing ideas back and forth in the course of writing their essays, which are somewhat related.  Robert is analyzing the effectiveness of the State Cooperative Commissions, and Carlos is analyzing how States compete for the loyalty of their citizens.  So those subjects, of a political nature, do interrelate a lot.  Then out of the blue, Robert said, "Emma, believe me when I tell you that Carlos really, really likes you.  Even now, in his mind, he is frequently reliving that weekend on the sailboat and your lifesaving swim out to Chris Memminger.  Has told me he wants to hug you and kiss you and just be close to you.  But says he is just a fellow from a Cuban family that lives and breathes growing, harvesting, milling and refining cane sugar.  Doubts a life like that would interest a fine lady who is working toward a Ph. D. in politics and government affairs.  I think he was encouraging me to make the first move on his behalf.  Goodnight."

Diary note by Robert Lee said, "Professor Davis gave us a brief overview of Confederate history from 1870 to 1890, an important twenty years of expansion in our economy and the start of our industrialization.  By this time, the Professor's ancestor, President Davis, was a respected and consulted elder statesman.  In so many ways during this twenty-year span his advice was sought and found worthy.  President Davis lived until December 6, 1889, just days before the beginning of those amazing 1890's.  From his beach house on the Mississippi Gulf Coast, named Beauvior, Jefferson and Varina Davis lived into old age, the senior statesman and senior first lady of the Confederate States of America.  President Davis lived to see his 81st birthday and to see the great success that followed his leadership of the first five years of our country." [270]

Diary note by Amanda Washington said, "We musicians rehearsed for our July 4th performance after supper while several of the other essayists sat around and listened.  All seemed to be enjoying the music.  Did I see Andrew Houston and Conchita Rezanov holding hands at a table in the far corner?"

---

[270] The note about Beauvior and death date of Jefferson Davis is truthful history.  And, in truthful history, the people of the Reconstructed former Confederate States greatly honored their fallen President in an amazing funeral observation, for the hatreds of war had largely subsided by 1889, and even the North was tolerant of the South paying farewell tribute to former President Davis.

# Part 3, Chapter 5, Day 23 – An Overview of Confederate History from 1891 to 1920 – Class Lecture, Tuesday, June 28, 2011

The twelve members of the Sewanee Project team were in their seats right on time looking forward to Professor Davis's lecture on Confederate history over the long span of 29 years, a generation, almost three decades. How could he cover such a vast history in a morning lecture? The twelve had begun to understand how Professor Davis managed to achieve the impossible. He simply cut to the core of the subject. And, to Professor Davis, the core of those 29 years of Confederate States history lay in the story of important inventors and industrialists who came to the Confederacy to lead in key innovations. In short, this morning's lecture was the story of immigrants who came to the Confederate States and made amazing contributions to our country. We now listen in.

## Henry Ford and the Evolution of the People's Automobile

Henry Ford (1863-1947) was born to an immigrant father, William Ford, who had fled the potato famine in County Cork, Ireland. Fled not just a failed potato crop, but, being English Anglicans surrounded by Irish Catholics, he had fled discrimination as well. He had arrived in America in 1847, went on to Michigan and settled near relatives. He married a lady who had been born in Michigan to a Belgium immigrant couple and soon sadly orphaned. William took a job on the railroad, saved his money and bought a farm ten miles west of Detroit. On his sixteenth year in America, a son, Henry, was born to William and wife Mary. As Henry grew it was apparent that he was not talented in reading, writing and arithmetic. His great interest in mechanics characterized his youth. At age 13, Henry suffered the death of his mother, a great blow to the teenager.

This was the year 1876. The Confederate States had long since experienced its Great Expansion and the McCormick's were well underway in producing reapers and new agricultural equipment drawn across fields by draft animals. Some folks were experimenting with putting steam engines on vehicles and farm tractors of various types, but prospects of broad success seemed limited.

By age 16 Henry Ford was an apprentice engineer in Detroit, but was soon fired. Perhaps difficulty reading and doing arithmetic limited his ability. He failed at other apprenticeships and, in 1883, at age 20, he found himself back on the Ford family farm. Five years later, having inherited the Ford farm from his late father, Henry married Clary Jane Bryant, 22, who lived on a neighboring farm. This was 1888, two years after Gottlieb Daimler of Germany had built his four wheeled gasoline engine vehicle. The French had quickly followed, but the United States was already far behind Europe in automotive technology. Hearing of such success elsewhere, farmer Henry Ford dreamed of developing and manufacturing horseless carriages. But first, build a farmhouse. Being good at building things, he took his wife's drawings of a house, cut the timber and built it. Then he took a job with Westinghouse servicing steam engines, bringing him a bit closer to the action. In 1890 he saw a stationary gasoline engine operating in Detroit. At this point he decided to try to design a gasoline engine and build it, but he hankered to be closer to the action. So, in 1891, Henry and wife Clara left the farm for Detroit and he took a job with an electrical power generation and distribution company, replacing a night supervisor who had been killed by electrocution. Henry and Clara's life began changing again two years later.

On September 20, 1893 J. Frank Duryea and brother Charles designed and built a four-cylinder gasoline engine horseless carriage and "sped" at five miles per hour down a Massachusetts street. Two months later Clara gave birth to the couple's one and only son, Edsel. The following month, on Christmas Eve, Henry fired up a one-cylinder gasoline engine he had designed and built. It was not impressive. He was two years behind a few Americans and five years behind Europeans. He could have bought a gasoline engine, such as the Sintz engine being made in Grand Rapids. Yet he kept working at making his own engine. He followed the progress of fellow Michigander Charles Brady King who had bought a gasoline engine and mounted it onto a vehicle he designed and built. Ford even rode a bicycle alongside King's vehicle during a demonstration in 1896.

Henry Ford, still intent on building his own engine, doubled the pace and recruited three fellow electric power plant employees to join in the adventure. Ford made some progress. He designed a carburetor and won a patent. He struggled with building a magneto and a spark plug, and made some progress there as well. He assembled a two-cylinder gasoline engine of four horsepower, installed it onto a light-weight vehicle he had built, and motored down the road, achieving 20 miles per hour. Pretty fast for a 500-pound vehicle without brakes. But Ford was no pioneer at this point. The trade magazine, Horseless Carriage, estimated that during the fall of 1895, perhaps three hundred people in the United States were building gasoline-powered vehicles using bicycle-like frames and running rear.

Although Henry Ford was not a major technology pioneer, he had inspired Thomas Edison during a brief encounter in 1896, and vice versa, when he had briefly talked with the great electric pioneer. Ford would later recall, "He asked me no end of details and I sketched everything for him, for I have always found that I could convey an idea quicker by sketching it. History records that Edison had then replied:

> "Young man, that's the thing! You have it. Keep at it. Electric cars must keep near to power stations. The storage battery is too heavy. Steam cars won't do either, for they have a boiler and fire. Your car is self-contained, carries its own power plant, no fire, no boiler, no smoke and no steam. You have the thing. Keep at it!"

And at that time Edison was experimenting with electric cars. That was 1896.

Three year later, by 1899, Henry Ford had raised enough money from several Detroit businessmen to start up the Detroit Automobile Company, the area's first auto manufacturing company. Ford quit his job at the power plant and headed up the new outfit. But his passion was to build a winning race car, not an economical family car. Perhaps a mistake. The Company directors objected to intense focus on a race car and, in February, 1901, they forced the company to close.

But Henry Ford continued with the race car passion. Childe Harold Wills was the brains of the effort. Others pitched in part time. It was mostly a volunteer effort, inspired by Ford's enthusiasm. Eight months later the Ford race team was ready for a challenge. Alexander Winton, a Cleveland car maker, invited everyone to race against his 40-horsepower "Bullet." Ford stepped forward. The race commenced at the one mile oval race track at Grosse Point. Winton's big heavy car managed the curves well and Ford was falling behind in his light 24-horsepower race car. Assistant Spider Huff jumped onto the inside running board and leaned out as would a sailor on a sailboat. Ford took the curves faster and made better headway. Then Winton's car started blowing smoke. Ford kept a coming and passed the ailing car to win the ten-mile race. The crowd of 7,000 cheered and Ford made history, widely recorded in newspapers. Ford had averaged 45 miles per hour. Very good!

Investors returned and the Henry Ford Company was born. Again Ford focused on a new race car. But investors brought in Henry M. Leland, of Connecticut, experienced at Springfield Armory and Sam Colt factories and precision machining. Leland pushed for luxury autos. Ford objected. He resigned under pressure in March 1902. But he kept the Ford name and some of his race car team stayed with him. [271]

Two weeks later, Ford received a letter from Thomas Edison:

"I remember meeting you six years ago and viewing your sketches and your ideas for gasoline powered automobiles. I was impressed then and am more impressed now as I follow your efforts building race cars – a great way to test and learn and to excite folks about your products – and your aim at manufacturing affordable cars and trucks for the pubic. Please come visit me in Tennessee. I am confident that investors in the Confederate States will be enthusiastic to back you in a joint race-car-people's-car venture. I have talked with Cyrus McCormick, III about a cooperative effort on gasoline engines for automobiles, trucks and farm tractors. He is eager to talk about that. Please come. The business climate here is favorable, especially toward people born to Irish-protestant immigrant families like you."

Henry Ford came to Tennessee two weeks later for a visit. Thomas Edison and Cyrus McCormick III persuaded Ford to relocate. And these two Confederate industrial leaders easily brought together the financial support needed to facilitate a quick startup by Henry Ford, Childe Harold Wills and others on the team. This was a major event in the history of the industrialization of the Confederate States, as is well known to us all.

From Europe, McCormick and Ford recruited key experts in machining and metallurgy technology and soon caught up with the European manufacturers of cars, trucks and farm tractors. McCormick already had well-established factories in several States across the Confederacy, producing his reapers, planters and other agriculture equipment drawn by draft animals, and Ford was to gain from that experience. In fact, McCormick's factories were soon making parts for Ford's cars. But the great contribution from Ford was the design and manufacturing efficiency needed to produce a very affordable car, the Model A, and later the Model T -- and the evolving assembly line production methods developed to produce the car using far fewer man-hours than ever thought possible. And farm tractors advanced in parallel. McCormick developed and produced the Farmall tractor and Ford followed a few years later with the Ford tractor. Together, these two tractors transformed Confederate agriculture from dependence on draft animals to dependence on gasoline tractors and shade tree mechanics. You probably sense that we are developing a theme here: the importance of immigrants, first and second generation, to the industrial expansion of the Confederate States. But these gasoline engines needed petroleum. And for that story we travel to Texas.

## Those Amazing Texas Oil Men

The story of Texas Gold starts with Antonio Francesco Luchic, born in 1855 in Croatia, then part of the Austro-Hungarian Empire. After graduating from the Graz Polytechnic Institute in Austria, he came to the Confederacy, arriving in 1880. Six feet two and strongly built, this intelligent, handsome and valuable immigrant gained Confederate citizenship in 1885 at Norfolk, Virginia, taking the English name Anthony Francis Lucas. Two years later, he married Caroline Weed Fitzgerald of North Carolina, daughter of a prominent physician, and declared his profession as a mechanical and mining engineer. Over the next six years he found important iron deposits in North Carolina, South Carolina, Georgia, Alabama, Mississippi and Louisiana. In

---

[271] Up to this point the story of Henry Ford is truthful history. But as we now proceed, the story becomes our alternate history. Ford will be moving to the Confederate States. We now tell about that. By the way, the company he resigned from in 1902 would become the Cadillac Motor Company and be the flagship luxury car maker for General Motors.

1893 he began work in the Gulf Coast salt mining region of Louisiana, with particular attention to Belle Isle, the former barrier island home base of the pirate Jean Lafitte. There, he strengthened his theory of the stratigraphy of deep down salt formations and how earth's oil deposits would collect under rising salt domes. Advised of oil seepages observed in Texas, he went to investigate. At the Spindletop region he observed a gentle swell of a broad span of land, which rose 15 feet above the surrounding Texas coastal plain, and he noticed slight oil, salt and sulfur leakage at the surface -- according to his theory, evidence of a rising salt dome below. But there were two problems: the oil reservoir was deep down (previous punch drilling in the area had only been able to go a few hundred feet and had come up dry), and the sand to be penetrated was prone to collapse into the drill-hole when flushed with only water, the conventional technique. So Lucas persuaded three Texas cattle ranchers to finance, on a 50-50 contract, a new drilling technique to go far deeper, and he hired experienced Texas drillers Al and Curt Hamill. Instead of the conventional punch drill rig, the Hamill brothers brought in a new-design rotary drill rig, utilizing the Sharps-Hughes hardrock rotary drill bit that had been recently invented by Walter Benona Sharp and Howard Hughes.

At Curt Hamill's suggestion a pond was dug nearby and cattle were set to stomping around in it to produce a steady supply of "drilling mud" to replace "drilling water" (a revolutionary idea). Drilling proceeded: 700 feet; 800 feet; 900 feet, 1,016 feet. Boom! On January 19, 1901, a gusher of Texas Gold (oil) shot up 150 feet and continued at a terrific rate for 9 days before it was finally capped. Running wild, it had produced 800,000 barrels. This one well had a production capacity of 100,000 barrels per day – more than the total production rate of all North American wells of that day. All over the world, Beaumont was the focus of oil production technology. Great world-wide oil companies were born: The Texas Company (Texaco); Gulf Oil Corporation; Sun Oil Company, Humble (later Exxon) and others. Texas Gulf Sulphur Company spearheaded a huge industry to supply sulfur, an important fundamental chemical. Large coastal refineries were built from Louisiana across Texas and along the Gulf coast of the former seceded Mexican States. The Confederate petrochemical industry was born, converting Texas Gold into the basic chemicals from which so many modern chemicals and plastics are made. The Sharp-Hughes Tool Company was born, enabled by the patent on its hard-rock drill bit.

Miss Tina Sharp, I know you understand this history exceptionally well, for Walter Benona Sharp was your great-great-grandfather.

"Yes, he was. I am descended from Walter Sharp through his son Dudley. Eleven years after the Spindletop discovery, Walter Sharp died. That was in the year 1912. Walter was only 41 years old at the time, and, with solid patent protection, the Sharp-Hughes Tool Company was a growing company with a bright future. My grandfather Dudley was only 7 years old when Walter died. His siblings were young as well. Walter had already made a lot of money by trading leases and contracting for oil wells, had founded the Moonshine Oil Company, and had acquired an interest in the Texas Company, which would become Texaco. Following the funeral, Howard Hughes must have been insisting that Walter's widow Estelle sell him all of her inherited stock in Sharp-Hughes Tool Company, and she must have felt overwhelmed with her responsibilities to raise the children and make sense of her late husband's other financial interest in the oil industry. So she sold the Sharp-Hughes stock to Mr. Hughes.

"After earning his college degree in 1928, my great-grandfather Dudley joined the Mission Manufacturing company in Houston, a maker of drilling equipment. He held various executive positions until he resigned to join the Navy soon after the Japanese bombed Pearl Harbor, leaving his wife Tina to care for the children with the help of her parents, who also lived in Houston. After the victory over Fascist Japan, Dudley held various administrative jobs, rising to Confederate Secretary of the Air Force from 1959 to 1961. So my father's family was drawn away from the oil business during the 1940s and 1950s. I chose to go into the nuclear power industry. Life goes on." [272]

Thanks for that personal story, Tina. It is personal stories like yours that makes our Sewanee Project such an amazing adventure for all of us involved here. I now continue.

For the first time in human history petroleum was cheap; in fact too cheap. To preserve Texas Gold for the uses of Confederates, to encourage vertical industrial expansion into oil refining and petrochemicals, and to encourage industries that utilized this valuable new energy source (for diesel and gasoline engines), the Confederate Government, in April 1903, imposed an 80 percent excise tax on all crude oil exports. [273] It worked. The Confederate petroleum supply was not grabbed cheaply by more industrialized nations, such as the United States, Great Britain and Germany, and a robust leading-technology Confederate automobile industry was enabled.

And this story naturally leads us to the airplane and Confederate immigrants Orville and Wilbur Wright.

### The Wright Brothers and the Birth of Confederate Aviation

Everyone is familiar with Orville Wright (1871-1948) and Wilbur Wright (1867-1912) and their invention of the heavier than air flying machine. Their flight experiments had begun in 1899 at the Wright Cycle Company, their bicycle manufacturing, maintenance and sales business in Dayton, Ohio, in the United States. But their work did not remain in Ohio. With visas in hand, they came to the outer Banks of North Carolina in the Confederate States in the Fall months of 1900, 1901 and 1902 to test the flight control concepts incorporated in each year's improved glider (none of those had an engine). The second glider was far improved over the first. The third was far improved over the second. By mid-October 1902, it appeared that the Wrights had mastered flight control. They were ready to install a gasoline engine on a flying machine that took advantage of all the lessons learned to date. [274]

It was at this time that Cyrus Hall McCormick II, son of the late Cyrus McCormick, Sr., observed the Wright's progress in controlled flight. [275] He was manager over the McCormick Harvester Machine Company's Eastern Virginia and North Carolina Division. McCormick had heard about the flying tests out on the Outer Banks and thought he ought to take a look. Anyway the fishing would be great in late September, earlier October. So there he was, observing and making friends with the brothers. McCormick was impressed by the Wright's obvious success. But more importantly, he was impressed by the brother's reliance on sequential experimental methods and measurements and step-by-step testing, and recognized that only by that total approach would man ever fly without killing himself in the trying. The Wrights reminded him of his McCormick ancestors and Henry Ford, who had been persuaded to immigrate into the Confederate States three months earlier. The brothers had not stumbled on the discovery of how to control flight. They had meticulously figured it out, by experiments and testing, and

---

[272] The story of the discovery of oil near Beaumont, Texas, Walter Benona Sharp and Dudley Cleveland Sharp, and the Sharp-Hughes Tool Company is truthful history. Of course, our essayist Tina Sharp is a fictional character as is her descent from Dudley Sharp. Dudley Sharp was United States Secretary of the Air Force during the Dwight D. Eisenhower administration.

[273] The Confederate taxation of outgoing exports to the United States and elsewhere is our alternate history.

[274] The story of the Wright brothers is truthful history up to this point except that North Carolina was not in the Confederate States.

[275] Our story departs from truthful history with the introduction of Cyrus Hall McCormick, II (1859-1936) who is a true son of Cyrus, Sr.

application of critical thinking. The Henry Ford Company could make a powerful light-weight gasoline engine. That was what the Wrights now needed. [276]

So, over a fine meal – McCormick-caught fresh red snapper, local sweet potatoes, baked beans and a fine fall-season salad -- the industrialist offered a deal the brothers would not be able to refuse. He offered to finance all of their work and give them the legal rights to all that they accomplished. He offered to connect the Wrights to Henry Ford and to help negotiate a contract for confidential assistance in aircraft engine development.

Back in Dayton, the brothers thought it over. They soon learned that Octave Chanute (1832-1910) had been trying to sell their aviation secrets. That made them furious, of course. A few years earlier, Chanute had tabulated Wright wind tunnel data to enhance its usefulness, and had been helpful in several ways. Now the brothers knew the truth -- all along Chanute had been spying on their work, seeking opportunities to use it to his advantage and to eventually discredit their accomplishments. They also knew that Chanute and a fellow flight experimenter, Augustus Herring, after witnessing many glider test flights at Kitty Hawk during the first days of October 1902, had left for Washington, DC in an attempt to secretly sell Wright flight technology to Samuel Pierpont Langley at the Smithsonian Institution. Fortunately for the brothers, Langley had not cooperated.

But Orville and Wilbur now knew it was time to get away from spying eyes in the United States and take the offer to immigrate to the Confederate States where they believed their work could be completed with honest confidentiality. Work at the Dayton shop was taking at least half of their time and did not earn enough money to permit hiring skilled assistants. They were quite proud of what they believed they could accomplish as aviation pioneers, but would they be the first to fly? Men in Europe and elsewhere in North America were working on manned flight. Even Langley at the Smithsonian Institution in Washington was financing development of a flying machine. The brothers feared they might waste too much time trying to figure flight out all by themselves. So they made a decision. They agreed to leave their father and sister in Dayton, turn over the bicycle shop to a trusted employee, and immigrate to Raleigh, North Carolina, the Confederate States, where they could work near the McCormick's Eastern North Carolina harvester manufacturing plant and be accessible to the Outer Banks flight test site.

Anyway, they needed a good light-weight gasoline engine to power their glider and Henry Ford's company was a good place to work on that next step in the invention of the heavier than air flying machine. Time was of the essence. Any month without progress was a big loss.

An airfield would soon be cleared not far from Raleigh. "Ironclad" contractual agreements between the Wrights, the McCormick's, Henry Ford and a small group of investors established and funded the startup of the Wright-Carolina Aviation Company. Lawyers assured the Wrights that they would be secure in the inventions that came from their work. And the deal was a blessing for the Wrights, for they were capable of inventing the airplane working alone, but not capable of defending their patents and launching a dominant aircraft manufacturing enterprise. Only the resources provided through a well-financed Wright-Carolina Aviation Compny, could accomplish that goal.

It worked. The Wrights invented the airplane and proved it flying their first powered flight design, where fight control was provided by "warping" the wings. The historic flight took place at Kitty Hawk on the North Carolina Outer Banks on October, 15, 1903. It was rather short, but within a week, the airplane was flying 1,000 feet keeping craft and pilot aloft for over a full

---

[276] In truthful history the Wrights would make their own light-weight gasoline engine over the ensuing months in Ohio.

minute. By the first week in November, with weather getting cold and nasty, the historic airmen were packing up their aircraft and heading back to Raleigh. [277]

But associates at Wright-Carolina, working alongside the Wrights, would be evaluating variations in flight control that achieved the same goal with concepts that were more simplified and manufacturing-friendly than wing warping. So "warping" of the wings was soon set aside in favor of ailerons, hinged segments at the trailing edge of the wings that pivoted up or down to cause the aircraft to descend or to climb, to pitch left or pitch right. Wright-Carolina also took advantage of gasoline engine expertise and manufacturing ability at Ford. Wright-Carolina became the world's foremost aircraft company and the Confederacy soon became the acknowledged world leader in aircraft design and manufacture – a leader in both design and efficiency in manufacturing – the latter being a gift from Ford expertise. The Confederate military quickly released a contract for Wright-Carolina aircraft for use in border and coastal surveillance and wartime. And plans were laid for military airfields along the Atlantic, Gulf and Pacific coasts, along the border with the United States, and within ten miles of every intersection of the main north-south railway express lines and the main east-west express lines. Congress approved a bill to purchase 500 acres of suitably level land at each such intersection for use by the Confederate Air Force, which was established in 1910. By 1914 serviceable grass or dirt landing strips were available at almost all of these sites.

As you know the Confederate States did not fight in World War I. But Confederate aircraft sure did! Over 3,200 Confederates were located in the British Isles and France teaching men to fly and to maintain aircraft. And 11,500 Confederate aircraft, manned by British and French pilots, were in the fight. By the armistice on November 11, 1918, it was evident that trench warfare was obsolete. Aircraft just flew over the trenches and took the war further beyond. But what made aircraft practical was aluminum. That story needs telling.

## Paul Heroult, Texas and the Confederate Aluminum Industry

Aluminum is a very common element in the earth's crust, and when found in high concentrations it is called bauxite ore. Fortunately, there was a major high-concentration deposit of bauxite in Jamaica. But how could metallic aluminum be economically recovered from bauxite ore? The first part was straightforward -- chemical treatment of bauxite ore yields aluminum oxide. Then came the tough part -- economically reducing aluminum oxide to metallic aluminum. Thankfully, in 1886, Frenchman Paul Heroult discovered a practical aluminum oxide reduction method using electrolysis and lots and lots of electricity. But where to get lots and lots of cheap electricity? Texas! So, a major chemical plant was built in the State of Cuba to produce aluminum oxide from bauxite shipped in from Jamaica. The aluminum oxide was then shipped to Texas to take advantage of the energy from natural gas that was being flared off at typical Texas oil wells. Instead of flaring it off, that gas was gathered into pipelines and burned in turbines connected to electrical generators to make electricity cheaply for aluminum reduction plants

---

[277] Efforts by Chanute and Herring to steal and sell Wright aircraft secrets is truthful history. In the United States, the Wright brothers would truthfully suffer from many legal court battles over patent infringement lawsuits. Following their demonstration of successful flight to the world, the stress of those patent struggles and the financial drain from fighting lawsuits would significantly slow the Wright's aircraft manufacturing business, both with regard to technical advances and with regard to manufacturing expansion. Wilbur would die rather early from stress and exhaustion, aggravated by eating seafood at a Boston restaurant, followed by contracting typhoid fever. He died in May 1912 at the age of 45 years. Orville took the loss gravely. He shunned business and took to seeking new inventions. In 1916 the Wright Company merged with Glenn Martin's company to become the Wright-Martin Corporation. When the United States entered World War I in 1917, the United States government forced a pooling of aircraft patents. Orville Wright was well to do, but did not build the vast aircraft enterprise that similar patent rights would have empowered another sort of man to achieve. Our alternate history presents a much happier ending for the two brothers who pioneered aviation.

located nearby.    Seems like wherever natural gas could be accumulated, a suitably-sized aluminum reduction plant sprouted.    That was the policy of the Aluminum Company of the Confederacy, headquartered in Houston, Texas.    By 1903, ACC was producing the cheapest aluminum on earth.    The Wright brothers invented the airplane at Kitty Hawk that same year.    Within a short time Wright-Carolina was producing the world's most advanced aluminum-block gasoline engines and aluminum aircraft bodies (aluminum skin over aluminum frames). [278]

## Thomas Edison's Electricity Empire

Returning our story to Nashville, Tennessee, we find that Thomas Edison was building an empire based on electrical technology.    How could one man do all that?    Well, it was more like three men: Thomas Edison, Nikola Tesla and Samuel Insull.

## Nikola Tesla, the Amazing Genius, Inventor of the AC Motor

Nikola Tesla (1856-1943) was a Serbian genius fascinated by science, mathematics and the emerging marvels surrounding electricity.    His father, Milutin, was an Orthodox priest and his mother, Duka, was also quite clever and creative.    Nikola received a good education in the Austrian Empire and learned many languages in the process.    He received his high school level education at the age of 16, took two years off, and then studied at the University for three years. But he did not finish.    You see, Nikola was not your normal genius.    His mind was exceptional to an extreme degree: he had a photographic memory; pictured complex problems within his mind without writing anything down; although polite, he found normal social relationships difficult; he was prone to bouts of gambling in excess; and he slept only briefly.    He never graduated from University.    In some ways he did not need to.

In 1881 he was chief electrician at the Budapest Telephone Exchange.    The following year he relocated to France and took a job with Continental Edison Company, designing and improving electrical equipment.    He was hooked on Edison. [279]

In June 1884, with visa papers in hand, he was in Nashville, seeking a meeting with Thomas Edison himself.    His mind was full of future electrical equipment designs and inventive ideas.    He wanted to be close to Edison to help bring his perceived electrical inventions into reality – Tesla had the amazing ability to conceive of an invention – Edison had the determination to take that conception forward to reality.    They were so different -- apart, they would be good, but haphazard – together, they would be focused and unstoppable, from conception to completion.    Tesla was almost 28 years old.

Edison gave Tesla a job redesigning the company's direct current electric generators and motors to improve service life and efficiency.    Edison was impressed, but did not quite know how to keep Tesla's genius under control.    The young man had worked day and night, seven days a week, on the generator and motor design.    Edison mentioned his concerns to the eminent chemist, August Wilhelm von Hofmann, recently retired from the University of Nashville and to William and Selene Jackson who raised fine thoroughbred horses southwest of the University on a lovely,

---

[278] The aluminum story is true to some extent.    Reducing aluminum in Texas using natural gas fired generation of electricity did not take place that rapidly.    The organization that would become the Aluminum Company of America built its first plant in Pennsylvania in 1903, and it used electricity from a nearby coal-fired power plant.    An inventor from Ohio, Charles Martin Hall, discovered the electrical process for reducing aluminum at the same time as Frenchman Heroult, and today the process is called the Hall-Heroult process (the French call it the Heroult-Hall process).

[279] The Story of Nikola Tesla is truthful history up to his arrival in North America in 1884.    In truth, he met with Thomas Edison in New York City that year and began working for Edison's company there.    In our alternate history Tesla meets with Thomas Edison at the same time, but in Nashville, Tennessee.    Our alternate history proceeds from there.

socially prominent and historic farm, of 2,800 acres called Belle Meade. From these conversations a plan was hatched. Keep Tesla at work on Edison projects three days a week, but add two diversions: give him a part time teaching post at the University of Nashville, complete with a laboratory, and give him a recreational outlet at the Belle Meade horse farm. Encourage female companionship. The plan was hatched and the plan worked. Teaching helped relax Tesla's hyper-active mind and improved his social ability. Sunday's at Belle Meade farm encouraged sorely needed exercise and light-hearted social contact. He loved working with the horses, and socializing with the ladies there. People who came and went found him interesting and vice versa. Tesla was getting more sleep and was more stable emotionally. He was 30 years old. [280]

By 1886 Edison and Tesla were working well together. Amazingly well! In 1887, at the Edison lab, Tesla invented an induction motor that ran on alternating current, called AC for short. In May 1888 Tesla received a Confederate patent on the motor. This was huge! Edison had been pioneering direct current (DC) power distribution systems, DC lighting, and DC electric motors. The DC motors were great for street cars because speed control was easy, but distribution from the generation station was only good for a mile or so because voltage was low and amperage was high, resulting in high transmission power loss due to resistance. As a result, direct current electric power stations needed to be peppered all over town. It was horribly inefficient. On the other hand, AC power distribution could include transformers -- which could step up voltage and reduce amperage, greatly reducing transmission resistance and thereby making long distance transmission practical -- and the process could be reversed, reducing voltage and increasing amperage for efficient and safe utilization at the customer's location. AC permitted one large electric power station to serve a moderate-size city. The Tesla patent was iron-clad. The Edison Company held the rights to the patent and Tesla would be receiving a portion of the royalties coming in from other companies seeking licenses to make AC motors. George Westinghouse's company in the United States soon came, hat in hand, to purchase patent rights for our northern neighbor. [281]

Tesla was acclimating to Nashville rather well, and learning to enjoy its Southern hospitality. A lady who frequented the horses at Belle Meade, considered to be quite good at controlling a particularly temperamental stallion, seemed to accept the challenge of socializing one Nikola Tesla. She must have succeeded, because the two fell in love and Nikola and Martha married in 1890. They were celebrities at the 1896 Tennessee Centennial and International Exposition, held that year to commemorate Tennessee's 100 years as a state. In one building, there was wife Martha Tesla showing champion horses in the agricultural pavilion to visitors' delight. Elsewhere, in the Science Building, Nikola Tesla was quite the showman demonstrating

---

[280] General William Hicks Jackson had married General Harding's oldest daughter Selene in 1868 and moved into the Belle Meade mansion. Belle Meade, a vast beautiful horse farm of 2,800 acres, was socially prominent, especially in the 1880's and early 1890's, and among the South's most prominent horse breeding farms. Today it is a lovely community of stately homes set upon sizable and impressive lawns.

[281] In truthful history Tesla invented the ac motor in 1887, a crucial invention that enabled widespread use of electric power to perform all sorts of work. US Patent 381,968 affirmed the rights of ownership in May 1888. Tesla had left Edison in late 1885. Two other men had financed Tesla's motor development work and shared in the patent rights, one-third to each man. In July 1888, George Westinghouse purchased exclusive rights to Tesla's patents on the ac motor and ac power transformers for $50,000 plus $2.50 per AC horsepower produced by each motor Westinghouse made – the $2.50 fee being an exceptionally high cost to bear. Nine years later, in 1897, Westinghouse persuaded Tesla and the other two to give up the $2.50 royalty for a lump sum payment of $216,000. Tesla and the other two made a grave mistake. If they had forced Westinghouse to keep paying the $2.50 per horsepower produced, they would have become among the richest men to have ever lived in North America. Tesla's patent was that fundamental!

alternating current motors and controls and promising to electrify the country with large power plants spread far apart across the Confederate States.

Tesla continued to teach part time and to lecture at the University of Nashville. He stayed with Edison throughout his career, until in 1822, at the age of 66 years, he decided to retire from teaching and work in order to better enjoy the grandchildren, a few fine horses, and travel. Trips back to his birth country, Serbia, he enjoyed immensely. [282]

Tesla and wife Martha had three children, a boy and two girls. They were bright but none had the amazing mental capacity of the father. They slept well. The Tesla's built a fine mansion on Belle Meade Blvd, a lovely residential area carved out of the old Belle Meade horse farm and kept horses for family and friends further out of town where land was suitably affordable. [283]

We now turn our attention to Samuel Insull the leader who made Edison so successful.

## Samuel Insull, Edison's Unstoppable Industrial Leader

Samuel Insull (1859-1938) had impressed Edison's chief engineer, Thomas Johnson, during his time in London, while the company was setting up London's first telephone exchange. So Johnson invited Insull to immigrate to the Confederate States to take a position in Edison's company. Insull accepted and arrived in Nashville, Tennessee in February 1881. He was at Edison headquarters before March, meeting the man himself. In those days, genius pushed a man fast at a young age. Edison, 34, and Insull, 21, working together, were to expand Edison's enterprises into a huge corporation named General Electric Company, while providing the Confederacy with cheap electricity to illuminate homes and factories across the country with Edison's newly invented incandescent light bulb, and later to drive machinery with Tesla's AC motors.

Like Edison, Insull was the son of an unimpressive middle class family in London -- his father a rather ordinary preacher and his mother, the more capable of the pair. And it was she who inspired the son to adopt an unbelievably tireless work ethic. It seemed that young Insull could handle any assignment. While Edison and others like Tesla took time to work on inventions in the laboratory, Insull was outside the laboratory, growing and growing the Edison enterprises.

When Tesla invented the AC motor, Insull was quick to persuade Edison to set aside his passion for DC power distribution and DC motors and switch as rapidly as practical to AC and

---

[282] In truthful history, Tesla, then 41 years old, found other financial backers and spent his own money lavishly in search of other inventions. In 1898, he used a radio transmitter to direct actuators on a model boat which allowed him to remotely control the boat's speed and direction. But the war department failed to see the value of the invention in directing torpedoes heading across the ocean to strike an enemy warship. So that idea fizzled. He advanced radio technology, but not as well as did Guglielmo Marconi. He stumbled upon x-ray technology, which would become so important in diagnostic medicine, but did not follow through with it. But his major failure was his blind and nonsensical belief that large amounts of power could be transmitted through the air, enabling a power station to power electric motors many miles away without any wiring to carry the electricity from the power generating station to the motor, say to the farmer's well pump motor. Fundamental laws of thermodynamics clearly showed that, although tiny bits of energy would be transmitted through the air to enable a radio station to broadcast music to a receiver that was plugged into the wall socket to amplify the sound thousands of times over, large amounts of power could not be delivered over miles and miles to run something as small as the farmer's water-well pump motor. It got worse. Around the year 1900 he thought he was receiving messages from aliens in other planets, such as Mars. He received his last patent in 1928, about a vertical takeoff airplane, which had no value. He never married or owned a home. This amazing genius died in a New York City hotel room in 1943, at the age of 86, alone, penniless, almost forgotten. Our alternate history socializes Tesla at Belle Meade and heals this compulsive character flaw. His name is famous today for its use by Elon Musk for his brand of electric-powered automobiles. By the way, the writer is now driving a Tesla Model 3.

[283] The author grew up on Lynwood Blvd, part of the Belle Meade residential development. Dad built our house in 1947. Was nice, but far from grand.

high voltage transmission. Insull clearly realized that a few large power plants distributing electricity over a wide area at high voltage was far more economical than a patchwork of small local generators delivering low voltage DC to nearby communities. And he realized that the new steam turbines being developed concurrently were far superior at turning electricity generators than the reciprocating steam engines then in use.

So Insull convinced Edison to change course and embrace high voltage alternating current distribution supplied by large, central, coal-fired steam power plants in which steam turbines turned the electricity generator and transformers stepped up the voltage prior to distribution and stepped it back down for delivery. As President of Tennessee-Edison, Insull oversaw the installation of steam turbines to power electricity generators at the Nashville-Edison Steam Station near the Cumberland River. The October 1903 startup shook with vibrations, but the equipment was soon balanced out and the success became obvious. These turbines had been imported from the United States, but turbines of equal performance would soon be manufactured in the Confederate States. Within just a few years, small local electricity generating stations powered by reciprocating steam engines would become abandoned technology. Thomas Edison born in Ohio, in the United States, a son of an immigrant from Nova Scotia, had been right about many things, but it took the genius of Nickola Tesla of Serbia and the industrial management skills of a 21-year-old immigrant from London to bring inexpensive electricity to the Confederate States. [284]

We now turn our attention to another pioneering invention of the era, wireless telegraphy, and then to radio.

### Guglielmo Marconi and Confederate Wireless Telegraphy

Guglielmo Marconi (1874-1937) is considered the man who invented wireless telegraphy, which evolved into radio. Our story begins near Bologna, Italy, when Guglielmo Marconi, at the age of 20, was inspired by his teacher, Augusto Righi, and reports of detections of radio waves by physicist Heinrich Hertz. Guglielmo, building his experimental equipment in the attic of his parent's home, within a few months discovered that the radio waves in his attic transmitter were being received a few feet away by his receiver. This was December, 1894. He set up telegraph keys and found he could transmit Morse code wirelessly. He figured he had something important. The following summer he set up a transmission tower and found he could receive Morse code two miles away, even with intervening hills. So he wrote Pietro Lacava, head of the Italian Ministry of Post and Telegraphs, seeking funding for further development. No response. Apparently, Lacava wrote on the letter: "to the Longara", a reference to the insane asylum on Via della Lungara in Rome. Then he filed it away. Receiving no reply from Lacava, Marconi spoke to a friend of the family who worked at the Confederate States Consulate in Bologna. This Consulate staffer sent a letter of introduction to Italy's ambassador to the Confederate States at Davis, Annibale Ferrero. Ambassador Ferrero arranged a meeting with Thomas Edison in Nashville. Edison immediately insisted that all efforts be made to encourage Marconi to bring his technology to the University of Nashville and pursue development there, with assurance that all patent rights would belong to him where applicable.

Edison took the Italian ambassador to meet the University's Chair of the Department of Physics, John Henry Poynting, who had emigrated from London ten years earlier and who had

---

[284] In truthful history, Samuel Insull immigrated into New York City and first worked alongside Thomas Edison at his New York City headquarters. Insull did favor high voltage alternating current power distribution from large central power plants, but his pioneering adoption of steam turbines over reciprocating steam engines took place at Chicago Edison's huge Harrison Street plant in the same year, 1903. General Electric Corporation was created in 1891-92 by the merger of Edison General Electric and Thomson-Houston Company.

worked there with James Clerk Maxwell during the 1870s. As we know, Maxwell, in 1873 had published "A Dynamical Theory of the Electromagnetic Field," which united all previously unrelated observations, experiments and equations of electricity, magnetism and optics into a consistent theory – the most important contribution to human scientific knowledge during the century of the 1800s. So there was no better place than the University of Nashville to anchor Marconi's work in solid physical science. [285]

Marconi came to Nashville in July 1896, expenses paid by Thomas Edison himself. He brought along his radio telegraphy equipment and demonstrated transmissions exceeding five miles over hill and dale. Financial support poured in. The importance to marine communication at sea was so obvious. Voice communication might somehow follow. Marconi established the Marconi Marine Telegraphy Company in July 1897 and set up a transmission tower at New Orleans in 1898 and in Charleston, Miami and Havanah in 1899. He demonstrated wireless overseas telegraphy between New Orleans, Miami and Havanah at year end. In 1901 he set up transmission/receiving towers at San Diego and Honolulu and proved communication between those distant places in December 1902. By that time he was successful in demonstrating ship to shore telegraphy for up to 1,000 miles during favorable night-time atmospheric conditions. By 1910 Marconi Marine Telegraphy Company was providing ship to shore, ship to ship, and shore to shore telegraphy services in Europe, North America, South America, Australia, Hong Kong, Japan and all Confederate States. Marconi telegraphy was a major factor during World War I. British, French and Italian aircraft, many being made by Wright-Carolina, were often homing in on German wireless telegraphy stations to silence them.

## Confederate Radio Development

Wireless voice transmission, what we call simply "radio," soon followed wireless telegraphy. But the technology was considerably different and Marconi was not a leader in its development – three other men earned that recognition -- Reginald A. Fessenden, inventor of the heterodyne principle (1901); John Ambrose Fleming, inventor of the diode vacuum tube (1904); and Lee De Forest, inventor of the triode amplifying vacuum tube (1906).

### Reginald A. Fessenden

Reginald A. Fessenden (1866-1932) was born in Quebec Province, Canada. His father was a minister in the Church of England, Canada. He received a classical education in Quebec Province and, at age 19, went to the island of Bermuda to teach in a small school. There he met Helen Trott of Bermuda, who would become his wife. Although his classical education had not taught him much about electricity or physics, he was excited about working in that field. So, in the summer of 1886 he wrote to Thomas Edison in Nashville in hopes of gaining employment as an unskilled technician. He wrote, "I do not know anything about electricity, but can learn pretty quick." Edison replied, "Have enough men who do not know about electricity." But the determined Fessenden persisted and landed a job that Fall as a tester at Edison Machine Works, which was laying underground cable in Nashville. His work impressed Edison and won an invitation in 1887

---

[285] The Marconi story is truthful history up to the point that Marconi contacts the family friend at the Confederate States Consulate. In truthful history, that friend was Carlo Gardini, Honorary Consul at the United States Consulate in Bologna. In truthful history Marconi was asking for help in arranging to take his work to Great Britain for further development. This resulted in Marconi going to London and there improving his equipment and demonstrating the viability of wireless telegraphy. Marconi never immigrated on a permanent basis to England. His main interest being marine telegraphy communication, he established the Marconi International Marine Communication Company and pioneered ship to shore and ship to ship telegraphy. He was slow to expand into voice radio transmission and receiving. He returned to Italy in 1914 and supported the Allied effort in World War I. He later supported the Italian Fascist Party. He died in 1937 of a heart attack, not living to witness the Germany-Italy-Japan alliance and World War II.

to work in the Edison Laboratories at Old Hickory as a junior technician. In 1892 Fessenden left Edison Laboratores to take a post as Professor of Electrical Engineering at Georgia Institute of Technology. At Georgia Tech he was free to pursue his own research and to keep for himself any patent rights that he might earn. It was in his Atlanta laboratory that Fessenden began to conceive of the heterodyne principle, where two signals combined to produce a third signal. He built a rotary-spark transmitter in 1900 and demonstrated successful wireless, but barely understandable, voice transmission for a distance of one mile. Later that year the Confederate Weather Bureau hired Fessenden away from Georgia Tech to work for them, providing for him financial support for laboratory and equipment expenses, while giving him all patent rights for inventions. The Weather Bureau put Fessenden and his equipment at Weir's Point, Roanoke Island, North Carolina, and there he demonstrated wireless voice communication over a distance of 50 miles, to a station beyond Cape Hatteras. Fessenden continued to work on wireless voice transmission using faster and faster rotary-spark transmitters, but that approach would soon be made obsolete by vacuum tube electronic devices. Yet, it was Fessenden who pioneered the heterodyne principle – demonstrating the route to eventual high fidelity radio and television. That path to commercial radio would be further advanced by John Ambrose Fleming. [286]

## John Ambrose Fleming

John Ambrose Fleming (1849-1945) was born in Lancaster, England. His father was a Congregational minister and John would be a devoted Christian all his life. He studied under the great physicist James Clerk Maxwell, mentioned earlier, and studied physics briefly at Cambridge. Beginning in 1897, he held the Pender Chair as Professor of Electrical Engineering at University College, London. His invention of the diode vacuum tube in November 1904 made modern electronics and computers possible. Vacuum tube diodes would remain a key component of most electronic circuits, such as radio and television receivers, until the invention of solid state electronic devices in the 1950s, which would be implemented commercially in the 1960s and 1970s. Fessenden worked as a consultant to Edison's company (beginning in 1882) and to Marconi's company (beginning in 1899). In 1907, encouraged by Thomas Edison and Guglielmo Marconi, he temporary took a leave of absence from University College, London for a four-year post as Distinguished Professor of Electrical Engineering at the University of Nashville, where he taught graduate students, engaged in research, and consulted with Edison and Marconi enterprises. His Confederate patent of the diode vacuum tube was upheld in courts and allowed Professor Fleming ample revenue to pursue his engineering and scientific career unfettered by worry or lack of financial resources. He lived to see his invention play a major role in Great Britain's victory against Germany in 1944. [287]

## Lee De Forest

Lee De Forest (1873-1961) was born in Iowa in 1873. His father was a Congregational Church minister and was active in the American Missionary Association. In 1879 De Forest took the position of President of the Association's Talladega College in Talladega, Alabama, a school for Confederate African American children. At this point Lee was six years old. The De Forest family retained their United States citizenship and lived in Alabama on a temporary basis.

---

[286] The story of Reginald Aubrey Fessenden is truthful with a few exceptions. In truthful history, he went to work for Thomas Edison in New York City, not Nashville. He became a professor at Purdue University and at University of Pennsylvania, not Georgia Tech. He worked for the United States Weather Bureau, not the Confederate Weather Bureau. The transmission from Roanoke Island to Cape Hatteras is truthful history.

[287] The story of John Ambrose Fleming is truthful history with a few exceptions. He did not take a leave of absence from University College, London to work in Nashville, although he did work for Edison in England. His patents were not as well respected as were those in our alternate history.

Although the father wanted the son to become a pastor, Lee had other ideas. He was excited about science and the amazing innovations being introduced almost yearly. He wanted to be a part of that. So, in 1891, at age 18, he declined to attend a boys' school in Massachusetts and instead left home for a boarding school in Nashville. This was a major turning point in his life. He was rejecting his father's dream of a son in the ministry and to some extent rejecting the code of conduct expected of that life-style (a handsome and "dashing" fellow, he would be divorced twice and married thrice). De Forest continued his education at the University of Nashville, earning a BS in Physics. He received his Doctorate in Physics at Georgia Tech in 1899 at the age of 25 years. De Forest became a career experimenter and promoter of his inventions. But most of the stockholder-owned companies he spearheaded went bankrupt and left investors with nothing. But he did hit on one very, very important invention: a derivation of John Ambrose Fleming's diode vacuum tube. In hindsight it would appear straightforward. But it awaited De Forest to hit upon it. He built a Fleming diode vacuum tube with a third element. In addition to the anode and the cathode, he inserted a grid-pattern wire between them. Whamo! The third wire performed as an amplifier. De Forest had rather stumbled upon the triode vacuum tube -- essential to practically all electronics and computers. Like the vacuum tube diode, the vacuum tube triode would be essential until replaced by the invention of the solid state versions (the transistor) beginning in 1948. [288]

## Confederate Radio Broadcasting

The first important radio station in the Confederate States was station CSM in Nashville, Tennessee (the "W" call letter was reserved for United States broadcasters; the "C" call letter was applied to Confederate broadcasters). It would become famous as the home of the "Grand O' Opry."

## Crucial Confederate Help in Defeating the German War Machine

It is sometimes hard to believe that a huge world war was triggered by a Bosnian-Serb named Gavrilo Princip. That horrible conflict began soon after Princip assassinated Archduke Franz Ferdinand of Austria in Sarajevo on June 28, 1914. The deceased Archduke had been heir apparent to the Austro-Hungarian throne. Princip also killed the fellow's wife Duchess Sophie. By August, war was spreading across Europe, involving Austria-Hungary, Germany, Serbia, Russia, France, Belgium, the United Kingdom, and the Ottoman Empire, to name just a few. It was mostly a land war involving troops in trenches and artillery. Many died in deadly gas attacks. But naval battles were an important part of the fighting – particularly attacks on marine shipping, inflicted by Germany's U-boat submarines. The war had been raging for 33 months prior to the United States entering the fight. It declared war against Germany on April 7, 1917. United States troops began fighting on European soil in early 1918.

The Confederate States never declared war on Germany or any nations allied with that country. Confederates were technically neutral and limited to marine missions. However, as a world leader in aviation and agriculture, Confederates helped by building and delivering aircraft to the British Isles, and by delivering food. Although German submarines, called U-boats, were a major threat to shipping, Confederates managed to make transatlantic deliveries with minimal losses by organizing merchant ship transatlantic crossings into convoys, which were protected by

---

[288] The story of Lee De Forest is truthful history except he did go to the boarding school in Massachusetts at age 18 and afterward received his BS and Ph. D. degrees at Yale. He worked and lived in Chicago, New York City and San Francisco. His work was mostly centered on wireless voice radio and ship to shore wireless communication. His invention of the vacuum tube triode was huge, but another experimenter would have surely soon discovered it. The story of Talladega is truthful history except it was, of course, a Confederate town when the De Forest family arrived.

Navy destroyers and other heavily armed Navy ships. Most of these convoy escorts were greatly helped by a centrally positioned Confederate aircraft carrier. When in dangerous seas, two to four surveillance airplanes were in the air looking for submarines on the prowl. When spotted from a ship or from the air, a destroyer gave chase. Some submarines were sunk. Some were forced to dive (when underwater below periscope depth, the submarine was "blind" and unable to see to launch a torpedo). Confederate aircraft deliveries began in March 1915.

By the end of the War on November 11, 1918, Confederates had delivered 11,500 aircraft to Great Britain and the Allies. Food deliveries to the British Isles also contributed to the Allied victory. [289] [290]

Another significant Confederate contribution to allied victory was the Tesla radio-guided torpedo. In 1898, Nickola Tesla had used a radio transmitter to direct actuators on a model boat, which allowed him to remotely control the boat's speed and direction. By the start of the Great War in Europe, the Tesla guidance system was secretly in use by the Confederate and British Navy, guiding torpedoes toward enemy warships and submarines.

## A Few Last Remarks

Before leaving stories about Confederate advances between 1890 and 1929, allow me to apologize for not presenting a comprehensive history. Available space did not permit it. But I do hope you can appreciate how diversity and emigrant recruitment played such an important role in Confederate success.

## Tuesday Evening Selected Diary Notes

Diary note by Chris Memminger said: "Had supper tonight with Tina Sharp. That was fitting because this morning's lecture was on the Confederacy's amazing technological and industrial expansion up to the year 1929. And Tina's great-great-grandfather was Walter Benona Sharp, the inventor of the Sharps-Huges hardrock drill bit that revolutionized oil well drilling and made possible the great Texas oil boom – key to jump starting the industrialization of the Confederate States -- and our rapid advance from steam engines to internal combustion engines – and essential to modern transportation. How about that! Now, Sharp's great-great-granddaughter is working to ensure that Confederate States electricity is mostly derived from nuclear power plants, like Comanche Peak. Tina is a brilliant young lady. Plays the French horn quite well, too. Told me that, while Professor Davis was out last weekend leading the backpacking trip, his wife Judith invited her over to the house to play French horn duets. Said Judith Davis is amazing and drives to Nashville to play first horn in the Nashville Symphony. Tina said she felt honored to play alongside a professional musician of her talent, even if just for the fun of it. Judith and Professor Davis have a small apartment on Music Row in Nashville to make it easier to be part of the Nashville music scene without killing themselves with the driving. Takes just over an hour and a half each way. She talked a lot about Allen Ross, how he loves his vast bison ranch and the

---

[289] Confederate military strategists realized that they possessed the world's most advanced aircraft technology and they foresaw the advantage of aircraft in naval warfare, far away from land. So, with fears of war growing across the Atlantic in Europe, and across the Pacific in Asia, the Confederate Congress authorized the design and construction of two aircraft carriers for the navy as well as sufficient aircraft to take off and land while underway at sea. The topside of these two Confederate aircraft carriers was a flat runway, 550 feet long by 50 feet wide with a narrow control tower rising up on the starboard side. Two elevators raised and lowered aircraft between the flight deck and the hanger deck below. Both Confederate aircraft carriers were launched in the fall of 1914.

[290] In truthful history, the German U-boat submarines inflicted severe damage to marine shipping, especially in the vicinity of the British Isles and in the Mediterranean Sea. The British did not organize convoys and assign Royal Navy warships to escort duty until May 1917, a move that greatly curbed merchant marine losses. In truthful history, Imperial Japan constructed the first aircraft carrier of the design noted in our alternate history. It was launched in 1922.

ranch crew that helps him and his family. Also said that, when Carlos and Allen play their guitars, it makes a great sound and gets the juices flowing in the music group that Marie Saint Martin started. Heard them playing this afternoon, too. They are having so much fun, and I enjoy listening in. Felt a little like Tina was smitten over Ross. But I cannot see how those careers could ever harmonize. Tina a nuclear engineer at Comanche Peak in North Texas; Ross a bison rancher in remote western Sequoyah.

Diary note by Tina Sharp said, "It's amazing how so few men enabled such remarkable advances in Confederate industrial expansion – whole new industries based on pioneering inventions – cooperative efforts among inventive geniuses. So much resulted from the decision by the McCormick family -- originially of Virginia, then of Illinois -- to relocate to the Confederate States. That encouraged Henry Ford to follow later. That encouraged Orville and Wilbur Wright to relocate from their Ohio bicycle shop to North Carolina at the point that their experimental work with gliders had taught them how to control an aircraft in flight, but before the light weight gasoline engine was built and integrated into the design. It was at that point, near Kitty Hawk, North Carolina that Cyrus Hall McCormick II happened to be fishing nearby, observed the Wright Brothers flight testing, served up a supper of red snapper, sweet potatoes and baked beans, and offered the help of the McCormick's and Ford's in speeding along their project to ensure they were the first to master the heavier-than-air flying machine. And we owe so much to Thomas Edison, who relocated to Nashville before he was successful in his amazing inventions based on electricity. He was like a magnet, drawing other electricity-related inventors to Nashville for cooperative efforts. Take Nikola Tesla for example. Working with Edison, he invented the AC motor, but suffered from emotional problems -- problems resolved out at Belle Meade. Amazing what time on a horse farm with the ladies can do to settle down a man of extraordinary genius."

Diary note by Robert Lee said, "Thank God we avoided being drawn into the Great War in Europe like was the United States. We helped the good guys with arms and airplanes, but did not put Confederate troops on the ground or become engaged in serious fighting in the Atlantic. Our help with military equipment was very important, perhaps crucial, but our brave boys were not over there in the trenches fight, surrounded by nerve gas and other horribles."

# Part 3, Chapter 6, Day 24 – An Overview of Confederate History from 1921 to 1938 – Class Lecture, Wednesday, June 29, 2011

When the Sewanee Project team settled into their seats this morning, they already knew that Professor Davis would be focusing on the history of Asia and Confederate relations with Asian countries and the peoples of Asia. This would be the first lecture when the twelve would be directed away from histories near the Confederate region to histories of regions far way to the west, all the way across the vast Pacific Ocean. On the other hand, they understood that, by the early 1920s, the Confederate States were among the world's major countries and understanding its history necessitated understanding the history of its relations to others around the globe. We now listen in as Professor Davis begins.

## A Fast-Paced Era of 17 Years -- Dealing with Economic Expansion, Economic Depression, Drought and Foreign Affairs

The decade following the Great War in Europe was a period of amazing economic expansion around the world as well as in the Confederate States. But this amazing technological and industrial advance was not followed by a devastating economic depression of equal duration as was experienced to our north, in the United States. We did suffer a sharp drop in our stock market soon after October 29, 1929, and an economic depression did follow. But, compared to 1930 and 1931 in the United States, the economic depression in the Confederacy was half as severe. And, by 1932, our economy was on the mend, while the Depression in the United States would be continuing through the rest of the decade. Available space in *The CSA Trilogy* prevents a detailed account of the reasons for our recovery success relative to our neighbor to our north. Major reasons for that success are believed to be: the lack of centralized economic power, such as existed in New York City; the lack of centralized government power, such as existed in Washington City; a more geographically diverse manufacturing economy with less concentration in big cities; the far less prevalence of demanding labor unions; the greater capabilities of the immigrant population, chosen, even recruited, because of their skills; the far greater racial diversity of the population enabling improved matches of skills to needs; better management of agriculture and relevant technology; a more diverse economy that was less dependent on heavy industry; an expanding vacation-resort-retirement economy from Florida to Cuba to South California, to the former Mexican states, to Hawaii; a growing entertainment economy, most notably in South California; a more resilient international trade that was less involved with Europe and more involved with South America and Asia; a culture of business management and expansion planning that looked beyond short term profits to focus on long term, sounder growth, and, finally, a more level-headed approach to monetary policy.

We often think of the drought years of 1934, 1936 and 1939-1940, when the great plains of North America experienced the "Dust Bowl." In those years, Confederate farmers fared much better than their neighbors to the north. The destructive plowing of deeply-rooted grass in the high plains did not occur in the Confederate State of Sequoyah and was not a severe problem in the State of North Texas, where agriculture was a mix of raising cattle and raising cotton.

Of course, much of the above history is well known and does not need to be detailed here. For that reason, we now turn our attention to events in Asia and Confederate relations with Asian people, because the major event in Confederate history during this generation will be the War against Japan, sparked by the attack on our State of Hawaii in 1941.

So let us acquire an understanding of the history of the three major nations of eastern Asia -- China, Russia and Japan -- and also other countries in the region, such as Manchuria and Korea, and those of the South Pacific. We start with Japan.

## Catching Up on the History of Japan, China and Korea

In a short 1868 Japanese civil war, the traditional shoguns, which empowered the Tokugawa regime, was overthrown by a "different kind of aristocratic elite, who decided that the way to repel Western imperialism was to embrace wholesale modernization." Thus began Japan's "Meiji restoration," in other words, thus begin a Japan ruled by "brilliant elitists." Christianity and firearms among the population were outlawed to discourage a counter-revolution. In record time, within only 32 years, the transformation achieved by this new fascist Japanese government was amazing: "By 1900, it had a disciplined, conscripted army, and a constitutional and parliamentary system, and it was Asia's most heavily industrialized society, exporting goods around the world. This relatively small island group had nearly 37,000 miles of railway tracks and 700,000 tons of shipping. It was already invading neighbors, looking toward an empire that would supply to it the industrial raw materials and fuels not available at home.

During 1894 and 1895 Japan invaded China to take to itself the traditionally subservient Korean Peninsula. The fight was swift and decisive: "twenty thousand Japanese troops assaulted the fort of Weihaiwe in China's northern Shandong province, seized the fort's artillery and, with this in hand, promptly sunk five of the finest vessels in the Chinese navy. Japan's claim to be thereafter in control of Korea went unchallenged, and she would formally annex it in 1910. At the same time Japan claimed control over the nearby Chinese island of Taiwan (Formosa), which also went unchallenged.

Japanese military confidence soared. During 1904 and 1905 it challenged both Russia and China for dominant imperialist influence in Manchuria, the very large northeastern province of China that lay not far north of the "Great Wall." Manchuria was bordered on the east by Russia and its seaport of Vladivostok and by Korea; on the north by Russia; on the west by Outer Mongolia and Inner Mongolia; and on the south by the Yellow Sea and smaller Chinese provinces. By the way, the Chinese capital of Beiping was only 125 miles southwest of Manchuria. Russia had already run its trans-Siberian railroad through Manchuria for more economical access to its Vladivostok seaport, so it resisted the Japanese invasion vigorously. Japan sent 1,088,996 soldiers to fight the Russians, suffering 81,455 dead and 381,323 wounded, but eventually defeated the Russian troops, thereby gaining dominant imperialist control. This was the first time an Asian power had defeated a European power since the days of the immense Mongol Empire (during the 13th and 14th centuries the Mongols controlled the largest contiguous land empire known to human history). In a treaty settlement, Russia was forced to hand over control of the Liaodong Peninsula which contained Dalian an important seaport city on the Yellow Sea.

Japan stationed a large military force in Liaodong -- the 10,000-man Kwantung Army. Over several decades, using resident Chinese labor, Japanese fascists would build up Dalian and Manchuria. Much of Japan's industrial expansion in Manchuria was facilitated by the Japanese-owned South Manchurian Railway Company (*Mantetsu*), which designed, constructed and operated company-owned railroads, mines and industrial factories.

Like elsewhere, Japanese economic expansion slowed severely following the 1929 worldwide depression, which persisted and dried up markets in Europe and the Americas. This setback encouraged the Japanese elites to advocate renewed military aggression against China, this time for complete, not just partial, control of Manchuria. Using a Japanese-contrived "incident" on September 18, 1931, Japan's Kwantung Army secretly blew up a section of *Mantetsu* railroad track near the Manchurian town of Fengtian and then assaulted the nearby Chinese military base. The Japanese press went along with the ruse, dispensing expanding propaganda and alleging that the Chinese were being punished for persistent banditry, devoting not one inch of newspaper column to the truth. When attacked across Manchuria by the

Kwantung Army, Chinese troops in Manchuria withdrew without fighting, as commanded by Chinese leaders hoping for condemnation from world powers. Suffering troop deaths of only 2,530 soldiers, Japan rolled on and on across vast Manchuria and, by July 1933, was in complete control, while the world stood by and did nothing more than booting Japan out of the League of Nations. To the elites of resource-and-land-short Japan, Manchuria was glorious. At only 146,000 square miles, Japan only matched the combined area of South Carolina, Georgia and Alabama. At 579,000 square miles, Manchuria matched the area of those three Confederate States plus the addition of Kentucky and seven more Confederate States (Virginia, North Carolina, Tennessee, Arkansas, South Carolina, Georgia, Florida, Alabama, Mississippi and Louisiana, as measured at the time of secession). The Japanese press crowed about the potential largess from occupied Manchuria, already the world's largest producer of soybeans: endless tracts of future farmland and virgin forests; untapped iron ore and coal deposits; huge harvests of wheat (5 million bushels) and sorghum (1 million bushels); many cattle (2.7 million head), horses (4 million head), and sheep (4.6 million head). In six years, Japan would attack much of remaining China in a thrust that would be a forerunner of the 1941 war that would involve Hawaii and the Confederate States. By then, resources from Manchuria would greatly enable Japan's impressive military might on land, at sea and in the air. Japan's military aggression was made possible by its modern navy transports, aircraft carriers, freighters and warships as well as by airplanes, trucks and tanks, all requiring petroleum fuels, etc. Japanese Fascists knew that, without petroleum and raw materials, Japan would be a powerless heap of economic stagnation.

## A Closer Look at Chinese History

We now turn our attention to the development of China, for it would be there that the Confederacy would do much to defeat the imperialistic Japanese Fascists and lead Asia into more peaceful years.

During the early 1800s China was huge. When including Inner Mongolia and Manchuria, China measured 3,704,426 square miles, which is 84 percent of the land area of the Confederate States and the United States combined. [291]

The Qing dynasty ruled China from 1644 to 1912. These rulers were Manchus from northeast China, their homeland being Manchuria. Like many foreign invaders of central China, Manchus adopted traditional Chinese customs, although they located the Chinese capital northward to Beiping, not far removed from the Manchus homeland. But not all of China was under firm Qing rule -- there were other powers in Chinese seaports. The British had control of Hong Kong by treaty and had much influence in Shanghai. Shanghai, the major trading center in Asia, protected foreigners in the sections of the city known as the International Settlement and the French Concession. But there was discontent. Chinese considered people of the European race who engaged in trade to be Imperialists and to be unfairly advantaged by past "unequal treaties." But Christian missionaries in China were looked upon as friends, helping hands and valuable teachers in fields of philosophy, medicine, industry and science. There were thousands of Catholic and Protestant Christian missionaries in China, many of them from the Confederate States, which had become home to the most dedicated body of Christians in the World, for the United States and Europe were experiencing a slow but persistent decline in Christian observance. More will be said about Christianity in China a few pages later.

Chinese history changed dramatically in 1911 as an admirable Republican revolution rapidly swept the land, concluding on February 12, 1912, the day the last Chinese emperor, six-year-old Puyi, abdicated with guarantee of a home and income. For a bit it looked like Sun Yat-

---

[291] In truthful history, China was almost exactly the same land area as today's United States.

sen would emerge as President of the Democratic Republic of China, complete with a bicameral legislature, but a military coup d'état would soon destroy that government. Sadly, much political and military turmoil would consume the next 35 years. At this time we introduce Sun Yat-sen.

Of all Chinese revolutionaries of the era, the most important leader of the drive to transform China away from an imperial dynasty was Sun Yat-sen, a physician and Christian, then 45 years old, who had been born in Guangdong province. In 1878, at the age of 13 years, Sun Yat-sen attended a Christian school in the Confederate State of Hawaii, living there with his older brother, owner of a 12,000 acre cattle ranch. There, at the Iolani school, he learned English, western history, mathematics, science and Christianity. He returned to China for additional schooling; then he studied medicine at Guangzhou Boji Hospital under Presbyterian missionary John G. Kerr, who had come from Ohio in the United States. Sun Yat-sen earned his medical degree and license in Hong Kong. He accepted Christ and was baptized in the early 1880s. So, Sun Yat-sen, considered the father of post-dynasty China, had strong roots in Confederate, American and British culture, science and values. Although licensed as a physician, he spent much time throughout his adult life advocating for various political revolutions and raising money overseas to help finance them. [292] We now look at Chiang Kai-shek and the Chinese Nationalists.

By 1926 the Chinese Nationalists were a formidable force. On June 5 Chiang Kai-shek was officially named senior commander of the Nationalist Revolutionary Army, the military force dedicated to advancing the aims of the Chinese Nationalist Party. Chiang would move the Chinese capital from Beijing to more centrally located Nanjing, situated upstream of Shanghai on the Yangtze River. From this point, Chiang would gain political and military control of the Nationalist Party and most of China throughout a decades-long confrontation with the Chinese Communist Party and the Japanese invasion forces.

Born in Zhejiang province in 1887, Chiang embarked on a military career at the age of 19 years, first attending the Baoding Military Academy in 1906, followed by the Imperial Japanese Army Academy in 1907. He served in the Imperial Japanese Army from 1909 to 1911, leaving that service upon hearing about the 1911 Chinese Revolution, which has been mentioned previously. Back in China, he supported the Revolution and became a founding member of the Kuomintang of China, known as the Chinese Nationalist Party. He thereafter rose in power in the Party's military wing, taking advantage of his excellent training and forceful personality.

Chiang Kai-shek's first wife, Mao Fumei, would bear him a son, Chiang Ching-kuo, who would take many leadership positions under his father's tutelage. [293] Chiang Kai-shek would divorce and remarry, his fourth wife being the famous and influential Soong Mei-ling. They married in December 1927. One cannot know the history surrounding Chiang Kai-shek without considering his fourth wife, the very capable and influential Song Mei-ling, known to us as Madam Chiang.

Soong Mei-ling was the daughter of Soong Jiashu, a very wealthy and influential Shanghai merchant and financial supporter of the Revolution and of Sun Yat-sen's efforts. A former Methodist missionary of Chinese ancestry and nicknamed "Charlie Soong," the father had five other children, many growing up to be very influential as the Soong name would pepper Chinese history going forward. Mei-ling spoke fluent English, and received a fine education at Wesleyan

[292] The history of Sun Yat-sen up to this point is truthful, except Hawaii was a State in the Confederacy.

[293] In truthful history Chiang Kia-shek would control the Chinese Nationalist Party and military through to the defeat of Japan in 1945 and for three more years until the impending Communist takeover of all of China would force his retreat to the island of Taiwan, with many supporters, in May 1948, where he would lead the Nationalist Party until his death in 1975 at the age of 87 years. Today the small island of Taiwan and the vast People's Republic of China remain divided, but China continues to claim that it is de facto ruler over the Nationalist island.

Female Institute in Macon, Georgia, the Confederate States of America, a Methodist school. She had begun her education in Macon at the age of 9 years, rooming with older siblings who were studying there, and gained her college degree in 1917, majoring in English, with a minor in philosophy. The Institute was renamed the Wesleyan College in 1917, the year of her graduation. She spoke flawless English with a charming Georgia accent for the remainder of her life. She returned to China, meeting Chiang Kai-shek in 1920. Mei-ling, 22, and Chiang, 33, were attracted to each other, but her mother forbade her daughter to marry such an old man who was married and professed to be a Buddhist. But, in the course of seven years, Chiang divorced his third wife and agreed to study the Bible and learn to become a Christian. The mother withdrew her objection and the Chiang-Soong wedding took place on December 1, 1927. The marriage would last 46 years, until his death in 1974. Mei-ling would live until 2003, to the ripe old age of 105 years. [294]

## Communist and Russian Influence in China

We now turn to the other political/military party vying for control of China, the Communist Party of China. The CPC had its origins in the May Fourth Movement by Beijing students in 1919, when Marxism and Anarchism ideologies gained traction among a group of Chinese intellectuals. It was modeled on Vladimir Lenin's political theory of a monopolistic "vanguard party." As you remember World War I had concluded the previous year, in late 1918, and Russian Communist factions had fought over control of Russia until gaining control in 1922, thereafter expanding into the Union of Soviet Socialist Republics. The following year, 1923, Sun Yat-sen led a movement to form an alliance between China's Nationalist Party and the Soviet's Communist Party. This led to China's Nationalists and China's Communists surprisingly working in alliance toward goals of uniting the country's provinces under a strong national government. Two years later, in 1925, Mao Zedong, then a young 32-year-old Chinese communist, took command of the combined Party's Office of Propaganda. But Chaing Kai-shek realized that the Soviets really intended to maneuver the Chinese Communists into control over the Nationalists. Fortunately, he won control over the Nationalists Revolutionary Army on June 5, 1926 and began a purge of the alliance's communists. Before long the Nationalist-Communist alliance was dead and the two parties were again adversaries, both seeking to bring all of China under a powerful central government, but with two distinctly different philosophies of how such a government would rule over the people. We now take a look at Mao Zedong.

Mao Zedong was born in 1893 to a self-made, wealthy farm family in Hunan province. His mother was a Buddhist but Mao abandoned the faith while a teenager. During the 1911 Chinese Revolution, he served as a rebel soldier for six months, resigning in 1912. He disdained physical work on his father's farm and moved from job to job, mostly spending time reading books and thinking about future Chinese politics. Desiring to become a teacher, Mao, then 21 years old, entered a Normal School in Changsha in 1914 and graduated in June 1919. By this time, already a determined revolutionary, Mao was well equipped to direct the Nationalist Party Propaganda Office when given the chance in 1925.

## Chiang Kai-shek and Chinese-Confederate Relations

It was at the Chinese capital city, Nanjing -- well-positioned on the Yangtze River, China's great inland waterway -- that Chiang Kai-shek's political philosophy evolved from favoring a strong centralized national government to favoring a constitutionally-limited decentralized republican government, being influenced by Confederate missionaries and Mei-ling. Several notable Confederate missionaries and businessmen resided at Nanjing and/or travelled through

---

[294] In truthful history, in 1913, Mei-ling left Macon, Georgia and entered Wellesley College in Massachusetts, the United States, to be near her brother, who was studying at Harvard College. So her graduation would be from that school. But her charming Georgia accent would remain with her afterward.

routinely. And, beginning in 1920, Soong Mei-ling loved spending time in the city and visiting with Chiang and influential people, including foreigners who came and went on business. She was quite an attraction and her command of Georgia-accented English charmed and disarmed. So she influenced them and in turn she and they influenced Chiang. [295]

The success of the Confederate States of America was a compelling thought. Could China emulate it? Were the Chinese people ready for decentralized democracy? Could the traditional war-lord and tribal warring factions be made to make peace and obey provincial and confederate laws? Could the mass communication tools of newspapers, magazines and books, supplemented by live radio, facilitate such a monumental transition from subjugation under an autocratic Qing Dynasty to a constitutional decentralized democracy in only one or two generations? Would the Christian evangelism sweeping across China from east to west contribute to the envisioned transformation? If Confederates could rapidly build a remarkably successful country containing a diverse society, could not the Chinese people, a more uniform society, do likewise? Would not the normal human desire for liberty win out over submission to a communist party dictatorship? These were the issues at hand.

Within political thinkers in the Chinese Nationalist Party, a faction gained ground that advocated a confederation of provinces united under a constitution that limited the powers granted to China's central government. It was with these thoughts in mind that Chiang appointed Mei-ling's brother, Soong Tse-Ven (known in the west as T. V. Soong), to the position of Ambassador to the Confederate States of America, instructing him to advance goals of strengthening the economic and mutual defense ties between the Confederate States and China. But Chiang and Tse-Ven believed that the envisioned evolution to limited central powers would have to be delayed until peace and security were achieved at home.

Chinese Ambassador Soong Tse-Ven arrived in Davis, the capital of the Confederate States of America, in June 1926. Ambassador Soong was already familiar with Davis and the southeastern states of the Confederacy. As already mentioned, his sister, Mei-ling had attended school in Macon, Georgia from the age of 9 through college graduation in 1917. Well Tse-Ven had received his early education at St. John's University in Shanghai and then, at the age of 20, had completed a bachelor's degree at the University of the South in 1915, here in Sewanee Tennessee, with a major in economics. Soong had then worked in international banking at Atlanta while pursuing graduate studies at Emory College. Upon returning to China he had worked for several industrial enterprises and, most recently, had helped Sun Yat-sen develop finances for his Canton government. Like his family, he followed the Methodist faith. So, Tse-ven was especially well equipped by 1926 to persuade the Confederate Government to support a strong alliance with the Chinese government of Chiang Kai-shek, even as the world suffered a fearsome economic depression and a growing Fascists military threat to peace. [296]

### Wednesday Evening Selected Diary Postings

---

[295] As we introduce Confederate States political philosophy to our narrative, we are departing from truthful history.

[296] In truthful history Soong Tse-Ven attended Harvard College for his bachelor's degree and worked for the International Corporation in New York while pursuing graduate studies at Columbia University. The dates are truthful, but the location of his studies and work has been revised to Tennessee and Georgia to reflect a logical family affinity for the Confederate States. In truthful history his leadership in various positions for the Nationalist government would be prominent: Nationalist Ambassador to Washington, D. C. beginning in 1940 and China's negotiator with Joseph Stalin over Soviet-Chinese issues. He headed the Chinese delegation to the United Nations Conference in San Francisco in April 1945, which later became the United Nations.

Diary note by Emma Lunalilo said, "I went to the Sewanee Olympic pool and swam laps for an hour this afternoon. Too much sitting. Had to burn some energy. The pool is very nice. Heard several commenting, 'Does she ever slow down? Does she ever get tired'? Of course those folks had never surfed the big waves in Hawaii. Perhaps I needed to exercise to prepare myself for tomorrow's lecture. We will hear all about the Japanese bombing of Pearl Harbor and the War to Defeat Fascist Japan. I know so many people in Hawaii who lost relatives in that war, both relatives in China and relatives in our State. Well, I am all swam out and ready for some sleep. Until tomorrow.

Diary note by Conchita Rezanov said, "Tennis doubles with Professor Davis, Robert and Marie this afternoon. Was good to get on the court. Nice day, too."

Diary note by Robert Lee said, "My family knew some of the Chinese and Korean Christians that came to the Confederacy during the 1920's and early 1930's. And they knew Soong Tse-Ven, too, when a young man here studying and beginning his career in finance. And it has always given me a good feeling to believe that we of the Southern States of the Confederacy managed to show by example how to build a country that works together in harmony, based on individual rights, and State Rights, and limited Central Government."

Diary note by Professor Davis said, "I always enjoy telling people about Soong Tse-Ven. Got his bachelor's degree in economics here at Sewanee, then his Masters at Emory near Atlanta. Yes, Tse-Ven was here in Tennessee and Georgia at a time when Europe was crazy, fighting the Great European War, which had also drawn in United States troops. So he was hearing reports of horrible war in Europe while observing peace in the Confederacy. I have learned from older professors' stories passed along to them by previous professors concerning Tse-Ven's days at Sewanee, at Atlanta, and at Emory. It is a small world. And how important were those bonds forged then between important Confederates and Chinese."

# Part 3, Chapter 7, Day 25 – Fascist Japan's Invasion of Korea and China, Its Attack on Confederate Pearl Harbor and Defeat of the Imperialists by Combined CSA-Chinese Militaries and the Confederate Atomic Bomb – Class Lecture, Thursday, June 30, 2011

Over the next eleven years, the threat from Fascist Japan to Pacific peace would become sharply apparent. As previously mentioned, Japan launched war to take total control of Manchuria in 1931. After success at that aggression, in 1937 Japan launched another, more threatening war against the Chinese provinces that lay south of Manchuria.

But the Chinese Nationalist Government had a skilled and persuasive advocate at Davis in Chinese Ambassador Soong Tse-Ven. At meeting after meeting, Tse-Ven explained that the Chinese Nationalists were considering a transition away from the vision of an all-powerful central government to a more decentralized democracy similar to that enjoyed in the Confederate States; and the people of the Confederacy ought to nudge China in that direction. What should Confederates do? Tse-Ven explained:

> Help bring peace and security to the Chinese people. Help bring agricultural and industrial expansion to China. Help develop China's natural resources, including oil and natural gas. Use development in China to sustain the economic expansion that Confederates have been enjoying during the "Roaring Twenties."

And Soong Tse-Ven did not just remain in Davis. He travelled all about the Confederacy, talking to leaders in government, agriculture and business wherever he went. Several times between 1927 and 1930 he was joined by his sister Soong Mei-Ling, by this time the wife of Chiang Kai-shek. Having spent many school-age years living in Georgia, her perfect English, complete with a distinct Georgia accent, aided her brother's efforts to win Confederate support for her husband's government.

Because of the able advocacy of Tse-Ven and Mei-Ling, and the logic underlying their arguments, the Confederate States did supply a great deal of aid to China between 1927 and the Japanese 1941 attack on Pearl Harbor. Confederate aid focused on building up Chinese air power, air defense, mobile artillery, anti-tank guns and modern infantry rifles and machine guns. You see, the Chinese had millions of people that could be called upon to fight to defend their country against foreign attack, but they could not be effective without economical, easy-to-carry modern weapons. In exchange, China would open its borders to commerce between the two nations, and to foreign investment in Chinese farms, mines, oil fields, steel mills, railroads, motor vehicles, and industrial plants. "Although China abhorred the imperialism of the British, Americans and French," Ambassador Soong advised, "the Chiang government believes it and the Confederates can negotiate an agreement that preserves the sovereignty of both parties."

There is insufficient space in this book to tell the story of all of the cooperative efforts between the two countries between 1927 and 1937, but suffice it to say that the result enabled the Chinese people to resist the Japanese invasion far more successfully than if that help had not been offered. [297]

A few pages back you were advised that the story of Christianity in China would be related in more detail. We do that now. First into China were the Catholics, most importantly those

---

[297] There are several reasons that the Confederates stepped forward to help China when, in truthful history, the United States did not. Most importantly, the Great Depression, which crippled the United States economy between 1929 and 1940, was far less restrictive to the Confederate economy, as presented in our alternate history. For Confederates, the depression was about half as deep and economic growth was on the rebound by 1933.

supported by the French. Many Chinese in rural China adopted Christianity, but only a few in the cities. Then came the British Protestants, who focused more on missionary work in the cities, especially the main trading cities, such as Macau and Shanghai. Robert Morrison of the London Missionary Society was first to translate the Bible into Chinese and have copies printed for distribution, finishing the work around 1820. Many urban Chinese adopted Christianity as a result of British Missions. Missions from the United States and Confederate States then came in large numbers, and their evangelism was similar to the British experience. But there were ups and downs in the spread of Christianity in China.

Earlier, the 1858-1860 treaty negotiations between the Qing Dynasty and Western nations had lifted official restrictions on Christian missionary efforts in mainland China, and this had allowed missionaries to move inland from the five seaport cities to evangelize broadly. The Great Confederate Missionary Movement had become significant during the 1870's and grew to primary importance by the 1890's. Confederates had become a confident people. They took their religious convictions seriously. They believed that Christianity was a personal relationship between God and each individual, and that government must respect that relationship and not interfere. Confederates compared their political philosophy with the various political philosophies of Confucianism, Buddhism and the branches of Islam and found all of them inappropriate. They believed that a Christian Chinese people would -- if they adopted the Confederate political model -- be most successful at advancing their homeland into a modern, peaceful, industrous country where individual rights would be respected, a strong moral and work ethic would be appreciated, and universal education would be promoted -- thereby creating an environment where even a diverse population would behave as responsible and respectful voters and government officials. It was with these hopes that missionaries came to China from various Confederate Christian denominations. From the original Confederacy came Southern Baptists, Southern Methodists, Southern Anglicans, Southern Presbyterians, Southern Pentecostals, Southern Assemblies of God, and African American churches such as the AME. From the former Mexican States came Catholics. From Russian America and Hawaii came missionaries of the Russian Orthodox faith.[298]

The expansion of Christianity across China had been impressive up to the time of the Boxer Uprising, which began during the spring of 1900. The Boxer Uprising had been centered in the capital city of Beijing and it targeted for destruction all western and Christian influences. Inside the city, many foreigners found protection, but half of the 450 Chinese Orthodox Christians were massacred. Beyond the city, there was widespread murder. About 250 foreigners and 30,000 Chinese Christians were slaughtered. In response, a large eight-nation military force came to Beijing in August and gained control. A year later, in September 1901, the Qing Dynasty signed the Protocol of Peking, which gave Western troops temporary control of Beijing and the seaport of Tianjin. Since the Uprising was centered in northeast China, its influence in central and south China -- the heart of Chinese civilization -- was far less devastating to Christian missionary efforts. And it was in those sectors that Confederate missionaries were seeking souls to save. Stretching through the heartland of China, the Yangtze River Valley extends from the seaport city of Shanghai, to the eastern city of Nanjing, to the east-central city of Wuhan, to the central city of Chongqing and far beyond toward the west to its source beyond the northern boundary of Tibet. It was along this river highway that Confederate missionaries were most effective. They were

[298] In truthful history the Confederate States were gravely devastated by the War Between the States and the subsequent Political Reconstruction, which left most well-to-do bankrupt. The faithful remained observant, but the resources to finance a vigorous mission outreach in far-away China was so limited that the Confederate contribution to winning Chinese souls was far smaller than presented in our alternate history.

also effective in missions out of Hong Kong and nearby Guangzhou (Canton) and westward up the Pearl River into the South China interior, north of French Indochina.

Without a doubt the Missionary endeavors of Confederates (Protestants, Catholics and even Orthodox) exerted a major influence on Chinese thought and culture. Confederates were viewed as a people of diverse heritage who had come together to build a moral, productive and happy country. Confederates were viewed as different from the British, or French, or Russian, people, or those "uppity, know-it-all" folks from the United States. Confederate influence was widespread, being felt by the rural farmer, the urban worker and the educated elite alike. When the Chinese people and their leaders began to weigh choices for a government over their country, they looked favorably upon the Confederate model -- a limited central Confederate government with most power held by the Provinces. China is huge. Although we of the Confederate States, think of all Chinese as being one people, one race, one ethnic group, the truth is different. Within China there resides a diversity among the population going back two thousand years, and that diversity is real and important. So this would be the situation at the time that China would be recovering from the Japanese invasion and the peace that followed the defeat of Japan. We now turn back the clock and look at efforts to defend the China that Chiang Kai-shek was leading.

In spite of its vast size, China had little petroleum capacity. There was only one producing oil field, at Yamen in Gansu Province in western China. It had a capacity of only 1,100 barrels per day. So it was obvious that China could not modernize and be self-sufficient without production from new Chinese oil fields and oil refineries. The idea of striking black gold intrigued scores of Texas oil men. Why? -- Because by the mid-1920's Confederate oil and gasoline was plentiful and, after 1929, markets for petroleum products shrunk. China looked to be just the place to go in search of oil. Equitable deals were struck to benefit both the oil men and the Chinese. So, Texans crated their drilling equipment and headed west across the Pacific.

About the same time, Confederates stopped exports to Japan of petroleum, refined lubricants and fuels in an attempt to curb Japanese militarism.

By the 1937 Japanese invasion of China, in addition to Yumen, domestic oil was being produced at wells in three central Chinese provinces (Jiangsu, Shandong and Tianjin). Refineries were operating nearby, located where cooling water was available. By 1937 these crucial facilities were protected by anti-aircraft guns and fire-fighting equipment. Strategic stockpiles of refined oil and gasoline were distributed across many hidden locations to prevent quick destruction.

Because China was vast and modern warfare was heavily dependent on air power, China needed new-technology air transports, bombers and fighter aircraft, and sufficient fuel to fly them, to train pilots and to fight off invaders. The Nationalist were willing to pay for aircraft on a lend-lease arrangement. In Davis, recognizing that a China aircraft deal would stimulate a sagging aircraft industry, the Confederate government agreed to finance it in exchange for future payments in Chinese goods, gold and silver. Some states with excess aircraft manufacturing capacity chipped in as well. Now, the Confederacy's aircraft industry was second to none. Remember it was in North Carolina that man first flew with practical control over the aircraft's flight.

By 1937 China had received 71 transports, 111 bombers and 410 fighters. Spare parts were on hand. Fuel was secure. Numerous air fields had been graded off and a team of 632 Confederates were engaged in training pilots and mechanics. Soong Tse-Ven's Bank of China handled the financing and paperwork, and his sister Mei-ling was involved as needed. At the head of the Confederate team was General Claire Lee Chennault of Texas (China paid the salaries of Chennault and his men). Confederate fighter aircraft, the Wright F-9, would be excellent at taking out Japanese bombers, such as the Mitsubishi G3M and be slightly advantaged in dogfights against the Japanese Nakajima Ki-27, if they came into eastern China from Japan. But when Japan would begin production of the Zero jet fighter in late 1940, Chinese pilots would be disadvantaged. Nevertheless, their high altitude bomber aircraft, the Wright B-11, had sufficient range to take a war to Japan from east China airfields and deliver incendiary and explosive ordinance on target using superior bomb sight technology unknown to Japanese aircraft designers at the time. And their transport aircraft could get the job done when flying at high altitude at night. [299]

Looking at China versus Japan from a military perspective, Confederate military advisers clearly recognized that China's strength was in its huge potential soldier population and in its vast land area, whereas Japan's strength was in its modern military machines. This indicated that the Chinese Nationalists needed to inspire patriotism among its population to facilitate recruitment of millions of soldiers; needed to have ample rapid-fire weaponry light enough for men to carry with them; needed to trained them in guerrilla fighting tactics; needed to have land mines and river mines, and armor piercing weaponry that men could carry (to stop tanks and river gunboats); needed to have anti-aircraft guns that men could carry; needed to have ample food and clothing for soldiers and the population; and needed to have a trained militia that could be called up on short notice to triple the size of the Nationalist army. Furthermore, China needed factories capable of providing most of the items on the list. Chinese Nationalists agreed to this plan, financing was secured, and Confederates set about producing and shipping those items they were to provide directly, while Nationalists set about setting up factories to make those items for which they were responsible. [300]

The world situation changed on August 23, 1939, the day Germany and the Soviet Union signed a pact dividing Eastern Europe between those two nations, complete with demarcation lines drawn on a map. That day, Germany agreed to not interfere with Soviet westward invasions -- into Eastern Poland, the Baltic States, Finland and much of Romania. In exchange, Soviets agreed to not interfere with German eastward invasions up to the demarcation line. So Fascist Germany and Communist Soviet Union agreed to divide between themselves the nations that separated them.

War broke out in Europe on September 1, 1939, when Germany invaded western Poland, magnified by the Soviet invasion of eastern Poland sixteen days later – the Fascists and the Communists were seizing their halves of Poland in accordance with the above-mentioned agreement. Poles would suffer greatly, especially as Soviets executed over 25,000 prisoners in the Kalyn Forest. This alarming aggression pact compelled the Confederate States and Nationalist

[299] In truthful history the Chinese Nationalists persuaded the Soviets to supply aircraft for the defense of China and 885 were supplied between October 1937 and January 1941. But the Chinese air force had only 230 aircraft at the time the 1937 Japanese invasion began with the attack on Shanghai, and Japanese swiftly advanced, month after month. So the Soviet supply simply came too late and fuel for those aircraft was too scarce to support training and combat. After the Soviet-Japanese Neutrality Pact was signed, no more Soviet aircraft could be obtained. The best of the Soviet fighter aircraft was the I-16. The story about Texan Clair Lee Chenault is true but he and his Flying Tigers did not arrive in China until just before the attack on Pearl Harbor in December 1941. Chenault oversaw three squadrons of 30 P-40 fighter aircraft each. These planes were painted with shark face nose art and the squadrons were called the "Flying Tigers." They were the most effective air defense available to the Chinese military, but they had come too late to push back the Japanese.

[300] By 1937, when the Japanese attack on Shanghai occurred, our alternate history presents the Chinese as far stronger than truthful history teaches. In truthful history, the Chinese Nationalists army was not able to withstand the 1937 Japanese attack and much of the reason for that weakness can be attributed to failure to succeed in a strategy like the Confederates proposed. In truthful history, the United States was far less attentive to selectively and heavily arming the Chinese Nationalists.

China to intensify and accelerate their respective military build-ups and mutual cooperation. The world was going insane over lust for military aggression.

Certainly, at this time, the Soviet Union military was totally occupied in the conquest of its half of the territory that lay between its border and Germany. So, for the immediate future it needed to ensure that Japan would not attempt to seize far-eastern Russian territory. On April 13, 1941, the two nations signed the Soviet-Japanese Neutrality Pact, pledging each to not encroach on the territory of the other. This pact was mere expediency, for the intent was to honor the pact only as long as it was useful militarily. Well, Soviets were certainly in no mood to mess with Japan, because, two months later, on June 22, Germany broke its non-aggression (divide up the countries between us) pact with the Soviet Union. On that day Germany began a massive invasion of Russia.

We now move forward to describe the War against Japan, [301] which broke out in December, 1941. Japanese attacked Pearl Harbor on December 7, 1941. During this same time period, massive Japanese attacks were launched against the Philippines (which was aligned with Spain), [302] Wake Island, Guam, Malaya, Thailand, the international sections of Shanghai, and Midway.

On December 8, the Confederate States of America declared war on the Empire of Japan. The next day, the Confederate States and the Nationalist Chinese signed a joint military alliance committing to the destruction of Japan until it agreed to unconditional surrender on the home island and at all Empire military forces worldwide. Cooperative alliances were also signed with France, The Netherlands, Great Britain, Spain and Australia insuring that each were dedicated to the unconditional surrender of Japan, the withdrawal and return of all territory occupied by Japan and committing each to provide military support toward the defeat of Japan consistent with their individual abilities to allocate those resources. Confederates also signed a Memorandum of Understanding, which stipulated that the neutrality and non-aggression pact between the USSR and Japan would include a commitment that the Russians would stay out of China including Manchuria and Inner Mongolia. [303]

Also, on December 10, the United States of America declared war on Germany and Italy and began the long process of engaging its full military strength toward Allied victory in Europe. Why did the United States decide to go to war in Europe in response to an attack on the Confederate state of Hawaii?

Apparently, Japan's aggression in the Pacific had persuaded the United States that a new World War against Fascism was underway, that it could no longer stand aside, so now, it's military had to participate in defeating that evil in Europe. Yet, it had felt no responsibility to help Confederates.

Since late 1938, the Confederate States had been supporting Great Britain and France by producing and delivering military equipment and other supplies helpful to their national defenses. And the people of the Confederate States were eager to help defeat Nazi cruelty as much as possible. As the world knows, no country was more helpful in rescuing Jews from Nazi terror

---

[301] In truthful history the "War against Japan" is called the "Pacific War," a theater of "World War II." In our alternate history the "War against Japan" is far less of a "Pacific War," since Confederate military strategy was far less focused on fighting Japanese across much of the Pacific, island by island.

[302] Because Cuba had won its independence and become a Confederate state, there was no United States war against Spain. In truthful history, the Philippines were a U. S Territory. In our alternate history it had remained with Spain.

[303] The Russian-Japanese nonaggression pact is truthful history.

than was the Confederacy. Over one million would be resettled in the Confederate States, many during the early years before the threatened gas chambers were operating.

You will recall that, during World War I, the Confederacy had been a major supplier of military equipment to the British, and you will recall that, although Confederates had avoided sending troops to Europe during that conflict, their commitment at home to developing and producing the most advanced military equipment had persisted from the days of the War Between the States.

But Confederates had to make tough choices to enable them to defeat Japanese Imperialists in vast Asia. Since late 1938, the Confederate States had been supporting Great Britain and France with military equipment, petroleum fuels and lubricants, and related supplies, in and effort toward peace in Europe. Now, by necessity, Confederates had to discontinue military shipments to European allies in order to focus entirely on the demands of the War against Japan. So, in January 1942, Confederates cancelled all contracts for military equipment that had been ordered but not delivered to the European theater of war. The Confederate States and The United States agreed to cooperate as much as practical. In the Davis-Washington Accord of January 1942, the United States pledged to patrol the Atlantic from Virginia to Florida and the Confederate States pledged to patrol the Pacific along the states of California, Oregon and Washington.

So, in early December 1941, the Confederate States went to war in the Pacific against Fascist Japan and the United States went to war in Europe against Fascist Germany and Fascist Italy. By December 1941 the war in Europe had greatly progressed. Nazi Germany had already conquered eastward to Austria, Poland and Czechoslovakia. Early German advances had gained a lot of ground across Russia during the summer and fall. But in early December, 1941, with the onslaught of frigid winter weather, the Germans were still desperately attempting to take Moscow. On December 2, 1941, German troops had advanced within 15 miles of Moscow, but then the first blizzards hit. Unequipped for harsh winter weather (vehicles stopped working, clothing was inadequate, guns jammed, etc.), the Germans were forced to retreat. But Russians believed the Germans would be returning in April, recharged for another onslaught. This was the situation when Confederate diplomats proposed a limited alliance aimed at protecting the Soviet Union from invaders from the East. Desperate in Moscow, the Soviets quickly agreed to the Confederate proposal and notified the Chinese Nationalists and the Chinese Communists of the alliance that promised to keep Soviet armies out of China and Japan.

It had been long obvious that East Asia was erupting into an ever widening war and the Confederate State of Hawaii and the western reaches of the Confederate State of Russian America were clearly vulnerable.

But the Japanese military bit off far more than it could chew when it attempted to demolish the Confederate Fleet at the State of Hawaii, at Pearl Harbor, on December 7, 1941, with an air attack by Japanese carrier-based aircraft. The sneak attack did considerable damage, but much of the fleet managed to get out of the harbor and the dog-fights between opposing aircraft destroyed many incoming airplanes before they could dispatch their bombs.

Although the damage at Pearl Harbor was limited, Japanese conquest of the South Pacific advanced rapidly elsewhere. Within four months, through to April 9, 1942, Japanese forces had occupied Burma, Borneo, Hong Kong, the Solomon Islands, Singapore, Java, Sumatra, Andaman Islands, as well as the Philippines and the international sections of Shanghai. Furthermore, Japanese had sunk a Confederate aircraft carrier and a major warship, the Houston. Confederates were faced with a major decision -- should they fight Japan island by island in an attempt to wear down its navy and cut off its supply of crucial military raw materials, or should Confederates exercise the "China Option." The "China Option" was a plan for a massive amphibious landing into China that would allow Confederates to join with Chinese troops, push the Japanese back onto their home island and force surrender. The "China Option" took advantage of the earlier Confederate support of China in its five-year resistance against Fascist Japan (1937-1941). And that option avoided many battles across South Pacific islands and many encounters at sea with Japanese submarines and attack aircraft.

The "China Option" was chosen. [304]

On April 9, 1942, Confederates withdrew from the South Pacific and consolidated at Hawaii to prepare for Operation Brotherhood, the amphibious invasion of China at the Guangdong Province coast between Hong Kong and Shantou. From there, they would swing west to liberate Hong Kong; then proceed northward up through China, pushing the Japanese toward Korea and Manchuria. Chiang Kai-shek and the Nationalists promised to field 1,500,000 troops and their limited aircraft to join with incoming Confederates. Confederates planned to land 300,000 troops in sequential waves, provide overwhelming air support and defend against a counterattack by the Japanese navy. There were at the time 900,000 Japanese troops spread out within the occupied areas of China plus 430,000 defending the border with the Soviets, its traditional enemy. The Allies calculated that it would be difficult for Japan to concentrate its army against advancing Allied troops without losing control of the large regions that its army had been assigned to occupy. Therefore, Chinese were organizing local militia and supporting aircraft to take control of areas being vacated by the Japanese occupation forces that would be retreating to confront advancing liberation armies. Intelligence indicated that the Chinese were eager to unite with allied Confederates to drive off the hated Japanese murderers and rapists. And there were considerable Chinese feelings of goodwill toward Confederates because Nationalists and Confederates were both viewed as standing for diversity and liberty. Japan had made a mess of its occupation over the past five years. Operation Brotherhood held great promise.

By late July, 1942, Confederates were pulling out of Hawaii and Russian America to converge on Guangdong Province, China. George Smith Patton was assigned to lead the Joint Confederate-Chinese Command army. A brief biography of General Patton is appropriate.

General Patton had been born in 1885 near Los Angeles, Confederate South California. He was of Irish, Scots-Irish, English and Welsh ancestry. His roots, like this writer's went back to George Washington's great great grandfather, making us far distance cousins. His Patton ancestors had fought in the American Revolution and for Virginia in the War Between the States. His father, George Smith Patton, Sr., had graduated from Virginia Military Institute, become a lawyer and had a fine career in Los Angeles County. The son, our subject, also attended Virginia Military Institute and then obtained an appointment to the Confederate States Military Academy. He was based in London in World War I as an observer and in logistical efforts to ensure that Confederate military equipment reached the British. [305]

The Confederate Navy was led by Admiral Chester Nimitz.

---

[304] In truthful history, the United States military was divided between the war in Europe and the war in the Pacific, and was pressured to give priority to liberating the U. S. territory of the Philippines, which had been acquired, along with Puerto Rico, during the treaty with Spain that had given independence to Cuba. So the U. S. fought in the Pacific, island by island, to slowly liberate the South Pacific and Southeast Asia, denying Japan essential raw materials until the atomic bomb was ready to finally force unconditional surrender. The United States suffered 110,000 killed during fighting to liberate the Philippines, the Pacific islands and Southeast Asia.

[305] The history of General Patton's life up to World War I is truthful except that he was trained at West Point. He did see important military service in World War I.

Chester Nimitz was a Texan of German ancestry, born at Fredericksburg, Texas in February 1885. His grandfather had been a Confederate officer during the War Between the States. He graduated from the Confederate Naval Academy in 1905 and became a career naval officer. He was expert in diesel engines, submarine technology and underway refueling technology. During World War I he was Chief Engineer of a Confederate refueling ship that was engaged in keeping the Confederate navy ships on assignment in the Atlantic as it protected Confederate merchant marine vessels engaged in delivering supplies to the British. Admiral Nimitiz took command of the Confederate Pacific Fleet ten days after the attack on Pearl Harbor and remained in that position throughout the war against Japan. [306]

General Claire Lee Chennault has already been mentioned as the early leader of Confederate aircraft based in China, the famous "Flying Tigers." He was promoted to commander over all land-based aircraft in the War against Japan, ie., over the Confederate Army Air Corps, China Wing. A bit about General Chennault is appropriate.

Claire Lee Chennault was born in Commerce, North Texas in September 1893. His father was John Stonewall Jackson Chennault. He grew up in Louisiana and attended Louisiana State University where he received ROTC training. He learned to fly airplanes during the World War I years but, because the Confederacy was not at war, he never engaged in combat missions. However he was a pilot in support of Confederate efforts to support marine shipping to Great Britain and was mostly based in Bermuda. He was also a Confederate Air Corps procurement officer in London, facilitating parts procurement in support of the British Army Air Corp. He remained in the Confederate Army Air Corps and advanced primarily on his skills in pursuit aviation and in instructing other pilots. He excelled as a test pilot. He had true grit and drew the best out of his men. He led the first team of Confederate airmen to China and from there built the Chinese Nationalist Air Corps. [307]

The sea-land invasion into Guangdong Province involved 90,000 Confederates on the first day of operations, July 6, 1942. By the end of the month, all 300,000 Confederates were on land in Guangdong Province where they were joined by 400,000 Chinese troops. Hong Kong was liberated on August 10 and efforts were underway to defend Hong Kong from Japanese counterattack. [308]

The sweep north through China took the rest of the summer and into the fall months. By February 7, 1943, exactly 14 months after the attack on Pearl Harbor, Confederates had cleared the Japanese from the Yangtze and Yellow river valleys and were within 200 miles of Beijing. They had also liberated the Island of Taiwan (Formosa), which Japan had controlled since 1895. The front between the Japanese and the Confederate-Chinese troops had narrowed to 250 miles wide. From new airfields in China, Confederates were bombing Japanese positions in Korea in anticipation of soon liberating that country. Korea was very close to Japan, and from there

---

[306] In truthful history, the story about Admiral Nimitz matches our story rather well. Since the United States was at war during World War I, his was fully a war-time position. Ten days after Pearl Harbor, President Roosevelt appointed him to the equivalent United States Navy position in the Pacific Theater.

[307] In truthful history, Claire Lee Chennault was passed over for promotion in the mid 1930's and decided to resign in April 1937. Almost immediately, he was hired by Chiang Kai-shek's government to lead a team of volunteer airman to China. These men became the Flying Tigers International Squadron of mercenary pilots.

[308] In truthful history, the Allied landings in Europe, referred to as "D-Day" would take place on June 6, 1944, but the Germans were far more dug in on the European coast and much more formidable across Europe than the dispersed Japanese occupiers, so far more preparation was needed to weaken Germany before risking an invasion.

Confederate bombing runs could rapidly destroy Japanese industry, fuel reserves and military facilities. In February 1943 the joint Confederate-Chinese force numbered 1,300,000 fighting men, well-armed and well supplied.

Fighting slowed for the Chinese winter and most advances were attributed to air power exchanges. But by April 1, 1943 the Japanese were being push further north. By August 1, Japanese troops and citizens had withdrawn from Chinese territory, including vast Manchuria. Next would be the liberation of Korea, which the Japanese had occupied since 1895.

While the Confederate and Chinese armies were pushing Japanese out of China, the Confederate Navy was interdicting shipping of raw materials from the conquered areas of the South Pacific and also defending the China coast from Japanese counterattack. Success at this was just as important as success on the Chinese battlefield.

Japan did not have many troops in Korea and did not value its occupation as highly as it had Manchuria. Furthermore, the Korean people were eager to help drive out the hated Japanese occupiers. Japanese troops were driven out of Korea by January 4, 1944. [309] Now a more intense bombing of Japan began.

The unrelenting bombing of Japan was a terrifying thing to behold. First priority was destruction of the Mitsubishi aircraft plants, for the Japanese Zero fighter plane was the most deadly in its air force. Zero production was eliminated by March 7, 1944, exactly two years and three months after the bombing of Pearl Harbor. The superior Confederate bombsite allowed more precise targeting, so results were quite good. Japan was resorting to suicide missions where the airplane itself was rigged like a bomb. Those were one-way trips.

On September 4, 1944, China and the Confederate States demanded unconditional surrender of the Empire of Japan. Leaflet drops were frequent, explaining to the people that further resistance would be terrifying, but that surrender would be like surrendering to "Diverse Brothers Seeking New Friendships and Liberty for All." Japanese propaganda was losing its sting.

Of course the Japanese did not know much about the Confederate's "secret weapon," a super bomb rumored to have the force of thousands compressed into one.

The discovery of nuclear fission by German chemists Otto Hahn and Fritz Strassman in 1938 revealed that an atomic bomb was perhaps possible and physicists Lise Meitner of Austria and Otto Frisch of Austrian-British citizenship worked out the theory of atomic fission. Hahn, Meitner and Frisch were Jewish and Strassman hated the Nazi oppression and would secretly shelter a Jewish friend. So all were careful to make sure that news of a possible atomic fission bomb reached the Confederate States, long considered a friend of Jews and a country where diversity was honored. News did arrive, punctuated by the advocacy of respected physicists Leo Szilard, a Hungarian-born Jewish physicist; Eugene Wigner, a Hungarian-born Jewish physicist; and Albert Einstein, a German-born Jewish physicist. Both Wigner and Einstein had come to the Confederacy to stay clear of the Nazis. Szilard and Wigner wrote a letter in August, 1939 warning of the potential of an atomic fission bomb and Einstein delivered it to senior officials in the Confederate War Department. The logic behind their warning was quickly perceived -- and doubly so because it was presumed that Nazi Germany already knew about a potential atomic bomb.

---

[309] In truthful history, the U. S. did not use the fighting capacity of Korea as much as would the Confederacy. In truthful history, this mistake would leave open the door for a Communist Revolution in Korea, which would later become a new war that the United States would be forced to fight. That war in Korea ended in a truce. South Korea has prospered. North Korea remains a grave danger to world peace.

So, on October 9, 1939, the Confederate Government launched a well-funded program aimed at building an atomic bomb, if it could be done. First priority was to recruit from Germany and its neighbors as many good Jewish chemists, physicists and engineers as possible so as to create a brain drain among the Nazis and a brain flowering in the Confederacy. Second priority was to engage a diverse team of scientists and engineers to arrive at the best path to building an atomic bomb. Third priority was to acquire as much of the world supply of uranium as possible to have plenty for us and to deny it to others. The recruitment effort had born good fruit. By May 1940, it was agreed that the atomic bomb would be based on the fission of uranium U-235, and the largest supply of uranium ore was being mined in the Congo for Confederate use.

Uranium U-235 is an isotope of uranium with an atomic weight of 235, which occurs naturally in concentrations of about 0.7 percent, the balance being uranium of mostly the 238 atomic weight. Refining of the natural uranium isotope mix from the rocky ore would be straightforward chemistry and did not present a very big challenge. But enriching the isotope mix from 0.7 percent U-235 up to 89 percent U-235 was an enormous challenge because all of the uranium isotopes behaved identically in chemical reactions, preventing any chance for enrichment through chemistry, and they differed by less than 1 percent in physical reactions. Yet, there was no way to build an atomic bomb with much less than 89 percent enriched uranium U-235. To explode in an instant in a nuclear chain reaction, about 22 pounds of 89 percent rich uranium U-235 had to be formed instantly into a solid spherical ball. That meant that the 22 pounds had to be kept in two or more separate parts to keep it quiet, then suddenly rammed together to set off the chain reaction explosion. That too, seemed reasonably straightforward. The big problem was uranium U-235 enrichment.

In July 1940 the site for the uranium enrichment facility was chosen. It had good access to electric power and water. It was in east Tennessee at a rural area to be called Oak Ridge. Land was acquired for the enrichment plants, 28,000 acres of it. The chosen enrichment concept would transform the uranium into a gas -- uranium hexafluoride -- and sequentially pump the gas through a long series of chambers. Each chamber included its gas compressor pump and the mesh barrier through which the gas was forced to struggle. Being of slightly lighter molecular weight, slightly more of the 235 gas progressed through the mesh barrier and made it into the next, slightly richer chamber. On and on the uranium hexafluoride progressed, the slightly heavier gas (mostly U-238) being recycled back to the beginning stage while the slightly lighter 235 gas progressed forward, stage after stage, until 89 percent U-235 gas passed through the last stage. The finished plant consisted of 3,000 stages and was producing 89 percent rich U-235 gas by May 1943. Now enriched to 89 percent, the Uranium hexafluoride gas was chemically reduced to uranium metal and stored in small lumps to avoid unwanted accelerated fission.

The small lumps of 89 percent rich U-235 metal were fabricated into a bomb in a research facility in a desert region of New Mexico. The bomb consisted of a modified sphere of 89 percent U-235 metal from which a cylindrical plug had been left void. Because the modified sphere contained only half of the 22 pounds of U-235 metal, it was insufficiently compact to spark a chain reaction by itself. Likewise, the cylindrical plug of U-235 metal was too long and narrow to spark a chain reaction by itself. But when the cylindrical plug would be fired like a rifle bullet into the void in the modified sphere, the combination would suddenly become a perfect solid 22 pound sphere and the instantaneous resulting chain reaction would detonate as a bomb of awesome power. [310]

By August 1944, five atomic bombs had been fabricated and one had been tested in the desert of New Mexico. [311]

Let us take a close look at the status of the War against the Axis powers in Europe during September 1944, the month unconditional surrender was demanded of the Empire of Japan. At this time the war in Europe was still raging, but Germany was clearly on the defensive and generally retreating. Of greatest concern for Confederates and Chinese was assurance that continuing German pressure on the Soviets was forcing them to remain fighting in Europe and to keep away from the War against Fascist Japan. In September 1944 the Soviets were fully occupied, on the offensive, moving westward against German positions. During late August and the month of September Soviets invaded Romania and took the capital, Bucharest, they agreed to a cease-fire with Finland, and they moved into Estonia and they took Latvia. Yet, much fighting remained. It would be seven months before Adolph Hitler would commit suicide and Germany would surrender. [312]

Our story now returns to East China, Korea and the buildup to the joint Chinese-Confederate invasion of Japan – an event that the Atomic Bomb would make unnecessary. During August and September, a combined Chinese-Confederate army was organizing to invade Japan at the northwest part of the main island, Honshu, along its Korea Strait coast between Nagato and Matsue. The invasion force would depart from the southern tip of Korea, from harbors such as Yosu, Pusan and P'ohangat, cross the Korea Straight (about 200 miles) and make landfall in various spots after heavy bombardment designed to take out shoreline resistance. This military buildup was no secret. Japan knew it was coming, and knew its ability to resist would, in the long haul, be futile. The Confederate Navy under Admiral Nimitz – a powerful force of submarines, destroyers, aircraft carriers and navy airmen -- had total control of the Korea Strait. The Army Air Corps, under General Chennault was punishing Japan with horrific bombing runs, softening up the region, including the manufacturing cities of Hiroshima and Nagasaki. Yet the Japanese were reluctant to surrender.

They needed to see what an atomic bomb attack would look like. Some argued for dropping the bomb on Hiroshima. Others argued for a demonstration attack that would kill a few thousand, not hundreds of thousands. The Confederates were making atomic bombs rather rapidly now, so it was decided that they should start with a demonstration attack and, if Japan remained defiant, then resort to attacking Hiroshima. A target was selected for the demonstration. It was in a rural area halfway between the towns of Nanso and Kasusa in the middle of the Boso

---

[310] The history of the atomic bomb is truthful with regard to the many key Jewish physicists involved, with regard to the enrichment of Uranium 235 at Oak Ridge, Tennessee, with regard to the sphere with hole and cylindrical plug, and with regard to the New Mexico site. In our alternate history, plutonium was not involved and the path to the atomic bomb was streamlined to accelerate the U-235 bomb schedule.

[311] In our alternate history, the Confederate development of an atomic bomb proceeded a little faster than it did in truthful history. Because of the danger of spies, the United States was not involved in the development of the atomic bomb according to our alternate history.

[312] In truthful history at this time the war in the Pacific was far from over. In September 1944, the Japanese occupied much of China, Manchuria and Korea as well as The Philippines, Iwo Jima and Okinawa. The Burma Road into western China remained blocked by Japanese troops and the first of 2,257 Japanese suicide airplane attacks had just begun. It would be seven months before Japan would surrender unconditionally in August 1945. In truthful history, on August 6, 1945, an atomic bomb would be dropped on Hiroshima. On August 8, Soviets would invade Manchuria and began a long process of supporting Chinese Communists in their upcoming war against the Chinese Nationalists. On August 9, an atomic bomb would be dropped on Nagasaki. On August 14, Japan would surrender.

Peninsula, across Tokyo Bay, 25 miles south of Tokyo. It would be a horrifying sight viewed from Tokyo and the extent of the destruction would be hard to hide from the public.

General Chennault's Army Air Corps bomber dropped an atomic bomb in the middle of Boso Peninsula at high noon on Monday, September 25, 1944. The Confederate propaganda campaign intensified. Continuous radio broadcasting spread the message and explained the concept of atomic power. "We do not want to kill you, but unless you surrender without conditions, the killing will be horrific." A rebellion began in many areas of Japan, among civilians and the military. Troops began to destroy their weapons, burn their uniforms and pretend to be civilians. Secret negotiations began in Nanking, China. A token concession was arranged to allow Japan to save face in its surrender: the Emperor was allowed ceremonial status and punishment of war criminals was limited to 10 years in prison and loss of citizenship.

On October 9, 1944, Japan surrendered without any other conditions. The formal transfer of power to the occupying Confederate-Chinese authorities took place in Tokyo Bay on October 16.

Although Japan surrendered at home without conditions, it understood that it was surrendering all of the land in the Pacific and in Southeast Asia that it had taken since beginning its military aggression in the Pacific in December 1941. Over the course of six months, through March 1945, all Japanese forces in the South Pacific and Southern Asia were gathered up and returned to the main Japanese islands. Generally Japanese returned to the homeland, but equipment, vehicles and supplies were left behind to be used by others. Facilities, such as rubber plantations, oil fields and refineries, were returned to previous owners or to restored local governments. Confederate military oversaw the restoration and were helpful in minimizing the in-fighting that so often follows a leadership vacuum. [313]

The political and physical reconstruction of Japan was overseen by the Confederate-Chinese Reconstruction Commission that was designed to place Chinese in the public eye but to reserve major decisions to the Confederates. In this way, it appeared that people of Asian ancestry were transforming Japan's political structure, but it was really people of European ancestry who were calling the shots. Steadily, Japan was organized into twelve states each of which held primary power, the remaining power residing in a Japanese Confederate government whose power was strictly limited by a firm Japanese Constitution. Most power resided in the states. Freedom of religion was assured. Japanese military was limited to defensive purposes. Japan would not be allowed to develop an atomic bomb although atomic electrical power generation would be permitted.

The next issue before the Chinese Nationalist government of Chiang Kia-shek was the transition of the Chinese government from a war footing to a limited Confederate government where most of the power resided in the provinces. This would take time. In fact, about two years would be required to take care of urgent needs of the people: to ensure adequate food, clothing and housing. The surrender of Japan took place in October 1944. It would take until October 1946 for China to begin serious debate about the Chinese Confederate Constitution and the constitutions for the several Chinese Provinces. Of course the Chinese Communists attempted to destroy these efforts by the Chinese Nationalists, but they were not successful, remaining

---

[313] In truthful history, the United States military adopted a strategy of sweeping the Japanese out of the South Pacific and Southeast Asia by force, island by island, naval engagement by naval engagement, ever growing closer to the major objective, launching its attack on Japan itself. In this alternate history, the Confederate Navy engages the Japanese at sea, eventually destroying their ability to resupply Japan, while simultaneously fighting alongside the Chinese to drive out Japanese forces in Asia. In both histories, the atomic bomb eventually forces surrender. In truthful history 4,000,000 Chinese troops perished as well as 18,000,000 Chinese civilians; 1,740,000 Japanese troops perished as well as 393,000 Japanese civilians; 111,606 American troops perished.

confined for the most part to sections north of the historic Great Wall of China. By July 1947, constitutions were approved for the central government of the Confederate Provinces of China, and respective provincial constitutions were in place. China declared itself a remade Confederation of Provinces on December 1, 1947. Chiang Kai-Shek was elected President.

But the Chinese Communists refused to accept defeat. With the help of Soviet Russia, they launched an internal civil war against Chiang Kai-Shek's Confederate government. The war was brutal, but rather brief. There was a consensus in the Chinese heartland that the people of the North ought to be allowed to go their own way. There would be a Communist country on the Chinese northern border either way: either Soviet Russia or a strip that would be called Communist China, or the Peoples Republic of China, which they liked to call themselves. So, in the peace settlement of January 1, 1949 the Peoples Republic of China was carved out of the northern rim of the Confederate Provinces of China, to become a Communist country unto itself, with obvious close political ties to Soviet Russia. The northern country included all land north of 38 degrees latitude and east of 110 degrees longitude. This meant that the Communist had control of their capital city of Beijing and its port city of Tianjin and all of Manchuria as well as part of the Yellow River Valley that lay east of 110 degrees longitude. The eastern portion of the Great Wall, built long ago to keep out the Mongols, was in Communist China and the western part was in Confederate China. West of 110 degrees longitude, the Confederate Chinese border extended northward to sparsely settled, Soviet-controlled Mongolia and further west to Russia. Going counter-clockwise from the Confederate Chinese northwestern border with Soviet Russia, the border briefly touched Afghanistan, then enjoyed a long boundary with Tibet, followed by borders with Burma, and then French Indo-China (now Laos and Vietnam).

The remaining country, known today as the Confederate Provinces of China, is a vast area of 2,565,000 square miles, and contains 24 provinces in which the individual governments (provincial and local) retain essential powers. It is home to 1,131,000 people who enjoy both liberty and economic success. The British returned administrative control of Hong Kong to Guangdong Province many years go. The Confederate capital is located on the Yangtze River in a small non-provincial region where the provinces of Jiangsu and Anhui meet. The capital is known as Sun Yat-sen.

Communist China, by comparison, consists of 700,000 square miles and 7 provinces. It is home to 230,000 people who lack liberty, and, except for those well-positioned in Party ranks, lack economic success. Central government control is absolute. The Communist Party is in full control. [314]

Although Manchuria became a major part of Communist China following the defeat of the Japanese occupiers, neighboring Korea regained its independence. There were efforts by Soviet Communists and Chinese Communists to incite a Communist revolution in Korea, but none ever gained traction. The Korean people seem to have been naturally drawn to the Confederate ideals of individual liberty and harmonious diversity. Confederate Christian missionaries had come to Korea in sizable numbers and exerted positive influence early on. The Korean government

---

[314] In truthful history, the Chinese Communists became too powerful for the Chinese Nationalists to resist, and they gained control over all of China, Manchuria and Tibet in a Chinese civil war that began in 1946 and ended with Chiang Kai-Shek and the Nationalist government retreating to the island of Taiwan. On October 1, 1949, Mao Zedong proclaimed the Peoples Republic of China. Our alternate history enables successful defense of all but northeast China because the Soviets were too occupied in Europe to rush into Manchuria and Korea before the first atomic bomb was dropped on September 25, 1944, and Chiang's forces were far more prepared militarily and politically to win the contest.

became much like the re-established Japanese government that was orchestrated by the Confederate-Chinese Reconstruction Commission. [315] [316]

Along the southern boundary with China, French Indochina transitioned to three independent Confederate-style countries: Vietnam, Laos and Cambodia. [317]

## Thursday Evening Selected Diary Postings

Diary note by Conchita Rezanov said, "Supper with Robert Lee. He is so very nice. Looked so pitiful complaining about being behind in figuring out an analysis of his essay, "Is Davis no bigger than it ought to be?" I guess that can be a tough nut to boil down into an analytical essay. I think he is taking it too seriously as a mathematical analysis of jobs, office space, square miles of land, public museums, government buildings, monuments and parklands, etc. I offered to help in the morning. He just needs to be less mathematical and more emotional. "Is Davis no bigger than it ought to be?" Answer: "It is only a big as it needs to be." We are not a nation. We are a Republic made up of 27 States, which are sovereign except for foreign affairs. Republics of limited constitutional authority do not need a big bureaucracy. He just needs the woman's touch."

Diary note by Robert Lee said: "I feel exhausted over this morning's lecture on the War against Fascist Japan. My grandfather, Robert Edward Lee, Jr., commanded a battalion of marines in the first wave of landings on the China coast and the subsequent advance northward

---

[315] Bertil Haggman, a Swedish historian with exceptional knowledge of world history, including the American Civil War, reviewed *The CSA Trilogy* manuscript prior to final editing and publication, and encouraged my work with the following comment concerning the chapter on Asia. He wrote: "The development in Asia during the Second World War in relation to the Confederacy is in my opinion one of the best parts of the manuscript. It is an excellent idea to let the Kuomintang government remain in power thanks to a Confederate intervention in China at an early stage, leaving Mao and his Communists with a small territory in northern China. In truthful history, the American government accepted Communist advancement in China at the end of the war. Millions were slaughtered in China in a civil war and millions suffered at the hands of the Communist regime after 1949. Earlier, Chiang had been described by the Soviets and pro-Soviet advisors to the Roosevelt Administration as corrupt, despotic and collaborating with the Japanese, which was incorrect. Among the pro-Communist advisors in Washington, DC at the time was Owen Lattimore. Then there was the "Ameriasia Magazine," which was concerned with U. S. Policy in the Pacific. Its publisher was businessman Philip Jaffe, born in Russia. For more see: M. Stanton Evans and Herbert Romerstein, *Stalin's Secret Agents – The Subversion of Roosevelt's Government*, published in 2012.

[316] In truthful history and with agreement from the United States, while its two atomic bombs (August 6 and 9, 1945) were forcing quick Japanese surrender (August 14), Soviet troops crossed into Manchuria (August 9), rapidly advancing and taking control from departing Japanese. Almost immediately, these Soviet troops continued into northern Korea, also mopping up remaining Japanese control. At the same time United States troops were moving northward from the southern tip of Korea. The two armies met at 38 degrees latitude, as agreed. But the Soviets were not satisfied to be overseeing half of Korea. They wanted all of Korea to be a Soviet satellite. Five years later, in June 1950, Korean Communists, now trained and armed by the Soviet and Chinese Communists, poured into the southern half of Korea. The United States resisted, landed a large army into South Korea and forced a boundary settlement in July 1953 (technically a cease fire armistice). The boundary, near 38 degrees latitude, remains today, separating a troublesome and tragic Communist dictatorship, and South Korea, a prosperous and rather happy democracy.

[317] In truthful history, the United States military was heavily involved in fighting the Japanese in French Indochina during the Pacific War. The United States Office of Strategic Services (OSS) supported the Vietnamese Communist leader, Ho Chi Minh, and his guerilla forces in their fight against Japanese occupation forces based on the theory that "an enemy of my enemy is my friend." Having suffered defeat by the Germans, the French were unable to fight the Japanese, but Ho Chi Minh's Communists could, and the OSS provided them with weapons and help. In the power vacuum that followed, Ho Chi Minh proclaimed, in September 1945, that North Vietnam was an independent country, not bound to French control. He pretended that his North Vietnam was to be a democratic country, but as the years went by and following the Communist takeover of China, Ho Chi Minh transitioned North Vietnam into a brutal Communist dictatorship. The French were forced to pull out of Indochina in 1954. Then Ho Chi Minh's troops, with Soviet and Chinese support, invaded South Vietnam and the United States became embroiled in the Vietnamese War. It begin on a small scale in 1955, escalated to a massive United States military engagement from 1963 to withdrawal in 1973, and concluded with the fall of Saigon to the Communist invaders in 1975.

toward Japanese invasion forces and Korea. My family has horror stories I would rather forget, if I could. But Granddad made it back home and that made me possible. Had supper with Tina Sharp. Now there is a lady that can tell you all about how the Confederates invented and constructed the world's first atomic bomb. I am just glad that atomic power, such as at Comanche Peak Nuclear Station, exploits the peaceful harnessing of the atom. Atomic bombs and Hydrogen bombs are too terrible to contemplate. But if the bad guys have them, we need them as a deterrent. Shows the importance of being sufficiently powerful at conventional warfare to enable the good guys to defeat the bad guys before having to resort to the horrors of nuclear exchange. I am so glad that we were able to force Japan's surrender by dropping a "demonstration" bomb in a relatively remote Japanese area (by Confederate measure that is; nothing in Japan is remote). Instead of a several hundred thousand, we got the message across by killing only about 25 thousand. Saved a lot of lives. Granddad told me the Japanese were so fanatical that they would have fought to the last person if the Confederate and Chinese armies had been forced to land invasion forces on Japanese soil to force their surrender. Granddad knew the score, for he commanded a battalion of Confederate marines. Granddad and Dad have both travelled to China since. Seen the places where major battles were fought. The Confederate Provinces of China are an amazing country. I want to visit once with Dad, before he passes on."

Diary note by Benedict Juárez said: "War is Hell and I know my great-great-great-grandfather thought it so. He had learned the importance of avoiding a devastating war in every way possible – the importance of strategic retreat, of being mobile but yet in control of that for which you are responsible. He always strove to sustain his legitimate Government of Mexico, even when it was reduced to only a few boxes of documents in a carriage drawn by horses, darting here and there. Then, when Confederates came forth with help and encouragement for Mexican State Secession and statehood within the Confederate States, my ancestor was positioned perfectly to act on the idea. He made it happen. I like to compare my great-great-great-grandfather to Chiang Kai-shek. Chiang moved his government when appropriate and avoided becoming trapped by either the Japanese or the Communists. He and key supporters struck deals with the Confederate States and its military and industrial leaders. The Confederate decision to support the Chiang government and join forces to defeat the fanatical Japanese by helping to drive them out of China and Korea was a good one -- but most importantly, it prepared the way for that great and massive country, the Confederate Provinces of China, whose people were the great and long-lasting key beneficiaries of that decision. The Russians were too tied down in Europe, fighting Nazi Germany for too long; they came east too late to effectively assist the Chinese Communist. By the time the Russians were in play in East Asia, it was too late. Today, Communist China is just a backwater in the story of the continent. What if China had been run over by the Communists and the Chiang government driven off the continent, say, onto the island of Taiwan? Goodnight diary!"

Diary note by Emma Lunalilo said, "Perhaps yesterday's long and hard swim helped me get through today's lecture. But it remains hard to recall what my Hawaiian family went through during the War against Fascist Japan. Thank God for the help of the Chinese Nationalists and for those Jewish scientists who enabled Confederates to be the first to produce the atomic bomb. What if Fascist Japan or Fascist Germany had done that?"

Diary note by Isaiah Montgomery said, "An important but seldom mentioned aspect of our War against Fascist Japan is how the Confederate troops were integrated within companies and battalions. In the same units were men of all racial backgrounds. This war was the first major military fight encountered by the Confederate States since the Great Expansion. Unlike the United States, we had avoided fighting in the First Great War in Europe, although our military weapons industry had a lot to do with the victory of those who defeated Germany. So, the War against Fascist Japan was the expanded Confederacy's first major military engagement. By 1940 there was little thought of separating soldiers into companies based on race. Integration was a good thing, and the Chinese understood it was a good thing, too. Perhaps it helped them to understand that people of diverse backgrounds can work together for the good of all."

Diary note by Marie Saint Martin said, "Good rehearsal this afternoon. Will be ready on July 4th."

# Part 3, Chapter 8, Day 26 – Overview of Underlying Confederate Principles, 1949 to Today -- Class Lecture, Friday, July 1, 2011

When the twelve young men and women arrived for Friday's morning lecture, they were puzzled at the outset as Professor Davis seemed to assume they had personally lived through the most recent 60 years of our history. They looked at each other as Professor Davis began, exchanging surprised expressions, thinking "I am only 25 years old" or something similar. But it was not long before they settled down and began listening to the morning lecture. Professor Davis had begun this way.

Many who will be watching you all presenting your respective essays, explaining what makes the Confederate States "The Greatest Country on Earth," will be old enough to have lived through the 1950's and on through the first decade of this century, a sixty-year span. For you and those who have not -- your parents and their parents -- probably did. Therefore, it seems wise to keep this chapter to a minimum and redirect the reader away from technology advances over the past six decades and toward underlying principles. After all, for those who have lived the history, there seems to be little need to retell it. So, instead of presenting a comprehensive narrative about the most recent 60-year experiences in Confederate society and governance, and about Confederate advances in technology, manufacturing and commerce over those six decades, I will be presenting some underlying Confederate principles that have supported the Confederate quality of life we enjoy today. We Confederates are a remarkably diverse society and we believe we have harnessed that feature to best advantage for all citizens. So, a bit more about Confederate diversity over the past 60 years seems appropriate.

## Human Diversity

A lot has been said already in this historical narrative about our Confederate States being home to a diverse population. A previous lecture presented the most recent numbers, based on the 2010 Confederate Census:

- Total Confederate population:  328,164,836
- People of European ancestry:  73.1 percent
- People of African ancestry:  16.0 percent
- People of Native ancestry:  10.2 percent
- People of Asian ancestry:  0.7 percent

The Confederate States have experienced far greater population growth than has our neighbor to the north. The population count in the United States 2010 census was only 175,426,391 – a number equal to only 53.5 percent of the Confederate population. When we look at population density, we find 328,164,836 Confederates living on 2,412,215 square miles (including vast and harsh Russian America), a density average of 136 persons per square mile. That is more concentrated than found in the United States, where 175,426,931 people live on 2,000,638 square miles – a density of 88 persons per square mile. Both population density numbers are comfortable, considering that the density in India is 953 persons per square mile and in Germany, 593 persons per square mile. In the Confederate Provinces of China, density averages 574 persons per square mile, and ranges from an average of 1,412 persons per square mile in Guangdong and Henan provinces, to 794 in Hubei Province, to 34 in sparsely populated far-western Xinjiang Province. By way of contrast, two notable countries support far less population densities than does the Confederate States or the United States: the density in Brazil is only 62, in Russia only 21.

So we Confederates still have a lot of room to grow, but growth rates over the next generation (2010 to 2044) are projected to decline. Family size is expected to decline further and the Confederate Congress has set a lower immigration target: a 12 percent 30-year immigration quota for the generation we are now beginning. Furthermore, having exceeded the diversity goal of around 70 percent of the population being of European ancestry, the immigration doors are now opened wider for other racial and ethnic groups. But emphasis remains on recruiting immigrants who have the skills and values needed to contribute well to our country, and we continue to ensure that our borders and coastlines are protected from unwanted illegal immigrants.

You have also read about how our country's success-with-diversity reputation has encouraged others around the world to replicate our experiences. An important example is found in the Confederate Provinces of China, home to the largest population on earth. To outsiders, China might seem to be populated by a uniform Asian people, but upon close inspection, there is actually considerable diversity there.

On the other hand, two Asian friends of the Confederate States manage to be successful with a rather uniform population: the Republic of Korea and Japan. So, diversity when well managed is a positive for a country. But countries where citizens are racially uniform, such a Korea and Japan, seem to do quite well without diversity.

Understanding human diversity is not that difficult for the average observer, but sometime the truth hurts. Why do people of African ancestry dominate in athletics? Why do Europeans and Asians dominate in mental excellence? Why do some groups embrace a strong work ethic and others seem not to care, eagerly accepting the dole? The more science studies the nature of diversity within mankind, the more it confirms that racial background is slightly more influential than family and community environment when it comes to determining the outcome of any one individual from birth to death. So what does this all mean to Confederates today, here in the year 2011? It means that Confederates are correct in demanding that the gift of citizenship in our country is a gift worthy of handing out with discernment. Our ancestors built this great country, and, to them, to their descendants and to future generations, we are obligated to ensure that our country remains successful and that it be a beacon of hope, attracting the especially capable from around the globe. It means that we are correct in designing our education system to fit the needs of our diverse population, matching challenges to one's ability and making every effort to help every citizen, growing up, become the best that he or she can be. It means that we are correct in asking that those allowed to vote contribute to the cost of operating governments at the local, state and Confederate level. It means that we are correct in honoring every Confederate citizen as worthy of our friendship and respect, no matter what he or she has or has not accomplished. All are worthy. Some are more successful than others. The gifted are honored. Those of few gifts are encouraged and helped as help can be given. For more on this subject, I recommend *The Nature of Human Diversity within the Confederate States*, by Karl Winestein, published by Atlanta Press, 2007. [318]

We are all looking forward to Isaiah Benjamin Montgomery's essay titled "The Importance of Understanding Human Diversity."

---

[318] In truthful history this book does not exist. However, two truthful books are suggested. One is *The Bell Curve, Intelligence and Class Structure in American Life*, by Richard J. Herrnstein and Charles Murray, 1994. The other is *Understanding Creation and Evolution*, by Howard Ray White, 2018.

# Individual Liberty and State Rights

It remains difficult to tell the story of Confederate Individual Liberty and State Rights without first clearing our conversation of concerns about the institution of slavery, which had begun in the early colonial days of North America and persisted in the Confederate States upon its creation. So let's cover that subject first. I refer to the original Confederate Constitution. [319]

Constitutional regulations over ownership of slaves of African ancestry are no longer applicable today. Of course, this issue was very important in 1861 when the Confederate Constitution was written and ratified. The basic concept was that the Confederate Government was not allowed to legislate over issues concerning ownership of slaves or obligations of the owner and of the slave, one to the other. Those issues were firmly to be controlled by the several States, each acting independently or through voluntary joint cooperation. The Constitution prohibited importation of bonded Africans from all areas in the world except from areas within the United States where slaves were permitted to live (The United States exception was allowed at the time in hopes that slaves and owners in Delaware, Maryland, Kentucky and Missouri would be permitted to relocate southward into a Confederate state.) The situation changed after the Montreal Treaty, which codified the boundary between the Confederate States and the United States and established the Confederate procedure for admitting African Americans into the several states, ensuring that those that were already free were successfully resettled, and overseeing the brief indenture and eventual emancipation of those that were not yet free. The Constitution stated:

- "The importation of Negroes of the African race from any foreign country, other than the slaveholding States or Territories of the United States of America, is hereby forbidden; and Congress is required to pass such laws as shall effectually prevent the same."

- "Congress shall also have power to prohibit the introduction of slaves from any State not a member of, or Territory not belonging to, this Confederacy."

The Confederate Government was responsible for one issue involving bonded Africans. As long as they accompanied their owner, they were permitted to travel among the several Confederate States. And any bonded African that ran away to a sister State was to be apprehended and returned to the State where his or her owner lived. But the Confederate Government would take no action to emancipate a slave or change the terms of his or her bondage, for the power to establish or change those regulations concerning bonded Africans resided in each State alone.

- "The citizens of each State shall be entitled to all the privileges and immunities of citizens in the several States; and shall have the right of transit and sojourn in any State of this Confederacy, with their slaves and other property; and the right of property in said slaves shall not be thereby impaired."

- "No slave or other person held to service or labor in any State or Territory of the Confederate States, under the laws thereof, escaping or lawfully carried into another, shall, in consequence of any law or regulation therein, be discharged from such service or labor; but shall be delivered up on claim of the party to whom such slave belongs; or to whom such service or labor may be due."

---

[319] All references to the original Confederate Constitution in this book are truthful history.

- "No bill of attainder, ex post facto law, or law denying or impairing the right of property in Negro slaves shall be passed." (This pertained to Confederate law, not State law.)

Another issue prevalent in the first years of the Confederacy was government control over the National Territories. That issue was covered in the original Confederate Constitution.

Regulations concerning governance over Territories, should any be acquired, were specified. These would be relevant when considering land between Texas and the Pacific, which became the States of New Mexico, Arizona and South California. This would also apply to the Indian Territory, which became the State of Sequoyah. The admissions of the Seceded Mexican States, Russian America, Cuba and Hawaii were all by individual treaties between independent countries, so territory law never applied. In the case of admission by treaty, the governing policy toward bonded Africans was to let each newly admitted State decide for itself. As you know the Seceded Mexican States, Russian America and Hawaii did not allow African slavery. The Constitution permitted division of Texas into four states with the approval of both the State of Texas and the Confederate Congress. A Territory held by the Confederacy was to allow immigration of African slaves and owners in the Territory Stage. Of course, once statehood was granted to a Territory its new State government would choose to allow or disallow slavery, if applicable, thereafter regulating the respective obligations of slave and owner and any pathway to emancipation. The Constitution said:

- "Other States may be admitted into this Confederacy by a vote of two-thirds of the whole House of Representatives and two-thirds of the Senate, the Senate voting by States; but no new State shall be formed or erected within the jurisdiction of any other State, nor any State be formed by the junction of two or more States, or parts of States, without the consent of the Legislatures of the States concerned, as well as of the Congress."

- "The Confederate States may acquire new territory; and Congress shall have power to legislate and provide governments for the inhabitants of all territory belonging to the Confederate States, lying without the limits of the several States; and may permit them, at such times, and in such manner as it may by law provide, to form States to be admitted into the Confederacy. In all such territory the institution of Negro slavery, as it now exists in the Confederate States, shall be recognized and protected by Congress and by the Territorial government; and the inhabitants of the several Confederate States and Territories shall have the right to take to such Territory any slaves lawfully held by them in any of the States or Territories of the Confederate States."

But this legal wording with regard to slavery in our Confederate Constitution only explains part of that history. The more important part of that history is the outcome. Every year following our successful independence, the percentage of persons of color who lived as slaves declined as more and more were put on suitable pathways to independent living. The result was a happy and successful population of Confederate citizens of full-to-partial African ancestry. And their contribution to our country has been, generation, after generation, consistently very important to our success as a whole -- a major reason we are considered the Greatest Country on Earth. Furthermore, they fully enjoy the benefits of Individual liberty and State Rights.

Without a doubt, the most remarkable fact about Confederate history over its first 150 years is the persistent adherence to the original commitment to Individual Liberty and State Rights in the face of a global transition to strong central governments and growing restrictions on personal freedoms, which became prevalent after the First World War and accelerated after the 1940's European War. During the last 60 years the citizens of the United States, living just to our north, have lost even more of the liberties enjoyed before the War Between the States -- by 2011 perhaps 90 percent of those liberties have been lost.

Permit me to begin by describing the limits on Individual Liberty and State Rights in the country to our immediate north, the United States. For them, over the past sixty years, the United States Constitution has become even more of a "living" document: a worthless piece of paper that seems sadly irrelevant to the rulings being handed down by their Supreme Court and their lower courts, where appointed judges often exert more lawmaking power than elected legislators. Much of United States industry cannot compete with foreign companies because of oppressive rules that regulate everything from the environment, to labor union authority. Individual and corporate tax policies are so manipulative that they stifle progress, while defeating the goals they claim to be supporting. Its "civil rights" movement has run amuck giving "protected status" to every minority class that politicians have been able to invent: race (of course), women (minority?), age (the young or the old), disabilities (physical, mental or self-inflicted), sexual behavior (every perversion), relative wealth (the so-called poor as government chooses to define that class). As a result, many in the United States find ways to manipulate the "system" and live off the "dole" – with lots of lawyers to help them, too. The legal profession dominates life there to a far greater extent than before the 1940's European War. There it seems like almost every issue is litigated, and lawyers get most of the money. Lawyers control the legislature and the courts, writing laws and handing down rulings that facilitate more and more litigation – and related profitable "legal work." A major cost of most businesses in the United States is the cost of avoiding litigation and paying attorney expenses.

Having now described the situation to our North, allow me to present the corresponding situation here in the Confederate States. The political/legal culture in the Confederate States is dramatically different. Even today, sixty years after the War against Japan, the Confederate Constitution still means what it says. If the Confederate Supreme Court rules in a way that appears to exceed the power granted by our Confederate Constitution, a State Supreme Court can challenge that ruling and can nullify its effect in that State for a period of seven years, giving ample time for the Confederate Congress or sister States to consider a Constitutional Amendment that would decide the contested ruling. The contesting State must only bow down and submit to such a ruling, if no disallowing amendment is ratified after seven years. Furthermore, in constitutional law, precedent is insignificant. Constitutionality questions must be considered against the language in the Constitution as amended without reference to precedent. As of 2011, the Confederate Constitution contains 43 amendments, added over time in recognition of advances in social, criminal and civil interactions, technological inventions, business practices, transportation advances, etc. By attentiveness to the need for amendments, the Confederacy has been successful in insisting that courts follow the letter of constitutional law and avoid legislating from the bench. In this way, Confederates have retained their tradition of Individual Liberty and State Rights.

Our final chapter features Marie Saint Martin's essay, "The Importance of Ensuring Individual Liberty and State Rights." This will complete the story for you.

A note to the reader is now appropriate:

During this morning, Professor Davis presented important information about all twelve subjects that the essayists will be addressing before the television cameras during Monday's celebration. But space in this book is only being allocated for his presentation on three of those twelve subjects. For the other nine, you will learn the essentials when you read the essays in the final chapter. The third subject taken from Professor Davis's morning lecture now follows.

## Confederate Schools, Colleges and Universities Focus on Educating for Student Success

Over the past 100 years, education in the Confederate States has changed dramatically. At the outset, most people in our country were rural, and, for most, to be educated meant having a modest ability with reading, writing and arithmetic. Today, education is comprehensive and tailored to meet the needs of a diverse population in which the vast majority no longer work in agriculture.

There is insufficient space in this history to tell the story of how Confederate education has evolved over these past 100 years -- we only have space to present the status of Confederate education today, in the year 2011. So only the basic structure of Confederate education will be presented below. For a discussion of why we believe ours is an exemplary education system, you must await Amanda Lynn Washington's essay on the subject -- the 12th and last of the essays to be presented. I now begin.

Confederate educational efforts today are diverse with regard to class organization; instructor talents; student goals, interests and capabilities; offered curriculum, and financial support. Perhaps most responsible for this diversity is the absence of control from the Confederate Government in Davis. This means that the highest level of governmental regulation stops at the various State governments, thereby introducing minor but significant variations when comparing a State to her sisters, which seems to facilitate healthy competition to serve best the needs of the people of each State. The natural racial and cultural diversity among young people of school age calls for diversity in educational methods and goals, while still affording every student the opportunity to achieve his or her highest educational potential. Of course, some children are home schooled, but discussion of that is beyond today's presentation.

Today, some students began attendance in preschool, but this not universal. All must begin attendance in first grade upon reaching the age of six years. In every public school, all first and second grade classes are composed of a student mix that reflects the community-wide student body as a whole. There is no segregation by perceived ability at that young age. On the other hand, in cities, busing students long distances across town is avoided, for the concept of community schools is followed, although this practice does result in different racial mix ratios among the communities that make up a city. Segregation by ability begins a mild intervention with grades 3 and 4. This allows the slow students to focus on mastering fundamentals and frees the brighter students to advance faster to more complex studies. The next segregation by ability takes place with grades 5 and 6. This is an important sorting out of the student body, for few who were placed in slow classes in grades 3 and 4 will ever leap frog into the advanced classes for grades 7 and 8, although there are exceptions. By grades 7 and 8 the student body has been sorted out into the slow group and the fast group. But the sort is never permanent. Students can always advance from the slow group to the fast group at annual testing. Likewise, students in the fast group must drop down into the slow group if annual testing shows an inability to keep pace with fellow students. Furthermore, over the course of their school career, students can be advanced as much as two grades when testing exceptionally high. Slow students can be retained in a grade as much as two times. This policy of class segregation on ability, for skipping grades and for being held back, results in a Confederate education that challenges the brighter students and nurtures the slower students. At the end of the 8th grade, student ages range between 12 years and 16 years, and 90 percentile ability ranges between a standardized grade level ability of 10th grade for the brightest in the advance classes to 6th grade for the slowest in the slow classes.

Now let us focus on Confederate high schools. Here, every student is classified as being advanced and potentially college bound or being average and probably trades bound. High schools are rather large when serving large communities, and this allows considerable specialization for the college bound, but even more so for the trades bound, for which the majority of education expenditures are allocated. Fundamental skills are required for graduation in either program. To graduate, the student must be proficient in reading; writing; arithmetic; Confederate history; responsible citizenship; the workings of local, state and Confederate government, and family skills (for girls, cooking, motherhood and domestic skills; for boys, shop skills, woodworking and home maintenance; for both, family economics, home economy and household book keeping). Now, every student does not master these minimum skills, so some never graduate. Attendance in school is mandatory for every student until he or she graduates or reaches the age of 17 years. Most high schools hold a mix of races, but that is not always the case.

Under certain conditions classes, or even schools, can be segregated to allow students of one race to predominate, and these situations are fairly commonplace in large towns and in cities with large populations of students of one race, particularly of the African race. In this situation, a class or school can be restricted to students of one race on an elective basis, given that every student has the choice to attend an integrated class or school. Today, students wishing to attended an African-race class or school must be, by appearance and known ancestry, of predominantly African (Negro) ancestry. "Colored" students of considerable non-African ancestry (mulattoes) are excluded from these elective African-race classes and schools because they are more European, Native or Asian in their ancestry than African.

Many non-college-bound students benefit from a wide array of hands-on teaching of trades and complementary off-site apprenticing. Over the decades, as technology advanced, training in some trades was discontinued to make room for new apprenticeship training in new industries and new technologies. Today, proficiency at touch typing, use of personal computers/tablets/smart phones, and internet-based inquiry is required of everyone, including trades-bound students. Of course apprenticing programs vary some among the states and between rural and urban areas within a given State.

College-bound students receive a classical high school education that is rather common worldwide, but with added emphasis on internet inquiry; science; mathematics; communication skills; world history; Confederate history; Confederate local, state and national government; music, and critical thinking. Instruction in a foreign language is available but not encouraged in public schools, but it is available in some private schools, in special language schools, and can be studied later in most colleges.

Athletics are available in all schools for students twelve years and older. Schools are grouped on ability into Class 1, Class 2 and Class 3 athletic associations to allow schools with few students of the athletically-gifted African race to find balanced competition. We now turn our attention to Confederate colleges and universities.

Even today, colleges and universities in the Confederate States are all privately funded and operate tax-free in a manner similar to religious institutions. In the early years, almost all began as church-sponsored institutions, and, even today, history teaches that the majority began that way. The remainder began as for-profit business ventures or through philanthropy. About 35 percent of today's students attend such schools. Since no college or university is supported by government, they have been historically frugal and focused on delivering a good 4-or-5-year college education at an affordable price. Five-year co-op education programs are very popular in the fields of science, engineering and pre-medicine, allowing students to alternate between work and study.

Research by college professors is limited by their personal entrepreneurial spirit and/or success in winning private-sector financial support. And college administrations frown on professors who spend too much time at research, thereby shirking their obligations to student education. State laws against collective bargaining also include a prohibition on grants of tenure to teachers and professors. So, when a professor hits upon an important discovery in, say, science or medicine, he or she generally resigns to enable full-time pursuit of the invention. Confederate college students have a realistic and pragmatic mindset about their college educations. They are going to college to gain an education useful in launching their careers. And professors and college administrations know that to be the case.

Confederate medical schools are always associated with hospitals. Here the shunning of professor research is relaxed and many teaching professors of medicine do conduct important medical research -- a natural outgrowth of the need for medical training to be near a hospital setting and because it is there that important research can be pursued.

You will learn more about Confederate education in Amanda Lynn Washington's essay presented in the final chapter. It is titled, "Because Confederate Schools, Colleges and Universities are Non-political and Emphasize Business, Science and Engineering and Attract the Brightest to those Fields."

## Class Readings of Essays and Group Comments

After lunch the essayists returned to the classroom to practice their essays before each other and before a television camera. Each presentation and all comments were recorded by the television camera to enable each essayist to subsequently review his or her performance. Delivery was judged as well as content. Three public speaking professionals and a speech therapist were also on hand to offer help with delivery were it might be helpful. But these twelve were already quite adept at public speaking, so issues of that sort were considered "fine tuning." On several occasions, suggestions were made to "deemphasize" this or "emphasize that" or "add this thought."

After supper most worked over their essays a bit, watched the video of their essay presentation and revised here and there for emphasis and double-checked some facts to ensure accuracy. By and large, Friday was work, work, work all day.

## Friday Evening Selected Diary Postings

Diary note by Andrew Houston said, "Supper with the beautiful Conchita. Lovely in so many ways. We play tennis in the morning. Will get to the court early before it gets hot. Hot weather is not so bad here at Sewanee, up on the Cumberland Plateau. Not as hot here as in Davis or in Nashville. Professor Davis delivered his last lecture this morning. Discussed the underlying principles that contribute to our greatness. Presented our 2010 population statistics. Our total population is now almost 330 million. Hard to believe. Could those settlers in the early days of Texas or those Natives that gathered in what became Sequoyah believe our country could support that many people? Hope to improve my delivery when we practice again in the Sewanee Concert Hall Sunday morning."

Diary note by Conchita Rezanov said, "Had supper with Andrew Houston this evening. Promised to play singles tennis with him tomorrow at 10 am, but we have decided to also play a doubles game afterward that includes Professor Davis and Marie St. Martin. Those two play well enough for a social doubles game and Andrew has become a bit too possessive of my time. Notice that I will be doing supper with Robert Lee tomorrow. He keeps asking me out and he is cute, although a bit too serious -- the writer's penchant to study all folks encountered."

Diary note by Amanda Washington said, "My essay will be on the importance of excellence in our country's schools, colleges and universities. Professor Davis discussed that at length this morning, which I found to be helpful. He believes my essay, the last to be presented, is the most important of the twelve. And he believes delivery before the television cameras is key to our effectiveness at explaining why the Confederate States are the greatest country on earth. Frankly, I believe he is right. My assigned essay is the most important subject. And being of African ancestry myself, I am expected to be the visual image of the success we have achieved within our diverse society. It looked OK on the television screen tonight."

Diary note by Robert Lee said, "Professor Davis presented information on many underlying principles that have made possible the continued success of our Confederate States. Among those was his discussion of how and why we have so doggedly continued to honor Individual Liberty and State Rights. In a way, looking out across the world since those war years of the 1940's, through struggles over Fascism, Communism and Socialism, it is hard to believe that we have remained true to the principles upon which our Confederacy was founded. In the early years we managed well the transition from slavery to independence for all people of African ancestry. We have managed well the transition from an agricultural economy to a diverse industrial economy. Those transitions, and others as well, could have redirected our country and our diverse society away from those principles. But we have stayed the course. So glad of that. Watched the video of my presentation given this afternoon. Going to ask an advisor in the morning: 'How can I put more passion into my delivery'?"

Diary note by Carlos Cespedes said, "Last rehearsal for our concert was this evening. Professor Davis plays a pretty good banjo. I think he, Allen and I will do just fine."

# Part 3, Chapter 9, Days 27 and 28 – Sewanee in Celebration Mode – Saturday and Sunday, July 2 and 3, 2011

I hope you have been enjoying reading *The CSA Trilogy*. We Confederates are sure proud of what we have created, so if one yourself, pat yourself on the back and say, "Well done." If a foreigner, take some tips from this book with you, to your home, and use to your advantage. If reading this book has prompted you to offer a suggestion about how Confederates could become even better at what they do, drop us a line. We are always eager to learn.

This chapter is quite short. But the writer does offer a little more insight into the thoughts and personal relationships among the twelve essayists.

Perhaps most of the essayists felt well prepared by Friday evening. And evidence seems to support that feeling. Anyway, the twelve, realizing that this amazing time together would soon be over, were especially eager to spend Saturday and Sunday pursuing non-academic interests together: music, tennis, swimming, running, riding, chatting.

## Sewanee in Celebration Mode -- Saturday

Saturday morning, Andrew Houston gave Conchita Rezanov a bit of exercise on the tennis court. What is meant by that? No way Andrew could beat Conchita in singles tennis, but he could hit back rather well in rallies when Conchita returned the ball within easy reach. On the other hand, Andrew stroked the ball rather well, back and forth, forward and rearward, to run Conchita all over the court. That was how one gives a superior player a "workout." That is especially true when the less accomplished player is the smitten one. In the adjacent tennis court Marie St. Martin and Professor Davis played a more gentle game of singles. They were rather well matched and kept score. After an hour of singles, the four joined to play two sets of doubles: Conchita and Professor Davis versus Andrew and Marie. Conchita relaxed a bit to make a game of it. There was an audience for a while -- Robert Lee, Chris Memminger and Benedict Juárez watched for a while and cheered the players on.

From the Memminger family's impressive horse farm, Chris's father had brought four fine horses up to Sewanee to participate in the Monday morning parade. Chris was going to ride one, outdoorsman Robert Lee another, bison rancher Allen Ross a third, and farmer Isaiah Montgomery the fourth. Although these were fine, well-bred stallions, these four young men looked to be up to the riding challenge. Anyway, Chris assured the others that these stallions had been in parades before and would not be spooked by the activity around them. The four riders got a workout with their steeds on Saturday after lunch and everything looked good.

Marie Saint Martin gathered her band together for a rehearsal Saturday afternoon. The band had been asked to fill a 15-minute slot in Monday's televised music program and was asked to take a 30-minute slot in the band shell on Sunday to entertain arriving visitors and participants. It was fun to be playing together and, as luck would have it, the six person band was actually rather good. Marie was steeped in New Orleans style band music and a good lead singer, embellishing her voice with genuine emotion. Allen Ross played his guitar reasonably well, with a pace-setting rhythm. And Carlos Cespedes occasionally added good accent licks on his Spanish guitar. Tina Sharp, a good classically-trained musician, sung harmony with well-chosen notes and spot-on pitch. Amanda Washington played the piano with gusto and mostly by ear, seldom looking at music -- somehow, it seemed, arranging occasionally as she progressed. Then there was Professor Davis on banjo. Not bad, but it would have been mean to exclude him. Anyway, he had his few runs and added some well-practiced twangs. But the most important aspect of Marie's band was the fun, the enjoyment that participants felt while playing together. Perhaps only musicians can fully appreciate that.

The six had agreed on the following 15-minute presentation for Monday, July 4th:

- "Diversity" (the Confederate anthem)
- "Amazing Grace"
- "My granddad was a country boy"
- "Don't mess with Hawaii and Texas too."
- "Dixie"

People in the Confederate States love to sing "Dixie," but with revised words that change the perspective from a person up north looking "away down south" to a "here at home" perspective. Anyway the fellow who originally wrote "Dixie" was from Ohio, writing music for a minstrel show being presented in the Northern States. [320] This is how Confederates sing "Dixie" today:

"We're . . .
Proud to be in the land of cotton.
Old times here are not forgotten.
Gon'a Pray.  Come what may.
Gon'a stay, in Dixie Land.

"In Dixie Land where I was born.
Early on one frosty morn.
Gon'a pray.  Come what may.
Gon'a stay, in Dixie Land.

"I'm so happy I'm in Dixie.
Hooray!  Hooray!
In Dixie Land I'll take my stand
To live and die in Dixie.

Hooray!  Hooray!
We Love, Love, Love . . . our Dixie!"

The final practice was fun.  All had agreed early on to keep the music within a range of difficulty each felt comfortable with.  That meant that Marie and Amanda, the most accomplished, would be the musical leaders.  It was fun and confidence improved.  A few other songs would be added for the 30-minute Sunday performance in the band shell.

The swimming pool was a popular afternoon spot.  Emma Lunalilo sped about the pool gracefully and, for a while gave Benedict Juárez and Isaiah Montgomery instructions on breathing and stroke improvements.  By five thirty, most of the twelve essayists were at the pool, most enjoying a beer or glass of wine.  It was a good day.

But the evening was "party time."  Professor Davis and wife Judy had brought in a country music dance band from Nashville that was really super.  They could play almost anything.  And

---

[320] Dan Emmett of Ohio wrote "I Wish I was in Dixie's Land" in 1859 for an opening walk-around during a New York City engagement of the minstrel group in which he sang.  Minstrel groups were White stage performers who blacken their faces and sang and acted in plays inspired by Southern Negro music. The message was Negroes longing to return to the South (leave the North).  A catchy tune, it became popular in the South in 1860 and became a traditional Southern song afterward.  But the original message of "longing to return to the South" soon gave way to a message of "celebrating living in the South."  For over 140 years, Confederates have sung the revised song, "celebrating living in the South."  Sorry Dan Emmett, but history does move on.

that was what they had come to do. They had come prepared to dedicate twelve chosen songs, each of which would speak in a special way to one of the twelve essayists. It would be fun. And each song, each special dedication, was going to be a surprise to each of the twelve.

There is insufficient space here to tell much about the evening, but we can report on each song dedication. So we now listen to the announcement preceding each of the twelve selected tribute songs:

"Our first song tonight is an easy dance song about beautiful surfer girls. Came out of South California, but let's think of it as a song about the place on our lovely planet where the sport of surfing began. Here's our toast to Hawaii and the beautiful, amazing, athletic, conqueror of mighty winds and mighty waves. Of course, this is 'Surfer Girl,' dedicated to our heroine, Emma Lunalilo. Let's get up and dance." [321]

"Now folks, among us here this evening, we have one fine young skipper who hails from a family with a long sailing tradition going back several generations. This skipper will be forever grateful that our heroic Surfer Girl was aboard his sailboat one stormy night off Cuba when the dreaded shout was heard: 'Man overboard'. Carlos Cespedes, this is dedicated to you. This one is called, 'Son of a Son of a Sailor'." [322]

"Now folks, we all know that each of you is immersed in history, in the history of our Confederate States. So let us now go back to the beginning and honor those soldiers in grey that enveloped those invading armies and forced surrender after surrender. Seems those northerners foolishly thought our defenders were measly retreating cowards. Surprise! That was our plan all along! So let's honor all of those men in gray and one of their prominent leaders, General Lee. Mr. Robert E. Lee, IV, we dedicate this one to your ancestor. Here we go with 'Wearing the Gray'. It's a spirited song. Let's get up a start to dancing." [323]

"I am certain that you all know that horses were mighty, mighty important in our victory over those invading armies from the Northern States. We all celebrate that. So let's pay tribute to Chris Memminger and his dad, who brought four fine thoroughbred stallions up to Sewanee for the Sunday morning parade. Here's to a real horse man, Chris Memminger, and about the toughest horse that ever lived: 'Tennessee Stud'. You probably know this song." [324]

"Folks, a feller can't think long about horses without musing over Texas cowboys and the men who ride over those bison ranges in Sequoyah. Sorry, Allen didn't find a bison boy song that seemed to fit the occasion. Will the song, 'Cowboy Logic' suit us for this evening? That cowboy was a stubborn sort of man. Ought to work for us tonight. Here we go essayists. 'Cowboy Logic'." [325]

---

[321] In truthful history, "Surfer Girl" was made famous by the Beach Boys of southern California.

[322] In truthful history, "Son of a Son of a Sailor" was written and made famous by Jimmy Buffett of Mississippi and Alabama.

[323] Since in, truthful history, Confederates were conquered and forced back under Federal control, there are no songs about the successful defense of the Confederate States.

[324] In truthful history, "Tennessee Stud' was made popular by Johnny Cash of Nashville, Tennessee fame.

[325] In truthful history, "Cowboy Logic" was written by and made popular by Michael Martin Murphy of Texas. In truthful history songs about buffalo seem to be about killing and skinning them.

"Now raising bison and cattle goes hand in hand with good old dirt farming. Isaiah Montgomery, you and your ancestors are and were farmers extraordinaire. So step up here and help lead us in this quite fitting song. Here is 'Down on the Farm'." [326]

"Now folks let's head to the far north, beyond Confederate farmland and serenade the beautiful and talented Conchita Rezanova with a song praising the mountain range named for that great Russian explorer, Ferdinand von Wrangell, a great leader of the Russian America Company and a great friend of Conchita's heroic ancestor Nikolai Rezanov. Take a ride on a bush airplane and let your spirits soar. Here comes the 'Wrangell Mountain Song'." [327]

"Wow! It was really cold up there in the Wrangell Mountains. So beautiful from that little airplane. Well, folks why don't we head far, far south and ponder those six States that emerged from the former Seceded Mexican States that Benito Juárez so amazingly led to freedom from domination by Mexico City rule. Although diverse in many ways, we Confederates have long been one, unified people. We are united as brothers and sisters within one huge Confederate family. God willing, we shall remain united within this one circle of brotherhood and sisterhood. Benedict Juárez, please come up here and help us sing 'Will the Circle Be Unbroken'." [328]

"We were just then, musically speaking, quite close to those four Texas states. So we in the band up here are primed and ready to sing 'God Bless Texas'. That's right folks, God had blessed Texas, and our Lord needs to hear a bit of celebration over that. Andrew Houston, your ancestor, Sam Houston, was such an amazing leader of Texas Independence, the Republic of Texas, and the State of Texas. We are all so grateful for his wisdom and leadership. So come up here and help us sing 'God Bless Texas'. Atta Boy, let's just do it, you all." [329]

"OK! We liked those Texas states so much we just need to sing some more about that great land. Let's see . . . I know. Let's sing about Texas Gold and the early days of the Texas oil boom. It at started at Spindletop, you know. An oil boom made possible by Tina's, ancestor, Walter Benona Sharp, inventor of the revolutionary hardrock drill bit. Also made possible by those tough men who worked those drill rigs, night and day, capped off those gushers and laid that pipe. They were called 'roustabouts'. They were also called 'roughnecks'. Tina, we thank you for your work at Comanche Peak, but why not turn the calendar way back and celebrate the beginning of Texas energy production, the Texas oil boom. Let's all sing 'Roughneck'. Come on. Let's celebrate that tough, tough Texas oil field man, that 'Roughneck'." [330]

"We've got two more songs of celebration left to go. Let's see. What ought to be left? OK. We are going to New Orleans and dance about. Amazing music there: gospel, country, jazz. Let's go marching for the people and for the Lord. Marie Saint Martin, we

---

[326] In truthful history, "Down on the Farm" was written by Jerry Lasseter and Kerry Kurt Phillips and made famous by Tim McGraw of Louisiana and Nashville, Tennessee.

[327] In truthful history "Wrangle Mountain Song" was written by and sung by the great Henry John Deutschendorf, Jr. of New Mexico, Arizona, Texas and Alaska. He performed under the name "John Denver."

[328] In truthful history, "Will the Circle be Unbroken" was made famous by the Carter Family of Virginia and Nashville, Tennessee and June Carter's husband Johnny Cash.

[329] In truthful history, "God Bless Texas" was made famous by the band "Little Texas" of Nashville Tennessee and written by band member Brady Seals.

[330] In truthful history, "Roughneck" was made famous by Johnny Cash of Nashville, Tennessee.

363

love your singing and know you know this one by heart, so come take the microphone and lead us all in 'When the Saints Go Marching In'." [331]

"Our last song of celebration concerns education, our schools and colleges, our teachers and professors. Part of one's life when going to school or going to college is that spirit, that school spirit, which includes the friends, the teachers and professors, and the sports teams. To me, and probably to you all as well, there is no more important school in Confederate history than Tuskegee Institute, and no more important education leader than Amanda's ancestor, Booker T. Washington. Amanda we all wish you great success in your future career in education and wish to now honor you with this celebratory song, 'Be True to Your School'. Here goes." [332]

The Friday night party was great fun and another event that would bind the twelve into a life-long lasting friendship.

## Sewanee in Celebration Mode – Sunday

For our Essayists and Professor Davis, Sunday morning was a day for haircuts, dressing up, a bit of powder on the cheeks, and nose and practicing delivering essays before the camera upon the stage in Sewanee Concert Hall. Every essay was downloaded into the computer that controlled the three transparent teleprompters, one to the left, one to the right and one straight ahead. Each essayist had to get comfortable with switching between teleprompters during delivery and speaking clearly to the 4,000 who would be packing the Concert Hall the following afternoon. All were thankful that they did not have to memorize their essay. Marie Saint Martin remarked to Emma Catherine Lunalilo, "Smarty-pants, a speaker who can memorize that much don't play fair." By noon the rehearsals were over and it was time for lunch. Where? At the Sequoyah tent for bison barbeque of course.

The parade began at 1:00 pm and Chris Memminger, Allen Ross, Robert Lee and Isaiah Montgomery were on their stallions raring to go (it took some horsemanship to hold them in place, for a raring stallion can be quiet a problem in a crowd). Each rider held his state flag on a pole anchored in a saddle strap. It all went well. They had practiced their essays first so they would arrive for the parade on time.

At 3:00 pm all were at the band shell to participate in or listen to the concert by the Essayists Band, which had been organized by Marie Saint Martin. Upon the stage was Marie Saint Martin, lead singer; Tina Sharp, backup singer; Allen Ross, guitar; Carlos Cespedes, Spanish guitar; Amanda Washington, piano, and Professor Davis, banjo. They did quite well considering their status as amateurs. The crowd appreciated it. Which song drew the most enthusiastic applause? Your writer was there. He says it was "Don't Mess with Hawaii and Texas Too."

Celebration was everywhere Saturday afternoon and Sunday. There were contests over sports, over music, over barbeque, over competition between stump speakers. Nobody was going hungry on Saturday afternoon or on Sunday, for a giant barbecue cook-off contest was held where each State's best barbecue cookers competed in hopes of winning the gold medal for the "Best Barbeque in the Confederate States." By the way, a vendor of bison barbeque from the Sequoyah tent would win the barbeque contest when the votes would be counted at 7:00 pm Monday. I did

[331] In truthful history, "When the Saints Go Marching In" is a long time gospel song. It was made famous as a popular song by famous jazz trumpeter Louis Armstrong of New Orleans, Louisiana.

[332] In truthful history, "Be True to Your School" was made famous by the Beach Boys of southern California. It was written by Brian Wilson and Mike Love.

not eat it, but was told it was very good chopped bison barbeque enhanced with sweet and tangy, vinegar-based, smoked sauce with fifteen percent pork added for enhanced flavor.

Sunday featured a comprehensive track and field athletic competition where each State entered its best in each event. The finals would be held Monday morning starting at 8:00 am and concluding at noon. Who would win the track and field contests? True to form, Confederates of notable African ancestry swept the field. Their advantage was genetic and other Confederates, humbly, admitted their opponent's superiority and warmly congratulated the many winners.

Who won the archery contest? Need you ask?

Who won the swimming and diving contests? Mostly those great Hawaiians. After the long distance swimming event, Emma Lunalilo turned to Conchita Rezanova and said, "My times have been almost that good. Maybe I should have trained harder and gone for that one."

Who won the equestrian contests? The one mile thoroughbred race was won by a horse from the Belle Meade stables outside of Nashville. The steeplechase was won by a great jumper from Virginia. The rodeo was won by about the most rugged West Texan this writer has ever seen or met. What a handshake.

Sorry, Russian American athletes. No snow and ice events.

Sorry, too, you sailors of the Atlantic, Caribbean, Gulf and Pacific. Can't do that in Sewanee.

Conchita Rezanov and Andrew Houston were disappointed, but understanding, that the celebration did not include competitions over golf, tennis and team sports. Cannot hold such competitions over just two days. But these two essayists were laying plans to get together in a few weeks and play tennis again. Perhaps doubles, thereby giving Andrew a chance to win one for the guys.

There was a Saturday evening through Sunday contest among Confederate brass bands to determine which would be selected for the Monday evening brass band concert, the next to last event of that night. There was one brass band that was not made up of Confederates. It was the Black Dyke Mills Brass Band from England, which had been featured in the 1870 Great Confederate Expansion Celebration. Would its current musicians win the weekend competition contest? Need to listen to them!

## Sunday Evening Selected Diary Postings

Diary note by Tina Sharp said, "I like Allen Ross a lot. Among the seven men in our group, I enjoy him the most. We are so different on the outside, but feel a kindred closeness on the inside. Where I am less than accomplished, he is accomplished. Where he is less than accomplished, I am accomplished. So together all of the gaps are filled and one gets the notion that, together, we could do anything we set out to do. But what would I do on a huge and remote bison ranch? Studied that puzzle as we ate supper together this evening. Answers? Not yet. But being around that cowboy (bisonboy, thank you) gets my juices flowing."

Diary note by Allen Ross said, "Supper with Tina Sharp. Her mind operates on a much higher plain than does mine. We seem so miss-matched. But I must confess I am attracted to that nuclear engineer. Who would have thunk it?"

Diary note by Isaiah Montgomery said, "Had a long chat this weekend with Robert Lee. I like him. From him one can learn a lot. No one in our group understands what my great-great-great-grandfather accomplished more acutely than does Robert. And he understands my people especially well. I think he is going to make a great writer."

Diary note by Professor Davis said, "Everyone did rather well on their essays during the practice deliveries before the television cameras. I am pleased so far. Comments within the group on the presentations of others were constructive, as I had hoped. . . . . Wife Judith listened to our rehearsals at one point and commented: "You all are not half bad." From her that is a complement. And she knows music of course. Rehearsed again Saturday. It is a good group. Good balance. On vocals, I am the bottom as a bass singer. Allen and Carlos play the guitar well, considering neither is a professional musician. Marie has a fabulous, distinctive voice and sings lead nicely; sings with that New Orleans passion. Amanda can play most anything on the piano, given a bit of time to work it out. Too bad our group cannot use a French horn. Judith said she has really enjoyed playing duets with Tina; they have gotten together for duets twice so far. But Tina sings well and has a good ear for harmony. I just dive in and play that banjo. . . . . Well, tomorrow is the big day for our twelve Essayists. I believe they are ready. That is great! What an amazing gathering of descendants of important early Confederate leaders! Among our twelve are descendants of a Cherokee leader and an African American education leader, as well as descendants from our Texas States and South Carolina. We have descendants from the most important leader of the Seceded Mexican States, of Cuba, of Hawaii and of Russian America. We have a descendant from our great military leader Robert E. Lee, a favorite of my ancestor, President Jefferson Davis. Great group! They are not the most expert in the subjects of their essays, but they know plenty about what they will be talking about, and they all have the ability to communicate those messages in a way that will really reach out to our youngest generation, in their teens, twenties and thirties. That is why they were recruited to participate in the Sewanee Project. And they will do a great job. And a romance or two might blossom from this month of togetherness. Never know. 'Til tomorrow, diary. Goodnight."

# Part 3, Chapter 10, Day 29 -- Confederate Sesquicentennial Day Celebration Day Events – Monday, July 4, 2011

On Monday, July 4, 2011, Confederate Bicentennial Celebration events were being held all day long throughout the Confederate States. There were celebratory events at every State capital, which generally included speech-making, parades, history lectures, church services, athletic contests, brass bands, country music and jazz concerts, awards ceremonies, cemetery decorations, stage plays and ceremonies honoring fallen heroes, and picnics and more picnics. And at the close of the day there would be fireworks – lots of fireworks. Nobody went to work on this very special day. Factories closed -- even chemical plants and refineries closed in spite of the difficulty in shutting down and restarting process industry facilities such as those. There were important celebrations at every city and most towns. Rare was the school band member who was not in uniform marching and playing along a parade route or at a celebration event. "Dixie" must have been played a hundred thousand times this day. School and church choirs were engaged in celebration activities all across the land. Chapters of the Sons of Confederate Veterans of the War Between the States were evident in every parade, proudly carrying today's Confederate flag, the Confederate Battle flag, the original Confederate National flag as well as their appropriate State flag. Veterans of the Defense of Secession conflict are now long gone, but great grandsons were evident everywhere. Veterans of the War against Fascist Japan were in the parades in small groups, for only a few remained and they were getting mighty old. But they were there too, many assisted by their relatives.

Perhaps the most heart-felt celebratory emotion was thankfulness that, except for the War Against Japan, Confederates had not been embroiled in a military conflict since the Defense of Secession. Considering the wars that had been fought elsewhere across the globe over the past 150 years, the ability of the Confederate States to avoid such horrors was being attributed to its military strength. Other countries knew better than to mess with the Confederate States. And today, when military aggression is most often tied to Islamic terrorism, Confederates are safe in our country and are engaged militarily only in a limited way, only giving military assistance to those being attacked. One Confederate said, "If we wait long enough all of the Islamic suicide bombers will have killed themselves off and there will be peace in the Middle East." [333]

Of course, the celebration at Davis was spectacular. But there was something special about the celebration at Sewanee. More reflective. Happy, but a bit more serious. Sewanee represented the essence of Confederate culture. Elsewhere, Confederates were celebratory and gleeful, parading about, engaged in activities resembling a summer picnic outing. At Sewanee, Confederates shouldered the responsibility of presenting to the country a reflection on our history and a discussion of why, yes why, ours was truly the "Greatest Country on Earth?" It was Sewanee's job to explain why Confederates were so happy and so able to celebrate a bicentennial with such unmatched pride.

The celebration at Sewanee began at 10 am and concluded with a music program that began at 10 pm and ended at midnight, complete with fireworks. How could so much happen at a

---

[333] In truthful history Americans of the Southern States have been engaged in several major military conflicts not suffered by the Confederate States as told herein. Truthful history includes the Spanish American War, World War I, World War II (the part fought in Europe), the Korean War, the Viet Nam War, and the more recent wars in Afghanistan and Iraq. The Confederacy was not drawn into wars in Europe. In our alternate history, Confederate success in teaming with China to defeat both the Japanese and the Chinese Communists dealt a major blow to the communization of Asia, negating the need to fight wars in Korea and Viet Nam. Unlike Europe and the United States, Confederates have not been especially dependent on oil purchases from the Middle East and have managed to avoid wars in that region, including those recently instigated by Islamic Terrorists.

university town high up on the Cumberland Plateau? Here are some answers. It was summer time and all dormitories had been vacated and cleaned to provide housing. Most student apartments had been sublet for the season. Extra cots were commonplace in every abode. This was a perfect gathering place for the young and it was especially for them that Confederates wanted to impart new knowledge of our history and our culture. Television and Motion Picture crews were on campus to present much of it to the country, and to the world beyond, and to record the event for a major documentary film. First there was the Colleges and Universities Parade across the campus, then through town, featuring small groups from 92 Confederate colleges and universities. Following that were speeches, wreath layings, outdoor dramas, concerts and military tributes. There were outdoor concerts featuring every Confederate music style, from Bluegrass, to County, to Jazz, to Popular, to Operatic, to Brass Band. The chosen Bicentennial symphony was the Nashville Symphony, so Judith Davis was there with her French horn making her contribution.

The Sewanee celebration was presented on television all day long, without interruption, with a special cable channel carrying every moment and other channels mixing segments from Sewanee with segments from elsewhere.

At 2:00 pm in the Sewanee Concert Hall, the Essayists Band, organized by Marie Saint Martin, presented the short 15-minute concert of four songs:

- "Diversity" (the Confederate States Anthem)
- "Amazing Grace."
- "My Granddad Was a Country Boy."
- "Don't Mess with Hawaii and Texas Too."
- "Dixie"

It was brief, but well received. These amateurs could not complain.

## Part 3, Chapter 11, Day 29 – Presenting the Twelve Essays – Worldwide Television, Monday, July 4 2011

The twelve essays were scheduled for presentation soon thereafter, from 3pm to 6pm, a span of three hours. The essays would be presented in the Sewanee Concert Hall, filled to its capacity of 4,000 seats. We now proceed to present the essay program. Professor Davis was the host of this segment.

### Why the Confederacy is the Greatest of them All

Professor Davis: "Greetings to Confederates everywhere, to those 4,000 with me here in the Sewanee Concert Hall, to those in our State of Tennessee, to those all across our Confederate States, from Virginia to Cuba, to Russian America, to Costa Sudoeste, to Hawaii. Over the next three hours you will be hearing twelve essays researched and written here at the University of the South in fulfillment of the "Sewanee Project," which was authorized and funded by the Confederate Sesquicentennial Committee in 2009. Each of the twelve "Analysts" in the "Sewanee Project" is an unusually gifted young man or woman whose heritage and background enables them to probe with special focus into our history and our culture in pursuit of answers to the question that has so mystified the world around us. The question, "Why are the Confederate States of America the Greatest Country on Earth?" But first just a snippet about me.

"My name is Joseph Evan Davis, IV, age 64 years. I have long been a professor of history and political studies here at the University of the South, situated on the beautiful Cumberland Plateau, within the lovely State of Tennessee, here in the Confederate States of America. My great-great-grandfather was Jefferson Finis Davis, the first President of our country. I stand before you today as a man humbled by his birthright, for no man ever contributed more to the success of our country than President Davis.

"Our Sesquicentennial Celebration today, July 4, 2011, begs for reflective thought, begs for renewed understanding -- not for just a few academics, not for just those among us who are naturally immersed in history, but also, and most importantly, for Confederates of all walks of life, of all backgrounds, of all racial ancestries, for, well . . . . for all of us. Greater understanding, not only for we Confederates, but also for people all over the world who admire our country's success and long to understand how they can use our experiences to advance the success of their respective countries and support sustainable happiness among their respective peoples.

"And it is primarily upon the young generation of Confederates, not yet in their 30's, that we will especially focus our attention today. They will be the leaders of tomorrow and upon their shoulders will rest the responsibility for continuing our success and ensuring that the happiness of our people does not wither in the face of unforeseen challenges, which the future will in due time surely lay upon us.

"So it is with great pride in our heritage that our 'Twelve Sewanee Project Analysists' -- each an outstanding descendant of a past Confederate leader -- has come to Sewanee for four weeks of study directed at helping all of us in this audience and across the globe watching on television, answer the burning question: "Why are the Confederate States of America the Greatest Country on Earth?" These twelve remarkable Confederate men and women will in turn answer this question from twelve different perspectives. Each perspective is relevant to the understanding sought, and each perspective is especially relevant to the contributions made long ago by each participant's heroic ancestor. These twelve 'Sewanee Project Analysists,' who will take the microphone in turn over the next three hours, are here on the stage now. Each will stand as I call out his or her name.

Mr. Isaiah Benjamin Montgomery of Mississippi, 27 years old, great-great-great-grandson of Isaiah Thornton Montgomery, whose family was so important in managing Jefferson Davis' large farm after Mr. Davis became obligated to redirect his energies toward serving the people of Mississippi in the United States Senate and, 150 years ago, serving as President of the Confederate States of America.

Miss Marie Saint Martin of Louisiana, 23 years old, great-great-great-granddaughter of Jules Saint Martin, nephew, of the Confederacy's first Attorney General, Judah Benjamin. Not just a nephew, but also an important confidant and helper in the office of the Confederacy's first Attorney General during those important first formative years.

Miss Emma Cathrine Lunalilo of Hawaii, 22 years old, great-great-great-granddaughter of William Charles Lunalilo, King of the Nation of the Hawaiian Islands during the transition from a monarchy to a democratic government -- the precursor to admission into the Confederate States of America.

Mr. Carlos Jose Cespedes of Cuba, 24 years old, great-great-great-grandson of Carlos Manuel Cespedes, leader of the Cuban peoples' successful fight for independence from Spain, and their country's subsequent admission into the Confederate States of America.

Mr. Chris Withers Memminger of South Carolina, 22 years old, great-great-great-grandson of Christopher Gustavus Memminger, the Confederacy's first Secretary of the Treasury.

Dr. Benedict Christian Juárez of Costa Este, 27 years old, great-great-great-grandson of Benito Juárez, who led the people of the northern Mexican states in their fight against the French Intervention and their fight to restore and sustain the principles of democracy against the evils of oppressive military rule out of Mexico City. Operating sometimes from a horse-drawn carriage, often on the move, President Juárez sustained a federal government limited by constitutional rules, and orchestrated the Mexican State Secession, its defense, its reorganization into six redefined states, and their admission into the Confederate States of America.

Mr. Allen Bruce Ross of Sequoyah, 26 years old, great-great-great-great-grandson of the Principle Chief of the Cherokee Nation, Koo-wi-s-gu-wi, often called by his English name, John Ross, who led his people from 1828 to 1868 and whose descendants played major roles in uniting the 'Five Civilized Tribes' in their campaign to make their new land, west of the Mississippi River, a State within the Confederacy that served their needs and ensured their happiness and protection -- the Great State of Sequoyah.

Miss Conchita Marie Rezanov of Russian America and presently living of South California, 23 years old, great-great-great-granddaughter of Nikolai Rezanov, the very important leader of Russian America during its colonial fur-trading days, and whose descendants played major roles in arranging for the people of the colony to purchase their land from Mother Russia with a loan backed by the Confederate States and paid off by gold mined from the land.

Mr. Robert Edward Lee, IV, of Alabama, with roots going into North Carolina, Tennessee and Virginia, 23 years old, great-great-great-grandson of General Robert Edward Lee, the most admired Confederate military leader during the Defense of Secession and a key advisor to President Davis.

Mr. Andrew Houston of South Texas, 23 years old, great-great-great-great-grandson of Sam Houston, known to the Cherokee as 'The Raven,' Governor of Tennessee, military leader of the successful struggle for Texas independence from autocratic rule out of Mexico City, President of the Nation of Texas, and Governor of the State of Texas, who died knowing that his legacy would be forever appreciated by all Texans and their friends across the Confederate States of America.

Miss Tina Kathleen Sharp of North Texas, 26 years old, great-great-granddaughter of Walter Benona Sharp, the leading Texas oil man whose invention of the Sharp-Hughes hardrock drill bit enabled the Spindletop gusher of 1901 and the Confederate petroleum boom that followed -- providing us with affordable fuels and petrochemicals, so important to our economic success and to discouraging aggressive notions from others around the world.

Miss Amanda Lynn Washington of Virginia, 25 years old, great-great-granddaughter of Booker T. Washington, pioneering educator and founder of the Tuskegee Institute. Like her ancestor, Amanda has embarked on a career in education that is grounded in the belief that, for an education program to be considered excellent, it must serve the needs, abilities and interests of a diverse population of students.

As our essayists again take their seats, we all thank you for that warm applause. Now we proceed.

# Essay 1 — The Importance of Understanding Human Diversity

## By Isaiah Benjamin Montgomery

Professor Davis:

Our first essayist is Mr. Isaiah Benjamin Montgomery. His essay is titled, "The Importance of Understanding Human Diversity."

Mr. Montgomery presently resides in Mound Bayou, Mississippi where he is a field supervisor for Section 8 of the Mound Bayou Corporate Plantation, where cotton, field peas, various legumes, soybeans, alfalfa and sweet potatoes are grown on 3,400 acres with careful attention to sustaining the soils through crop rotation, chemical analysis and supplemental additives. Overall, Mound Bayou Corporate Plantation owns and operates farming operations on 110,000 acres along the Mississippi River between Natchez and Vicksburg. Since the 1860's, MBCP has been owned and operated by Confederates of African Ancestry. They work the land and reap the rewards. Fellow Confederates, I present to you a man who knows what he will be talking about, a man who has earned the admiration of everyone in the Sewanee Project -- Mr. Isaiah Benjamin Montgomery.

Isaiah Montgomery:

Thank you, Professor Davis for that warm introduction, perhaps more generous than deserved. Thank you.

Why are the Confederate States the "Greatest Country on Earth"? I believe that question cannot be fully answered without recognizing that the Confederate people, by and large, understand the importance of human diversity and they are respectful of fellow Confederates of all walks of life.

We of the Confederate States are in many ways a broadly diversified citizenry. We are diversified with regard to race and mixtures of races; diversified with regard to physical and mental talents; diversified with regard to inherent drive to excel; diversified with regard to strength of family relationships; diversified with regard to being self-directed versus other-directed and with regard to optimistic outlook versus pessimistic outlook; diversified with regard to eagerness to accept government and private charity versus pride in being self-sufficient and fully in control. And, to an extent much greater than observed elsewhere on earth, the people of the Confederate States embrace our diversity and its origins, and generally endorse government policies, at local, State and Confederate levels, which are designed to optimize the welfare of all classes within our diversity, while also ensuring guarantees of individual liberty, every individuals right to work without limitations, and the right of every young person to a government-financed and appropriate education through high school.

Now I want to quantify the diversity among our citizens with respect to each person's Confederate heritage. And here we will be classifying a citizen's heritage according to the prevalent ancestry in the family tree of each.

Fourteen percent of our citizens are primarily descended from colonial families that successfully won the war against Great Britain known as the American Revolution.

Twenty-eight percent of our citizens are descended from families that arrived after the Revolution and came to live in land that would become the seceded Southern States or came south into the Confederate States during the time of the demarcation of the boundary between the USA and the CSA.

I have mentioned 14 percent and 28 percent. That adds to 42 percent. These are today's citizens primarily descended from our original Confederates. Of these original CSA descendants, 25 percent have noticeable African ancestry and 3 percent are partly descended from Native Americans.

Twenty-two percent of our citizens are descended from families who came into the Confederate States through Mexican State Secession or through the successful Cuban Revolution followed by Cuban statehood. Of these, 20 percent are of nearly pure European ancestry, 20 percent of nearly pure Native American ancestry and the remaining 60 percent are of various mixtures of Native American and European ancestry, plus, for a few, also a degree of African ancestry.

Three percent of our citizens are descended from families who came into the Confederate States through the successful purchase of Russian America, followed by statehood. Of these, 70 percent are of nearly pure Native American ancestry.

Three percent of our citizens are descended from families who came into the Confederate States through the successful transition of the Hawaiian Islands from a Monarchy to a Republic, followed by statehood. At that time the population was half Polynesian and the remainder was European or Asian. These peoples rapidly transitioned into a mixture of those races, the Polynesians benefiting from the disease resistance acquired from European and Asian parentage.

We have now accounted for 70 percent of the ancestry of present-day Confederates. Now you probably find this presentation confusing. You ask, how can all people today be classified into the groups listed above? Are there not ancestry mixtures? Good question. What we have done is identify the predominant ancestry of individuals and classify them on that basis. This means that many people trace their ancestry to a mix of the categories listed above, but we take the predominant ancestry and place the person in that group in order to simplify the analysis.

At this point only 70 percent of the population has been described. What about the remaining 30 percent, not yet categorized? These are people descended from foreign immigrants who had successfully obtained visas to enter into a State to engage in work and, three years later, had won the right of citizenship for themselves, spouses and children. You see, foreign immigration into each State was carefully controlled by said State, as was the right to citizenship after the three-year work permit ended. As it has turned out, foreign immigration has swelled the population of Confederates such that the population is of predominately European ancestry. Since around 1870, States have been particular about recruiting immigrants who were thought to be capable of making noteworthy contributions to Confederate society and to the Confederate economy. Furthermore, Confederates have insisted on merging immigrants into existing society, insisting that they make every effort to learn English and to think of themselves as full members of their adopted country, leaving behind notions of the society from which they had come. This "Learn English" policy was accepted as a worthy goal by Spanish speaking peoples of the Seceded Mexican States and of Independent Cuba, as well as of those brought in from Russian America and the Hawaiian Islands. So Confederates are a remarkably diversified society with regard to many criteria, but not with regard to language. There, uniformity is sought and English is the language of the country.

What about diversity in physical and mental talents? The racial diversity of our population ensures that we also have diversity in physical and mental talents. Strength, agility and general athletic superiority is evident among the most talented Confederates of significant African ancestry. Intellectual excellence seems to be predominant among Confederates of nearly-pure European ancestry, although it is also seen in the small population of Asian immigrants whose history in our States dates after about 1870. Musical and entertainment talent is widespread among Confederates of all backgrounds and is recognized around the world as the best that exists. Most heralded are the entertainment centers in South California, Nashville, Tennessee and New Orleans, Louisiana.  Country Music and Jazz are hallmarks of Confederate music.

What about the characteristic drive to excel observed among Confederates?  The drive to excel is more prevalent in the Confederate States that anywhere else on Earth.  Here we see the results of several factors that contribute to our people's "drive to excel."  One factor is the nature of the Confederate population.  In the early years, ancestors of the original Confederate States were recognized as the great pioneers of westward expansion across North America, across the Appalachian Mountains, through the Ohio Valley, out to the Mississippi River and on Texas. Those genetic and cultural traits are evident even today in the great agricultural, industrial and commercial businesses their descendants have created.  Among Confederates descended from people from the Seceded Mexican States and from Independent Cuba, who gained liberty through great effort, we observe a pronounced "drive to excel."  (Many Mexican families from south of the Seceded Mexican States who treasured independence and opportunity immigrated north before the border was closed in 1880, thereby adding to the general ability and "drive to excel" among that population.)  But that is only the ancestral factor in Confederate excellence in this human trait of "drive to excel."

Another factor that has influenced the Confederate personality is the culture of opportunity that has, from the beginning, been a noted characteristic of our governments -- from local governments to State governments to the limited overall government in Davis.  When every State is required to compete for the loyalty of its citizens, each naturally strives to create opportunity to excel and to provide various pathways to enhance personal success.

What about the "strength of family inter-relationships" among Confederates?  First and foremost, the heart of Confederate success beats in the family.  Of Confederates between the ages of 30 and 50, 86 percent are married and 91 percent of these have given birth to children and are raising, or have raised them.  Divorces are not common, as presently only about of 13 percent of marriages end in divorce.  And these marriage and divorce numbers do not differ much among Confederates of the various racial backgrounds.  Confederates continue to be noted for their large families, which was especially remarkable in the 1800's where families of 10 children were often observed.  Today the average family size in the Confederate States is 3.8 children per couple.  And the immediate family of mother, father, children and grandchildren is often broadened to include uncles, aunts, nieces, nephews, and in-laws and their families.  Summertime and holiday reunions are commonplace and traditional.  It is within the family grouping that morality, religious views, expectations, work ethic, and other values are developed and maintained.  In more socialized political systems to our north in the United States and in Europe, one observes far more political involvement and government involvement in allegedly attempting to infuse the values mentioned above.  But in the Confederate States, those values are mostly encouraged within the family and family groupings -- and Confederates insist on maintaining that social norm.

What about key Confederate personality traits: are they self-directed or other-directed; is their outlook optimistic or pessimistic?  Of course no two people are alike, so within the Confederacy are people with personality traits that span the full range in the two categories mentioned here.  But, when compared to people in the United States and to those in Europe, we observe that Confederates are predominantly more "self-directed" and shrug their shoulders at notions of going along with the crowd, without asking questions, by just embracing the prevailing viewpoint.  Confederates are prone to investigate and then make up their minds and proceed on a course that represents a "self-directed" approach to engaging whatever issue they encounter.  You see, Confederates are seldom accused to following a "herd instinct."  And they are generally optimistic in their view of the present and the future.  The past?  The past is the past and that will not change. Optimism deals with handling events in the present and anticipated in the future. The personality traits discussed here seem to be distinctly Confederate and seem to be the result of experiences in our Confederate history, in our success with diversity, in our family grounding -- success, from generation to generation, with advancing our way of living and our way of relating to one's fellows.

What about the Confederate people's pride in being self-sufficient and fully in control of their lives and the lives of their families, immediate and extended? Well, among Confederates, pride in one-self and in one's family seems to be deeply ingrained, going back to the days when most lived on farms and worked them as best they could, good years and bad, accepted as a normal result of weather and economic swings. When handsome profits occurred, a part was set aside for a drought year (the concern is "drought," not saving for a "rainy day"). So frugality and forward financial planning is considered a Confederate trait, and because of that, it takes a near disaster to convince a Confederate to come seeking charity, private or government dispensed. Today only 17 percent of Confederates depend on the agricultural economy; yet Confederate agricultural exports remain huge. Although most are no longer on the farm, they embrace lessons learned by grandparents and great-grandparents in the days when so many did work the agricultural economy. Private charity is a major source of relief for Confederates needing assistance. Many are church-based. Many are local neighbor-helping-neighbor assistance groups. Beyond that, town, city and county government charities are available. There are medical charities, for no Confederate in need of medical help is turned away because the patient or his or her family would be unable to pay (even so, most obtain minimal insurance that covers big-ticket cost so as to ensure the best care without facing bankruptcy).

In closing, I will make a comparison. In the United States labor unions have long been prevalent in both the private and public sector, and over the course of decades, they have bargained for luxurious medical benefits, resulting in a huge medical care economy, complete with lavish hospitals and physician offices and thousands of medicines demanding and getting very high prices per dose, the latest and greatest being heavily advertised on television. And in the United States, their Federal Government dominates in dispensing medical, living and retirement charity. Furthermore, the United States is full of lawyers and much health care litigation, creating an environment that results in extravagant costs for health care providers, expensive defensive medical practice protocols, and high-cost insurance premiums for families.

Not so in the Confederate States. Here hospitals are adequate, but not lavish, litigation is minimal, and defensive medical practice unnecessary. This results in good medical care at a cost that is only one-third of the cost in the States to the north. Health care is a small part of the Confederate economy.

When it comes to retirement funds, most are private. But each State operates a retirement fund for its citizens should they want to take that path. Unlike the United States with its near-bankrupt Federal Social Security Fund, the States within the Confederacy seem to have their citizen's retirement funding needs under good financial control. Furthermore, the high birth rate in the Confederate States and the strong and caring core family unit contributes to plenty of folks out there working in support for every person of retirement age, today normally defined as age 68 years and 6 months.

That concludes my essay. Thanks for your attention. Professor Davis now returns to the podium to introduce my friend, Marie Saint Martin.

Professor Davis:

Thank you, Mr. Montgomery.

# Essay 2 — The Importance of Ensuring Individual Liberty and State Rights

By Marie Saint Martin

Professor Davis:

Fellow Confederates, our next essayist, Miss Marie Saint Martin, hails from southern Louisiana with ancestral ties to the early French Creole people of that region. Accomplished in many endeavors, including athletics and music, Miss Saint Martin aspires to become an entrepreneur, and the past four weeks with her convinces me that she will succeed in that as well. From the land where Andrew Jackson of Tennessee led Americans in the decisive defeat of the British in the war of 1812, I am proud to present to you Miss Marie Saint Martin, who will enlighten us on 'The Importance of Ensuring Individual Liberty and State Rights.'

Marie Saint Martin:

Thank you Professor Davis and thank you all in the audience and on world-wide television for your attention to a brief essay on what I consider perhaps the most important facet of our Confederate culture – The Importance of Ensuring Individual Liberty and State Rights.

Jules Saint Martin, my great-great-great-grandfather, was Judah Benjamin's nephew who worked alongside him during his term as Attorney General in the Davis Administration and as the leader of the Confederate Secret Service during the Seceded States' successful defense of their independence. And their writings and my family culture provided me a degree of guidance as I studied for and wrote this essay. Fellow Confederates, perhaps nothing is more important to our success, security and happiness as sustaining Individual Liberty and State Rights. So I began with a question; "Why, yes why, do Confederates cherish their Individual Liberty and State Rights?" I will be attempting to help you understand the answers to that "Why?".

First it is important to understand that these two characteristics of Confederate society go hand in hand. Human nature prevents a society from having Individual Liberty without State Rights, thereby preventing a society from sustaining Individual Liberty where the central government can trump State Rights and dictate its will upon one, several, or all of the States and the people who live in each. You see, in a democracy without sufficient constitutional restrictions on power grabs by the majority, humanity will naturally and foolishly evolve its limited central government structure into a rather unlimited central government where power is consolidated, thereby creating a "Monopoly of Government," where political demagogues and their supportive voting majority can dictate policy that erodes both State Rights and Individual Liberty. By this method, over several generations, a constitutional guarantee of State Rights can be systematically minimized, bit by bit, to such an extent that Individual Liberty gradually withers on the vine. This was on the verge of happening in 1860 when the Northern States Republican Party gained control over the governor's office in every Northern State as well as the Federal House and Senate and the office of President. Republican leaders decided that they could slowly but surely expand Federal power with the belief that they would remain in control and make government serve them and their supporters at the expense of the others who lived in the country.

The Southern States, realizing the danger of Northern States Republican Party rule, and, seeing no benefit from remaining in the Union, decided to secede, which was approved by eleven States -- a legal prerogative of those seceding States. The Lincoln administration attempted to force the seceded States back under its control by military means, but failed in that attempt. A peace treaty was drawn and a boundary between the North and South was established, defining the extent of the Confederate States of America prior to the additions of the Seceded Mexican States, Russian America, Cuba and Hawaii.

For some of you who are listening to my presentation, the message going forward will seem unnecessarily legally technical. Yet, that is the language that underpins our country's legal system. I will continue.

At the beginning of its existence, the Confederacy was established on a foundation of State Rights, a foundation even more stringent than was the union from which its States had left. And, while State Rights in the North thereafter steadily withered into almost nothing, in the South, stringent limits on centralized power persisted and are alive yet today.

So why and how has retaining broad restrictions on central power contributed to making the Confederate States of America the "Greatest Nation of Earth?" I will explore that with you.

To me a key to our understanding remains with the original Confederate Constitution. [334]

In the Preamble of their Constitution, Confederates, at the outset, assured that each and every one of their States was initially "sovereign and independent," and each was only delegating specific and limited powers to a central government, reserving all the remainder to itself and its citizens.

"We, the people of the Confederate States, each State acting in its sovereign and independent character, in order to form a permanent federal government, establish justice, insure domestic tranquility, and secure the blessings of liberty to ourselves and our posterity, invoking the favor of Almighty God, do ordain and establish this Constitution for the Confederate States of America."

The States were insistent that the central government not be allowed to boost the economy of certain states over others or disproportionately empower a favored population class, a favored industry or a favored section over others.

- No "duties or taxes on importations from foreign nations can be laid to promote or foster any branch of industry."
- No "clause contained in the Constitution, shall ever be construed to delegate the power to Congress to appropriate money for any internal improvement intended to facilitate commerce; except for [coastal navigation and harbor works]."
- "No preference shall be given by any regulation of commerce or revenue to the ports of one State over those of another."
- "Reserving to the States, respectively, the appointment of the officers, and the authority of training the militia" according to the discipline prescribed by Congress.
- Important rights of citizens were enumerated. These included the right to religious liberty, trial by jury and personal gun ownership.
- "Congress shall make no law respecting an establishment of religion, or prohibiting the free exercise thereof; or abridging the freedom of speech, or of the press; or the right of the people peaceably to assemble and petition the Government for a redress of grievances."
- "No religious test shall ever be required as a qualification to any office or public trust under the Confederate States."

---

[334] The quotations from the original Confederate Constitution in this book are all truthful history. The original Confederate Constitution was carefully constructed to ensure and to perpetuate State Rights and Individual Liberty for all citizens, including those of African ancestry who were free, but not those who remained bonded to a master.

- "A well-regulated militia being necessary to the security of a free State, the right of the people to keep and bear arms shall not be infringed."

- "The enumeration, in the Constitution, of certain rights shall not be construed to deny or disparage others retained by the people of the several States."

- "The powers not delegated to the Confederate States by the Constitution, nor prohibited by it to the States, are reserved to the States, respectively, or to the people thereof." This means that the central government, the Confederate States of America, can only exercise those specific powers authorized by the various States.

In the original Confederate Constitution, the right of each Confederate citizen to due process of law was firmly stated.

- "The right of the people to be secure in their persons, houses, papers, and effects, against unreasonable searches and seizures, shall not be violated; and no warrants shall issue but upon probable cause, supported by oath or affirmation, and particularly describing the place to be searched and the persons or things to be seized."

- "No person shall be held to answer for a capital or otherwise infamous crime, unless on a presentment or indictment of a grand jury, except in cases arising in the land or naval forces, or in the militia, when in actual service in time of war or public danger; nor shall any person be subject for the same offense to be twice put in jeopardy of life or limb; nor be compelled, in any criminal case, to be a witness against himself; nor be deprived of life, liberty, or property without due process of law; nor shall private property be taken for public use, without just compensation."

- "In all criminal prosecutions the accused shall enjoy the right to a speedy and public trial, by an impartial jury of the State and district wherein the crime shall have been committed, which district shall have been previously ascertained by law, and to be informed of the nature and cause of the accusation; to be confronted with the witnesses against him; to have compulsory process for obtaining witnesses in his favor; and to have the assistance of counsel for his defense."

- "In suits at common law, where the value in controversy shall exceed twenty dollars, the right of trial by jury shall be preserved; and no fact so tried by a jury shall be otherwise reexamined in any court of the Confederacy, than according to the rules of common law."

- "Excessive bail shall not be required, nor excessive fines imposed, nor cruel and unusual punishments inflicted."

- "Every law, or resolution having the force of law, shall relate to but one subject, and that shall be expressed in the title."

- "The trial of all crimes, except in cases of impeachment, shall be by jury, and such trial shall be held in the State where the said crimes shall have been committed."

- Amendments to the Confederate Constitution could be initiated by any three States or by Congress. Ratification required approval by two-thirds of the States.

- "Upon the demand of any three States, legally assembled in their several conventions, the Congress shall summon a convention of all the States, to take into consideration such amendments to the Constitution as the said States shall concur in suggesting at the time when the said demand is made; and should any of the proposed amendments to the Constitution be agreed on by the said convention -- voting by States -- and the same be ratified by the Legislatures of two-thirds of the several States, or by conventions in two-thirds thereof -- as the one or the other mode of ratification may be proposed by the general convention -- they shall thenceforward form a part of this Constitution. But no State shall, without its consent, be deprived of its equal representation in the Senate."

It is a key Confederate constitutional principal that limits on Confederate power are unassailable and rates of taxation in each State must apply equally for all citizens and corporations within that State. This obligation upon every State ensures that a State cannot compete for loyalty by shifting tax burdens from one class to another. Tax rates on individuals and corporations must match. The Confederate Government has no power to set tax rates in a State simply to ensure a State is not imposing favoritism. But every State is obligated to apply the same tax rates, within its borders, equally to all classes.

Another key characteristic of Confederate life is the uniform rule that every citizen has a right to work without constraints imposed by labor unions. Employees of private companies and corporations can form unions to advance their group interests, but no employee can be forced to participate in union activities or to pay union dues. Of course, no government employee at any level of government can belong to a union.

Also civil court lawsuits must cover valid issues between plaintiff and defendant and monetary settlements must be restricted to compensation for proven loss. This means that a court cannot impose additional punitive damages, such as damages related to alleged pain and suffering, etc.

Thanks again for your attention. I am afraid my time is all used up. I could go on for hours, but now turn the podium over to Professor Davis, who will introduce our third essayist.

Professor Davis:

Thank you Miss Saint Martin. Such an important subject and so well done.

## Essay 3 — Because Individual State Governments Compete for the Loyalty of Her Citizens and Because Powerful Local Governments Ensure Local Control.

By Emma Catherine Lunallilo

Professor Davis:

Yes, it is time to introduce Miss Emma Cathrine Lunalilo of the great Pacific State of Hawaii, who will present her essay on how local governments and State governments compete for the loyalty of the citizenry and why honest competition is good for our people and for our country. Miss Lunalilo's great-great-great-grandfather, the last King of the Monarchy of the Hawaiian Islands, did much to facilitate transforming his kingdom into a democratic nation and then into a State within the Confederate States of America. All this time he retained the loyalty of his people, making the political transformation peaceful and successful for all involved. Miss Lunalilo's college and doctorate work on Political Science and Diversified Government, coupled with her unique personal heritage, affords her special insight into the subject of which she is about to speak. Fellow Confederates, I present Miss Emma Cathrine Lunalilo."

Emma Catherine Lunallilo:

Thanks to you Professor Davis and thanks to this wonderful audience and those watching on television, wherever you are. My essay explains why the Confederate States are the "Greatest Country on Earth" from a third perspective – from the perspective of citizen loyalty. Loyalty to our country is considered a given fact of Confederate life. But what about loyalty to one's State or to his city, town or county. What keeps Confederates from moving about frequently seeking "greener pastures" and depleting some places and enriching other places? What about competition among all of those governments for our loyalty?

Marie Saint Martin's essay about Individual Liberty and State Rights naturally leads us to questions about local and State governance. It leads us to questions about interactions among the various State governments today, in the year 2011. Without a powerful Confederate Government forcing States to behave alike and cooperative, and when considering the amazing new inventions and advances in manufacturing and world trade over the past sixty years, would not advantaged States have become strong while disadvantaged States became weak? Well, there is some evidence of that, but the result is moderate, not severe.

So, my study these past few weeks and the essay I am presenting tonight will concern the importance of ensuring that each individual State competes for the loyalty of her citizens, for citizenship is first to the State, second to the country."

First, let us examine government within a typical State, much of which remains mostly local, including control over schools, roads, water, sewage, garbage, and property taxation. Of course, within a State, people sometimes vote with their feet, moving within the same State to a different county to seek a better life, a better job, better schools, lower taxes, a more suitable life style, etc. The ease with which people can relocate within the same State limits bad behavior by governments at the local county level. Furthermore, every State competes against sister States for the loyalty of its people by making itself attractive for industry, commerce, sought-after schools, quality of life, etc. Confederates have learned that a State that is advantaged in resources, transportation, schools, weather, topography, and/or quality of life does benefit in this competition, but there are limits.

There are limits because, when people and industry flock to an advantaged State, its cost of living rises and applies a break to slow down overly rapid expansion. A disadvantaged State fights back by enhancing what people find attractive there, be it low land cost, low taxation, attractive rural life, or by recruiting industry not needing certain advantages that might be deficient in their area, but benefitting from lower wage costs.

That's where the Interstate Commissions and the Governor's Councils play key roles in negotiating reasonable, mutually beneficial policies among neighboring States. If the Confederate Government in Davis was far more powerful with regard to regulating States, these Commissions and Councils would not be a factor in guiding various States policies. But, given our emphasis on State Rights, these Commissions and Councils are very much needed and very helpful. The Interstate Commissions help negotiate cooperative programs that facilitate a more level playing field, especially in transportation planning and attracting industry that is best suited to each State in a given region. Today, in the year 2011, Confederates still believe that this cooperative spirit is still working well for them. A few argue for a stronger central government, especially in dictating welfare programs and special benefits, and protections for so-called minorities, but such advocates have yet to find success. The firm restriction of voting rights to empower at the polls only those who "contribute" to government still acts as a barrier to the political efforts of the "Centralizers."

Allow me to define a term you have heard before. That term is "Monopoly of Government." This is a critical concept. We have long feared being dominated by a monopoly within an important industrial sphere. But what about government monolopy? This could apply to a Monopoly in the Central Government, in our case the Confederate Government in Davis. But it could also apply to Monopolies in certain State governments, or even all of them. In either case – with a Monopoly at the Central level or at the State level -- local government and individual citizens would lose many of the rights that had been envisioned for them long ago, at the creation of the Confederacy. There is good news. In the Confederate States of America, "Monopoly of Government" is absent, although it yet remains a future risk we strive to avoid. You see, over the 150 years of our existence, we have so far avoided succumbing to encroaching "Monopoly of Government." If you are a student of world history, you recognize that our situation has no parallel on earth. Absence of "Monopoly of Government" is uniquely Confederate. Of that we are thankful. But how have we avoided that pitfall?

Over the past 150 years there have been many efforts to, step by step, move our country toward certain monopolies. As transportation technology has advanced, many advocated central government control of and management of railroads, highways, waterways and airports. But State governments said we can work those issues out among ourselves, utilizing regional Interstate Commissions that report to the governors. As education advanced toward high school for just about everybody and college for more and more, the States said, "We can handle that, funds and regulations out of Davis are not needed." As industrial growth outstripped agriculture, creating new concerns about labor laws, work-week hours, collective bargaining and other issues, the people said, "We can handle that at the State level; we do not want to empower politicians at Davis to gain important control over the economy." And the restriction on import taxation (tariffs) that was embodied in the Confederate Constitution has remained in force. Davis does not manipulate taxation on imports to give advantage to any industry. Trade is not without tariffs, but the rates are modest and uniform, and the spirit of the Confederacy is "can do." We can compete world-wide given a fair chance. And we do.

But what happens when the government of a State grows too big and maneuvers its taxation to gain an advantage over others? We now explore that issue.

Several Confederate States are famous for attracting large populations of retired people and vacationers. Most noteworthy are three: Florida, Cuba and my State, Hawaii. Given their amazing year-around beaches, sun bathers, swimmers, sailors, fishermen and beach lovers in general are drawn to these States – not just Confederates, but people from all over the world – the United States, Canada, the British Isles and Northern Europe particularly. To be accommodating, these three States maintain a large vacation Visa program that controls foreign vacationers coming and going, and these State-specific Visas do not permit travel beyond the granting State boundary. It works well – an example of how State Rights works for Confederates. Visa's can be purchased for 8 weeks duration or 30 weeks duration, but only once per year. The 30-weeks Visas enable a large population of foreigners to come to these three States and spend six months in condominiums and houses they have purchased with the expectation of many years of use, each year, during the season that appeals to them individually.

Generally speaking, county, town and city taxes are derived mostly from taxes assessed on real estate. But the various States have adopted a mix of revenue collection concepts to augment property taxes – some rely heavily on sales taxes, some on income taxes, and some on a bit of both. As a result, some States have become havens for retired wealthy people with large incomes who choose to live in a State that relies mostly on sales tax revenue.

This variety of State taxation concepts works reasonably well. Confederates sort it out and simply leave a State that becomes abusive in its taxation of a certain class within the population. Some States do not need to tax residents much at all. Russian America is most noteworthy in this regard. Russian America's oil tax revenue is sufficient to fund all State needs and most of the local government revenue needs as well.

Manufacturing industries are a major part of the economies of the former Mexican States, and taxes on manufacturing corporations and their real estate fulfill most State and local revenue needs there, affording a lighter tax burden on the citizens of those States.

These are just examples. And some States are more balanced in taxation policy because of topography and tradition. North Carolina comes to mind. Lovely from the Outer Banks Atlantic coast to the Blue Ridge Mountains and westward to the Great Smoky Mountains, North Carolina contains lovely rural areas, rivers, lakes and expansive cities. She is a State that appeals to every Confederate desire somewhere along its vistas. Balanced in climate and tax policies, she attracts Confederates to work in textiles, furniture making, banking and investment finances, agriculture, and a variety of other manufacturing industries. A lot of those retired Florida folks come to the North Carolina Mountains for cool summer climes.

On the other hand, corporations that do business in several or all of the Confederate States cannot minimize income taxes by locating headquarters in a low-income-tax State. Why? Because Confederate law requires corporations and companies to report income in a way that fairly allocates it to the various States. This allows each State to tax a fair portion of the income reported by every relevant corporation and company.

This principle also applies to individuals with high income that maintain homes in several States and move about during the year. They must allocate their reported income to each relevant State based on the days lived there.

This concludes my presentation on efforts that governments within our Confederate States make to seek and retain the loyalty of their respective citizens. But one more comment before leaving the podium. You all, if you haven't ever come to the Hawaiian Islands to visit us, please make an effort to do that. Our islands, the ocean surrounding them and the people who live upon them are beautiful and eager to welcome you. Professor Davis?

Professor Davis:

Wonderful presentation, Miss Lulanlilo. Folks, I did not mention that Emma is an expert swimmer and surfer and that our essayists consider her a true hero. Three weeks ago six of our essayists spent a weekend break on an overnight sailing trip off the coast of Cuba and encountered a night-time "man overboard" crisis that might well have become a disaster had not Emma dove into the water and swam out through stormy seas to deliver a life jacket and flashlight to her fellow essayist.

## Essay 4 — Because The Right to Vote is Restricted to Citizens who Contribute to the Welfare of their Respective State.

By Carlos Jose Cespedes

Professor Davis:

Fellow Confederates, Mr. Carlos Jose Cespedes of Cuba will be presenting our next essay. I might mention that Mr. Cespedes is especially grateful for Miss Lunalilo's heroic swimming rescue because he was hosting the overnight sailing trip on his family sailboat that weekend and was striving to bring the craft about in the stormy seas and navigate back to his two fellow essayists before the crew lost sight of them in the dark stormy seas.

In Carlos Jose Cespedes' upcoming essay on voting rights in the various Confederate States, you will learn about how the right to vote is restricted to adults who contribute to the welfare of the State and excludes from voting those who live upon the welfare of the State. Ours is a culture that says, "If you are a contributor to the welfare of the state, you vote; if not, you are not a bad person, but should refrain from giving direction to the government that is helping to support you." Even in 2011, this long-standing rule still governs who gets to vote and who does not.

Mr. Cespedes is the great-great-great-grandson of Carlos Manuel Cespedes, the famous leader of the fight to win Cuban independence from Spain and the subsequent inclusion of the State of Cuba in our Confederate States. Please welcome Mr. Cespedes.

Carlos Manuel Cespedes:

Thank you Professor Davis. I will forever be grateful for Emma's heroic rescue. I have never known a human being who displayed such selfless bravery and risked so much for another person. And I thank fellow Confederates here today before me, and the millions watching on television, for your attention. My essay speaks to the question of, "Why are the Confederate States the Greatest Country on Earth" from the perspective of rules in each State concerning who is permitted to vote in any given year.

As Confederate citizens, you know that all voting rules are specific to a State and none are regulated by the Confederate Government, save the most basic of concepts. Perhaps this guidance has preserved the historic Confederate culture more than any other.

Voting rules vary a bit from State to State, but differences are minor. The State of Cuba is the most relaxed about limiting welfare recipients' access to voting. The four Texas states are perhaps the most stringent about limiting. But the differences between Cuba and the Texas States are not large. On the other hand, in the United States, people dependent on government largess are "organized" by "political machines" into voting blocks and often control elections in major metropolitan areas where they congregate to secure their government benefits and sustain them through their votes.

The right to vote, as defined in each State, is designed to ensure that the policies of every government within that State's boundaries is sufficiently reflective of the voting decisions of the citizens therein who enable its existence, whether that government covers a town, a city, a county, the entire State or election of Representatives and Senators to represent it in Congress.

Unless you are a Confederate yourself, you are probably living in a country where the right to vote is controlled at the national level. Not so in the Confederate States. At the outset, each State established it rules regarding voting rights. That has never changed. You see, overall immigration policy and is controlled by the Confederate Government in Davis, but, concerning voting rights of citizens living in a given State, it is that State that controls those issues. We observe that control over who votes at the State level is a powerful constraint on unwise growth in centralized power. By controlling voting rights, the individual States can exert important influence over the power and policies of the Confederate Government. It was like this throughout the United States before 1860, before the rise of the Northern States Republican Party, and the subsequent secession of eleven Southern States. But one consequence in the North of its war against the Confederacy was passage of an Amendment to the United States Constitution which centralized in Washington regulations over voting rights. [335]

So, with each Confederate State in control of voting rights, who is allowed to vote and who is not? Are the rules similar in each State? Yes, the rules are similar in most regards in each State. So we first look at the general rules that States have decided ought to apply all across the Confederacy.

Of course no person who is not a citizen is allowed to vote. And identification of valid citizenship is carefully ensured everywhere. Nobody is successful at pretending to be a citizen when that is not so.

The Age Requirement.

Every citizen upon reaching the age of 21 years is qualified to vote if he or she passes the tests defined below. [336] If presently in the Confederate military, a man or woman can vote at age 18 years.

The "Net Contribution Test."

To vote, a citizen must contribute to his or her State, county and city governments in an amount that clearly exceeds any benefits received from government welfare programs. Every five years, an accounting is made and if the person passes the test, he or she is approved for the next five year period. Each five year period begins with the first year of voter registration and repeats every fifth year thereafter (the test update is applied by the State of current residence). That means that everyone who pays taxes and receives no government welfare benefits easily passes the "Net Contribution Test." For those receiving government welfare over the previous five years, an accounting is made by the elections board to determine which is the greater – taxes paid or government welfare received? If the greater is taxes paid, the "Net Contribution Test" is approved. If government welfare exceeds taxes paid, the person does not pass the test and voting is not allowed for the upcoming five year period (it will be refigured five years later).

The "Good Citizen Test."

No person who is sentenced to prison is allowed to vote until 10 years following his or her release. A second sentence to serve prison time results in loss of voting rights for the remainder of that person's life. Even military veterans are not exempt from this limitation.

The "Military Service Test."

Regardless of age, every man or woman who has served two years or more in the Confederate Armed Services is allowed to vote, even if he fails to pass the "Net Contribution Test."

---

[335] In truthful history following the conquest of the Confederate States, the United States centralized control over voting rights throughout the states, ending forever local control over that key State Right.

[336] In our alternate history the voting age in Hawaii was raised from 18 to 21 years 20 years following statehood.

The "Capability Test."

A person who is judged to be incapable of understanding the workings of government is not allowed to vote. When a person, normally upon reaching the age of 21 years, applies to be registered to vote, he or she is interviewed by an election official who is trained to fairly judge competency. This is a once in a lifetime event for most. Every State accepts the judgement of another State's competency judge, so moving about during one's lifetime is not an issue. Only the most mentally handicapped are ruled unfit. The applicant must be able to read aloud a basic and brief story in simple English about the fundamental workings of the Confederate Government. Looking ahead to old age, devastating sickness or accident, the voter may encounter another need for testing. Here, his or her doctor is asked to evaluate the person for competency. There are appeals available in every case. In the early years of the Confederacy, applicants not minimally proficient in English were allowed to prove competency in their native language. But on the 100-year anniversary of the Confederacy, the States agreed to require sufficient competency in English to pass the "Capability Test." Today, this seems like a harsh hurdle for new immigrants, but Confederates expect immigrants to adopt the culture and language of their new homeland and believe that becoming sufficiently capable in English and the workings of their government to pass the voter test is a strong incentive for them to work to achieve success at it. Confederates believe today that, to intelligently cast a vote, a citizen must be able to understand appeals by candidates expressed in English.

The "Identity Test"

Every voter carries a "Voter Registration Card" to the poll to prove identity. The card, resembling a driver's license, contains a photograph and a thumb print. A copy of every card is retained by the State Registration Office and lost cards can be replaced at any post office after filling out a request. When a person moves, the "Voter Registration Card" continues to be good. On the back of the card is room to record up to 8 polling location codes, meaning that a card need not be replaced when a person moves about. The States have agreed on the format for the card so they all look similar. The original State of issue is identified. When mailing in an absentee ballot, the card is enclosed in the envelope. It is mailed back after the election.

The "Marriage Test"

A married couple is evaluated as a whole. If one passes the above tests, then the spouse is considered to be passing as well. Of course, the exception is criminal behavior; the spouse of a criminal is not denied the right to vote for that reason.

## Concluding Thoughts.

What does the above list of rules mean? It means that the Confederate voter will understand the workings of government and contribute to its success. It means that voters take pride in being qualified to vote and take the responsibility seriously. It means the vote is not corrupted by people not deemed worthy of the privilege, such as criminal behavior, incompetency, inability to comprehend arguments expressed in English, and/or excessive dependency on government welfare. And it means that those overly dependent on government welfare are incentivized to strive to do better for themselves -- that society wants more from them. Furthermore, it recognizes that married couples and stable families are the backbone of a prosperous and successful society. To further that goal, the married are given a qualification advantage by being treated as a couple.

People from foreign countries often complain that the several States in the Confederacy are too restrictive on qualifying people to vote. Some say voting should be allowed by a teenager upon reaching the age of 18 years. Well, he or she can vote at 18 if in the Confederate military. Not so otherwise. And that overall policy has proven to contribute to voter wisdom. Young people acquire a lot of wisdom between the age of 18 and the age of 21. Trust me on that. A lot of growing up takes place in those three years. Some say the Capability Test discriminates against recent immigrants and young people who have done poorly in school. They cite a disproportionally high percentage of colored people in the disqualified group. That is foolish. The prevalence of colored people is only moderately higher than of others. Education in every State in the Confederacy is of high quality and students of every race and background do rather well, especially with regards to the fundamentals needed to qualify as a voter. Among twenty-one-year-olds, less than one percent of voter applicants are disqualified for Insufficient Capability (of people over 80 years of age the disqualification is 3 percent). Thus criticism of our voting rules is unrealistic and very few elections would be decided differently if the Capability Test were discontinued. On the other hand, the Capability Test is a meaningful restraint against political demagoguery -- an ever-present danger to good government in a democracy.

The "Net Contribution Test" is the most criticized. It is tough. But Confederates are determined to avoid the rise of a welfare state mentality within society. Restricting the vote to people who pay more in taxes than they receive in welfare from their State and local governments is a sound concept that prevents a culture of "taxation without representation." Only those that pay the taxes (and/or serve in the military) are allowed to vote for candidates to "represent" them in government. In the old days government welfare did not exist, so a computation of taxes paid versus welfare received made no sense. Now, State and local government welfare programs exist, although to a much lesser extent than in most developed nations. So, Confederates simply ask: "Do the math: if tax payments exceed welfare receipts, please go to the polls and vote. If not, we encourage you to try harder." We have even heard complaints about the voter identification card with photo and thumb print. That complaint is ridiculous. Just get a life! Now we come to the Marriage Test. Well, evaluating a couple as a whole is simply good common sense. With that, I close my case.

There are small differences in voting qualification rules among the several States, but there is insufficient room in this essay to list those differences. They are small and impact election results very little.

What is the bottom line for this essay? The "proof is in the pudding", as my grandmother often said. The Confederacy is the greatest country in the world. That is a given. Why? Well, control over voting rights at the state level and the rules each State has established for voter qualification is surely a major contributing factor to our success. Want more proof? At state elections where voters choose their governors and legislators, the average turnout at the polls is 67 percent. Compared to other countries, that is a great rate of participation. This proves that our contributing citizens are engaged in ensuring that government works for them.

I thank you for your attention. I hope you have found my remarks helpful in furthering your understanding of how the voting rules in our respective States have contributed to making our Confederate States the greatest country on earth. Professor Davis?

Professor Davis:

Folks, what you have just heard presented by Mr. Carlos Jose Cespedes explains much that a person needs to understand in answering the question, 'Why are the Confederate States the greatest country on earth? Thank you Mr. Cespedes.

## Essay 5 — Because International Trade and Low Tariffs Encourage a Vibrant Economy

By Chris Withers Memminger.

Professor Davis:

Our fifth essay will be presented by Mr. Chris Withers Memminger of South Carolina. Chris was the "man overboard" person so heroically rescued by Miss Emma Lunalilo of that fateful over-night sailing trip off the coast of Cuba. Chris, our audience probably wants to know how you fell overboard?

Chris Memminger:

First, let me say that I am probably standing before you all today only because of the heroic swim by the amazing Emma Lunalilo. In the darkness she impulsively grabbed a life jacket and flashlight and dove into the turbulent seas and swam toward me, not because she could see me, but because we were shouting back and forth to determine direction by sound. It was that dark. OK, why the heck was I in the water in the middle of the night? I had been seasick for much of the trip. Never been sailing on the open ocean before. I was trying to get some sleep topside near the helm when I just had to vomit. I stood up and leaned over the side of the boat to vomit into the water when a gust of wind struck the sails and tilted the boat way over. I lost my grip and fell overboard. All that in just an instant, at the onset of an incoming storm. So Emma Lunalilo is my heroine.

My essay today answers the question, "Why are the Confederate States the Greatest Country on earth" from the perspective of international trade and our tariff structure and how our Confederate trade policies have encouraged, and still encourage, a vibrant Confederate economy. Professor Davis assigned that topic to me because my great-great-great-grandfather was Christopher Gustavus Memminger, the Secretary of the Treasury in the Jefferson Davis Administration. So I now began.

Confederate attitiudes toward international trade and low tariffs originated in the days of State Secession and the creation of the Confederate States of America. So I should start at the beginning and, from there, bring us forward to recent times.

Much of the 1850s political disagreement between the American States, North versus South, originated from opposing views on the schedule of tariffs imposed on imports, the vast majority coming from overseas. Industrialists in the Northeast, struggling to complete with imports from Europe, campaigned for high tariff walls to discourage imports and allow for big domestic price increases. Agriculturalists in the South -- being by far the biggest purchasers of imported goods, seeing little of the tariff revenue being spent in their region, and being a major exporter of cotton, which sustained the value of American currency -- believed that international trade should be conducted over low tariff walls and, for some products, no tariff at all. So, upon its creation, the Confederate States instituted a minimal tariff schedule. On the other hand, immediately after State Secession, the United States Government dramatically raised the rates on its tariff schedule. In fact, to a large extent, the Lincoln Administration decided to wage financial war on the Confederate States to force merchant ships entering our seaports to pay the United States Government the high tariffs it had enacted immediately after our State Secession.

Well, following the Treaty of Montreal, the Confederate Government retained the low rates on its tariff schedule for two reasons. First, Confederates were exporters and were actively negotiating trade deals: seeking low tariff rates on cotton shipped to other nations in exchange for low rates on imports arriving at Confederate seaports. Second, Confederates wanted their central government at Davis to be distinctly limited in power (the Confederate Constitution limited import tariffs to only that needed to raise revenue, protectionism being outlawed). Also, the long boundary between the Confederate States and the United States (similar to Canada's long southern boundary) suggested that the costs of catching and punishing smugglers and the costs of manning tariff collection stations along the border were not worth the revenue received.

Of course, at the time of our beginning, there was a tremendous need to develop industry within our borders. But Confederates were tough and resourceful and they were determined to succeed with industrialization without protective tariffs. How did they do that?

- The War had made Confederates intensely patriotic: they were willing to pay more to buy local to advance the country's industrial economy.

- From the outset, Confederates encouraged immigration of mechanics, machinists, iron and steel workers, boilermakers, pipefitters, shipbuilders, railroad men, farm equipment manufacturers, textile engineers, and individuals who were expert in scientific studies or in starting industrial enterprises of all types, as well as entrepreneurs with access to capital. And those valuable immigrants came by the thousands; from Europe and from the United States. These courageous men perceived the Confederacy as a golden opportunity: a new land, relatively free of existing competitors and political restraints, where they would enjoy success.

- Early on, the Confederate States encouraged the startup of trade schools and engineering schools, often loaning money to school and college startups with easy payback terms. But, beyond high school, Confederates never set up a system of State supported colleges or universities. The Confederate economy benefited from the private enterprise approach to expanding education toward the practical arts, science and engineering, with less emphasis on a classical education.

- We also need to recognize the contribution of Confederates of African descent. New farm equipment and methods were making it possible to get greater yields with fewer workers. And the population of people of African ancestry was expanding. Furthermore, there was great interest in progressing individuals from bondage to independence. By contractually assigning a slave to work in industry for wages, he gained valuable skills and the money he earned in excess of the cost of his upkeep often went toward paying his owner an amount sufficient to gain independence for him and his family. Programs like these rapidly advanced people toward freedom and independence. Another essay will cover that in full detail. It was not unusual for such "work for freedom" contractual arrangements to be fulfilled in five to seven years. [337]

- There was a parallel contribution from Confederates of European descent. Confederate farm families were typically very large, a couple often raising five to eight children to adulthood. Subdividing the farm for the family's married children typically reduced their standard of living. Moving west to establish new farms was a great solution for many, but not for all. So, from these large farm families, many children, upon reaching adulthood, sought careers in industry and commerce.

- Finally, we come to the nature of and capabilities of the broad diversity within the Confederacy, a land populated by ancestors of Northern European immigrants, Spanish American immigrants, Natives, imported Africans, and others -- and to a lesser extent a land containing Russian Americans and Hawaiians. In such a mixed population one sees

---

[337] Indentured seven-year contracts between an established colonist and an arriving immigrant from Europe were commonplace during early colonial days in America.

broad genetic and cultural skill sets. Some Confederates are skilled at physical labor; some are skilled at mental tasks; some are skilled at creating substantial businesses and corporations; some are exceptionally inventive, and the list goes on and on. Many set career goals that ensure they will be comfortable and successful at raising their families, but not much more. And those goals are worthy and necessary. Others set career goals that strive for more -- to reach a higher level of excellence -- and these are often leaders in their chosen fields. And these goals and achievements are also worthy and necessary. Yet, beyond that second group, are the truly exceptional Confederates who have remarkable skills and talents and the drive and passion to make the greatest contributions. It is among this last group, that the Confederacy derives its greatest success in science, industry, innovation, new business ventures, and new products -- ranging from that new hybrid tomato that has better flavor and longer shelf life, to that robotic device that increases manufacturing efficiency, to that new cancer drug that is curing some and extending the life of others. Confederates recognize that is it among those in the last group who are making the greatest contributions to the advancement of our country. Yet, those of the last group could never achieve such success without the contributions of all the other Confederates in the workforce, striving to make their individual contributions toward maintaining and expanding the Confederate economy. That is the nature of diversity. We are all different and we can all make worthy contributions.

At this point I need to fast forward to more recent times, to our experiences over the past, say, sixty years.

When viewing international trade in the modern era, one observes that much, much has changed worldwide over the past sixty years up to 2011. Yet, diversity within the Confederate States has continued to keep our country competitive in this global economy. Over these six decades, Asia has changed dramatically -- especially in the Chinese Confederacy and in Korea and Japan, where manufactured goods are both of high quality and inexpensive. Although Confederates do fairly well in meeting this competition, it puts our neighbors to the north, the United States, at a great disadvantage, because they must struggle with excessive government regulations, strong labor unions, lawyers, discouraging taxation, etc. Because those issues are far less prevalent here, manufacturers in the Confederate States are not disadvantaged nearly as dramatically.

Over the past sixty years, the United States has accumulated too many lawyers (58 lawyers for every other wage earner), too many accountants, auditors and supporting clerks (27 for every other wage earner) and too many Federal Government workers (59 for every other wage earner). The Confederate States have far fewer of the three classes mentioned above (less than half the US number per other wage earner). Why? Because many of those people are not needed in the Confederate States. But, how -- in today's world-wide economy and commercial complexity -- have Confederates avoided burdening their economy with inordinate legal and bookkeeping overhead expenses? There is insufficient space here to give all the reasons, but the most important include: far less government rules and regulations to be met; a far simpler tax code; the burden is on plaintiff to pay the legal expense of defendant if it loses its lawsuit; absence of "punitive damages" awards in court cases, and far fewer lawyers elected to State legislatures and Congress – eager to enact laws that enrich lawyers. On the other hand, the Confederate States have far more engineers (3,000,000, a number triple that in the United States), far more skilled manufacturing and construction employees, and far more skilled manufacturing managers.

More than ever before, United States manufacturing corporations are managed to maximize profit only on a quarter-by-quarter basis, always looking to the near term bottom line and tomorrow's stock price. There, growth is too often through acquisitions and moving manufacturing out of the country. On the other hand, Confederate manufacturing corporations are managed for the long haul, with a view five years or more into the future. Owners of stocks in Confederate corporations understand this philosophy and take comfort in it. So, Confederate corporations focus on product improvement, new products, more efficient production methods, robotics, and computer-controlled machines to increase productivity per employee. When a new manufacturing plant is built in a Confederate State you can be assured it will be the most efficient of its kind anywhere on earth in terms of units of product per man-hour of labor.

Now, over the years, the Confederate idea of free international trade has moderated in response to competition from other counties, but the tariff structure for Confederate imports and exports is modest and negotiated on a country-by-country basis to bring equity to the balance of trade, enabling money flow between trading partners to approach breaking even at year-end. Confederates are net exporters of petrochemicals, agricultural products, information technology, synthetic fibers, and many more classes of products.

An example of a Confederate-negotiated balance in trade can be observed in finished clothing: a deal is struck whereby Confederate companies export cotton, synthetic fibers, dyes and finishes and the trading partner returns those in finished clothing. Compare that to our neighbor to the north, where the so-called trading partner goes elsewhere for all raw materials and still exports to the United States the finished clothing – no deal struck there.

In closing, I submit that these policies and programs contributed greatly to successful expansion of industrialization in the Confederate States, without relying on the crutch of high tariff walls.

Fellow Confederates, I thank you for your attention and now hand over the podium to Professor Davis.

Professor Davis:

Thank you Chris. We believe that over the past 150 years the Confederate States have managed international trade policy successfully, with proper attention to the needs of all concerned.

## Essay 6 — Because Immigration Policy Emphasizes Enforcement and Selecting Applicants Most Beneficial to Confederate Advancement

By Benedict Christian Juarez

Professor Davis:

Our next essay will be presented by Benedict Christian Juárez of Costa Este, one of the six States that resulted from Mexican State Secession. His great-great-great-grandfather was Benito Juárez, the great Mexican leader and revolutionary of which we have already said much today. Doctor Juárez recently earned his Ph. D. in Philosophy at Juárez University in Ciudad Juárez in the State of Central Norte. Perhaps my mentioning the name 'Juárez' three times in the same sentence explains the scope of the historical importance of our next essayist's ancestor. So I proudly turn the podium over to Dr. Benedict Christian Juárez.

Benedict Juárez:

Thank you Professor Davis and my thanks go out to everyone here and those watching on television. I am grateful for being here and for being given an opportunity to present an essay on a subject that is so dear to me. Perhaps I am not as thankful over being here as was the previous essayist, but thankful just the same. I was not on that sailing trip. How about another round of applause for the amazing Emma Cathrine Lunalilo?

Fellow Confederates, my study and subsequent essay will concern the importance of ensuring that Confederate immigration policy emphasizes enforcement of our borders, and selection and recruitment of skilled and productive people and families who were encouraged to become legal immigrants.

I begin with a review of the history of Confederate immigration in the early years. So we first examine the long-standing Confederate policy that no person is allowed to enter the land of the Confederacy without a government entry permit. Enforcement of this policy was not completed immediately following the establishment of boundaries. But the intent to establish such a policy and to establish firm enforcement did come rather quickly. By 1870 border enforcement was well established. The first line of defense was the "Confederate Identification Card," what a fellow called his CIC. There were three versions of the CIC: a citizen CIC, a temporary resident CIC, and a visitor CIC. A person needed his or her CIC to do just about anything. You could not buy property without your CIC; could not buy a train ticket without one; could not marry; could not get credit for having paid your taxes; could not get through a traveler's check point; could not get a job without your employer getting into trouble; and the list went on and on. By 1890 all CIC cards had photos and thumb prints. The photography cost considerable money, but being a Confederate was something to be proud about and those in our country illegally were to be shunned. A person caught without a CIC was either found to be qualified to receive one or was deported and allowed to carry away only the minimal essentials (the fine for tardiness in getting a CIC stung a bit, but was not thought excessive). A temporary resident CIC was required for a limited work term or to attend school, these being purchased before departing for the Confederate States. A citizen CIC was issued to all citizens free of charge and was easy to obtain locally with proper documentation, most often the birth certificate.

Since a Visitors CIC was required to be carried by everyone who visited the Confederacy to visit friends and family or to vacation and sight-see, they were issued and paid for at the port of entry. Often a visa was obtained by the person prior to the start of his or her travels, and that made the issuance of the Visitors CIC quicker and smoother.

Now we get to the "National Fence." Yes the "National Fence." By 1910 the list of folks who wanted to emigrate into the Confederacy greatly outnumbered the list of available openings for persons who had skills that, unfortunately, were not in demand. People with great qualifications of education and skills in demand were not having trouble immigrating, for those were sought, even recruited. But the rest, the laborers and farm hands, were having a hard time qualifying for immigration. Thousands were sneaking across the border, especially from Mexico and South America. Apprehending them and sending them back was becoming very expensive. The solution was the "National Fence." Sounded like a huge drain of available Confederate labor. Images of the Great Wall of China were tossed about. It would take a lot of workers to build a barrier as restrictive as the "National Fence." Who would pay for it? Well, a solution was obvious. Immigration officials quickly realized that the laborers they needed to build the National Fence were right before their eyes. Instead of deportation, illegal immigrants were organized into work gangs and put to work building the "National Fence." It consisted of a leading masonry wall 2 feet thick and 15 feet high and a parallel masonry wall of the same dimensions. Barbed wire, and eventually electric wire, topped both walls. The two walls were separated by a 40-foot wide no-man's land where trained dogs often warned of intrusion. Since 1940, it has been brightly lit every night. Today it is monitored by cameras, underground digging listening devices, and an assortment of clever devices to further discourage breaching. Built primarily by illegal immigrants, the "National Fence" is a wonder to behold. It symbolizes the principal that the Confederate States is a country of laws and permission to become a Confederate citizen is a treasured gift.

Having discussed the CIC card and the National Fence, we now turn our attention to the Confederate Immigrant Recruitment Program. The process begins with a Sponsor's recruitment Application. A Sponsor seeking an immigrant or a group of immigrants might be an individual, a college, a corporation or a civic organization, such as a farmer's association, a trade gill or a chamber of commerce. A government organization could not act as a sponsor, but that was the only meaningful limitation. Advertisements for sought-after immigrants normally listed a specific skill set or skill sets needed, such as mechanics, chemists, textile engineers, college professors, scientists, people with railroad and steam engine experience, industrialists qualified to start businesses for which demand existed, etc. The possibilities were endless. But not all advertisements were forwarded to foreign embassies – when the desired skill was readily at hand somewhere in the Confederacy, the advertisement was returned. Farm worker advertisements were returned except for special skills, such as vineyard horticulture and wine making, or cultivation of new types of crops or orchards. Why? Confederates were already world leaders in agriculture. The Sponsor submitted the advertisement at the county seat; it was forwarded to the state capital where it was endorsed or questioned, and from there it was forwarded to Davis where it was accepted or returned. Davis forwarded the advertisement to selected embassies at countries where the desired skills were plentiful. At those embassies the advertisements were posted.

Organizations in those countries often facilitated communication between interested persons and Confederate embassies and helped with drafting responses in English for persons who felt qualified and wished to emigrate. Often resumes of hopeful emigrants were already on file at embassies, thereby permitting agents to match advertisements to resumes and return the matched file to the Sponsor If the Sponsor accepted the resume, the process was upgraded to a Sponsor-Emigrant Contract. Details varied, but the contracts covered how the cost of transportation was to be paid or reimbursed, acceptability of family members, the nature of the housing and job conditions at the Sponsor's locale. The number of years of contractual obligations was defined, and afterward citizenship was normally sought. Many emigrated from the United States and Great Britain. More came from Europe, especially Germany and France, and as far east as Russia. In the early years, the greatest priorities were given to emigrants who showed promise in inventing, developing and manufacturing labor-saving farm machinery and textile machinery. From north of the Ohio, England, Scotland and Germany came many who proved to be key to the impressive expansion in the Confederate farm machinery industry. From the northeastern United States, England and Scotland came those who were key to the rapid expansion of the Confederate textile industry. Major priority was given to the Confederate Immigrant Recruitment Program and papers advanced through channels rapidly. As the years went by, this program kept pace with emerging technologies, facilitating the growth of the Confederacy into the most advanced economy in the world.

Prior to the 1890's, emphasis was directed toward recruiting emigrants who would bring technological capability, for labor was readily available. But, by the mid-1890's, solid Christian families capable of strengthening the backbone of Confederate society were also encouraged to emigrate and the quotas allowed were generous. But emigration by several classes continued to be discouraged. The door to emigration by African Blacks remained closed with few exceptions. Because Muslims -- according to their religion's original fundamental doctrine -- were of a militant, conquest-driven, intolerant, state-church religion, they were viewed as incompatible with the voluntary religious culture and government philosophy of the Confederate States. Therefore, emigrants from Muslim countries were denied access unless they were considered to be Christian refugees from Islamic persecution. The quota for emigrants from Asia was small, but did allow for some activity, Hawaii receiving the most, primarily Chinese. Confederates never embarked on a policy of admitting emigrants who were fleeing tyranny in mother countries as a form of charity.

Yet, there was one exception: In response to the persecution in Nazi Germany, over one million Jews were brought into the Confederacy between 1937 and 1944, clearly saving many from the gas chambers, and many survivors followed in the decade afterward. My, how those Jewish immigrants have benefitted our country. Amazing!

Over the past sixty years, concluding in 2011, Confederates have continued to insist that all immigrants arrive legally and at the invitation of sponsors. Seems like people all over the world have hoped they or their children will someday live in one of the Confederate States. One class of the hopeful is characterized by people who seek to flee persecution by religious fanatics and to flee civil wars. However, Confederates do not open their doors to wholesale immigration of such asylum seekers, but they do encourage sponsors to find among those desperate people the few that promise to make important contributions to Confederate society. So, over the past sixty years, inviting people capable of making important contributions has been the focus of Confederate immigration policy. Many immigrants were also from among those who managed to escape the former Soviet Union. Some have been and are even now from among those who managed to escape Communist China.

An impressive number of the leading scientific, medical and engineering pioneers over the past sixty years have been and/or are immigrants who were sought out and sponsored to immigrate into the Confederacy. And they have made major contributions to Confederate prosperity and global economic competitiveness.

A contrast can be drawn between Confederate States immigration policy and United States immigration policy. In the United States, elites in the Democratic Party configure immigration policy with an eye on enlarging the Democratic Party vote, and hand out government largess to win those votes. Not so in the Confederate States. The Confederate people agree that their's is a cherished country whose borders deserve firm enforcement and whose invitations to immigrate should be given out to only the most worthy applicants.

That has continued to be Confederate policy over the past sixty years, and looks to be so into the foreseeable future. You may have read in the news that the Confederate immigration target for the 30-year generation beginning in 2010 and ending in 2040 has been reduce in recognition of the maturing growth experienced over the past 150 years. The target through 2040 is an immigration quota equal to 12 percent of the 2010 population. And the doors will be opened wider than before for people seeking to immigrate from Africa, India, South America and Asia, since our 70 percent minimum European ancestry diversity target has been surpassed.

The net result of our Confederate immigration policy has been the development of a diverse society committed to State Rights, a Responsible Electorate, and Individual Resourcefulness. Diversity is a good national trait, for a prosperous and vibrant society needs varied skills and varied industriousness. It needs people good at hard physical work just as surely as it needs people good at challenging mental work. It needs good managers just as surely as it needs faithful workers. It needs creative scientists and inventors just as surely as it needs schooled technologists to bring those discoveries to market. It needs both good teachers and diligent students. The very bright find routine boring; the less bright find routine comforting. A few become leaders; many become followers. A few start up and run their own businesses; many become employees. Many base their happiness on a good home and family life where Mother is the focus of activity (If mama ain't happy, ain't nobody happy). And women engaged in the homemaking career are commonplace, even today. So the list goes on and on. Another essay will say more about family life, children, population expansion, and so forth.

Ladies and gentlemen, that concludes my essay. Thank you. Professor Davis?

Professor Davis:

Thank you Dr. Juárez. No other essayist on the Sewanee Project team would have been more fitting as you have been for studying and presenting this very important facet, which is so very important for understanding why the Confederate States are the greatest country on earth.

# Essay 7 — Because the Two Major Political Parties Compete by Appealing to an Informed Electorate

By Allen Bruce Ross

Professor Davis:

Fellow Confederates, our next essay, number seven, concerns the importance of sustaining an informed electorate. Folks, in Confederate elections from the local school board, to the mayor, to the Governor, to the Congressional Representative, to the Confederate President, candidates seldom gain traction in our country through political demagoguery and trickery. Why? Because a substantial majority of Confederate voters are well informed and quick to reject such politicking tomfoolery. And I am pleased to tell you that Allen Bruce Ross will be presenting the Sewanee Project essay on this aspect of understanding why we are so great.

Allen Bruce Ross is of mixed European and Cherokee ancestry. His family raises grass-fed bison on a large family ranch in western Sequoyah, a 4,500 acre spread named "Ross Brothers Buffalo Ranch." But Allen is more than a bison rancher. He is also a degreed attorney who specializes in Native American law. In fact he holds a degree in law from the University of the South. Yes, right here. I have known Mr. Ross for several years now and have always admired all that he has done. Allen descends from an important Cherokee that was very important in the history of the Five Civilized Tribes and the State of Sequoyah. I am speaking of his great-great-great-great-grandfather, Principle Chief of the Cherokee Nation, Koo-wi-s-gu-wi, also known by his English name, John Ross.

I now turn the podium over to Allen Bruce Ross. Allen?

Allen Bruce Ross:

Thank you Professor Davis for the introduction. Yes, folks, I am descended from the great Cherokee leader John Ross, and it is partly through knowledge of my family history that I feel able to present with a special warmth of feeling the essay that I have prepared over the past four weeks. Fellow Confederates, I firmly believe that the Confederate States are the Greatest Country on Earth partly because, and to a significant degree, "The Two Major Political Parties Compete by Appealing to an Informed Electorate."

My essay will concern the political parties over the 150-year history of the Confederacy and the extent to which citizens have demanded and secured for themselves an electorate that is exceptionally well informed and wisely wary of the evils of political demagoguery.

A previous essay discussed the composition of the Confederate electorate, the age limit of 21 years, the Capability Test and the Net Contribution Test. These rules, and others, go a long way in ensuring an informed electorate. Young men and women below 21 years of age usually still need to mature significantly. People unable to pass the Capability Test, because they are so few in number, are more symbolic than impacting. But the Net Contribution Test is very important, for it removes from the electorate a large block of citizens whose interest is likely selfish rather than patriotic. But this is only part of the story about how Confederates ensure an informed electorate.

First, I should mention that much of the sorting out of political issues takes place within our two major parties, which field the more important candidates for office. Called the Democratic Party and the Peoples Party, these two hold meetings and primaries where candidates vie for nominations. Of the two, the Democratic Party is the more conservative and the Peoples Party is the more progressive. And, like throughout the world, with television and internet readily at hand, the potential for political demagoguery is prevalent and the voter needs a good sense of history and wisdom to sort truth from fantasy, and identify the candidate best suited for offices in the city, county or State government or in our Confederate Government.

Confederates understand that being "informed" and being "educated" are very different concepts. But this fundamental truth is rather ignored in the United States. Many, even most, people living to our north are "educated," but they are poorly "informed." There, public schools through grade 12 seem to be turning out students who lack the ability to separate propaganda from meaningful facts. There, teachers and school systems have a "political or social agenda" to "teach" students a certain philosophy of political or social thought, and adroitly discourage critical study – instead, feeding them a pabulum of nice-sounding nonsense. Even in colleges and universities, the spoon feeding of the pabulum continues. When an inquisitive student looks deeper into a question in search of social truths that contradict the politically correct dogma, he or she is criticized and discouraged. The United States policy of educating toward "political correctness" is enabled by five notable features:

1. High schools that focus on college preparation and omit teaching life and trades skills.

2. Colleges that put far too many in classes that do not contribute to useful careers.

3. High schools and colleges that fail to teach entrepreneurship and running one's own business.

4. An education culture that encourages harmful student debt, and finances it with burdensome student loans.

5. High schools and colleges that fail to turn out young men and women who are critical thinkers and analysts of the world around them.

As a result, in the United States, many young people with only a high school education have not learned a skill, have trouble getting a good job, and become discouraged. And many with a college degree are burdened with debt, have acquired little useful training, and settle for a job that only requires a high school education. For many U. S. college graduates, it is off to graduate school, more debt, more disappointment and deepening frustration. The very weak manufacturing economy in the United States compounds this problem further, because good jobs are not plentiful.

For the most part, a person's "good sense of history and wisdom" is acquired from parents, teachers, trusted associates and selected reading. So let us look at each source of political wisdom in turn. We first look at parents.

Confederate society is a world-leader in the prevalence and emphasis on the importance of strong families. So, it naturally flows that parental guidance in matters of history and politics establishes a foundation upon which further knowledge is constructed. Most important is the father, who normally imparts leadership in matters of morality, social interactions and functions of government. But mothers, grandparents, uncles, aunts and older siblings are also influential. It is in listening to family discussions that the youngster first acquires a sense of what ought to be the proper roles of government and how to recognize good leadership.

We now look at teachers, and their role in making Confederates an informed electorate. Part of the story is the Confederate culture of "no nonsense" in education. Confederate men and women are adept at critical thought and at analyzing the information they encounter. In public school, students are trained to be critical thinkers, to search out the truths behind a question and to debate the question in search of the truthful answer. Another part of the story comes from positive work experiences for young men and women entering the work force and beginning to raise families of their own. They acquire a positive thinking, can do attitude, a byproduct of the strong Confederate economy, with good manufacturing jobs and appropriate training. This has been the situation over the past sixty years and continues to be the case today.

When school teachers work for the government, as is the case worldwide for most, there is a normal bias to teach the idea that big government is good government, for that promises more teacher jobs and higher teacher pay. And that bias surely exists, but it is tempered in the Confederacy by the fact that college and university education is not government funded, and it is there that teachers learn to be good teachers. So, unlike in countries with government-funded colleges, like the United States, Confederates do not suffer the handicap of a teacher education bias advocating big local government at all levels from local to Confederate. Furthermore, teachers unions do not exist in public schools, for no State government employ can organize a union to bargain for employee's wages and benefits. Our Constitution bans collective bargaining by Confederate Government employees, and all of the States have established like rules. Compared to most other countries, Confederate parents are more engaged with the schools and teachers where their children attend, and act as a policing factor, spotting and denouncing untruthful and biased instruction when observed. And when parents advocate solutions to perceived problems, local school boards listen. So, by and large, these factors work together to produce an educational culture in public schools that imparts a good and balanced knowledge of history and government responsibilities. Finally, in every State, the last year of high school features two important courses that seniors must pass to graduate: "Comprehensive and Comparative Confederate History" and "Government, Politics and Responsible Voting." We now turn to the influence of our culture, and of trusted associates.

Another part of the story is our culture, which believes there is no, yes, no "politically correct" answer to issues within society. The correct answer to an issue is the correct answer because it is the correct answer -- one that can be proven, by logical, scientific-style analysis, to be the correct answer. Concerning debate over a specific issue, Confederates often have different opinions, some emotionally driven, on what ought to be done to solve the problem -- but they seldom manage to shout down and cut off intelligent debate by demanding a desired answer simply because it is "politically correct".

There is a tendency in other democratic countries to condense political campaigns down to slogans, and to spend far greater effort in denouncing the opposition than in advocating the aspiring candidate's forward-looking policy or program for government. This is amply reinforced by the influence of television and the internet where, if unchecked, negative campaigning would rule.

Two Confederate cultural traditions work against a predominance of negative campaigning. First is the voters' tradition of ignoring predominantly negative advertising that demeans the opposition. A sense of fair play governs. The other is the strict libel laws, which can cause significant legal trouble for a candidate who recklessly and falsely engages in slamming the opposition while omitting mention of what he or she is advocating. Because of our informed electorate, candidates mostly lose votes when presenting abusive negative campaigning. We now look at selective reading and related thought.

Campaigns in our country emphasize the programs that the candidate advocates, his or her past political success, and the past success of prior party programs. And they emphasize this in concise campaign pamphlets that, in straightforward language, explain the platform of the candidate and his or her political party. Furthermore, education does not end upon graduation. Popular among Confederate parents and grandparents are the many well-written and factual books, pamphlets, newspaper and internet studies, and compact books, all presenting in everyday language factual analyses of various government programs at the local, State and Confederate level, as well as policies in foreign affairs. The Democratic Party maintains a commercial-free documentary-style television program. The People's Party does as well. These are biased, of course, but firm libel laws prevent excessive demagoguery. The Confederate motion picture industry is centered at two locations: Hollywood in South California and north-side Atlanta in Georgia. Admittedly, movie producers are trending toward sensational, violent, and frankly vulgar films, and the last decade has been the worse. But compared to movies produce in the United States, the Confederate film industry remains far more family-friendly and supportive of a good-government culture, personal responsibility and moral behavior.

I close with emphasis again on the Confederate family. Family tradition is exceptionally strong here, single parent families are relatively uncommon, and our youth acquire much of their traditional ability at critical thought and analysis from their parents and siblings. By the time men and women become twenty-one years old, this in-home teaching experience has equipped them to analyze political debate with a critical eye and to measure political parties, candidates and their agenda with good discernment. The difference in the consequential political campaign styles in the United States and in the Confederate States is readily observed. In the United States political demagoguery prevails; short, negative, and often merely hateful, campaign advertising peppers television. In the Confederate States the political demagogue is readily figured out and defeated. Combine that tradition with the limits on voter qualification and you have a country that is governed by an "informed electorate."

This concludes my essay, and I greatly appreciate your attention. Professor Davis?

Professor Davis:

Thank you Allen Bruce Ross. I have so appreciated spending time with you over the past few years during your Ph. D. studies here at the University of the South, and especially during the past four weeks of our Sewanee Project effort. We members of the Sewanee Project team wish you well in the future and look forward to future meals featuring your amazing bison steaks and buffalo burgers.

## Essay 8 — Because the Confederate Capital at Davis is no Bigger than it Ought to Be

By Conchita Marie Rezanov

Professor Davis:

Our eight essay will be presented by Conchita Marie Rezanov, whose ancestry goes back to the colonial days of Russian America. Folks, when the Sewanee Project was conceived two years ago, those involved decided early on that it would be essential that it be made up of descendants from all aspects of our country's heritage. I believe we have succeeded at meeting that goal, and we thank Miss Rezanov for representing the amazing, hardy and determined people of colonial Russian America and their descendants in the Confederate State of the same name. And our next essayist is so aptly prepared. She is presently working toward her Ph. D. in Political Philosophy at Argüello University in San Diego, South California. And my respect for and admiration of Miss Rezanov goes far beyond the academic world, into the world of competitive tennis. Some of you already know of Conchita as a highly ranked amateur tennis player. She deserves that and more.

Miss Rezanov's essay will help us understand that the Confederate Capital at Davis is no bigger than it ought to be, and to understand that smallness at Davis is a benefit to us, and, in fact, contributes to the greatness of our country.

Miss Conchita Marie Rezanov:

Thank you Professor Davis. Folks, as a senior player, this man plays a fine tennis game, proven to me on several doubles matches we have played over the last four weeks. So please keep it up, Professor Davis. Well folks, I am proud of my ancestor Nikolai Rezanov and his wife Concepción and the role they and their descendants played in leading the settlement of Russian America and in facilitating the colony's independence and subsequent inclusion into the Confederate States of America.

And that pride and family experience has contributed to my study for, and drafting of, my essay: "Because the Confederate Capital at Davis is no Bigger than it Ought to Be." Well, the answer is partly because our capital at Davis is no bigger than it ought to be. But how can smallness be great? Let me explain.

Over the past sixty years, across the globe, the capital cities of most countries have grown by leaps and bounds. Not so much Davis. It's amazing how compact is the capital of the "Greatest Country on Earth". Facilities for the Executive, Legislative and Judicial Branches have expanded only about 35 percent over the past 60 years. Confederate Military headquarters remain in Davis, but military facilities are even more decentralized than they were sixty years ago, following the victory in the War against Fascist Japan.

For comparison we look, at the size of the United States Federal capital that occupies the District of Columbia and the spill-over into neighboring Maryland and Virginia. Now that is big! Real big!

The various agencies within the United States Federal Government employ 1.0 percent of that country's workforce and 25 percent of those people work in and around the District of Columbia. Within the 18 non-defense Federal agencies (Agriculture, Commerce, Education, Energy, Justice, Labor, Interior, Treasury, Health and Human Services, Social Security, Veteran's Affairs, etc.) employment totals 692,000 persons, equal to one percent of total United States employment. And these employees consume a lot of building space, about 500 square feet each. The Federal Government long ago outgrew the 68 square mile confines of the original District of

Columbia. Today what is called the National Capital Metropolitan Statistical Area covers 3,060 square miles -- home to 3,350,000 people. We are quite different here in the Confederate States.

As you know, the Confederate Capital at Davis was carved out of land donated by Tennessee, Alabama and Mississippi. It measures ten miles east to west and fifteen miles north to south. Here we find the President's Residence, the Cabinet Building, the Congressional Building, the Representatives Building, the Senators Building, the Supreme Court, the Department of State Building, the Joint Military Command Building and nearby buildings for the Army Command, the Navy and Marines Command, the Air Force Command and the Special Forces Command. But the administrative offices of the Confederate military are not concentrated at Davis; only the senior offices are there. Designated locations around the country are responsible for weapons systems development based on weapon class, with the intent of provisioning all military needs. For example, Manned Aircraft Development is administered at Fort Worth, Texas; Guided Missile Systems Development at Atlanta, Georgia; Land Vehicle Development at Nashville, Tennessee; Naval Surface Vessel Development at Mobile, Alabama; Space Vehicle Development at Huntsville, Alabama; Naval Submarine Development at San Diego, South California; Artillery and Firearms Development at Richmond, Virginia, and Special and Other Weapons Development at Charleston, South Carolina. Military training facilities are dispersed about the Confederacy: Marine and Guerilla training is in Cuba; Desert warfare training is in Arizona; Artic training is in Russian America, and Special Forces training is in Hawaii. Experience shows that organizing military operations in this decentralized and weapons-specific manner results in economy, and moderates service rivalries. Although military defense is a major Confederate Government responsibility, efficiency in military matters keeps operations at Davis to a minimum.

The other major responsibility of the Confederate Government is regulation of International Trade and Foreign Relations. These functions are administered out of Davis with associated offices at Charleston, South Carolina; New Orleans, Louisiana; Puerto Vallarta, Costa Sudoeste; Los Angeles, South California; and Honolulu, Hawaii.

Unlike the United States, the Executive Department of the Confederate Government does not have a Department of Education, a Department of Labor Relations, a Department of Medicine and Healthcare, a Department of Pensions and Public Welfare, a Department of Transportation, a Department of the Interior. But it does have a Department of Postal Mail and Communications, and a Department of Border Security and Immigration Control. And the Confederate Department of State Relations is rather extensive and contains a large staff, for, although the individual States coordinate many public projects through Interstate Commissions and Governors' Councils, Federal staff is often involved as consultants in giving guidance.

Because the reach of the Confederate Government remains limited by the Confederate Constitution, much of what goes on in the United States capital takes place in our country at the State level (Agriculture, Education, Energy, Transport, Environmental Protection, Health and Human Services and Social Security) or is perhaps not even needed as a government function (Labor, Housing and Urban Development). Left for the Confederate Government are those important agencies (Commerce, Homeland Security, Justice, Interior, Treasury, Veterans Affairs, General Services Administration, and the State Department).

But that is not the full story, for the Confederate Government is not so heavily burdened by regulations that consume the time of huge bureaucracies. Therefore, Confederates are far more efficient at administering the responsibilities of their central government, because regulatory laws are not extensive. As a result, we see that government work at Davis remains within the boundaries of the 89 square mile district and about one third of the employees live in the District of Davis and the reminder live nearby in Tennessee, Mississippi and Alabama. Instead of the

692,000 Federal Employees needed to administer the terribly complex and expansive Federal governance of the United States, Confederates manage quite well with 341,000. So instead of the central government consuming 1.0 percent of the workforce, it only requires 0.25 percent in our country.

So, considering the limited scope of Confederate responsibilities, we ask the question, "Is Davis no bigger than it ought to be?". The answer is in the affirmative. Considering the vast size of the Confederacy, it is remarkable that its capital is small, with a population about ten percent of that observed in the United States. But it works remarkably well. Large bureaucracies are sluggish, inefficient and prone to make stupid decisions, those often being "too little, too late".

This concludes this essay, folks. Thanks for your interest in this fascinating explanation of how "smallness" enhances "greatness." Professor Davis?

Professor Davis: "Thank you Miss Rezanov. Although the years are creeping up on me now, I do hope to keep playing tennis a bit longer. Time spent on the court with you and other essayist has motivated me to stick to it.

# Essay 9 — Because the Councils of Confederate Governors Ensure Interstate Cooperation on those Regional and National Issues which are beyond the Authority of the Confederate Government

By Robert Edward Lee, IV

Professor Davis:

Fellow Confederates and television viewers around the world, we have four more essays to present from the Sewanee Project team. All twelve have addressed and will address, from different perspectives, answers to the question before us that is so very important for gaining the understanding we are seeking here today. Our next essay examines the role of the Council of Confederate Governors and the many Governors Multistate Commissions. Folks, how can a great modern country succeed without a centralized powerful central government? Well it can. And we Confederates have proved that to be so. Our next essayist, Robert Edward Lee, IV, is about to step forward to explain how we, as a people, are able to do just that.

Although only 23 years old, Mr. Lee is already working as a Confederate employee in the Department of Interstate Affairs, a consulting agency at Davis. He prepared for this career by earning a degree in Political Science at Jefferson Davis University in Jackson, Mississippi, and a Master's degree at The Calhoun School of Government Studies in Athens, Georgia. His great-great-great-grandfather was General Robert Edward Lee of Virginia, an important military leader of our Defense of Independence. Ladies and gentlemen, I present Robert Edward Lee, IV, born and raised in Montgomery, Alabama.

Mr. Robert Edward Lee, IV:

Thank you Professor Davis and thanks to all before us today and around the world watching on television. Professor Davis suggested that I was prepared by education for my new job in the Department of Interstate Affairs at Davis, but in truth, as of now, I remain at my new job more as a student than as an advisor. But, just being there these past two years, among the seasoned staff at DIA, gives me useful insight into how the Councils of Confederate Governors work, how the many Governors Multistate Commissions coordinate projects, and how competing interests are negotiated in good faith for the betterment of all States within our Confederacy. But, speaking particularly today to the young men and women within earshot of my remarks, I am hopeful that my youth helps all to understand the culture of cooperation that has been and remains a hallmark of Confederate political discourse -- for nothing is more important to Confederates than avoiding conflict that might destroy the State Sovereignty we have enjoyed over the past 150 years.

My study and subsequent essay will explain the importance of the Councils of Confederate Governors and the many Governors Multistate Commissions. Through the governors acting jointly in Councils, and through people they appoint to the various Multistate Commissions, we Confederates cooperate to ensure that each State retains its constitutional rights, while, as technology and populations expand, effective coordination is maintained with regard to the necessary regulations and programs of State and local governments. In this manner, we manage to coordinate internal matters without involving the Confederate Government at Davis.

Unlike in our Confederate States, governments around the globe have added more and more regulatory functions to their perceived responsibilities, and have centralized and expanded bureaucracies charged with oversight. Over the past 60 years, the contrast with the Confederate Government has become more and more striking. Within our country, with few exceptions, regulations handed down by governments are State regulations. States issue environmental regulations where needed. States regulate education as needed. Welfare is a State matter. Labor relations are generally not a government responsibility, because workplace unions are voluntary and right-to-work laws prevail in every State. Furthermore, no government employees are allowed to unionize. All States have enacted a 40-hour work-week, and time-and-a-half for overtime hours for non-management personnel. However, generally speaking, work-place regulations are not extensive in the States.

The Confederate Department of Interstate Affairs is an important branch of the Executive Department and is under the overall direction of the Confederate President. It is rather extensive and contains a large staff, made up mostly of experts in important fields of knowledge. But it holds no power, for individual States make decisions on matters beyond Confederate control. These decisions are made by the many Governors Multistate Commissions, with oversite provided by the Council of Confederate Governors. The Council of Confederate Governors, made up of every Governor and the Secretary of the Confederate Department of Interstate Affairs, meets for one week every three months, at a different location each time. This Council is helpful in clearing disputes within specific Governors Multistate Commissions, whose members, frankly, cannot always agree on a project plan. Thankfully, all in all, this decentralized structure for project planning gives good results and can be credited for delivering good project plans that are responsive to the needs of the individual States, while avoiding the inefficiency and loss of liberty that is observed in nations controlled by all-powerful centralized governments. I will now further explain the nature of the many Governors Multistate Commissions.

When cooperation with sister States is wise, as in planning major express highways and transportation networks, specific Governors Multistate Commissions, composed of commissioners and staff from affected regions, negotiate and develop plans, which are eventually endorsed by affected governmental bodies. These Multistate Commissions handle assigned tasks rather well, generally resulting in designs, budgets and cost-sharing specifics that win approval in affected State legislatures.

The list of currently active Governors Multistate Commissions is quite large, and has grown by 45 percent over the past 60 years. Our Confederacy is composed of 26 States. Presently, in the year 2011, there exists 520 Multistate Commissions. On average, a State is a member in about 80 Multistate Commissions. They normally only involve neighboring States, for there is rarely need for the governor of Virginia to be involved with the governor of South Texas – those two States are too far apart to benefit from a Multistate Commission involving transportation planning, economic development, education, health care, environmental concerns, water resources, mining, drilling, etc. For the most part, the governor of Virginia and his staff focus on Multistate Commissions that include North Carolina, Kentucky, Tennessee and, on occasion, a few other States in its region.

Some Governors Multistate Commissions have long lives; some are created to address one problem, finish that task, and are then dismissed. Some involve only two or just a few States. A few involve every State in the Confederacy. And some credit for the success of Governors Multistate Commissions can be attributed to the guidance provided by the Confederate Department of Interstate Affairs, located in Davis.

Over the decades, managing governmental and regulatory issues involving more than one State has been a challenge for governors and legislators going back to the early decades of the Confederacy. But we have met the challenge with openness and honesty. Officials with governing responsibilities still naturally seek the best deal for their constituents, and that innate ambition has not lessened over the past 60 years. But, the tradition of inter-state cooperation has become more and more fixed in the minds of Confederate voters, and here we are talking about a discerning and informed electorate. Confederates understand that, for the most part, what is best for neighboring States is probably best for them and their State as well. And they, the voters, expect elected officials to act in that overall interest.

This concludes my essay about the importance of the Councils of Confederate Governors, the many Governors Multistate Commissions, and the guidance available through the Confederate Department of Interstate Affairs located in Davis. Thanks for your attention.

Professor Davis?

Professor Davis: Thank you Robert Edward Lee, IV. Political observers beyond our Confederate States profess disbelief when pondering how our country can prosper in peace without a strong central government to oversee the goings on among the several States. Listen up, you all. Mr. Lee has explained it rather well I think.

# Essay 10 — Because Confederates Excel in the Transportation Network

By Andrew Houston

Professor Davis:

Our next essayist is Mr. Andrew Houston of South Texas, who obtained his degree in petroleum engineering from the Hughes-Sharp School of Science and Engineering in Houston and is presently on a leave of absence from the Texas Oil Company while working on his Masters of Business Administration at The University of Austin. Folks, petroleum is the key to economical transportation and has greatly contributed to the greatness of the Confederate States. So it is fitting that Mr. Houston will be answering the question, "Why are the Confederate States the Greatest Country on Earth?" from the perspective of our excellence in our transportation networks. We are also blessed to be hearing this essay from a Texan and a descendant from the greatest Texan that ever lived, the amazing Sam Houston. It is with great pride that I present to you the great-great-great-great-grandson of Sam Houston. Ladies and Gentlemen, Andrew Houston.

Andrew Houston:

Thank you Professor Davis. You are right. Petroleum played a pivotal role in the growth and efficiency of the Confederate transportation network. Pivotal with regard to automobile and truck transportation, with regard to railroad transportation, and with regard to transportation on our waterways and across the Gulf of Mexico, the Atlantic Ocean and the Pacific Ocean. You ask, "Why are the Confederate States so Great?". Much of the answer lies in our excellent transportation networks. I now begin.

The manufacture of locomotives and railroad cars was begun in earnest by an English company at Columbia, South Carolina in 1865. Other railroad manufacturing soon started up near Mobile and Houston. Of course, there was an immediate and great need for iron and steel. Many an ocean ship carried cotton to England and returned with iron and steel rails, bars and rolled sheets. Folks considered the iron for cotton trade essential to the advancement of Confederate industry. The Confederacy was becoming a balanced export-import economy. And the strong Confederate dollar encouraged confidence in international commerce.

By 1914, the year war broke out in Europe, the Confederate transportation network was remarkably well prepared to meet the country's defensive needs. And from that point forward to today, it has improved steadily.

Our express railroad network remains in place today, much improved in terms of the track's capacity for safety at high speed. Today, the trains on the Confederate triple-track express railroads normally cruise at 100 miles per hour, allowing long-haul diesel train couplings to travel cross country in under two days. Extensive switching yards have been built everywhere the south-north express lines intersect with the east-west lines.

A 50-car train can be broken apart and reassembled in one hour, and cargo sent along its way. Computers keep track of every rail car. Today, 75-car couplings of 104-foot flat-bed railroad cars each carry two 50-foot rail-containers along Confederate railroads (equal to 150 highway trucks). When in the vicinity of a rail-container's destination, a crane lifts each container off its rail car and sets it down upon a waiting highway transport trailer to be hauled by truck along the highways and roads to its final destination. Omitted from Confederate highways are long-haul tractor trailer trucks, often with two drivers, moving goods long distances across our country. Confederate railroads are moving freight by rail at one-tenth the fuel consumption and one-twentieth the manpower that would otherwise be applied to the task. Long haul tractor trailer truck carriers are far too expensive to be competitive. Furthermore, States have saved huge sums of taxpayer money in expressway construction, because omitted is the need for extra lanes to make room for intense and heavy tractor trailer traffic, and omitted is the frequent repair that would be needed to fix pavement damage from the pounding of unnecessary heavy trucks. Finally, roads are safer to drive upon. We now turn to roads, automobiles and short-haul trucks.

Diesel and gasoline powered automobiles and trucks were pioneered in Germany, and quickly expanded to France and Great Britain. Of course manufacture soon exploded in the Confederate States and the United States. In parallel, the Texas oil boom provided abundant fuel to meet the rapidly rising domestic and export demand. By 1910, automobiles and trucks were being produced at many small manufacturing sites in the Confederacy. But it was in 1919 that the concept of parts made to precise dimensions, labor specialization and paced assembly along converging and diverging conveyor lines became the standard of manufacture. With this innovation, pioneered by Henry Ford, "mass production" enabled a vast supply of vehicles at prices the middle class could afford.

Over the past sixty years, Confederate producers of automobiles, trucks and locomotives/railcars have achieved world-wide prominence. As you recall from reading history books, those industries had been a bit more robust in the United States prior to 1930. But Confederate manufacturers had begun to catch up during the 1920's, the decade when employee unions began troublesome work stoppages in the North. During the 1930's the Great Depression dealt a severe blow to producers in the United States, prompting some producers to relocate to the Confederate States. From that point going forward we Confederates are views as the leaders in these industries. Let us look at the Confederate road network.

Following the boom in automobile and truck manufacturing, Confederates realized they needed improved graded and paved roads. Thankfully, Governors Multistate Highway Commissions enjoyed great success in the planning and construction of a network of express highways that would eventually crisscross the country. Road construction remained the responsibility of local and State governments. The Confederate Government never became involved in financing highway construction. It was not necessary, because the Multistate Commissions hammered out routes that made the best sense for the regions served.

Over the past sixty years, the central Confederate Government has still refrained from building roads for vehicular traffic. To the north, the United States has Federal motor expressways called "Interstates" and a large network of Federal highways. In the Confederacy these roads remain a responsibility of the various State governments. Even so, Confederate motor roads were good sixty years ago and today are clearly excellent. One reason for this excellence is the absence of long-haul truck traffic. If a tractor-trailer load needs to go more than 500 miles, much of the trip for that trailer will be aboard an express "piggyback" railroad car. This reduces traffic on expressways and reduces the pounding on expressway pavements. It also reduces transportation costs compared to trucking the load all the way (a railroad diesel locomotive use one tenth of the fuel consumed by a tractor-trailer). [338] Confederates conceived a railroad network early on, in the 1880's, and this concept has resulted in a steadily expanding railroad network. Railroads remain the most efficient means of transporting freight long distances, but, for personal long distant travel, Confederates prefer to fly: ours is a very large country.

We now turn to aircraft and airfields.

Over the past sixty years, Confederate commercial airlines have grown to become the most popular carriers in the world, dominating travel between Europe and North America, between

---

[338] The cited superior fuel efficiency of rail transportation is truthful.

Asia and North America, and between North and South America. To our north, in the United States, a heavy tax burden is imposed on foreign airlines, including Confederate airlines, in support of that country's union-dominated airline industry. That allows domestic carriers to dominate air travel there. On the other hand, right to work laws limit the power of employee unions in the Confederate States, giving our airlines a competitive advantage, not to mention those lovely Southern belles who wait on passengers travelling on Georgia-based Delta Airlines, serving the very best sweet tea. Another advantage for Confederate airlines derives from the robust Confederate aircraft industry. As of 2010, the three major commercial Confederate aircraft manufacturers – Wright-Carolina Aircraft Corp., North Texas-based Houston Aircraft Corp., and South California-based Douglas Aircraft Corp. – delivered 31 percent of new worldwide passenger aircraft (This figure is based on the seat count, meaning large aircraft count more than small aircraft). [339] But what about ocean transport?

Over the past 60 years, Confederates have lost some ship-building business to Korea and about half of the merchant vessels owned by Confederate marine shipping companies have been constructed in vast Korean ship-building yards. But Confederate marine shipping companies still carry 63 percent of the freight that enters or leaves Confederate seaports. Most of that is containerized freight. As you recall, Confederates pioneered containerized ocean freight transport and efficient container loading/unloading at major world seaports. Major shipbuilding sites in the Confederate States are still located in Norfolk, Virginia, Charleston, South Carolina, Mobile, Alabama, Port Arthur, Texas, San Diego, South California, and Tampico, Costa Este.

That concludes my essay on the excellence of our transportation network. But that is only half of the story. Our next essayist will focus more directly on our excellence in producing abundant energy at minimal cost. Professor Davis?

Professor Davis:

Thank you, Mr. Andrew Houston. You are right. Transportation requires energy and Confederates have been pioneers in developing abundant energy at minimal cost. Our next essayist tells that story.

---

[339] The Confederacy's share of the worldwide market for new commercial aircraft is obviously fictional, but is a reasonable projection of what might have been. Douglas Aircraft Corp., was based in Long Beach, California and produced the famous DC-3 and DC-10, and merged with Boeing in 1997. Boeing has a major aircraft assembly plant in Charleston, South Carolina.

# Essay 11 — Because Confederates Excel in Producing Abundant Energy at Minimum Cost.

By Tina Kathleen Sharp

Professor Davis:

For the Confederate energy story, we proceed to our eleventh essayist, Miss Tina Kathleen Sharp of North Texas. You know, it is fitting that these two essayists are from two of the four Texas States, which laid the foundation upon which we Confederates have built our energy and transportation success.

Miss Sharp is a nuclear engineer at the Comanche Peak Nuclear Station north of Fort Worth, North Texas. And we thank her and all others in the Confederate nuclear power industry for the terrific growth in the electrical generating capacity of this industry and for the sustained safety and reliability of this technology. Confederates pioneered the development of nuclear power and the Sewanee Project is please to present to you, as our eleventh essayist, a young woman from that industry who fully understands the technology. Ladies and Gentlemen, Miss Tina Kathleen Sharp.

Miss Tina Kathleen Sharp:

Thank you Professor Davis. It is quite fitting that I follow Andrew Houston in our presentations of essays. My career is centered on nuclear power, and this essay will cover Confederate greatness in my chosen field. But I will spend considerable time on Confederate development of energy from coal, oil and what we call renewable sources. Ample, inexpensive energy is essential for a country to be considered "great." And "why are we great?" is our question of the day. So let me tell you about Confederate energy.

Walter Benona Sharp, my great-great-grandfather, of Tennessee and Texas, was a leading Texas oil man and inventor of the Sharps-Hughes hardrock drill bit. His pioneering work made possible the Texas oil boom, which began with the Spindletop gusher in 1901 and helped make the Hughes Tool Company a leader in design and manufacture of oil field drilling equipment. I now continue.

After our ancestors' successful Defense of Independence, the people of the States of the Confederacy understood better than ever the importance of developing energy resources. The first important fuels were hardwoods and coal, both abundant east of the western plains. These fuels fired steam engines which were put to work powering railroads, ships and boats, and a great variety of machinery. Water power was also important and its development was accelerated further. After the invention of diesel and gasoline internal combustion engines, motor cars and trucks proliferated, skyrocketing the demand for petroleum-based fuels. And here the Confederacy led the world in petroleum and natural gas production and oil and gasoline refining, which soon gave birth to a diverse petrochemical industry, and its offspring: resins, plastics and synthetic fibers. Over the same decades, electric power generation and distribution followed, enabling previously inconceivable technology advances. Now we look at various aspects of these advances.

Wood for all conceivable uses had always been a terrific asset of the southern colonies and the southern states. And coal was abundant for mining in western Virginia, eastern Kentucky, Tennessee, and northern Alabama. Some coal reserves remain in the United States, but, today, we consider imported coal to also be a Confederate resource. So Confederates have been secure in our reserves of fuel wood and fuel coal.

For water power, Confederates first impounded large creeks and small rivers to turn water wheels that powered small mills devoted to grinding corn and wheat, ginning cotton, running spinning and weaving textile machines, and even some sewing machines. But Confederates were also blessed with large rivers. Many were impounded to enable the pressurized water to turn large turbines linked to large electric generators, thereby cleanly producing abundant electric power. Most important were the series of power dams that impounded the mighty Tennessee River and that impounded the mighty Colorado River. Other major impoundments were built in the Carolinas, Arkansas, Oklahoma, West Texas, New Mexico, Costa Este, Costa del Sur, Central del Sur and Costa Sudoeste.

Our biggest energy story of all is the history of Confederate nuclear energy development. It began with European nuclear physicists and the horrors of Nazi Germany and World War II. No country was more active in aiding the persecuted Jews of Germany and Eastern Europe than was the Confederacy. Scientists at the Georgia Institute of Technology in Atlanta had for many years retained close contact with important Jewish nuclear physicists and they helped facilitate the immigration of many of the most capable. Confederates will be forever thankful for the seven nuclear physicists who made sure that the newly-discovered horrific potential of an atom bomb was handed over to the Confederate Government while making sure the discovery was kept secret from Nazi Germany and anyone else that might leak it out to others. I am speaking of physicists -- Otto Hahn, Fritz Strassman, Lise Meitner, Otto Frisch, Leo Szilard, Eugene Wigner, Albert Einstein.

I will now go into important details that will help you understand the underlying reasons for our success in energy production.

Confederates need energy for transportation, for building heating and cooling, and for industrial processes. Coal was the most important energy resource in the early days of the Confederacy, but, by 2011, its primary use is in industrial processes and electrical generation, and it continues to be replaced by natural gas. About 40 percent of energy used in the Confederacy goes to heating and cooling homes and buildings. Of that, natural gas and propane gas are the primary sources of heating for hot water, for homes and for buildings, with heat pumps accounting for only 20 percent. Electricity is the primary source of cooling for homes and buildings, and 60 percent of that is provided by nuclear power plants. Overall, electrical power generation today is 60 percent from nuclear plants, 25 percent from gas-fired plants, 5 percent from hydroelectric dams, 5 percent from coal-fired plants, and 5 percent from solar arrays.

Looking at transportation, we find that petroleum-sourced liquid fuels (diesel fuel and gasoline) provide almost all of that need, but battery power usage is growing in automobiles through hybrid technology and plug-in battery charging technology is on the horizon.

What allows Confederates to bring these energy resources to consumers at minimal cost?

We first look at litigation and regulation. You already know that the Confederacy is not considered a litigious society, especially when compared to the United States. The payoff here is in reduced cost to deliver energy. Concerns about an energy development project in a Confederate State are brought before legislative bodies, not before courts. The elected representatives decide what ought to be done. Issues are boiled down to common sense considerations, cost benefit studies, risk studies and property right legalities -- and decisions seem to crystalize readily. This saves lots of money and time, both contributing to minimizing cost to the consumer.

Regulations within the Confederate States seem to be ample, but not overly burdensome to progress. In the United States, printed regulations fill a tractor trailer truck. In the Confederate States a pickup truck suffices. This means that project planners can get right to the point in planning and designing an energy sourcing project. That saves time and money, and both benefits help deliver energy at minimal cost.

Major delays, where they exist, are most often encountered in nuclear power plant planning and designing. In the United States, a nuclear power plant takes 10 to 15 years to win approval for the beginning of construction. In the Confederate States, 5 years is normally sufficient. Plant design in the Confederate States can focus on what is needed for the particular plant site in the judgment of the engineers assigned to the project. Redundancy is provided, but not excessive redundancy, thereby speeding design, construction and start-up. This planning agenda seems adequate. Keeping the time-frame efficient saves a lot of money. There has never been a serious nuclear power plant failure in the Confederate States, and the industry is the backbone of the Confederacy's base-loading electricity supply.

Hydroelectric generation also benefits from minimal litigation and minimal regulation. The people, through their representatives, make the call on what hydroelectric projects should be given the green light and how much land is to be flooded behind power dams. This certainly speeds planning, land acquisition and construction. Hydroelectric power is often what is turned on in the afternoon to provide extra electricity for peak air conditioning demand on hot summer afternoons because it is very efficient to bring hydroelectric turbines online and modulate them in response to demand fluctuations.

Natural gas is another major fuel for electrical generation, and it can be readily fired up and fired down in response to demand changes. Again, minimal regulation and litigation enhances the economy in Confederate natural gas production and pipeline distribution networks.

Economy can also be measured in terms of utilization of Confederate energy. If a building is designed with well-placed insulated windows and with enhanced insulation, innovative natural ventilation, and high efficiency heating and cooling equipment, less energy is needed to ensure comfort. Many Confederate buildings are relatively new and built to standards enacted in the 1960's and more recently. These more recent superior designs improved the overall Confederate average energy efficiency. Confederates emphasize building standards, and planning for the long haul. A builder can sell a cheaply built house cheap, but the owner suffers afterward in inefficient fuel and electric bills. We see well-conceived building standards as a good thing for our country. And States take responsibility for implementing intelligent standards.

Our transportation economy can be measured in terms of energy consumed per ton mile. Here we see the benefit of Confederate regulations that require long-haul truck loads to swing by a container transfer rail head to allow the load to continue by rail or water. This saves in expressway construction and maintenance and also saves in fuel. This Confederate regulation, fairly uniform across the States, requires a tractor-trailer to divert to a container transfer rail head or pay a substantial "express" tonnage fee to carry the long-haul load directly by tractor and driver by way of express highways. Container transfer rail head facilities and sea-land container port facilities are well positioned across the Confederate States and the standardization of the "Confederate Container" permits consistent and quick transfer soon after the truck driver arrives. Today so much of that activity is computerized and controlled by satellite communications. Every Confederate Container has a communication chip aboard that permits satellites to keep track of its location and its unique CC identification number. Computer-assisted dispatchers keep the freight moving amazingly well, and truckers can often quickly give up a delivered load and quickly take on a new load, avoiding excessive idle time. This system was developed over the years in the Confederacy, but is still in its infancy in the United States because of a long history of trucker union resistance.

This completes my essay about the contributions of the Confederate energy industries to the greatness we believe we enjoy. Professor Davis?

Professor Davis:

Thank you Miss Sharp. We greatly appreciate your passion for keeping our nuclear power plants safe, and share your pride in your ancestor enabling the amazing Texas oil boom.

## Essay 12 — Because Confederate Schools, Colleges and Universities are Non-Political, Emphasize Business, Science and Engineering, and Attract the Brightest to those Fields

By Amanda Lynn Washington

Professor Davis:

Fellow Confederates we have arrived at our twelfth and final essay. Could this one be the most important of them all? Could this one explain, more than any other, "Why our Confederate States are the Greatest Country of Earth?" Could our system of education here in the Confederate States be the essential key to our success?

Folks we are especially blessed to have on our Sewanee Project team an ancestor of the pioneering Confederate educator, Booker T. Washington. Yes, his great-great-granddaughter Amanda Lynn Washington is about to step forward and discuss the importance of excellence in our country's schools, colleges and universities. Miss Washington earned her Education degree at Jefferson Davis University in Jackson, Mississippi, spent a year as a classroom teacher, and is presently working on her Ph. D. at Washington University in Lynchburg, Virginia. Her Ph. D. thesis is being titled "Achieving Excellence in Educating a Diverse Population." How fitting! Ladies and Gentlemen, please welcome to our podium Miss Amanda Lynn Washington.

Miss Amanda Lynn Washington:

Thank you Professor Davis and my thanks go out to everyone here and to all people watching on television. Thank you. Are we not a diverse society? Diverse in so many ways? Think of the eleven essayists who have preceded me at the podium today. Do they not represent much of the diversity that characterizes this "Greatest Country on Earth?"

By your applause, I believe you agree that to be the essence of our greatness.

My essay will explain that, to a degree, we are "Great" because Confederate schools, colleges and universities are non-political and emphasize business, science and engineering and attract the brightest to those fields. But that is only part of the story. To understand all of it one must know the educational diversity that encourages everyone to be the best he or she can be. I now begin.

Booker T. Washington of Virginia and Alabama, my great-great-grandfather was a leading educator of African American students, notably at the Tuskegee Institute, which he founded. His pragmatic approach to teaching people of African ancestry and his advocacy for student-targeted educational programs all across the Confederacy had much to do with the successful training of our people to succeed at working in many diverse fields of endeavor -- ranging from agriculture, to manufacturing, to transportation, to construction, to medicine, to education, and so forth. And, as we all know, the pragmatic training of which he pioneered has been a major contribution to the excellence our Confederacy has enjoyed in intelligent and capable craftsmanship across diverse fields of endeavor.

My study and subsequent essay will concern the importance of excellence in our country's grammar schools, high schools, colleges and universities. I will explain that our education culture, from first grade to graduate level, is strictly non-political. You will be impressed over how Confederate teachers encourage every student to become the best he or she can be, leaving high school with a skill set or prepared for college. And our educators encourage the brightest students to study and succeed in the important fields of business, technology, medicine, science and engineering -- fields key to the economic progress of everyone in our country.

Following the successful defense of State Secession on the battlefield, the Confederate public education movement emerged as a direct, pragmatic starburst of necessity. The needs were awesome, and only an enormous effort would suffice. The 15-year span from 1864 to 1879 was extremely challenging for a newly expanded diverse country of 18.5 million people.

From Virginia to Texas -- the core Confederate States – the population of 14.0 million was in great need of a basic education. Spread out among them were 700 thousand people of a noticeable degree of African ancestry, still grouped as families, who had been accepted from the North for resettlement as independent people. English was spoken by about 90 percent of the population, so the necessity of learning a new language burdened only a small minority and enthusiasm among those people for striving to learn basic English was admirable. But most were not able to read, write or do basic arithmetic, so, early on, the need was focused there.

On the other hand the six seceded Mexican States – Costa Noroeste, Central Norte, Costa Este, Costa del Sur, Costa Sudoeste, and Central del Sur – and the State of Cuba were home to 4.5 million people who only spoke Spanish or a mix of Native and Spanish languages. Except for those trained by Catholic Church schools, ability in reading, writing and arithmetic was rather rare. But these States had pledged to educate their people in English in exchange for admission into the Confederate States of America. And without exception, all seven States launched ambitious programs to teach English in addition to teaching reading, writing and arithmetic.

The other two States, Russian America and Hawaii only contained about 120 thousand people, few of whom spoke English, so language training was the obvious focus of education programs there.

With goals established, and without exception, every Confederate State undertook a broad public education program of community schools dedicated to teaching English-speaking children and their parents basic skills in reading and writing and basic arithmetic (addition, subtraction, multiplication, division, and home and farm book-keeping), plus the fundamental concepts of their respective State and local governments and of the Confederate Government. To such programs was added teaching the English language where needed, and placing that need at the highest priority. All programs were customized to fit the needs of the community, and to each individual, recognizing that "one shoe does not fit all." Programs ensured that every student deserved and received the opportunity to achieve his or her highest educational goals. Of course, to be successful, a student had to work at his or her studies. But, and this is important, no student was allowed to excessively retard the opportunity that his or her classmates cherished toward achieving their respective goals. How was this accomplished in practice, considering the diversity of ability and interests within the student population?

Targeted teaching methods were established for students of mostly African ancestry because educators in the Confederacy observed that, as a practical matter, many of this group predominantly learned in a manner distinctly different from students of mostly European ancestry. So, where appropriate, schools and/or classes were geared to that specific learning method, which is more demonstrative, physical, hands-on, and more by rote. The greater uniformity of interests and capabilities within the African-race schools and classes allowed the teacher, often also of African ancestry, to focus in on the needs of his or her students, producing good results and advancing the class together.

Schools and classes designed for students predominantly of a Native race were commonplace in the Spanish-speaking States of the Mexican secession, and from South Texas to South California, as well as in the Native State of Sequoyah. There, priority was given to teaching English. Most teachers were likewise of the relevant Native race and were free to focus their instruction on the particular learning styles that worked best for those rather uniform student groupings. [340]

In both situations described above, students appeared more cheerful and more focused on school work and healthy friendships, far more so than if they had been thrust into an integrated class or school. So that is the story of the formative years of education in the Confederate States. We now jump forward to the subject of Confederate education today, in the year 2011.

Pre-kindergarten and kindergarten half-day schools are offered in some communities, but not all that many, and those available are poorly attended. Why? Because educators, through testing, have concluded that parent instruction of children prior to age six years, is superior to class-room instruction. By the third grade, students who received parent instruction were more advanced than those who attended classes prior to age six years. The only exception is children of immigrant parents who are struggling to learn English themselves, because the minds of the very young are especially "wired" to learn language. Here we observe another example of the axiom, "one shoe does not fit all."

As you recall, the concept of designing schools and/or classes to group students of like ability and like needs was imperative in the early years of Confederate grammar school education. Although not a necessity today, it does offer advantages to parents and students who prefer that arrangement. And for most making that choice, the positive outcomes validate those decisions. My late great-great-grandfather, Booker T. Washington, would understand why some choose that path, and I encourage you to study the issue with an analytical mind.

My great-great-grandfather would also approve of the long-standing decision to advance remarkably bright students a grade or two during their years in grammar school, and likewise to hold back underperforming students a grade or two over that same time span. This philosophy of education for students in grades 1 through 8 ensures that all are able to "be the best they can be" and to allow the teacher to focus on teaching a classroom made up of students of fairly similar levels of attainment. As a result, a typical eighth grade class might be made up of students ranging in age from 12 to 16 years. But the advantages of uniform ability far outweigh the alternative of classes of uniform age but discordant ability.

---

[340] The reader is encouraged to compare the alternate history told in *The CSA Trilogy* to the truthful history of the United States. In truthful history the Political Reconstruction that followed the conquest of the Confederate States created a political divide in the South between Blacks (organized to vote Republican) and Whites (would not vote Republican for 100 years). This political divide resulted in rigorously segregated schools everywhere, designated seating in railroad cars, and in larger towns and cities such inconveniences as designated toilets and water fountains. In truthful history, these so-called "separate but equal" practices were endorsed by the U. S. Supreme Court in 1896 in a 7 to 1 decision on the Plessy v. Ferguson case. Voting to endorse "separate but equal" were Chief Justice Melville Fuller (of Maine and Chicago and Harvard, Democrat nominated by President Grover Cleveland), Justice Stephen Field (of California, Republican nominated by President Abraham Lincoln), Horace Gray (of Massachusetts and Harvard, Republican nominated by President Chester Arthur), David J. Brewer (of Connecticut and Kansas, and Yale, Republican nominated by President Benjamin Harrison), Henry B. Brown (of Massachusetts and New York and Yale, Republican nominated by Benjamin Harrison), George Shiras, Jr. (of Pennsylvania and Yale, Republican nominated by Benjamin Harrison), Rufus W. Peckham (of New York, Democrat nominated by Grover Cleveland), and Edward D. White, of Louisiana, Democrat nominated by Grover Cleveland). Voting against endorsement was John M. Harlan (of Kentucky, Republican nominated by Rutherford Hayes). Stated another way, in truthful history, the "separate but equal" endorsement was enacted by the U. S. Supreme Court by an almost unanimous decision during the time of Grover Cleveland's second term as President, when the South (very much a minority in American political and economic power) was still struggling to recover from 1860s and 1870s devastation and Political Reconstruction, and when the North (by far a majority in American political and economic power) was reacting to the substantial northward migration of people of color. In our alternate history, the racial divide promoted by Political Reconstruction and the economic devastation suffered within the conquered states did not occur, and the consequence is the far happier story you are enjoying in *The CSA Trilogy*.

Even more than ever, Confederates understand that high schools have two distinctly different objectives – to prepare some for four more years in college while preparing the others for post-high-school careers. Why not try to prepare all for college? Because, for most, those four years would be a waste of time and money, unnecessarily delaying by four years their entry into gainful employment, or in starting a business of their own or in partnership with others. So, today high schools educate toward two alternate career paths: 1), preparation for college, or 2), teaching skill sets helpful in entering the workforce, practicing a trade or starting a business. Those two paths are often abbreviated as "college-bound" and "non-college bound," the latter a handy way to describe relevant programs without engaging a long string of words, while never intending to demean those taking the non-college path. Some feel ready to call high school a "done deal" upon reaching the age of 17 years, and that is OK. Prior to that age, school is compulsory.

Further discussion of programs for students on the "non-college bound" path is appropriate, but please understand that a full-size book would be necessary to fully tell that story. So examples will have to suffice. Programs in support of the oil and petrochemical industry are important in the Texas group of States, and training in the manufacture of fibers, textiles and garments is important in the Carolinas and the seceded Mexican States. South California and Virginia emphasize computer technology and manufacture of semiconductors. Georgia, Alabama and Mississippi emphasize agriculture and animal husbandry. Approximately 35 percent of non-college-bound boys choose high school apprenticing, as do about 25 percent of girls. In typical apprenticing programs, funding is shared 50-50 between the State and the apprenticing company. Major programs today include machining, welding and metalworking; home and commercial construction; travel and leisure; clerical support in finance and banking; understanding wholesale and retail systems; robotics, including their programing and maintenance; railroad, automotive and truck maintenance; maintenance of manufacturing machines; electrical power generation and distribution; process control applications and systems maintenance; and entertainment, media and printing technology. Confederate apprenticing programs are universally cited as a major reason that Confederates lead the world in productivity. Germany comes in second.

We now look at high school students on the "college bound" path. For the most part they receive a classic education, leaving specialization to future college years. Ability at "critical thinking" is a hallmark of Confederate "college bound" education. As mentioned before, the culture in Confederate schools is firmly distanced from political advocacy. Each student is encouraged to think "critically," "logically" and "objectively" about an issue and by that process of reasoning arrive at a decision. That was perhaps the most important skill I learned in high school and it enabled me and other students arriving at college to quickly identify and avoid a professor who was overly pushing his personal point of view.

Of course, in high school those on a "college bound" path can choose between the "arts" and the "sciences" and many have by then made a choice for themselves regarding choice of a career beyond college.

Foreign language instruction is seldom offered in public high schools, and, in my opinion, that serves us well. Why? Because English predominates in business and communication worldwide; the world is awash with many languages (on what basis would a student select one over the other?), and, from its beginning, the Confederacy has emphasized advancing citizens to proficiency in English. So teaching a foreign language in grades 1 through 12 seems counterproductive. Learning a foreign language is relegated to private schools, special language school and colleges.

Athletic programs are an important aspect of a high school education. But Confederates are careful to prevent African-race schools from overly-dominating competition in the popular sports of football, basketball and track. So, schools are grouped on ability into Class 1, Class 2 and Class 3 athletic associations, without considering race. Popular programs include football, basketball, soccer, track, tennis and gymnastics. My school was a member of the Class 1 athletic association in Henrico County (Richmond) where I attended high school. I was a pretty good athlete: enjoyed playing basketball and running on the track team. I fully agree with the Confederate culture that prevents schools blessed with better athletes of African ancestry from dominating over schools without that advantage. Works best for all concerned.

I also enjoyed participating in the music classes and music programs at Douglas Freeman High in Richmond. Most students of African ancestry find science and mathematics rather difficult, but when it comes to music, as a whole, no racial group is better. So, many of us like to sing and play musical instruments, and, in that ability, we take special pride. In summary, the Confederate culture of ensuring students can "be the best they can be" is supported by careful attention to providing outstanding opportunities in athletics and music, from sixth grade through the final high school year.

Now, this essay would be incomplete without mention of students who are educated at home, at religious schools or at private schools. Home schooling for several grades, or all the way through high school, is fairly common in the Confederate States, especially for parents that stress proficiency in agriculture, in a trade, or preparation to work in the relevant family business. Standardize testing ensures that the home schooled meet academic standards of proficiency, so that path gives no evidence of being abused – outcomes are admirable for all but a few.

I have friends who live in the United States who ask me, "Why are there no public colleges and universities in the Confederate States?" I reply, "Why do they exist in the United States?" You see, my "critical" study of higher education in the United States, as part of my current Ph. D. work, persuades me it may be impossible to provide public colleges without enabling abuse. You ask, "What sort of abuse?" Let me explain. When government provides the money to enable an enterprise, that enterprise is naturally supportive of its financial "sugar daddy" and advocates for more and more money – more buildings, more students, more professors, more of everything. And that abuse is readily observed to our north. There, far too many "students" are "going to college;" far too many high schools are failing to prepare students for success in careers that do not benefit from college training; far too many professors focus on their so-called "research" and "publishing" endeavors and are protected in that by "tenure" rules; and far too much college instruction is directed at "brain-washing" students into believing that big, powerful government is wise and beneficial to mankind. Confederates recognize this to be a systematic feature of government-funded higher education and simply "do not go there."

Anyway, education at private and religious colleges and universities need not be prohibitively expensive for the young Confederate man or woman. There are scholarships for the exceptional and those without financial means, and there are "college loans" that help defer the cost. Since Confederates go to college to enable a successful career, earnings after graduation are generally good and loan payment is normally manageable -- they get good jobs in the career for which they studied. Furthermore, colleges are managed as efficient enterprises, enabling the student to receive a good education without spending heavily on the frills. And the student pays by the class, not by the semester. Widely attended lecture hall classes are the least expensive. Other classroom studies are rather affordable. For the sciences and engineering, lab courses cost more, as they ought to. The student is billed according to the cost of providing any given class or lab. Grants to private and religious colleges by benefactors and gifts reduce the cost billed to the student as well – the 2009 survey, the last available as I write this, revealed that 43 percent of the cost of a college education in the Confederacy, on average, was covered by the contributions of benefactors, gifts and foundations. Finally, co-op programs allow about 25 percent of students to pay for much of their college education by apprenticing in their chosen field for pay, and completing the 4-year degree in 5 or 6 years, graduating "ready to go," and debt-free or with minimal, easily managed debt.

As mentioned earlier, college professors are not paid to do research, and that ensures they are focused on the task at hand -- providing a good education to the students in their charge. More research by professors is found in programs leading to a Ph. D., but, even then, the levels of research are modest when compared to government funded colleges and universities in the United States and Europe. You may ask, "How can the Confederacy be a leader in science and medicine without extensive independent research in universities?" I suppose experience in other countries has shown many great inventions and discoveries have arisen in government-funded research at universities. But that is not the only way for a society to achieve such success. Because the culture in Confederate business is to manage the corporation for long-term success, fundamental research is a major part of research and development budgets in Confederate companies. Confederate patent law, which grants exclusive rights for 17 years, also encourages fundamental research. Several major Confederate corporations have grown from small research endeavors into giants in their field, merely on the strength of a fundamental discovery. The Confederate stock market has historically supported corporations whose major strength is in research and development.

Few Confederates go to college to become more "broadly educated." Perhaps that was worthwhile a generation or two earlier, but today, with the availability of books and the internet, all a young person needs to do to become "broadly educated" is to research relevant subjects and to read about them. And that is relatively free of cost and so well fits into profitable use of one's leisure hours. So college courses of study that cannot contribute to career building continue to shrink, and those that meet the needs of companies seeking college-skilled entry employees continue to expand, thereby assuring a continuation of the country's culture of honoring pragmatic education.

Teachers colleges focus on training teachers and college professors, and they are successful in that role, garnering 90 percent of students seeking such careers. I can assure you of that principle because I am a descendent of the late Booker T. Washington and that is my chosen field.

Today, 95 percent of Confederate students graduate from high school -- 40 percent graduating from non-college bound course work without benefit of apprenticing; 30 percent graduating after benefiting from apprenticing programs; and 25 percent graduating as college-bound students. Of that 25 percent, those graduating from college with a bachelor's degree represent 18 percent; those receiving an advanced degree represent 2 percent, and those receiving a degree in law and joining a State bar representing 0.5 percent.

I like to think that my great-great-grandfather, Booker T. Washington, was helpful in instilling the long-held pragmatic approach to our Confederate education culture. Before State Secession, education was classical and Christian in its course of study, and was pursued by only a few. Soon, thereafter, Confederates faced the challenge of the Great Confederate Expansion and of accommodating a very diverse population with huge needs for basic education and skills in English. At the same time they faced the challenge of accelerating industrial development. These urgent needs were met by building a pragmatic public education system through high school and a pragmatic private college education network. Look around. You see, the hands-on pragmatism of Booker T. Washington continues to be applied in various ways as the needs of the modern world unfold before us.

That's all folks. Thank you. Professor Davis?

Professor Davis:

Fellow Confederates, were not our twelve essayists spot on? You can read their essays and view videos of these presentations tomorrow and for many future years by going to the internet. We of the Sewanee Project hope you do that. And let us make these essays a foundation upon which we all build a firmer understanding of ourselves, our ancestors and the culture in which we live.

Thank you.

# The Celebration Continues

Professor Davis:

I believe we are about to listen to some amazing brass band music. [341]

And the celebration continued.

Two hours later, the celebration in the Concert Hall concluded with the singing of the Confederate States Anthem by all in attendance, supported by a 200-person mass choir and the Nashville Symphony. Among the singers were the 12 essayists. Among the French horn section of the Symphony was Judith Davis.

### The Confederate States Anthem

We are one.
We are free.
We are the Great
Diversity

From Carolina's sandy beach,
Westward to the Pacific shore,
From Artic ice beyond our reach,
To warm Gulf waters we adore.

We are one.
We are free.
We are the Great
Diversity.

Asia, Europe and Africa --
The roots of our family tree
It was God's plan -- shout out hurrah --
That we could live in Harmony!

We are one.
We are free.
We are the Great
Diversity.

The Lord knows of our faithfulness
And leads us toward prosperity.
His love enables our toughness,
Honor and generosity.

Diverse, Diverse.
We are Diversity

It was a glorious celebration, capped by the grand fireworks display over Sewanee. The Reverend Billy Graham, the world-famous evangelist from North Carolina, was 92 years old and in declining health at the time of the 150th Confederate celebration. So, his son, the Reverend

---

[341] Shucks! The Black Dyke Brass Band won the contest and closed the program. Well, the English started brass band music. So we Confederates have to be humble and let them shine. But when it comes to country music and jazz. That is a story for another day.

Franklin Graham, gave the benediction as other Christian clergy stood nearby, having had taken part at other times during the celebration.

"Our heavenly father, we praise you for the . . ."

And that is the way Confederates and people all over the world were reminded of **Why the CSA is the Greatest County on Earth**.

A final comment by the writer: Dear reader you will be pleased to know that on July 4th, 2012, all twelve essayists and Professor Davis held a reunion in Sewanee to renew friendships and catch up on what everyone had been doing.  Amanda Washington and Isaiah Montgomery did travel to West Africa together so she could conduct research needed for her Ph. D. dissertation.  But no romance was detected.  On the other hand Andrew Houston and Conchita Rezanova walked in together sporting a big surprise.  The lovely Conchita was wearing an engagement ring.  An annual repeat of this reunion was the uniform pledge made by all upon departing for their respective residences on July 6th.

The end.

## About the Author, Howard Ray White

Howard Ray White was born Howard Ray White, Jr. in Nashville, Tennessee on August 4, 1938 to parents Howard Ray White, Sr. and Martha Bell White. The father had always been called Ray White, so it was easy for the boy to always be known as Howard White. Ray was a school teacher as a young man, but his main career of 25 years was to lead the Nashville Boys' Club, and oversee the building of Nashville's fine Boys' Club facility on Thompson Lane, which was dedicated by Richard Nixon in 1965. Martha was a high school teacher for 26 years, primarily teaching home economics and English at Hillsboro high school. Ray built a house in the Belle Meade community of Nashville when Howard was 9 years old. Howard attended Hillsboro high school and then Vanderbilt University, also in Nashville, where he earned a degree in chemical engineering. After completing his junior year at Vanderbilt, Howard married Judith Hunt Willis, also a Vandy student. Howard and Judith celebrated their 52$^{nd}$ wedding anniversary in 2011, the year of the 150$^{th}$ anniversary of the creation of the Confederate States of America. Ray died in 1979, after which Howard dropped the "Jr." in normal use of his name.

Howard's wife, known as Judith Willis White, and a native of Nashville, was and still is an excellent musician and French horn player. She played in the Nashville symphony and later in the Roanoke, Virginia symphony and the Charlotte, North Carolina symphony. Her parents were Dr. Larry Jordan Willis and Edna Hunt Willis of upstate South Carolina. Her father was for many years Supervisor of Nashville City Schools. Howard and Judith have three sons, two living. Howard and Judith have lived in Charlotte, since 1972.

Howard became interested in history in his early fifties and eventually focused on a study of the politics before, during, and after the War Between the States, a horrific period in American history of which none other compares. He generally set aside the study of military aspects of the conflict to more clearly focus on the political and cultural aspects. He went way back in time, several centuries back, and moved forward to truly understand and to quantify the background history prior to that era. By the mid-1990's he realized he was writing a book. It would involve four volumes and tell the relevant American history, much through the lives of important leaders of those times. These four volumes are titled, ***Bloodstains, an Epic History of the Politics that Produced and Sustained the American Civil War and the Political Reconstruction that Followed***. Being a new historian and outside of the academic community, Howard decided to self-publish, the first volume becoming available in 2002, the fourth finishing the job in 2012. (See www.amazon.com). [342]

Soon after the completion of ***Bloodstains***, Howard and Dr. Clyde N. Wilson of Columbia, South Carolina jointly founded the **Society of Independent Southern Historians**, a web-site based, nation-wide organization of folks interested in reading and writing truthful American, Southern and Confederate history. A bit later, Howard and Dr. Wilson co-edited a publication by the Society that included fourteen other writers, all Society members. Published by the Society in 2015, and titled, ***Understanding the War Between the States***, this book of only 80 pages, is considered by many to be the most effective resource available today for teaching truthful history concerning the War Between the States, especially regarding political and social aspects. The book's target audience is "middle school, high school, college and beyond." A variation of this

---

[342] Other books self-published by Howard Ray White include his mother's autobiography, *Springfield Girl*, a Memoir; his grandfather's poetry, *Understanding Granddad through his Poetry*; his father-in-law's Ph. D. thesis, *Advancing American Reading Achievement During the Great Depression*; Howard's assessment of Biblical teaching, *Understanding Creation and Evolution*; Howard's study of the Fort Sumter incident, *Understanding Abe Lincoln's First Shot Strategy*; and Howard's study of abolitionists propaganda, *Understanding 'Uncle Tom's Cabin' and 'The Battle Hymn of the Republic'*.

book was published in 2018. Especially for home schooled students and parents, it is titled, *American History for Home Schools, with a Focus on Our Civil War.*

Howard's background has been presented above to help the reader of *The CSA Trilogy* better appreciate his understanding of truthful and relevant American history -- essential to conceiving of an alternate history where the South wins a negotiated settlement of the War Between the States. That accomplished, Howard was then free to construct an subsequent world history. The emphasis in *The CSA Trilogy* on Confederate political deception and delaying tactics derives from Howard's understanding of the 1861 and 1862 political and cultural situations. Believing that, after the 1862 elections, defeating Federals by conventional warfare would have been impossible, he constructs a concept of "retreat, envelope, capture and imprison." It further logically flows that the negotiated CSA-USA boundary wins approval by east-dominated Republican leaders. The French Intervention in Mexico is easily transformed into a story of the secession of northern Mexican states, their independence from Mexico City and their inclusion into the Confederate States. With CSA help available, the Cuban Revolution is easily transformed from Spanish victory to victory for Cuban Independence fighters, and inclusion into the CSA as the state of Cuba. Far to the north, the purchase of Russian America by the United States Federal Government, at the time protested as "Seward's Folly," is transformed into independence for Russian America and inclusion into the CSA. And, to complete the story of the Great Confederate Expansion, adding the mid-Pacific Hawaiian Islands as a CSA state so nicely blends with the Russian American story, that the reader feels naturally strong and satisfying emotions. After that, the story of the war against Fascist Japan -- and how the Confederates and Chinese Nationalists supported each other so effectively to drive the Japanese out of mainline China and Korea and force unconditional Japanese surrender -- is very different from truthful history, yet plausible and far more satisfying. Howard enjoys telling happy stories, and *The CSA Trilogy* is surely one to admire. Howard was inspired by the great histories written by the late, great Texan, James Michener (*Hawaii, Texas, Centennial,* and so many more). He remains ever grateful to Michener for teaching the world how to tell truthful history as a story of many generations, of families, and of heroic men, in a style that resembles a compelling novel, but teaches supremely. One final thought: Howard Ray White allows you to live the history – a trademark of his story telling talent.

# Closing Commentary and a Few of the Historical Resources Utilized in Preparation of this Alternate History/Historical Novel

The following is a sampling of resources that helped the author understand the truthful history from which he departed in creating his fictional alternate history/historical fiction novel. For twenty years the author studied, wrote and sequentially published his four-volume history series, *Bloodstains*. These twenty years of study enabled him to formulate a logical alternate history of 1860 through 1862 that was consistent with many of the sectional North-South cultural, political and racial passions -- passions that were, at the time, driving the truthful history along the course it, in fact, did take.

There is historical precedence for a Confederate victory over invading United States troops. In truthful history, the first major battle of the war was the Battle of Bull Run, in Northern Virginia. There, truthful history shows defeated and panic-stricken Northern troops abandoning their weapons and running back to Washington City. Our alternate history draws on this nature of a first battle between untested invading troops and untested defending troops.

The author realizes that much of the story involving attitudes toward slaves, slavery and race, as presented herein during the 1860's, is hard for people today to understand. He realizes how difficult it must be for people today to believe that, in 1862, the people of the North did not want Negroes living in their communities, and that people of the South were accustomed to it and were agreeable to accept immigration of Negroes from the North into the Confederate States, both those that were free and those soon to become free. The idea that the Party of Abraham Lincoln would give up what would become Oklahoma (Indian Territory), and arid New Mexico, Arizona and Southern California for far less, but bountiful, land in northern and western Virginia is also hard to believe for most. But the author reminds these people that, the North was eager to get rid of Indians, and the far away southwestern land was mostly occupied by people of Mexican ancestry, plus a few Southerners, and was extremely dry. Republican leaders wanted to ensure they retained Northern California and the States of Oregon and Washington, and believed that shedding the arid southwest would prevent any future agitation for a Western State Secession movement. Although this eventually gave Confederates four additional States, it greatly reduced the likelihood of a future State Secession movement. And, preventing another State Secession movement was very important to political, financial and economic leaders of the Northeastern States, who dominated the Republican Party at the time.

After creating the fictional story of the successful military defense of the Confederate States and the subsequent boundary separating the two countries, the author recognized that this major alteration in the history of North America readily facilitated a much happier history for Northern Mexico, Russian America, Cuba and the Hawaiian Islands. So, happily, he then proceeded to create these four alternate historical outcomes, all in the flash of only a few years. By this rapid inclusion of nine additional States, the Confederate States created a truly multi-racial society, including a large population of persons with significant native ancestry, and/or Spanish ancestry, and/or African ancestry, plus a few with Asian/Polynesian ancestry. These people added to the original Confederate people of European ancestry, yielding a multiracial society of divergent and complementary skills and talents.

The reader is probably amazed that the South, as described in this alternate history, was able to rapidly build an industrial economy. How could that have happened? First, the author realized that, in this alternate history, the South is not devastated by war. There are resources and capital in the South to advance industrialization. Second, the many Southern people who died as a result of the war, in truthful history, remain alive and are stepping up to advance their new country. Third, the author realized that much of the industrialization in North America, as we know it in truthful history, was the result of inventive immigrants, because Scotland and England were the world-leaders in invention and industrialization in the 1860's, 1870's, 1880's and 1890's. In those years, in truthful history, new technology and inventive leaders were immigrating into the Northern States because the economy of the Southern States had been destroyed and was only very slowly recovering. In our alternate history many of these same inventive immigrants are recruited into the Confederate States, enabling a rapid advance in industrialization and the introduction of new technology.

This new industrialization in the confederate States rapidly reduced the number of laborers needed on farms, making retaining slaves far too expensive and accelerating arrangements for their freedom and inclusion in society as free Persons of Color. In truthful history, Brazil was the last country in the Western Hemisphere to free all slaves: the final date was 1888, and no war was involved. So readers are encouraged to understand that, in our alternate history, emancipation in the Confederate States was accomplished before that date, even though some elderly slaves might have remained with former masters voluntarily to ensure their care during old age.

The author apologizes that more of the story in *The CSA Trilogy* is not devoted to heroic and accomplished People of Color. They were very important to the success of the Confederate States, providing vitally needed talents and energy. Their cooperative attitude during and after the war enabled successful emancipation and living as independent persons afterward. The reader should realize that, in truthful history, Political Reconstruction, which was implemented by the Republican Party for ten years following the conquest of the Confederate States, drove a lasting wedge between the races in the South that forced Southern Whites to contrive methods to rescue their towns, counties and States from ruin under Carpetbagger rule.

As the Confederate States advanced into the twentieth century, it followed naturally that, in our alternate history, the Japanese attack on Hawaii was an attack on a Confederate State, this drawing Confederates into a War against Japan. In our alternate history, the CSA only fights in the Pacific and the USA only fights in Europe. So the military strategy for defeating Japan does not involve the Philippines. An alliance with China is secured and facilitates the CSA's major war plan: interrupt supplies such as oil coming to Japan, drive Japanese out of China, prepare for a joint Confederate-Chinese invasion of Japan, but demonstrate the Confederate's new atomic bomb to persuade unconditional surrender of the Imperialists.

Much of the historical information gathered in support of creating *The CSA Trilogy* was obtained through internet searches and small books and essays, too numerous to mention. But it does seem appropriate to list several of the major resources utilized in the writing of this work. That list follows:

Concerning American History from the America's earliest colonial days to 1885, the author's published history is *Bloodstains, An Epic History of the Politics the Produced and Sustained the American Civil War and the Political Reconstruction that Followed.* This is a large work in four volumes. Volume 1: *The Nation Builders* (2002), Volume 2: *The Demagogues* (2003), Volume 3: *The Bleeding* (2007), and Volume 4: *Political Reconstruction and the Struggle for Healing* (2012).

Inspired by *Bloodstains*: The author co-founded the Society of Independent Southern Historians in 2013 and helped the membership cooperate in writing a teaching aid for schools, colleges and parents. This concise but comprehensive book of 80 pages is titled *Understanding the War Between the States, a Supplemental Booklet by 16 Writers that Enables a More Complete and Truthful Study of American History (Middle School, High School, College and Beyond)*, 2015. A recent variation is titled: *American History for Home Schools.*

Concerning Fort Sumter, see: *Understanding Abe Lincoln's First Shot Strategy (Inciting Confederates to Fire First at Fort Sumter)*, by Howard Ray White, 2011.

Concerning Abraham Lincoln and the Republican Party of the North, see: *Lincoln*, by David Herbert Donald, 1995.

Concerning Abraham Lincoln's parentage, see: *The Genesis of Lincoln*, by James Harrison Cathey, 1899.

Concerning Stephen A. Douglas and the Democratic Party of the North, see: *Stephen A. Douglas*, by Robert W. Johannsen, 1973.

Concerning Jefferson Davis and the Democratic Party of the South, see: *Jefferson Davis*, by Hudson Strode, three volumes: *American Patriot*, 1808-1861 (1955), *Confederate President*, 1861-1864 (1959), and *Tragic Hero*, 1864-1889 (1964).

Concerning Native Americans of Southeastern North America, see: *The Southeastern Indians*, by Charles Hudson (1976), *History of the Choctaw, Chickasaw and Natchez Indians*, by H. B. Cushman (1899) and *After the Trail of Tears, the Cherokees' Struggle for Sovereignty, 1839-1880*, by William G. McLoughlin (1993).

Concerning Sam Houston, the Cherokee Nation and Texas, see: *The Raven*, by Marquis James, 1929.

Concerning Judah Benjamin and the Confederate Government, see: *Judah P. Benjamin, Confederate Statesman*, by Robert Douthat Meade, 1943.

Concerning the races of Mankind, see: *Understanding Creation and Evolution*, by Howard Ray White (2018).

Concerning people of African ancestry after the end of slavery, see *Up from Slavery*, by Booker T. Washington (1901), *The Negro Problem*, a collection of seven essays, edited by Booker T. Washington (1903). Note: in *The CSA Trilogy*, the author is happy that People of Color are perceived as being far happier and successful.

Concerning Mexico, see *A History of Mexico*, by Herbert Weinstock, 1938.

Concerning Mexican Leader Benito Juarez, see *A Life of Benito Juarez*, by Ulick Ralph Burke, 1894.

Concerning Russian America, see *Russian America: The Great Alaskan Adventure, 1741-1867*, by Hector Chevigny, 1965.

Concerning Natalia Shelikohova and the Russian America Company, see *Natalia Shelikhova, Russian Oligarch of Alaska Commerce*, by Alexander Yu. Petrov, translated into English by Dawn Lea Black, 2010.

Concerning the Hawaiian Islands, see *The Hawaiian Kingdom*, by Ralph S. Kuykendall, in two volumes: *Foundation and Transformation, 1778-1854* (1938), and *Twenty Critical Years, 1854-1874* (1953).

Concerning Cuba, see *The Pearl of the Antilles*, by Antonio Carlo Napoleone Gallenga (1873), *The Book of Blood . . .* , by Nestor Ponce De Leon (1873), *Sugar and Railroads, A Cuban History, 1837-1959*, by Oscar Zanetti and Alejanndro Garcia (1987), translated by Frankin W. Knight and Mary Todd (1998), and *Cuba, a New History*, by Richard Gott (2004).

Concerning China and Japan, see *A New History of Christianity in China*, by Daniel H. Bays (2012), *China's War with Japan, 1937-1945, The Struggle for Survival*, by Rana Mitter (2013), and *Japan's Total Empire, Manchuria and the Culture of Wartime Imperialism*, by Louise Young (1998).

Concerning how English and Scottish pioneered the industrial revolution, a sample is provided here in *Brilliant! Scottish Inventors, Innovators, Scientists & Engineers Who Changed the World*, by Andrew G. Patterson. The sections about years 1750 to 1899 illustrates the importance of encouraging immigration of such men into the Confederate States.

52553378R00233

Made in the USA
Columbia, SC
05 March 2019